THE LAST
LEGWOMAN

THE
LAST
LEGWOMAN

A NOVEL OF HOLLYWOOD, MURDER...AND GOSSIP!

PENNY PENCE SMITH

ISBN: 978-0-578-65740-0

Cover image: logoboom/Shutterstock.com
Cover design: Cynthia Gunn
Interior design: Robert Barclay
Pueo logo: Glenn Freitas

45-720 Kea'ahala Road
Kane'ohe, HI 96744

For Marilyn and Carol...what a ride!

CHAPTER 1

BEL AIR, 1983
EARLY TUESDAY

Every weekday morning by eight-thirty, Bettina Grant sits at her desk, arranging a hard-to-get interview, negotiating a tough exclusive story or simply cementing a critical relationship. The most widely read Hollywood columnist in the country, she's typically on the phone, the morning's cigarette dangling from her fingers or smoldering in a chipped ash tray.

So, when her assistant, Meredith Ogden, found a dark and silent home-office as she arrived at work on a rainy Tuesday morning in December, the young woman paused uneasily in the doorway. No smoke trails curled from the desk, and neither the TV voice of *Today Show's* Jane Pauley nor *Good Morning America's* David Hartman played in the background. There wasn't even the dependable aroma of fresh coffee.

Looking around the quiet four-office suite, Meredith remembered that Monday nights and Tuesdays were days off for Ito, the houseman. She checked the garage and saw Bettina's Jaguar in place, then looked out the front door to Bel Air's perky Bright Leaf Lane. Showers had brightened the green hedges and yards where winter flowers were tucked into tight little beds along the road and around the throats of the well-kept homes. The van belonging to Sonia, the secretary, was absent from its usual place—not surprising due to an argument with their boss the day before. She'd show up later. Only Meredith's beloved bright red Mustang punctuated the street.

She switched on lamps in Bettina's den—the columnist's personal office—then in Sonia Schaeffer's adjoining box-like enclave, and finally in her own work center, pleasant with large banks of windows. Slender and athletically built, the thirty six-year old journalist dropped her brief case and shed her raincoat. Her copper-blond hair was twisted back off her neck, and she wore a tailored grey pantsuit with a creamy white blouse, a silver necklace and earrings. Her work uniform.

She punched answering machine buttons, listening to messages left since Bettina Grant had checked the lines at end of day before leaving for dinner out. Bettina's sister Luanne, a sales pitch for a local police circus, and Sonia's throaty voice reporting that her van had not started. She would arrive at work whenever she could. It was neither uncommon nor unexpected. The last two calls—one at nine p.m. and the other at eleven, a frustrated and wrathful "huff followed by a grumbled "fuck you"—were perplexing and a little worrisome. But Bettina's crammed schedule often left her unavailable, and callers annoyed.

Meredith penciled the phone messages on sticky-notes and pinned them to Bettina's keyboard, adding exclamation marks to the last one. The den was Bettina Grant's professional control center, furnished in overstuffed chintz, modern glass and rosewood furnishings. Two TV monitors sat within easy eyesight, the walls adorned with celebrity photos in casual conversation with Bettina, most autographed. Yellowing photos of three 1950's starlets hovering around a microphone; a reminder of Bettina's trio singing days with her two sisters, Luanne and Rachael.

The columnist's calendar showed no early morning meeting, only an afternoon interview. Meredith walked the elegantly comfortable private quarters—living room with its trendy antique furnishings and art, powder room—looking for signs of activity and went to the kitchen and made a pot of coffee. The dishwasher was full and clean.

Returning to her own office, she began to sort out the day's business, tending to phone calls and mail. Her mind went to preparing for her noon exclusive interview with a prominent actress finally returning to the set of a multimillion-dollar movie after an extended absence following a temper tantrum over script quality. It had taken Meredith weeks to negotiate the meeting and an agreement that she would be the only press member allowed on the set.

At nine, the silence of the house weighed on her, and she began to feel a little paranoid. Bettina, not generally a late sleeper in any case, always phoned the office if she was away, fearing she would miss a good story lead. Maybe she picked up a new "interest" at the dinner the night before? Meredith dismissed the thought. At fifty-five, Bettina seemed to have lost interest in coupling—even recreational mating. Of money, power and sex, the columnist found the former two more satisfying than the latter, and over time even money had lost its luster. Power, however, was never a disappointment.

"Bettina, you up there?" The young journalist called up the stairs. She heard no response and hesitantly advanced up the staircase. "Bettina, get down here. Your public calls. And Sonia's out!" Her more aggressive yell was answered only with silence.

Meredith climbed to the top of the stairs, crossed the small hallway and rapped on the door to the master suite. When no one answered, she cautiously opened the door and saw the languid form of Bettina Grant sprawled in uncompromised repose against smartly-colored sheets and pillows. Filtered window light highlighted the drowsy scene: a milky arm curled gracefully above Bettina's tumbled ash blonde hair, face free of the theatrics and make-up of her public life, looking serenely at ease.

Meredith smiled mischievously. Some dinner party, she thought as she stepped lightly to the edge of the bed. She leaned in closer to Bettina and said, "Get up, lazy!"

Strands of Bettina's hair quivered from Meredith's breath, but nothing else moved.

"Oh shit," hissed Meredith, stumbling back into the room. Instead of looking relaxed and lazy, Bettina Grant looked waxy, and dead.

CHAPTER 2

Two policemen hunched over the small kitchen counter along with Meredith. Her hands shook as she clung to a mug, now empty, and tried to stay calm. The cop made notes and directed the activity of other law enforcement people who suddenly filled the house, arriving quickly almost as quickly as the death was labeled, "high profile."

"I should have tried some CPR," Meredith whispered, mostly to herself. "Maybe there was time…." The thought was short circuited by Bettina's dead image. "God, she looked like something out of Movieland Wax Museum…is that still open?"

"So, she went to a dinner party last night?" A voice from the outside pried its way into her consciousness and Meredith turned to look at a weathered officer sitting opposite her.

"I think so. I know that she was planning to go to the dinner—but I left her at about six o'clock and didn't talk to her afterward," she said wondering if she was being unduly accurate. Maybe she'd watched too many TV law and order series. Never volunteer any information of which you aren't certain, she reasoned. Or for which you can be blamed. Or held accountable.

Meredith's reverie was interrupted by the sounds of the doorbell and conversation at the front door. She looked up to see Allan Jaymar, Bettina's neighbor from across the lane, pushing his way into the kitchen.

"What's happened, Merri?" he asked, his face etched with concern, and calling her by the nickname known only to those closest to her. "Where's Bettina?"

She realized this would be the start of many, many inquiries and with a catch in her throat, Meredith answered, "Allan, Bettina...passed away...last night."

"I saw her at a dinner party, she seemed fine. What happened?"

Allan was one of Bettina's oldest personal and professional friends, a retired entertainment industry artists' agent/manager who shared as much show business history as Bettina. Meredith chose her words carefully. "We don't exactly know, Allan. I found her in bed this morning just...dead."

At that moment, two law enforcement technicians came down the pristine staircase carrying camera and equipment bags. They clumped indelicately into the kitchen.

"She just died—but it's hard to tell exactly how or why," said the older of the pair.

"No obvious signs of any kind of struggle—just a decorative pillow on the floor—maybe tossed off the bed before she climbed in. But there was some miniscule scratching on her nose and what looked like a tiny bit of caked blood. Fancy bedding can be dangerous to your health," he joked. No one else was amused.

"Because it's such a high profile...person...we've been told to be thorough. A Special Cases investigator and the medical examiner are on the way and will be working in the bedroom very shortly. Other rooms later. We'd appreciate it if you would all stay on the first floor for now. We'll know more later and after an autopsy."

The younger of the pair held up a Polaroid print. "There's a booklet—looks like a manuscript—next to the bed. She was probably reading it before she went to sleep."

"What is it?" puzzled Meredith, reaching for the print. "Huh," she looked closely at the photo, squinting to see the details. "It's a manuscript from Cassie Ainsworth—my predecessor. I wonder when Bett got this. Dated December 1... only a few days ago. It must have arrived last night after we all left. Sonia always date stamps material of any kind. Bettina wouldn't have bothered. And I know she would have said something about this—we all know Cassie. I wonder what this is all about." She was silent for a moment, then looked around, feeling deflated. "What about all of this?"

"Meredith, say nothing to anyone about Bettina's death for now. Nothing. Same instruction for Sonia and Ito!" Allan spoke up in rapid dialog, looking around the room. "And nothing to anyone from anyone here. Bettina is well enough known that we could have a media circus and there'll be repercussions with her editors across the county, and we don't know enough. Not a word. I'll be right back." And he trotted from the room, out of the house and across the street to his own home.

Now retired, Allan had managed some of the biggest names in the entertainment industry, weathered most of their life crises including untimely and questionable deaths, addictions and proclivities. It was a drill he knew well.

Everyone fidgeted for a few minutes. Meredith responded to more questions from the police officer until his radio buzzed and he stepped out of the room. As he returned, he announced, "Hey—we're in a communication lock down. Don't use Mrs. Grant's name or the address on any of your radio communication—or in conversation. Word from the above." He quickly asked everyone to remain in the kitchen while they processed the office areas. Allan had quietly returned to the group. Meredith recalled he had friends in the mayor's office.

☆

"We're supposed to tell the officers about the people who didn't like Bettina Grant?" mused Sonia, her one-time Valley Girl accent subtly creeping out. She had arrived around noon, as most of the law enforcement people were leaving or already gone.

Ito had been snatched back from his weekly visit to relatives. He perched on the edge of the couch in Meredith's office, dressed in street clothes instead of his usual houseman jacket. The office had been released after the police had fully probed, pushed, peeked into every nook and file cabinet and exercised all other activities requisite in clue-hunting.

Meredith had changed from the morning's professional suit into a pair of worn jeans and an oversized pink sweater which she kept in the office for days when she could slip off the exterior facade and slump comfortably over the Selectric keyboard. Lunch with the movie star was long cancelled and forgotten.

"Should I clean up?" asked Ito nodding toward the living room and the rest of the house.

"What should we file for today's column?" Sonia asked.

"Bettina isn't just out of town," Meredith reproached her colleagues. "She died. She's gone and she was the core of this place, its heartbeat. This is more than an inconvenience."

The twosome looked at one another and then at Meredith.

"What will New York do?" added Sonia, referring to the headquarters of *American Media Syndicate*, the company that paid their salaries and distributed their work.

"I don't know," said Meredith. "Russ is at 'lunch'—a characteristically long New York lunch."

"Did you have to break the news to Bettina's dad?" persisted Sonia seriously, referring to Bettina's aged father.

"No, thank God. But I had to deliver the sad news to Bett's sister Luanne, and she graciously agreed to tell their dad and

Lorraine and Lea." The latter referred to the columnist's two grown children.

By then, the trio of characters now occupying Bettina's house had been carefully instructed in which rooms they could move about, and those they were to avoid. The entire upper floor of the house was off-limits and now loomed at the top of the stairs like a chamber of whispered secrets. Fingerprint dust and other remnants of the tech team's investigation still remained throughout the house.

The hyper blip of the phone was a welcome interruption. When Meredith replaced the receiver, she looked at her two companions seriously. They caught the glance and were silent.

"A 'senior' investigator named T.K. Raymond is coming over here in a few minutes to talk with each of us. I think that bodes poorly for the fate of Bettina. And, he's again reminded that we not talk to anyone about this now. To defer all questions to the police. He said, 'It's in your own best interest.'"

"Let's not be misquoted—or taken out of context," mused Sonia.

"If we haven't before, we will soon," sighed Meredith. "But look, be careful what you say or how you say it. We don't want to prejudice any case that might come out of this—or jeopardize the outcome of a future trial by too much speculation. That's assuming Bettina didn't suffocate herself, which is entirely possible…but…."

"So, Meredith, what you plan to say about Bettina in tomorrow's column?" Sonia continued to probe.

"There may not even be a column tomorrow. Unless Russ decides to keep it going—under my or someone else's by-line—there may not be any more *Hollywood Dateline*. I've pulled an emergency back-up column, but the lead has to be about Bettina and I'm still struggling to figure out the best way to write it. I'm still shaking and beginning to feel the reality, the sadness. I need to find some balance."

A cloud passed over Sonia's face. "I figured they'd hand the column to you and you'd keep it going—just like you've been doing for the past ten years."

Meredith laughed, welcoming a lighter moment. "Now you've even got me to the point of a chuckle," she said. "I'm a feature writer, remember? So yeah, I also cover a lot of movies and TV and parties and stuff for Bettina and yeah, I come across pretty good gossip—well celebrity 'news.' But I don't have the killer instinct Bettina does. Never will. Don't even want to."

"And that's why people liked you better than Bettina, Sonia interjected, "I know because they talk to me. I'm no threat and they can be honest. I keep hearing what a nice person you are, what a good writer..."

"And that, with a dollar bill, might buy you—or me—a cup of coffee," said Meredith. "Good Hollywood gossip columns—like Bettina Grant's—go for the throat. I don't."

"It is possible," said Ito quietly, "someone decided to target the throat of the good Mrs. Grant? She must have a long list of people who'd like to do that by now after 25 years of antagonizing."

"What about her weekly gig on the TV show?" quizzed Sonia, changing the subject.

Meredith shrugged, "I guess Russ will talk about that from New York. We're all on emergency notice for now—with nothing really settled for the future."

"Well, it seems out of the question that the newspaper syndicate would give that column, or the TV spot, to anyone but you, Meredith," Sonia insisted. "After all, no matter what you like to say or call yourself, you ARE Bettina's legwoman."

"Was…," said Meredith. "And you know I hate that label—it's so 1950s! The name is now 'field reporter.'"

☆

When Russ Talbot returned Meredith's call, his refined voice was heavy with either sadness or resignation. She wasn't sure which. Bettina was a long-time associate and friend, but also an important and lucrative asset to the *United American News Syndicate* he managed. Her loss, especially in the manner in which it came, posed heavy problems with no easy solutions. "I'm so sorry about Bettina," he said haltingly. "She was a friend."

They discussed the day's unfolding events, then he turned to business. "Look, Meredith, I'd like to keep the column going —mostly in tribute to Bettina—for the time being. We have so many papers that carry the column and who will want to follow the story. In fact, I'd like you to write it up and we'll put it on the wire tonight under your by-line. We'll announce that you'll be maintaining the column for the subscriber papers until we have decided the best plan of action."

"How much should I say, Russ?"

"You're a good journalist, Meredith. Cover the situation as you would for anyone else so prominent. Please include the respect we all felt for her…will all miss her…and so on."

"And what about the *Morning Coffee Show* TV slot? She's not due to appear until next week again—but what will we do with that one?" The silence on the other end of the line was telling. Bettina was a celebrity. Meredith was a respected and familiar name in international celebrity journalism, but no red-carpet contender with any kind of celebrity of her own. She'd been the quiet behind-the-scenes operative in the partnership for years.

"We'll talk more about that later," came the sophisticated voice. "I talked with Allan Jaymar today. He called to express his condolences and we talked about this situation. We are both thinking about the best way to address the show and feel that the guest spot should go vacant until after the holidays. A quick shift of personalities would be puzzling to the viewers. I think the producers agree."

Meredith acknowledged her understanding, relieved and glad to have Allan in the picture with his standing in the industry and willingness to guide everyone through the confusion. She wondered what other unimagined surprises the day would bring. In Bettina's office, a "High Profile" Special Cases detective was talking with Sonia. Their conversation caught Meredith's attention as she said goodbye to Russ.

"Sure, Bettina alienated people—columnists do that. I think it's their job," Sonia was explaining. Meredith felt her heart race and she gulped for breath. She inhaled deeply, reminding herself to take things one step at a time. After a few minutes sitting quietly, listening, she turned to her Selectric keyboard and began to type out the details of Bettina's death. It was late afternoon but felt like three days had passed since she arrived that morning.

A while later, Meredith closed down the typewriter and went to the den. "Excuse me," she interrupted the conversation. A lanky man sitting uncomfortably in one of Bettina's overstuffed den chairs looked up. Rain had flattened his dark curly hair against his head. A pleasant but serious face looked well-lived in and striking.

"Are you considering Bettina's death to be a homicide?" asked Meredith.

The detective glanced at his notes with intent dark eyes. "Why?" he asked, finally looking up at her.

"I have to write a wire story about this. I need more of the details."

He grimaced. "Our witnesses are members of the press. Worse yet, the Hollywood Press. Maybe the PR department should be investigating this case," he finished with humor, "Just say, we're not ruling anything out at this point."

"Does that mean that you do think Bettina Grant could have been murdered?"

"Murder" had been only a vague word in the very back of her thoughts until that moment.

The detective, standing up to his full six-foot-two frame, turned away from Sonia and toward Meredith. "I just ask the questions. Here," he pulled a card from his inside coat pocket and handed it to Meredith. "This is our PR gal. Call her. Put her neck on the line. I'm only the crime investigator and really only here because this death is one considered 'high profile'."

Meredith took the card and turned back to her office. Then she looked back at the detective, "PR gal?"

"Image formation professional?"

"I think the term is 'Public Information Officer,' and she'll have her work cut out for her with this case," Meredith snapped, turning back toward her own office.

The sound of the large screen television set mounted high in the corner of Bettina's office had been turned to a low din and the various news and information shows droned. A smaller version of the monotone broadcasts filled Meredith's office as she kept a wary eye for any mention about the death of her famous boss. So far, law enforcement had managed to keep the story under wraps. Meredith was grateful. Only one or two very discreet calls from close industry friends had interrupted an otherwise disastrous day. Tomorrow, however, would be another story.

She picked up her phone set and punched in the number of the "PR gal." Surprised by the friendly attitude of the public information officer, Meredith felt confident working through a credible and noncommittal statement about the death.

She hung up as Ito made his way through her office, vacuum in hand. The slightly built Japanese man handed Meredith a few crumpled items: a mother-of-pearl button, a folded cleaner's receipt and the tab-end of a machine-generated airline boarding pass. "What's this?" she quizzed.

"Bounty from under your couch cushions. Just vacuum debris from a little while ago, after the techs left, something worth keeping," he answered before heading for the door. He'd resumed his role as the steward of the house earlier that day, his usual day off.

Forty-five minutes later, Meredith curled into Bettina's other chintz-covered chair for her turn to be interviewed by the detective. The day's light had disappeared entirely, Sonia had left, and only the flickering from the TV screen kept the vigil, except, of course, for the persistent cop who sounded as weary as Meredith felt.

"Sorry to keep you so late," he said.

"Part of the turf here," she replied. He explained that he was part of a unique investigative office that was called in to manage "high profile" cases—those involving notable public figures and celebrities in ambiguous situations where criminal investigation might be required. "We coordinate with all of the police and sheriff departments on these kinds of cases. Saves them a lot of hand-holding."

The day's stress was etched across Meredith's face as she rubbed a knuckle across one of her large, brown, eyes and ran a hand over her expressive, almost too large, mouth. "Okay. Special handling. What does that look like?"

"Let's start with the idea that you knew Bettina Grant about as well as anyone. Any idea what went on upstairs last night?"

"Not a clue…Sorry…bad pun."

"Bad puns are part of my turf," he said, a barely noticeable grin flickered over his face.

"I couldn't even fake a good story about last night. Bettina is so consumed by what she does for a living that she rarely even invites guests into her home. She said she had an easy schedule for the evening—dinner about ten minutes away, home and bed. Not an unusual agenda for her."

"Family? A kid, or parent who might have stopped by, or may have talked to her?"

"By phone, maybe, but otherwise…," Meredith shook her head. "Let's see: her youngest daughter Lea lives in Massachusetts and is estranged from Bettina for all practical purposes. The older daughter Lorraine lives with husband and children in New Mexico. She had two sisters, Rachael and Luanne. Rachael died about ten years ago. Luanne lives with her family in the Valley and only comes over for special occasions, and Bettina's father, Pop, is in a retirement home and doesn't leave unless someone drives him here or Bettina picks him up."

"Men friends, some male company last night?"

"A date?" Meredith restrained a chuckle. "Not that she mentioned, and not likely. She's long-divorced and has a couple of real 'friends' who are men, but she's been discouraged lately because even they've all married younger women and haven't been available as escorts or even pals. It's hell being glamorous and visible and 55! She was married for many years, but her ex rarely comes around and when he does, we all usually hear about it. And we know that Bettina was at a dinner party last night. Allan, the neighbor, saw her, said she was fine when she left."

The detective sighed his acknowledgment, which sounded like disapproval, and made notes as Meredith turned off the television and switched on the den's overhead lights.

"She wrote about movie and TV stars. She was Hollywood. She believed in it. She was one of them, a celebrity that is. She had been for a quarter of a century."

"Would you mind talking again about what happened when you got here this morning?"

"Well, first thing was a strange and a little bit scary phone message for Bettina from last night." She told him about the message. "We've gotten unpleasant messages before. It's the nature of our business. But the timing was a little un-nerving. I saved the message on the recording."

"Note to check out the phone records. What else?"

Meredith tucked her feet underneath herself and recounted the morning's activities. As she finished the story, she realized with both a deep sense of loss and some trepidation that she was sitting in Bettina Grant's den—surrounded by the heart, soul, dreams and triumphs of the flamboyant woman who was suddenly gone. She sat up and looked around. The place felt empty and strange, obviously would never be the same experience as it had been for the past ten years.

"Are you cold?" asked the detective, noticing the change in her demeanor.

"No, it just occurred to me that I'm sitting here talking on blithely about Bettina Grant—in her own home, as though she's away on a book tour or vacation, and you're suggesting that someone may have…killed…her last night just upstairs. She's someone I've basically lived in concert with, in a manner of speaking, for years, laughed and cried with—well, she's just disappeared. And besides that, now I seem to be in charge of this—this place—for the time being anyhow. That, in itself, is a terrifying thought. I'm frightened, not cold."

"Then let's get this thing over with," said the detective with more warmth in his voice than she had expected, "so we can both go home. Try to think about the events of the past week and what, if anything, might have compromised Bettina Grant in any way."

Meredith settled back into the chintz chair, unwound her hair, let if fall to her shoulders and tried to reconstruct the typically frenetic previous week.

The day before Bettina Grant died, a winter breeze stirred the rose bushes outside the window as she fumed about expectations. The gentle quiver of the leaves, combined with the hard edge of Bettina's voice, had lulled Meredith into a daydream as she sat in the meeting with her boss and Sonia.

"…made me look like a fool, an ignorant idiot!" the columnist spat in a final exclamation, grabbing Meredith's attention.

Sometimes, Bettina sounded the credible and focused journalist Meredith knew her to be. At that moment, she sounds more like one of the petulant celebrities she wrote about. The columnist sat at a desk in front of a wall of beveled windows overlooking the small rose garden, chastising Sonia for photocopying incorrect issues of the daily column which Bettina had subsequently tried to use as a hand-out while lecturing to a college journalism class.

"What was on your mind?" Bettina raged on. "You've got your head up your ass. Get it out! Or find a real job!"

Sonia's lower lip was hard set, but she sat unmoving in the overstuffed chair at the edge of the imposing roll-top desk. It was a rare, but not a new drill. Meredith allowed herself the luxury of a tiny, mental sigh. She knew from past experience it would take at least two weeks and an expensive dinner to get Sonia to forget this episode.

The phone rang and Sonia gratefully scampered to answer it at her own desk.

The scene was Hollywood news at its best in December 1983, Meredith knew. The columns and features known as the *Hollywood Dateline* were the most widely read material covering the entertainment industry through the *United American News Syndicate* (UAMS). Bettina Grant's daily gossip column was the core and along with the team's feature stories appeared in more than 400 newspaper around the world.

Bettina also had managed to capture one of the rare "news" spots on the National Entertainment Network's popular *Morning Coffee Show* seen across the country, edging into a new era of broadcast Hollywood gossip destined to become a major American news delivery platform of the future.

As Bettina Grant's "legwoman" for the past decade, Meredith's job was a far cry from the by-the-book news chasers who trained her at Northwestern University a generation earlier. Answering phones and correspondence, tracking down "news" about the movie, TV and music industry was a role known in earlier decades as "Legwoman" to a gossip columnist. Meredith rose from that to the ranks of feature correspondent and Los Angeles UAMS Network Bureau Manager. Sometimes her biggest task was to mitigate the mood whims of her famous boss.

"For you Bettina. Charlie Marek," called Sonia, sounding surprisingly calm after the dressing down she had received. She often surprised Meredith with her ability to quickly recover from Bettina's rebukes.

Bettina sat up sharply against the thick, cream-color leather desk chair, reached for the cigarette languishing in a chipped ashtray that bore the signature of the long-closed Ciro's nightclub, and picked up the receiver.

Meredith took the opportunity to return to her own work. She shrugged at Sonia as she passed through the small office. Sonia shrugged back and thrust her middle finger in Bettina's direction. Maybe a San Francisco weekend for the loquacious brunette, Meredith considered. Whatever the cost, it would be far less than trying to break in another innocent to the mercurial and often scythe-like whims of Bettina Grant.

"Paul DeMarco on line two," called Sonia to Meredith.

"Paul?" said Meredith as she picked up the line.

"Here's your lead for tomorrow's column," he said, with a smoker's rasp and a rush of words. "Ask your buddies at NBS where their really hot late late-night talk show host spent last night."

"And where was that, Paul?"

"Joey enjoyed the hospitality of the county sheriff last night—for punching out a fan."

"I thought he was cured of all that," Meredith joked and reached quickly for a pen to take notes.

"What I hear is that he was being followed by a couple of fans. Guess they, like the rest of the hip generation, think he's cool, although I can't figure why. Anyhow, one of them apparently approached Joey, said something stupid, because Joe just hauled off and punched him out. Again and again."

"Where did this alleged assault take place?"

"Pacoima."

"That's a long way away from Joey's fancy West Side turf."

"And—it was in a biker bar."

Meredith smiled, toying with the information and wondering how Paul DeMarco, a Hollywood fringe player who worked for Reverend Bobby Michael's *Christian Celebration* TV Show, came across this type of news.

"A secret side of our nightly hip TV star?" she said cynically. Celebrities, a glittering illusion, was seldom what it appeared.

"Maybe. One of the Reverend's chaplains was called to the jail in the Valley to talk to a troubled inmate. He watched Joey getting booked. Anyhow—it's your story. Use it with grace and remember where it came from."

"Sure, Paul. If anyone asks, I'll give you a great recommendation to the Pearly Gates."

Meredith pulled the long sleeves of her sweater down over her hands and folded her arms. She tucked her jeans-clad legs under a well-proportioned figure and contemplated the notes she had just taken. Telling Bettina about the story before it was fully developed would be a mistake. Bettina tended to get hyper over news like this. She would often pace the office all day until she captured the whole story, her frosted red/blond hair looking like an electrified nettle bush, hands tucked under her armpits, elbows flapping like a stricken chicken.

The Joey O'Neal story was intriguing. The fast-talking comedian and his *Dark Streets Show,* had become the darling of late-night talk shows in the past three years. He was a study in 'hip', thirtyish, with fashionable long hair pulled into a ponytail at the nape of his neck. He wore designer fashions and talked the jive which was threaded through MTV as well as the nation's young professional culture. His ratings were not threatening to Johnny Carson, and only sniped at David Letterman—but then again, both had many years' head start on Joey. "Not to mention more intelligence, talent and class!" Meredith had once written. Most of the editors had deleted it from her story.

She chewed on the end of her pen as she figured out who could be trusted to unravel the details of the story without giving the whole thing away to one of the other voices of celebrity news. Sometimes even the regular TV news program took on certain stories that involved mainstream celebrities, or the daily papers, but the biggest concern was the weekly rags—the *Celebrity*

Parade (called "the barf" by other more "respected" journalists), *Hollywood Insider* (known to insiders as the "the scab") or one other tabloids that provocatively raised the skirt of celebrity-dom for the steady stream of shoppers at supermarket check-out counters.

The tabloids, according to Bettina, had one big advantage over the more "professional" Hollywood news outlets: an increasingly illiterate population. But, disgusting as they were, the barf, the scab and their look-a-likes were big-time competition to the few remaining newspaper columnists and feature writers who covered the movie and television industries, she grudgingly admitted.

Meredith pecked out the home number of Bill McLaren, the network publicist assigned to the *Dark Streets*, a good friend since she had joined Bettina's ranks ten years earlier.

"Just wondering what I would say when you called," said Bill.

"It didn't take a genius to know you wouldn't be taking calls at the office today. Phone been ringing off the hook?"

"No, you're the first—that's the good news. How and what did you hear?"

"You'd never believe it."

"Try me. Who's the snitch?"

"Let's just say I was meditating and got a divine inspiration," said Meredith. "What's the deal, Bill? A biker bar in Pacoima? We got a closet Hell's Angel here or what?"

"Or what."

Meredith uncurled her legs and hunched over her desk, pushing papers aside and focusing on the notes she was taking.

"What can you tell me…and don't give me a no comment. I can find out more from the Sheriff's office where our star spent last night. Give me something more positive to print."

Meredith chewed on her pen, and discovered she was holding her breath. It was a finesse she had learned many years before. Phone-line silence made most people uncomfortable.

"Okay," sighed McLaren finally. "You'll have to confirm what little I know somewhere else, piece by piece, because you can't quote me—and it's far from over yet. You know I'm going to have to tell my boss I talked with you. I'll tell him that you tracked me down and forced me to talk or else you'd print pictures of our nightly news anchor with a collie!"

Meredith smiled and quickly ended the call, then dialed the local Sheriff's office to confirm the report on Joey O'Neal's arrest. Deeply focused on organizing her notes, she was surprised when Sonia knocked on her door frame to say, "good night." A felt hat was pulled down over the secretary's head of thick curly hair and a poncho, a poor re-creation of the 70s, was tossed over her shoulders. Meredith thought about initiating a fashion discussion then quickly dismissed it.

"We'll talk tomorrow," she mouthed, glancing furtively toward Bettina's office.

"Sure," Sonia replied passively as she turned to leave. Meredith realized it must be five o'clock. Sonia had two time disciplines: punctual and tardy, the former at quitting time, the latter, any other time.

"Ito!" Bettina's shout pierced the late afternoon quiet.

The slight man dutifully and silently appeared at the office door seconds later, adjusting his glasses as he arrived. "What?" he asked, his face immobile, his voice, a flat tone of compliance.

"Coffee, please, Ito, then go take your night off!"

He bowed only slightly and disappeared toward the kitchen. Meredith settled back into the chair across from Bettina's desk.

"Now, what's this major break you've been on this afternoon?" Bettina stood up, turned her chair around and straddled it backward. Meredith was always amazed at the pretzel-like ability she displayed when she was on the trail of a hot story. Straddling her leather and chrome desk chair was the only physical activity other than smoking and typing that Bettina had ever displayed in front of her staff. "A substitute for sex" Sonia called it. In public Bettina added sipping champagne and making very big entrances at Hollywood parties.

"It's a big story—but it's not complete yet and we have some decisions to make," Meredith began.

Ito reappeared bearing a tray with two steaming cups of coffee. For four years Meredith had explained that she never drank regular coffee and for four years Ito had persisted in delivering it to her desk at least three times a day. Sometimes she drank it, usually she tossed it down the bathroom drain. Today she accepted the china cup with resignation and took a sip.

"Joey O'Neal had a major altercation with a fan last night, apparently two young guys followed Joey…"

"An ardent fan story?" sighed Bettina.

"I've always admired your ability to cut to the lead" said Meredith. "But stick around, you'll like this one. The couple apparently followed Joey to some biker bar in Pacoima…" Bettina's raised her eyebrows, her curiosity piqued.

"When one of the men tapped Joey on the shoulder and asked for an autograph, Joey exploded—you know how big he is. He apparently pummeled the little guy right into the ground. Or at least into the hospital. The bartender doesn't watch late night TV—at least not *Dark Streets*—and didn't recognize Joey. He called the cops, who arrested Joey and tossed him into jail!"

Beads of moisture appeared on Bettina's upper lip. Her dark eyes had taken on the famous Bettina Grant intensity. She leaned forward to hear more.

"Like it so far?" smiled Meredith.

Bettina waved a hand impatiently. "Tell me the rest of it. Then type it up for me so that I can get it onto the wire tonight."

"There is no 'rest' of it yet. The young fan is in Angel of the Valley hospital. Doing okay but has a security detail. No one's talking. I got a beat on his home phone and tried to reach his family but no one's answering. Joey's lawyer Myron Bernstein paid bail and picked him up less than an hour after he was booked. Bernstein is not available and no one at the network is talking.

"Way I see it we have two choices. One, we can run the story as we have it and turn the rags on to it. They'll get the rest of it, the juicy stuff, when it unravels tomorrow. Advantage for us—we broke it first. Or, we can sit on it, hope that there's not a leak and file it tomorrow night with more of the details. Advantage—bigger, better story, nothing left but the sniper fire for the rags. Disadvantage—someone else may get wind of the story and break it before us."

Bettina ran an anxious hand through her hair. "We don't know why Joey turned on the kid or what he was doing in the biker bar, right?"

"Right, and we don't know if there might be a relationship between Joey and the kid that no one may know about. Maybe he wasn't just a fan following an idol."

"What about the hospital? Can we find a nurse or an orderly who'll talk?"

Meredith shook her head in frustration. "Get Real. You know as well as I do the havoc that kind of hearsay wreaks. Fodder for the lawyers. Leave that for the rags—it's not our style. Or policy."

The two veteran Hollywood journalists had a filing cabinet-full of information from fringe sources. In an earlier era, Elizabeth

Taylor had been in the hospital and a talkative orderly had crocheted a fanciful tale about orgies in Taylor's ward. A rare and uncatalogued illness threatened the film star's life and, according to the orderly, had already left her without eyesight. Photographers milled around every entrance to the hospital, reporters disguised as visitors and delivery people skulked down hallways. The news stories were so fanciful that the real truth behind Taylor's hospital visit was never revealed. Her publicists and agents may well have figured there wasn't any reason for an official story. Hollywood was having too much fun making up its own.

"Then what's the next step for Big Joe," Bettina asked.

"I think you, personally, should call the producer of the *Dark Streets*," said Meredith. "They'll be taping the show right now. You know him. Maybe he'll level with you."

Bettina thought about it. "You know they'll talk to Joe about this. What do you think he'll do? Release a statement? Deny? Threaten to sue? All the usual behaviors?"

"It's late in the day and the show is already in progress. Whatever he does will be done later. I think we're safe with whatever part of the story we do have. I've confirmed it all."

"Can you hang around?"

"Sure," said Meredith, feeling a familiar frustration. Late hours forced by Bettina's special stories were nothing new and this would have been the only night of this week when she was not pressed into service covering one or another Hollywood party, screening or other excuse for wining and dining the press. The months of November and December were Hollywood's busiest months with rush screenings of films held for release until the end the year in order to be considered in the year's Oscar contest, and a myriad of other holiday parties.

Bettina swiveled her chair back to the desk and picked up the phone. Meredith sat in silence trying to think of another source she might call to learn more about the unfolding drama of Joey Neal. Ito passed silently through the room heading toward the outer offices to empty waste baskets before he left. Meredith idly followed him into her own cocoon. She sat down at her desk and began to scan her phone lists for inspiration. Ito quietly replaced trash cans he'd emptied, his backpack over his shoulder as he was on his way for his weekly time off.

"Hot story? "he asked, startling her.

"Tough one."

"Good. The boss lady's happier when she's on the trail of a hot story."

"You two have the most unusual relationship? Do you even like her?"

"More or less. But she eats stories—and people—for breakfast," said Ito. "No other life in this house," he went on, "once you and the one with the big mouth are gone for the day."

"Good grief. What do you call me when I'm out of ear-shot?"

"Cutie." He grinned.

"Why do you stay here? You're too smart for this kind of job." Meredith whispered loudly after him.

"The job is interesting. Fan stuff! I love Hollywood," Ito turned to answer. "And besides the food is good."

"You should know—you cook it." Meredith's mugged.

"Exactly," he said with a totally uncharacteristic wink.

"Shit, shit, shit," barked Bettina. Meredith jumped from her desk and made a fast trip through the other offices to the columnist's den. Ito had disappeared into the darkening shadows of the large house.

"This is a big one," whined Bettina, "but I can't get it—not yet, at least."

"What'd you find out?"

"Your pal Bill McLaren prepped Franky Faraday, Joey's producer, for my call. He took it. But there's more to this thing than I can get to right now. It's so frustrating—I'll bet even the FBI is involved—and God only knows who else. Franky asked me to be patient, promised us the whole story exclusively if we wait."

"For how long?"

"'As long as it takes,' he said. But I got the impression that he is going to talk with Joey about it. Then anything is possible. God, I just hate to sit on a good story. A throw-back to the good old days of scoops."

"So, what's so different with the good new days of scoops?"

"Mary Hart," Bettina simpered.

Here was the most widely syndicated newspaper columnist in the world with the best inside contacts to Hollywood, the best reputation for integrity in the business, thought Meredith. And, like a child, Bettina still wanted all the candy in her hand at once. And she knew it.

"Well, let's figure it out—the *Insider* doesn't go to press until Friday afternoon," Meredith reasoned. "Today's Monday. Advantage—us. The scab and the barf have a Saturday press time, and the TV tabloids are daily. Advantage—us. So, it's the TV tabloids we have to worry about. And of those, *Hollywood Today* is taped a day in advance. CNS's entertainment news segments are always at least a several-hour delay. Also, our advantage. So, what we really have is the NBS local news and network news shows that tape on the same lot with *Dark Streets* and may hear rumors."

"But," interjected Bettina enthusiastically, "the five o'clock news is on the air now and the ten or eleven o'clock news is already in the can for the national feed. The local show—well, that's the only gamble."

Both women sat quietly in the darkening room. "This is why you're the bureau manager here and I'm the lowly columnist," said Bettina as she reached for a cigarette and turned to her typewriter. "What the hell, let's tell what we know. It gives us column leads and additional story fodder for tomorrow. I'll get it to New York before I go out tonight. Tomorrow will be a hurricane!"

And, I can go home now, thought Meredith appreciatively as she jumped up quickly to retrieve her coat and purse before something else delayed leaving for the day. She knew the next day would bring a different type of bedlam.

CHAPTER 4
TUESDAY EVENING

Meredith told the story to the detective. "Bettina called Joey's producer once more that evening but couldn't uncover any more information and, not surprisingly, wrote up the story as a special feature, and sent it out before she left for her dinner party at seven. It broke over the wire service this morning. We still didn't know what Joey was doing in a biker bar and why he took out after the kid who was his fan. All we could get was a comment that 'he over-reacted.' With that, some information from the producer about the show going on as usual, and the few details available on the public record, we broke the story. There are still lots of unanswered questions. You may have read the story by now."

"I don't normally see show biz gossip," said the detective. "I'm just never home in time to watch that pretty Mary Hart lady on *Entertainment Tonight.*" He had not looked up from his notes but had a slight grin on his face.

"But I suppose when you do watch TV, you only watch Public Broadcasting, right?"

"No, ma'am. MTV. Madonna's my fantasy." He regarded her with either a smile or a smirk. Meredith wasn't sure which. He continued, "Would there be or have there been repercussions as a result of the story?"

"Like what?"

"Angry phone calls, threats. Are there still parts of the story you are researching?"

"Well, there was the one call I told you about, but I don't know who made it, and it isn't like we haven't had insults and threats before over stories. We haven't found out what Joey was doing in a biker bar. That was the big question we kept getting stonewalled on. Our phone rang all day, but no one had hard facts and information. More questions than answers. And no direct comment or contact from anyone associated with Joey."

"Was Grant still chasing down the story last night?"

"Doubt it—if so, only subtly. She left for dinner with close friends, and apparently got home late. I'm still digging out the story today—what there was of today as a work-day, anyhow."

"Can you give me a thumbnail description of who Bettina Grant was as a person? Not the celebrity."

Meredith thought hard before answering. "Well, she described herself as a typical San Fernando Valley housewife who fell in love with writing, was at the right place at the right time and found herself at the top of not only her own game, but the Hollywood gossip game. She insisted family came first which was why she never moved out of her house into more business-like offices. Once her kids were grown and gone, and Bettina was divorced, this was her whole life. And she devoured it. She was incredibly generous to those she respected, ethical as it gets, and yet a cunning strategist in her business. But not at all hesitant saying what she felt or believed. She could be harsh, and lots of people were the recipient of that. She worked hard to be a good working mother although the kids found their lives elsewhere and didn't seem to care much for this…world." Meredith swept her hand around herself, indicating the office.

"Your secretary says Bettina had a lot of enemies. is that a true statement?"

Meredith snorted out a hint of a laugh. "Sonia would probably view them that way, but most of them weren't really enemies. Semantics. When a Hollywood columnist writes about the dark side of an otherwise glittering image, people get pissed. Still, Bettina's had a lot of power, and her ability to spread the name and good news about people creates instant forgiveness for the bad."

"Anyone who hasn't had the recent opportunity to experience the forgiveness part?"

Meredith considered the question as the detective regarded her intently. She massaged her forehead as stories filled her memory. She mentioned the anger and sense of betrayal publicly expressed when Bettina had, in print, dismissed as "psycho-babble" a deeply candid interview with the best-selling author of a sensitive book, soon to be a film, about child abuse.

"The truth of the matter is that for all the talk about breaking the Joey O'Neal story and scoring another exclusive, beating out the competition, Bettina's column has taken a much softer line than it ever used to. Like she's lost the heat. I mentioned it to her a few weeks ago and she said the movie and TV industry had become an industry of balance sheets and suits. That the juice and fire was all in the ledger sheets, not the bedroom sheets now and her column only reflected that. She whined that she couldn't make a silk purse out of a sow's ear."

"Was she right?"

"I wasn't around during the early days of the movie magazines and when living in sin was racy stuff. The days of Hedda Hopper and Louella Parsons. I kind of like the business part of the intrigue, find it taking a more center stage with the celebrity stuff. Bettina came from another generation of columnists. Most of the studio or network 'business' issues in her column have come from me."

"You're writing her column now?"

"No…yes. Well, sort of. We have always kept a week's worth of generic emergency columns on hand in case something happened, and we weren't able to file a fresh column over the wire to our offices in New York. Bettina had today's column written and filed at five last evening. We'll use those extra columns for the next few days. Then, well," Meredith shrugged, "that's up to the newspaper syndicate. I think I'll be writing the column for a couple of weeks at least until we decide who will replace Bettina."

"Isn't it logical that you'd be lobbying for this opportunity? Your secretary says you're Grant's legwoman and the natural heir to the throne."

"The throne?" laughed Meredith. "Sonia would say that. And by the way—the label of 'legwoman' went away about the time the *Brady Bunch* left the airwaves. Gloria Steinem would have your head."

"Huh. That would be interesting. Well, Sonia also said Bettina Grant was the Queen of Gossip. And that you were the lady-in-waiting."

Meredith shook her head. "I'm a feature writer at best and bureau manager and editor doing my best, Detective Raymond. There's a big difference. It's true that I dig out news for Bettina. I even write her column when she's away, her TV scripts often, and sometimes her major movie star features. But at heart I'm too tame for the gossip ranks. I write good feature stories about people and other more industry-related subjects."

"But doesn't the Bettina Grant column run five days a week to your two stories a week? And doesn't she make a lot more money than you?"

"That's a fact, detective. But it still doesn't qualify me to step into her shoes. Not many could fill those shoes, believe me.

And by the way, in case it should come up—last night I was having pizza with my neighbors until about eleven-thirty and then went home to bed. I had a phone call about three a.m. from a ... friend...who is on a movie location out of state and doesn't adhere to normal sleep hours. I'm sure there's a record somewhere of it. I'll give you Ted and Marcy's names and also the 3 a.m. caller's contact information before you leave." Raymond nodded his acknowledgment and made more notes. By the time he closed his notebook, the antique grandfather clock in Bettina Grant's entrance hall chimed seven soft bells.

Other than the office, the house was silent and dark. As Meredith walked the detective to the door, she pulled on her raincoat, left over from the morning's drizzle. She collected her unworn clothing from its hanger on the back of the office door, tucked the worn brief case under her arm, and looked around sadly.

"When will we know more about the cause of death?"

"Maybe tomorrow," he said. "Call me then. Whatever the cause, even something as un-Hollywood as a heart attack, I should know more about it. And try to keep folks out of the upstairs—it's taped off for now. Tomorrow I'd like to look through the bedroom with you to see what, if anything, seems out of order. I won't bother you tonight." He handed her his business card.

"One last thing," he said as an aside. "I take it you are continuing to work from the house?"

"We have no alternative—in our business, we have to keep operating."

"It'd be better if you didn't but be alert and cautious. Just because...."

"Thanks. Tonight, I don't think I could even go upstairs," she shivered. "I'm feeling a little overwhelmed," she continued, unaware the man was not engaged in her anxious monologue. "Look around here. Tomorrow Sonia and Ito and I will be expected to perform as though nothing here has changed. And everything has. By then, this place will be a madhouse, the ringing phones, other reporters and colleagues, will make us all crazy, the family will descend on us with all kinds of demands.... and officially, we don't really have the right to be here. This is Bettina Grant's home. No matter what has happened, I'm really the wrong person to be in charge!"

"You sound tired, Ms. Ogden. Take a deep breath, go home."

"The sooner the better."

Meredith watched the detective's undistinguished blue car disappear down the street as she was carefully hanging her spare clothes in the Mustang. Suddenly, she was interrupted by a familiar voice.

"Merri, lovey!"

Porter, "Potty", Osborn, waved his stubby sweater-clad arms at her from the front curb of the house across the street, two doors down from Bettina's. Meredith looked around to see the barrel-shaped actor beckoning to her.

"What's been going on over there since this morning, lovey?" he called. "So much traffic."

Meredith paused to gather her wits, realizing that this was only an early salvo in the barrage of inquiries that would be fired at her and Sonia in the next few days...weeks. She quickly reminded herself to coach both Sonia and Ito on how to answer questions. Car doors locked, she shoved her hands deep into the pockets of her jeans and walked across the dark street toward the traditional red brick house where Potty stood in front of a white colonnade over the front porch.

At night, the small elegant street was posed in its manicured finery like a formal table set for a festive occasion, the glow from the street lamps illuminating the details like quietly flickering tapers.

"Hi Potty. You probably know more from Allan than I do about my day," Meredith called as she reached the front walkway of the house across the street.

He reached out and wrapped his arm around her shoulder and said, "For heaven's sake, come in and tell us about it."

"I should go home, Potty. It's been a long day, and I'm hungry and tired." As she entered the pleasant foyer of the house, weariness flooded every fiber of her body.

"Then have a drink and some of Allan's magnificent chili and tell us about it. We're dying to hear. And you won't get better chow anywhere—not at home, not from your pantry for sure."

Meredith had to laugh aloud. "You've known me for too long, Potty."

Potty Osborn, well-known character actor, exuded the aristocracy and accent of East Coast wealth. But it was wrapped up in a pear-shaped package. The image had served him well with TV and movie comedy directors, and he had enjoyed a twelve-year run with a popular detective series on which he had played a wealthy benefactor of a free-living playboy sleuth. The dozen years had given him financial security and his primary role these days was as bridge partner and household manager of Allan Jaymar, Hollywood agent, and Potty's long-time companion.

Meredith enjoyed the couple. Allan was one of the entertainment industry's gentlemen. He had guided and managed the careers of a select handful of its "nice" albeit powerful folks and had never failed to live up to a certain code of integrity exhibited rarely by his peers. Allan had lived across the street from Bettina for as long as Meredith had worked for her and had become a close friend to both women.

The foyer of the house was, as always, seductive. A large oak table preened with holiday spirit under an arrangement of red carnations, white gardenias and evergreen. The other rooms were furnished in bold pastel sofas, love seats and chairs—all overstuffed and homey. Light-colored wood accented the rooms, and the burnish and luster of authentic antique mahogany and oak added dramatic punctuation.

The rosy glow of the fireplace added to the hospitality, and poinsettias were placed at every corner and niche to add holiday emphasis. Had she not been as tired as she was, Meredith might have swooned at the sight.

"Allan, put another bowl on the kitchen table and pour this girl some sherry," called Potty.

"Ah, the news-hen," Allan said with a smile as he came from the kitchen, uttering another now-discarded term for a female journalist. His silver white hair, thinning atop his proudly held head, matched the well-trimmed beard on his long face. He wore a camel-colored cashmere cardigan over an impeccable silk sport shirt, and gray flannel trousers. Even the tassels on his polished moccasins stood at attention. He embraced Meredith in welcome. "I'm sorry about the events of today," he said.

A hug from Allan was always a visit to a fatherly and reassuring place for Meredith. As she smooched his cheek the familiar spice of his aftershave lotion was comforting, and Meredith felt the frenzy of the day melting away. In the meantime, Potty had fetched a pair of oversized slippers and was guiding her into the fire-lit den. "Sit down, for goodness sake, and have some sherry. And put on these silly slippers. They're just for overstressed feet."

She willingly accommodated him and was surprised at how comforting a pair of over-sized furry slippers could be. Allan followed them into the room, wiping his hands on a towel. "I can tell a news-hen with news on her mind," he winked at her. "Tell us what's new since I saw you this morning."

"If you don't," Potty interrupted, "we'll be impossible. You know that."

"I do," said Meredith, slumping into the thick sofa cushions with a sigh. "Talking about it is the easy part. Living through it wasn't. Allan—thanks so much for your help and guidance today. And for talking with Russ in New York. Whew. I'm a bit overwhelmed and just hate to spoil this lovely occasion." But she nevertheless told them of the afternoon's happenings, then sat back and gazed down into the small amount of golden liquor left in the bottom of the sleek goblet.

"So far, we really have no cause to believe that Bettina was struck down by anything more than a bad heart or a bad mood," ventured a sobered Allan.

Meredith shook her head. "Except that when someone dies of natural causes, the reports are out almost immediately. And no one dusts for fingerprints."

"Not always," Allan countered quietly. Meredith regarded the proud but sad aging face and remembered that Allan had been close friends with more than one celebrity who had died unexpectedly and under questionable circumstances.

"Any celebrity death is always considered out of the ordinary," he explained. "And Bettina, for all her insistence that she was 'just a journalist and not a celebrity,' was in fact just as much a part of show business as any of the actors or singers she wrote about."

"We saw her last night, you know," Potty said. "At Lou and Miriam's. For dinner."

"Yes, of course you would have. How did she seem? Was she with anyone—an escort? What time did she leave?" Suddenly she slapped a hand over her mouth and laughed. "Sorry. I just spent several hours under the scrutiny of a 'high profile' detective. I guess his attitude was catching."

"She seemed fine—same old Bettina. A solo act. She talked business, as usual, and spoke confidentially about Joey O'Neal. She was still hot on the trail of his story—trying to figure why he'd be hanging out in a biker bar in the Valley." Allan rose from his chair, walked to the sideboard and picked up a cut crystal sherry decanter. When he returned to the conversation area, he refilled the three glasses, then sat down. He set the decanter on the glass coffee table.

"Are you taking over the column, Merri?" he asked nonchalantly.

"I've thought a lot about it. How could I not, with everyone and their brother bugging me about it?" Her words were biting, she realized, and she quickly apologized.

"It's all right," said Allan. "Taking over the column is a big decision. You shouldn't make it lightly. Being a columnist is entirely different from being a normal journalist."

"I know it. And I know that if I take on the column, I lose the ability to bury myself in a single story, to research it to completion and weave it my own way."

"The way I see it," said Potty philosophically, "the best thing about being a columnist is the commission check from the syndicate every week." Each journal that subscribed to the column paid according to how many times a week the column was used. The columnist was paid a percentage of the amount papers paid.

Bettina had a large and ardent following of entertainment section editors throughout the world and pocketed a generous sum every week. Meredith, as the syndicate's feature writer, was paid a flat fee for her services, bonuses for multi-part features and special projects for specific papers—generally foreign ones. She also covered the field for Bettina Grant who preferred to conduct the big star interviews and leave the day-to-day news gathering to a "field reporter." She paid Meredith monthly to be that "legwoman." The Newspaper Syndicate funded the office operations including Sonia.

"Yes, the column money is very lucrative, the police have already reminded me of that," she added ruefully. "Fortunately, no one is under suspicion for anything at the moment, since we don't yet know what killed Bettina Grant."

"With that cheery bit of conversation and before I serve the chili," said Allan, "let me offer to help in any way I can. I'm a pretty good negotiator, you know." He winked at Meredith. "You have great momentum right now, a good reputation— and you're very good at what you do. You should try to leverage that. Now I'd like to forget—for the next two hours at least—that I have lost another good friend. Isn't it odd," he looked back into the living room? "People are born, die, live through victories and tragedies every hour of the day and we acknowledge them with seriousness and respect. Except when the victim is a celebrity, even by a muse—then no matter how hard we try, we make the situation the subject of jokes and cynicism."

His words chilled the atmosphere, even the crackling fire. Allan himself had frozen in mid-step to ponder the thought. "And we, the members of that already over-humored community, tell the very first jokes."

He disappeared into the kitchen and announced only seconds later that chili was ready.

☆

The air was bitingly crisp as Meredith left Allan's house. She looked around at the quiet, dark street and said to the twosome bidding her good night, "Keep an eye out. I'm feeling very vulnerable and not the least little bit paranoid right now. Being cautiously aware can't hurt." They agreed.

Fifteen minutes later, she pulled her car into the garage in her six-unit garden townhouse complex in Brentwood, a verdant section of Los Angeles' Westside. She lugged her belongings in, pushed the door shut with her hip and fumbled to open the downstairs door to her unit.

Her silver-and-gray alley cat, Paco, greeted her in the kitchen and followed her into the bedroom as she hung the suit in the closet, and returned to the kitchen. She hurriedly fed the feline who vocally reminded her that the dinner hour was long overdue. Then she reached for the silvery cold bottle of Stoli. It had no company other than ice in the freezer—or the refrigerator.

"Paco, how come Potty knows me so well? Am I that transparent? He's right: square meals—-or decent snacks—aren't part of the menu around this household anymore." The clock above the stove indicated midnight. "No wonder I'm exhausted."

She swallowed the small shot of vodka then crawled into the shower to rinse off the day's grimness—but realized as the steam from the shower filled the bathroom, familiar voices filled her head.

"Who will look after you now?" they asked. Bettina Grant was harsh, flamboyant, stubborn, arrogant. But fair to a fault, and generous to Meredith.

Leave it alone, Meredith warned. You've been an adult for a lot of years. You crossed the "adult" bridge a decade ago when you left the Hollywood Zephyr behind. You're thirty-six years old and heir-apparent to the most powerful columnist in Hollywood! Grow up!

"You traded the Zephyr for Bettina Grant but who's your Hollywood travelling buddy now? Who'll fend off the predators?"

Meredith rubbed the rough surface of a large bath-towel angrily over her body and pushed the voice out of her mind while she brushed her teeth. Sleep finally anesthetized the sting from their words.

CHAPTER 5

WEDNESDAY

"If these phones drive me any crazier, someone'll have to pay worker's compensation for my nervous breakdown," shouted Sonia at the top of her voice the next morning, shortly after the breakfast she had tried twice, unsuccessfully, to eat. A peanut butter sandwich, one lone bite evident, sat amid the chaos on her desk.

"Thank God for the extra columns. And our temp," said Meredith smiling at the motherly-looking typist sitting at Bettina's desk, answering phones and taking messages. "If yesterday was a barren desert of writing and news for us, today's as bad, that's for certain."

News of Bettina Grant's death had broken publicly internationally that morning and the phone calls had never ceased. On CNS's *Morning Coffee* where Bettina had been a regular part of the weekly format, the tone and mood was respectful and somber. Every news show included at least a brief, reverent message about "the long-time Queen of Gossip."

The news had the most impact in Bettina's own town— Los Angeles. Before the daily air quality warnings or the traffic conditions could be forecast, show business folks were dialing Bettina's office number to express shock, sadness, curiosity, and concern. Most delicately asked how the grand dame had died.

The Police Department's official statement was still, "No information is currently available on the cause of death." It prompted Meredith's call to Detective T.K. Raymond at his office before ten a.m.

"M-mph…," he answered.

"Detective?"

"Donut."

"Detective Donut?"

"Eating a donut." He coughed. "Well, I'm a cop. It's what you'd probably expect."

"I expect some answers. Like what killed Bettina Grant? I have a lot of people pushing me and you promised information. Maybe I should just call your PR gal."

"It's too early to be snide. Besides, our PR gal hates this kind of stuff as much as you do."

"Not quite as much."

"I actually have more to discuss, but I think it would be good to sit down and talk about it all. I was about to head your way. I want to re-look at the upstairs—with you this time. We have some other questions and we need another walk though."

Meredith shuddered. "Okay, but it's a circus here—and soon to get worse. We're all looking fearfully over our shoulders toward the stairs and then lapsing into a kind of lethargic grief. I have a temp answering the phones which never stop, Sonia's totally absorbed, and the family arrives from all over in about two hours. Can you get here before that? I can't guarantee the state of anything once they converge."

"Are they staying there?"

"No. Lorraine, the oldest daughter, and her husband are staying with Bettina's sister Luanne, And Lea, her younger daughter, I think, will stay with her cousin. Thank God. Still, the scene won't be pretty in any case."

"I'll send my partner, Marty Escobar, over right now—be there in about fifteen. Make sure he has access to all of the house, including the houseman's quarters, and please walk the upstairs with him. I'll get there as soon as I can."

Marty Escobar arrived soon. He was a stocky young man with a brown-black military crew cut and wore an ill-fitting sports jacket, blue shirt and chinos. Meredith asked Ito to show him through the house, leaving the two to work on their own until she was needed upstairs. She went back to pounding out the week's celebrity article and updating one of the spare columns for the day's wire post.

Marty Escobar and Ito explored the interior of Bettina's Jaguar in the garage. "For someone who was as mobile as she was, this woman kept a very clean car," exclaimed the investigator.

"Well, I make sure of that," replied Ito. He adjusted his glasses to peer into the passenger-side floor.

"So, you take care of the house, keep it picked-up and clean, wash the car, and…what all else are you responsible for?"

Ito smiled. "Keeping her personal books, doing her taxes, paying the bills, the grocery shopping and planning, cooking… probably more. I'd have to think more about it."

"So, you basically run the household?"

"More or less, but not the office. Other than cleaning, it's off limits."

"How'd you land in this job, anyhow?

"I read about these types of positions and was curious. I came to UC and got an MBA on a student visa from Japan. Interned for one of the big accounting firms for a while— boring. Got a work permit and heard about working in the homes of rich movie folks. For fun, I registered with one of the agencies and met Bettina Grant. Wow—movie stuff, an elegant home and she 'let' me do the cooking. I'm a very good cook. I thought it wouldn't hurt to experience the life for a while. Four years now."

The detective smiled. "Interesting story. Hooray for Hollywood. I'll need the names of the relatives or friends you stay with on Monday nights and Tuesdays." Ito agreed. Making their way from the garage, Marty inquired, "Sonia? What's her story?"

"All-American, think she's from the Valley, struggling single mother. A twelve-year old son. Both live with Sonia's mother. Sonia's loud and brassy, but I find her quite nice when she's not getting yelled at. Very patient. Wants to write." He chuckled. "And I want to direct movies." Both men laughed at the cliché.

"Your boss ever entertain men at night?"

Ito chortled. "Only a couple of times since I've been here, but not in a long time. My quarters and even the doors are well insulated. In the evenings, after dinner, I never wander out unless called upon. But whatever she did socially, at night, was normally obvious in the morning. Mrs. G was not much for doing dishes or glasses, so the remnants of the evening were usually in the sink the next day. Except on my night and next day off. She nearly always picked up the glasses and dishes and put them in the dishwasher. They were always clean when I got back on Tuesday night. This week was no different. Except that she died after she cleaned up."

"Huh. Ever see her take diet pills or Valium or any kind of sleeping drugs?"

"Never. She was always proud that she didn't 'play with those poisons!'"

A few minutes later, Detective Escobar knocked on Meredith's door frame and asked her to join him to explore the bedroom and second floor. She tensed as she followed him up the stairs. "I'm not very comfortable with this," she said.

"I don't blame you. Death scenes aren't my favorite, either, but they come with the job." They walked through the guest bedroom and bath. Meredith saw nothing that caught her attention as unusual or out of place. They entered the master suite. She shook her head as she recollected the room and the shock it had brought the day before. She stood in the archway into the large bathroom and closed her eyes.

"You all right?" asked Escobar.

Meredith nodded yes and then walked to the glass shelf over the spa-tub. She inhaled deeply. "Bettina wore one fragrance—something floral—of course expensive. But she apparently also liked another scented bath gel or shampoo—spicier, like cinnamon. Can you smell it? I'm not familiar with it, but I'm hardly ever up here." Her smile was sad.

Escobar sniffed and said, "Yeah, I can. Faint, but like Christmas!"

They made their way downstairs. "Nothing catches your attention—nothing you can identify as unusual or missing?" asked Escobar. Meredith shook her head no. Escobar made his way to the outside to explore the yard and patio, and Meredith returned to work.

Sooner than Meredith expected, Bettina's youngest daughter Lea arrived from Boston, pushing the front door open, then slamming it and tossing her suitcase into the living room. Shorter than Bettina, with dark curly hair and slightly rounded features, Lea seemed to have moved through her thirty-two years with a continual chip on her shoulder. Her face was a mask of impassivity with a hint of anger. "Wouldn't she be cute," one of Bettina's cronies had once whispered as an aside to Meredith, "if she had ever learned how to smile?"

"Lea—hi. I'm Meredith, if you didn't remember me." Meredith extended her hand. Lea ignored it.

"Hi—is my dad here?"

"I'm so sorry about your mother," Meredith said. "And, no, I haven't seen your dad, nor heard from him, but he's probably at his office, waiting to hear from you."

"Nice jacket," said Sonia, standing at the office door. She had only heard stories of the daughter, her disdain for Bettina, and about the legendary yelling matches between them.

"Thanks." Lea said. She moved toward the telephone on the sideboard. She dialed her father's office number, ignoring the trio watching.

She snapped comments into the phone, finishing with, "…tell him I'm here at mom's but I don't want to stay in the house." When she hung up the phone, she turned to see Meredith, Ito and Sonia still fixed on her.

"Lea, your Aunt Luanne called and said your cousin Nicole is expecting you to stay with her," said Meredith.

"Oh great. With all Nicole's nasty little yuppie kids."

"Well, that's up to you, of course. But you might call."

Lea huffed and reached for the phone again. Ito turned silently and returned to the kitchen. Meredith and Sonia disappeared into the offices.

The office phone rang a heartbeat later and Sonia called quietly to Meredith, "Larry Grant would like to talk with you."

"Hello, Larry. What a sad time. I'm so sorry."

"For what? The fact that my ex-wife is dead or that my daughter is a menace to nice people?"

"You choose, there's plenty of chaos to go around."

"My secretary said Lea sounded 'strung.'"

"Actually, she's pretty rational. She kind of said hello, but then again, she hasn't screamed or hit anyone or even called Ito a contract gigolo—yet."

"Well, it's early," said Larry. "I know you have a world of stuff on your own shoulders right now. Thanks for your help." Moments later the house phone rang, and Meredith heard Lea quickly engage in a heated conversation with her father.

"What's her story," said Sonia. "I haven't been around here long enough to understand how one kid from a privileged family like this can get so nasty?"

"Who knows?" said Meredith. "When Lea first finished college, she wanted to be in show business. Bettina got her a job with one of the publicity agencies, but it only lasted a few months. Lea said her superiors didn't understand her. 'They' confirmed it by firing her. Bettina was humiliated. After, there was a PR job with some resort hotel in Newport Beach, followed by a similar post in Miami. The break with the family came after Newport. Lea moved to Boston and eventually married a wealthy developer guy who seems to idolize her. He put her into interior design, I understand. She always was creative."

"I just heard her tell her dad she thinks the family should take control of the office and the 'product coming out of it—right now—before someone steals it all.' She called it intellectual property and worth a fortune. Said they should have taken control before it was a crisis."

"Good. That lets me off the hook. Now she can be Russ Talbot's problem! And he thought Bettina was a handful!"

Marty Escobar finished his walk through of the property and slipped quietly into Meredith's office. "I'm done. Detective Raymond should be here soon. Nice to meet you and I'm sorry for your loss...and well, all the rest of it. I'm leaving now." Meredith shook his hand absently as he left through the back door, and she heard more voices in the front of the house. Lorraine and her husband Max had arrived. Meredith rocked herself back and forth trying to refocus.

Finally, she gave up and left her office to greet the family members, guiding them into the living room. When everyone was assembled, Meredith explained what was known at that point about their mother's death. A somber air permeated the house, and conversation was subdued.

"Doesn't anyone have an idea what caused Bettina's death?" asked Max a well-built dark-haired man who looked travel-weary in a University of New Mexico sweatshirt and jeans. His wife Lorraine, Bettina's older daughter, sat tearfully in the corner.

"I'm told we should know more today, but it seems like Bettina went to bed and died. Why, seems to be the question everyone is working on. You'll be meeting with the investigator from the Police Department, probably later today. They'll contact you to arrange a meeting, I'm sure."

"Shouldn't we be going through things and making some decisions?" probed Lea.

"Lea!" snapped Bettina's sister Luanne. She looked angrily at the younger woman through red, saddened eyes.

"And," added Max, "we should be appraising the house and figuring out what to do with it? I'm sure it would sell quickly."

"The investigators have asked that you wait until they have a better take on it—leave everything as is for the moment," Meredith answered.

"When will you be packing up all of this stuff?" sniffed Lea, whipping her head toward the offices.

"When all of the T's are crossed, I's dotted, and your mother's legacy is secured. You know your mother wouldn't want to dismantle all the work she's spent her life building."

Bettina's ex-husband Larry Grant, Lea and Lorraine's father, quietly entered the living room. Meredith looked at him gratefully. The family surrounded him with greetings. Lorraine and Luanne hugged him. Lea looked on impassively. Larry Grant was a sixty-year-old man about five-foot-nine, hair greying and thinning. His face was not really handsome but comfortable and accessible. His gray suit was well-tailored. But amid the din of conversation, he looked tired and troubled.

"The police just left—again—and have more work to do here," Meredith offered.

"Thank goodness you're not in Vegas, dad," said Lea.

"Come on," said Larry, slightly peeved. He picked up his daughter's suitcase, still in the middle of the living room. "We need to convene in a neutral spot—somewhere without memories or ghosts or crime scene drama—and plan the next step. We'll get everyone's questions answered in due time. Meredith—you'll be a part of that, you know. But right now, I think the kids need to get settled with the rest of the family so we can deal with the loss and take care of some necessary arrangements. We have a lot of decisions, and I'm sure you've had enough excitement anyhow. We'll be over at Luanne's for the day."

Ah, an adult, Meredith thought.

As the family piled into the cars along the curb, Meredith barely had time to sigh in relief before Sonia called, "That detective on the line."

"Do you know the Java Jug down on the boulevard at the bottom of the hill?"

"Yes," said Meredith.

"I think I'd like to talk away from eager ears. Can you spare an hour?"

"I guess I'd better," She reached into her desk drawer for her purse and turned off the typewriter.

"Let me ask you something," said Raymond, sitting in the coffee shop fifteen minutes later, stirring a cup of dark blend java. "What kind of drug kick was your friend on?"

"Drug kick? You've got to be kidding. Bettina was compulsive about a lot of things— but not about drugs. Cigarettes and Hershey bars were her passions." Her own cappuccino swirled around the milk pattern on its surface.

"The M.E. tells us she also liked amphetamines, Valium and booze."

"You're nuts. Bettina drank very little and had a real attitude about Valium. I can't believe the amphetamines."

"Was she dieting?"

"Forever. But not with diet pills anymore."

"Are you sure about that?"

"Pretty much. She was kind of obsessive about her dieting. But she said gave up diet pills years ago. She was more into the chocolate protein shakes and personal weight trainers."

"Well, the reason for her death is still confusing and uncertain, but from the first reports, it looks like she had enough chemicals and alcohol at war in her system to allow her to simply lie down, go to sleep and not wake up."

Meredith scowled into her coffee and dipped a spoon into the symmetrical pattern.

"Then there was an issue with the pillow. Her nostrils were internally contused—only very slightly. And you might remember there was a scratch on the top of her nose and a trace of caked blood. That was mirrored on the throw pillow on the floor—a minute spot of blood—and some spittle. There was also a small thread from the pillow in her mouth. That suggests the pillow was pushed against her nose and mouth. But it didn't kill her. They tell me she would have already been unconscious from the drug cocktail in her bloodstream. And, in her drugged state she could have rolled against the pillow, knocking it to the floor."

Meredith sighed heavily. "What do I say about this?"

"Cardiac Arrest. That's as accurate as you can get for now."

"And about as unbelievable."

"True," he agreed. "But then since when has the reading public cared about the truth?"

"People aren't dumb," Meredith reminded him. "They've seen too much police stuff on TV, and they'll ask what caused the cardiac arrest."

"You could tell them she dieted herself to death."

"Very funny, Detective Raymond. Or not so."

"Well, I'm sorry but the reality hasn't changed. Cause of death is unknown at this time. You might give it some thought, though. Our officers found nothing on the premise—in her bedroom or bathroom or kitchen, anywhere—to indicate that she was taking any of the drugs found, so far, in her system. Did you and Marty notice anything we should know about?"

Meredith shook her head. "Did you check her purse?"

He grunted an affirmative. "Did you find out anything about where she went that night?"

"Yes, she was at Lou and Miriam Feinberg's dinner party over on Maple Drive. There were about twenty people there. I'm sure the Feinbergs will be happy to provide you with a guest list as well as any other information you want about the party. Do you know the approximate time of death?"

"Medical examiner says between one and three a.m."

"I was just thinking about that phone message."

Raymond scowled and shook his head. "We have the recording and phone number, but it was local and from a pay phone on La Brea. Nothing else definitive. Yet."

"What about fingerprints—there must have been some?"

"Oh yeah, tons of them but you'd expect that in a home office as open and busy as yours—which is a problem in itself. Lots of people come and go—staff, family, friends, visitors. The lab is still on it but so far there's nothing surprising to indicate anything or anyone obviously suspicious. We've all enjoyed discovering a couple of well-known folks who apparently visited on the first floor."

They both sat quietly, staring into their drinks. Finally, Raymond spoke up, "Was anything missing—jewelry, equipment, cash—that you know about?"

"Nothing I can tell. I know the jewelry she wears normally, but I don't know everything in her jewelry case. And apparently her purse and wallet content were intact. All the office equipment and her household stuff, antiques seem to be in place. But Bettina's kids reminded me that the most valuable thing in the house is our files. There are twenty-five years of them, some with intimate and potentially damaging information. We have one of the most complete sets of celebrity files anywhere. That's why we keep it in that large closet in my office, under lock and key.

"I lock it personally when I leave at night. Only Bettina and I have a set of keys, plus one kept hidden in the office. Sonia knows about it—but is instructed to touch it only when one of us is not around. We keep our facsimile machine in the same closet along with the very futuristic carry-along phone-in-a-bag, and the photocopy machine. But they're all accounted for. Our files are indexed," said Meredith. "A huge, ongoing headache—but I can ask the temp to check the cabinets against the index. It still won't be perfect—and it will take some time."

"Why would the kids care about your files?"

"Maybe sell them? One daughter emphasized how valuable they are."

"And what about the book manuscript from her former employee? The one found next to her bed when she died? What can you tell me about that?'"

"Nothing. I'd never seen it before, and I don't think Bettina had it until sometime later that day. I can look up Cassie Ainsworth's contact information in New York for you. I think she was, or is, here at the Beverly Hills Hotel."

"This seems personal, not professional," said Raymond. He took the last gulp of his coffee. "I'll be in touch probably tomorrow morning."

Meredith sighed I frustration. They both rose and collected their belongings from the table.

"Watch your own back—just to appease me, if nothing else. This isn't some TV series script and we don't know the extent of it yet." Meredith rolled her eyes.

Back in her office, Meredith phoned the Police PR person again and confirmed an official statement. Then she contacted Russ at the newspaper syndicate. Together they constructed the least compromising news comment possible about Bettina's cause of death. Meredith advised Sonia and Ito, then Bettina's sister Luanne, by phone, how to answer inquiries. She dreaded the meeting that would come soon with the whole family.

☆

T.K. Raymond sat at his desk and fanned out the reports around Bettina Grant's death. "Not suicide, not accidental," he muttered to himself. From the adjacent cubicle, his partner Marty Escobar chimed in, "lot of moving parts."

"But not much clarity. If this case was a train, Meredith Ogden would be the engineer. Working side by side every day— lots of nights. Seems almost as much of an addicted workaholic as Grant, shoulder to shoulder with her most of the time. I feel like she should know a lot more…but there doesn't seem to be much more, as far as she can remember."

"Do you think she's honestly telling you everything she knows?" Marty asked.

Raymond shrugged. "Seems genuine. Has a pretty honest reputation—for a Hollywood journalist—I think she's sad and scared. I've checked out her whereabouts Monday night. Apparently, she really was at home."

"The houseman, Ito," said Marty, walking over to Raymond's desk and sitting down in the side chair. "He practically ran Grant's personal life. Much savvier than he leads you to believe. MBA, accountant, knows all about Grant's finances…"

"And totally an outlier," added Raymond. "No role in the public or active life of the Hollywood circuit. Total access to the deceased and the house. Why would a smart MBA grad, obviously a competent accountant, take on—much less stick with—a 'houseman' job?"

"He says it was the aura of Hollywood and movies, but I wonder. I'll check him out more completely. I have his relatives' contact information. See if there's an alibi that holds up, try to find out more about his legal status here as well, maybe education? What about the family?"

"I'm hoping to talk to the ex-husband later today," Raymond reported looking at his growing list of people making up the puzzle. "How about taking the sister Luanne? You're so good with grieving relatives." Marty pursed his lips and blew a loud raspberry. "Sure," he said, pulling himself from the chair and moving back into his own office.

"Lab expects to know a little more later on today," called Raymond. Escobar grunted his acknowledgment.

Raymond pulled together the list of players in the drama, regarding each name. Sonia, Ito and Meredith all checked out. Family—Larry Grant, Luanne, kids—due in later in the day. Cassie O'Connell Ainsworth, perhaps the last person to see or talk with Bettina Grant before she died? Was there more? He figured he'd better peruse the manuscript left with Bettina by

Ainsworth. Allan Jaymar, dear friend, neighbor? Interjected himself into the investigation from the beginning. Did he fit in? His partner Potty—closest proximity, yet saw nor heard nothing? Late night TV star Joey O'Neal? Tangential or connected? Russell Talbot and the syndicate? Had the columnist become "too" special? Who else wanted that coveted column position and enough to kill for it?

Then there was the miles-long list of professional contacts, celebrities, studio, music, TV people, some of who revered Grant, some of who would love to see her gone, maybe even avenged? Raymond gathered up his papers, shoving them into his case, pulling on his coat, grabbing his radio and gun, to go talk to Larry Grant.

Meredith woke up abruptly by the shrill ring of the phone at five-thirty in the morning. Sleepily, she mumbled, "hello."

"I'm sorry to waken you. Don't you return phone calls?" The voice on the line was affable and familiar.

"Only when I feel like it," she answered, recognizing Detective T.K. Raymond. "And I never feel like it in the middle of the night! I went to bed very early last night and must have missed it."

The cat jumped onto the bed, rubbing against the phone receiver, curious about the untimely conversation.

"I need to talk to you this morning."

"Just doing normal detecting—at five-thirty in the morning?"

"I wouldn't be working now if this wasn't important?"

"I thought you'd drawn the swing shift," Meredith yawned.

"Not exactly. My desk is full of other cases. Surprising! And, I've drawn a pain-in-the-ass case, a Movieland case," he said. "You're the movie expert, so I hope you'll help me solve it."

"Pass. I'm a reporter, not a detective." Meredith sat up against the pillows and rubbed her eyes with one hand.

"It's all just research except you go to movies and parties, see celebrities and glamour. I go to burglaries and murders, see criminals and dead folks. In any case, I have to talk with you about some information I've come across. What time is good for you?"

"Early as possible, and away from the office," sighed Meredith. "Today is Bettina's memorial service. The entire Grant family will be passing through our lives, and I don't think you'd want to be around it. Unless you need to talk to them all."

"I've been talking to them. And I'm sure I will again. But not until I get straight on a few questions that have come up. What's a good time?"

"Breakfast. But give me 90 minutes. And somewhere close. How about up the street in Brentwood Village. The Skillet. They open early."

"High rent district. Sure."

"Wear your sunglasses."

"Hey, cat. Who left my clothes on the floor again?" Meredith dropped the phone into its cradle, pushed Paco aside, untangled herself from the bedcovers to hustle into the shower.

☆

Raymond stood up from the red vinyl booth to greet Meredith as she arrived at the small cottage-like restaurant. "You're all dressed up. I'm always at a loss to figure out how you women can pull yourselves together so fast," he said.

Meredith did a subtle model's pose before sitting. She was wearing a navy-blue silk St. Angelo with a white cashmere coat. Her day carried a heavy agenda including Bettina's service.

"We still have columns to produce, so I have to keep the activity going. I have a lunch interview with Melanie Connors. She's back on TV again, and she's one of the 'nice people.' We're lunching at the Polo Lounge."

"Drudgery," smirked the detective.

"You're a vision, too, Raymond. 'High profile' high style?"

He was wearing a gray UCLA sweatshirt and a pair of well-worn jeans. His dark curly hair hung a little too long around his ears. A scratched leather bomber jacket was tossed over the back of his chair. "The sneakers are new," he said, holding out one foot.

Meredith looked down at the large pair of feet housed in athletic technology on the end of a pair of long legs that stuck out from under the table. "Impressive."

"Changed them just for you. I've been on a case up in the Canyon, climbing around in the dirt, and up all night. So maybe try to be nice."

"What's so important?" Meredith scanned the menu. A waitress in a blue uniform and a blue and white gingham apron with a tidy bow in the back bustled about the tiny dozen-booth coffee shop. A name tag on her shoulder read "Sandi."

Sandi materialized next to the table with her order pad poised. "Waffle, side of ham, a bowl of berries and decaf coffee," said Meredith.

Raymond looked at her in wonder. "Where do you put it? Oatmeal with nonfat milk and strong coffee for me." As Sandi moved away, he looked around at the glass cases bearing trays of large and lustrous baked delicacies. "Sure you don't want one of those dinner-plate sized cinnamon rolls, too?"

"Maybe later. Your own menu is an assault to a hedonistic way of life, Raymond."

"That's what I'd like to talk about," he said. Meredith scowled. "Not yours," he quickly added. "Bettina Grant's."

"Hedonistic isn't the word I'd use, but let's not quibble over semantics."

"Of course not."

Coffee arrived. Meredith inhaled the steam from her cup while Raymond toyed with his spoon. She noticed fingers that were muscular and precise in their movement. Mature, she thought, then smiled self-consciously to herself, wondering why such trivial facts occupied her mind.

Sandi the waitress arrived laden with breakfast plates. She placed the dishes in front of them, her starched uniform swishing as she moved on to the next table.

"I talked with the Feinbergs yesterday," Raymond began. "As you know, Bettina was at their home Tuesday night. They say she was the model of decorum, had a whiskey sour before dinner, a glass of wine with dinner and then excused herself earlier than we assumed—a little after nine o'clock. She told Mrs. Feinberg that she had a late coffee date with an old friend. Ring a bell?"

"Not at all. She never mentioned a call from anyone to me. I can't imagine…" Her mind began to thumb through the list of "old friends" Bettina might be seeing. Then she thought about her own phone messages from the night before.

The detective watched her, posed to make notes in his spiral notebook.

"Cassie O'Connell Ainsworth. Bettina was reading her manuscript, remember? She was Bettina's former 'legwoman.' I replaced her ten years ago. Time flies. Anyway, maybe it was Cassie. I had a message from her last night, too. I haven't returned it yet. But she's at the Beverly Hills Hotel—like all good show biz folks. Her network must be picking up the tab. She's been living and working in New York for the past few years, News Editor for one of the local TV stations. She could have been Bettina's surprise visitor."

"Does it fit? Could Cassie and Bettina have met at the house?"

Meredith hesitated then grimaced. "Maybe but there would have been some evidence in the kitchen or living room—dirty ashtrays, used coffee cups. Bettina was willing to take dirty dishes and ashtrays only as far as the sink. But I was the first one in the house the next morning and didn't see anything. Even the dishwasher had clean dishes. But there was the manuscript."

"I'll talk with her since she's apparently still here." He took a drink of coffee and sighed. "You're sure Mrs. Grant didn't have a habit?"

"I'm not sure of anything, anymore. Ito mentioned that Bettina seemed to get into the brandy bottle when no one was around to notice—particularly on his nights off. I never knew about that. Maybe she did take diet pills and Valium. Again. Once, years ago, when she was working on a couple of book projects, along with writing her column and all the other things Bettina did, she pumped herself up every morning with diet pills, then knocked herself down at night with Valium. But that was ten years ago, and she spoke eloquently about cold-turkeying and having learned an important lesson.

"Besides that, Bettina would have nothing to hide if she did acquire a habit. She'd love to be able to describe, in print, being one of the first to check into the new Betty Ford Clinic. Beating addiction has become trendy in Hollywood, and Bettina always loved a good trend."

Raymond poked a spoon into the oatmeal sitting in front of him. "Would you eat this?" Meredith shook her head. "My son says it's good for me," he said and took a bite.

Meredith absently registered "my son."

"So, Bettina Grant drank a little. And used to pop pills," he continued. "She'd have to do a lot of both to accomplish the state she was in on Wednesday morning. The lady had been partying—in every sense of the word. She must have gotten lucky somewhere."

Meredith grimaced again, torn between her surprise at the news and embarrassment. "How do you know? What did you find…I mean…."

"Like pubic hair or cum tracks?"

"If you were a little more clinical," she suggested, blushing.

"Semantics," said Raymond. "Semen deposits or cum tracks. They're all the same thing and fortunately, I don't have to write about them, just identify them. And no, there were none of either in the bed covers, but our medical examiner had no doubt that Bettina got lucky somewhere that night. Not in her own bed, however. There, for all intents and purposes, it looks like Bettina Grant brushed her teeth, washed her face, hung up her clothes, drew the drapes and crawled into bed with her alarm set to wake up at her usual hour. Any new inspiration about candidates? Newly discovered lovers?"

Recollections of private conversations with Bettina over the past year washed through Meredith's thoughts. She couldn't think of a single instance when her boss had mentioned a "date," much less suggested a sexual tryst with anyone. The last romantic episode Meredith could remember Bettina recounting was four or five years before with the star of a talk radio show, a pop psychologist on whose show Bettina had guested.

The relationship was short-lived but intense, beginning flirtatiously in the studio, escalating over dinner the same night. Bettina called the office and left word on the answering machine that she was staying over in New York for a few extra days. Returning to California, she looked "played out," as Meredith assessed the situation.

"She said little about it except that it had been a wild escapade that would lead nowhere but was fun while it lasted. He called her quite a few times at first, even flew out to visit. Once. The day after he left, Bettina seemed down. She said her initial instinct had been correct and the reprise had 'nothing but a nice distraction'. Other than the radio psychologist, her last involvement—that I know about—was the two-year relationship she had with a magazine editor from Canada. But that was at least five years ago."

"Tell me about the ex-husband."

"Larry Grant. Attorney. Nice looking, not terribly smart. Trial lawyer, kind of an ambulance chaser, but does okay. Partner in a small law firm in the Valley. Nothing spectacular but makes an okay living. Likes bimbos, apparently. Lived with a couple of them after the twenty-five years with Bettina. Lives in a small townhouse complex in Encino. Seems to spend most of his time on a sailboat in the Marina—or in Las Vegas. Likes to play cards, I hear. We don't see much of him and I never did know him well. He's been at the house for a few special family occasions. He was around more when Cassie was working for Bettina."

"Tell me more about…Cassie…."

"Attractive brunette, bright. Worked for Bettina for eight years, started when Cassie was only twenty-two. She was more than Bettina's right arm. Bettina knew how to choose her support. People say Cassie was her crutch, her best friend, her alter ego. She saw Bett through her divorce from Larry, the drug problems of the daughter, helped her grow from a minor fan magazine writer into a major columnist. Of course, Bettina did as much—or more—for Cassie."

"Why'd she leave?"

"Grew up, I guess. Got bored writing about the pretty people. Discovered that there wasn't enough room in the office for two ambitious people. See, the way it worked with Bettina was that she would move Heaven and Earth for her number two person. As long the number two person didn't hunger to be a number one person. "

"Was there any danger of that?"

"I doubt it, but Bettina was always honest about her insecurities. She told me, and I'm sure told Cassie more than once, she wanted an associate who had talent, persistence and balls—when it came to news and writing. When it came politics and promotions, she wanted someone who wasn't aggressive because aggressiveness was Bettina's strong point and she liked to exercise it. She said she believed that while her own writing talent was a little shy, she could provide the money and security to hire and keep a talented support staff happy for a long time. Cassie reached a point where she needed to grow, and Bettina had no place for her to grow. They parted amicably."

"And remained friends?"

"For a while. Cassie enrolled in a graduate journalism program in New York and more or less disappeared. We'd hear from her at Christmas or once in a while when she was in town. Bettina seemed to develop more and more animosity towards her every year. When Cassie got her first on-camera news job— hard news, not entertainment—in Philadelphia, she sent a tape of an award-winning investigative report to Bettina, along with a thank you note for all the teaching, inspiration and stuff. Bettina refused to watch the tape. When Cassie took over as News Director of the network's nightly news in New York she sent a tape of her first show. It's never been played, as far as I know."

"Funny," said Raymond, scraping the last of the sticky cereal from the bowl.

"Eventually Cassie quit corresponding. And it was too bad. She'd had a nice enthusiasm and energy. I never worked with her, but we talked a bit in the first few years. I'd like to have known her better."

"Maybe after this is over, you can read her manuscript. Do you trust Cassie—the little of her you know?"

Meredith shrugged. "I hardly know her at all, but I do wonder what is in that manuscript."

"You never outgrew Bettina?" He looked closely at Meredith.

"I'm a good behind-the-scenes command. I fit Bettina's profile. As long as I wrote well, won and kept people's confidences and candor, Bettina Grant saw to it I was rewarded well and never got hassled. I never needed to be her. And she never needed to be me."

"So, what now? There aren't many Bettina Grants in this world. Which brings me back to the question—what about the column, anyway? I've been told by lots of people there's a real run for the gold among your writing friends. Would any of them take preemptive action against Bettina—like, well, killing her?"

Meredith thought about it and shook her head wearily. "I don't know."

"Are you in the race?"

"I think," said Meredith, exasperated, "I'll go to work. I'm tired of that question being asked over and over."

She laid a ten-dollar bill on the table, rose brusquely, picked up her coat, looked quickly toward the bakery cases, then walked out, leaving a bewildered Detective Raymond holding a spoonful of oatmeal midway between the bowl and his mouth. He wondered as she left why she had been staring at his hands so intently.

Meredith was still peeved from Raymond's question as she arrived at the office earlier than usual. She felt sad and apprehensive coming into the empty house where death had so recently taken place. Before the phones began to ring, or Sonia arrived or the patter of the day accelerated, Meredith wanted to spend time revisiting the decade she had spent with Bettina Grant. There were private memories and trade secrets among the books in the floor-to-ceiling bookcases. Meredith decided they should remain the property of Bettina Grant: personal inscriptions in celebrity-authored books, a few intimately autographed photos and some paperwork from Bettina's divorce that should not be shared with others. Knowing about them only attested to the depth of the trust between the two women.

She also wanted to search for a leather journal Ito had mentioned casually, a journal Bettina sometimes wrote in at night on a quiet evening. After an hour of sifting through drawers, shelves and cabinets, the former legwoman had managed to load only two shoe boxes full of papers she felt merited further examination. For a few minutes she thoughtfully fingered the colorful button Ito had found amid the sofa cushions in her office. She remembered Bettina's pleasure in finding the fashionable dress from which it had fallen. Bettina had planned to debut the outfit at the Feinberg's dinner.

When Meredith reached into the back of a low built-in cabinet in the den bookcase, she felt the scarred leather of an old briefcase. It was not a fashionable case, bearing no recognizable logo, but it had been a cast-off of Larry's and was the carry-all that Bettina had relied on during her nascent career thirty years before. She had refused to discard it, even though she had been gifted with a succession of more fashionable totes over the past 20 years. She had dutifully carried each until a new one arrived from a studio chief or publicity firm the next Christmas.

She examined the desk, cabinets and other niches and receptacles in the den, then Meredith sat down in Bettina's well-used office chair and focused on the personal computer housed in a custom-built cabinet atop a dedicated rosewood table. She pressed the power switch on the machine's back panel and the screen illuminated. In seconds the directory listed those the subjects to which Bettina Grant had given her thoughts.

No surprises were found as Meredith pried into the electronic alter ego of her late employer. The boxy personal computer had been delivered to the office by the newspaper syndicate only a few months before, encouraging the team to learn its promising efficiency and power. But its complex operations mostly intimidated them and took more time than anyone had to devote. Bettina had commandeered the machine for herself and used it only for the simplest word processing functions. Yet she salted her conversation among peers with the few words of computer jargon she had learned. Like personal trainers, rain forests and cosmetic surgery, Bettina enjoyed a good trend when she found one. A few months later, the media syndicate had provided a computer for Meredith which she kept at home for work away from the office.

That afternoon, Meredith sat down in Sonia's small cubicle and talked candidly with her. "Lock the file cabinets—all of them," she instructed. "And let's put the column material we're working on into the bottom drawer of one of them. I don't want anything left around for idle fingers to pry into over the weekend."

"What makes you think those same idle fingers will respect a locked cabinet?" asked Sonia.

"I doubt anyone will have the time or opportunity right now to break and enter here unless someone really wants something from our files we don't even know about."

"You don't think anyone would lift the equipment, do you?" asked Sonia earnestly.

Meredith considered the possibility for a minute, then shook her head. "I hope not. But when it comes down to it, we don't have any legal or official right to any of this—not the file information, not the phones, not the facsimile machine."

"Why would anyone want to disrupt our work? What possible benefit could they get from doing that?" Sonia persisted, then caught herself. "Well, I recall Lea mentioning how valuable—'worth a fortune'—the files might be."

"None of the family has ever done a thing to suggest that they would approach you and me and the office here with anything but deepest respect—for Bettina if nothing else. But still, the house will be open, more or less, over the weekend. As I understand it, the entire group will be meeting here on Sunday for the reading of Bettina's will."

"She had a will?"

"Oh sure. Bettina was nothing if not absolutely clear about who would receive her legacy. But anyway, I think it makes good sense for me to take home the column materials for the next couple of days—just in case we aren't invited back into the place for start of business on Monday."

"We can always send the columns for Monday and Tuesday from a commercial fax place."

Meredith nodded, still thinking. "I still wonder who, legally, owns all these files. They are valuable, you know. There's thirty years' worth of background on Hollywood's biggest and best. Bettina told me that years ago, for a short time, she and Cassie O'Connell worked for some outfit that was sold to a small-time publishing company. The day the sale was announced, Cassie took all the files home, hiding them in a basement locker until it was certain no one from the new firm was going to confiscate their material."

"I would never have thought of that...but then...," her voice trailed off. "What about Lea? She had this idea that the family owned the office. What if she takes the files hostage? She seemed totally focused on them when she was here earlier."

"I can't imagine why she would be interested in these files, considering that she's been estranged from Bettina for a long time, and they have nothing to do with her work or her life now. But let's not drive ourselves crazy. Bettina's not here to approve moving all that paperwork out of the house—and it's grown out of three filing drawers to ten three-drawer cabinets. I think we're going to have to take a few precautions, to be smart, and then, trust."

"What stars do you think will show up for Bettina's service?" Sonia changed the subject with a question she had obviously waited all morning to ask.

"Hard to tell. Hollywood stars have an interesting penchant for honoring the living—the ones who can help with today's career. But it has only been a few days and the family set up the service so quickly it's catching everyone by surprise. If I were to guess, the crowd will be small and mostly close business friends. Maybe one or two of Bett's close celebrity friends—if they are in town or even know about it."

Sonia nodded, apparently satisfied as well as excited at even the prospect of stargazing. She opened her desk drawer and took a small chain holding several tiny metal keys from the back. "Some of these have never been used," she commented as she began to secure the banks of beige metal data drawers lining the closet at the end of her office.

Meredith watched the small brunette work her way across the closet and was proud of the Sonia she saw today. The secretary wore a simply cut deep purple dress that was neither extreme nor showy, yet it clung nicely to the curves of her tight body. Gone were the kitschy fashions she generally wore—skin-tight jeans with spangly tops, thigh high boots, or whatever else was the latest in bad-taste fashion of the day. Sonia tried so hard to be a member of the glamour set she managed to prove just how far out of it she really was. Meredith had long ago learned that as an official observer, a "fringe player," as she called herself in the game of celebrity, dressing classically and with understatement served her far better than trying to compete.

"You can't compete with a celebrity," Bettina had advised. "If you out-dress the people you are interviewing, they'll fixate on your clothing, concentrating on something other than talking to an impartial, transparent observer they feel they can trust and confide in."

The fashion lessons had been important to the personal style for Meredith who was, intrinsically, a lover of color and statement. She loved color and interesting styles. But she had learned the art of subtle fashion.

A few minutes later, Meredith and Sonia left the offices and met Ito at the back door. He, too, was uncharacteristically well dressed in a tailored blue suit, crisply laundered white shirt with his initials on the cuff, and a silk tie appropriate for any executive club. He smiled almost sadly at Meredith and Sonia.

"Strange day for all," he said.

"Is this your last day here?" asked Sonia.

"No, the family has asked me to stay on until the decision has been made about the disposition of the house," he answered.

The threesome made their way to their vehicles and each discretely looked back to regard the house, home to them for many years. A mixture of curiosity and sadness in their faces.

Bettina Grant's memorial service was held in a small, formal chapel at a well-known cemetery and funeral park. The remains had been cremated at Bettina's own request, and she had also opted against a traditional funeral service. "Staging her last public appearance here is exactly what I would expect Bettina Grant to do," said one former movieland columnist who had written her own memoirs five years before after she turned in her press pass.

The mortuary on the slopes of Mount Hollywood offered all the wizardry possible to create a silver-screen atmosphere, a filmland memory. Meredith imagined a Gossip Hall of Fame in which Bettina could rest along with her peers, the likes of Hedda Hopper, Jimmy Fiddler, Shelia Graham and Louella Parsons.

A surprisingly small crowd congregated to pay last respects to that Queen of Gossip. But for the group's relatively small size, it was comprised of the entertainment industry's heavier hitters. Bettina would have been proud, thought Meredith. Quality not quantity, Bettina's by-words—a legacy that rested without peace in the forefront of Meredith's mind each day as she sat down to recreate the word patterns that Bettina Grant had stamped out as her own.

The chapel was small but ornate, a cavern brushed thickly with the dark and rich style of the Flemish masters, like a living Rembrandt or Van Dyke cavern. Meredith reflected that, in many ways, the shadowed environment ran counter to the flamboyance and brightness with which Bettina Grant had lived.

Mourners arrived in small groupings. The CEO of Landmark Films was accompanied by the head of Production for one of the TV networks. A half dozen celebrities with whom Bettina had maintained an on-going interview relationship over the years stood reverently in the shadows. Sonia's curiosity would be satisfied. Several journalists and publicists with whom Bettina had worked closely and two competitors who were probably in attendance out of sheer relief, were also sprinkled throughout the group. Then there was the publicity industry, with the heads of the three largest entertainment public relations firms talking somberly together. A few of their younger press agents stood close by, wondering uncomfortably why they were required to attend the last services for someone they barely knew. But it was the way of the industry.

Meredith caught sight of Cassie O'Connell Ainsworth, dressed quietly in a dark blue suit and no coat. Cassie waved discretely to Meredith and held an imaginary phone receiver to her ear with one hand while dialing in the air with the other. Meredith nodded her understanding, a silent agreement to phone Cassie after the service.

The tall deft figure of Detective T.K. Raymond stood discretely in the rear corner of the room. Meredith was surprised to see him, then remembered he was investigating the death. She guessed there were clues to be found here. His weathered looks carried a sadness she had not seen before. Sonia had described him as "a cross between Tommy Lee Jones and Richard Widmark." Meredith wondered how Sonia even knew who Richard Widmark was—an older actor who played mature, heroic leading men, but not a fan magazine cover star. Raymond had caught her expression and Meredith turned away, embarrassed.

The family, a dozen strong and not as imposing as Meredith had expected, sat quietly in the front seats of the chapel. Sonia had integrated into the throng in the back seats, and Meredith searched hard for an apt group of mourners with whom she could associate. She noticed Larry Grant talking quietly in the back with a striking older brunette and a tall, balding man, neither of which Meredith recognized. Larry soon made his way toward the family and the other two sat down far in the rear of the church.

Meredith felt a familiar sense of standing on the outside looking in, something she had dealt with throughout most of her years with Bettina. She moved slowly along the wall to the right of the seats, inching her way quietly toward the front. Suddenly the voice of Bettina's sister-in-law Luanne broke the stillness in the room as she began to speak from the podium about her sister. Meredith stood alone next to the front row of seats, wishing fervently to be invisible or disappear into the wall.

Close family and friends—a few of whom Meredith herself had contacted—recited a short fifteen minutes of eulogies. Suddenly it was Meredith's turn to step up to the lectern to remember the woman she had known so well, and yet suddenly seemed a stranger. She felt removed from the words she had assembled but articulated them precisely, with ease, focusing on the generous, supportive and human Bettina.

When she concluded, she stepped away from the podium and returned to the support-giving wall next to the first row of chairs. As the assemblage stood together to say a murmured prayer, she felt a hand slip into her own—a soft, tiny hand that shook, palsied. When she shifted her eyes discretely to see who stood next to her, she saw the silver etched silhouette of Bettina's antique father, Arthur Amalfi, now ninety. The wizened hand squeezed hers confidently, and Meredith was grateful to be acknowledged. At the end of the prayer, Mr. Amalfi looked over sadly and Meredith could see that he, too, held on to courage far longer than was necessary. Tears only brimmed at the edges of the old eyes, but not one spilled over. Meredith leaned forward and kissed him on the cheek before she disengaged her hand and became the public persona at which she was so polished.

"Valley Obituaries
Bettina Marlys Grant—famed celebrity confidant, journalist and columnist

Internationally renowned entertainment columnist and journalist Bettina Grant died at her Bel Air home on December 7, according to her sister Luanne Carter. Grant was "the most widely distributed and read Hollywood columnist across the world," according to Russell Talbot, Managing Director of the United American News Syndicate that disseminated Grant's work. Born in Van Nuys, CA, to Arthur and Maria Amalfi, Grant attended local high schools and California State University at Northridge. While in college she developed a love of journalism, met and married husband Lawrence M. Grant, and began writing celebrity news for the Valley Chronicle. She subsequently joined the Valley Star Magazine as a reporter, became West Coast Editor for fan magazines Movie World and Star Beat, then national columnist for the news syndicate World News Features. In 1969, her column was acquired by the prestigious United American News Syndicate. For several years, Grant performed with her sisters Rachel and Luanne as the "Awsome Amalfis," singing in local clubs.

Grant is survived by sister Luanne Carter, daughters Lorraine Harven (Max) and Lea Bolstoy (Oscar), and former husband Lawrence. Services were..."

Meredith suffered from the sting of Bettina's death and the sadness of the funeral service that afternoon, but she also continued to worry about filling columns in the days ahead. Against her own better judgment, she ventured out to an industry gathering in hopes of learning something new about local happenings which had become only background noise in the confusion.

"Courageous of you to come out tonight," said a heavily made-up aging blonde, Linette Bluesman, a producer of the local/social segment of an L.A. TV news show. "Tough loss. Sorry for you." Meredith smiled graciously. She tried to remain unemotional and impassive, and again chastised herself for attending the too-touted birthday celebration of Richard Voner, a veteran producer-director. Voner's publicity agent was spotlighting his client and his recent film in order to encourage Academy Award attention during these sensitive months just before Oscar nominations took place. The private party was filled with distant friends of Voner's—many of whom happened to be press members.

The party was held at the Crystal Decanter, one of L.A.'s preferred eateries. Sculpted rosebush trees formed a tight hedge in front of the building, a stone and brick quasi French countryside manor.

"Your story on Joey O'Neal was surprising," said Linette. "He was supposed to be here tonight but well, the publicity and all. He can be pretty vocally abusive and he told Richard he felt 'aggressively' bitter toward you folks. Just a lot of drama, he said." Meredith's shook her head to minimize the subject, and to staunch the spike of fear she felt from the comment.

"It's always nice to see Fred Barton," Linette added.

"Fred's an old friend," said the public Meredith, amazed that she was called upon to justify a social outing with an old working pal. "We've known each other since we worked together at the TV station."

Friends most often compared Fred physically to Billy Crystal, the slight, trim forthright comedian who appeared often on late night TV and co-stared in the series *Soap*. Fred was now the editor of one of the two major film industry daily trade publications and had been so for a decade. He was a diminutive man with an unassuming air and a deep enjoyment of the movie industry, or at least the lifestyle it afforded. His pay had never quite matched his position, but he was accorded a great deal of power, which he enjoyed and occasionally used. He wore impeccable suits and now boasted a head of curly and distinguished silver hair. But he drove a 12-year-old Rambler, so Meredith usually volunteered to drive when they accompanied one another to events. Valet attendants at glitter-town restaurants preferred to let Fred park his own car. They never turned away the Mustang.

Meredith and Fred stood at the curb on Melrose Avenue, waiting for the parking attendant to bring the car around from the parking lot behind the building. Linette air-kissed the duo as she retreated back through the restaurant's etched glass doors. Meredith turned to wave good-by when the small black purse she carried tumbled from her hand and spilled its contents onto the sidewalk. Impulsively she stopped to retrieve them, scampering toward the doorway, hardly hearing the sound of a car speeding toward the curb. She looked up at the same moment there was a "thump" and Fred seemed to fly from the curb, not under his own power, into the flower bed in front of the restaurant windows.

She ran over to where the little man sat on the ground, grasping his knee. A large, newer model black car sped down the street, squealing as it crossed the nearest intersection, disappearing into the night. Meredith reached down to help Fred, at the same time trying to stuff her belongings into the tiny beaded clutch bag,

Two parking attendants, several other restaurant patrons and Alfredo, the maître d', rushed to Fred's side. The scowl on the Alfredo's face was a direct contradiction to the usual patronizing smile that was his trademark. He squatted to the ground, puffing in his overstuffed tuxedo, and steadied Fred.

"What went on here?" he asked in his dramatic French accent. "Who was driving that car?" he demanded. "I know Disney was pissed off about the story we ran about them today, but…this is too much." Fred joked. The grimace on his face was no joke. And Alfredo didn't miss a minute of it.

Fred's grimace grew deeper. "I hardly even saw the car. It just jumped out at me and sped away."

"A drunk," commented a patron. A larger crowd was gathering at the spot. Fred struggled to his feet self-consciously with the help of Meredith and Alfredo. He tested his legs and found that he could stand, then brushed off his suit.

"Shouldn't we call the police?' Meredith asked.

"I'll call 911," said Linette, materializing like a bad habit.

Fred shook his head adamantly. "Don't! It'll only bring a lot of negative publicity to this place. They'll never comp me again for a meal. And honestly, I couldn't identify that car if my life depended on it. Could you?"

Meredith thought about it. She knew it was black or very dark blue, and for some reason she knew it was a Cadillac although no matter how hard she tried to picture it she could conjure no visible image that confirmed it. She also flashed on the comment about Joey O'Neal being "aggressively bitter."

"Don't you think we should at least take you to the emergency room," she persisted. "You might have broken something."

"Nah. I'm just bruised. If something was broken, I couldn't walk. I'll be good and keep an eye on it. I promise. Right now, though, I'd like to go over to the Laser Disque and have a drink.

Fred's typical evening pattern was to stop at a trendy night spot to cap off his evenings out. He didn't mind that his age belied the tony image he strove to exude. He liked to consider himself part of the new music scene. Meredith had hoped to beg off the night cap but considering Fred's mishap, she thought better of idea, and accepted the car keys from the attendant.

Alfredo was smiling more easily now, and with extreme solicitude he again brushed off Fred's suit with a small, soft brush, and wished them both a good evening.

"Nice guy," said Fred.

"Worried guy," Meredith corrected him. "Someone else might have sued the restaurant."

"For what?"

"Anything. I'm sure that somewhere in that crowd of people was at least one attorney who could put a case together for you."

"Going to Hollywood parties is getting complicated, and I'm a simple guy."

Meredith headed for Sunset Boulevard and the Laser Disque. "I can't help but think about that car," she ventured a while later as they sat at the bar in the darkened night club. Ultraviolet black light illuminated a small dance floor. The band was mercifully on a break, although the lounge was jammed with social chatter.

"Don't think about it," he said. "I'm trying not to. Mind over matter. Maybe I won't hurt tomorrow."

"Poor thing," cooed Meredith caustically. "So fragile. Maybe you can find someone in your apartment building to watch over you tonight."

"I'll probably make a phone call or two and find someone to do that when I get home," said Fred, sounding for all the world more like a small boy than a sophisticated adult.

"We'd all rest more comfortably if you did," purred Meredith, recognizing that calling out for one of the lithesome young neighbors to fill the evening was always in his rhetoric, but probably never happened.

"What I started to say," she said aloud, "was that I keep realizing that if my purse hadn't fallen to the ground, with me scampering after it like a crippled frog, that car would have hit me, not you. Have you realized that?"

"No, but thank your guardian angel, Merri. Neither your pretty dress nor your dainty bones would have stood up as well as my wool suit and bulging muscles."

Meredith thought about the incident long after she had dropped Fred off at his apartment and returned to her own home. Once again, it was midnight when she drove into her own complex and noticed the silver Jeep parked in front of her house. She grinned warmly as she walked over to the car and rapped on the window. A sleeping head snapped up and the figure inside lowered the window.

"It's about time," he grinned.

"Dusty, when did you get here—I didn't think you'd be in town for a few more days?"

"About two hours ago. We wrapped the shoot nearly three days early."

"So, you decided to come directly here—to surprise me?"

"After two months on location I figured what's another night?"

He climbed out of his car, captured his backpack from the rear seat and followed Meredith into the townhouse. She went straight to the bedroom and kicked off her pumps, dropping down heavily on the edge of the bed with a loud sigh. "I have to feed Paco," she murmured.

"I'll do that," Dusty said. "You shake off the day." He stood up to confront the feline now standing in the bedroom door, meowing loudly. The process was not a new drill.

Clothes shed on the floor, hair damp from a quick shower, Meredith joined the solidly built athletic man who bore a resemblance to a slightly graying Burt Reynold. Stretched out atop the quilted bedspread. His thick tousled salt and pepper gray hair and perennially sun-tanned face looked even more boyish than usual.

"Glad to see me?" he asked.

"You're the nicest thing that's happened to me all week."

"Should I be flattered or was it a terrible week?"

"Well, what do you think? Bettina dies on Monday night, the entire Grant family swoops down on us—after all, the office is in Bettina's home. Now Sonia and I are the interlopers! I've got a troublesome story that has to be resolved on Joey O'Neal, a persistent detective who seems to think I have the key to all of Bettina's secrets, and, by the way, a possible motive to kill her. Then there was the memorial service this afternoon and at least three hundred and fifty phone calls of condolences, a major screening to cover, and Richard Voner's 60th birthday party at which I was nearly run down by a car and missed only because Fred Barton was standing in the wrong place at the wrong time and took the impact instead. I'm still feeling shaky."

"Probably not as shaky as Fred."

Meredith laughed. "He's fine, in need of TLC which I'm sure he'll find from one of the starlet neighbors in that singles building he's lived in forever. Fortunately, he managed to roll to one side and only seemed to bruise a knee."

"What an 80's woman!" chuckled Dusty, reaching over to turn on the lamp. He leaned forward and kissed Meredith's well-toned shoulder.

"Pretty dress," he said, looking at the midnight blue knit cocktail dress in a mound on the floor.

"Thanks. It's new and somber. I had to fight with myself to even go to the party tonight."

"Why did you? Are the Voners all that vital?"

"No, but I feel compelled to keep on showing up, pushing for column material, stuff to write about. God only knows why. I'm too shell-shocked, sad, numb and exhausted to make rational judgments. And tonight, someone mentioned O'Neal was feeling vengeful."

"Well, you're safe now. How about jumping under these covers with me. I guarantee you'll forget about being rational." She did.

CHAPTER 10

SATURDAY

Morning started out later than usual in the airy Brentwood townhouse. For the first time in a week, Meredith slept late and wasn't thinking about murder, Bettina and work. Dusty yawned as he pulled a pair of jeans over a slight but muscular body and padded barefooted toward the kitchen to start breakfast. He had offered to make a Spanish omelet. He had managed to stop for ingredients on his way the night before. The offer was a good idea, he realized as he surveyed the vacant shelves of the refrigerator and cupboards.

Meredith absently began to pick up the neglected clothes from the bedroom and hang them up in a walk-in closet off the bathroom.

"Things really must have been busy around here," commented Dusty eyeing the littered floor. "And to think, this woman has a housekeeper!" A lacy slip landed on his head.

The piquant tomato/pepper omelet sauce simmered on the stove, and Meredith made coffee. Dusty, still barefooted padded through the living room to retrieve the newspaper from the front steps. He always felt comfortable in the place. Soft beige walls boasted well-positioned pastel paintings and bold burgundy and aqua hues splashed throughout a textured sofa, chair and draperies. A pile of fat throw cushions surrounded a beige marble fireplace.

"Ugh," he said as he caught a glimpse of his own reflection in the hall floor-to-ceiling mirror and pulled in his stomach. "It's good to be back from Mexico and the starchy foods company's catering wagon serves." He wished he could stay home longer than a couple of days.

"Were you ordering room service last night for breakfast this morning?" he asked moments later. He held a large bakery box with a plate-sized, heavily glazed cinnamon bun staring out from the glassine box window.

He handed it to Meredith, a look of comic puzzlement on his face. On top was the business card of Detective T.K. Raymond. "You forgot your cinnamon bun. Sorry."

A blush crept over Meredith's neck and face. "I told you he was intense. I walked out on him in the middle of a question/answer session yesterday morning."

"Must have been some question he asked," Dusty mused. He eyed the thick sauce bubbling on the stove and then the cinnamon bun. "We could warm it up for breakfast?" he suggested.

"I can think of a couple of things I might do with it—but breakfast sounds better," she murmured.

When they finished eating and the dishes were tucked into the dishwasher, Dusty and Meredith huddled over the butcher block table in the bright circular alcove and finished their coffee.

"I have to get home to the house. My oldest son and two friends stayed there a few days while I was away. God knows what surprises await me. You know how twenty-year-olds are about mountain cabins!"

Meredith smiled at Dusty's reference to his "mountain cabin," a redwood house built on a cliff overlooking the Santa Monica mountains with a view to the ocean. She had enjoyed weekends in the secluded hide-away, but not this weekend. A phone conversation with Cassie O'Connell Ainsworth after Bettina's memorial service had prompted the two to spend the day together. Meredith was curious about why the woman was in LA to begin with, the manuscript and how she ended up at the funeral service.

"We've met briefly and talked casually a number of times," explained Meredith. "But never really spent any time together. We're going to have lunch and remember Bettina. She has a book manuscript in which I suspect Bettina plays a big role. I'm curious what it is. Besides," she added without guile, "who knew you'd be home this soon?"

Theirs was an easy-going relationship, three years old at that time, and never based on demands or expectation. The lightness of it worked well for both. Meredith was admittedly shy of long-term commitments.

Dusty smiled agreeably, as always, promised to call her the next day and left, pulling his bulging backpack over his shoulder. He turned to kiss her good-bye, then looked at her with concern. "Have a good day but try to let go of some of this drama over Bettina. Mysteries are fun, but most often they're not even really mysterious. And if they are, they can be dangerous. I'm betting Bettina Grant can haunt with a wicked vengeance."

"You're just worried about competition from a detective who sends cinnamon buns," said Meredith, pushing a strand of copper blonde hair away from her face, grinning flirtatiously.

"That, too," said Dusty as he kissed her casually on the mouth then turned and left. Meredith watched him lope casually down the steps and to his car, and thought to herself, speaking of buns, a terrific set on that man.

The first order of business was a call to Raymond's office, which Meredith dialed while she poured a final cup of coffee and made a list for the housekeeper who was scheduled to clean the unit that afternoon. She didn't expect to reach Raymond, but to leave a message and get on with a much-needed day away from pressure and work drama. His voice was a surprise not altogether welcomed.

"I didn't think you'd be working on a Saturday, Raymond," she said. "This is Meredith Ogden and I called to thank you for the cinnamon bun and to see if there's any news from your investigation."

"Yes, it's Saturday, Ogden, but that doesn't stop the flow of crime in the beautiful Hills of Beverly," he said drily. "Thanks acknowledged, but before we get on to the business of Bettina Grant—it's your turn."

"My turn? For what?" asked Meredith, puzzled.

"For apologies. Or is walking out on an uninformed and well-intentioned detective standard behavior for the hoi-ploy of the movie industry?"

"'No, it isn't typical behavior—well, maybe it is typical, but not of me and I am sorry. I'm a little tired of being asked the same question. That's all."

"Just remember, Ogden, whoever inherits the column does figure into this situation. In fact, the column is turning out to be a big issue. Maybe you're too close to it to notice that plenty of others would like to be in your shoes. I hear that everywhere I go."

Meredith had not considered that thought. "I see your point. Does that mean I am a suspect, detective?"

"Probably not—I worry you're more of a potential target, under the circumstances. But to answer your question, here's where I use an old and cliched line," he chuckled, "Miss Ogden, everyone is suspect until we solve the crime."

"Was it a crime? Or just a poorly intentioned dose of medication?"

"Since there's nothing to show that Bettina Grant typically took pills of any kind, and there were no other identifiable artifacts. Sorry—medicine bottles, prescriptions and such. And suicide seems very unlikely…there's no motivation or indication…we're tending in the direction of foul play."

"I was hoping to feel relieved—like no real predators were out there after Bettina. I've been a little worried because last night someone nearly ran me down and did manage to knock my date to the ground before speeding off into the night."

"Where was this?" Raymond's voice turned serious.

Meredith explained the circumstances of the freak accident to him. He listened as she told the story. Then she added the rumor that Joey O'Neal had "aggressive bitterness" at her on his mind. Instead of pursuing the accident, Raymond said, "Tell me more about the Joey O'Neal story? I'm trying to tie up connections here and so far, the only loose end with regard to people fearing Bettina or you might be someone connected to Joey—or the circumstances involving his visit to the bar."

"I don't know any more yet," Meredith reported. "In fact, I want to drive out and visit the bar sometime today or tomorrow and talk in person with the owner. I'm out of leads otherwise. No one's talking. Not even my usual contacts who tend to be loose cannons."

"Please don't do that. Leave the crime investigation to the police, Ogden."

"This isn't police work, Raymond," she said angrily, emphasizing his last name. "It is called good reporting."

"Look," he said with an exasperated sigh, "you say vengeance is on O'Neal's mind, and someone just tried to hit you with a car—and now you're telling me that there's no harm in peaking underneath the covers of one of Hollywood's most glamorous beds. And the bed of a guy who's already been arrested for beating up a fan! You're not dealing in glamour issues any longer. And if you plan to go out there, at least call me so one of my people can go with you."

"Maybe," said Meredith before bidding the detective a cool farewell and hanging up the phone.

CHAPTER 11

SATURDAY AFTERNOON

West Los Angeles and Beverly Hills wore one of its rare cloaks of natural splendor on that Saturday as Meredith drove the short 15 minutes from her townhouse to the Beverly Hills Hotel. It was not a "critical" day in the estimation of the Air Quality Board, meaning one could actually see the skyline of the various L.A. basin commercial centers—each its own cluster of high-rise buildings—or at least an outline of the mountains North or East. These were the days when out-of-towners took mental snapshots of Southern California and subsequently used them as motivation to pack up the family belongings and follow the sun, not realizing such crystal days were the exception, not the norm.

It took determination for Meredith to push away thoughts of the murder and any danger they threatened as she drove up to the imposing hotel. Kitschy in its pinkness, it was surrounded by overgrown greenery and palm trees stretching languidly into the sky. She marveled that the place had not changed at all in the 12 years her life had wound around it in one way or another, and that when she drove up to the front coach entrance, the year could just as easily have been 1951 or even 1991. That was the kind of consistency and hospitality that kept the place always in high vogue.

Crossing through the intimate lobby, she smiled as she always did at the garb and demeanor of the patrons. A familiar-looking elderly figure was cuddled up to the registration desk conversing in near-whispered tones. Big sunglasses shielded much of the woman's face, and a thick turban covered equally as much of her head, leaving only a few shards of skin exposed to the public eye. She wore long silver slacks and a knee-length sable coat. She clutched a worn crocheted handbag under one arm, under the other, a Siamese cat stared impassively at an unknown subject.

Meredith dialed Cassie from the house phones, moments later making her way down the corridor to the room number Cassie had given her. Before she had a chance to knock, the door swung open and the tall, well- appointed brunette greeted her enthusiastically.

"It's been a long time," said Cassie.

"Years if you don't count Bettina's service yesterday."

"A scene from a 1960s Fellini movie. I stepped back into a world I left behind. All those people—like I remembered them—except most of them I had never met, and the others were a lot older than I remembered!"

She waved Meredith into the room's interior, a sunny place with furnishings reminiscent of early Hollywood but well maintained with modern pastel fabrics and accents. Smiling in from outside the windows was the verdant and incessant tropical plumage that characterized the Hotel.

"Definitely Fellini," said Meredith, tossing her purse and gray leather bomber jacket onto the chair. "The difference between your era and mine is you had all those people around—most of the time, from what I've heard. I hardly ever see them. Imagine how strange it was to be at Bettina's funeral as a part of them."

"Look, the network is picking this up today," Cassie interjected. "What do you say we take ourselves down to the Polo Lounge and have some lunch and check out the action?" Meredith quickly understood Cassie's plan.

The famous Polo Lounge had been one of filmland's waterholes for four decades. During the week, agents and managers fought for well-positioned tables in order to be seen by and to see the key players and with whom they were lunching. A seemingly casual mealtime dalliance could well mean a motion picture deal in the works, a new romantic alliance, or a new agency-client relationship in the formation. All were good to know about.

"Nice outfit—perfect for the Polo Lounge," said Cassie as the two found their way to the maître d' post.

"You're looking well, yourself," said Meredith, slightly intimidated by Cassie's frankness. Meredith, in khaki walking shorts, a fuzzy white sweater with a paisley scarf, and large gold hoop earrings, mothered the question nagging at her.

"Just curious," she began, "when did you see Bettina this week? To give her your manuscript?"

Cassie paused for a moment and then replied, "I didn't see her. I called her late Monday afternoon, hoping to stop by later if she had a rare night at home. But no such luck. She said she was finishing her work and about to leave. Told me to put the manuscript at the back door by the office. I did a couple of hours later. I guess she never got a chance to read it."

"She tried," said Meredith, looking at the menu. "Didn't get the chance. You see anyone or anything going on in the house when you got there?"

Cassie regarded her closely and replied, "No. All I noticed was a light on in the back patio around the office door. A dim light upstairs. Was someone supposed to be there?"

Meredith shook her head. "Just trying to fit the puzzle together." She again remembered Bettina never left outside lights on after eleven o'clock—had motion-sensor beams in the garage for when she drove in at night.

"What's your book about?" she casually inquired.

"It's really kind of a composite of the early days of entertainment news and celebrities," said Cassie also nonchalantly.

"You're not burning Bettina, are you?" Meredith worked hard to continue the casual tone.

"No, of course not," Cassie shrugged, then smiled. "There is no burning that woman."

"I hate the thought of someone dissing Bettina in light of everything that's happened."

"Well, figure that no matter whether living, or now a legend, a sizzling book about her life would only increase the value of the name Bettina Grant," shrugged Cassie, then quickly added, "but that's not what my book is about—at least not most of it!"

Meredith winced inwardly and reminded herself to calm down. "Did the police talk with you?" she changed the subject.

"Sure. Marty someone. Told him pretty much what I told you. He said 'thanks.'" Cassie, in tailored black jeans and a red gnarled-knit V-Neck sweater, dismissed the conversation. A red satin biking cap sat on top of her thick, curly brunette bob. Her dark eyes danced about the room taking in every movement, face and grouping.

By the time pink linen napkins were ceremoniously placed on their laps, Meredith's eye was drawn to a couple who had arrived shortly after she and Cassie. The latter noticed the attention and asked, "You know those people?"

"I'm not sure. He looks familiar. I've met him somewhere. She's familiar, too, and kind of staring at me. I think I may have seen them at Bettina's service—in fact I kind of remember them talking to Larry Grant. Never mind. I'm sorry. I'm a little shaky and paranoid. Keep wondering if I'm being followed."

Soon the two women chatted in the non-stop staccato of two diligent woodpeckers at work on a common tree. As dessert was offered, both had mellowed and set aside any distrust or distance. Two gin fizzes had assisted in disarming the pair.

"I think you had the fun Hollywood," said Meredith, eyeing a piece of cheesecake on the dessert tray held before her. She pointed at it resolutely and continued, "Hollywood journalism today is more about production deals and directorial debuts and schedules. When I thumb through the stuff you and Bettina were involved in, sometimes I'm a little jealous. We hardly ever see a real scoop. The TV hard news shows get those. And any real glamour stories go to the TV magazine format like *Entertainment Tonight* or *People Magazine*.

"Even the big star interviews are dry. Stars like Kevin Costner talk about their next directorial assignment and live out of California."

"If you hanker for the old days, you could join up with the *U.S. Star*," chuckled Cassie. "That's what our original days were like. Our subsidizers were movie magazines—the old-fashioned kind. I chased down more wedding stories, wrote articles that left barely a dry eye in the place."

"Network news must be a refreshing change," observed Meredith.

"Ha," Cassie retorted pointing to a piece of strawberry cream pie languishing on the dessert tray. "An espresso for me..." Meredith held up two fingers indicating one for herself as well.

"News in general is changing or haven't you noticed the infamous 'sweeps' months lately," Cassie continued. "Every news organization in the country leans on the luster of the movie and TV industry and the popularity of celebrity exposure on their shows when they need to seasonally pump ratings. The way I see it," she leaned forward on her elbows and spoke intently, "what you do, what I used to do—at least we were honest. We were writing about people—their passions and flaws and miseries and triumphs, true. But we were in a very parochial world, not the mainstream of the news business."

Meredith exploded into cynical laughter. "Since when? You were trained under Bettina Grant just as I was. Did you ever even suggest to her that what she did was trivial?"

"Parochial, not trivial—but even so, God no," said Cassie. "I didn't know it was trivial until about my eighth year with Bettina. Suddenly I felt as vital as a career counselor in a hospice ward."

"But it was fun for a long time, wasn't it?" prodded Meredith.

Cassie smiled nostalgically. "Yes, it was. It really was. In fact, the fun of those years kept me from being serious about anything real until I was at least 35 years old."

Meredith felt an uncomfortable heat simmering quietly within her ego but was drawn to the conversation because Cassie was so persistent about the subject. And deep down inside it struck a familiar note.

"Who's your favorite star?" Cassie quickly changed direction.

"I…well…." Meredith tried to remember the long list of stars she had met and interviewed. "That's hard. There are so many."

"I used to fumble for an answer, too," said Cassie, "until I'd been away from it for a couple of years. Then those answers seemed crystal clear."

"Okay then, who was your favorite interview? Your favorite star person?"

"John Wayne—most memorable. Probably because I spent time with him on location in a dusty little town in Mexico where he always filmed, a long way from Hollywood. Ultimate reporter role playing," smiled Cassie. "Riding in jeeps across rugged plains, traveling by horse to a location. He was always a gentleman, called me 'Little Lady.' Once saved me from stumbling into a cactus patch, said, 'Imagine me trying to explain to your bosses why you came home punctured up by those things?' Nice, no hiding from the political criticism that dogged him, hidden skeletons…"

"Besides real super stars, you got the 60's and start of the 70's…Vietnam wind-down, Watergate, the emergence of rock music. I've got stars talking about being producers and directors."

"Wait five years and look back," smiled Cassie, raising an eyebrow. "You know how fast things change. A new war—probably a new criminal president—new diseases and cures, the world moves a lot faster than it used to. You have to stay on roller skates to keep up much less ahead of it."

"No, there's a difference. The stars don't seem to be much involved in those events."

"Not now, maybe, but they will. Like a roller coaster. It's 1983. There's a lot of news ahead. There's AIDS and the homeless issues," persisted Cassie.

"It's really not the same as helping to disrupt a war or fell a hubristic president," sighed Meredith, reaching for her fork to attack the creamy dessert placed in front of her, but keeping a curious but elusive eye on the couple sitting nearby.

Several hours later, lounging on the patio of Cassie' hotel room. The two continued their conversation. "Five British rock stars were living in a nasty squalor—trash and dirty clothes all over the place, a month's worth of unwashed dishes and empty tequila bottles strewn throughout every room—in a rented Bel Air Mansion—a leased Rolls Royce parked out in front—scathingly criticizing the American values system. But living and enjoying the very heart of it as visitors. The sixties!" Cassie shook her head.

"Today all the rock stars talk about is their record deals, who's directing or co-staring in their videos and the lawsuits over lip-synching. Maybe a little culture disintegration would be more interesting."

"Ask me anything about Lawrence Welk!" Cassie challenged Meredith with humor in her voice. Meredith opened her dark eyes coyly and innocently asked, "Who's Lawrence Welk?"

"Touché. But be not smug! He's back on cable in all his 1950's style. And a lot of his former band members and entertainers play the nationwide fair circuit!" She fell silent for a moment. "We saw their romances, their weddings, their babies born, their contract disputes with Welk. And we saw their sorrow when a deranged fan stalked the father of his star juvenile singing trio—for a long time—threatening violence, and in fact, finally shot him dead. It was a sobering moment, yet no one even remembers it."

"I'm working on an interesting, but very different, story right now, when I'm not swept away by Bettina's death." Meredith said with a smirk. "I could become a real reporter again if I weren't careful." She outlined the series of events that had unfolded over the past week. Cassie listened intently, nodding from time to time, as the story lengthened.

"I 'm going to ride out to the Valley sometime this weekend and talk with the bar owner myself. I can't get through to him by phone and no one else is talking."

"Want some company?" asked Cassie.

"So long as you remember that it's our story here and doesn't find its way elsewhere."

"Cagney and Lacey, Starsky and Hutch…" said Cassie, as she nodded her accord.

"Hopefully not Rosencrantz and Guildenstern," said Meredith. "Remember what happened to them."

"I have to do something," she told Cassie. "But it will only take a second." She phoned Raymond's office, feeling much relieved that he was not around. She left a message for him then hung up hurriedly.

"If we're talking going inconspicuous," ventured Meredith as they walked to Cassie's rental car, a rented silver Honda, "how about losing the cap?" She cringed in anticipation of Cassie's response.

"Well if it's biker-girl authenticity we're concerned about," said Cassie, "what about that cute little preppie outfit you're wearing? Ankle socks? Can we stop at a Walmart and get you some jeans?"

"Okay, okay. Keep the damned hat but be prepared to catch the full attention of everyone inside the Happy Harley. And no need for Walmart—I keep jeans and t-shirts in my trunk for when I need them."

"Go get them," said Cassie as she handed her keys to the valet, and discretely removed the little red cap. The couple sitting near them in the restaurant walked by, stopped to talk for a moment, then headed toward the street.

CHAPTER 12

LATE SATURDAY AFTERNOON

Raymond had missed lunch and in late afternoon, walked into a sandwich shop a block from the office, deciding between a healthy turkey on whole wheat versus a seductive Reuben. His son Will's voice echoed, admonishing him for eating poorly. He shook his head and went for the Reuben, reasoning he'd run four miles that morning and it was very late for lunch, anyhow, nearly three-thirty. He considered it part of dinner.

"Smells good," said his partner who arrived at the headquarters at the same time as Raymond.

"What're you doing here on Saturday," asked the older detective. Marty Escobar laughed. "Same thing you are... catching up for an hour or so with the paperwork while it's quiet." Raymond grunted, "Never quiet enough."

"By the way—talked with Grant's sister, Luanne, and associated family yesterday." Escobar shook his head. "Lots of tears, no idea who would want to kill sister...except for a few thousand actors, producers, directors...but none she knew would actually do it. And she's not involved at all with Bettina's world. Luanne's husband, Herb, came in while I was there. Kept shaking his head and muttering things like 'Just bizarre. Bat-shit-crazy world that woman lived in. Different planets.'

"Grant's daughter, Lorraine, and her husband Max weren't around, had gone off to Universal Studios before they drive home tomorrow. Luanne said Max was trying to start a new real estate business and apparently had asked Bettina for money a few months ago, but she turned him down. They live in Albuquerque and haven't been in LA in a year. Everyone could confirm their whereabouts. Lea, the younger daughter wasn't there either. I'll catch up with her tomorrow or Monday. The others told me there had been real fireworks between her and her mother, almost fisticuffs at one point.

"They all say that the good Ms. Ogden should have more answers because she was closest to the source. No help."

Raymond recounted his conversation with Larry Grant. "Not much help there either. Says the split with Bettina about a decade ago was rough and tumble for a while but they managed to smooth it out—he said for the kids' sake. But that's what daughter Lea's animosity is about. She blamed her mother for being too 'addicted to fame and power,' driving her dad away, but is now angry at her father for his hedonistic lifestyle. He says he's changed, got along great with Bettina, even allowed her access to the house for as long as she wanted. Is engaged to Vivian Malden. She's a psychotherapist and daughter of the guy who runs one of the studios. She's already alibied him on the night of Bettina's death."

Raymond sighed and turned to his desk when he noticed a phone message there. "Sonofabitch," he blurted out.

Marty Escobar looked up. "So much for the quiet."

"How can a girl so smart and apparently talented, be so dense at times?"

"Ah—you mean the elusive Miss Ogden. A *woman*, by the way—unless you want to get hurt. What now?"

"One minute she'd sad, next one scared, next insightful, always willful—and then really naive about what a homicide is about." Escobar was puzzled.

"How about catching a beer in Pacoima?" Raymond snapped. His partner shrugged. "I'm not expected home until dinner."

The two men rose, Raymond tossed out most of his sandwich as they headed toward the garage. "I'll explain on the road," he said, not happily.

☆

It was four-thirty and Meredith and Cassie had anonymously phoned the bar to confirm the presence of the owner. They were in Cassie's rented car heading north on the San Diego Freeway. They chose the rental car in lieu of the Mustang, which still sat in the hotel parking garage, reasoning that they would be less conspicuous in a plain colored Honda. Meredith explained to Cassie the background of the unfolding Joey O'Neal story, echoing the detective's warnings.

"So, who is this detective guy you have to check in with?" asked Cassie a few miles further along the freeway.

"Detective T.K. Raymond. He's the 'High Profile Crimes' investigator on Bettina's, um…demise. He wasn't pleased when I told him about the car hitting Fred, and even less enthusiastic about me going out to the Happy Harley."

"Am I doing a stupid thing?" asked Cassie. "Is death and disfigurement involved?"

"I don't think so, but we ought to watch our backs. These are biker boys—the big, mean kind."

"No week-end yuppie riders here—lawyers and dentists?"

"Only if they're really stupid. The cool ones hang out near the cappuccino bars in Encino and Manhattan Beach!"

"So why hasn't this detective guy done this stuff himself?"

"Because he's investigating Bettina's death—not the Joey O'Neal story and there's nothing to connect the two. At least right now. So, this is my gig, not his."

"Then why's he so worried? He interested?"

"Not hardly—he's an older guy. Mostly he—and everyone else—think I probably know something or am the key to information that will help lead to whatever happened to Bettina. But he did send me a cinnamon bun," Meredith chuckled.

"You have designs on this cop?"

"Uh—no! He's about a decade older than me and 'personally' disconnected from the case. I think he's just concerned about my health and well-being in the shadow of a murder—and he seems to think I have information that I haven't. I don't even know if he's single, married, gay or whatever."

"Is he cute?"

"Cute? Too old for cute. Sonia calls him a cross between Tommy Lee Jones and Richard Widmark."

"Quiet, strong, tough, sensitive? I'm surprised Sonia even knows who Richard Widmark is."

"She's surprisingly aware of anything celebrity," Meredith mused as the Happy Harley Bar sign loomed high to the right off the freeway.

Cassie turned off at the exit, looped back on the next major street and pulled in front of the dirty, run-down building, neon beer advertisements flashing in the dusty windows. Scruffy or not, it boasted a long row of heavy, massive motorcycles along the front curb.   Most were black, many gleaming under the dazzle of newly polished chrome. A fake hitching post ran along the sidewalk in front of the building and there were shoddy, paint-needy swinging doors, at the entrance.

"Not a yuppie in sight," whispered Cassie as the two women pushed the doors aside. Meredith acknowledged the fact through clenched teeth.   The bar interior looked and smelled like ten years of bad hangovers.   Wooden tables and chairs were strewn without pattern across the dusty room. Chairs covered mostly in vinyl, were split and stained. The massive wooden bar was scarred with the petroglyphs of a hard drinking, hard talking, hard fighting era. Even the floorboards were eloquent with a history of tough nights and scrappy people.

A dozen patrons stood around a large TV screen hanging at the far end of the bar, watching a late afternoon football game. One or two of the crowd were female but dressed in the same leather or denim motorcycle garb as their male companions. And, they were built similarly—thick and hard, often with long, mostly wind-matted hair. A blonde with an exaggerated multi-hued Mohawk clung to the beefy arm of a man who not only wore his hair to his waist but sported a midchest-length buckshot-colored beard as well.

"What, exactly, do biker chicks drink?" whispered Cassie.

"Not mineral water," murmured Meredith under her breath. "Not the Polo Lounge, is it?" she added sweetly as the bartender, a fleshy man with a large belly overflowing his belt stepped up to face them. He wore a Hawaiian shirt that stretched the integrity of the buttons holding it together in the front. The nose bridge of his glasses was held together by a band aid.

"A beer," said Cassie confidently.

"Two," Meredith spoke up quickly.

"Any particular brand?" asked the thick man, eyeing the two with amused curiosity.

"Oh, anything… Heineken."

The bartender looked at her oddly, shrugged and said, "Sure."

"Heineken?" purred Meredith. "You might just as well have said, a white wine spritzer with a pink umbrella, please."

"Well, it's all I could think of on such short notice!"

When the bartender returned and poured their beer, Meredith spoke up.

"We're looking for Pat Dowley. Is he here?"

"He is, right in front of you," said the bartender.

"Well," Meredith began uncertainly, "I'm Meredith Ogden. I've tried to call you a few times about the night Joey O'Neal was arrested in here. Last week."

The big man eyed her closely, surveying every inch of her compact figure, then said, "Well, it's a cinch you ain't that pretty TV lady Mary Hart."

Meredith tamped down a snide response. "No, I'm a newspaper correspondent. I broke the story about the arrest."

The big man began to wipe down the bar around them with a dingy rag. "Lady, I don't know a thing you don't already know from the cops. Like I told them, and the others, this big celebrity comes in here to have a beer. A couple of seconds later a couple of baby-faced teenagers wander in and walk up to him and before they have a chance to say anything, he takes on one of the kids and pulverizes him. I call the cops and they're here in a second—a lot faster than when I need them for Saturday night fights—and then it's all over. I don't know nothing else. And the cops told me to keep quiet on even that much."

"Why'd the cops tell you that?" asked Cassie. "Most of this is public record."

Dowley shrugged. "Who knows? The guy from the Feds said silence was golden, was in my best interest...and all that stuff."

"He remind you about your liquor license?" asked Cassie.

"Not in so many words."

"Why would the Feds be involved with this?" asked Meredith. "We are talking about the FBI?"

Dowley ran a fat hand across his lips imitating a zipper.

"Joey come in here often?" Meredith asked. Dowley shook his head no. "Ever even been here before?" Another head shake, then the big man shrugged and walked away.

"Well, how about that?" whistled Meredith under her breath. "So, there is more."

"Yeah, but how..." Cassie's words were cut short by the sudden appearance of a large presence moving between her and Meredith.

"Hi girls! Let me buy you a real beer. We can make it a party."

Meredith wrinkled her nose. She sensed the intruder before she actually saw him. What she saw was a hard, round body, massive in its grimy jeans and battle-worn leather vest and a face, ruddied like a fast food hamburger patty. A weather-bleached green bandana was tied around the broad forehead securing a thinning mane of greying, limp hair. He looked at Cassie and grinned merrily—his yellowed front teeth showing in the dim light of the bar.

"Thanks, but we're just leaving," Cassie smiled.

"You go on ahead," the man said to Meredith, placing a thick arm on the counter, cutting off articulation between her and Cassie. "I'll talk to this young lady for a while."

"Thanks so much," said Cassie politely, "but our husbands are waiting for us, and we do need to leave." She leaned forward around the thick elbow propped on the counter and lifted troubled brows, quizzical eyes toward Meredith.

The brawny biker exploded in a loud guffaw. "Girls, it's Saturday evening and you're hanging out in this bar. There's a hubby waiting at home? Kids, too? I'll bet."

"Four of them," purred Cassie demurely, suddenly aware that her arm was locked in an iron grip of the big man. He plopped against the bar, his big form looming.

Meredith thought frantically, searching for an easy way out.

"Jackie, come 'ere," bellowed the big man. "Come talk to these two nice girls with me." A dozen eyes turned from the

TV set at the other end of the bar and fixed on the trio. A few boots scuffled in their direction. The bar manager Pat Dowley was nowhere to be seen.

"Actually, sir we're here from America's Most Real People," chirped Meredith, two light fingers tapping the big hand resting on the bar. Distracted, the biker lessened his hold on Cassie who slipped her arm out of the iron grip.

"And you could be the perfect subject for us to put onto video for our next show," Cassie added. Both women glanced at one another in a mutual appreciation.

The intruder suddenly relaxed his stance, his attention and interest obviously piqued. "Video," he said loudly. "This young lady wants to make a video."

Oh, oh, thought Meredith.

"There you are, Trixie. We wondered where you went." A gruff male voice suddenly cleared the air. "We thought we told you to meet us in the bar down the street. Dan and I have been over there waiting for you two. Did we give you the wrong address?'

All eyes turned to the solid forms of Detectives Raymond and his partner Marty Escobar, standing at the opposite end of the bar from the TV. Marty rested against a bar stool, his arms crossed against his chest, and Raymond perched a foot dramatically on the floor railing, propping open his leather jacket, baring the pistol in his shoulder holster.

Seconds later, Raymond stood outside on the sidewalk barking admonitions at the two women. "What the hell do you think you're doing? Look at you two. The Beverly Hills newsgirls after their big scoop. And the headlines would have been, 'Two West L.A. women beaten and raped in Pacoima bar!' Is that the scoop you're looking for?"

"We were doing just fine by ourselves!" snapped Meredith.

Marty started to laugh into his hand. Raymond drew back from her, regarding her with raised eyebrows. Cassie began to chuckle. "Come on, detective. Were you really going to shoot it out with the boys in there?"

He looked down and chuckled softly. "Maybe." Suddenly all four were laughing.

"Trixie?"

"Look," said Raymond after the laughter had settled, "I don't want either of you screwing around in this situation any further. Let me check out the FBI thing. I have more contacts to do it and I'll get answers a lot faster than either of you. Believe me, it's safer if I do it! You can just say thank you if there's anything to it.

"In the meantime, seeing's how it's dinner time on a Saturday night and Marty and I had to cancel the evening's plans because of this lady's phone message at my office, can I buy dinner for you two hot shot reporters? I'll buy—but it won't be at the Polo Lounge!"

Meredith looked at him suspiciously then at Marty, standing off quietly with a knowing smirk on this face, "How did you know about the Polo Lounge...?"

"Goes with the turf," he said, turning away from them with a wave. "Let's go to Gino's in Santa Monica. It's good Italian, close to everyone and not fancy."

"Gotta beg off," said Marty, shoving his hands deep in his pockets. "Not that I wouldn't love a nice dinner out on Raymond's dime—but I'm expected home for dinner, and I don't think I can use Gino's fettucine as an excuse. Sorry. Drop me at the station?" Raymond agreed.

Meredith and Cassie shrugged at one another, bid Marty good night, and found their car to follow Raymond.

"What was the message you left for him anyhow?" asked Cassie. "It made him cancel his plans."

"He's just being a drama queen. I said I was going out to the Valley to have a beer with a couple of bikers."

Three hours later Meredith, Cassie and Raymond had returned to the room at the Beverly Hills Hotel. The two women were sprawled on the floor, well into their third bottle of red wine. Raymond was the most sober because before going to the restaurant he had decided to drop Cassie's rental car at the hotel and drive the two women in his own car to the restaurant. He suspected wine would be involved so he volunteered to be the designated driver. Something else that came with a cop's turf.

"Hope the neighbors don't think I'm having a wild orgy in my room," laughed Cassie after a spirited exchange of cop jokes. Raymond smirked.

"I think we've all drunk too much," said Meredith.

"Well, some of us, anyhow," chuckled the detective. He looked at Cassie with wary eyes and asked, "By the way did you see Bettina on Monday night"

Cassie shook her head. "No. I told Meredith that I talked with her just as she was about to leave for dinner hoping to catch her and deliver my manuscript. But she said to leave it at the door, and she'd call me the next day. Well, I guess she couldn't... you know...I called her that morning but didn't know about the situation. The secretary just said she wasn't available." The silence in the room was heavy.

Raymond turned to Meredith. "Have you read the manuscript?"

"No, you have the only copy in a plastic bag in your evidence room." She looked at Cassie, who began fidgeting with her glass.

"I read some of it," he said. "I put on vinyl gloves, I should say, for more reasons than one—it's…well…intriguing." Noticing Cassie's obvious discomfort, he quickly changed the subject. "So, what made you escape the wondrous world of Bettina Grant, anyhow?" He slipped off his running shoes and settled into one of the overstuffed chairs in the well-appointed hotel room.

"I think," said Cassie, measuring her words, "it was just time to go. You know? I couldn't grow anymore, and I couldn't live in Bettina's shadow any longer. She knew it. She was great about it."

"If that's so," interjected Meredith. "What in the world made her change her mind so completely about you?"

Cassie took a long drink of her wine, leaned back and sighed. "I don't know. I thought you might, Meredith. One minute we're friends and confidants, the next not even speaking. I think, two years before I left, Bettina divorced Larry after 25 years, and I guess she went through a hard, emotional phase. I didn't recognize it, never experiencing a serious break up of my own. I simply didn't understand or appreciate her pain. Bettina, as you know, would never open up about personal pain. Talk generally about it, talk about others who have experienced it— sure. But not her own. And even I bought the facade.

"When I left, I think she felt abandoned, maybe like a daughter turning her back on mom. But it was a two-way street, you know. I remember sitting in my dingy little studio flat on the edge of the campus at Columbia one night when Bettina phoned to ask why we weren't friends any longer. 'What do you mean?' I asked in shock.

"'Well, you never call me and ask me how I am,' was her answer. I stuttered out some sort of shocked response that seemed to appease her for the time being. Then she told me all her problems with the column, with her new assistant, with her life in general. When I hung up, I realized she had never once asked me how I was doing—or even what I was doing. I was the one in uncharted waters, terrified of a new world away from mom and Hollywood. I even kind of hoped she would put in a good word for me in some of the network circles. Never happened, and she was hurt because I wasn't tending to her needs.

"But then you came along." Cassie's voice turned cheerful, "with great writing skills and apparently more patience than I ever had with Bettina's ego—which, I've heard, became a work of art over the years."

Meredith hesitated before answering, then offered, "Like you said, it was a two-way street."

"How did you get along with Larry?" Cassie suddenly focused on Meredith, turning the conversation away from the detective.

"What do you mean?"

"Did he...well, harass...you? He sure did with the rest of us."

Meredith sat up in alert surprise. "He was gone by the time I came aboard. I hardly ever saw him. Bettina talked about him, or course, and he would occasionally stop in to see her. A couple of times he brought along the ding-a-ling of the month, but I only talked with him a few times. It always surprised me that he would flaunt his ladies in Bettina's face—in her home, but I didn't know anything more than that. He's always been pleasant. Has a good sense of humor on the phone."

"In this day of sexual harassment," smiled Cassie, "he'd be in jail by now if I—or our former secretary Carolyn—had any say in the matter."

"What did this guy do?" Raymond sat up at full attention.

"Mostly he made a terrible pest of himself and put us all

in a very awkward situation. He'd come into the offices early in the morning. Our offices were cut off from Bettina's, as you both know, and she couldn't see or hear what was going on back there. He would start to nibble the back of our necks, our ears, sometimes stroke our hair, our noses.

"We tried everything to convince him to leave us alone. We asked nicely, pushed him away—very hard at times—we got up and walked out of the office. But he'd be back the next morning. I swore at him and threatened to tell Bettina. He'd look at me with a twinkle in his eye and say, 'Oh really?' Of course, he was right. Neither Carolyn nor I was willing to risk our job—at first—and we didn't want to hurt Bettina. So, we put up with it. Until he cornered Carolyn one morning when both Bettina and I were out of the office, and practically drug her into the bedroom. He'd forced his hand down the front of her jeans and had pushed her half-way down the hallway when she hauled off and slugged him in the face. Larry's always been a little vain. He released his hold on her. That afternoon she quit—quietly—no notice or drama. Bettina never knew why, and I never broke my promise to Carolyn to keep the incident a secret."

"Wow!" said Raymond. Meredith was staring at Cassie, still in shock.

"Yeah, wow! Right down to the last line on the divorce settlement. Does he still own the house?" Asked Cassie. Surprise shook Meredith to her core. The detective pulled his supple body into a sitting position, fully engaged.

"Bettina wanted to stay in the house and Larry wanted to travel and live unencumbered for a while," Cassie continued. "So, he moved into one of those singles complexes that had it all including furniture, maid service and nubile neighbors. The house was refinanced so that Bettina could use the cash for a TV talk show pilot which she'd been trying to raise the money to produce and star in. She never got it off the ground, by the way, but was allowed to stay in the house and pay the mortgage. She was supposed to relinquish it to him in five years, or anytime thereafter when he felt he needed it. I guess he hasn't. Anyhow, she banked the cash from the refinance—must be a nice nest egg by now. And she's still in the house. I don't remember all the particulars, but it was too good to be true, knowing Larry as we did," she waved her hand dismissively and reached again for the wine bottle. Raymond was making mental notes. Meredith sat quietly, staring into the large glass of wine she was finishing off.

"I think it's time for me to go," said the detective. Meredith shook her head to clear the numbness from sitting in a folded position and of drinking much more alcohol than she was accustomed to. Then she expressed her own intention to leave, and Cassie pulled herself from her own sprawl on the floor.

"It's been fun, Meredith. Can we do it again sometime?"

"You liked the feel of the old grind?"

"That's why I'm here," said Cassie absently, lifting her slender body from the floor.

"Really. Like how?"

Cassie's face slowly reddened. "Don't you know? Mort Agee, my agent, has proposed me as Bettina's replacement."

Meredith mouth fell open. "I don't understand. She wasn't even…dead…when you arrived. And then, the network, your husband…"

"God this is awkward," winced Cassie. "Mort said you'd turned down the column, you'd made it clear you weren't interested." Meredith continued to stare at Cassie numbly. The brunette fumbled to continue the explanation." I originally came to town to meet with Mort about the book I'm writing. He called me when he heard the news about Bettina—and then called Russ at the syndicate. I stuck around to explore the situation. Here's the thing: I'm 42 years old, the politics and pace of network news are a killer. Bob has been offered a good job opportunity right here in L.A. I'm looking for something for myself as well. Maybe even one kid before I'm old and noticeably gray."

"Great," snapped Meredith. "Just what this industry needs. One more housefrau who wants a glamorous part-time job in Hollywood and thinks she can write a column with a kid on her hip and two free theater tickets in her pocket. Damn it, Cassie, you know better than that!"

"Is this a done deal?" interrupted the detective.

Cassie shook her head. "No, of course not, but…"

Meredith waved her hand defensively and said wearily. "I'm tired and I drank too much. And I need to think. Mostly I need to sleep. It's been a long week."

She squared herself to face Cassie, and pointed an angry finger, "One thing—the O'Neal story is mine! No discussion. That's the deal, no matter what." Cassie nodded in timid agreement.

"Well, she's just one of a long line," said the detective as they crossed the hotel lobby, nearly empty except for the bell captain and night clerk. "She hasn't any more chance of getting the job than any of the others. And you have the lead. You know that."

"This is too much. I'm getting old, or maybe just falling apart," Meredith sighed.

"No, you're tired and confused. And hurt."

"Yes, I am. But she didn't need to come three thousand miles to sign the deal with Mort Agee. Why was she here? I wonder what's really in that book of hers. Maybe Bettina really wouldn't have wanted to read it! Maybe it drove her to drink! Have you checked out Cassie's where abouts last Monday night?"

Raymond sighed. "I didn't associate her with the murder. It seemed like a long shot, but I'll have to follow up on it. Can you get home by yourself?"

"It's not far." Her voice sounded fragile.

"Leave your car here and I'll drive you."

Meredith looked at him with innocent sleep-hungry eyes. "Okay—but my car…"

"Stand here and I'll take care of that." He walked over to the front desk staffer and spoke for a moment, reaching into his pocket and leaving a $10 bill behind.

"There's a police car a block away. I'll have one of them drive it to your house," he said as he rejoined her and waited for his own car. She looked at him with a disjointed expression.

"If you think…not happening," she barked, climbing into the passenger side of the car when it arrived. "I'm not an easy pick up, detective. And you can stop calling me Ogden. I have a first name…" She stopped her tirade and laid her head back against the seat.

"That's not at all what I had in mind, believe me!" he gestured to the valet with open palms and a shrug. "She always leaves mad," he said to no one in particular, handing the valet a tip and climbing into the driver's seat. The car was silent all the way to Meredith's Brentwood townhouse.

Raymond pulled up in front of the walkway to her unit. She sat against the car's seat without moving, so he quickly opened his own door, got out and walked to her side. She looked at him with blank eyes through the window. "I hear your teeth gnashing all the way out here. Come on, let's go inside," he urged, opening her door and taking her arm to help her out.

"I'm sorry," she murmured as they reached the front door. "I'm just so tired—and sad and confused. What happened to my life?" Without comment, she handed him her house key. He reached around her and opened the door, steering her into the pleasant confines of the condo. She walked into the living room and collapsed onto the sofa. "I'll just lay down here for now."

She curled against the back cusions, her coat, gloves and scarf still on.

"No—you go to bed. I'll let myself out and leave the key under the matt. Your car should be back in the driveway soon and someone will be around to check on the place every couple of hours. Keep your doors and windows closed and locked."

She lifted herself with effort and headed for the floating stairs to the second floor. Then turned around, "Paco—my cat. Will you please feed him?"

"I guess," he said, surprised, looking toward the kitchen.

"Food in the fridge, cat on top of the fridge, bowl in the sink, and thanks," she responded to the unasked question that hung in the air. Then, she moved up the stairwell.

Raymond perused the refrigerator and given its spare contents, easily found the cat food. "Hello" he said to Paco on his perch overlooking the kitchen. "Just how much do you eat?" guessing how full Paco would want his bowl.

Returning the left-over can of food to the fridge, the detective rinsed off the spoon and watched Paco slurped his dinner loudly and gratefully. He felt a sense of accomplishment seeing the feline's pleasure. "When you finish, get up there and comfort your human," he directed the cat who looked at him blankly and went back to his bowl.

Raymond picked up the kitchen phone and punched in a few numbers, spoke quietly and quickly and hung up. He snapped off the kitchen light whispering, "There, cat, take that! Eat in the dark!" He heard no noise from the upstairs rooms. "Everything okay up there?" he called. No answer.

"Ogden? Meredith?" No answer but a slight mumble. He advanced the stairs hesitantly. At the top he could see into the master bedroom and that she had simply flopped on the bed still wearing her coat, scarf and even her knit gloves.

"At least take off the gloves." He made his way into the bedroom and helped her sit up, removed her coat and tossed it on a nearby chair. "Look," said Raymond, "It's no wonder you're exhausted. You've had a pretty devastating loss. They aren't easy…"

"Oh, Raymond, I know loss," she sighed, "believe me, I KNOW loss." She flopped back onto the bed, her eyes already closing. He pulled a throw from the bottom of the bed, tucking it around her.

"I like your hands," she whispered barely audibly.

"Why?"

"Lock the door when you leave."

He checked all the windows, sliding door locks, and front door, then he turned the key and placed it under the matt, joining the full set of keys also there belonging to Meredith's car. He waved to the two uniformed cops who had parked it in the complex's driveway, not far from the entrance to Meredith's door.

"What am I doing here?" Raymond wondered.

CHAPTER 14
SUNDAY—BEVERLY HILLS

Meredith had stripped off her clothes and crawled back under the covers during the night. But between anger toward Cassie and the past week's anxieties, she found sleep elusive and finally got up early. Paco blinked, confused by the hour.

By seven-thirty she was warming up in the earliest Sunday morning aerobics class at her health club, reasoning exercise was the best way to both work the alcohol from her system, and temper the anxiety tightening her body and mind like an over-tuned bow string. She retreated into the high beat aerobics music, moving across the wooden floor with the handful of other early morning exercisers. Pushing into the escalating rhythm, Meredith realized a need to clear not only her mind but her calendar for the week ahead. Anticipated intrusions would, without a doubt, interfere with writing a lucid column and articles each day.

She gathered her belongings as quickly as the class ended, then hurried home to shower and focus on work. It was the Sunday of the annual Christmas luncheon sponsored by the Hollywood Women's Press Club. Meredith had made reservations and arranged to attend the event with two publicity agent friends. But she felt compelled to write a column before she joined the festivities.

Surprising even herself, she had assembled material for and written two columns by eleven-thirty, record time, then turned out in a new white wool and silk ensemble for the holiday luncheon. A plan was shaping vaguely in her mind, but until it surfaced more clearly, she was uncertain about what the day would bring.

The Hollywood Women's Press Club Christmas Luncheon was always the most colorful way to welcome the holiday season. Each year the women who participate in the making of entertainment industry news honored a handful of celebrities. Some celebrated for perpetuating Hollywood's golden image, others for besmirching its now-mythical image once considered golden during the early days of movies. One of the club's founders had been a Hollywood gossip columnist to top them all, Louella Parsons.

Whoever the honorees and no matter the year, the luncheon was always one of the bright moments in an otherwise competitive and hungry business environment. Meredith found her friends Bebe and Regina at the check-in table behind the human wall of paparazzi photographers and newsreel cameras poised at the hotel entrance waiting for celebrity arrivals. A buzz of excitement and self-designated importance and opportunity typical of a celebrity event energized the large crowd.

As usual, Meredith and her two friends, both long-time members of the Hollywood publicity mill, had been assigned a prime table graced with two television stars who were among the presenters for the short but glittering program. Creamy young voices from a nearby college choir blended together to fill the ballroom thronged with holiday celebrants.

At the conclusion of the carols, the crystal chandeliers were suddenly emblazoned, and jolly red and white snowmen centerpieces on each table grinned mischievously. Meredith excused herself from the table before the start of the ceremony and hurried to the bank of public phones outside the ballroom. She made a quick reservation for a late afternoon flight putting her into New York's La Guardia airport at midnight, then booked a hotel reservation.

took to the podium to open the ceremony, Meredith whispered farewell to her two friends and table mates and hastened to her car. She lamented having to leave the luncheon. This year Tom Selleck was among the nominees for Golden Apple. She had interviewed him several times in Hawaii for his hit TV series.

On her way home, Meredith made a mental list of the tasks that needed attention before she could leave town. She called Sonia to report that columns for Monday and Tuesday were written and she would file them in person at the newspaper syndicate in New York. She also asked Sonia to call Detective Raymond and made a phone conference appointment at some specific time the next day. She had no idea where she might be at any particulat time in New York but wanted to talk with him. Finally, she told Sonia how to leave messages for her in case of emergencies—like being invited out of the Grant home now that the owner was no longer in residence there.

As Meredith packed a single bag, expertly from years of short and quickly planned travel, she felt heightened urgency about the trip. A pot of coffee brewed while she worked, then she sat down to phone Dusty. The amiable stuntman-turned director answered with a quick "hallo."

"Sorry about the change in schedule," she said at the end of the conversation.

"Sounds important," said Dusty, sounding unconcerned. "I'll be up north until next week-end. But in case whatever the latest scoop you're chasing down runs into Christmas, remember

I'd really love to have you join me at the ranch in Sedona. It would make for a great holiday."

"I don't know what the coming days will bring," she sighed. "In fact, I wish we could leave now. I could use the rest." The Arizona ranch, long time in Dusty's family, was neither large nor elegant, but offered a simple lifestyle always providing a tonic for when she visited.

"Maybe you can sleep on the flight," Dusty suggested. "Anyhow, have fun in the Big Apple," he bid her farewell.

She dressed for the long night flight, put two cans of cat food on the counter, bunched up an old sweater on the bed where Paco felt secure when she was away, walked quickly to the townhouse next door and rang the bell. A round, ruddy-cheeked white-haired man with horn-rimmed glasses and a bushy white mustache opened the door. Meredith sheepishly handed him a house key, pleading, "Please, Norman. Feed Paco for me tonight and tomorrow night if I'm not back by then? It's an emergency."

Norman chuckled jovially. "Another pesky emergency! Poor, little latchkey cat! Don't worry, we always have a good time together, Paco and me."

CHAPTER 15
SUNDAY NIGHT—IN FLIGHT

The flight was not completely full, but still bore a sizable crowd of Sunday night commuters on their way to Monday morning business meetings on the other side of the country. For most of them, including Meredith, such later afternoon/ early evening flights were part of life. They were the space-age travelers who approached a hectic travel process with the same stalwart resignation with which they approached a lengthy freeway commute or tasteless food in a company cafeteria.

Long ago Meredith had decided to travel first class whenever possible. Mostly it was one of the perks of her own particular position, the one luxury her newspaper syndicate provided and the one requirement she placed as well on travel arranged and paid for by a movie studio or network. She funded the first-class treatment herself for this trip, grateful for the large number of frequent flier miles and coupons she had earned over the years she flew on business. She settled back in her seat, drained by the weariness of the past week.

Shortly after take-off she was awakened by the cabin steward who offered cocktails to the handful of front cabin passengers. Meredith requested a glass of white wine, and then smiled at scolding Cassie about ordering a Heinekens at the biker bar. The recollection brought her back to the real world. She took out a small stenographic notebook and settled in to face facts for the first time since Bettina Grant died.

Meredith realized her decision paralysis during the previous week had cost her a great deal, witnessed by the fact that Cassie O'Connell Ainsworth already had time to fly to California, meet with an agent, and probably be presented to Russ Talbot at the Newspaper Syndicate. How many other proposals in addition to Cassie's sat on Russ's desk, Meredith wondered?

She reviewed her options. She could take over Bettina Grant's hard-won post and become the columnist she had always been pleased not to be. To do so meant Meredith would have to sacrifice a writing style and the time to exercise it that she greatly valued. She could remain a "legwoman" (she shuddered at the name) to whoever else might take over Bettina's column and continue in the same manner as she had for the past ten years. The plausibility of that option seemed unlikely considering that whoever became the columnist would probably want his or her own staff and, in any case, may not even want an assistant.

She could seek fresh employment. Her long-time dream had been to write for the *Los Angeles Times*. It was also the dream of every writer on the west coast, most of whom would kill to accomplish it—especially in the growing entertainment section. Finally, Meredith had to honestly admit chasing down everyday stories in regular news environments was no longer appealing.

There were different newspaper syndicates she could approach, but most did not offer full-time opportunities to cover entertainment news, welcoming instead freelance submissions. Other syndicate writers Meredith knew were generally subsidized by other day jobs, spouses who worked real jobs, alimony checks or trust funds. Many were just poor. Making a livelihood from freelance journalism was seldom a lucrative endeavor for the majority of writers. Most women's magazines were based in

New York and had a reputation for a certain amount of brutal arrogance toward West Coast writers, Meredith among them. She had once made a trip specifically to introduce herself to the various editors of several of the magazines. They had been bitingly blasé. One said, "Oh, we save our Hollywood articles for our special writers as a reward." When Meredith explained that she was an expert in such journalism, the editor had looked at her through dusty glasses, scratched her head with a blood-red chipped fingernail and said, "Well, then you have plenty of work out there on the coast and won't mind so much having someone else cover the beat from here."

And finally, there were the rags. Meredith had been approached three times by one or another of them over the past five years. She could be a Bureau Chief for the *Glitter Parade* making a handsome salary. But she would wake up each morning feeling like a fraud, and worse, most of her friends would never speak to her again. Idly she wondered who did speak to "those" reporters? They seemed to get around in Hollywood just fine. And they showed up at all the functions just like the "real" press. She was told, off the record of course, that the networks and studios had a tacit agreement to cooperate with the rags whenever possible because their news stand circulation numbers were ominous. All those shoppers who were lured into purchasing the tabloids in the supermarket check-out lines also watched TV or went to movies, and ratings, after all, were the name of the game.

Then there was the option of changing fields completely, maybe moving away from Los Angeles. But the show biz capital of the world had always been as seductive for Meredith as it had for the multitude of others who hovered on the edges of the celebrity stage. Not that it was such a bad fringe to stand in— Hollywood journalism had very nice perks. Indeed. Fred Barton was an example of that. What he lacked in salary, he made up for in free trips, movies and plays. A short hotel mention in a column in the trade publication he edited, a brief article in one of the two or three other small journals for which he freelanced, and Fred traveled as "guest of the house" throughout the world. Sometimes he was even allowed to bring along a friend, which made him enormously popular with the starlets he met during his normal editorial beat.

There was a strong journalism ethics movement afoot to forbid studio-funded travel, even lunches. But everyone wondered if it would ever become the norm.

Dim lights here and there throughout the airplane cabin indicated a few awake passengers, but most had snapped off their overhead reading lamps and were at least attempting to sleep in the in all-encompassing blackness of long night flight. Meredith welcomed the neutrality of such extended flight. It imposed a certain type of distance from the pulse of the worlds she was both leaving and approaching and established a limbo which never failed to provide a certain amount of perspective and relief.

She appreciated that opportunity on this particular night to think more about the events of the past week and about Bettina. With all the drama and activity surrounding the murder, little time had been available for Meredith to simply reflect on the woman who had been so vital in her own life. She settled back and allowed herself to picture the Bettina as the "other" persona she'd come to know so well. A small smile etched her lips as she thought about dinners, long talks on the patio, even a few comical sailing and tennis attempts by the two women who were inadept at both. As the mental home movies of their friendship rolled, Meredith settled into the more poignant moments of writing and editing advice, romance and social mentoring, and close-up personal support through difficult times. Tears gathered and delicately spilled. She was glad the cabin lights were low. It was a moment long overdue.

Meredith then began to think about the activities ahead for the single day she would spend in New York. She had an ambitious schedule but barring major setbacks such as hopeful appointments being away, she felt comfortable she could accomplish the meetings and results she had in mind. The urgency of the agenda amused her and was reminiscent of the many urgent New York overnighters Bettina had made on their behalf during the past ten years.

Bettina Grant had possessed an uncanny instinct for her own professional well-being. The tone of an editor's voice could inform Bettina when there was discontent with a story, and Bettina had no qualms about demanding candor. Such candor prevented heavily edited work that could be a grating surprise to the author when published.

Bettina's canny also saved a good deal of shock and embarrassment resulting when a syndicate forced a new trendy addition to its existing Hollywood line-up, or brought aboard a totally new writing team in place of a veteran staff such as Bettina's—simply because new blood continually approaches syndicate editors offering cut-rate talent in order to score a respectable affiliation. In Hollywood press circles, the size and stature of the "affiliation" dictated the position on the guest lists—for movie screenings, concerts and premieres, and parties.

Meredith remembered how often Bettina had run interference during Meredith's own career. Bettina's days as Meredith's writing coach had been long over, but the younger woman had never stopped learning from the columnist's negotiating skills. Skills based mostly on from-the-hip reactions and a near sixth sense of predator activity.

Ideas the two women discussed, Meredith recalled, always lost fatuousness, gaining momentum and form. Seedling stories grew into acorns and eventually oaks. What was missing from the Joey O'Neal investigation was Bettina. She knew how to call in a card here or there or nag an arrogant source to the point where some detail would be dropped, and Bettina could pick up the full story as a result. And always, Bettina adhered to the ethics of good journalism: confirm a third-party story with a credible source, give a subject a chance to respond to a rumor or allegation, never use a pure gossip item that has not been witnessed by others, collaborated by an independent source, or name the source.

I'm alone in this now, Meredith reminded herself, opening the doors to the committee of voices that harangued over the what ifs in the middle of the night. She mused over what lured so many into the Hollywood world, and how she, herself had floated into it. It was a tough life no matter how exciting and made her wonder why Cassie had thought it to be less stressful than network news.

Cassie O'Connell Ainsworth was trying to nap in a first-class seat on the New York bound flight of another airliner. She, too, was finding difficulty in relaxing. Also accustomed to long fights, she had slipped off her shoes as quickly as the flight had left Los Angeles, and now tried to visualize her own bedroom at home and the type of instant comfort she felt when she turned off the bedside lamp to sleep.

But conjuring wasn't working. Her mind wandered over the events of the past four days and the recent happenings disturbed her. The trip to Los Angeles had evolved in a confluence of dilemmas which drenched Cassie in a shower of the past— reminding her of Hollywood's own unique acid rain which at one time or another caught even the most innocent visitor.

Only a few days before, Cassie talked with her book agent Mort Agee about work opportunities in California. Her husband, Bob Ainsworth, currently the Photo Director for a major TV news operation, was seriously considering accepting an offer to be Chief of Photography for an international news magazine with its graphics headquarters based in Los Angeles. If he did accept the position, Cassie would have to find a new job in California as well. She hoped Mort would be instrumental in securing a good post for her.

"Too bad there isn't a gossip column or a TV spot on celebrity gossip available," Mort told her. "As I have been networking and making the rounds here about type of work and opportunities for you, I keep getting that word. Too bad Bettina is still around and kicking."

Cassie snickered. "She'll never die, Mort. She's an institution."

"Well, she is getting older," he said. "and the industry is changing. Maybe it's time for new blood."

Cassie thought about that and decided to scope out the LA turf personally, arriving Monday. Late on Tuesday evening, Mort had called to report that Bettina Grant had died and, curious about the successor to the gossip columnist, he had phoned his close friend Russ Talbot, president of the *United American News Syndicate* for which Bettina had written. In the course of the conversation, Russ had confided that Bettina's legwoman said she did not care for column-writing as such and mentioned she preferred field reporting and feature articles. Russ did not know what plans he would make to replace Bettina.

So, Cassie had decided to stay in Los Angeles a few days, initially to attend Bettina Grant's memorial services. Bettina had been her boss for many years, and was, at one time, a good friend. When Cassie had learned that the Hollywood Women's Press Club Party was scheduled for the Sunday after the service, she quickly phoned an old friend who was a member and asked to tag along. With some additional time on her hands, Cassie also had decided to spend some time with Meredith which prompted the Saturday adventure to the Harley Bell Bar.

"Swear to God it wasn't to undermine her." Cassie had explained to Bob early Sunday morning from her hotel room. Her room was not being subsidized by the network, after all, but rather by Mort Agee as the keystone of an image he insisted Cassie maintain while she was in town. He felt she should present herself on all fronts as one of the pretty people. She shuddered to imagine the price tag on that "image" when Mort's invoice arrived.

"Mort told me Meredith said she didn't want the column job and so I thought for sure she would know people like me would be going for it."

"But how do you feel about the column, itself, now," asked her husband, amused at the energy and drama Cassie could ~~inject into the simpler situation—like talking with her agent~~ about a new job.

"Oh, I think I could have a lot of fun with the column," she said over the phone.

"Remember, you don't have to do this," Bob reminded her. "We have plenty of alternatives staying right where we are for now. Or, we could move to the Coast, and you could stay home and write more novels. You have a good agent. That's half the battle."

"Don't start," she cut him off. "This is a good opportunity, and since we both agreed that the New York lifestyle isn't what we want anymore, this column could be perfect. I just have to toughen the steel armor on myself and remember that I'm looking out for number one."

"Sure," Bob answered with a quiet chuckle at the other end of the line. "Be careful about armor, though. Remember, going into battle with or without armor can be fatal. Maybe this isn't a war you want to fight. There are plenty of others. Mort already has one novel of yours to sell."

Setting aside the dictates of war, Cassie had packed her suitcase, and met her old friend Betty Lars, her former national publicity contact from one of the major networks, now retired. Betty was delighted to have Cassie accompany her to the Press Club gala. A little young blood was important, said the veteran, at a table full of old cronies. But the Press Cub was a little like that—a blend of Hollywood's old and new guard—blue and white/blonde hair mixing it up with the Hollywood's newest generation, currently strutting about in taut leather mini-skirts, large earrings and generally big hair.

Cassie was snapped back to reality at the event by a large contingent of the holiday celebrants. These were the folks Meredith had called "the fringe players" who circulated on the outside edges of Hollywood's celebrity core, doing whatever jobs allowed them luxurious proximity to the glow. Some, thought Cassie, were dowdy, simpering little people with bad complexions and greasy hair, who'd sell their sisters in order to capture a place on the "A" invitation list. They spent their time around the studios, record companies and press agents in order to win acknowledgment. This was the Hollywood contingent with which Cassie had the most difficult time identifying.

When Betty reintroduced the striking brunette to the few familiar faces that Cassie remembered from her long-discarded Hollywood Rolodex, only one person remembered or recognized her. One male press agent with whom she had worked closely for a decade had somehow sprouted silver hair and was wearing a camera around his neck. He looked at her blankly as though he had never set eyes on her before and acknowledged her only with an absent nod of his head. She soothed her ego telling it there were at least a thousand people attending the luncheon and of those, she had once known less than a dozen. She sauntered up to one publicist, once a frequent contact from her Hollywood days, and suggested an appointment to catch up. Short, egg-shaped, hair sprayed into place, pristine suit, and rimless glasses, she was amazed at how much he had changed, and thought he resembled an aging toad. She wondered how he had managed to snag a super-model turned TV glamor girl as his wife. He looked at Cassie with no evidence of recognition and said he had no job openings. Deflated, she still felt the pull of desire to be one of the ones who was recognized, part of the pack.

Cassie and Meredith never ran into one another during the awards program at the celebration, but Meredith had left early, and Cassie stayed until the last announcement was made and the lights were turned up full. Then she dropped Betty off at her West Hollywood home and drove directly to the airport.

As she reflected on the Press Club party, she again thought back to the days at Bright Leaf Lane in the shadow of Bettina Grant. In all, they were good days, Cassie thought. Best in the earliest times when Bettina, Cassie and their newly hired secretary Carolyn were still struggling as a team for acknowledgment and had not yet been touched, themselves, by the wand of celebritydom. Bettina's family took center stage and the kids' high school activities and eventually college concerns were paramount. The entire office staff was somehow engaged in the process of the Grant family.

Cassie remembered an afternoon when rain torrents had grown so fierce the electricity blinked off throughout Beverly Hills, and the rivers of runoff waters swelled the streets making driving close to impossible. Bettina's husband, Larry, was away at a lawyers' conferences, and Carolyn called home to say she'd be staying as long as the weather conditions remained torrid. The three women settled in to drink wine and catch up on personal gossip in front of the fire. Ito's predecessor, a heavy Latin woman named Theresa, had cooked up a Mexican-spiced stew and made biscuits for them, murmuring her thankfulness for the availability of a gas range during an electrical black-out.

"Who's the sexiest man in Hollywood?" Carolyn had asked Bettina. Dressed in stretched-out stretch jeans and a large UCLA sweatshirt, Bettina leaned back against the coffee table and lit a cigarette. "Dan Rowan," she said, blowing a smoke ring into the soft light and referring to the host of the then wildly popular comedy TV Show "Laugh In."

"What about guys like Chuck Heston or Gregory Peck," urged Carolyn.

"Dan Rowan," insisted Bettina. "He's funny, bright and sensitive, and…"

"James Garner…now there's the charmer," mused Cassie.

Carolyn had pulled the sprawling sheepskin rug over her chilled legs and murmured, "I think you're both getting senile. Charles Bronson—he's the one. Peter Fonda—maybe a close second."

One office evening just at the five o'clock wind-down time, a messenger arrived at Bettina's front door with a crate of live lobsters, a gift from a Maine-based singer promoting his first network TV special.

"What the hell do I do with a half dozen Maine lobsters?" groaned Bettina. "They won't sit around waiting until tomorrow to be cooked. And I'll be out of town, anyway. Let's cook them now and have a little dinner party tonight." And they did.

From TV magicians leaving promotional rabbits on the doorstep to elegant parties such as the wedding reception for Liza Minelli and MGM Chief Jack Haley Jr. at the re-opened Ciro's night club on the Sunset Strip, all the events shared with the flamboyant columnist brought a smile to Cassie's heart. She wondered when the whole "family" feeling gave way to high-stakes Hollywood star-climbing.

She stared into the blackness of the night attempting to numb her mind until a soft tug on her arm brought her back to the low-lit interior of the first-class cabin. She was staring up into the face of a short Japanese man with a gray crew cut as precise as any she remembered from the 1950s and dressed in a crisp business suit. He smiled, bowed slightly and said, "My friends…we wish to play a game of bridge but cannot without a fourth partner." He looked at her expectantly.

"I'm sorry I didn't understand your question," said Cassie confused, struggling to return from her reverie.

"Would you be so kind as to join my friends and me for a game of bridge," said the small man in halting English.

Cassie was disarmed by the question and it took her two seconds to accept. Bridge was better than trying unsuccessfully to visualize the comfort of her own bedroom for hours.

Three hours later, as she followed the line of sluggish night stragglers disembarking from the jet and saw Bob in the waiting area, she still had a grin on her face. This time it was a smug one. She hugged her sturdily built husband whose dark hair was still damp from the light snow falling outside. "Good trip?" he asked shifting her carry-on bag from her shoulder and to his own, then slipping an arm around her waist.

"You take your successes where you can find them," she said with amused wryness. She held up a wrist that sported a man's shiny Rolex Watch, and pulled a wad of twenty-dollar bills from her pocket. Bob looked at her, perplexed.

"Bridge," she chuckled. "Nobody should ask me to play bridge for money."

"Every night, Toots, I pray to God you don't run across a sore loser."

CHAPTER 17

MONDAY MORNING—NEW YORK

Russ Talbot arrived at his office at United American News at nine-twenty Monday morning and found Meredith sitting in the tiny waiting room. It took him a moment to recognize the attractive blonde as she stood before him, reaching to shake his hand. He had met her on a half dozen previous occasions but had actually spent very little time with her.

"I was in the neighborhood, Russ. Thought it would be a good idea to say 'hello.'"

"It's always nice to see our writers, he said genially but with even less commitment than Meredith had expected. "Follow me through the labyrinth and let's have some coffee."

She trailed after him through a maze of drab and cluttered cubicles. His gait was long and quick. The syndicate offices were typical of a newspaper business environment; functional and generally ten years out of style. It wasn't until they reached the closed door which bore his name, that the pervasive power of the newspaper syndicate became obvious. Not that the office was luxurious, but by its organized clutter, maps and awards, it spoke eloquently of the massive network of correspondents, photographers, artists, analysts, even cartoonists engaged in the global business of information dissemination. A teletype and fax machine sat side by side, both grinding out pages as Russ and Meredith entered.

Russ punched the intercom button on the desk and commanded his secretary to bring coffee, while at the same time waving Meredith to a seat in one of the stuffed leather chairs opposite his own behind the large, weathered but imposing desk.

"How are you doing without Bettina? Have they uncovered any leads on the case?" he asked as he hung his overcoat in a small closet on the opposite side of the room. Meredith reached into her satchel and pulled out the column that would usually be faxed to Russ's editorial office—one of the series of cubicles outside his door—at five that evening.

Meredith sighed, "No definitive leads, some ideas. We're doing fine, considering the situation, but it's so unnerving and it's frightening to me. People keep telling me I know more than I realize, and I can't figure out what that is. But I keep looking over my shoulder. Even here in New York I feel like I'm being watched or followed."

"And what brings you to New York?"

"Just this," she said, handing him the column. "And to talk with you about being Bettina's replacement."

Russ sat down behind the desk, leaning forward. "I didn't think you were interested in being a columnist. You told me that yourself, something, by the way, that Bettina found very comforting—as you can imagine." He settled back, folding his hands in his lap, behind him, a panorama of Manhattan spreading across a wide expanse of window.

A thick but well-proportioned man in his sixties, Russ Talbot had white hair, a ruddy Irish complexion, intense blue eyes and a cultured Boston accent. Meredith found it difficult to imagine him in the battlefields of Indochina or Korea—both hot spots where he gained his early newspaper experience—or as a field reporter for a major television network in the earliest days of the medium. The Russ Talbot sitting behind the executive desk in the offices of one of the world's most powerful news syndicates exuded the presence of a man who had acquired his post by divine providence.

Meredith always found talking with him to be intimidating. More so now than even before. "Times change, and people grow," she said. "I wanted you to know I am serious about being considered as Bettina's replacement. I think I'm the most qualified person to assume the role, and I'm fully prepared to learn whatever I need to learn to make that happen."

Russ sat back and looked at her with interest. At that moment the door opened, and a tall, grey-haired woman dressed in a blue suit entered the room carrying a tray with a carafe of coffee and two china cups and saucers.

"Cream or sugar, Meredith?"

She shook her head. The secretary put the tray down on the corner of the desk and left as efficiently as she had entered. Russ maintained his curiosity as he regarded Meredith from his chair. She felt uncomfortable.

"Can we talk about this at lunch?" he finally spoke up. "Are you free? I have a meeting in fifteen minutes and I'm not prepared for it. We have a lot to talk about and I'd like to do it without feeling pushed."

"Sure. I can arrange that."

"Good," Russ said rising brusquely, an indication to Meredith she would have to take her coffee into the lobby if she expected to drink it at United American News. Choosing to leave the coffee on Russ's desk, she reached for her bag and coat and moved toward the door. Russ followed her, slicking his hair with one hand while picking up Meredith's column with the other. Outside his door he handed the paperwork to the secretary and instructed, "please make certain that Don in Editorial gets this." She nodded and rose to deliver the document.

Meredith found herself suddenly in the elevator not certain what had happened during the brief ten minutes she had spent in the inner offices of United American. Outside the air was chilled and the sky was overcast, threatening snow once again. Meredith pulled her old but dependable "Eastern" coat around her body, grateful for its thickness.

She walked the dozen blocks back to the hotel with hurried purpose, returning to the neutral comfort of her room. Once inside, the dry heat challenged the effects of the temperature outside and stung her cheeks and fingertips. Pondering her shaky connection with Russ Talbot that morning, Meredith wondered, "What would Bettina do?" Then she reminded herself, "She'd be one step ahead." So, she sat down on the bed, pulled the thick phone book onto her lap and began thumbing through the pages. Finally, she found the name she sought and picked up the phone.

Ten minutes later she was again heading into the chill, walking again toward Midtown. She headed to a meeting with Doug Manning, Director of the Newland Radio Syndicate, a subsidiary of the massive Newland Broadcasting Corporation that owned and operated radio and TV stations throughout the country. Meredith had met him seven years before covering a movie about a sensitive political scandal in Louisiana, and due to a lack of anything else to occupy their time between interviews in the sleepy backwater town, the two had become good friends over beer and boiled shrimp.

When the assignment ended and each were headed in different directions in the small airport, they independently realized the short friendship could have become more—if there had not been such distance between their respective homes. Since then, they had run into one another on a variety of occasions, and typically each would phone the other when on the other's home turf. They would have a drink or lunch. For a reason neither admitted, but both recognized, they avoided dinners and late-night socializing.

Doug had moved up the management ladder quickly at Newland. And as always, he was delighted to hear from Meredith. She found the good-looking, pleasant-faced man waiting for her in the building lobby. As always, he was dressed well but without inspiration. Meredith vaguely wondered if there wasn't someone in Doug's life who could put a little color in his wardrobe, then warned herself off.

He invited her to lunch, but she begged off, deferring to Russ. Doug said he understood, and suggested coffee at Newland's cafeteria. "It ain't elegant," he said, "but it is convenient."

"What's the gig that brings you to the Big Apple?" he asked her as they wound down a set of stairs to the cafeteria.

She giggled. "Why is it, Doug, that we always meet in these beautiful buildings, monuments to contemporary architecture, the latest in whiz-bang construction technology—and always choose the back stairs to get around? What's wrong with elevators or even escalators?"

He stopped and looked at her, his voice serious. "Practice, Merri. Good reporters mustn't ever stop practicing how to snoop around the back stairwells."

"Of course," she answered. Their destination was an only nominally modernized version of an old company cafeteria. Holiday decorations were strung across the doorways and food lines, and background music droned bland Christmas carols.

"I'm considering some new directions in my career, new options," Meredith explained, amused as she filled a paper cup with industrial-strength coffee from a large vending machine. It wasn't United American's dainty china cups—but the atmosphere was far more congenial.

"I heard about Bettina," said Doug. "Everyone was shocked. But why aren't you taking over her column?"

"I haven't decided one way or the other yet, Doug. That's why I'm here—to talk with the syndicate. And to pick your brain."

"Your timing's good. Another day and this brain would be skiing for the holidays."

"Sorry I didn't phone ahead. With so much happening back at the office, I didn't make the decision to come East until yesterday."

"It's just as well. There's so much going on I'd probably have put you off. This way you caught me unaware, and I was able to make time for you. The programmers are working on new concepts—radio products—for the stations, ours and others—and we've been up to our asses in statistics and paperwork."

"I don't understand," said Meredith.

"Every year we re-examine the syndicated shows we offer to our own network and to the other radio stations that subscribe to our programming in markets where we don't have a station. We look at the ratings, how many stations are using the material, at the costs—all those things—and decide which programs to keep and which to drop."

Meredith felt a jolt of anxiety and opportunity. She had not anticipated that approaching the subject of a syndicated entertainment radio show would be so available.

"Well, it's certainly something think about," said Doug a half hour later. In front of him were copies of entertainment columns and feature stories from the major papers across the country, a biography on Meredith, and most importantly, an outline of the proposed radio show—outlined in pencil on a cafeteria napkin.

"You're right. There are plenty of TV shows and news segments focusing on entertainment, but not much specifically produced for radio. And Newland certainly hasn't any Hollywood product, so you're offering us something competitive that we don't already have. I wish we had a voice tape on you."

"Could I make one?"

"Sure, but where and when? We're putting next year's programming together right now and waiting until the holidays are over would be a mistake. When do you fly back to the Coast?"

"First thing in the morning," Meredith answered, smiling inwardly at the East Coast label for California, "The Coast."

"What if I could arrange an hour for you in our test studio this afternoon? No one would have to know the particulars." Meredith was surprised how quickly the project was developing.

"I'd need to prepare a script," she said, thinking quickly. "How long a tape would I need?"

"Three good minutes. Enough to give us a strong sample of your voice and presentation."

"I've never thought about how I <u>sound</u>. People have told me I have a good speaking voice, but how good is good?"

"We'll see. I'll ask our engineer Will Hurd to work personally with you, as a favor to me. Let's go back up to my office and see what's available on the studio schedule."

"Doug," Meredith caught his arm as he stood. He looked back at her, "what's this going to cost me. No one puts themselves on the line like this without wanting something in return."

He smiled at her mischievously. "Just be good. No, be great. You'll make me a hero, and a lot of money for both of us."

"Money?" laughed Meredith. "Is that involved, too. I thought it was just for fame."

"In the media biz, honey, fame is money."

CHAPTER 18

T.K. Raymond wondered about money, as in net worth, as he stepped from the elevator in the stylish Wilshire office building in Los Angeles, and found his way to the offices of Vivian Malden, Psychotherapist. An innate distrust of people who tinkered with other people's minds made him hesitate as he reached for the door to the office suite. A tall well-appointed brunette, he figured to be about forty-five, was waiting for him just inside, in the "Waiting Room."

"Detective Raymond," she said matter-of-factly, extending her hand. Her grip was strong and determined. "Come in— let's talk back here. They made their way through a comfortable sitting room to a modern office. "Sit," she commanded pointing to a leather chair opposite her desk. He complied. She excused herself to take a phone call. He looked around the office, noticing photographs with apparent clients and one on the desk with Larry Grant. Others showed Vivian in theatrical yoga and karate stances, and at horse riding events. He also noticed a small cabinet of certificates and trophies confirming she excelled in those activities.

"Now, what's this about?" Vivian asked, returning to the conversation. "I get that it has to do with the death of my fiancé's ex-wife. How can I help you?"

"Well," he began, suddenly intimidated. "There are a few questions we have, to follow-up conversations with others involved with the case." She stared at him, expression flat and without comment.

"Did you know the deceased, Bettina Grant?"

"No. I saw her at a party or two where we were both guests, never talked with her." She offered neither inflection nor emotion.

"Has Larry Grant ever mentioned anyone who might have been a threat to her, or to him, for that matter?"

"No," she answered. "Larry hasn't any enemies I know of. I couldn't say about Bettina."

"Were there any troublesome…issues…between the two of them?"

"Heavens no! He's been remarkably generous with her about use of the house. And, she's been very civil and open with him regarding the children…and all the rest of it."

"Several people have mentioned that you and Larry spend quite a bit of time in Las Vegas."

"Larry has clients there. Hotel and casino executives. And sometimes he likes to play cards there because he knows a lot of people. I've only accompanied him a couple of times. Vegas is not my favorite."

"Does Larry have a gambling problem?"

Vivian laughed. "Not that I know of."

"How about the Bel Air house. Will you two move into it?"

"No. We've found a nice place in Pacific Palisades."

"Already purchased?"

"Yes. But escrow won't close for quite a while. All of the issues around his former wife' death have complicated things a bit."

"Think back a couple of weeks to Monday evening, December fifth. Can you recall where you were and where Larry was?"

Vivian put a well-manicured finger to her lips and thought. "That was the evening of the local law association holiday dinner party. Larry went. I did not. I had a migraine coming on. The dinner started at about six at the Beverly Hilton, I recall. I think it ended around ten, but Larry went on to a private party in the same hotel with a group from his firm. He and another colleague were in charge of it this year. I took some migraine meds and went to bed. He came in a little after midnight."

Raymond tried not to show his surprise at the answer. He'd been told Larry was at home with Vivian.

"Did he waken you when he came in?"

"Yes, of course. Larry isn't a very quiet man. His own firm planned the after-party. They rarely have time to socialize around the office, and the party was an annual tradition. They always expect to break up at midnight, but he said sometimes it was later. Larry says that the young woman who worked for Bettina, Meredith something, knew more about her life—both professional and personal—than anyone. I hope you've talked with her."

Raymond nodded his yes. Then asked, "Black belt?"

Surprised, the therapist answered, "Yes. These days a woman needs to be able to take care of herself in any situation."

"My son was into karate before he left for college. Now he's into Lacrosse."

Vivian smiled and nodded impassively.

"You have nice offices, Ms. Malden. How long have you been a therapist?"

"Forever," she smiled slightly." Got my master's degree fifteen years ago and opened this office about seven years ago."

"I seem to recall you had a call-in radio show for a while," he said, calling on the information he'd uncovered before making the appointment.

"Well, yes, I did."

"But you aren't still broadcasting?"

"No. I stepped away. I'm not a celebrity type and the political issues involved with being a public persona made me very uncomfortable. My work is with individuals and some companies who require that their troubled personnel seek counseling." Raymond nodded, reminding himself to check out what those issues might have been.

As he left the office, Raymond thought it was time to stop in to see his Malibu neighbor who was on the board of one of the professional psychological associations. He wondered about the full story behind the radio therapist leaving her own show. He also thought there was some kind of hole in the timeline but couldn't really find it. He'd also have to confirm Larry's attendance at the association after-party.

There was only one thing Doug had forgotten to mention to Meredith until the last minute before she left him that morning. The column.

"Keeping the column would be a big help," he told her as an aside. "Your name would be automatically promoted in all the cities where your by-line appeared. I'm not saying there's no chance without it, but your chances are a lot better with it."

Meredith felt a sinking sensation. She knew that she would have to be persuasive during lunch with Russ in the next hour. When she emerged from Doug's office it was only eight-thirty a.m. on "The Coast." She decided to hold off calling Sonia until after lunch, giving the secretary time to round up the information Meredith had requested. She took a long hike down Fifth Avenue and perused the shops she had browsed so often over the years during business trips to New York. The holiday decorations in the store windows and along the streets winked at her, helping to lighten the mood. In her spare hour, she finished the Christmas shopping left on her list, feeling she'd accomplished something special whether or not she ended up employed.

Later, on the way to lunch and walking down the sidewalk with Russ Talbot, the tail of his well-tailored overcoat creating its own wake, Meredith felt optimistic. She was glad she had worn her favorite suit—a blue/gray silk tweed with a creamy midnight blue silk blouse. She knew she looked great and that realization gave her confidence. Russ took her to lunch at what she considered a typically New York restaurant. French, cramped, arrogant but boasting excellent food. The maître d' knew Russ by name and showed them to a quiet table away from the main traffic flow.

Lunch went well, the conversation well enough. They talked about Bettina, both somber and savoring the opportunity to share the memory of the woman they had known well. Then, the discussion slid into operational subjects—from new office possibilities to promoting the new columnist. Meredith participated in the discussion with guarded candor, wary that she might be giving away more than she may be getting from the meeting. She reminded herself that Russ may be planning to hire someone other than her.

Finally, Russ began the expected conversation, also exercising candor so his general interest wouldn't be mistaken for a serious offer. "Here's where I think we are Meredith," he said as the waiter poured a stream of steaming coffee into his cup from a polished pot. "You certainly have the tools and the system down to become the new Bettina Grant. And in spite of the fact that the industry itself knows you well and would find it quite comfortable to continue working with you, there are people who are more promotable than you. People who could bring…," he paused to find the proper words, "…more cache than you bring right now."

"Can you give me some examples," she asked, summoning her most professional non-threatened tone.

Russ showed discomfort in the discussion. "Roger Golden, the columnist from *Hollywood Variety*," he said. "Phyllis Armstrong from the *Dallas Journal*. She has two books on the shelves, does a local TV show and well," he paused again, "she's one hell of a columnist. I wouldn't give you a nickel for her feature material, but she knows how to turn a column phrase!"

Meredith knew she was bucking two formidable veterans in entertainment industry information circles. Her name on a list alongside of theirs made her feel uninitiated and insignificant. So far, however, Russ had not mentioned Cassie O'Connell's name, but he hadn't mentioned a half dozen other entrants Meredith knew had declared their intentions to run in the race for the by-line. Already she was beginning to battle voices in her head, shouting at her to run completely away while the running was good. Shut up, she commanded uncertainly.

Russ was smiling at her in a quiet, fatherly way. She wasn't sure if that made her feel angry, or in some way comforted. "You always told me—and everyone else, including Bettina—you weren't a column writer, you enjoyed doing Bettina's field work. You weren't interested in devoting your life to 'three paragraph news stories' is the way I remember you putting it. You have to be careful what you ask for, my dear."

Meredith winced. "I said it before, Russ, and I reiterate it now: I'm willing to learn whatever is necessary to make this work because frankly, I need to expand my own abilities and to grow. And you'll see that whether I do it with UANS or elsewhere, I'll for sure do it!" Russ's silvered eyebrows rose as he regarded her words.

When they parted at the corner near the syndicate offices, Russ promised Meredith that the column would remain "Bettina Grant's Show Business by Meredith Ogden" until January 31. Six weeks would give Meredith a chance to show him the kind of writing she was capable of as a columnist and give him a chance to test whether the hundreds of editors who had trusted Bettina Grant would be willing to trust Bettina's ingenue.

Meredith returned to the hotel room to redraft the column she'd just turned in, to make it a radio script, and to call Sonia before the four-thirty recording appointment. When she dialed the office number, a sophisticated male voice answered, "Good morning, editorial offices."

"Who's this?" asked Meredith, checking anxiety in her voice.

"Ah, it's you Miss Meredith, it's Ito."

"What are you doing answering the phone?"

He chuckled over the wire and said, "Miss Sonia has her hands full with too many calls this morning, so she asked me to help out. And I have important messages for you." Meredith shook her head and laughed at the picture.

"First, Mr. Austin, Mrs. Grant's attorney, would like you to call him today at your earliest convenience." A feeling of dread rose up in Meredith's stomach. She feared it meant she and the office would be asked to relocate soon.

"Larry Grant would like you to call—thought you might have lunch with him. There are some topics he wishes to discuss. Then, Detective Raymond said although he can't promise what his schedule will be, he will try his best to be at his desk at three o'clock your time to answer the questions you have. Mrs. Masner called to remind you of the party on Friday night. She said, 'black tie, as usual,' and she can't wait to see your dress and has bundles of gossip for you.

"Mr. Dusty phoned to say he realized he'll miss Friday night's gig. Apologies and he'll talk with you at the hotel tonight."

A soft sigh came from Ito as he said, "And your neighbor Norman called, a bit hysterical it sounded, and said to tell you someone had broken into your townhouse. He stopped by to feed the cat this morning but didn't want to touch anything, so he just shut the door and said to tell you to call the police when you return."

The silence on the phone line was resounding. As Ito's words registered in Meredith's mind, she exploded, "He shut the door?

What about my cat? What about fingerprints? What happened in there?"

"He didn't say," Ito answered. "He seemed frightened, and it seemed to me, a little angry. Would you like me to go over and check it out?"

"No, thank you, Ito." Her heart pumped and she felt light headed. "Please call Detective Raymond and tell him about it."

She paced the hotel room furtively for a few minutes, fighting to control the fear pounding her entire body. Finally, she sat down to focus on the script she had to write. She continued to remind herself that even if she cancelled the rest of her time in New York and flew home as quickly as possible, she still wouldn't get home before morning the next day.

MONDAY—LATE AFTERNOON—NEW YORK

"Calm down, Ogden," came the slightly impatient voice of T.K. Raymond. "Until we see the condition of your townhouse, we can't tell who might have been in it or why. And your neighbor is right. Until you personally go through the place and tell us what's missing, we can't tell anything—a burglary, someone searching for something, or maybe just a scare tactic."

"If the objective was to scare me, they've done a mighty good job? Why me? Wasn't Bettina enough?" Meredith's voice quavered, distressed.

"For a lady who delves into people's lives and the unfolding mystery of it all, you sure can be naive," said Raymond. "You've been playing with fire in several flammable situations: The Joey O'Neal investigation, Bettina's death and the inheritance of her column and probably a half dozen other situations I—and maybe even you—don't even know about. Someone tried to run you or your friend down the other night and you didn't even call the cops! When do you get back here?"

"I have a flight booked for tomorrow morning early because I have a couple of important appointments in New York this afternoon, but I think I'll try to take a red eye out of here tonight to get there as fast as possible."

"Don't," said the calm voice of the detective. "Getting here at three o'clock in the morning won't do anyone any good, least of all you. Finish your business there and get some sleep tonight. There's nothing at this point that can't wait another twelve hours."

"What about Joey O'Neal? Sonia said you had something on it." She heard an exaggerated sigh at the other end of the line.

"Not for now, that's my deal," said Raymond. "It, too, can wait until tomorrow."

"Tell me," Meredith implored, impatience straining the phone. "It's the least you can do." She checked her anxiety and apologized. "T.K., I need a win right now. Okay?"

"Okay, but the deal's still the same—you sit tight on this until tomorrow. I did some checking. This is tough stuff, Meredith, even for a cop. The FBI is in the picture, and apparently sat by and watched O'Neal go to jail in order to protect something bigger. I only have sketches—I can't go any further on my turf. You'll have to put your own sources on it when you get back. All I have is that Joey O'Neal is being blackmailed. Something about his past. One thing more—there's someone in a convalescent hospital in New York—Long Island, I think—that plays into this. I don't know who or how, and my sources are tapped out. And—final terms—you never heard any of this from me."

Meredith sighed. "It is the Johnny Carson case from twenty years ago, all over again, maybe even bigger. A young couple on their way to the laundromat saw Johnny Carson drive into the same shopping center. They couldn't believe their good luck, so they followed him. Too bad for them. Carson was the target of a blackmail scheme and at that moment was leading the cops to a point where he was instructed to drop a pay-off. Everyone confused the couple with the blackmailers and in the process of arresting them, someone beat up the young man."

The Los Angeles end of the phone line was silent. "Okay, Raymond, I'll sit on the story for tonight, but I won't like it."

At the same moment she was trying to figure out how to survey the convalescent hospitals in Long Island for more information.

Raymond read her thoughts. "Don't even! You have enough on your plate for the moment."

"But if we know this much, so will the rags…"

"I doubt it," snapped the detective. "And so what? This is one you can afford to lose. It's better than losing your sanity—or your life."

"My cat," said Meredith unexpectedly, feeling weary and vulnerable. "I wish I knew what happened to my cat." Raymond groaned at the other end. She also wished she could concentrate better on revising the script for her test tape, but she had shifted into a well-learned survival mode she'd know from a childhood engaged in juggling domestic dramas with the other demands of school and adolescence.

Detective Raymond agreed to meet at her office the next day as soon as she arrived, and to drive home with her to survey the damage. He was also pushing for her to spend a few days with a friend, away from the place people knew she lived, for her own safety—just in case.

She was already feeling like a frightened, homeless waif. As well as having to leave her own domain for fear of being targeted and worse, her offices could also be packed up when she returned. She had forgotten to ask about that and wasn't up to more bad news so didn't phone back. She had returned Larry Grant's call and agreed to a lunch date on Thursday, three days away.

She also set a meeting with Marvin Austin, Bettina's attorney to discuss the terms of the will. Bettina had, apparently, stipulated a few things about the office and the files. Thank God, thought Meredith. Then reminded herself that anything was possible, and she shouldn't thank anyone just yet until she was sure there was something for which to be grateful.

☆

The recording session had gone surprisingly well and fast. By six o'clock, Meredith was in Doug Manning's office, handing him her "demo tape," in time to catch him before he left for the evening.

"I'm not promising anything, but I'll give it my best shot," he told her. "I'll present it to the Programming Group tomorrow morning. There's a meeting at eight-thirty and believe it or not, it's my last opportunity to offer any new additions to the schedule. I like this idea. I hope they will too."

"When will we know something for sure?" asked Meredith.

"Mid to late-January. No one will be putting in any worthwhile work over the holidays, and we'll reconvene the first week in January to finish up. I'll keep you posted—whatever decision is made."

She hugged him and said, "Let's get famous and rich."

He gave her a "thumbs up" gesture. "And Merry Christmas."

"Oh, right," she said absently, as she closed his office door behind herself.

"That was rude of me," she said aloud in the elevator, surprising the other passenger. But she knew her rudeness had more to do with the need to pull off a major finesse than with overlooking the season. She had to convince Russ that she had won a nationwide syndicated radio show on Newland to press her promotional visibility. At the same time, she had to keep Doug thinking that she had won Bettina Grant's column spot in order to support the visibility he, too, demanded.

It's a house of cards, she thought, remembering that only thirty-six hours before she had been innocently working out in her Sunday morning aerobics class, considering the holiday schedule. And seven days earlier none of the current worries were on the horizon. Her life was upside down and dependent upon an unpredictable set of circumstances that could spiral off into the galaxy leaving her stranded without a space suit. She longed for the days of being Bettina Grant's number two person, directed by the iron will of her boss, appreciated for and required to produce only her talent.

Weren't those the days, she thought sardonically as she stepped out into the frozen air, the winds goading the falling temperatures into icy predators. She hurried to the corner and flagged down a cab, giving the driver an address.

A doorman at the coop building, Meredith's destination, phoned upstairs to the resident. "No," Meredith said, she wasn't expected, but was certain she'd be welcomed. Welcomed might not have been the word for it, but the doorman received affirmative instructions and put Meredith into the elevator bound for the seventh floor.

CHAPTER 21

MONDAY NIGHT—NEW YORK

"Expected" wasn't the word Cassie O'Connell would have used for Meredith's unscheduled arrival, either. When the doorman had buzzed and announced Miss Ogden, Cassie moved to the rush of adrenaline, compulsively running to the bathroom to primp, making a quick tour of the living room to tidy up.

"Tidy" was an understatement about the cooperative apartment Cassie and her husband Bob Ainsworth shared. The place was not only tidy, but a snapshot of a lifestyle captured through eclectic furnishings, rugs and artwork, souvenirs of work assignments in foreign lands, visits to isolated outposts, dusty marketplaces, and shopping meccas throughout the world. The co-op's large picture windows overlooking the entrance Lincoln Center entertainment palace was a note of irony, Cassie suspected, and would not be lost on Meredith.

When the buzzer sounded, Cassie pulled her tall frame into a portrait of composure and opened the heavy door. An awkward moment passed between the two women before Meredith said, "I was in the neighborhood…"

The entry hall walls, covered by photographic montages recording Bob's and Cassie's various assignments, caught Meredith's attention as they did all visitors to the apartment. The wall was a black and white fresco of the lifestyle and adventure only imagined by most journalists—real ones or wanna-be's.

"This is real journalism, Cassie. But … you know that."

Cassie was at a loss for words as Meredith scanned the photographs. "In a way, I guess. All my J-School friends in college intended to go to Vietnam. Those who went don't remember a lot about the exhilaration and the great writing opportunities, but they do remember the impossible deadlines and clogged communications channels, the fear and panic, diarrhea, the malaria, the mud and the heat and how the glamour seemed to disappear in the blink of an eye, and only the jock itch was left. Or the bills because expense accounts were woefully slow getting reimbursed in the jungle."

Meredith laughed. She told Cassie of a young woman she had run into in a show business PR firm who, angry that Meredith had not used material about her client, retorted, "Well, if I considered myself a serious journalist, I'd be in Nicaragua or Saudi Arabia."

"So would I," Meredith had told her then changed the subject. "I'm not interrupting dinner, am I? I promise not to stay long," she said.

"But Bob's working until midnight. The evening news is in the can. So, I'd planned to unpack, do some wash, all the rest of it." She looked at Meredith and shook her head. "It's hard to believe that we were in that biker bar less than 60 hours ago."

"Sixty hours of crazy," said Meredith.

"You need a drink." Meredith nodded without hesitation. When Cassie returned to the large living room with a tray bearing two tumblers, a small ice bucket and a bottle of Glenlivet, Meredith smiled. "A woman after my own heart. I was afraid you'd serve me Heinekens."

"Only in California."

A moment later Meredith lifted her glass and said, "Here's to Hollywood and journalism and broadcast news and that fact that a career in librarianship is looking better and better."

Cassie toasted and took a drink. Then she looked at Meredith curiously. "You sound not only discouraged, but bitter and sad. Am I to blame for that?"

"Maybe partly. I got a little too complacent going 'round and 'round under the carousel lights of Hollywood. When the music stopped because the organ grinder died, I discovered my own little legs aren't powerful enough to keep the big menagerie moving."

"You're being hard on yourself," said Cassie. "Things kind of happen the way they happen."

"Maybe for you," Meredith mumbled. "I have to kick start this machine and it's a huge undertaking. By the way, my friends at home say the same thing—I'm hard on myself."

Cassie, surprised at the unexpected vulnerability of the talented young woman sitting across from her, said, "I think you're just tired."

"People keep saying that, too."

"Probably because it's true. It's been less than a week since you found Bettina Grant. Have you had one full night's sleep yet?" Meredith shook her head.

"See," said Cassie.

"But I won't get one soon, either. There's so much at stake right now—and someone just ransacked my house. I haven't even been home to see the damage yet."

"What in the world are you doing here, then?" Cassie asked, eyes wide.

"I'm here to talk to you. And to find out just how serious you are about the Bettina Grant column."

"I'm very serious about it—and not because I want to take away something that's rightfully yours. Doing people out of their livelihoods isn't my thing. Believe me. But Bob has a perfect job offered to him in California and I wasn't kidding about the possibility of starting a family. But I have to keep working. Having something—a life for myself—is critical because Bob's work is so absorbing and when he's not here, he's really not here. Besides that, my dad's in California and he's on the downhill slide. I'd like to spend some time with him while I can.

"If I'd known that you were still considering taking over the column, I wouldn't have bothered to look into it. But everything I was told pointed to the contrary. I have to confess I met with Russ this afternoon and he says he's still open to suggestions."

Meredith winced at the news. It wasn't surprising, nor was it comforting. "I know that, too," she spoke back. "But I also know that the two top contenders are neither you nor I." They talked about the various column contenders and the odds, and then out of convenience, discomfort or simple courtesy, both allowed the topic of conversation to shift elsewhere. Finally, Meredith set her glass down, stood up and walked to the large window overlooking the dramatic, brightly lit buildings across the street.

"It's perfect," she chuckled. "A view on Lincoln Center. If I were going to live in New York and love the entertainment industry as I do, this is where I'd want to live."

"It works well for me and Bob," said Cassie quietly.

"Where'd you ever meet a character like Bob?" Meredith asked, still staring into the lights of the view outside.

"In Guatemala. Six years ago. I was sent there on a special assignment from the TV station I was working for. I was doing on-camera reporting in those days. Bob and I were both holed up in the same hotel during a riot."

Cassie's mental picture of Bob was still as compelling that night as it had been when she first noticed him leaning against the badly painted portico column at the hotel, cameras hanging from his shoulders, a small black cigar dangling from his mouth and a cynical grin on his face. Cassie had been arguing with the hotel proprietor about the number of rooms reserved for her camera crew, discovering that she seemed to be losing the argument. That, in itself, was uncertain because of her own poor command of the language.

Bob casually wandered over and in perfect Spanish negotiated on Cassie's behalf with the proprietor, a sweaty little man in a soiled beige suit. Soon Cassie had everything she needed including the services of the "special hotel porter," the proprietor's brother.

"This will cost you," Bob said as an aside. "The rule here is carry lots of bills and spend them effortlessly." As casually as he had appeared, he disappeared into the thick but straggling row of potted palms lining the arched walkway to the bar.

In the course of the next four days, Cassie frequently crossed paths with the tough and stocky photographer—in the hotel, the marketplace and wherever there was graphic activity. Cassie wasn't a seasoned war and riot reporter. She was awed by the cool demeanor with which he moved through the morass of red tape and gritty action.

One night he found her in the bar after a long and dusty day. "Buy you a cool one, Toots?" he asked. She glowered at his use of the word "Toots." He knew it and ignored it. Instead he ordered two beers. Bob Ainsworth was darkly attractive in a rugged way. His solid build was that of a boxer, and his hands, thick and hard, still moved with the grace of an artisan. He wore his dark hair short around his beefy face from which intense blue eyes regarded the world carefully, as though every view was through the all-telling lenses of his cameras.

They talked about combat news coverage and Hollywood. He was amused although at the same time impressed by Cassie's background in the movie industry. "I'm a big fan, grew up in a tough L.A. neighborhood with movies as my best friend," he told her. "But never had the balls to intrude upon a celebrity's space. I could never do paparazzi work."

Cassie, on the other hand was totally in awe of his field record as an award-winning photographer. When he told her he wanted to leave the field work and move into management, she doubted it. Not many hard-hitting news pros could imagine life without the cameras around their necks.

"Being a sixty-year-old war photographer isn't my idea of the perfect golden life," he told her. "I think we have to make changes within ourselves and by our own choice. The state of the world won't make them for us any longer because there always seems to be a war somewhere nowadays. Nobody rewards old war correspondents with desk jobs after the war is over. The war is never over."

When she herded her crew to the Quonset-hut airport to catch their ride on the convulsing little aircraft sitting on the steamy tarmac, Bob appeared in the dirty waiting room among the cackling throng of locals also vying for space aboard the craft. He walked up to Cassie and nonchalantly handed her a manila envelope. She accepted it hesitantly.

"Just a memento, Toots, of your war reporting days," he grinned. She opened the envelope to find a handful of photos, each a candid shot of her as she moved through the complex routine of putting together a special report in the troubled Latin community. Laughter bubbled to her lips when she saw the first photo, one of herself jumping in terrified surprise, her dark hair flying, as a scorpion scurried across her shoe as she began an on-camera narrative. The other photographs were as comically provocative.

"You're a good subject," said Bob Ainsworth drolly. She blushed as she realized how much time he had spent watching her, intimately, close-up. Before she could compose words to respond, a rapid Latin voice crackled through the drone in the waiting area and she was being rushed to her airplane by a sweaty customs official. She looked over her shoulder to see the photographer, cheroot in his mouth, saluting her with his index finger. She waved hastily back to him and the moment was over.

It had taken Cassie days to soak the dirt and grit of Latin America from her skin. She was sprawled languidly in a bubble-filled tub in the bathroom of her small brownstone flat three evenings after her return when the doorbell downstairs buzzed. She pulled herself from the warm water, wrapped a towel around her body and went to the intercom.

"It's Guatemala Bob," said a voice from outside.

"Who?"

"Bob Ainsworth, from Guatemala."

"Oh. Okay." She pushed the buzzer that would release the downstairs door to him. Her apartment was located on the second floor, so she had no time to dry her hair or run for a bathrobe before he knocked on her door. She opened it cautiously, not sure she had understood the voice from the outside. But the swarthy character from the dusty city was standing in her doorway looking as tough and determined as ever, the famous cigar hanging from his lips. His khaki pocketed jacket was travel worn and soiled, and he drug his camera bags over his shoulder as well as a bulging travel pack. He looked at Cassie through lined, weary eyes, eyes nevertheless intense as he regarded her standing with the long-wet hair clinging to her face and neck. And the fact that she was wearing only a towel.

He stepped into the flat, kissed her on the mouth and said, "Can I use your shower. I've had a long trip." She nodded, dumfounded, and pointed toward the bathroom where the bubblebath still steamed in the tub. As an afterthought, she called, "Get rid of the cigar. I don't allow smoking in here." He turned to look at her, grinned and tossed it into an ivy plant.

"It's your place," he said, heading again in direction of the bathroom.

"We haven't been apart since then," Cassie concluded the story of her courtship with Bob Ainsworth. "We got married six months later under a big oak tree on a hillside in Montana. It just kind of works."

"Good story," said Meredith, a little envious. "I'm jealous of love stories like that."

"What about the detective?"

Meredith looked at Cassie, amused. "You're kidding. He's way older than me. And as far as I can tell, I'm a real pain in the ass. Because he's assigned to a 'high profile' death and I'm intertwined with the victim, I'm his ward. Besides, I'm too busy chasing after a livelihood to have time to chase after a man."

"Well, it has only been a week, I keep forgetting that," said Cassie.

Meredith was blushing. "Don't forget the stuntman-turned-director."

"Of course." said Cassie.

"Look, I really came here to ask a favor. Maybe you owe me. But in any case, I'll share the take if you'll work with me." She outlined to Cassie the small bit of information she had collected on Joey O'Neal and the mystery person in the convalescent center. Cassie's news interest was hooked, and she fetched a yellow tablet and a pen to make notes.

"Will you investigate the situation from here? If we turn up something, you can have it the same day the Syndicate runs it—as long as you credit my story and the syndicate wire."

Cassie thought for a moment, then looked straight at Meredith and said, "Done deal."

"One other thing," Meredith began, hesitantly. "What's your book about? Is Bettina skewered in it?"

"Skewered? No—but they say, 'write about what you know.' I did. And I figured she'd never read it anyhow, like she never looked at my tapes."

Meredith thought about it for a moment, then retorted, "Yeah, but this is different. If you've put her into the center of it....?"

"She probably would have been flattered to be featured in a book about Hollywood, even though that wasn't the intent, but so what? She can't read it now, anyhow."

Meredith nodded her head slowly as Cassie looked away, her face impassive. It wasn't the time to argue.

Bidding a weary goodnight to the brunette by eight o'clock, Meredith returned to her hotel room, ordered a steak and baked potato from room service, and returned a call from Dusty. After the conversation with Cassie and the story of Bob Ainsworth, Meredith felt a rare need for more romance and even more stability in her life. The images of Dusty Reed that filled her mind didn't exactly resonate with the lifetime pictures she coveted, but talking with the amiable character was comforting.

Looking at the clock, she made a hasty decision to call Allan Jaymar. She needed his calm and knowing perspective. When he answered she heard his competent and calm connection as she explained her dilemmas.

Placing the room service cart outside the door, she finished a glass of white wine, left a wake-up call at the front desk and went to bed, surprising even herself by hearing no voices pestering her during the short moments before she fell asleep.

CHAPTER 22

A sleep-deprived Meredith left the hotel by four-thirty the next morning and was on an airplane heading to the West Coast by six. In the isolation of the aircraft cabin she began to ponder how she ended up on the chase: Bettina Grant's legacy—and killer, the chaotic story about a truly non-vital TV celebrity, and simply a job. Her last job-hunt was a dozen years earlier and landed her with Bettina. That realization took her on a mental journey bringing her to that morning's flight. It also reminded her she continued to identify herself, personally, as a "widow."

Meredith nostalgically recalled the Hollywood sojourn began when she was armed with a brand-new Northwestern University journalism degree and lured to Los Angeles by the seduction of the entertainment industry. Her ally was Gloria Carter, a former school roommate with a small apartment and an extra bed—and a job at a television network.

Soon after her arrival in LA, Meredith was a network temp worker, sometimes typing scripts, sometimes answering phones and sometimes photocopying documents. She ultimately landed permanently in the publicity office of the network's local station where her boss, Fred Barton, was a pleasantly nebbish man who reminded her of the actor Billy Crystal. Funny, smart, unassuming and supportive of his staff. In his New York accent, he complimented her on her writing and gave her extra projects because he could see she was capable of handling them.

At the station she met junior news producer Trevor Phillips. Tall, red-headed and bespeckled, his booming voice demanded, "You're new? You'll have to come to lunch with us in the executive suite." She nodded, slightly embarrassed.

"Should I go?" she asked Fred Barton. "Sure," he answered. "Phipps" he said using the normally-used nickname for Phillips, "is one of the good guys and whatever you do, it'll be an adventure. Which he'll probably film. That's his mission in life, maker of movies."

The "executive suite" was a taco truck a block away and their lunch companions were two old buddies of Phipps, both in TV production, who met there most every day. Lunch eventually evolved into movie screenings, or concerts, or art openings once or twice a month. Meredith was often the only female in the "crew" of three men, but increasingly more often simply with Phipps. Both their jobs gave them access to local events, including theater tickets and symphony performances, and Phipps' love of filmmaking inspired road trips to capture other excursions such as the florescent blooming of the wild flowers in the desert, or the annual return of the swallows to the graceful ancient mission at San Juan Capistrano. The "crew," Phipps and his two friends Geo and Thad—childhood pals, sons of filmland executives—shared his hunger for "making movies." Together they had enlisted and managed to land a plumb role in the Vietnam-era US Military, making and splicing together news and film footage—their posting, a back office in the wilds of the San Fernando Valley.

Meredith's journey with Phipps moved gradually and occasionally into the bedroom of her own one-bedroom apartment not far from the studio. They shared an attitude or acceptance that it was all simply part of the Hollywood adventure. Between the two of them they always had a new venue to explore—all of it laced with and colored by the excitement that whatever they did was part of the fabric of life in Hollywood—splendid, vibrant and sitting on the edge of the world. It might be the thrill and breath-taking moments of the Romero brothers' classical guitars ringing in the Hollywood Bowl on a balmy night with a large moon and a picnic. Another, sliding subtly backstage at the Greek Theater after Neil Diamond's stunning "Hot August Night" concert that set the singer up to be one of the generation's icons

She never once asked, "Where is this relationship going?" It was already "there." It was a bird's eye view of all the possibility Hollywood had to offer—belief that someday the work would equal the momentum and promise that the life around it was providing. Neither made large salaries and their adventures were not Red Carpet experiences, but those around and behind the spotlight. Meredith managed her own one-bedroom apartment. Phipps shared a house in the Hills with Geo and Thad. It was enough.

One evening, two and a half years into the journey, Phipps invited Meredith to his parents' house for dinner. They lived in an older, eccentrically antique house in one of the LA's traditional luxury neighborhoods. She'd visited before for a birthday or two and had occasionally been at events at Phipps older brother Larry's newer, trendier home. The "crew" had almost always been in attendance. Dinner that night, however, included just Phipps and Meredith and seemed to have only a purpose of "catching up" with Magda, his aging mother, a widow of a dozen years. Suzie, the housekeeper/caretaker, served dinner and busily cleaned up. After desert and coffee, Magda excused herself, explaining it was her bedtime. She leaned over to kiss Meredith on the cheek and smiled. "So sweet," she said. She smiled at her son. "Don't get up," she said, waving her hand dismissively as she left.

Meredith and Phipps took their coffee into a living room that seemed out of a 1940s Sunset Boulevard noir film. She sat down on a chintz and slightly worn couch and he pulled up a matching chair to face her. "I think," he said, "it's time we got married."

"Married? You mean like...wedding and stuff?" She found herself stammering in surprise.

He grinned his huge grin and said, "Well, yeah... that's usually how it starts."

The proposal was incongruous to everything the twosome seemed to be and over the next few seconds life images with which Meredith could not resonate flashed: weekly suburban schedules, kids, school lunches. She couldn't picture life outside of the world they knew as "Hollywood"— the movie, TV and music world—and she couldn't picture life Inside Hollywood without Phipps. So, she said, nearly whispering, "I guess you're right." Because this was Phipps, her companion in adventure, and that's how they were.

"Isn't this just the greatest!" he practically shouted.

"Sh! Don't wake your mom."

"Well, we have some planning to get to," Phipps said as they opened Meredith's apartment door a while later.

"Weddings, you know, are about the only time you get to write, design, produce, direct and star in your very own production," he chuckled. She laughed lightly, grabbed his hand and pulled him into the bedroom.

"Let's worry about weddings another time," she said. Idle conversation about "planning" was the only wedding topic that arose in the next several days.

Two weeks later, on a Friday afternoon, Fred appeared at Meredith's office door just at the end of the day. She was organizing news releases for the following week. "Got time for a drink, Merri? Let's run over to O'Banion's across the street."

"Sure," she agreed, realizing that Fred looked somehow downhearted. She gathered her purse and jacket, double checked the desk once more and turned out the lights. At O'Banion's they slid into a red leather booth, tiffany shaded lamps overhead, she asked, "What's up, Fred. You seem sad..."

He signaled the waitress and ordered two scotches. "Wow really serious with scotch! No beer today?" He shook his head and looked at his hands and then at her.

"I am serious Meredith—I have sad news and have been asked to pass it along to you." She felt a jolt of anxiety, and fear crept up her spine. Losing her job? He shook his head. "No—it's Phipps."

Confusion overtook anxiety for Meredith.

"This morning. I'm sorry, he stood up at his desk and collapsed with a heart attack. It was two hours before anyone noticed...he was writing, and everyone left him alone. It was too late. He's gone Merri." Tears ran down Fred's face.

"But he's only thirty-four! He's too young to have a heart attack," she blurted out, trying to make sense of the news. "He was fine when I talked to him this morning. He didn't say he was sick or...anything."

"Totally unexpected," said Fred. "No symptoms, nothing unusual, from what I'm told. His brother Jerry called Theo who called me...no one knows a lot except that he's.... gone." Meredith felt reluctant tears trickle down her cheeks, but she wasn't even sure what they were about. Friend, lover, pal, collaborator... fiancé?

Fred drove her home, shared a beer until her friend Gloria arrived from her own apartment a few blocks away. As he left, Meredith kissed Fred on the check and hugged him. "Thank you—I'm sorry the task had to fall to you."

He smiled meekly. "Better me than the personnel department."

Two days later, Meredith visited Phipps' mother at the older woman's request. Magda opened the door and tears ran down her face as she took Meredith's hands in her own. "Phipps' timing was never very good," she commented, attempting to lighten the moment. Meredith agreed.

"We called him the Hollywood Zephyr Express—always riding the dream express through the galaxy," said Magda as they shared a cup of tea. After a very silent moment, the older woman opened a drawer behind the table and extracted a small box tied with a light blue ribbon. "You should have this," she said. "Trev—Phipps—asked me to have these cleaned so he could give them to you this week-end. She wiped her wet eyes.

Meredith slowly opened the box to see a lovely antique ring, platinum with a large diamond in the center and filigree work holding it in place. Tucked next to it, a simple matching platinum band. She looked up at Magda.

"His grandmother's—intended these to go to him for his future wife," she said barely softly enough to be heard.

Meredith shook her head. "No, I can't do that. You should keep them." Magda put her palms up refusing the exchange.

"Phipps' cousin should have this," insisted Meredith.

Magda continued to refuse the box. "You keep them—for now," she said to the younger woman. "Savor how he felt about you and what he, at least, saw for your futures. Someday you may decide to close the book, but not now. They will bring you comfort. And just knowing you have them brings comfort to me and the family."

As Meredith hugged the woman at the door and turned to leave, Magda said, "You're so young and he was so emotionally driven—you may not have felt the depth of commitment he felt but let yourself grieve. You'll feel the loss. Know that we will always consider you part of our family. Please visit us and stay in touch!"

She was stunned others knew more about the fledgling engagement than she did. It would be several years before she could adequately parse the depth of her feelings, or the nature of them toward the charismatic "Hollywood Zephyr." At Phipps' celebration of life, his sister-in-law inadvertently introduced her as his "widow." The words stung Meredith deeply, but she did nothing to correct them. She knew that in his eyes and heart, they were as true as they could be. And often felt they had indeed managed to define her.

Meredith resigned from her job the next week. She packed up, slung a backpack over her shoulder, prepaid the rent, and spent the next three months hiking, traveling and dreaming in Europe. Upon her return to the Hollywood bubble, she phoned Fred, explained it was time to write—however she could find that path. A day later she drove into Beverly Hills to meet Bettina Grant. The years to follow brought dates and dalliances including an actor, contractor, restauranteur, banker and Dusty the stuntman-turned-director. And always the rings tucked away in the safe deposit box.

A dozen years later she was still thinking about loss when she felt the wheels of the plane touch down at Los Angeles International Airport: loss of two loving parents during her college years and how their insurance had allowed her to continue following a dream; loss of Phipps who defined part of that dream; Bettina who engineered another part of it. Meredith acknowledged that the shackles of loss, reinforced by guilt, had indeed imposed a kind of "widowhood."

Resolutely, and wearily, she stood up and collected her bag from the overhead compartment.

As Meredith's flight winged across the continent, in New York the crunch of the gravel under the tires of Cassie's car served as pegs further tightening the already taut strings of her nerves. Many years had passed since she had personally investigated a story such as the one that had brought her to the small but tidy residential nursing home in the rustic suburban neighborhood on Long Island.

The world has changed, she told herself, reviewing how she would introduce herself. Earlier in the day she had casually checked with a paralegal friend in the station's legal offices to make certain she understood how much leverage she had in this particular project.

"Trespassing? What kind of a story are you chasing?" asked Mary Bolyn, the paralegal.

"Nothing serious. Just wanted to make sure we do things by the book."

Mary regarded her warily then smiled. "By the book? In news? Since when?"

"So, if I understand you," said Cassie a few minutes later, "we have to correctly identify ourselves as news reporters before entering. I know that, and I know that we can't legally conceal our cameras on private property. If we are given permission to enter private property—as news reporters, with cameras—what can we run or show on the air?"

Mary shrugged, "Anything you get until they throw you out. Once you're asked to leave, you have to exit, or the property owners can call the police, and have you thrown out—or arrested for trespassing."

Cassie had also summoned the junior-most intern in the news department and instructed her to track down information on Joey O'Neal: where he was born, the schools he attended, any marital information, anything that would give them a key to his involvement with a private hospital in Long Island.

"Just be cautious," Cassie had warned. "Don't get us sued this early in the development of the story. Getting sued over a block-buster story is one thing, getting sued before you even get the details is something else."

An ambitious girl, Veronica the intern, had developed a complete dossier on O'Neal by eleven o'clock that morning. Cassie was pleased and amused. The kid had both ambition and intuition, both musts in the news business.

"I found out Joey's real name from a friend of mine who works for one of the celebrity services companies. He was Joseph Herman Ornstein from Philadelphia when he started out. Attended University of Pennsylvania for about two years. I got his home address from the university—don't ask how—you won't get sued, honest. And then I called Philly information. His parents still live at the same address. Can you imagine? I don't know who answered the phone, sounded elderly. I told her that I wanted to run out to the 'home' in Long Island to visit but I had lost the address. Guess what?"

Cassie had regarded the intense young woman with curiosity.

"Here's your address. I don't know who's out there, though. I ran out of ideas on how to ask that question since I'd implied I knew the party. This could be a series of unrelated coincidences, of course. And the information could add up to a big fat nothing."

"Great work!" Cassie realized how difficult it was for fledgling reporters to nudge their way into other people's lives and coax the truth from them. Such gall usually came only with experience, she mused cynically.

She walked into the news studio control room and found her assistant reviewing video footage for broadcasts later on the day. "I'll be back by noon," she said to the young man. "You have all the footage for now. When I get back we'll plan tonight's program." He nodded in affirmation and Cassie headed for the door and her car.

Ninety-minutes later, she arrived at the well-appointed red brick structure. She shivered in the afternoon cold and pulled her wool coat closer. A bitter breeze whipped her curly dark hair into her face. If the atmosphere held true to its promise, there would be flakes in the air before evening. She did a quick survey of the building, surrounded almost entirely by a brick wall. The best chance she had to take a photo of O'Neal's relative would have to come from within the building. "And legally, that means I have to have permission."

She wished young Veronica had enough additional gall to uncover at least a name about which she could inquire. She opened the back door of the car and removed an elaborate floral arrangement. She locked the car door and trudged up the walkway carrying the flowers in front of herself like a shield against impending danger.

The prickling heat inside the home's small, orderly foyer made her nose itch. She wrinkled it and looked around at the entrance and the hallway leading to the rooms. Everything was spotless and painted in warm, bright colors, looking new or at least well-maintained. Quiet efficiency pervaded the entire place.

A brass name plaque was affixed to the wall next to a small doorway, indicating the office of the director. Cassie stepped inside. The round matronly figure of a woman was bent over a file cabinet in the rear of the long room. She looked up, surprised when Cassie entered. Running a self-conscious hand through short gray curls, she asked, "How can I help you?"

Cassie smiled and said, "You can help me correct a very stupid oversight." The older women tilted her head to one side quizzically and said, "Well, I'm only a temporary clerk-typist, but try me. The director's on vacation and her administrative assistant had to run an errand—should be back any minute. But maybe I can help. I'm Bernice."

Cassie's hopes fell dramatically, but she persisted, hoping she might get lucky. "Well, I work in the news department for one of the New York TV studios. A cohort in TV, Joey O'Neal, has a relative living here. I'm here to deliver this floral arrangement to her. Unfortunately, in my own rush to finish a dozen different errands before I drove out, I didn't bring the slip of paper with the person's name on it. I think it was Ornstein, but I'm not sure."

The woman looked at her blankly, then bit her lip. "I don't know any of the patients, but we can look in the residents' file here and maybe we'll learn something from that. She opened a black binder and ran her index finger down the list. "Ornstein—there's a Rebecca Ornstein. Could that be it?"

"I'll bet it could," smiled Cassie, amazed she had crossed the first major hurdle so effortlessly. Sometimes you get lucky. "Do you think I could see her and deliver these in person? It would be such a big help."

The clerk shrugged and said, "Why not? We sure wouldn't want to disappoint Joey O'Neal. What an exciting job you must have! Let's find her. Lots of our patients are out on short-term visits, for the holidays," she lowered her voice, "when it's possible you know. Some aren't…well, they can't cope on the outside, you know. I haven't worked here long—only a few days from the temp agency. Most of the patients are in the solarium at this time of the day. Why don't you wander down there and see if she's around? Ask Wally, the attendant, for her. I have to stay here."

Cassie passed only one other person as she made her way down the long pristine hall. She came to a wide, round room with windows that overlooked the outside yard, now enshrouded in winter. Skylights brought more brightness into the space filled with potted palms and other greenery. She spotted a solidly built man wearing yellow pull-over and white trousers and a name tag that said, "Wally." She asked for Rebecca and he pointed toward a drawn-looking woman sitting in a straight-back chair in an isolated corner of the room, among palm leaves. The woman looked about forty, but empty face and eyes gave her an ageless, translucent quality. Limp brown hair hung to angular shoulders that were wrapped in a blue sweatshirt. She stared blankly into the dim grayness of the winter sky outside the window.

"Rebecca?" Cassie asked gently. The woman did not move. "Rebecca," Cassie repeated. She imagined she saw a minute flicker in the frozen eyes, but in fact there was no acknowledgment of Cassie's. Walking closer, facing the seated figure, Cassie held out the floral arrangement. "These are for you. Aren't they pretty? They're from Joey."

Still no movement, no acknowledgment. Cassie felt a deep sadness looking at the face that should have been youthful but wasn't, and the lifeless eyes staring into secret chambers of their own prison. Slender hands lie formless in the gaunt lap, fingernails clipped clinically short and straight. On the fourth finger of the left hand was a thin gold wedding band.

"She doesn't respond," said a voice from behind, startling Cassie. "That's why she's here." Cassie looked up to see Wally watching the action. She froze in uncertainty.

"I'm just delivering these…" she began then stopped. Wally shrugged and said, "Suit yourself. Leave them but she won't even know they're here." He walked away and Cassie breathed a sigh of relief.

"I'll just leave them here on this table," Cassie said to the inattentive ears of Rebecca Ornstein, and looked around to see no staff members close by. She discretely removed from her handbag a small thirty-five-millimeter camera loaded with very high-speed film to accommodate any light conditions. She quickly lined up the image in her viewfinder and snapped off a half dozen shots, re-setting the shutter and lenses speed each time to make certain she compensated for all light possibilities. Slipping the camera back into her purse she said, "Enjoy your flowers, Rebecca," and hurriedly walked back into the hall.

"I can't tell you how much I appreciate your help on this," Cassie said to the temporary typist, Bernice, when she reached the office. Thankfully, the director's assistant still had not returned. Cassie again chose to finesse the clock—and Bernice. "Who do you think Rebecca is?" she asked the woman. "Don't you just wonder if she is Mr. O'Neal's relative—a sister or cousin perhaps?"

"I was curious about that," confessed the woman. "But I thought it probably didn't matter and maybe you knew anyway."

"Not me," confessed Cassie. "But, am I ever curious now, guess it's the newswoman in me. Aren't you still wondering?" Cassie was eyeing a computer terminal sitting on a desk not five feet from where they stood. She knew that the electronic data bank held the answers to any questions they might have.

"I bet we can find out easily enough," said Bernice conspiratorially. She went to a file cabinet with exterior locks protecting the drawers. "They're not locked during the day," she said as if reading Cassie's mind. She opened the top drawer, fingered through the row of file folders and pulled one out.

She opened it, laid it down on the nearby desk and then began thumbing through the stack of paperwork from the folder. Cassie once again held her breath. Stapled to the inside of the front file cover was a bright red notice: 'Confidential.' Bernice hadn't noticed it, or perhaps didn't understand its importance. Or didn't care, so curious was she about personal data on a glamorous Hollywood celebrity. Instead, she located what appeared to be the basic admittance sheet on Rebecca.

"Oh, here it is. But it isn't very interesting. She was admitted here five years ago by her husband, a Joseph Ornstein. Doesn't mean a thing to me. Does it to you?"

Cassie shrugged innocently and said, "Can I see?" She looked over Bernice's shoulder to see the form for herself. Age 35, address 908 West Birch Street, Philadelphia. She memorized the information, patted Bernice on the shoulder and said, "Well, it was a fun fantasy, wasn't it. Thanks for all your help. Oh, by the way, I snapped a picture of Rebecca with her flowers in case Joey O'Neal wants to see it. I'm sure no one will mind, but why don't you take the flowers home if Rebecca doesn't want them?"

"How nice of you," said Bernice. Cassie never heard the answer. She was out the door, trotting down the red brick steps and striding briskly to her car trying not to be obvious about a desire to be miles away from the place very rapidly. In the parking lot, she saw an officious looking brunette moving almost as quickly as she was but heading into the building. Cassie's intuition told her to make fast tracks. She barely avoided meeting the nemesis who would have prevented her from accomplishing the difficult mission as painlessly a she had.

"What's the Ornstein address in Philly," Cassie asked the intern from a public phone booth just off the roadway. "908 West Birch Street," said the voice at the other end of the line. Cassie was struck with another jolt of adrenalin and she moved quickly to the car, anxious to return to the office, call Meredith and turn the information over to her own news people for the next day's program. She had photographs and had accomplished it all legally.

☆

"You're kidding," said Meredith. "You are good."

"No, I 'm foolish—and very lucky," said Cassie. "And to give you an idea how foolish I really am, I actually arrived at the home entertaining thoughts about breaking into the office after dark."

"What...?" Meredith responded with a loud guffaw. "Cassie, the network news director turned cat burglar! What headlines that would have made!"

"What a law suit it would have created! Don't think my knees weren't knocking over that possibility. But I was egged onward by our mission into the biker world. As it was, the typist opened the gates to King Joey's mines without even noticing the 'no trespassing' sign. If she had accessed the same file on the computer, she'd have been locked out, I know it. There had to be internal security codes on the electronic files. But we sailed right passed them by never even turning on the computers. I told her I was in TV news and even took a photo. She never batted an eye."

"You are a lucky lady," said Meredith. "I need one more day!"

"Why?" croaked Cassie, eager to hand over the hard-won story to the network's morning news crew so they could, as agreed, break the story as part of their "people in the news" segment of the morning program.

"Because, it's the right thing to do," Meredith responded. "We don't even know if she's still married to Joey. The big story is that he announced his engagement to Mandy Martell, the rock singer, a couple of months ago. No wedding date set yet, of course. But when I check out the files, I'm sure I'm going to read this will be his first marriage. So, in the interest of fair reporting I have to get a comment from Joey, or his camp, about this. I can't run anything until I at least put the question to him. You'd do the same thing."

"You're right, damn it," sighed Cassie. "Think you'll have something by tomorrow?"

"Count on it. If I fax the information to Joey's manager, then say that I'm running the story 'today' with or without a statement from Joey, I'm bound to get at least a 'no comment.' And speaking of that, we're still one link-up short of an explanation as to why Joey was in the Harley Bell. And why he beat up the kid."

"This could be Joey O'Neal week in the press. But with his ego, he may well love it."

Cassie took a deep breath as she hung up the phone, then locked the freshly printed photographs, discretely developed only minutes before in the news department's film lab, along with her notes in the bottom drawer of her desk. Her day had been over for hours and darkness had long ago fallen on the city. Bob was working again. But they were planning to finish Christmas shopping the next evening, enjoy a rare dinner out together, buy a Christmas tree and decorate it. After the day of investigation and then work, Cassie intended to get a good night's sleep which she hoped would put her back onto a normal schedule after the strange and unnerving week behind her.

As she straightened her desk and slipped on her coat once more, she had second thoughts about leaving the O'Neal material in her desk. She unlocked the drawer, placed the prints and notes in her purse, then left the office.

CHAPTER 24
TUESDAY AFTERNOON—BEL AIR

"The prodigal sister returns, and not a moment too soon," announced Sonia as Meredith dragged herself and her luggage into the office mid-morning on Tuesday. With the three-hour time difference, she had already spent a half-day in transit from New York, going directly to the office, arriving almost in time to do a full day's work on "The Coast." The break-in of her home weighed heavily on her mind.

"You have a dozen calls to return," Sonia began the morning's litany, but a card table set up next to Bettina's desk distracted Meredith.

"What's that?" she asked.

"Ito's desk," said Sonia, self-consciously.

"Ito's desk?"

"He's helping out since there's nothing else for him to do around here except keep the moving boxes in order. And, his time is already paid for." Meredith reluctantly took the cue and wandered from the offices into the house proper. She was unnerved by what greeted her. Every cupboard, drawer and closet had been emptied, the contents packed away into boxes or stacks on the floor. The perpetual orderliness of the well-decorated rooms was now unraveled just as the stability of Bettina Grant's life and legend was slowly disintegrating. Meredith felt sad again, grief beginning to blossom after the days of chaos and confusion.

She turned quickly back into the offices just as Ito came from the kitchen. Now he was dressed in a long-sleeved sport shirt and broadly cut trousers. His hair was brushed back off his face, no longer the bowl-shaped elfin cut he had worn as Bettina's houseman.

"Put your things down," he told Meredith congenially, relieving her of the carry-on hanging case still burdening her shoulder. "When you're ready, we'll give you the run-down from yesterday and today."

She nodded robot-like and walked into her own office. Thankfully nothing there had been disturbed. But the thought of dishevelment of personal belongings made her remember the condition of her townhouse.

"I have to call Raymond."

Ito shook his head. "I hope you don't mind, but I took the liberty to do that. He's on his way over here. ETA about forty-five minutes."

"How about marrying me and taking care of me for the rest of my life?"

Ito shook his head. "You are too tall for me. Besides you aren't rich enough. But I will fix you some coffee—decaf?"

Sonia sighed, "He's been a God-send."

Meredith shivered and turned to survey the work piled up on her desk. To her surprise there were not the usual clumps of paperwork covering the surface. Instead there were four neat piles, organized with explanatory notes on the top of each. She looked at Sonia, who shrugged and said, "So he's a better organizer than me."

"First things first, you are supposed to interview the new member of *Sarah's World* tomorrow at lunch," Sonia said as the three settled in around the coffee table in Meredith's office. "And then just to make things a little more exciting, the publicist from the new Nick Nolte film is expecting you to do a set visit. Oh, are you going to continue to do set visits or just concentrate on the big interviews like Bettina did? The publicist says she can't promise Nolte tomorrow, but she can arrange a luncheon off-set next week."

"One thing at a time," said Meredith. "Confirm the *Sarah's World* luncheon, and yes, the set visit. I need copy for the columns, and yes, I will continue the visits—I have to keep writing the column."

"I could help," Sonia offered tentatively.

"Yes, you probably could. That's another issue. What else?"

"I've gone through the news items sent to you from the publicists to see which look interesting enough to use. I've called for more information on those that needed it." Meredith sat up in surprise at Sonia's newly exhibited enterprise.

"I, too, have some things for you," said Ito, and began a self-conscious rundown of the phone calls to be returned. He cleared his throat and concluded with, "Finally, we have about one month's possession of the offices and then we will need a new home. If you agree, I'll start looking, but I would like some direction on what to look for."

"It certainly feels like you guys are in control here. I'm glad someone is. Which brings me to my news—or lack of it," Meredith began the slow, non-newsy report of her trip, careful not to mention the meeting with the radio syndicate or with Cassie O' Connell. "And what this all means, Ito, is that I can't give you any reason to look for new office space because I don't know that any of us will be involved with the column after January 31. Awkward as it is, that's a week after we're due to vacate these premises."

"If you approve, I'll check on an extension," he said calmly.

"Have we heard what's going to happen to the house? Is the family putting it on the market?"

Ito spoke up, "I'm told they were waiting for you. Maybe that's what the appointment with the attorney is about tomorrow."

"That's tomorrow, too," said Meredith. "Another full day." The group disbursed in time to return a phone call before the figure of T.K. Raymond appeared at the office door.

"And, she's back," he said quoting an obscure TV show source which Meredith could not remember.

"Darn, I'm at a loss for the author of that quote," she said, reaching for the hanging garment bag and her other belongings, adding, "and she leaveth with the good detective to assess the damage done unto her home, and to scorn the forces that done it!"

She drove absently to the townhouse determined to remain businesslike whatever the circumstances. She opened the garage door from her car remote and pulled in. Raymond pulled into the driveway and parked behind her. A black and white police car sat in front. Two uniformed officers got out and walked down the driveway to meet Raymond and Meredith. Together they entered the house through the garage entrance.

Meredith steeled herself for the sight to come as the group walked into the kitchen and then into the living room. Every drawer, cupboard, closet, hamper and other possible receptacle had been opened, the contents disgorged. From knives and silverware in the kitchen to panties and hosiery in the bedroom, everything was heaped ungraciously on the floor. Meredith's jewelry box lay upturned on the carpet, finely entwined strands of silver and gold caught up together in hopeless webs, dozens of pairs of earrings scattered throughout the room.

Meredith shook her head and closed her eyes at a sight too complex to comprehend in one glance. Cold fear grasped her stomach and she looked around frantically. "Paco, where's Paco?" she cried. "He has to be here somewhere. No one would really..."

A firm hand on her shoulder stopped the rising emotional tide. Raymond turned her shoulder to face him and said, "Relax. After I spoke to you yesterday, I took the liberty of borrowing a key from your neighbor and coming over to survey just how drastic the situation was. C'mon." He walked to the half-bath located off the living room and opened the closed door. A large gray cat sat on the counter against the wall, glaring. When he saw Meredith, he jumped to the carpet and strolled toward her as though nothing had happened.

"How'd you do with all of this?" she asked as she picked up the furry animal and hugged him close to her chest, nuzzling his neck. Paco looked at the three others with patient disdain. Hugging and kissing in public wasn't his strong suit.

"There's the guy with the story," laughed one of the cops, reaching out and stroking Paco's back. "If he could talk."

For the second time in a week Meredith watched as law enforcement performed its scientific best to uncover damage done the evening before. This time they were in her own home. She prowled through the mess when permitted, absently picking up clothes here and there, stuffing utensils back into drawers when and where possible. The rest would be attended to more meticulously later when there weren't a dozen eyes and ears focused on her.

She initially guessed that nothing was missing. "There's not much of great value here anyway, except for the electronics, and it's intact," she explained. "All my really good jewelry, the little of it I own, is in my safe deposit box. Any paperwork here is a duplicate of what's in the office and no one touched my checks or credit cards that were in the desk drawer. I travel with only a couple of them."

Books had been pulled from the tall bookcase in the second bedroom, but even the signed first edition celebrity volumes had been left behind.

"Someone was obviously looking for something specific," said Raymond to the other officers. "And probably personal. Are you sure there's nothing missing?" he asked Meredith. "Think hard about that."

She ticked off a mental check list, her hands wrapped around a cup of coffee she'd managed to brew for everyone amidst the rubble. Paco sat on the corner of the counter observing the activity with reserved interest.

"Could someone have wanted something you had with you?"

"I only had a couple of columns with me. Bettina's old brief case along with two shoe boxes of paperwork of hers was in my car trunk. Most of it will go over to Luanne who is the executor of her will, but I brought a few documents home that looked work-related. We'll see."

Raymond pointed toward the steps down to the garage. "Let's look through them. It can't hurt." Paco jumped to the floor from his perch and followed them down the steps, still trailing when they returned a few minutes later, arms clutching the boxes and the briefcase from the office.

"Some divorce stuff," said Meredith by way of explanation as she set the contents onto the living room floor. "A couple of pictures of all of us together which I doubt anyone else would want, a love letter from an admirer," she said sheepishly. "I didn't think the world needed to see that or even know about it."

"Some famous star we might know?" sniggered Raymond.

"Why yes, detective, you probably would."

The two sorted through the papers in the box then Meredith separated the handles of the well-used briefcase and pulled a half dozen scraps of paper from the three pockets. She reached deep inside and found an old tube of lipstick and a half-dozen unused tissues, now yellowed with age.

"More of the same, I guess," Raymond said, as a heavy-set uniformed policeman came into the room. "Doesn't look professional, the method of entry was too sloppy. They broke into the bedroom window from the balcony. It's an easy climb from the back. No obvious prints. I'd say whoever did it watches the same cop shows everyone else does. Probably wore gloves. The guys are about wrapped up here."

"Sorry," said Raymond, looking apologetically at Meredith.

"We seem to be striking out on all fronts," she said.

"It's not over yet."

"I just want this thing to go away and to get on with my life."

"Have you eaten lunch?" Raymond asked, offering a hand to help Meredith from the floor.

She shook her head. "I'm not hungry and I have a lot to do." She looked around the room. "Any reason why I can't clean this up now?"

"Not one," Raymond answered. "But eat something and try to keep an eye out for anything you notice that may be missing—something you overlooked before. And one more thing…."

She looked up at him. "I don't think you should stay here alone tonight," he said. "I've already told you that, but I want you to listen to me this time."

"Great. I should invite a friend in?"

"Maybe better, go stay with a friend."

"Sure," she said absently, absorbed in thoughts about the job ahead of her. Raymond followed the last uniformed officer out the front door, calling, "Talk to me tomorrow—and find a friend to stay with tonight." He figured she'd dismiss the order.

"The guy couldn't have waited until the place was dirty," muttered Meredith. "He had to do this right after the housekeeper had been here!"

☆

Meredith spent nearly four hours putting away the belongings that were strewn about the unit and then, because she felt like her private domain had been so painfully violated, scrubbed down the counters and floors and vacuumed the rugs. It was nearly six when she finished, but the adrenaline pumping through her system had not calmed down. She changed into a pair of gray workout togs and drove the five minutes to the health club for an aerobics class.

On the way home she stopped at the Brentwood Village market and collected three bags of groceries including a roasted chicken and a half dozen deli items to tide her over for a few days. An excellent cook when she needed to be, Meredith had long before given up the need to prove her culinary capabilities to herself on a nightly basis. She and scores of other working women found gourmet and deli take-out as the TV dinners of the eighties.

Against all advice to avoid being alone at home that night, Meredith ended the long day heading to the shower before sleep. Stepping into the tiled enclosure, she remembered the detective's warning. She had never before considered anyone breaking into her home, but now she was feeling invaded and vulnerable. As she heard the shower running, she thought of the grisly scenes from the 1950's movie classic "Psycho" in which the heroine is murdered grotesquely in a motel shower. Meredith turned off the water, pulled on a bathrobe. She went from window to window throughout the entire house checking locks and latches. Only then did she feel comfortable enough to step into the cleansing, cascading water and let the needle-like points wash away the long day that had begun a continent away in Manhattan.

Hungering for a little pampering, she pulled on a pair of pink silk pajamas, a seriously femme gift, unused until now, from her friend Gloria. Moving into the kitchen to see about dinner, she fed Paco, re-heated deli-chicken and opened a cardboard container of three-bean salad. When the chicken was warm, she pulled white meat from the bones and piled it onto her plate with an unusually large dollop of mayonnaise, defiantly reasoning that she deserved the calories.

She then took the dinner and a freshly poured glass of sherry into the living room and settled onto the rug in front of gas log's glow in the fireplace. Paco curled up a few feet away, his eyes sinking gradually into deep sleep, his purring a comforting backdrop.

When Meredith had finished eating, she idly reached over and pulled Bettina's old briefcase closer. The case evoked bittersweet memories and Meredith allowed herself to explore the moment of nostalgia. The love letter to Bettina had come from a world-famous composer who the columnist had met while visiting the set of a movie he had been scoring. Meredith looked at the date and was surprised to see that it was written only six years prior. She read on curiously, because in the entire time Meredith had worked with her, Bettina rarely interviewed anyone but the "star people," leaving all others to Meredith.

She obviously did more than interview this guy, thought Meredith, then smiled. She had a vague recollection of a large gift box of autographed CDs arriving by messenger one afternoon, and later an arrangement of tropical flowers into which was placed the latest CD album of the composer. Bettina had left on an unexpected trip to Cancun three days later, a rare "R 'n R" break, Bettina had called it.

Meredith expected that the trip was more than that, but she would never know. Bettina's romances were seldom, and even more seldomly talked about. Those discrete trysts had gone to the grave with the woman who had partaken of them.

Meredith reached deep into the brief case in a final gesture of curiosity. Her fingers wrapped around a small cylinder which she tugged to dislodge from the bag's seam. It was a gold Cross Pen with Bettina's name on it. Meredith smiled sadly, recognizing the gift from the Publicist Guild many years before, honoring Bettina as the guild's favorite member of the press that year. The pen had been lost a year or so later, disappointing Bettina to no end. For a moment Meredith forgot that she would never see how pleased her boss would have been when she handed it to her the next day. Then she wondered, again, idly, what Cassie had written about the columnist and how the famous woman might have taken it.

She unfolded the few inconsequential pieces of paper from the case, mostly actors' biographies or fact sheets from now old movies or TV series long since cancelled. Her fingers happened on a stapled-together group of yellowed receipts apparently from the Hyatt Regency Lahaina, Maui, signed by Larry Grant with a room number scribbled on the bottom; records of an earlier, perhaps happier time in Bettina's life.

Flattening each fact sheet, Meredith read them closely by the light spilling from the fire. As she explored the background information from a 1980 Jack Nicholson psycho-thriller, "The Shining," she heard a barely audible crunch on the front porch. Meredith sat upright, her entire body prickling, her neck and spine locked in apprehension. Raymond's words echoed in her mind. She heard a light knock at the door.

Slowly and quietly she brought herself upright, tucking the briefcase and its contents behind the log carrier next to the fireplace. She moved warily toward the entry hall and the front door. The knocking sounded lightly again.

Turning on the front lights, she peered through the small window in the door. T.K. Raymond's face stared back at her, fish-eye lenses-wide. Relieved at a familiar, nonthreatening face, she opened the door, taking the blast of cool air from the December night, quickly reminding her of her lightly silk-clad body.

The detective, being no fool, noticed it as well. She shivered and slipped behind the door as she opened it. He was obviously warmer than she was, dressed in a thick wool jacket over a dark blue turtleneck sweater and jeans. He looked more like a stockbroker at leisure than a homicide detective.

"If you'll turn your back, I'll put something more on, and we can close the door," she said nonplused.

"Good idea," he answered, embarrassed, turning his tall frame away from her. She pushed the door closed hard and dashed up to the bedroom to emerge seconds later wearing a white fleece robe over the pink silk.

"I feel like a delinquent who's just been caught by the truant officer," she grimaced. Her face was unadorned by make-up, hair pulled into a shower-damp ponytail.

"Because I caught you in your pajamas, or because I told you not to stay here alone and you did anyway?"

"Okay, both."

"I figured you'd do just about what you wanted to, and that wouldn't include having a slumber party. So, I stopped by."

"Well thanks. Not really necessary. You know, I could have followed your instruction and had company."

"You could have, and I would have tipped my hat and said goodnight, knowing that you were in safe hands."

She laughed. "Well, at least not alone, I guess! Come in, please. I'm drinking sherry. Can I interest you in a glass?"

"Against rules—but, well—I'm off duty—beer instead?"

"Light?" He nodded okay, and she padded into the kitchen to retrieve a bottle and a beer mug.

"Bottle's fine," he called.

"So, what's the story? Why are you here? Make sure I'm still upright?"

"Checking in, is a better way to look at it. I can't stay long but I have arranged a police car to drive by every half-hour or so."

Raymond pulled up a chair across the coffee table from the sofa and sat down. Meredith slouched onto the sofa, tucking her feet under her robed body.

He told her that his partner's investigation he had come up with a partial license plate on the dark car that had knocked Fred to the ground. "A bus boy from the restaurant was just getting off work, coming around from the back of the place on the way to his bus stop. He saw the car, caught a part of the plate, but then nobody asked him for it, and he dismissed the whole thing. We're lucky he has a good memory."

"Does it correspond with anything else you've found. Maybe a Mafia or cartel car?" asked Meredith, trying to humor the detective.

"Not yet, but we're working on it."

"What about Bettina's appointment the night she died?"

"Nothing there, either. But we're still working on that."

"Your most popular response seems to be 'But we're working on it.'"

"'Defensive' isn't a great look on you." he frowned.

"Sorry. Just tired. It's been a long week. Between angst, grief, chaos…The O'Neal story building daily. Still in limbo but a heavy challenge…along with everything else."

"Is there anything I need to know about that story?"

"Not yet…still working on it." She grinned mischievously.

"You've had a lot going on. Did you resolve your future with the newspaper syndicate?"

She shook her head no. "I have a lot of competition—not the least of whom is Cassie. By the way I saw her in New York. She says, 'hello and thanks for dinner.'"

He smiled.

"We both apologize for intruding on a family weekend."

He flinched, surprised at the comment, then smiled. "No problem." But the embarrassment on Meredith's face prompted him to add, "Widower. 48-years old. One 24-year old son. Other questions?"

"No" she laughed. "Not really. We were naturally curious, being women and all."

"And the silver Jeep that we've seen at the curb off and on...?" Raymond was grinning, almost paternally.

She held up both hands, both ring-free, and shrugged. "Unencumbered. I'm—it's hard to explain and for another time." Uncomfortable in the silence and feeling a need for closure, she said quietly, "I kind of think of myself as a widow. Long story over a martini at some point." She pictured the image of Phipps's rings in her safe deposit box.

Raymond nodded. "We'll do that. Meanwhile," he lifted himself from the chair. "The cop car will continue to patrol past your door, and it's not smart for you to go anywhere without someone—preferable bigger than you, hopefully stronger—accompanying you." He handed her his card. "Let me or my partner Marty—his phone number is on the back—know where you're going if you're doing something away from home or office publicly. 'Kay? And please, no seedy bars or South-Central clubs or...."

"Well, okay on the bars and clubs and I will be moving around for work during the day," Meredith began defensively. "But, here's the thing. I'm going to a big black-tie party Saturday night. Both of my normal escorts are out of the picture: on location and otherwise promised, so I'll be going alone. Not a big deal, with my work, I'm used to a solo social life. It's my friend Gloria Masner's annual holiday party, the one personal thing I do each Christmas season and, the group is hardly the murderous type. No cameras, politics, deal-making...but I wouldn't miss it. And if necessary, I'll stay at Gloria's for the night." She shrugged dismissively. "So, if I am required to have an arm piece—unless one of your buddies out in that black and white is available ...," she snickered.

"George Masner's wife?"

"You know them?"

"Lots of people know George," he answered. He stood, uncomfortably, thinking, for a moment, then sighed, "I'll have to dig out the tuxedo I guess."

"Really?" Meredith quizzed, looking at him suspiciously. "Well, you won't be uncomfortable. It's not a big public thing with photographers and fan stuff. It's a nice party for good friends."

"'Arm piece.'"

He pulled on his coat. At the door, he smiled, regarding the white robe with the pink trim, and said "Lock your door." Then left. She saw the black and white slow down in front of the place and watch the detective wave to them.

Closing and locking the door, she settled back in front the of fire and wondered why in the world she had made the "widow" comment to this guy. She thought the identity had disappeared with the advent of maturity.

☆

Raymond waved at the two police officers in the black and white car. He climbed into his own vehicle and started down the street toward the highway, but in an impulsive moment, pulled into the parking lot of a nearby trendy bar and grill and parked. Inside, he made his way to the quiet end of a mahogany bar, exotic and artistic bottles of liquor lit dramatically along the back wall. He ordered a beer and stared at a TV monitor hanging above, for a while, seeing but not paying attention to the football game in progress. He thought about Lilli. What life might be like if she were still alive, waiting for him at home in the Malibu house they had worked so hard to buy and renovate.

Now, no one waited. Raymond lived there alone, rarely entertaining because he had chosen work as his substitute for the energetic woman who had been his wife. He had raised his son Will—thought he'd done a pretty good job. Will came home from college a few times a year, but wasn't around much, being a social and bright kid who seemed to love life. Like his mom, thought Raymond. The university semester was over for Will, but he'd gone on a ski trip with friends until a few days before Christmas—still a few days away. Recently, Raymond said to the boy, "I wish you'd spend more time here."

Will's answer was simple. "You're working so much now I hardly see you. And it's sad around here. The house is exactly as it was when mom died ten years ago, dad. Isn't time to move on. I'd be happy to move along with you, but you have to want to."

"He's a smart kid," thought Raymond, standing up from the bar stool, leaving money on the counter along with a half-finished beer.

CHAPTER 26
WEDNESDAY—BEL AIR

Meredith started the next day much earlier than usual, detouring to the office via Allan and Potty's house at their insistence. Savoring rich chicory coffee and a fluffy, buttery croissant with orange marmalade, she talked about the sadness and guilt in not having time or focus to grieve for Bettina. "We'll do it for you," soothed Potty. "You'll have plenty of time soon to deal with it."

They talked quickly about the case and about business. "Remember, Merri," Allan reminded her as she left, "I'm here for you and know a lot about the way these types of things work. Let me help you."

"I honestly don't think I could do it without your guidance, Allan."

"Don't try," he smiled paternally. "But your trip to New York tells me you are certainly capable of taking care of business. I have a few more years under my belt and a couple of good contacts…but you're doing fine." As he spoke, a black and white police cruiser made its way slowly down the lane.

"Everywhere—they follow me everywhere," moaned Meredith.

"Good," Potty and Allan exclaimed simultaneously.

When she let herself into the office it was still earlier than other arrived. Meredith felt hesitant and not just a little emotional again, wondering how it would be to simply sit down at home and let the reality of it all overtake her—even for a day or two. She was surprised of how little had changed in the four rooms defining the business environment over the past week since the death of Bettina Grant. Anyone unfamiliar with the happenings of the past seven days would not have realized that a major upheaval had taken place.

The evidence of upheaval was apparent, however, where it most counted. In Meredith's opinion, the columns were weaker than Bettina's, due in part to the fact there were concerns other than piecing together a "go-for-the-gold" gossip column occupying the concentration of the writer. She was blatantly frustrated about that, and realized it was imperative she right the oversight by making the next month's columns provocative and vital. Quality writing and reporting would be the only way she could hope to win the loyalty of the editors.

The Joey O'Neal story could go a long way in accomplishing that task for her. And she would devote part of today tracking down any and all response possible from Joey's various spokespeople. She also knew there would likely be other time-gobbling interruptions to a normal workday that she would have to take in stride. One of those was an eleven a.m. meeting with Bettina' attorney. She recognized Ito's neat, precise handwriting and was grateful for it, amused by it. He had also noted the lunch with a major network comedy series star, as well as the movie set visit in the afternoon hours. She instinctively knew the day was too full, deciding to postpone the set visit until the next day, the day when she was supposed to meet Larry Grant for lunch.

Ito moved around in the kitchen, no doubt fixing coffee—this time decaf without his usual sarcastic, "Why bother?"

Meredith thought about Larry Grant and the stories Cassie had told her, the information she had about the house. She wondered what he wanted to discuss. Probably telling us we should move out of our offices ASAP, she mused. Ito had volunteered to handle office arrangements and Meredith fully intended to allow him the pleasure. He seemed surprisingly capable. She didn't need logistic problems as well as the other challenges she faced.

Soon after the morning began in earnest, Meredith's schedule changed once more, and she reinstated the set visit for early afternoon. She juggled the constantly ringing phone with the demand to get a column written before five o'clock filing. In the midst of it, Sonia called to Meredith, "It's William Roland, Joey O'Neal's Manager."

Meredith braced herself for what she thought might become negotiation and answered the phone with a friendly but business-like "Meredith Ogden."

"What is this bullshit, Miss Ogden?"

"Excuse me, but I'm not sure I understand your question." Meredith kept her voice cordial.

"What is this bullshit about Joey O'Neal and a previous wife and a biker bar. I think you've been dreaming up tales, my dear."

"Not according to the records of the Morningside Care Home in New York. They believe that one Rebecca Ornstein was admitted by her husband Joseph Herman Ornstein in 1986, AKA Joey O'Neal, of 908 West Birch Street, Philadelphia, Pennsylvania, the home of Joey O'Neal's parents."

A protracted silence overtook the phone line. Meredith silently tapped a thumb against her desk nervously, waiting for the agent to speak. Finally, he accommodated her. "You're dancing with disaster here, young lady," he said.

"Why?" asked Meredith. "Because of Joey's recent engagement to the rock singer. Does she know about Rebecca?"

"Of course, she knows everything about Joey," snapped the agent.

"That's good. So, she must know when Joey divorced Rebecca. There was no indication in any official documents. And what does all of this have to do with Joey's altercation in the bar out in Pacoima, or his arrest? That's already old news."

"I'm not going to answer any more of your questions," said the agent in a tone that had not mellowed.

"Look," said Meredith, "why not ask Joey to talk with me personally. Can't you see that having a loved one stricken with a debilitating mental disease is nothing to be ashamed of. In fact, there are a lot of people in the country who would probably embrace Joey even more if they knew what a generous and loving friend he has been to a woman who no longer responds to the world. People can learn from Joey."

"I'll call you back later!" The agent's voice dripped with rancor.

"Wait," Meredith cautioned. "Do it before the end of the day because I'm going to press with this story at five o'clock this afternoon. If I don't have a statement from Joey, I'll go with what I have from you."

"That's blackmail."

"No, it isn't," Meredith retorted, feeling comfortable and strong in her words. "And, it would be good if Joey could shed some light on why he was in the Harley Bell and beat up that fan. He's never talked about it and I know it must have something to do with Rebecca."

"Don't be surprised if you get no answers, but a lawsuit instead."

"Are you saying on the record that Rebecca Ornstein is NOT Joey's wife or ex-wife? And that there's no connection between the incident in Pacoima and Rebecca?"

"I'm not telling you anything, on or off the record, my dear," said the agent as he hung the phone up.

Seconds later Meredith's network contact rang her. In a hushed voice he said, "I don't know how you did this one, but you really did it big time. Half the network executives are running around trying to calm down Joey O'Neal, appeasing him and trying to make him understand that suing only makes sense if the information is untrue. What the hell do you have Meredith?"

"You're not going to call your own entertainment news division in on this are you?" she asked, proud that she had thought of the competitive aspect before trusting even as good a friend as Bill McLaren.

"Give me a break Meredith. When have I ever rolled over on a story of yours?"

"I just wanted to hear it from your own lips," she grinned as she outlined the information she and Cassie had pulled together. There was a deep and frustrated sigh at the other end of the phone.

"Look, let me give you this, unattributed, of course: the fan thing in Pacoima happened because the kid interrupted a sting the FBI had set up to squelch an extortion threat against Joey. I guess the FBI got involved because I heard a blackmail threat came from out of state, but none of us here knows what the information being used against him was or is. I rather suspect you've uncovered it."

"Well, good for me," sighed Meredith, then added, "And Cassie O'Connell."

"Nothing like stereophonic clubbing," said McLaren.

"There's no need for anyone to feel beat up or threatened by this, unless Joey is doing something illegal or unethical. Why's he so paranoid about Rebecca?"

"Maybe just ego and image. He is known as an icon for the 80's hip generation, you know. Probably hates the thought of having to come back to reality from the cloud nine he's built around himself. His life looks pretty perfect. Hell, maybe he even believes it. He's making so much money he probably has his manager write a check each month to his wife's care home, and that assuages any guilt or concern—or lack of either—over her condition."

"Whatever his reason, he's certainly been enjoying the ruse," Meredith said. "I asked William Roland for a half dozen explanations. If you can provide any of them instead, I'll owe you one. I'll even interview one of those icky kids from your dozen or so family comedies, if you ask nice."

"Listen if I can squeeze out any answers from Joey O'Neal, you may owe me a lot. In fact, you may have to hire me as your legman, Meredith. But I'll try. Because that's what I get paid to do. Some call it public relations. Others of us know it as slow suicide."

"Thanks—really," said Meredith as she hung up the phone.

"I have to get out of here," she told Sonia. "but stand by for bear! They're rumbling through the woods today. Keep Detectives Raymond and Escobar's numbers on hand and use them if necessary. I'll leave the numbers where I can be reached, and I'll check in at least once an hour. I'm taking that huge, field ops excuse of a cellular phone with me so I can talk with anyone pertinent to the Joey O'Neal story if I need to. I intend to be back here by three-thirty, and we'll put the column—however it looks by then—to bed at five."

Sonia saluted and added dramatically, "Oui, oui mon commandant!"

"God, am I beginning to sound like her?"

"Never."

CHAPTER 27

WEDNESDAY—BEVERLY HILLS

The law offices were in one of Beverly Hills' newest and ultra-modern high-rise buildings. A young secretary ushered Meredith into a living-room style conference room with a corner view of L.A.'s west side. When the attorney himself entered, Meredith was amused. He must be the last vestige of the original law firm that occupied these many names on the door, she thought. White-haired and ruddy cheeked, he was inconsistent with the stark offices.

It was no surprise to her that Larry Grant would be assuming his rightful ownership of the house and planned to take possession on February one. The attorney was surprised that Meredith knew these details. She grinned at him and said, "I'm a reporter."

He was amused by her statement. He reached across the conference table to push away a disruptive candle and pinecone holiday decoration and apologized. "One of the interns won it at the law association party. I left early, by nine o'clock to avoid all the falderal—but the young man who won it apparently didn't want it at home, stashed it in here." He shook his head.

Down to business, Meredith was surprised that Bettina had left the complete files and the office equipment, desks, computers, copy and fax machines—the lot—to her. In whatever agreement she had with the Syndicate and any other news outlets which she had served over the years, Bettina had insisted upon ownership of the source material. Meredith was flattered by the gesture then fascinated by it.

"When did she write this will?" she asked.

The attorney motioned to turn to the front page and note the date. "October 31, 1983, last Halloween, just a few weeks ago," he pointed out.

How appropriate, she thought, then suspecting that Bettina must have had some instinctive motivation for putting her affairs into order so recently. "Did she tell you why she was putting a new will together," asked Meredith. The old man folded his hands and leaned forward. He looked uncomfortable with the question.

"She merely told me she hadn't updated the will in a very long time and felt it might be a good idea. Her age and all. Of course, most everything went to the girls, you know. She left her housekeeper, Ito, her Jaguar if he, and the car, were still around when she passed. She also left him all the kitchen equipment. Can you imagine?"

Meredith grinned, noting that Ito's rusted, decade old Chevy, was generally parked out of sight in the alley behind the house. He loved the Jag and Bettina often allowed him to drive it. Refocusing, she carefully scanned the will once again. "But oddly enough, it says nothing about the house here. What you're telling me about Larry's ownership is not from the will?"

"No, it's court records, my dear. You see the house was refinanced at the time of the Grant's divorce ten years ago. Bettina was given the cash and Larry the house. But Larry didn't want to deprive Bettina of her home and her place of work. So, he allowed her to stay there until such time as he wanted to return, or it was to be sold." The older gentleman smiled suddenly. "Ironic that the first time I've seen Larry in years was the night

Bettina died—we were both leaving the law association dinner at the same time at the valet stand."

Meredith smiled, still surprised that there was no mention of the house situation in Bettina's will, if only as a seal on the agreement. Bettina was nothing if not compulsive about sealing agreements. As she was leaving the office, Meredith thanked the courtly old gentleman, taken her copy of the will and other documents pertaining to the office with her. She pointed the Mustang toward Universal Studios off the Hollywood Freeway where she would grab a sandwich and spend an hour on the set of the new movie, "Keeping Up."

The cellular phone had not rung, so she placed a call to the office from the pay phone outside the coffee shop she had chosen close to the studio. Sonia reported no action from the O'Neal camp. Meredith was disappointed. She climbed back into her car and drove to the studio's working entrance.

A uniformed guard checked her name from the guest list, handed her a paper permit to park on the lot, and waved her off in the direction of the sound stage. The publicist was waiting for her arrival, presumably with a few good interview subjects: the producer, the director, an underling celebrity or two. The star had been promised for a lunch interview several days later.

When she walked over to the designated sound stage, its massive windowless facade blotting out the sunlight for a square block, as expected, the publicist was standing by, press kit in hand, ready to escort Meredith through the web of fantasy within the movie making machine. The two women stood outside the metal door to the stage for a few minutes while the red light was on, indicating cameras and sound rolling inside. As quickly as the light blinked out, they pulled on the heavy door and entered.

Meredith made quick work of the usually tedious set visit. Her questions were precise and to the point, no warm-up niceties today. When the producer ambled over to the set, she quickly suggested they huddle outside the sound stage in order to keep the conversation moving and uninterrupted by the incessant quack of the buzzer indicating that cameras were rolling again and calling for silence.

When the director took a five-minute break, she cornered him hastily as well. Her questions were ready: "What makes this film special? How come such a large budget? Have you found the star difficult to work with—he hasn't worked in eight years? What about the rumors of a walk-off? Is the star's relationship with his leading lady causing delays or any problems in the portrayal of the characters?" And so on, and on. "Star babble," Meredith had labeled it to Cassie who had laughed heartily in agreement.

Seventy-five minutes later Meredith bid an appreciative farewell to the publicist, reclaimed her car from the parking area and headed to the office. She drove the Ventura Freeway to Coldwater Canyon and took the winding verdant street over the top of the hill to enjoy the open air of the canyon. She was pulling off the freeway onto the Boulevard when the bulky much-touted—and rarely carried—cellular phone rang. Sonia alone had the number. It was seldom used because it was cumbersome, expensive and didn't always transmit or connect.

"Hope you're close to the office," said an intense Sonia through static-laced air. "Joey O'Neal in the flesh is on his way over here right now and he sounds mad!"

"Is Ito in the house?" asked Meredith.

"Yeah, why?"

"I think it might be helpful to have a male presence around with the macho ego of Joey about to descend upon us."

"Good point," said Sonia, then she chuckled. "Ito? Macho? Well…"

Meredith had scant minutes to push the Mustang over the Canyon through the complex maze of Beverly Hills streets. She parked and ran from the car to prepare to meet up with one of America's favorite late-night stud-muffins. She was in her office no more than five minutes reviewing the facts of the story when she heard the limousine pull up and the driver ring the front doorbell. She waited while Ito answered the door, then directed O'Neal into her office. She stood up and extended her hand cordially.

"Joey, it's nice to meet you." Joey O'Neal, all six foot two of him, did not speak at first, but rather glanced around the room, as if confused, and then glared at her with anger in his eyes. He was perfectly coifed and dressed in a gray brushed silk sports jacket, wide, loosely cut black slacks and a black shirt with a multi-patterned tie. He was the vision of the tony single guy.

Meredith withdrew her hand and gestured toward the couch. "Please sit down, won't you?"

He moved toward the couch, still silent. Well, she thought, at least he's obedient.

"What the hell do you want from me?" he asked suddenly, contained rage straining from his barely controlled voice. Meredith sat down in a side chair.

"Just the truthful story," she said. "Coffee? Tea?"

He waved an impatient hand. "Do you have any idea how you're fucking up my life?" he said, nearly shouting.

"Tell me," she directed him without rancor.

"I'd like to tell you where you can fly your broomstick to," he growled. "You're one big busy-body, aren't you? And who gave you permission to walk into a private rest home? That's trespassing, you know!"

She folded her hands slowly. "I had nothing to do with that. The person who visited with Rebecca identified herself as a TV news person and was told to make herself at home. No one even suggested there was a restriction on Rebecca's guests."

Joey suddenly became quiet, glaring at Meredith as he slowly pointed an angry finger at her face. "If you so much as say one word about any of this…"

"Someone else will," she finished the sentence for him. "As I just told you, I didn't find Rebecca. A news reporter from the East Coast did. She saw our original story about the altercation in the bar and called me. But if I don't use this, you know she'll sell the information to the *Glitter Parade* or one of the other rags. And when that happens, no one will ask for your side of the story. Give me credit for at least calling your agent. I could have gone to press without doing even that."

"You're nuts if you think I'm going to thank you for this," he said standing up and pacing up and down in front of the coffee table. "Everything goes along under control—for years—and then you blow it out of the water. Lady, if you had any idea what a mess you're causing me, how much pain this will inflict…"

"Joey, why don't you just tell me. So far as I can see, the only people who will be pained about this will be your new fiancée—who you will have to level with sooner or later if you haven't already—and your fans, who may just love you even more if you have a vulnerable side to show them. And of course, your blackmailer who now has nothing to hold over you."

Again, he was shaking a finger at her, bending intensely from his tall stance to where she sat, to make his point. "You sound like little Miss Cream Puff, dearie. I got the Feds all over me for this extortion thing and I'm sworn to silence so they can track…." suddenly his face grew florid as he realized his mistake.

"Don't stop now," said Meredith. "We're finally beginning to get somewhere." With that Joey O'Neal swept back his hand and slap-punched her hard across the face. She reeled backward, not so much from the strength as from the shock of the blow. Her hand slipped up to her cheek instinctively. She could feel a searing sting, a throbbing sensation in her head. Her eyes were wide in surprise.

Sonia burst through the door, "I'll call the police, detective Raymond..."

"No!" Meredith commanded. "I'll do that! Or, we'll talk this out, won't we Joey?" Sonia stood for a minute more than quietly withdrew.

Joey O'Neal was as stunned as Meredith by his action and he, too, reeled. He began to apologize through gnashed teeth and angered expletives. "See what I mean, see what you've done to me."

"I believe, Joey, that anything I've done to you is nothing compared to what you've just done to me, and right after your arrest for assault in Pacoima!" She stood up with angered intention and moved brusquely toward the phone.

"Ah, come on!" he cried out, sounding like a small boy. "Give me a break. Consider what I'm going through." She leaned against her desk, perching on one hip and faced him squarely. Her mind boiled with anger.

"Okay," she began, holding together the storm inside of herself, "stop me when I'm wrong. You're out of control, Joey. You've been carrying around this secret of a sick wife who you've never divorced and who will probably never recover and you're trying to live the life of the well-heeled celebrity you are and feel you deserve, but you're drowning in guilt and intrigue because you can't be open about things. Then someone else—not a reporter, that's for sure—comes up with the real story about Rebecca and is blackmailing you. Threatening to expose the sham and your entire lifestyle and image. So, tell me, Joey, what have you got to lose by telling the story yourself?

"Surely you don't believe that once the guy is caught, the story will stay under wraps for very long. Don't you know that the worst-cases of press leaks trickle out of any of the fed organizations—take your pick!"

Joey O'Neal ran a shaking hand through his thick dark hard and sat down wearily on the couch.

"And the fan in the Harley Bell Saloon—an innocent by-stander, I understand, but why the Harley Bell?"

"I was supposed to meet the blackmailer there! As soon as he saw an entourage arrive, the meet was dead. I knew it when the kid and his wife showed up out of the blue to ask for an autograph, and I exploded. The creep phoned me later to confirm that I was right."

"So, we've saved you a bunch of ransom money by telling the story. And probably given you the gateway to a long sit-down article with *People* Magazine after it all settles down, where you'll be painted as a caring, conflicted super-star. What now?" asked Meredith, working hard to ignore the throb coming from her right jaw, and the urge to scream obscenities at the man sitting opposite her.

"You tell me. We're right back to square one. You got a crystal ball or something? I don't know any more than I did ten days ago. And you're saying that I'm supposed to go to millions of people and say, 'Hey, just kidding,' and tell a woman who thinks she's going to marry me the same thing?"

"If you don't, Joey," said Meredith in measured words, looking him hard in the face, "and even if I don't, someone else will. Word is out—it's why you were being exploited—before I ever caught it."

He rose and walked to the door. "Thanks for nothing, sweetheart." And he left. She sat unmoving, paralyzed until she heard the limousine door close and the car drive off. She looked up to see a wide-eyed Sonia and hesitant Ito standing in her doorway watching her cautiously.

"Wow—you handled that better than I would imagine anyone would," whispered Sonia tentatively. "Will he let you use it?"

"Let me? Where does he come off hitting women," hissed Meredith, ignoring Sonia? "He probably beat Rebecca. No wonder she's under lock and key. Well, he can't do this to me— I'll take it to court! Or at least press charges!"

"He never once said 'Off the Record.' I listened," announced Ito triumphantly.

Suddenly Meredith's jawbone ached all the way to her ear and she jumped from her chair and yelled. "God-damned, that hurt!" She ran into the bathroom to look at the now darkly reddened spot on her cheek.

"Now I'll have a big bruise on my face for Gloria's party!"

To say that her success in capturing the O'Neal story had been sweet for Meredith would have been an understatement. Russ Talbot was not only impressed by her investigative thinking, he had been surprised by the fact that she had planned a strategy to promote the story via Cassie's network exposure and more, and provided a list of foreign papers for him to contact about buying an in-depth special feature on Joey O'Neal. Russ had offered the same opportunity to the American subscribers as well. Meredith would be writing an in-depth Sunday feature which would be put on the wire to purchasers on Thursday night. The extra exposure also meant extra money generated—just when she could use it, at Christmas.

She felt guilt tugging at her again—all of this done with the spirit of Bettina Grant hovering, but no one was mentioning the name because life moved so fast. And no one knew what to say.

"Are you going to press charges or sue Joey?" Cassie asked jokingly when the two had talked late in the day after Meredith had composed her information.

"I don't know, probably not, but I'm certainly going to mention in the story that he hit me. If nothing else, it adds some character dimension to the article, don't you think?"

"Ha-ha," was all Cassie could manage, then she added, "This thing with Joey doesn't have anything to do with Bettina's murder, does it?" Her voice had become serious.

"I don't know, but I doubt it," Meredith replied, then thinking as she spoke, added, "He'd only have had a very brief glimpse of what was coming on the night Bettina died. Just a report of the arrest from the public record. But...there were a couple of hang-up phone calls on her line late that night. One sounded exasperated with no words. And someone did hear him talk about vengeance. I still don't think he would be that stupid."

"How's your jaw, by the way? I hope you had it checked out by a doctor."

"Urgent care and x-ray," said Meredith. "Nothing broken, but there's going to be a whopper of a bruise."

"Well, get some tender loving care," Cassie laughed.

"Not likely," said Meredith, baiting her tone slightly. "My friend's having a big party Saturday night, and I hope I don't look like a clown."

"Business or pleasure?"

"Hard telling, the way things keep turning out these days."

"Just to keep the record straight," Cassie said, her voice suddenly full, "My book sold."

"That's just great," said Meredith, "I still want to read the manuscript when the police release it—and at the rate I'm going—the last legwoman you write about may well be me!"

"Not yet, please. I've got an option for a sequel."

"Congratulations! That just about sets you up securely for a move out here with Bob, doesn't it?"

"Well...I wanted to mention something to you about that. See, the publisher thinks I'm a shoo-in for Bettina's column."

"Where'd he hear that?" asked Meredith, curious but no longer angry or frustrated by the competitive situation with Cassie. "He knows something we don't?"

"He heard it from me. It was a finesse, what else."

"And when or if you don't get it?"

Cassie laughed. "Hopefully, by then he'll be so committed to the promise of my book he'll just forget how helpful it would be for me to be visible every day in papers across the country."

"If the New York media got together and compared notes on how many of us have been finessing other opportunities with the promise of being visible every day in Bettina Grant's column spot, we'd all be in big trouble," said Meredith.

She felt relieved and a bit heady over her O'Neal success and more comfortable that she could trust Cassie. She kicked her feet up on the desk and explained how she had wooed Doug Manning and the radio syndicate with the promise of Bettina's exposure. Then she outlined how she had wooed Russ with the promise of the radio show as a support mechanism to column spot.

"I don't care what they say about Roger Golden and Phyllis Armstrong and all their supposed cache, if they could roll you and I into one person, the syndicate would have a powerfully invincible columnist!" Cassie chortled.

"If…and if…and if…," echoed Meredith before signing off and wishing Cassie good luck on the morning news break recapping what newspaper readers were reading that day from her on Joey O'Neal!

"It's been fun," said Cassie.

That evening Meredith was back in her pajamas for an early dinner, pampering herself after a long bath. She had forsaken pink silk for a pair of old flannel favorites that revealed nothing and were more comfortable than anything else she owned. The fact that bright cartoon pictures of Mickey Mouse were splattered all over them was of no concern. What was of concern was her badly bruised and aching face.

She settled down with a chicken sandwich, her Joey O'Neal notes, and an ice pack which she held against her jaw. When she had examined the spot in the mirror, earlier, she saw the bluish-purple welt that had begun to rise next to her eye.

"It looks like I got punched in one of your western movies," she told Dusty later that evening when he called in from location. He sounded mildly amused while at the same time slightly nonplused at her attitude.

"Why don't you come on out here for a few days and let all this shit settle down," he suggested.

"It is settled down," she said, "It's over. The only thing left up in the air is if I have a job after January thirty-one, and if I do—where will we work, and then of course, who killed Bettina Grant? That should be the primary concern—but there's so much to think about. By the way, did you get a call confirming our phone conversation the night Bettina died…the one you made at about three a.m.?"

"No, should I have? Are they checking you out?"

"I thought they already did. No one seems to put me in the investigation crosshairs, but you are, after all, my alibi."

"You know, Merri," sighed Dusty, "I think I'd retire while I was ahead if I was you. Why don't you go on out to my place in the mountains and stay out of sight for a while, if nothing else?" he offered.

She laughed again, wishing she could take him up on his offer, then said, "The only incentive I'd have for doing that, Dusty, is if you were there to brew up a really good margarita for me and keep me warm."

"Then it'll just have to wait a few days. But keep the thought. I like a ready woman!"

She brewed a cup of coffee hoping it would keep her awake long enough to watch the Joey O'Neal show later and thought about being a "ready" woman. She felt a little guilty and maybe even some embarrassment because her own insecurities made her wonder how "ready" she was for anything but compassion—and sleep. These were the times when she wished she had a parent living, or, God forbid, a husband to whom she could come home and unload the traumas of the day. Dusty never appeared in her mind in that thought. The echo of "widow" haunted her again, particularly after a day like the one recently completed. Her jaw throbbed as she mused over the folly of marrying just to have someone around on whom she could unload her troubles.

She began to structure the in-depth feature on Joey O'Neal when the phone rang again. This time is was a more cheerful version of T.K. Raymond. "I hear congratulations are in order on breaking the Joey O'Neal story. And you got belted in the face!"

"Where'd you hear that?" she quizzed, wondering how he'd found out.

"I kind of find things out. It's what most people expect of a detective. And Ito called me. How's the face?"

"Purple and ugly," she said, then added, "Ito called you? Since when do you and Ito have a conversational relationship?"

"Since Joey O'Neal was punching you out, and we researched Ito's background and brought him in for questioning. Don't ask about that. It's confidential—part of the detecting we do."

"Ito," she murmured. "Huh. And by the way, how come you didn't check out my alibi. My three a.m. caller. He said no one ever confirmed it."

"Didn't need to. We had the phone records. And, put a frozen pack of peas on your face."

"Well, I'm thinking that eating a frozen container of ice cream might be more satisfying, but as usual, my freezer is void of either, so plain old ice will have to do!"

"Tell you what—I could supply an ice cream cone if you're up to conversation."

Meredith didn't have a quick answer and found herself thinking out loud with excuses. "I have a long feature due on Joey O'Neal by tomorrow at five. Besides I'm in my pajamas already and want to watch Joey's show tonight."

The detective cleared his throat and asked, "The pink ones?"

"No, as a matter of fact. My old Mickey Mouse flannels."

"In that case, how about a rocky road cone in front of tonight's Joey O'Neal Show in your living room? I need to see what he has to say, as well."

"I like rocky road ice cream."

When she opened the door a half hour later, she still wore the child-like pajamas. Raymond stepped back and directed her to turn around once. "Fetching," he said.

"Fashion forward."

"Well, I did show you my favorite running sweats. Now let me see that bruise."

She turned her face to give him a full view of the welt on her cheek.

He whistled. "That's nasty. At the party Friday night, I hope your friends don't think I did that to you."

"Don't remind me. I've already thought of that."

"Well, in an effort to not sound too much like a broken record, you're lucky that's all you got from Joey O'Neal. Remember, he ended up in jail in Pacoima. What you do for a living…." He shook his head.

"What I do?" she jibed. "I'm just a journalist—mostly writing about celebrity fluff. I go to parties and hang around with pretty people, remember? You get the crime and dead bodies. Take off your coat. I have fresh coffee." The detective slipped off his jacket and handed her a brightly colored sack that held a pint of rocky road ice cream and two empty waffle cones. He followed her into the kitchen and held the cones as she scooped the sweet confection into each.

"I have to re-ask you a question you've heard before," he said somberly as they settled into the living room in front of the TV. She looked over at him curiously. "In the farthest stretches of your imagination, can you give me even the wildest possible hint of someone Bettina Grant might have been seeing, or at least saw and slept with the night she died?"

"I've thought and thought about that. Ito and Sonia and I have beat ourselves raw trying to come up with some idea of a wild card for you, but nothing. We've given you every name we can think of—and none of them seem probable. And yet...I think you're right, that I probably do know something I don't even realize I know about Bettina. That little bombshell of a fact is lying down there obscurely in my subconscious and I just can't identify it. Kind of niggles around in my mind. The more I think about it, the more I agree that I'm the one person who was closest to her—socially, logistically. But my mind is... constipated!"

Raymond sighed, licking the melting cream from the remainder of the cone. "It all comes down to that late appointment. Obviously, it was someone she's either been seeing or wanted to see. But there was no indication of any socializing before they went to bed, no wild and crazy foreplay. Her clothes were hung up, her make-up washed off. I'm totally perplexed."

"Could she have gone to bed with the guy before she came home?" Meredith wiped her hands on a napkin, ice cream long devoured.

"Maybe," said Raymond thinking hard, "but there's not enough evidence on any level to tell us anything for sure, and the timing doesn't seem to work."

"You mean no cum-tracks?" giggled Meredith. Her laughter turned into a grimace and she put a hand to her jaw. A tear squeezed from her right eye.

"Hurting?" asked Raymond. She nodded and reached for the ice pack. He picked it up for her and shook it.

"Lukewarm water." He took the bag into the kitchen, emptied it and refilled it with fresh ice cubes. He returned to the living room, sitting down on the couch and handing her the cold bag. She gently put the pack against her face and slumped back against the cushions with a sigh of sheer exhaustion. Neither of them spoke, and soon he heard her breathing the rhythmic and relaxed cadence of slumber, her head nestled back against the sofa cushion. He let her rest.

The late show leading into Joey O'Neal's program was winding down. But soon, *Joey O'Neal's Dark Streets* began, and Raymond shook Meredith gently to waken her. "Sorry to disturb your dreams, but you wanted to watch Joey tonight." She shook her head groggily and was painfully awakened by the throb in her head. She settled against Raymond to watch the show.

"Awake?" he asked a few minutes later, fearing she had dozed off again and would miss whatever announcement to the world Joey would make about his hidden life. She sat up.

Thirty minutes into Joey's hour show he made light joking conversation with his musical director about how a nefarious past, supposedly his own, had been uncovered by some nosy gossip reporter, and how ludicrous it was that anyone would think such sordid details of a guy's life would matter to anyone but the guy himself.

"That was it?" Meredith sat at full attention.

"He did that badly," said Raymond. She agreed.

"I can't believe that's all he's going to do. He's just set up my story for even more attention that it would have otherwise received. Viewers will be looking for it. He did it beautifully for me, but you're right, he surely did it badly for himself. He really looks like the fool now."

"There's nothing like doing things right," said Raymond standing up and bringing Meredith to her feet. She looked up into his face. The depth in her eyes seemed endless. He slipped an arm around her shoulder, turned her around and pointed her toward the stairs.

"And the right thing for you is to take your pain killer and go to bed. There'll be a police car outside off and on tonight. If I have to be in perfect form Saturday night, so do you. Tomorrow, however, you'll be a big celebrity. Be rested and enjoy it. I'll lock the door."

She was too tired to protest. He lightly touched her bruise then turned and left. She thought vaguely of Dusty's comment about "Ready women," and went to bed too exhausted to consider the possibilities.

Raymond left Meredith's house and walked slowly to his car, once again pondering his role—law enforcement protector, patriarchal mentor, attracted paramour. And he wondered, what hers was: a vulnerable journalist in danger? A frightened and lonely ingenue in need of a father-figure? Or a lusty, attractive and determined young woman who saw him with better eyes than he saw himself?

THURSDAY—BEL AIR

Raymond had been directly on target when he told Meredith she would become an instant celebrity for her coverage of the Joey O'Neal story. From the moment she entered the office the next day, albeit a half hour late, her phone rang incessantly.

"Great bruise," remarked Sonia.

In the midst of the calls, Sonia called out, "Better take this one. It's from Hawaii. One of our favorite TV stars is in Honolulu for a charity appearance, got drunk and put on quite a side show for the patrons of the black-tie event. Doti Larson from the hotel is calling to give you the info."

Meredith smiled and took the call. Doti was an old friend, a former network publicist who had moved to Hawaii to handle publicity for one of the series that was filmed in the tropical paradise for nearly six years. She decided to stay and took a public relations job with one of the larger hotels. She was always a good source of celebrity goings-on because she had a rare opportunity to deal with vacationing stars who had lowered their public guard and allowed their true personalities to emerge. Doti was careful to only pass along activities that had been public.

The story would have to be handled with great care, if used at all, because the celebrity was a well-respected long-time actress from various hit TV series. A drinking problem had been kept carefully under wraps for years, and only when she occasionally lost control—as she had done at the black-tie affair—did the problem come to light.

"It was a dead give-away when she fell out of her chair as she was getting up to be acknowledged. Who would have known?" laughed Doti. "Yes, there were a number of event guests and staff who witnessed the situation."

"You really get the best of them, don't you?" chuckled Meredith, remembering that the year before, at a similar event, another TV series star had flown in accompanied by his teenage girl friend. Before the three-day stay had concluded, they had trashed the room in various drug-induced episodes, the celebrity had deserted the girl after being called back to California by his agent for an audition. The hotel and charity organization finally put her on an airplane before the hotel room was demolished beyond repair.

Doti bid a cheery "aloha" to Meredith before ringing off. Meredith wondered vaguely how she would handle this story, if she used it at all. Stories like this, she thought to herself, are so tough. Interesting, but hard to use without sounding like the ultimate bitch. And always required contacting the subject's representatives for response.

"Your face hurt? Want an ice pack?" Ito inquired mid-morning.

At noon she drove to Larry Grant's small but well-appointed one-story office building in Santa Monica. He met her in the reception room, noticing the side of her face immediately. "You need a new boyfriend," he said, directing her to his car.

Meredith carried an oversized tote purse and, reaching for the back door, she asked, "Okay if I put this in the back seat?"

"Sure…just push that stuff aside…when the kids are here, we play some tennis." Meredith brushed tennis balls and a racket, a couple of coffee cups and a jacket to the other side of the back seat, tossed her tote in and closed the door. She climbed into the passenger side next to Larry. Meredith grimaced as she noticed that the car interior floated in a cloud of a cologne or air-freshener. She wondered vaguely if Larry, or any other guy who filled the air so thoroughly with fragrance, had some evil odor to hide? They drove to a nearby restaurant for lunch.

He had chosen La Poulet Rouge, an older but respected French restaurant that was quiet and easily tolerated private conversations. Meredith was amused at Larry Grant—all charm and business. He had aged well. Dressed well in a gray silk suit and a monogrammed shirt, his still-substantial head of hair, now salt-and-pepper, helped what had been fairly ordinary facial features take on character over the years.

"I wanted to thank you personally for putting up with all the activity around the house and treating my ex-wife's image so well now that she's gone," Coffee was set before them at the conclusion of the lunch. "You've even put up with Lea remarkably well."

Meredith demurred with an acceptable amount of humility, then asked him, "What's with Lea's attitude? I never really saw the rift between her and her mother, because she was gone before I arrived."

Larry shook his head slowly. "Lea seems to have always had anger issues. We never knew when or why they started. After her stumble through school and college—give her credit she finished—she just had terrible trouble finding a path. At Lea's request, Bettina found her a role in 'show business.' It was a disaster. Lea blamed Bettina. That repeated itself several times on both coasts and then Lea seemed to find some grounding when she met her husband and settled in. He took care of her, put her in a creative place. He was a condo developer for high-income owners and Lea did the interior design for his units. Then, something happened to his business and he lost a lot of clients and money, one of his big developments went bust, and Lea came to Bettina for money to help shore things up. Bettina turned her down, offered to let them come back to California and help them here. Well…" he took a sip of coffee. "That idea crashed like the Hindenburg."

Meredith toyed with her spoon as he explained, then she asked, "I was under the impression she blamed Bettina for your divorce."

"She did blame Bettina. Said Bettina 'had her head so high in the sky she kicked me right out of the picture.' Not really true, but it served Lea. As I said, she had anger issues, and blaming others was part of the rhetoric. She had already been embarrassed by her own failures in Bettina's world she figured it was Bettina's fault for putting her in that world. During one of Lea's visits, Bettina called and asked me to pick up the girl. She'd become so frighteningly agitated—threatening to hit her mother. Bettina was afraid she would turn even more violent." He stared into his cup.

"All of that had nothing to do with the divorce and now she thinks I'm the playboy of the western world. If it sounds like I've thought about this a lot, believe me I have. That's how I met my fiancé, Vivian. She was my therapist. She's been a huge help."

Interesting background thought Meredith. Helpful, but he's answered every question artfully with no clue to his own real feelings about Bettina. Since there are no free lunches, I wonder what he really wants?

"Don't feel pressured about moving out of the offices immediately," he responded without her asking about the working quarters. "Stay put until February first or a couple of weeks longer-if that works best for you. Just let me know."

Meredith smiled with relief. "Won't it be awkward for you to move back into the house you shared with Bettina for so many years—where your kids were born? And where she died?"

He smiled confidently. "Not at all. Lots of water under the bridge since I lived there. The place has been renovated and redecorated so many times I hardly recognize it any longer. In fact, I would redecorate, myself, if I moved in. But Vivian and I will be getting married, and plan to sell the Bel Air house to buy something more our own."

Vivian's name was familiar to Meredith. "I know her father, I believe," she ventured, realizing that Frank Malden was a well-known television producer with several hit series to his name.

"Most people in these parts do. Vivian's very independent, and different from most of the shallow women I've hung around with. Except, of course," he added cordially, "for Bettina."

"Of course."

"I'm anxious to get our life together underway," Larry went on solicitously. "We made plans to buy a house—had to put that on hold—when this thing with Bettina happened."

"You mean Bettina's death?"

"Well, yes. It's hard to put it that way yet. You know, it's hard to imagine her gone."

"Yes, I know."

"I imagine you're all keeping the office humming 24/7 to keep ahead of the deadlines."

"We're doing fine, actually," Meredith responded. "I try to get everyone out of the office and house by five o'clock just in deference to the house itself. I think it deserves some time to grieve on its own! Even Ito's been spending some evenings and nights with friends—some new freedom. He's going to a movie, tonight! Probably the first time in all these years."

"Have there been any new developments on the investigations into her death? I haven't been able to get a single line from the cops, except questions about Bett's medication habits. How about you?"

Meredith shook her head no. "Me either. 'Still investigating' is their official line. They're back to repeating the same questions they started out with. And I'm still puzzled about the pills she took," she said, baiting Larry. "I can't believe she had started playing with that stuff again. Particularly after she'd had trouble with them before."

Larry agreed absently, his mind obviously wandering elsewhere until he directed his attention back to Meredith either out of courtesy or good play-acting. "Particularly with her allergies and all."

Meredith nearly let the inference slip by, then focused quickly. "I can't remember what exactly she was allergic to."

"Nothing unusual," said Larry quickly gesturing to the waiter for the check. "Taking diet pills and alcohol together is usually dangerous. Bettina had an especially bad reaction to the combination—maybe not exactly an allergy but certainly a bad reaction. The Valium, of course, was the worst."

"I guess I never saw her under those circumstance, but those combinations are never good."

Larry nodded in agreement then turned his attention fully to Meredith. "There's one thing more I wanted to mention to you—the signed first edition books. I understand that she left them all to you?"

"Yes, well, she apparently felt that we had shared so many of the interviews and relationships with the stars who wrote those books…I guess. I plan to pass a few along to Cassie O'Connell Ainsworth. She was as much a part of Bettina's life in Hollywood as I was."

"Yes, of course, Cassie O'Connell," said Larry again absently. "There are one or two of the books I'd kind of like if you wouldn't mind parting with them," he continued. "The one from Richard Burton. You know, Bettina and I spent a lot of time together on Burton's set in Mexico and I think he meant the book for us both."

Meredith nodded and made a note on her napkin. "What else?" she asked.

"Well, I thought if you'd gone through the box of Bettina's books you might have run across a leather journal with some personal notes. For a while, we kept a journal—in the leather notebook—together and I know she'd want me to keep it private. We were in counseling a dozen years ago, trying to save our marriage. She may have continued the notes elsewhere. She mentioned she might. She could work so much faster on the keyboard than in longhand."

"Twelve years ago—that seems so long ago," Meredith probed. "I'm surprised you'd really want to dredge up all that unpleasant stuff again."

Larry smiled placatingly. "We were married for more than twenty-five years. Feelings don't just disappear."

"Of course not. Ironically, Bettina used to say the same thing about you."

"What else did she have to say about me?" he asked lightly, jokingly. Meredith smiled. "Nothing much, Larry. You'll recall that Bettina was always as fair as the facts allowed her to be." Her mind was distracted. She was anxious to get back to the office.

"Well, if you do come across the journal…thanks so much," he said, reaching for the check, a noncommittal look on his face.

"I'll watch for it—There are still some of Bettina's nooks and corners to explore, but here's the thing, Luanne and Lea went through the drawers, and every paper stack with me to sort out Bettina's personal documents and material from the work stuff. Not easy with a woman who is one with her work…but, most every scrap of paper, envelope, bill, receipt was collected. Luanne's the Executor of Bett's will, as you know. And I think she turned everything over to the attorney and CPA in a meeting just this morning. At least, that's my understanding. Sonia scoured the work files but hasn't found anything else that's personal to Bettina—aside from her work compulsion," Meredith half-chuckled.

Larry smiled, almost nostalgically, in appreciation.

As the parking attendant opened her door, Meredith thought, what a waste of a perfectly good lunchtime. He could have asked all those things on the phone, but maybe he just has a personal need to woo women into agreements. Who knows? She sat back and brooded discretely while Larry drove back to his firm and her car.

She collected her tote, bid Larry a cordial farewell as he was greeted in the parking garage by a familiar-looking man Meredith later recalled from the funeral and the Polo Lounge. Anxious to return to her offices, she dismissed the encounter.

Lea, her sister Lorraine, and their aunt Luanne were moving around the house, dressed in jeans and sweat-shirts, busy in the final stages of sorting and packing up Bettina's belongings. Although Ito did his best to remove himself from the activities, the women would call upon him from time to time to lift a heavy box, or direct them to a cupboard, or move a piece of bulky furniture. Mostly he was staying at his "desk" next to Sonia's. He now seemed to prefer paperwork to people-sitting Bettina's relatives.

Over the past ten days, Lea softened to the point of sharing deli sandwiches over lunch without resorting to angry outbursts or the usual litany of four-letter labels for those she did not like—which was just about everyone in the room. Such pleasantries had even Lea's family wondering what had caused such a mellowing of this ordinarily peevish personality.

Meredith entered the offices and walked through them into the living room just as the affable luncheon enclave was breaking up. "Anything we can do to help?" she offered, expecting a "no thanks" and not disappointed when she got it.

"We're nearly finished here," Luanne explained, pushing a strand of graying hair into the bandanna she wore around her head. "The trucks arrive tomorrow morning early to pick up all this stuff and send it off to wherever it's being directed. Lea gets most of the furniture. My husband and I are taking some of the pictures," She grinned and added, "Ito gets the kitchenware. Larry, of course, has a stake in some of this. There's stuff the Goodwill truck will also pick up tomorrow. The office furniture—mostly the desks and side chairs—will stay for you all. If you don't mind, we're planning to take the sofa in your office—it was one of Bettina and Larry's original pieces and he seems to want it."

"Of course, but I hope one of you will be here to tell the drivers which boxes and furniture goes where?" Meredith asked, concerned.

"Oh, sure," Lea answered. "You'll have us all in your hair tomorrow. Even my dad. We should be out of here by one o'clock at the latest and then the cleaning team arrives to really shake the place down. Dad says Ito can finish off the offices the day you guys move out. Dad and Vivian are going skiing for Christmas. Hope she can keep him away from the tables at Tahoe."

"What about Ito?" asked Meredith, suddenly concerned about her part-time helper. "I thought he was here until at least the middle of January."

"He is," Luanne spoke up, stooping to pick up a stack of linens. "His room stays intact for now, furniture and all. And, of course, he has the kitchen stuff."

"And the coffee maker," Ito added drily. "I also have my own cookware." That surprised Meredith. She never knew.

Meredith wandered idly into the kitchen merely to observe the dismantling that had taken place. Packed boxes lined the counters and some cupboards. She smiled, remembering ten years' worth of coffee from those cups and also remarking that, "we'd better remember to bring in our own cups tomorrow."

"Not necessary. I have it covered," said Ito from the office area. His was an organized mind, mused Meredith and she returned to her desk to get on with the day's writing, most of which had to be completed by five o'clock filing time.

First, she finished the day's column, including a personal comment on Joey O'Neal's public lack of interest in the story about himself, evident by his lackadaisical attitude and comment about it on his show. She found a nice way to talk about the Hawaii incident without identifying the hotel, or the celebrity— only the incident—and brought in one of the interviews from her set visit the day before. She reviewed and re-edited the three pages twice before handing the pages to Sonia for final proofing, pencil correcting and faxing to New York. She also assembled material for the next day, realizing that she would have to write columns ahead again because she intended to take four days off over Christmas, two of them weekdays when columns would have to be filed. The task was not troublesome considering holiday material sent to her by celebrity publicists about the stars was always plentiful, if not particularly vital.

Eventually she began the second rewrite on her Joey O'Neal special feature story drafted loosely on her home computer the night before. It was longer than usual, and she spent the better part of the afternoon cleaning up the content, taking as few calls as possible in order to capture complete concentration. Ito quietly brought in a cup of fresh decaf coffee which Meredith drank without ever realizing Ito had been there.

At four forty-five, as she was finalizing the article to give to Sonia, also for the five o'clock faxing, Allan Jaymar's even, quiet voice came on the phone line inviting her to stop by for a drink after work. She hesitated for a moment, then accepted.

"But only for a moment, Allan. I'm as frazzled as I was last week when I saw you, with holiday preparations of my own only half-finished and Christmas barely a week away. But I always enjoy your company and a drink might help me decompress. So, give me forty-five minutes to an hour to finish up here and I'll be there. Thanks."

Allan signed off with his customary "Ciao."

A few minutes after five Sonia stuck her head in the door to report the column and feature had been received in New York and would be on the wire, as planned, before midnight.

"Before I go, here's something important. I think it'll be safer with you than here," said Sonia in a whispered voice.

"Look what I found in the back of the bottom file cabinet we used for storage—ironically in a folder behind our 'dead' files." Sonia opened her bottom desk drawer and handed Meredith two computer disks. "They're titled 'What if,' but the few pages I scoured on Bettina's computer were definitely Bettina's own thoughts—and romance was only a part of the stuff she wrote about. And no, I didn't mention them to anyone."

Meredith accepted the two floppy disks, looking at them with disbelief. "Don't tell anyone you found these. Our lives may depend on it!"

"Okay, boss—that's a good reason! Happy reading, but I want to hear all the spicy details tomorrow!"

"Thanks for taking care of that," said Meredith, now organizing notes to include in Joey O'Neal's file. "Have a good evening and I'll see you tomorrow. Maybe we can get our routine back to semi-normal."

"Fat chance," said Sonia cynically. "It's not our style. 'Night." Meredith slipped the disks into her brief case and in a moment of insecurity, quickly followed Sonia out, locked the case in her own car trunk and returned to the office.

Five minutes later Ito knocked lightly on the office door frame to announce he would spend the night with his cousin in Westwood and return early the next morning before the day's activity began. "I'm going to that film showing at the Village."

"Have fun," Meredith answered, realizing that in the past Ito probably had to compress all his entertainment hours into his one night off. She was glad he had this opportunity, making a note on her "to do" pad to urge him to take more time to find a place to live as well as enjoying the other vestiges of a more independent life. Especially now that he would have a decent car.

She hardly noticed that Lea, Lorraine and Luanne had already called out "Goodnight." She had uttered a truant, "see you tomorrow." Her attention was focused elsewhere. Suddenly she looked up to realize that her office light was all that illuminated the large house. She wandered into Bettina's now dark office and switched on the small desk lamp, all that remained standing on the modern wood and glass desk now that all else was packed up. The small pool of golden light spilled only slightly and without energy into the living room.

Meredith stood in the archway leading into the living room, her eyes sweeping across the ghost-like hulks in the shadows. Her vision adjusted to the darkness and she sought out the mantle she remembered was usually adorned with the bright foliage of the holiday season at this time of the year. It was bare but for mere recollections of the antique icons and crystal candlestick holder placed artfully by a high-priced decorator years before. As she glanced toward the now-darkened kitchen she felt a moment of prickly Deja vu, a recognition of something so fleeting it escaped before she could identify it.

A feeling she couldn't identify, a morbid curiosity welling from deep within, pulled her attention toward the upstairs bedroom. A noise, a creak? A shadow on the stairwell. Except for her brief visit to the second floor with Marty Escobar, she had been unable to convince herself to climb the stairs again after finding Bettina dead the week before.

She walked softly, avoiding the boxes and covered furnishing, toward the stairwell and looked up. She hesitated, remembering a comedienne's line about the world's dumbest women being "the ones who hear a noise outside in the middle of the night, and go out to see who it is!"

The suggestion of sinister presences in the upstairs suite drove her to retreat to her own office, welcoming the flood of overhead light and the assumption of normalcy. She did a quick sweep of her desk to make sure all the notes and resources on O'Neal were filed away, opening her top desk drawers, patting the papers in each one unconsciously. Her attention was briefly snagged by the presence of the extra button, the torn boarding pass and receipt that Ito had found in the couch cushions. "I must remember to really clean out these drawers next week," she made a mental note, and declared herself finished for the day.

As she reached under her desk for her purse, she felt a sharp jerk against her throat, pulling her body backward against the flexible back rest of the desk chair. She gasped and strained against the force, now becoming a single blade-like sensation cutting off her breath. She beat her fists at an unseen predator who she instinctively assumed was above and behind her, but the desk chair's back caught most of the blows. Yet, one fist apparently struck home. The strain against her throat lessened for a single second, long enough to permit her one long gasp of breath, a lifesaving one. It enabled her to summon enough strength to heave herself sideways to the floor. Her attacker, and the chair, fell along with her, rolling a body harder than her own on top of hers, only slightly lessening the grasp on the line around her throat.

Her well-toned, exercised body attempted to flip him over, but succeeded only enough to push him again off balance and surprise him enough to loosen the line around her neck. In the scramble of bodies and the chair, confusion reigned. Elbows and knees were entangled and scraped, and a heavy thud bounced against the back of Meredith's head. What had been a warm glow of office light quickly dimmed to a strange orange then brown flicker.

"Damn," she thought as the light dimmed, "I'll be such a mess for Gloria's party."

☆

When Meredith opened her eyes, she was surrounded by darkness. She thought she was still unconscious, or maybe blinded by the blow to her head. She blinked her eyes and moved her head from side to side, finally noticing that there was a sensation of vision as her eyes adjusted to a lack of light. The pain in her head spoke eloquently, flooding over Meredith's consciousness. Dizziness accompanied it. Tears welled in her eyes in response to the slightest movement, and she felt the sensation of a warm wet trickle creeping down her neck toward her back. Idly she wondered what time it was.

She tried to lift her body from the bent position it seemed to have fallen into, but a wave of dizziness and the wash of pain stopped her. She realized that she was wedged among solid, stationery objects in a very small space. Groping over her shoulder with one hand and then the other she finally deduced that she was in the narrow, tight file closet along with the ten three-drawer file cabinets and various technological equipment. The door was obviously locked. And, she quickly guessed that someone also would have secured the sliding wooden doors from the outside.

In exhaustion, pain and resignation, she lay quietly without moving in her unnaturally folded condition, hoping a solution would materialize. She remembered someone in a moment of inspired spirituality commenting that "when you're in trouble, if you're still and listen to your intuition, the universe will provide."

Heavy, she thought. What the universe was providing was a distinctive odor she didn't bother to identify. She was fading in and out of consciousness—or was it sleep. She couldn't tell the difference. In her momentary inventory of her life's experiences, she could not remember ever being unconscious before.

Then the universe did provide a vague half-world dream that identified the odor as smoke. Something burning. The office. Someone is torching the office! Her mind roiled in confusion. Why? She meandered in and out of grayness trying to answer the question—before the reality hit her. "Why" didn't matter at all. "Continue living—that's what matters," she muttered to herself.

Struggling to right herself and gain leverage against the closed doors, she managed to regain her footing, but even her full weight against the doors would not budge them. The heat from what she could only assume was a nearby bonfire would soon take over the wooden doors and the rest of the room—if it had not already.

"Think!" she verbally commanded her brain. "Think hard."
It did. To no avail.

"What's on the top shelf?" she asked herself out loud, trying desperately to be a methodical problem solver. Nothing but highly flammable paper. "How about in the file cabinets? Nothing else but easy-to-burn paper and…and…Think, Meredith!" Then she recalled that the bulky "high tech" cellular phone was kept in the bottom of the farthest file cabinet, along with an electronic dictating machine, the fire extinguisher the fire department insisted they keep on the premise, and the copier machine. But it would take a contortionist to reach the furthest of the ten file cabinets. She thought again of her spiritualist friend who in addition to telling her the universe would provide, also used to say that anyone could transcend pain by willing it away.

"I'm willing," she hissed aloud. She pulled herself tight against the file cabinet and, jumping and squirming with difficulty, tried to climb on top of it. She edged around in order to use the front cabinet handles to boost herself up, cringing against the metal so as not to bump her head on the closet shelf. She squirmed across the top of the cabinets, flattened against the hard steel, and then slid laboriously feet first down between the immovable door and the front of one cabinet in order to reach, unseeing, to the bottom drawer of the next to try to open it at least far enough to slip a hand in and retrieve the phone or at least the fire extinguisher. The strain was painful and awkward and as she bent sideways, sinking her hand into the scant six-inch opening of the drawer. "Thank God for yoga!" she proclaimed aloud

Finally, her fingers felt the metal extinguisher, dragged it through the small opening and dropped in on the floor within reach. Sliding her hand back into the drawer she felt frantically for the hard piece of technology they called a telephone, trying to recall if she had returned it to the cabinet the day before and whether its battery was charged. Her fingers landed against what she knew was the vital piece of equipment, wrapped in its ugly fabric bag. "Someday they'll figure out how to make these smaller," she murmured.

Pulling it out she fumbled around the mechanism with a now stiff hand and grappled with it in order to punch 911.

Meredith remembered little else. There were image flashes of trying to use the extinguisher but not knowing if that was even necessary, of a severe headache and incredible weariness, and finally the sound of banging in the room outside, the closet door crashing open and hands catching her as she was released to the floor.

Three hours later she was pushed in a wheelchair out the door of the nearby Hospital Emergency Room, a bandage around her head, by Sonia. Allan Potty, T.K. Raymond and his partner Marty were in tow. No one looked pleased. Least of all Meredith.

"We were so worried about you," said Potty. "And then we got your call."

"My call?" Her voice was small.

"You said you'd just called 911 to report a fire in your office but you didn't want us to think you'd stood us up."

"Who or what hit me?"

Sonia started to snicker. "Some guy—with that huge antique dictionary on the stand by the window. We all know that words can kill."

"You aren't really going home, not in this condition, are you?" Allan scolded. "I wish you would have stayed here at least for the night."

"No way," said Meredith, straightening up. "I spent enough time in hospitals when my parents passed, but never, personally, stayed in a hospital. I don't intend for this jerk—whoever he is—to put me in one at this point. I'm going home to my own bed and my cat and my security!"

"Why don't you stay with us instead?" asked Potty. "You shouldn't be alone in this condition and with this madman on the loose."

"She won't be alone," Raymond spoke up. "I've got a patrol person lined up to stay with her for the next couple of nights. This has all gone way too far."

Meredith looked over at him, almost amused. "Really."

CHAPTER 31
FRIDAY

Against the objections of the female officer who had stood nightly guard over the numbed journalist, and the outright demands of Detective T.K. Raymond, Meredith dragged herself from the cocoon of bed and staggered into the bathroom to make ready for the office Friday morning. Later than normal, she realized, but was determined to stay focused. She could still hear Raymond's teeth gnashing over the phone when she told him where she was going—and pleasantly told him where to go and how to get there.

"You're feeling a little better, I can tell," he said.

Arriving at her office around ten-thirty, tight-muscled, cautious and dazed, Meredith was chauffeured by the policewoman who continuously encouraged her to go back home and rest. She reminded the woman that column deadlines don't wait for people to be rested. Besides, she was compelled to see for herself the extent of the damaged office. To her surprise, the mess was far less than she imagined, but the sight of the closet doors torn out by the firemen in their efforts to free her, made her curious.

"Whoever did this sure did it badly," Sonia commented. Even in the red haze of an oppressive headache, Meredith knew she had heard that phrase before. She recalled something about Joey O'Neal and T.K. Raymond. She couldn't remember which had said it.

But the statement was appropriate. Whoever had slipped into the house and assaulted Meredith had done it badly, witnessed by the fact that she was back in the office walking around, and the office suffered only one scorched corner as well as one set of burned drapes. No furniture, paperwork files were damaged by the blaze which had apparently been set in a waste basket.

"Thank God for all of you," Meredith whimpered. Sonia had risen to the chaotic occasion and drafted a column, and though it would win no prizes for writing excellence or even great gossip, it contained ample material with good-enough punchlines to allow Meredith to polish it quickly.

Sonia and Ito had stood by as the second law enforcement team within two weeks assaulted the house leaving gray dusting powder on doorknobs and sills, on the phones and desks looking for any hint of the attacker. An hour after the team arrived, they were gone, but in the meantime, a phalanx of movers was now on the doorstep. The exodus of personal property from Bettina Grant's former home had begun.

Sonia had contacted both Larry Grant and Luanne the night before to report the attack on Meredith, and the fire. She was careful to let them know that the fire had done little damage. Luanne had arrived early the next morning after conferring with Larry who said he was already enroute to Lake Tahoe with Vivian for the Christmas holidays. He would deal with insurance issues and repairs when he returned. The entire family expressed their shock, sympathy and offered to help Meredith and the others in light of the assault.

Each bump and thunk of a box or a chair felt as if someone was beating on her head. She flinched again and again. She sat down next to Sonia's desk. "Thanks for putting this column together. You guys are holding up like real heroes. I wish I could say the same, but I feel like garbage and I'm going to have to go home. My head is like a piece of raw hamburger—on the inside this time. I wish people would leave that part of my anatomy alone next time. I'd much rather have a broken arm or leg than a broken head!"

"You're fortunate you have any head left," scolded Sonia. "We all should have listened to that detective more closely. Before you go, here's a new item that just came in from Consuela at that resort in Fort Lauderdale."

Meredith listened half-heartedly.

"She hosted an engagement party for 78-year old Jack Morgan, the old-time western star?" Meredith nodded her recognition of the long-time celebrity's name. "He arrived with a younger-than-springtime lady, Miss All-American College Girl—no kidding, that's her beauty queen title—on his arm, telling the world they were getting married in a month or so. Consuelo confirmed it with the western star, and threw a small cocktail party, complete with press, of course, to celebrate. On the beach at the hotel, Miss College Girl was telling everyone including the press that she was sorry to spoil Jack's fantasy, but she was marrying some theatrical agent on Valentine's Day and nobody in their right mind would think she would waste her future on a decrepit old actor."

"How's Jack taking the news?"

"Hasn't heard it. He flew out directly after the party. Miss American College Girl is supposed to meet him in L.A. next week."

"So, it's up to the press to break the news to him?"

Sonia shrugged.

"Find out the name of Jack's agent, call him, tell him the story we've heard and get his reaction. It's a good column lead for Monday."

"That's nice—at least get his response—maybe warn Jack."

"It's the right way to do things. Bettina's way. Write it up for Monday. I'm going home."

☆

There was not much new in the way of crime development for Raymond that Friday afternoon, so he left the office early while the sun was still shining. He usually made the trip back and forth to Malibu after dark this time of the year. As he pulled into his driveway, he was reminded of Will's comment about moving on and how sad the house seemed. Entering the living room from the garage below, he looked around. Will was right, he could have been arriving in the same room at the same time ten years earlier and heard Lilli's voice calling "hi!"

But it was 1983, and Lilli only lingered in the aging furniture and the trinkets and souvenirs from travels and adventures long ago forgotten. He changed into sweats and took a run down the beach. When he returned, he was energized and picked up a used grocery bag and swept nonessentials from the tables and moved through the house, discarding trinkets, unneeded ashtrays from long forgotten vacations. He couldn't recall looking at them in years. Lilli had been an adamant clutter-hater. She cleaned closets, cabinets and drawers at least annually to remove life's unused left-behinds and make room for the new. He hadn't followed her lead very well and began to walk through the rooms.

He took in the contemporary simple furniture and décor, still enlivened by the warmth of color and charisma. Clean lines remained, but the place needed polishing and updating after all the years. Framing it all—floor to ceiling windows overlooked the ocean. Raymond stood absorbing emptiness, walked to the front-most window and opened it, swinging it wide over the surf below. The snap chill of the breeze began to clear his head. Years before, with the help of family, they had bought the house from a failing client of his father's management firm where he had worked right after college and his and Lilli's young marriage. She was a nurse and he struggled to be the perfect theatrical agent in a world he disliked. Will was born and then Vietnam intervened and when it was over for Raymond, his family was a different family. Pressures from his own parents goaded him into a law degree, but before the Bar's letter of acceptance arrived, Lilli's was in hospice fighting breast cancer, and even sooner, was gone.

T.K. Raymond joined the Police Academy sixty days later and chose his own path in law enforcement, making as few changes as possible to life as it was when Lil was alive. He went to work, progressed through the ranks, and spent the hours away from the job raising and doting on Will until the boy went off to Vanderbilt three years before.

Now standing at the open window, taking in the moon's highlights on the waves below and the points of light along the coastline, he imagined himself to be blown into the tumult of the ocean. The exhilaration was freeing, and he imagined that's where Lilli had gone—blown out the window and into the wild. He was envious of the freedom, but he still had ground under his feet and realized it was time to notice it.

Which made him think, in some disjointed way, about the wily houseman, Ito, and his inconsistent traffic citations and travel puzzles. And Ito's house-keeping skills. Shaking the thoughts from his head, Raymond went to the utility closet and decided to clean the house. Will would be home in a few days.

CHAPTER 32

SATURDAY MORNING

Saturday morning, the light bled through the mini-blinds in the large airy bedroom creating a limbo-like glow over the canopied bed. Meredith, curled messily in the sheets, noticed nothing. She had been asleep since eight thirty the night before, and it was the weekend.

She pulled herself from disjointed dreams a half-hour later when Dusty called. The female officer keeping vigil in her living room answered the phone and knocked on the bedroom door. She had tapped gently on her door at first, then rapped harder until Meredith yelped, "What?"

The cop was leaving for the day, a patrol car was in front if she needed help. Meredith sat up gingerly, quickly aware that the past three days had been spent in pain of one type or another. The headache from the blow on the back of her head was a dull ache, leaving stiffness in her neck and shoulder joints. But the soreness throughout the rest of her body reminded her of the acrobatics with the attacker and tense struggle in the closet. She sunk into general weariness and returned Dusty's call.

"Someone should have stopped me from going into this business," he opened he conversation. "We're hung up here because of a 'misunderstanding' between the local driver's union and the studio. Over two vehicles. A good misunderstanding runs a shoot over schedule and over budget. Oh, that's off the record."

His affably gruff voice was a pleasant awakening for Meredith. He also was quick to relate his own displeasure about her activities over the past thirty-six hours.

"Look, it's bound to be over soon," she countered. "How many times can this guy continue to do things so badly?" she asked.

"Until he succeeds. He may not have burned the office down, but he left some scars behind—on you."

"But we're so close to solving this. This guy has to have made some mistakes along the way and I'm probably the one who would notice. I just haven't recognized them yet."

"You're playing the heroic victim role too well. Are you sure it isn't getting in the way of the investigation?"

Meredith was glad he could not see the blush creeping up her cheeks. "I can't imagine that," she said defensively.

"Well, you have a way with your independence if they haven't figured it out already," His chuckle was welcomed. "I can give them some clues about a lady who feels that no one can do the job as well as she can—no matter what the job!"

"Woman, Dusty."

"Right. Well, just don't romance the cops into relying on that woman more than is necessary, or helpful. You're a writer, not an investigator. Maybe if you got out of the way, they'd make a better effort of it, not wait on you to find their evidence."

She sighed, rebuffed, and admitted to herself that in some way he was right. "I'll just hang in here for a while longer. A big ending will make great copy."

"Well, darlin' I'd hate for it to be the copy for your epitaph, that's all."

"I truly think this whole thing will fizzle out into nothing."

"With an attempt on your life? The break-in of your townhouse? Bettina's death, get real!"

"Coincidence," she shivered, not believing it herself.

"Right." There was no conviction in his voice.

"Look, you have enough to worry about. I'll be careful, and thanks for checking in with me. It's a nice assurance." she told him then sent him back to his "misunderstanding." She was sorry she couldn't use that misunderstanding in her column—production hang-ups were good column material. But Dusty's work was off limits and she often felt guilty about his warmth and support even in light of her own normal emotional focus elsewhere. He didn't seem to mind. She promised to check in with him Sunday night, and wished that life was back to its normalcy of two weeks prior.

Meredith admitted to herself often over the past three days how sorry she was she had never taken the self-defense classes available to her at the gym. She knew she had not been prepared to ward off attackers—the face-slapping or the head-beating kind.

Only my hair-dresser—and my make-up artist will know, she thought ruefully. Looking at herself in the mirror, gingerly touching her purple face and the knot on the back of her head, she decided it was not the day for a high impact aerobics class.

She decided it was, however, a good day for pampering. Gloria's party was that evening and she intended to have a good time—banged up head, bruised cheek or not. She padded into the kitchen to make coffee and read the newspaper which she found on the table, already perused by the cop who'd been her guard for the night.

An item in the paper reminded her of the disks, and she retrieved them from the trunk of her car where they remained forgotten and uninterrupted for a day and a half. Their discovery had come in the flurry of activity before the fire. Those activities flashed through her memory as she turned on her computer. She silently but profusely thanked the newspaper syndicate for it. She knew only how to use it for basics—read, limited writing and saving pages. It was enough.

Before anything else demanded her time, Meredith slid the first disk into the computer. The inner thoughts of Bettina Grant began to unfold. Meredith scanned the material, starting at the first entry apparently copied from an earlier journal written by hand before the computer arrived. But time was short and there was far too much to read in a couple of hours. And so far, nothing was revealed anyone else needed to know.

She knew there were bound to be entries shedding light—or at least inspiring more specific memories—helpful in the case but, pressed for time, she turned off the computer to continue the project later. She showered and moved around the townhouse picking up and cleaning, dogged that some forgotten thought was still lodged deep inside her memory.

"This must be ESP," she told Raymond as she answered the phone to his unexpected call. "I wanted to talk to you. I was thinking about the case."

"That's good." said the Detective somewhat flatly. Meredith puzzled over the response but continued. "There are some things that come to mind I need to pass on. I'm not feeling very analytical today, but maybe you are. If so, maybe we can put together another piece of this puzzle."

"Go on," the voice remained distant and flat.

"I had lunch with Larry Grant on Thursday—before the afternoon's excitement."

"I remember you saying something about that."

"He said that Bettina had bad reactions to Valium and also the combination of booze and diet pills. No surprise. But give me a good reason why she would be taking it again knowing about that?"

"Habit. Compulsive behavior. What else…?" A change in the tone of Raymond's voice stopped Meredith. In a one-second decision, she decided not to reveal discovery of the electronic journals.

"That's all," she said. "I told you before that I feel like there's something important lurking deep in my memory, but I can't identify it. It keeps slipping away, eluding me. I was hoping you'd have something enlightening to flush out my recollection."

"Dream on," he laughed, lightening up. "Enlightenment is the one thing I'm short of in this case—along with a lot of other things." His candor was as disturbing as the lack of buoyancy in his voice. Meredith remembered Dusty's caution about getting in the way of the investigation.

"Like what?" she probed.

"Nothing critical," he laughed feebly, "it's just that our key witness has had her apartment broken into, was assaulted, yet continues to go on about her routine like nothing ever happened, and I'm beginning to feel like I haven't had my thinking cap on since this case started. Like I need to go back to ground zero. But that possibility keeps eluding me."

"Like how…?"

Raymond cut short her words, "You haven't noticed? There have been other…distractions…competing with the logic of the case."

"And…?"

"We need to talk about tonight…I've been thinking about it…"

"Great! First my face gets bruised, then my head gets smacked and now you're going to tell me I'm going to spend hours in the beauty salon, put on my pretty new dress and go to Gloria's party with my wounds disguised—alone? Or do I have to take the guys from the black and white with me?"

"Meredith Ogden you would never be alone, anywhere, in any situation! And, I wouldn't miss the opportunity for a real Hollywood party," he quickly countered. "Of course not. I just want to caution you that there's some feeling, mostly my own, that I may have crossed a line here from objective investigator to invested participant. It's not particularly healthy in the detecting business. Tonight, let's try to think of me as a protective LAPD cop doing his job watching over a threatened witness. At least that's what I'd like the guests to think. After that, well…."

"I got it," she said measuring her words carefully, wondering what prompted the change of the tone, a distancing from the open dialogue and banter they had shared. She felt like a child being scolded. "But you're not reneging on the martini!" she snapped.

So what? she told herself. If Raymond weren't here, I'd be going off to Gloria's alone anyway. Or maybe with Fred. Instead, I have a good-looking karate-trained bodyguard for an escort. I could do worse.

"You do whatever you need to," she told him flippantly. "As for me, I'm off to Robert Herman's salon on Beverly Drive. Resisting is futile—that's from some sci-fi film but take it to heart! I'm taking the day off. Go rent your tux for tonight!"

"What self-respecting Beverly Hills stud would *rent* a tux?" he asked just before he hung up.

☆

The cadence of Christmas was never more visible than it was at Robert Herman's Salon. One of Beverly Hills' most fashionable centers for beauty, Robert Herman had also contracted one of the city's prominent artists to decorate the entire facility. A jewel-studded Christmas tree adorned the corner of the large main room, with tiny twinkling lights and transparent glass ornaments draped dramatically, and gem-stone-like glitter. Every workstation boasted a matching mini tree.

Meredith found herself thinking about her long friendship with Gloria; roommates in college and for a time in their earliest days in California, then after Gloria had become an attorney, practicing with a large law firm, and Meredith working in Hollywood. Together they gossiped, went to parties and drank a lot of wine. Then one day a few years ago, Meredith took a call from her old friend. It was a curious one.

"What do you know about George Masner?"

"The theatrical agent?"

"That's the one."

"Powerful, a mover and shaker. I don't know much else—he's not a glitz character. Apparently rules his fiefdom with a strong hand."

"Is he a player?" asked a curious Gloria.

"Like how?"

"With women?"

"Not that I've heard. As I said, he keeps his personal life out of the limelight. Most of these agent-types are out on the town at least every week with one or another of their starlet clients. Frequently marry them—a Pygmalion thing, I guess. I've never heard stories that this guy is one of those—in public, at least."

"That's good news," said Gloria.

"Why?"

"I'm thinking about marrying him."

Meredith gulped and quickly demanded the hows and whys.

Gloria answered, "Who knows why. He likes me. I like him. He's older—ten or twelve years—that's not so good or bad, but he's an incredibly vital man, he's good in bed—and God, is he rich. We want to be together. Those are the pluses. What would you do?"

"I'd let me be a bridesmaid at an elegant-beyond-elegant wedding."

So, Gloria did, and Meredith was. And Gloria was still her best friend in the world, gave one of the best Christmas parties of the year, and continuously told her dear friend she needed to let go of her loyalty to a dead ghost. Every time the subject came up. Meredith remembered the ring still languishing in the safe deposit box.

Under the spell of a vigorous massage before her hair appointment, Meredith told herself nothing about the ring mattered, and nor did Raymond's distancing himself from her. Even the cops waiting outside at the curb were inconsequential. If she was a ready woman, it was only for a good time among good friends.

She laughed heartily, shocking the masseuse—and herself.

CHAPTER 33

SATURDAY EVENING

The Neiman Marcus dress hung regally against the dressing room door, its web of minute silver strands and sequins covering the simple long-sleeved top, the deep purple luminescence of the form-fitting skirt catching the low lights of the dressing table. Meredith spirits brightened every time she glanced at the dress, one she had coveted the holiday season before, finally bought after Christmas, but not yet worn. No event special enough had come up since then—until now. Elegance was always in fashion at Gloria Masner's Christmas party.

She was pleased with her copper blonde mane, and happy that she had convinced the hospital attendants to shave only a small patch of hair from the back of her head when they put four stitches in her scalp. The image looking back at her in the mirror was pretty good, she had to admit, band-aided though it was. Small wounds covered cautiously by an upswept style, a little professional make-up technique, an aspirin for luck—and pain. Who'd know the difference?

She glanced at the computer and the two disks as she went about her preparations and pondered what to do about them. So far there had been nothing to indicate who might have killed Bettina. Only a great deal of very personal thoughts about family and her role in the super-attenuated Hollywood atmosphere and culture. All personal and revealing, but no insight into why someone would murder her. Finally, the pull of the glittering social event ahead seduced Meredith away from ruminations of Bettina Grant.

Meredith felt a jolt of anxiety when the doorbell rang. She was surprised at the promptness of the detective, and her own anxiety about the evening. She had struggled to quell a feeling of vulnerability from the not-quite two weeks of constant crises—and her own embarrassingly and curiously flirtatious attitude, in spite of the rules Raymond had set down earlier in the day.

She opened the door and whistled. The lanky six-foot-two frame looked entirely different wrapped up in a well-tailored Armani tuxedo, hair freshly cut, and shoes formally spit-shined.

"Wow," she said.

"Likewise," he responded with a shy smile.

As they drove to the Masner's, Meredith explained that Gloria was her best friend, former classmate at Northwestern, and a Hollywood participant until Gloria went to law school, became an attorney, met George, and became a trophy wife. She was also law firm senior partner at this point. Each year, the Masner's put on the kind of holiday party that had filled Gloria's own youthful fantasies; a formal, sit-down dinner, champagne, jazz quintet in the ballroom of the Holmby Hills mansion. Each Christmas, Meredith was once again pleased that she was one of Gloria's best pals, and that the evening always also enlivened her own youthful fantasies of what life in the fast lane should look like. What made the evening even more special was the many other long-time friends that Gloria included, because Gloria valued the friendships, and, it was a mutual feeling.

A valet attendant opened the door of the black BMW, Raymond's personal car. To Meredith, the ride seemed incongruous with the detective's usual low-key persona. The Masner's sculpted iron door was open with a black-tied manservant greeting arriving guests. He took Meredith's coat, handing it to a tall woman dressed in a starched uniform.

Gloria, in her own trophy splendor, greeted friends and directed them to the bar. Her blue-black hair was swept into an array of gemstones and she wore a stunning midnight blue velvet strapless gown that fell elegantly to the floor. She waved enthusiastically at Meredith and beamed as Meredith introduced T.K. Raymond.

"Teke! Great to see you, buddy. And decked out in Armani!" laughed George Masner, suddenly appearing next to Gloria at the entrance. Both Meredith and Gloria looked at one another with surprise. "How's Will? And your mom?" asked Masner.

Raymond answered Will was great, visiting shortly from Vanderbilt after a ski trip with friends, and his own mother was fine and sent her regards from Laguna Beach where she traditionally spent the holidays. "Well, you tell her hello," said Masner.

"Teke? How do you know George Masner?" asked Meredith as they worked their way toward the bar. She tried to be casual about the surprise acquaintanceship of the two men.

"My dad used to work with him."

"What did your father do?"

"He was the Business Manager for the Williams Creative Agency. One of its founders, actually."

"So, you're a show biz brat!"

"Sort of. My parents kept me as far out of it as possible until they didn't. I was expected to join the legacy firm. I did, then didn't. But still…I ended up in Beverly Hills and generally assigned to 'high profile' cases, so Hollywood crime solving has drug me back into the hot spot."

She continued to be amazed as a handful of the older guests paid their respects through "Teke" to the Raymond family.

Meredith and Raymond circulated among the begowned women and penguin-dressed men, a swirl of fashion and formality for which an impressionistic brush would have done glorious justice.

A realization began to take over Meredith's thoughts. Joey O'Neal and the key information about the Long Island convalescent home had come from Raymond. She suspected who his sources must have been but thought better of bringing up the subject. She realized he had gone beyond his standing in the police force to obtain the information for her. And she considered the wisdom of Dusty's concern that she was obstructing an otherwise objective investigation. She also reconsidered Raymond's earlier admonishments and thought they may really have had little to do with a personal relationship, but maybe more with the web of investigations she was doing with the O'Neal story.

Dinner was served at round tables set up in a heated tent over what usually served as the tennis court. Candelabras lit each table, silver and crystal picking up the glow then frivolously tossing it back and forth across the room. After dessert, one of the popular Beverly Hills society jazz ensembles played. Some couples danced, other sat on the settees around the dance floor and at the small round cocktail tables talking, laughing and sometimes singing to the occasional Christmas songs offered by the musicians.

Meredith sought out the handful of old friends who tended to congregate at one table throughout the evening and catch up with each other's lives. It was one of the few times during the year the five women were at the same table together. Three including Gloria were married, one recently divorced and alone at the party, and Meredith. Her detective escort was cordial and friendly, but kept a discrete distance from his date, and spent a lot of time with the host and mutual friends.

As the evening progressed, he appeared at her elbow, extending a hand and saying, "Come and dance with me?" Surprised, she joined him without a word. "I didn't want you saying that no one danced with you at the season's most elegant party."

She felt light as the sparkle from the chandeliers highlighted the deep luster of the skirt as she moved along the dance floor. She was surprised they continued to dance, totally comfortable, until the end of the jazz trio's set.

Inevitably, however, after multiple martinis, succumbing to the seductive glow of the holiday candles and the sultry embrace of the jazz, she lightly chuckled and said mixing business and pleasure was not so bad.

"What part of this is business?" Raymond asked.

"Nothing, really," she answered. "Just thinking about the past couple of weeks and those disks."

"Disks?" he probed.

"We found Bettina's diaries on disk."

"When? Did you look at them?"

"Only briefly but so far there's only a lot of very personal ruminating about life. Nothing that merits public scrutiny." She could sense Raymond tensing and wasn't sure she should have brought it up.

"When did you find these?"

"Sonia found them the afternoon I was attacked. I forgot about them until today. I looked at them for a few minutes this morning but didn't see anything—so far—that seemed relevant."

"Is there somewhere somewhat private around here where we can talk?" He looked around. Meredith knew exactly where to go, but she was reluctant to leave the festivities and it was obvious.

"Hey," Raymond said, careful not to scold. "I took the time to get pretty, put myself on the arm of the loveliest and smartest woman here, dance with her, toast to the holidays with her, but in the end, I still have to worry about crime-stopping. And, protecting her by finding a murderer."

Meredith led him across the pool esplanade, to an out-of-the-way small studio office. She tested the door, found it open, as she knew it would be. Gloria never locked her own office. She switched on a lamp that sat on the desk. One wall devoted to law books quietly reflected the soft light. Raymond settled his tuxedo-clad figure into a floral-patterned side chair and waited. Feeling somewhat contrite and expecting chastisement, she stammered out finding the disks, and explained how little pertinent information she had found. Her voice was low and subdued.

"How late exactly did you plan to stay at this party?" he finally asked, looking up apologetically at her. Her eyes took on a new determined curiosity. She had emerged from the glow of the evening and was back to business.

"No exact time. I had originally entertained vague thoughts about champagne at dawn. But after your lecture this morning, I hoped at least champagne at midnight."

"How about champagne at…," he looked at his watch, "say eleven and then…."

"We go back to my place," she cut him short, "and look at the disks."

"How disappointed would you be?"

"For someone who's just the ward of a macho-cop? Why would I be? I'm getting a ride home, aren't I?"

"Okay," he said, resigned, and pulled himself clumsily from the overly feminine chair. He cleared his throat. "We could, instead, go back to my place, drink champagne and do wild things in the night—but then whoever may be implicated on those disks could trash your place again, or skip out to Mexico.

Twelve hours ahead of the law, because the law was busy doing wild things in the night."

She was taken back by both his words and their adamancy and found herself without comment. She turned to leave the small den and dismissed a barrage of errant thoughts with a wave of her hand. "It's all right, honestly," she said. "Remember, I'm used to tinsel town and a world of illusion. If I believed that everyone I talked with who showed extra attention to me was serious, I'd be one very disappointed lady."

"As it is, you're just a pissed off one—at me. But we will have that martini—if you are in the game. By the way, you were the one who brought up the journals."

"I'm in and silly me," said Meredith, perky again.

CHAPTER 34

Raymond followed her into the townhouse around midnight. Meredith turned on the computer and printer and retrieved the disks from their hidden location under the fireplace log holder. The detective searched the cupboards until he found coffee beans in the freezer and, a few minutes later, turned them into a rich brew. Paco watched from the top of the refrigerator.

When Raymond returned to Meredith who sat at the desk in the corner of her living room, she was staring intently into the monitor screen. She wore horn-rimmed glasses he had never before noticed. He set a mug down next to her as she scrolled from one page to the next, scanning the words for mention of people or activities that might be connected to Bettina's strange death.

Raymond had shed his tux jacket and rolled up the sleeves of his formal shirt. Meredith's new suede plum-colored pumps lay discarded next to the sofa, her beaded bag tossed aside on a chair. Raymond read over her shoulder, a process that continued for some time before Meredith suddenly stopped the scrolling and froze the screen.

"Look, this part was written about two years ago, Raymond. She talked about an evening with Larry—her ex-husband. A very sexual evening."

He read for a few minutes, then huffed, "It sounds like this isn't the first of them during this time period. She must have been sleeping with him for a while."

Meredith stopped reading and thought for a few moments. She remembered something she had seen earlier and looked up to Raymond. "In Bettina's old briefcase—I found a bunch of receipts—credit card slips and an itemized bill from the Hyatt Regency in Lahaina, Maui—for Mr. and Mrs. Larry Grant. I thought it was from a long time ago, but I just realized the hotel has only been open a couple of years! I didn't even look at the date. Why would she have a copy of them unless she was there with him?"

"Keep reading," said Raymond. Meredith began slowly scrolling the screen again.

Forty-five minutes later the two sat staring at the screen, a final entry from Bettina Grant before the stream of consciousness ended as the life of its author flickered out.

"Almost every Monday night, in the last three years, when Ito was off, Larry Grant came home to Bettina," said Raymond matter of fact.

"If he was there the last Monday night, she was alive—the night she died—it's no wonder she prepared for bed as usual and slipped quietly into a sleep as though her nightly routine was never interrupted. It barely was," murmured Meredith.

"And we know how she got lucky before she went to bed," said Raymond. "Did he or she ever mention reconciling—or even seeing each other romantically again?"

"Uh-uh. In fact, Larry is engaged to marry someone else. Maybe Bettina was only a comfortable convenience who he hadn't even told about his coming marriage. Or maybe the engagement was just a story for me. I haven't read about it anywhere and his fiancée is rather visible. Or, maybe Bettina did know about it and was despondent over it to the point…"

"Or maybe there is more to it than that, Meredith," said Raymond, pacing the living room.

"Didn't you question him?"

"Over and over. Her—Vivian—too. But there is no reason at all to suspect him any more than any of the rest of you. Of all the people Bettina saw regularly—publicly—he had the least contact with her that we knew about. And he said he was with his fianceé the night Bettina died. His story checked out. He was at the law association party until midnight when he went home to Vivian. We confirmed he was at the party and she confirmed he came home around midnight."

"Did you ask the neighbors about any cars in Bettina's driveway the night she died?"

"Of course. No one reported seeing any cars arrive. Not even the one your pal Allan Jaymar and his friend drove as they pulled into their own garage across the street at eleven-thirty after the dinner party where they had seen Bettina. But we're talking about an elderly community, and most of the folks were long asleep when Bettina met her maker, and many were away for the holidays…we're still working on it. But this is old territory, Meredith. Where's the briefcase? Let's look at the hotel receipt again."

Meredith retrieved the case from its hiding place under the bathroom linens, feeling a little silly for hiding it. She handed it to Raymond and took a sip of her coffee as he began to systematically take it apart. Suddenly the coffee swirled into her nostrils and something about the aroma hit a nerve of recollection. She sat upright as though jolted by an electrical shock. Raymond glanced at her, surprised.

"I can't help it," she smiled embarrassed. "A Deja vu type of feeling—like there's something else I know but I just can't find it; a name that's just on the tip of my tongue or a comment someone made, but I can't bring it into memory. Maybe I need hypnosis."

Stapled to the yellowed hotel receipt and the credit card slips was a travel folder from the hotel. Raymond impatiently dug into his coat pocket for a latex glove, slipped it on and then examined all the contents—an itinerary from the travel agent, another receipt—this one from a Hawaii restaurant, several loose pieces of hotel note paper with phones number jotted down on them, and one more small folder from the hotel with another paper folded and stuck into it. He unfolded it, laying it flat on the desk and smoothing it out with his large gloved hand. The words on it were hand-written but precise and well-organized. Three signatures, each dated, were executed on the bottom.

As he read it, Meredith followed over his shoulder. Then both fell silent.

"Big time," said Raymond. "Bettina lent Larry a lot of money and used the house as collateral," he whistled. "Until he repaid her—by next month—he would have no claim on the place. It became her property. The agreement is even witnessed, with an address in Las Vegas. But I don't recognize the name."

"Unless he repaid her. Isn't that what you'd call motive?"

"At least it gives me the leverage to get serious about him. We still don't know for sure that he was with Bettina the night she died."

"He surely had every opportunity to tell someone—anyone or everyone—to keep himself in the clear from murder accusations."

"It also gave him an incentive to look for this note and destroy it—at your house, at the office. He probably figured that if anyone found it, you would, Meredith. No one else had access to Bettina's secrets and their hiding places as you did."

"Can't you just pick him up?"

"We don't have evidence that he was even near Bettina's house the night she died. Now, he's out of town skiing. We've kept tabs. Just because. We've kept tabs on others as well. And there's warrants and paperwork. I have to put the law enforcement machine in gear."

"So, you have to be able to prove the killer was at Bettina's house? Motive doesn't count for anything?"

"I need to talk with my boss and the DA's office. We probably can get a warrant to search his house, car and so on. But we'll need more."

"Well, that's it, then," said Meredith, dropping her glasses on the desk, and stretching her back against the chair. "Case solved? My days as a ward of the police are over?"

"As a ward? We don't know that yet because this isn't finished. I have to get these disks down to the office now. I want them under lock and key—after you make copies and put them out of sight. And, I need documents to pick up Larry Grant for questioning as soon as we can locate him. I need to use your phone." He hastened into the kitchen and made a hurried call.

Meredith overheard the surprising words, "…and while you're there, look into the thing with the Japanese house guy. Sorry to hit you with this just before Christmas, but I think that's the place to finish it."

"What about Ito?" She demanded.

"Just some follow-up in Las Vegas. Everyone seems to be going there these days."

"Ito?" she asked to no response. She bent to pick up her party pumps from the floor. "Bettina left her car and other stuff to him. You'd better get going. Time's a-wasting."

Raymond laughed. "Not a chance. You're coming along. You said something about champagne at dawn. After the station, we could make that date. Processing the paperwork will take some time—maybe until Monday."

"Should I change clothes?" Meredith looked around, confused.

"Nope. If I go into the cop station in formal wear, so does my date. Something has to explain this clown costume I'm wearing."

Nevertheless, Meredith hastily stuffed spare clothes—jeans, pullover and sneakers— into a cloth duffel bag. Bejeweled gowns were known to be cumbersome at some point—no matter what the circumstances.

"You sure about this? I'll probably just be in the way."

He toyed with the papers in his hands and finally looked at her, directly and intently, "You talk about 'champagne at dawn.' Can you give me some idea what that involves or includes, please?"

"Everything," she said without hesitation.

CHAPTER 35
SUNDAY—MALIBU

At first, the sound of the surf confused Meredith and she thought she was again dancing to the music's deep throb at the Masner's party. She soon became aware of the comforting cadence of the waves outside the small beach house belonging to T.K. Raymond. She listened to his steady rhythm of sleep, remembering the heat of the hours before. Her body felt sated, spent and relaxed. She had forgotten what relaxed abandon felt like.

She turned toward the sleeping figure and touched the tip of her tongue to his shoulder, tasting the salt that she knew had dried there. She was reminded of how uncompromised his 48-year old body was. Unexpected, she recalled. A hesitant sun was trying to brighten a predicted overcast morning on the ocean's horizon outside the second story window casement of the replicated saltbox house.

When they had arrived at the detective's house in Malibu sometime before dawn, its contemporary elegance surprised her—as did its location on the beach. She was amazed at a framed diploma from UCLA Law School in Raymond's tiny den, and the wall full of photographs taken with his family and familiar faces—faces many times more famous than even she had enjoyed the opportunity to meet. Mostly she had been surprised at the grace and finesse with which Raymond had waltzed her "ready" body in the king-sized feather bed looking out to sea, the poetic confidence of his hands and lips, the gentle demanding of his caresses, and finally the fire and urgency in his penetration of her senses. She had given up and surrendered in harmony, dismissing all ancient concerns and baggage of her own. If her body never spoke to his again, the night would be recorded as one of moon-struck madness, and a kind of acceleration into a new phase of adulthood.

"Ready woman," she winced, carefully climbing from the bed to regard the morning more closely. It was nearly eleven according to the digital clock on the nightstand. She quietly explored the room and found a dark blue robe hanging in the closet and slipped it on. The hem brushed the tops of her feet, but it was warm. She found her way into the kitchen, looking for coffee—the real stuff—to kick-start the day. T.K. Raymond had not stirred. She wished it was Saturday instead of Sunday so that there was more of the weekend left. She was, at the same time, grateful to have even a casual morning, calm, safe and secure, with no work demands.

As she located cups in a logical cupboard, she was flooded with thoughts that had languished unconnected for days within her memory. She was jolted into reality by an aroma. Coffee—linked to coffee cups, linked to the coffee cups on the back seat of Larry Grant's car. She sat down to explore the realization. She remembered that her turquoise dress exuded an unusual odor and recognized it: smoke combined with a very familiar spicy fragrance. Larry's? He probably did not expect Meredith to be around to remember the cologne odor in his car.

Other images flooded her memory.

Meredith rose hesitantly and wearily from her seat at the kitchen window to awaken Raymond. The word "arouse" came to mind, and she rued the fact it would be used only in reference to the case, once again.

A few minutes later, a gull squealed overhead, calling to a companion also hovering high above the surf outside the house. Raymond was slouched into a wood lounge chair on the deck above the sand, wearing a pair of rumpled gray sweatpants and sweatshirt, regarding the morning with a troubled squint. He ran a hand through his unruly hair, askew from sleep, and accepted the cup of coffee Meredith handed him.

"Not what I expected," he murmured as he blew on the steaming liquid to cool it down. "You've drug us both out of bed, with only a few hours of sleep, and you expect me to be lucid. Dream on, you really are too young for me."

"If I'm dreaming, then thank my subconscious for handing you Larry Grant on a platter. And age is only a state of mind—and I didn't notice the difference earlier."

Raymond transferred his sleep-sodden squint from the horizon to Meredith.

"Oh," he said absently, "Nice view."

"Thank you." Meredith felt suddenly self-consciousness.

"Now, tell me how I can have Larry Grant on a platter. Somehow, after last night, if your thoughts are on Larry Grant, I have to wonder just how much this old set of bones disappointed you."

"This isn't about your bones or—that's for a later discussion—maybe over those infamous martinis. When I reached for the coffee cups today, I remember some things. I can place Larry Grant at Bettina's house the day she died, and when I was beat up."

"Don't let me stop you." Raymond yawned.

"There were a couple of coffee cups on the back seat of Larry's car on Thursday. I didn't pay much attention to them, but what just came back to me is the realization they were Bettina's. I know it because Ito has served me coffee in one from their set of four this week."

"Left over from before the divorce—or maybe Larry took a cup of coffee for the road after another visit to the house?"

"A visit to the house, yes, but a very recent one. Those cups were a promotional gift that arrived the afternoon Bettina died, a Christmas gift from one of the PR agencies."

"Okay, so maybe Larry stopped by after that."

"How and where?" said Meredith. "I was with her until nearly six. She was at the Feinberg's from seven until somewhere after nine. Larry only stopped by once after Bettina's death—and that was to collect the family the day they arrived. The remaining two cups were packed up the next day. I watched as Ito did it. What does that tell us?"

"Larry Grant made his usual Monday night stop at Bettina's house."

"After nine-fifteen-ish"

"…and before one-ish a.m. around the time she died. You're sure about those being the same cups?"

"Yeah—not many coffee cups around with the face and slogan of a prominent comedian—and the year 1983—glazed on them." A moment of thoughtful if reverend silence settled over the deck as the two considered the impact of the revelation. A sadness washed over Meredith.

"What do your forensics experts say about the time Bettina actually took the drugs?"

Raymond shrugged. "Two—three hours before she died. Hard to say exactly. Could have been more."

"No sign of a struggle or distress so Bettina probably took that stuff without even knowing—don't you think?"

"Or else on purpose. But from all I know about the lady, it doesn't sound like she was on a self-destruction course, no matter how despondent she may have been over Larry—if she even was. And what we know about her knowledge of pills and their effect, especially to Valium, makes it hard to imagine that she would knowingly ingest that much..."

"There's something else lurking in my memory—my dress."

Raymond cringed as he glanced over his shoulder into the house. "I'm sorry—I know it was special, sparkly, we didn't treat it very well, did we?"

Meredith laughed. "Relax, Raymond. This dress will live to dance again. But the one I was wearing the day I was attacked won't. I couldn't stand to put it on again, even though it was turquoise—my best color, and even if I had nothing else on earth to wear."

"Cannot imagine that," he murmured.

"Listen to me! When I handed it over to the forensic guy on Thursday, I remember cringing at the odor in it. I realized this morning I was smelling more than smoke. It was the same fragrance both Marty and I noticed in Bettina's bathroom after she died. We commented on it. I don't know how I missed it. Larry Grant's car was saturated in it the day we had lunch. It was so strong he nearly closed up my sinuses for good and definitely wrecked the taste of my lunch. If I had to guess, I can't remember the brand or name of the scent, but it's familiar—spicy. You guys will have to check that out."

Raymond yawned and stood, looking out at the ocean. "Well, Cinderella, if I spoiled your fantasies about dancing until dawn, you've certainly disrupted mine about enjoying a very rare Sunday that might hold some fairly personal surprises."

"And you said I was just a ward of the Police Department! You told me that just yesterday. On the phone, Raymond."

"Unexpected consequences," he sighed, resigned, continuing to stare at the sea, hands on his hips. "There's work to be done. I'm sorry your memory didn't come back sooner. The day could have been used for better things that solving crimes."

"Maybe a night with an older man was what I needed to clear my memory. A lot's happened you know—and stress... well, you know the rest." Raymond found himself shaking his sleep-tousled head vigorously.

As he helped carry Meredith's bag and formal clothes into her condo, an express delivery packet was propped against her front door. With it was a note from her neighbor explaining that he had accepted delivery for her.

"What now?" she implored. "What else could possibly complicate my life—the one I hoped was about to settle down?" She ripped open the cardboard envelope to find a hand-written note from Allan Jaymar.

"You've been out all day, and we need to talk," it read. "Much has happened very quickly. Cassie is on her way back here. Please come to breakfast on Monday morning at my house—the enclosed proposal, from Cassie, is only half of the story. I have the other half to propose. You'll like it."

"Crap," said Meredith.

Raymond practically jumped aside. "Don't even tell me. I got problems of my own. I'll call you tonight." He brushed her forehead with his lips and was gone.

As Raymond walked into the investigators' room, checking the mail slots for whatever waited for him there, his desk phone rang. He was greeted with Marty Escobar's hurried voice. "I'm here with Mrs. Greenfelt in Vegas, Raymond. I have a Polaroid of her with her copy of the loan agreement the Grants signed. She's an all-night waitress at the Lantana where they apparently wrote this up in October. They asked her to witness and she did, but she wanted a copy, said she felt a little vulnerable. They made a Xerox at the business office. I also have her on tape talking about the whole conversation. I can use the Las Vegas PD's new fax to send the photo to you and I can play you my recording which you can record. The quality might suck, but we'll have it now. I also have that stuff on Ito. Interesting."

"Good work," Raymond exclaimed, "thanks for being willing to take the hang-over shuttle…" But Escobar cut him off. "I have to run—I have an appointment in 30 minutes with the manager at the Sand Dune Casino. The manager at the Palmetto told me Larry racked up a big heap of debt, but the casino kind of allowed it because Bettina had given them all so much publicity over the years. We know she was aware how big his debt was. Gotta go. I'd like to get wrapped up—if possible—in time to get home tonight."

Raymond sank into his desk chair as he signed off. Finally, it was coming together. But "it" was still a mystery. Larry Grant? Ito, who had some questionable uses of Bettina's Jag and other issues? And what about Cassie? Her book manuscript would have set Bettina Grant in flames had Bettina been alive, and she should have been except that someone killed her.

Pulling out his satchel, he began to organize and process what he had learned and what to do next. Thirty minutes later his phone rang again. "It's Sunday," he hissed." No crime allowed on the Lord's day!" Then he answered, "Raymond."

"Okay, so there's more." Meredith's voiced seemed a little embarrassed.

"More what?" asked the detective.

"I just remembered something else. It may be nothing, but...."

"But...what?"

"You said Larry Grant's fiancée alibied him along with friends from the law association dinner. When I talked with Bettina's lawyer, he said he left the dinner early, by nine, himself, because he was too tired to stay. He also said he saw Larry at the valet stand, leaving, at the same time. I think you said Larry got home around midnight."

"I don't know what we unleashed last night, but your memory is a good start."

"So, do I get my martini?"

The loud guffaw coming across the phone lines made her smile. "How about a week of them in Paris? "

"Okay."

"After we wrap all this up."

☆

"Well, the cops on TV are always working," Meredith told Gloria on the phone a while later. "Raymond had made good on his promise of champagne at dawn. But not very much of it. He told me about the death of his wife, Lilli, and the challenges of raising his son alone as a pressured, over-scheduled police officer, of fending off control by, and interference from his parents and in laws."

"You obviously told him about your own life," Gloria fed the conversation. "What about the widowhood you can't seem release?"

"Well, I have to admit I felt a little guilty and frivolous listening to his real story of widower-hood. I decided that's for the conversation another time. It's kind of self-imagined isn't it?" She was silent for a moment then added, "White bread, Gloria. I told him I was white bread. Remember that's what you called us—you and me. And honest to God, that's how I sometimes feel in this carnival-like world here. Unspectacular, predictable. White bread."

"I never cease to be amazed at how hard you are on yourself Meredith Carol Ogden. Take a nap, Merri. Better yet, take a vacation. You need one," said Gloria just before she hung up the telephone.

As she said, "Goodbye" to Gloria, Meredith's glance fell on the proposal sitting on the floor. More than anything, she was confused by what Cassie had constructed. And hopeful about the contributions Allan would make the next morning. At first, when she saw the document with a cover letter to Russ Talbot, Meredith was angry and threatened, and a sense of unfair advantage. But she thought better of the accusation when she realized there was no such thing as unfair advantage in the game of career roulette, especially in the state-of-mind called "Hollywood."

When she finished reading, she had put the document down and opted for a nap instead of an anxiety attack, preferring to savor some of the glow from the early morning hours.

"Anything for normalcy again," she sighed, knowing that normalcy would take a long time to establish especially without Bettina Grant to dictate what it should be.

Meredith looked in the mirror as she headed for the bedroom. The bruise on her cheek was now turning a sour shade of yellow without make-up over it. She grimaced at its ugliness. And her hair was unruly and tousled around the shaved patch— an ache emanating from around the stitches—and more. What a treat for a guy to wake up to.

So what? she thought. They're my bruises. I earned them and I'm proud of them.

Paco curled up next to her on the bed as she drifted off into the afternoon, dreaming of gulls calling overhead, and coffee cups.

CHAPTER 37
SUNDAY/MONDAY

"I can tell you're furious with me for going ahead with this without your permission. But I had the opening and I decided to take it. I knew Russ was meeting Phyllis Armstrong this week and had been in conference calls with Roger Golden twice. I didn't think it could wait."

It was Sunday evening, after Meredith's nap and Cassie's last-minute flight west. The two women sat opposite one another in a tiny stucco-covered Mexican restaurant only two blocks from Cassie's good friend Betty Lars' West Los Angeles house where the dark-haired journalist was staying on this unplanned trip. The stroll to the cantina was strained and mostly silent, and the conversation less spirited than when the two had last met and talked.

"You couldn't have called me before you talked to Russ on Friday?"

"I knew I'd have to sell you on the idea, and the timing was ripe to get to Russ. And, when he told me that Allan had stepped in, well…" She shrugged.

"What balls you have, Cassie," sniped Meredith.

"But what do you think about it?"

"It's quite a concept," Meredith admitted, trying hard to let go of her anger toward Cassie, and direct her comments to the proposal. "Not one I would have put together. What in the world gave you the idea that you could take such a liberty with my life?"

"You did," said Cassie. "You talked about the house of cards we were building, and I got to thinking how much stronger the foundation would be if we combined the elements. It could work."

"But Cassie, this is even more of a house of cards. Actually, it just makes the entire web even more complex."

"Yes, but we can make some of it happen, Meredith. You know that. Some of it already has happened. My book sold, with an option for the next one. So, I there's a definite for Russ. Your chances at the radio syndicate are good. Russ can't lose. We can't lose."

Meredith gritted her teeth and asked the one shaky question about the proposed merger of the two aggressive talents into a single Hollywood entity. "So, who's the columnist and who's the legwoman?"

"There isn't one, Meredith. You were the last Hollywood legwoman. You must know that. No self-respecting journalists of the '80s would allow themselves to be called a 'legwoman' or 'legman.' They're all 'field reporters' or 'assistants' now. That aside, here's the way it breaks out. We'd share the column— under a double by-line. That way neither of us is required to do all the screenings, all the parties or the set visits. We'd set up a schedule each week or month, with enough time to freelance for other outlets or do more features for Jay, write books or do a radio show. This would be a witty, stylish, intellectual form of gossip—not the 'confidant to the stars' from the 1950s. If we market this concept well enough, we shouldn't lose any of the existing revenues, and believe me, with the amount that came in to Bettina we both could live as well or better than we're used to, maintain the secretary, and pay for a small office."

"Sonia, the secretary, is growing up. For reasons of which I am not sure," conceded Meredith. "She's matured by leaps and bounds since Bettina died. She's becoming a real editorial assistant. And there's a new 'secretary'."

Cassie gave Meredith a puzzled look. "Ito," said Meredith, trying to maintain her coolness, to give the impression she was still uninvolved in the scheme. "Bettina's former houseman. He's brilliant at organizing and running things. I suspect he'd been running Bettina's life for a long time. He'd extend our activities so much..." Meredith caught herself as she let slip a hint of interest. "What about the TV slot? Who's doing that?"

"I hope Allan can help us with that, he has the contacts." Both women went silent in thought. "Let's look at the numbers again," Cassie said with a discrete, private smile, pushing aside a now spent plate of enchiladas and reaching into her purse for a pen. Meredith followed her example, reaching for a napkin on which to make notes. An hour later, they were talking more easily about the plan.

"A real issue," said Meredith, "is whether you and I can work that closely together."

"Maybe with a well-written understanding and support from Allan and Mort, we can make sure we have some kind of framework to make sure we can work together." Both women fell silent, considering the options ahead, a possible future.

"We have to sell Russ on this. I'm still not sure we have his serious attention," Meredith broke in.

Cassie shook her head. "That's why Mort Agee spent an hour on the phone with Russ on Friday, and why we're scheduled to have breakfast with Mort and Allan tomorrow. And, you can be sure they have some revisions to make."

"You did all of this around me, though. That bothers me. Will that stuff really stop at this point, Cassie?"

"It stops on the dotted line. Mort and Allan could pull this off when neither you nor I could. And yes, Mort's already put in some discrete inquiries at the radio syndicate. The president's an old friend of his and the prospects look great. Look again at the number—and at the opportunities. Then tell me you can't make this work comfortably."

"I'll meet but I'm not promising anything," cautioned Meredith.

"You're just pissed off because I went around you."

Meredith shook her head. "Give me time."

It was a troubled sleep in spite of the need for a full night of it. At eight a.m. she and Cassie arrived at Allan's portico entrance on Bright Leaf Lane. Meredith glanced over her shoulder, surprised to see that both Sonia's and Ito's cars were already visible at the office/house across the street.

"Ladies," welcomed Allan as he swung wide the heavy door. "Life's about changes, it seems. Hello again, Cassie. It's been a long time." Both women grunted their hellos, uncertainty on their faces. Mort Agee with his thinning, slicked back hair and black silk suit, was seated in the living room, a mug of coffee already in his hand.

"Hi Cassie," he stood up, setting down the mug and extending his hand. "Meredith, your reputation really precedes you. I'm Mort." She met his hand with her own. Both women registered their surprise as Russ Talbot stood to welcome them. Dressed uncharacteristically in brown pull-over sweater and tan slacks, tasseled loafers in place of his usual shined wingtips, he acknowledged Meredith then Cassie. "Nice to see both of you."

Meredith quickly reached out to shake his hand. Cassie murmured "Hi, Russ."

"You didn't really come all the way out here for us," Meredith said looking at him dubiously.

"Well, yes I did. Between the two of you, and these two," nodding at Allan and Mort, "I needed to get this whole situation resolved. Not just for the column and syndicate, but for my own peace of mind. You two," he pointed at the two women, "can scare the hell out of the most sane and confident person in the world."

Meredith and Cassie looked at one another and small grins formed on both faces.

"Determined is the way I look at it," said Meredith.

"No shit," chuckled Russ as Allan waved them into the dining room where Potty and a young female helper were placing food on the table.

"What do we know about the police investigation into Bettina's death? Have they identified a suspect yet?" asked Russ.

Meredith shook her head. "They are closing in, I'm told. There are several 'people of interest,' but no arrests yet." Frustration was the only response by everyone at the table. Small talk ensued before Allan advanced the conversation to the topic at hand.

Russ opened the discussion with an important announcement. "We're taking things a little differently at the Syndicate now. The public's media preferences are changing, and the concept of 'gossip' is changing as well and is more pervasive. People are getting more—eventually most—of it from TV. But the interest is no longer only in who is sleeping with whom, but everyday goings on in the broader industry. We want to take a more universal look, cut a large piece of the entertainment pie."

All eyes were on him. Meredith was caught between enthusiasm at the idea, and trepidation that her role was over. Cassie quickly realized her proposal was only bare bones of the changes that were about to take place.

"So, here's the full picture," said Allan, speaking up. "The columns will be broader, more industry and people oriented, not just celebrities acting out, but more behind the scenes, movie production news and so on. Much of what you and Bettina have been doing for a while has come close to this concept," he addressed Meredith. "Now, there'll be daily columns, and weekly features—your by-line Meredith. For the newspaper subscribers, Cassie, you'll add special features once a month and a Question/Answer column weekly."

Cassie felt a crushing disappointment. Her role was diminished greatly, it seemed. But Russ picked up the conversation. "You'll both be covering the scene because the syndicate has created a new department with a weekly TV slot that features you both but produced by Cassie. *Morning Coffee*, of course, is the first subscriber, but we have a half-dozen more we expect to close in the next few days. So, you'll both have to cover the news, events, productions and so on. Equals, sharing the work. Needless to say, those TV segments will be time-consuming and very, very visible. Cassie, you'll have your work cut out for you. You'll alternate the in-front-of-the-camera roles. Meredith, learn to love the lens." Cassie smiled confidently, figuring she could pass the Q/A column onto Sonia, who would love the opportunity.

Then Russ spoke up again. "You all need to understand this is a new direction—and it is still a risk. We can't promise the concept will be as successful as the tried-and-true print column, but we also believe that we have to expand into a different direction to stay ahead of the market. If it doesn't pan out, you all will be the first to know, so in some respects, we are all partners in this new endeavor. Please understand that it might not work.

"The Syndicate will keep the office open here in Los Angeles, in new quarters, of course. We have a budget for rent and facilities, but it won't be a lovely home in Bel Air. It will however, become the L.A. Bureau of the Syndicate and pump out weekly movie 'packages' with a short feature story and photos—yes, they can be stock photography—for our foreign as well as domestic subscribers. You two can figure out who should write those—as well as any requests for special features from any one or more subscribers. We've already had those kinds of requests. Now we can fulfill them. We will continue to fund the staff. When Bettina was…with us…we funded her, one writer, a secretary, freelancers and photographers when needed. Allan and Mort can work through the budgets and finances and work out the details."

Again, Russ commanded the conversation, "Meredith, your radio deal is your own. Play it how you'd like, and I know you'll make sure it happens well. Cassie, you have a book to promote with what I understand may be a sequel so that's your own project, but the TV segments and Meredith's radio spots will begin in April. Everything else starts on February 1. Gives us time to promote the new look and packages. Until then, it's business as usual."

"As if Bettina were here, just across the street," murmured Meredith. It was a sobering moment amid a heady atmosphere.

Meredith felt positive about the interaction, and once questions were answered and contractual issues discussed, the group began to move toward adjournment. Russ was going to play golf with a friend before returning to New York. Cassie was enroute to the airport. Meredith hugged Allan and whispered to him on the side, "You're my manager now, you know. We need to talk about how to compensate you."

He smiled. "It won't hurt your pocketbook much—I'm retired you know. And I have your back—I promised Bettina."

She pulled back to look at him in question. "You promised? When?"

"A couple of years ago. She told me, 'If anything happens to me, or I'm just being an asshole, make sure that girl gets a decent career. She's smart, talented and maybe a little too loyal. Help her out of it.'"

Meredith choked back tears and Allan was doing the same.

She waved goodbye to the various individuals and told Cassie to let her know the plans for the move from New York. Then she crossed the street to the office. As she pushed the back door open, she took a deep breath. Soon there would be no more mornings at Bright Leaf Lane where she had arrived every morning for a decade. Mort and Allan would help them find a new office, move, and she'd step into a new role she'd agreed upon. But, there was daily material to be written between now and then, and columns and articles prepared in advance of a four-day vacation over the holidays. And, she needed to recruit both Sonia and Ito, convince and engage them in future office and work plans.

"And my dinner-dance card is really full," she reported to Gloria later that day by phone. Dinner with Dusty had important place in the calendar. She owed Fred some time and an update. And then there was a dinner with Raymond before closing down for Christmas for four days.

"And you give me a bad time about my trophy lifestyle," Gloria gibed. "Seems to me that your romantic escapades make the drabble in the romance novels look positively anemic."

"It's not intentional, hardly even 'romantic.'" insisted Meredith. "I'm basically a monogamous, sentimental lady."

"Tell it to the High-Profile office of the LAPD," snickered her friend warmly.

That evening, she was again enjoying Mexican food, in another part of town, filling Dusty in on the developments. He was amused, regarding her with the quiet interest that had become part of the long-time friendship. "Sounds to me like you got yourself a new career," he said, biting into an enchilada.

"Well, I'm not totally convinced yet, but it could work…."

"You're not totally convinced, but I'll bet you signed a contract this morning," he grinned.

"Not until tomorrow."

"You sure you can't come over to Arizona for a quiet Christmas on the ranch?" he asked.

Meredith shook her head wearily. "I'm exhausted from fending off the drama, and I'd love the respite and solace of your ranch. But…"

He looked at her knowingly. "But?"

"Too much going on—and I have a couple of other commitments I can't overlook right now." She wanted time to herself to flow into the next phase of life, needed to make that jump without feeling guilty or fraudulent about any personal involvement. And while Dusty might well be in her world in the future, she couldn't imagine retirement any time soon, as Dusty would like, nor life among the cacti, far from the energy and activity of her current world. Both understood they had a very comfortable relationship as show business lovers, with no lens needed to the future.

Two more focused, busy days of work and productivity were divided by a promotional screening of a movie rushed into public release in time for December 31 Academy Award consideration deadline. Meredith accompanied Fred for an after-movie dinner at his favorite restaurant, Musso and Frank, and filled him in on the plans. He shook his graying head and said, "Wow, kiddo. I go from one single employer to another—usually after a long stay in each—but you seem to weave the most complex environment around yourself and make it work. When I sent you out to meet Bettina Grant so many years ago, I wondered how it would all come together." Meredith laughed and took a sip of her drink.

"Now look at us both," she chided. "Neither married, neither rich—not very famous—both still more excited about work than anything else on the horizon."

"You've tragically lost a lover and a boss. I just lose girl friends in average ways."

She instinctively knew Fred would be there as a friend and hoped she could be as helpful to him as he'd been to her over the years. She mentioned it, he chuckled, telling her, "So long as you are willing to go to a few Hollywood gigs with me in the Rambler—or better, drive whatever car you own—make me look good with a gorgeous blond on my arm, and not be embarrassed, we're good."

She rose early the next morning and dressed in jeans and a striped sweater. Raymond arrived at seven-thirty bringing lox, bagels and cream cheese. She fixed coffee and orange juice, feeling apprehensive, not knowing what to expect from his call the afternoon before, requesting a private talk before their dinner date later in the evening. But he arrived, also in his jeans and a pullover and the expensive athletic shoes. When Meredith opened the door, he was gazing out to the street, turned around and smiled. Food sack in one hand, he squeezed her arm affectionately with his free hand.

Settled in around the small dining table, food spread out between them, they made small talk for a while. Then Raymond wiped his mouth and sat back. "I wanted to give you the full rundown before it's released and made official." She swallowed hard, expecting the scenario they had worked through a couple of days before.

"We really looked closely at Joey O'Neal because we found that the phone number of the two calls late the night of Bettina's death was from the club where he hangs out," Raymond began. Meredith's eye widened in surprise.

"We also looked at Cassie. I don't think you ever read her manuscript, but I still can't imagine she would release that book while its primary subject was alive. And we thought maybe Cassie thought that way, too. No, she was just not thinking at all at the time. Then, there's Ito. We checked out his papers—visa, and so on—because we found two speeding tickets. One on the route to Vegas in Bettina's Jaguar and the other in a rental car the night she was murdered."

Meredith stared at him, confounded. "Bettina apparently allowed him to use the Jaguar, if she didn't need it, some Monday nights and Tuesdays." Raymond explained. "He loved to drive it instead of his old clunker. Last Monday night, she needed it, but wanted to make sure he left for the night, so gave him a $100 bill and told him to rent a car. She knew Larry would be visiting."

The mention of Ito in Bettina's Jag brought a smile to Meredith's face. "He loved that ride!"

"Now, do you recognize either of these people?" He pulled two photographs from a manila envelope, laid them on the table. She stared at them.

"I saw them both at Bettina's service, chatting with Larry Grant. Then, I saw them again the day Cassie and I were at the Polo Lounge. They seemed to be staring at us. And I noticed him at Larry's firm the day we had lunch."

Raymond replaced the photos in the envelope. "Hard to say what they had in mind at the restaurant, if anything but coincidence, but I'm glad you two drove Cassie's rental car to the Valley that day, and not the Mustang. I'm guessing they were planning something. He's a document processor and delivery guy for Larry's firm. She's Larry's fiancée. Really an odd partnership.

"Now, here's something for you to consider. What would the implications be if Larry and Vivian had traded cars the night Bettina died?"

Meredith thought for a moment, her brow knitted tightly.

"Seriously—think about it." Meredith puzzled the question then shook her head.

"So, here's the scenario—stick with me. Larry and Vivian often traded cars. Her work was mostly in her office. His was out with clients and potential clients. He has a six-year old Mazda, she, a two-year old Mercedes. Her Mercedes made him look more successful. She only drove his to and from her office. He drove her car to important appointments and also the night of the law association dinner."

"And…"

"The night Bettina was killed Larry was driving Vivian's Mercedes and she was driving his car. Think about in which car you saw the incriminating cups. Think about the cologne smell in Larry's car." Meredith was trying to keep up with the unfolding story, still analyzing the facts.

"Larry goes to the law association dinner in the Mercedes. He leaves early and goes to Bettina's house, has a drink, sex and probably conversation, but has to leave earlier than he usually does on his Monday night visits so he can return to the party which he's in charge of and has to close out at Midnight. Gets home a little after that, as confirmed by Vivian. All of his activities that night are in Vivian's car.

"Vivian, meanwhile, recovers miraculously from a migraine, after Larry leaves for the dinner, drives Larry's car to Bettina's house late to make sure she's home. We don't know what transpired, but we know that the evening ended up with cups of tea and some pretty lethal chemical additives. We also know that Bettina had been drinking alcohol, and probably never noticed the bitter taste in the tea. Cups are quickly collected, dumped in the car, and Vivian is back home before Larry arrives."

"Oh, come on. That's a little too convoluted, even for me."

The detective got up and went to the kitchen to refill his coffee. Meredith sat patiently.

"Everything you and I and Marty uncovered is true, factual. Here's the difference between reporting and detecting," Raymond said. "We have corroboration from the association folks and the hotel about Larry's first departure from the dinner, his return, and final departure after midnight—in the Mercedes. Even the valet. The Daltons, who live around the corner from Bettina's house, said they noticed a silver Mercedes parked on their street that night when they took their dog for a walk around nine-fifteen. We were finally able to talk with them Monday."

Sipping his coffee, Raymond continued, "They also saw Larry's dark blue Mazda as they were going to bed later that night after the Mercedes was gone. So, silver Mercedes earlier, about nine-fifteen p.m. Mazda at eleven-thirty p.m."

"But how did Vivian know when Larry would leave Bettina?"

"She didn't," said Raymond. "Pure coincidence. Vivian didn't even know about Larry's weekly visits to Bettina. Wouldn't have known until Bettina told her. Vivian took herself independently to Bettina's house at eleven, we don't know what transpired between the two of them. No struggles nor violence indicated. But she was home by midnight, about a mile away. And Bettina went to bed and died."

"I can't imagine the conversation. But if she didn't know about the romantic liaisons, why did she go to see Bettina, anyhow? Why would she kill her?"

"The usual," sighed Raymond. "Money. Let me tell you about Vivian. Privileged childhood and a series of misdirected career attempts finally settled into psychotherapy after many years of study. She worked for an established practice for quite a while, then opened her own, bolstered by a radio talk show she managed to land. But she was a little too outspoken and got into a harangue with a caller, used some verboten language on the air, and worse, also inadvertently mentioned the problems of a well-known client. No names used, but it was obvious who it was. Of course, he sued, she was fired from the show, and most of her clientele jumped ship. She was deeply in debt, had to sell her home and move into a high-rise condo. Long before, her father had cut off any financial support.

"Then she met Larry—and they both assumed a bigger net worth of each other than was real. He moved in with her and as they planned their future, she saw even bigger bucks lurking in the background through Bettina. Larry had told her just enough about the original arrangement involving the house in Bel Air. Vivian put a deposit on a new minimansion in Pacific Palisades, assuming that Larry could borrow the down payment from the cash Bettina had saved from the earlier house refinance.

"When she told Larry her plan, he had to confess that he had already borrowed the cash from Bettina to pay down his gambling debts—which Vivian knew nothing about. Larry now owed Bettina a lot of money—around a quarter of a million dollars. And then, as he also finally confessed to Vivian, he had used the house as collateral for the loan, and if he didn't pay Bettina back by January one, she would take ownership of the place." The detective stood up and paced around the room, tapping on his coffee cup.

"Vivian went to Bettina, she says, to 'convince' her to refinance or renegotiate the Las Vegas deal. We can only imagine Bettina's type of refusal. But Vivian had already assumed Bettina's response—and figured that if Bettina died, no one would know about the collateral issue. No one would know Vivian had been at the house. Larry had told Vivian no one else had a copy of the agreement, so the house would return to him. He could refinance, sell or whatever he chose. But it was critical that the loan agreement was never discovered. They both assumed you, alone, would have access to that piece of paper."

"So, who assaulted me? And ransacked my home? And ran down Fred?"

"What evidence did you find in your dress?"

Meredith shook her head. "I don't think a woman would be strong enough to pull off an assault that big."

"Vivian is a Black belt karate expert, and an all-around athlete. And, she's determined. Don't underestimate her. The car incident with Fred was Larry's gofer and so was the break-in on your apartment, working with Vivian. All to keep you from finding any evidence of the Las Vegas deal. You undoubtedly would have been the only person to know—or discover—any copies of the agreement."

Meredith sank back into the sofa. "Geez, I thought Larry was smarter than this. Why didn't they all just down and talk about it?"

Raymond laughed loudly. "If only."

"They confessed?"

"Well, Vivian broke. Talk about a woman scorned. Said she was sorry she hadn't done Larry first. Larry really had nothing to do with the criminal parts of it, but admitted the gambling, the loan and the relationship with Bettina."

"I keep thinking of how badly they did it all. And stupid. You mentioned earlier even the guy who hit Fred rented the car under his own name. Assaulting me, trying to burn down the office—and me—but failing. Except for killing Bettina. But isn't this all too simple, Raymond? All of it too coincidental?"

The detective laughed hard. "Most crimes are simple. Committed by first-time novices through passion and anger or frustration or vengeance, romance scorned…"

"…or greed?"

"Or greed. Or stupidity. Larry wasn't all that much different. Except…" His words were stopped by the puzzlement on Meredith's face. He grinned confidently. "The guy took the state bar exam three times before he passed—and then only barely passed. What does that tell you?"

"You checked that out! Now, you're just arrogant? The majority of the people who take the bar exam have to retake it more than once, you with the fancy law degree!"

"Look who he chose as his new soul mate. Think about Vivian. She conceives of a very viable murder concept, and would have pulled it off—but screwed up by not bothering to dump the murder vessel, by hiring an incompetent to run you down in a place someone couldn't help but notice and rent a car with a credit card in his real name, by trying to strangle you herself and when she failed at that, failing again by proving herself to be the worst pyromaniac in the western hemisphere. When someone said, 'that was done badly,' they weren't kidding."

"Based on the button Ito found in my office couch, that otherwise benign little sofa was the scene of all that passion."

"Passion on that couch for several years, it seems from the evidence forensics finally retrieved from the cushions."

"Where's Larry now?" asked Meredith.

"Spending the holidays with his daughter Lorraine in New Mexico. And no plans to move into the house which the two daughters will inherit."

"Why did Bettina and Larry keep up the relationship? Sex?"

Raymond shook his head and shrugged. "He says that their friendship and attraction to one another never left. But their individual attitudes about life and how they should live it became too different. Once divorced, it all just worked. Obviously, part of his lifestyle included other women. I guess Vivian learned that."

The room was quiet for a few moments until Meredith spoke up, "Murder vessel, Raymond?"

"Detective talk."

"Oh." Silence fell between them. Raymond stood and started to pick up the breakfast debris.

"Gotta go—work calls. I'll meet you at five-thirty tonight and you can tell me about your day, and about your new deal. Our Public Information Officer—isn't that better?—can give you our official release."

"I'm going to work for the last day in the world as I know it," Meredith sighed and looked away. He noticed a tear slipping down her check and reaching across the table, gently wiped it away with his thumb.

"Thanks. I'll need to save those tears," she murmured quietly. "I'm going to hike to the top of Tahquitz Trail in Palm Springs, sit on a log, look out over the desert, and cry for however long it takes to finally release the past few weeks. I need the time and space—which I haven't had."

"Not all of it was bad, I hope?" Raymond looked at her.

"No, not all."

CHAPTER 30

WEDNESDAY

On the day before the office was closed for Christmas, Meredith went into work about ten, later than normal. She was organized for the four days away but needed to write the Bettina Grant murder wrap-up articles before leaving. Sonia was finalizing the files and paperwork, anticipating the break. Ito had worked with Allan to locate new space and finalize both the office and his own move from the lovely but, otherwise sadly empty house on Bright Leaf Lane. Luanne, Bettina's sister, would bring in a cleaning crew after the holidays and put the place on the market when it was empty in February.

The police were about to close the book on the murder investigation, but questions were still being asked of everyone. At that point, no information had been released about the prime suspects. It was the limited knowledge of only the police, and now Meredith, Sonia and Ito. Meredith walked across the street to share what she knew with Allan and Potty who were surprised, nonplused and saddened.

"We're about finished here," Meredith announced. She and Sonia were putting the daily and advanced columns and features on the fax to New York that afternoon. "We have four days with a week-end to restore our sanity. Can we do it?" They all shrugged.

"Hollywood is all about drama," said Ito. "Would we expect anything else?"

That evening, the office locked up and work put to bed, Meredith met Raymond for dinner. She was grateful he was not dressed up, glad for comfort clothes and no adornments. They met at a diner, because Raymond would leave directly to join his son and mother in Orange County for the holidays. As they sat down in the trendy Santa Monica Grill, sawdust on the floor and bare wooden rafters above them, Raymond said, "It feels like the weight of Hollywood is off my back. Now, tell me about your new deal."

Relieved to have the conversation focused, Meredith summarized the new arrangement with Cassie and the various media organizations. "Then, today I filed a long story about solving the murder of a prominent gossip columnist…met two TV stars, wrote two columns, filed charges against Joey O'Neal—I don't know how serious I am—but it seemed the right thing to do. He shouldn't have the right to beat on anyone, especially me…and then…"

"Should we worry about retribution?" Raymond interrupted.

"Legally, everything we wrote was one hundred percent verifiable truth, and I would think he'd let the matter drop rather than call more attention to his anger issues. The extortion never took place because it was interrupted by the fans and the fight in the bar, and the extortionist—an orderly in the care home—has been identified and arrested. I think we're clear."

"Until the next one."

"Until…well, we do have a line on some Cartel funds invested in…well, you shouldn't know about that," said Meredith, stopping short, then smiling. She quickly continued her report, "Last night I went to a private screening of a new film up for Oscar consideration—it wasn't all that good—but the interview with the producer has to wait until after Christmas because I was going to be tied up tonight."

"This should prove that I don't work all the time."

"…and the newspaper syndicate is partnering with Cassie's publisher to throw a big introductory reception for us both here and in New York in February. It's going to be a very high-profile party locally at the Beverly Hills Hotel!"

Raymond toyed with his food for a moment, then looked at her intensely. "Do you really trust Cassie? Do you think she'll be an equal and complementary partner?"

Meredith thought for a moment, pursing her lips. "I have to. Remember that we are all players in this big strange, predatory world of show biz. Between Allan and Russ, we should have a mediation core. Who knows where Mort sits, but Cassie and I do think alike—we were trained by the same ringmaster—and we enjoy working together. My own belief is that we will strive as hard as we can to make it work because it's a good plan and we both can benefit from it." She shrugged. Raymond nodded slowly.

"Your schedule leaves me breathless," he said. "It's good to see you on the upward swing. You're wearing it well."

"I feel good—finally. Especially without uniformed cops following me everywhere—even to the hair salon! My yellowed bruises are fading. And, I'll be even better after the holidays with some time off!"

"I'm sorry we're going to Laguna Beach. Will came home two days ago and goes back in time for New Years at school. Want to come to Laguna?"

She shook her head. "Tempted for sure. But I have a couple of things to take care of to really clear my head—and heart— before stepping on to the new path ahead. I'm going to Palm Springs to visit an old lady friend who has soothed my brow way too many times for all the wrong reasons over the years. There's a gift I'm taking back to her and am taking ownership of my own brow and all the emotion and consternation that goes with it."

Raymond looked at her with some amusement and shook his own head. "You are an enigma for this old guy—I never met a tornado in Mickey Mouse pajamas."

"You're not old—you just think you are. I know better," she grinned slyly. "And being the curious type, I intend to study more about old guys like you—after the holidays."

"Maybe then you can tell me why you have such fascination about my hands," he smiled a little embarrassed.

She shrugged. "Dunno—they seem strong and…mature… maybe in control." He shook his head.

A while later they found their way to their respective cars in the parking lot. The Pacific Ocean surged on in the darkness and the lights of the coast were sparse but bright. It was obvious the evening was over, and Meredith rose on her tip toes to kiss Raymond lightly before she eased into the driver's seat of the Mustang. As he closed the door for her, she caught herself considering a different scenario for the night, then quickly dismissed it.

Raymond stooped down and knocked on the window. She lowered it, looking up expectantly. "Hey, gossip columnist, call me when you get home. And you'd better invite me to your party. We still have a martini to drink and some stories to tell. Merry Christmas."

Meredith laughed easily and called out, "Get your tux cleaned, Raymond, and Merry Christmas," and started the engine. Just before she snapped the car into reverse, the detective stepped back, then called out, "By the way, I have a real first name, too! It's Tucker!"

Raymond shoved his hands into his pockets and walked to his car as he watched the taillights of the Mustang disappear down the street. What kind of parents would name their kid Tucker? He wondered.

The next day, Meredith rose early, packed her car, handed her key and a big Christmas basket of gourmet snacks to the neighbor, mentioning simply, "Paco." Then she drove to her bank, entered the safe deposit vault, retrieved a small ornate box from the drawer, placing it gently and lovingly into her purse where it would ride until it reached its rightful owner. She pulled away from the bank, headed to Interstate 10 toward the desert.

ACKNOWLEDGEMENTS

A mega-watt spotlight on so many who helped this story unfold, but especially, my patient and always supportive husband Dixon Smith and my gang of story weavers: Deborah Baker, Dana Barnum, Cynthia Gunn, Jean Timmons, Gay Tsukamaki, Ruth Walden and Jane Hoff. Thank you for your time, interest, insights, and encouragement! And to Robert Barclay at Pueo Press for his knowledge and assistance in the publication process.

ABOUT THE AUTHOR

Penny Pence Smith began writing professionally as a teenager for the local Indio, California, daily newspaper. Later, after college graduation, she covered the entertainment industry as a movie magazine editor, as assistant ("legwoman") for a well-known gossip columnist, feature correspondent and bureau manager for the *New York Times Special Features Syndicate*, and as correspondent for the *Hollywood Reporter*. With a Ph.D. in communication, she has taught journalism and communication at UNC Chapel Hill and Hawaii Pacific University. Her *Under A Maui Sun* and *Reflections of Kauai* were best-selling tourism books in Hawaii.

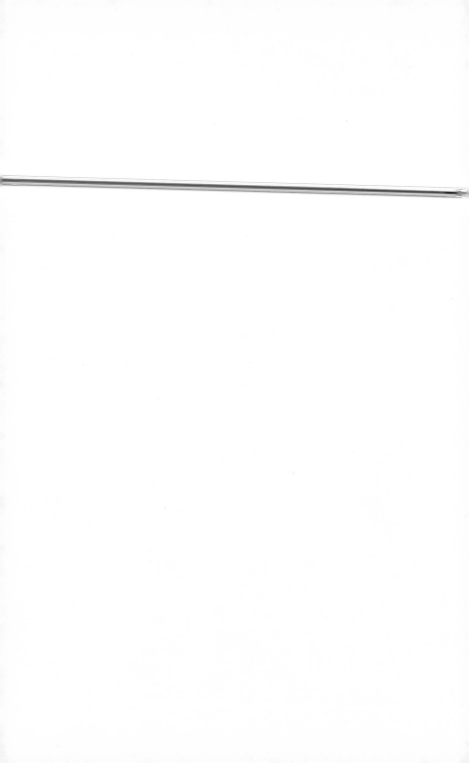

STRANGELY

FUNNY

SARAH E. GLENN

EDITOR

Mystery and Horror, LLC
Tarpon Springs, FL

Strangely Funny

First Trade Paperback Edition

All stories in this anthology have been printed with the permission
of the authors.

This is a work of fiction. Any resemblance to any actual person
living or dead, or to any known location is the coincidental
invention of the author's creative mind. This includes historical
events and persons who may have been recreated in a fictional
work.

ISBN-13: 978-0989007603
(Mystery and Horror, LLC)

ISBN-10: 098900760X

Printed in USA by Mystery and Horror, LLC
(www.mysteryandhorrorllc.com)

Dedication

To: Kassiani P. Glenn
Thank you for believing.

STRANGELY

FUNNY

_____

SARAH E. GLENN
EDITOR

Mystery and Horror, LLC
Tarpon Springs, FL

Table of Contents

The Best of Taste by Edward Ahern........................ 1

Once Upon a Gnome by Gloria Alden 9

The Taste of Copper by Alex Azar 21

Indricotherium by Rosalind Barden 33

County Water by David Bernard 45

Something Plucked This Way Comes
by Leslie Carmichael 51

Tom & the Roadside Café by Kimberly Colley 65

Criticus Ex Machina by Sarah E. Glenn 71

Happy Anniversary by Laura Huntley 77

Window Watching by Joseph Jude 89

Ruby by Jon Michael Kelley 95

Deadbeat by John Lance 101

Jake Blossom, Pixie Detective
by Ken MacGregor 111

A Proper Job for a Lady by Gwen Mayo 123

Tommy and the Trolls by James McCormick 135

One Scareful Owner by Catriona McPherson 141

What Were You Drinking by David Perlmutter 155

No More Blue Pills by Suzanne Robb 173

The Homunculus Caper by Joette Rozanski 189

Aunt Bessie and the 'It' by Norman A. Rubin 197

If You Can't Trust a Rhyming Demon, Can You Trust a Demon not to Rhyme? by David Seigler 203

Turtle by A.P. Sessler 217

We Bring Them Back. For You! by George S. Walker 233

I Must Be Your First by Paul Wartenberg 251

Down for the Count by Ted Wenskus 267

The Best of Taste
by Edward Ahern

Subj: WEB BLISS Introductory Membership
From: BCartright@WEBBLISS.com
To: harscaramanga@aol.com

Dear Mr. Scaramanga,

Welcome to WEBBLISS, where you will be guided to your perfect relationship. Your introductory level membership entitles you to my personal attention while we evaluate your needs and help you into your ultimate relationship.

I will walk with you through the initial relationship stages, and remain with you in your search for a perfect partner. Incidentally, unlike many other services, we welcome same-sex and alternative lifestyle inquiries.

Harald (May I call you Harald?) please excuse the delay in this initial note, but we have only just confirmed your introductory payment of $199.99. We appreciate your resolving the issue of an apparently invalid credit card with our credit department. As mentioned when we talked, we will continue to bill your account for $204.50 per month while we help you into your perfect match.

Attached please find our introductory questionnaire. Some persons find our 200 questions a little daunting, but I'm sure you can handle them. Please answer the questions honestly, even the embarrassing ones about your sexual tastes. An inaccurate understanding of your psyche could mean inappropriate contact with another person. Please also include a picture of yourself.

As part of your introductory level membership, you are entitled to call me twice per week for the first six months with any questions or comments. Any additional telephone sessions will be billed at a very reasonable $129.99 per session.

I have enclosed my picture and biographical information so that you will be able to better identify me as we carry on this process. I'm sure we will find a match for you that will exactly dovetail with your qualities and life style. I look forward to receiving your completed questionnaire and discussing the results with you.

Sincerely yours,

Bernice Cartright, relationship counselor

Date: 2/25/2008 11:27:54 A.M.
From:bcartright@WEBBLISS.com
To:harscaramanga@aol.com

Dear Harald,

Thank you for your completed questionnaire, lengthy letter and picture. We will process the questionnaire and provide you with the results shortly.

I do have to ask that you resend us a head and shoulders photo, as nude photographs, however tastefully done, are not postable to interested respondents.

I also perhaps need to clear up a misconception about our service. We have no expertise in the three part or four part relationships you describe and would not be able to develop that interest for you. We feel there are still many other interesting individual choices available!

How clever of you, incidentally, to try and find my location and personal telephone number from the data I provided. However, we find it is best to retain a little distance in our relationship, and a few of the facts I provided were masked to achieve this. Please don't take this as any indication of a lack of trust, it's just company policy. Whichever Bernice you called at 2 a.m. must have been quite surprised. We can always talk during business hours by scheduling a time and your calling 1-900-GET-MATE and asking for me. I hope you do call, as I very much want to learn more about you.

I have shared your detailed letter with staff members expert in alternative life styles. They rarely have a chance to experience the kind of frank honesty and graphic detail which you provided, and appreciated your candor. We feel you are a most unusual and complex man.

2

I hope you'll schedule a call.
Sincerely Yours,
Bernice Cartright, Relationship Counselor

Subj: Keeping sane at work
Date: 2/26/2008 9:37p.m.
From: BerniceC@comcast.net
To: Merryweather@edgygourmet.net

Heather,
    Another go-round dealing with an abnormal. If the money weren't so good I'd revert to selling love potions. Fortunately I have the gatherings to keep me functioning and well fed. Without you twelve women and our ceremonial dinners, my life would be misspent coping with the kinkies.
    Thank you incidentally for the update on the next banquet. I'm already prospecting for a suitable entrée.
    There's the phone, gotta go and make another quick $75.

Stir the pot
Bee

Date: 3/06/2008 5:43p.m.
From:BCartright@WEBBLISS.com
To:harscaramanga@aol.com

My Dear Harald,
    Thank you for your phone call yesterday. Your vivid descriptions were enlightening. I was not aware of several of the practices you elaborated on.
    Please accept our sympathies for the prior relationship which you described for me. It must be horrible to have a partner commit suicide. We feel that your immediate effort to find another soul mate is a sign of a robust psyche.
    We are also sorry that the initial meeting which we arranged for you turned out so badly. We have explained to the woman that because of the disclaimer she signed she is not able to sue you for psychological trauma as she had threatened.

3

I do also have to make sure that you understand that I am not a candidate for that partnership. Given the closeness we are developing your graphic fantasies are completely understandable, but cannot happen. I am only your counselor.

Your reaction to the charges for a 900 prefix call are also understandable, but as you in particular can understand, the intimate and graphic nature of our conversations require the privacy and lack of restrictions which are assured by making a 900 prefix call. However, for three or more calls per month we do offer a volume discount, something you want to keep in mind as we go forward.

Harald, I know that as we begin to better understand each other we will focus in on your best relationship. I look forward to your next phone calls, so please schedule more.

All Best Regards

Bernice

Date: 4/06/2008 6:47:45 a.m.
From: BCartright@WEBBLISS.com
To: harscaramanga@aol.com

Harald Dear,

You certainly have our analysts talking to themselves. They've told me informally that they have never encountered as complex, even convoluted a person as you. I've attached their findings, which they admit does not do justice to your persona.

You clearly have special needs that will not be satisfied by a prissy Mary Jane type of woman. To verify this we presented your specifics to an internal panel of three women who serve as our benchmark for offbeat cultural mores. To a woman they felt that they would not be able to relate adequately with you, nor begin to satisfy your needs.

Harald, you are one of a rare breed that requires our more special attention. In order to accomplish this, we will need to move you to our advanced group. This requires an upgrade in your membership from our Web Bliss category to Web Ecstasy, but I know you will find the additional $200 per month worth the expense. We will be able to tap into networks of sophisticated, progressive women who are interested in (and capable of!) interacting with your complex nature. We expect to have you involved with a woman who can satisfy these needs within a month. Because of the more sophisticated and complex nature of this level, the cost of our being together on the telephone must also go up, to $250 per hour.

We also will arrange for you to provide a sample of your blood for screening. This will reassure your prospective partner that she can frolic without fright. Should we find any niggling problems we will also advise you how to remedy them.

We hope this is agreeable to you, as we cannot proceed further at the introductory level, and I would hate to lose contact with you. I've attached a more intimate questionnaire for you to fill out, as well as an invoice for the first month's advanced servicing.

And thank you so much for last week's phone call. Your ability to bundle expletives and scatological comments is remarkable. Thank goodness we are in the privacy of our 900 number context. I do recommend, however, that you shift your focus from what you and I might do physically to your new relationship with the woman we find for you.

Please don't trouble yourself to send me another present. When you told me you were sending me a stuffed toy I had no idea that you had stuffed it yourself. The ferret's menacing teeth and arched back make it quite life like. I'll have to find just the right place for it.

Fondly,
Bernice

Subj: Banana nut/absinthe bread recipe
Date: 3/29/2008 10:43p.m.
From: BerniceC@comcast.net
To: Merryweather@edgygourmet.com

Heather,
Thanks so much for this recipe. You were right; using the real wormwood tinged absinthe was the key. I actually made two

5

loaves, one as indicated and one with a generous leavening of weed. Both were delicious.

Incidentally I think I have zeroed in on an excellent dinner entrée, but will need to prepare it on site. Would you be available a few hours early to help with the usual grunt work?

And yes, the lonely hearts club is still paying the rent for me.

Yours,

Bee

Date: 4/30/2008 4:56 p.m.
From:BCartright@WEBBLISS.com
To: harscaramanga@aol.com

Dearest Harald,

Welcome to Web Ecstasy! Thank you for continuing and developing our relationship. We've processed your advanced placement questionnaire, and your blood sample. The traces of marijuana and cocaine are of no concern, and attached is a form for you to take to a local medical office for treatment of the venereal disease.

Once you're certified we will arrange for a meeting in a public place so you and your prospective partner can begin to get to know each other.

I've also attached the results of your second questionnaire. I'm sure that the results will be no surprise. You already know how complexly sensual you are, open to practices which the timid would shun and which our antiquated legal system would not approve of.

And thank you so much for your phone calls. I've come to relish these early morning explorations of your sexuality. Please do keep in mind, darling Harald, that these conversations, no matter how intense, are just foreplay for the relationship we will be finding for you. I am constantly amazed at how you can make a normally gross description seem like a term of endearment.

I'm just delighted to hear about your dining and exercise habits. It's unusual to find a hearty recreational drink and drug user who takes such care with his diet and muscle tone. I pride myself on also being a fussy diner. I'm sure the woman we connect you with will find you toothsome.

Speaking of the phone calls. We seem to have maxed out the credit card which you're using for our calls together. Please provide the operator with a new card for your next call; I would hate to not hear from you!

Most Fondly,

Bernice

Date: 5/28/2008 9:27a.m.
From:BCartright@WEBBLISS.com
To:harscaramanga@aol.com

Darling Harald,

We know each other so well that I feel that I can be completely honest with you. The two women who you met unfortunately did not share the feelings and impulses which you have so candidly expressed to me.

They both held you in the highest regard, but felt that their idiosyncrasies and kinks did not quite match yours. You probably assumed this about the first woman, with whom I gather you had a bit of a food fight in the restaurant. The second woman I'm sure appreciated your fondling attempts at intimacy, but alas didn't click with you either. She indicated she would resume her relationships in the motorcycle club.

This is not your fault! We often find that intricate personalities such as yours require a special effort to find a unique solution.

Unfortunately also, we seem to have run out of credit resources to continue the search. The cash payment you made last week did not quite cover your costs to date. We appreciate that you have no other resources, and certainly don't want you to again hold up a convenience store.

We do feel we have an obligation to bring this to fruition for you. Despite these setbacks there is one group of women I'm aware of which should be uniquely suited for you. I will telephone

7

shortly with specific instructions on how you should meet with one of them. Please especially pay attention to the dietary restrictions for 24 hours in advance of meeting, she has allergies that must be accommodated.

We really appreciate your dedicated effort with us, and I am amazed that you have helped illuminate some dark places in my mind. We will arrange this meeting at no cost to you, and hope that it becomes your ultimate experience.

You will be unforgettable.
Always
Bernice

Subj: Edgy Gourmet banquet feedback
Date:6/24/2008 10:34p.m.
From: BerniceC@comcast.net
To: Merryweather@edgygourmet.com

Heath,

Thank you so much for forwarding the positive feedback you received from our recent banquet. And thanks again for all your help in getting the entrée dressed out and prepared. You were right; the traces of marijuana and cocaine were plusses to the taste experience.

As to leftovers, I really don't need any, so please give them away to our usual charities, perhaps The Little Sisters of the Poor.
Yours in Good Taste
Bee

Ed Ahern resumed writing after forty odd years in foreign intelligence and international sales. He has his original wife, but after 45 years they are both out of warranty. Ed dissipates his free time fly fishing, shooting and attending French, German and Japanese language groups.

Once Upon a Gnome
by Gloria Alden

Betty Brunsweiger, an older woman in jeans and plaid shirt with short gray hair, patted Jack on his head. "You're still my favorite boy," she said fondly as she moved him a little closer to the front door. He had been a birthday gift from her husband, the last of the children he'd given her before he died two years ago.

Jack gave her his gaping grin with missing teeth and didn't reply, but she felt he understood.

"Good morning, Betty. Quite warm for so late in October, isn't it," Mary Belle Jones called out over the white picket fence that bordered Betty's property.

"It certainly is," Betty said. "Perfect weather for the trick or treaters tomorrow night."

"What's that you say?" The tiny white-haired lady shouted.

Betty walked over to have a little chit chat with her neighbor without shouting, although even up close she had to raise her voice since Marybelle had trouble hearing. She was always trying to adjust her hearing aid.

Marybelle stared toward Betty's front porch squinting through her glasses. "I see you brought Jack out to help with your Halloween decorations."

"Yes, I thought he'd enjoy being part of the festivities. He can't pass out candy, but he can watch and listen."

"I don't pass out trick or treats anymore," Marybelle said. "I can't afford to buy the candy, and I like to be safe inside my house when it gets dark. I marvel at how brave you are sitting out there on your front porch after dark."

Betty laughed. "We don't exactly live in a dangerous neighborhood, Marybelle. Besides, Halloween is my favorite time of the year. I like dressing up and being a part of it."

"Don't you worry someone will try to break in and steal something from you?" Her face puckered with anxiety over her foolhardy friend.

"Jack will protect me," Betty said with a smile.

She cocked her head and frowned. "Who'd you say will protect you?"

"Jack." Betty said raising her voice a little.

"Oh." She smiled. "I know how much he means to you. That's why you usually keep him beside your bed at night. Sort of like having a dog sleeping there, I imagine," Marybelle said, "although I never could abide having a dog in my house. No, my cat, Hillary, is more than enough company for me. She's company and don't need taken for walks, neither."

Betty chuckled. "Jack doesn't need taking for walks, and I don't need to clean a litter box, either. In fact, with Marvin gone, he's the most important person in my life now – my treasure, so to speak, and I keep my treasure in my bedroom where I can keep an eye on him nights. Oh, here's the mailman already."

Betty left Marybelle and walked towards him as he came to her front gate.

Mr. Paulson, slightly stooped from the heavy bag over his shoulder, opened the gate and met her halfway to her porch pausing first to wave at the neighbor "How you doing, Mrs. Jones?"

"Tolerably well with this nice weather, Mr. Paulson. Arthritis is not much trouble today."

"And good morning to you, too, Mrs. Brunsweiger. Nice day."

Betty smiled at him. She liked this affable mailman, who was always cheerful no matter what the weather was like. "What do you have for me today? Anything besides bills?"

With a smile, he reached into his bag to bring out her mail. "Hard to tell, but it does look like you have a couple of greeting cards of some kind. Is it your birthday?"

"It will be tomorrow on the thirty-first. I was a Halloween baby," she said, smiling.

"Well now, Halloween must be real special to you."

She nodded. "It is."

"So that's why you have that ugly whatchamacallit on your front porch. You sure have a lot of those things around the yard," he said as his eyes wandered around her lawn and gardens looking at gnomes tucked in here and there and everywhere he could see. He figured she probably had them in the back yard, too.

"They're gnomes," she said. "Some people think they bring good luck."

He laughed. "I find that hard to believe. Myself, I think they're pretty ugly."

"Maybe in your eyes, but I consider them my protectors."

"In my opinion, you'd be better off with a dog or a gun, especially at your age since you live alone. A lot of older people are preyed upon for the money they keep hidden in their house, you know."

She scowled. "I don't have any money hidden, so I'm perfectly safe with Jack as my protector. I don't need a dog or a gun, thank you very much."

He smiled. "So you say. I hope Jack can do his job, Mrs. Brunsweiger."

She watched as he went down the walk and returned the wave he gave her before he continued on his route. She went up the porch steps to put her mail inside, but stopped beside the orange gnome with green vines and leaves wrapping around his short stalky body. "Ignore him, Jack. He doesn't understand."

Two teenagers came racing down the road before stopping their bikes in front of her house.

"Hey, Mrs. Brunsweiger, I like the ugly Jack O' Lantern gnome. I've never seen him before," the freckled red-headed boy said.

"Normally, I keep him inside, Billy, but I thought he'd look nice out here for Halloween." She liked Billy and had watched him grow from a toddler when he'd moved in some years ago to the fifteen year old he was now. Sometimes he helped her around the house with yard work or lifting heavy things.

"Who's your friend?" She asked.

"Oh, this is Josh Tyler. He's kind of new to the neighborhood."

11

She looked at the taller, older, dark haired boy. "It's good to meet you, Josh."

"Same here." He looked around the yard at her vast collection of gnomes in various sizes and shapes and rolled his eyes with a derisive look on his face before turning to Billy and jerking his head towards the road. "Let's go." With that he started off without a backward glance to see if Billy would follow.

Billy looked embarrassed as he gave Mrs. Brunsweiger a slight smile before peddling off trying to catch up to his friend.

A little disturbed, she watched as they disappeared around the corner. There was something she didn't like about this new friend of Billy's. Her sixth sense told her he wasn't the best of friends for him. She hoped they didn't become too close because she had a feeling he might be bad news.

"Jack, maybe I should move you back inside." She'd hate to have anything happen to him. Normally, it was a safe neighborhood, but there was something about Josh she didn't trust. Maybe she was making an unfounded judgment, but it was better to be safe than sorry, she always felt.

So she propped open the front door, put the waist high Jack on a dolly and wheeled him down the hall to her bedroom and placed him once again beside her bed where he normally stood. She stepped back to look at him. Satisfied, she smiled and said, "There you are, Jack. I know you'd much rather be on the front porch watching the world go by and especially there for the trick or treaters, but you'll be safer in here."

The rest of the afternoon, she worked on decorating her front porch for Halloween. She draped fake spider webs from the posts and porch ceiling and fastened rubber spiders on them. A particularly large one was up in the corner. She was just anchoring Charlotte, as she called the large spider, firmly in place when someone coming up the steps spoke, causing her to almost fall off the ladder.

"You shouldn't be up on a ladder, Betty," the elderly gentleman with a cane said.

"I guess not if someone's going to sneak up and startle me." She scowled at him as she came down the ladder and turned towards him.

12

"I keep telling you to let a man like me do the hard work," Mr. Johnson said.

"You think with your arthritic knees you could do better than I do, Henry?" she retorted.

"I saw Billy and another young boy here a short while ago. Why didn't you get one of them to do it for you?"

His eyes glared at her or at least she assumed they did from his frown, but his glasses were too smudged for her to tell if he was actually glaring.

She gave an exasperated sigh. "I keep telling you I'm perfectly capable of taking care of myself."

"That's what Mrs. Peabody thought." He nodded his head several times. "And look what happened to her. Fell and broke her hip and now she's in a nursing home."

"Mrs. Peabody was ninety-three and blind as a bat. It was that stupid little yappy dog of hers that tripped her. You'll notice I don't have a dog, and I've some ways to go before I'm that old."

"I don't know why you think you have to act like you're still a youngster," he grumbled. "Why are you still decorating for Halloween at your age? You must be having your second childhood or something. I always thought Marvin spoiled you by buying you all those stupid statues just 'cause you like them. They're an eyesore is what they are. A blight on the neighborhood."

She toyed with the idea of snatching his cane away from him and hitting him on the head, but her better sense won out. Even if she just tapped him on the head, he'd be bellowing and tell everyone in the neighborhood she'd beat him. He'd probably call the cops, too, and maybe even file a lawsuit against her. Who knew what the old coot would do?

"You've had your say, Henry. If you have nothing positive to add, I'd just as soon you'd leave so I can get back to decorating for Halloween."

He turned and shuffled down the walk muttering. Betty heard "stupid old broad" but that was all. She started to chuckle and turned so he wouldn't see her laughing if he looked back. She'd known him for more than fifty years now, and he'd always been a complainer and someone who thought he knew best about everything.

Going around the house to the back yard, she wrestled a bale of straw from the garden shed into a wheelbarrow then took it back to the front. Tugging and pushing while muttering a few cuss words over the effort, she finally got it up onto the porch and in place by the front door. As she straightened up and arched her back to relieve the strain, she glanced across the street and noticed Henry rocking on his front porch watching her. She couldn't see his expression, but she could imagine his smug look. She was tempted to give him the sign of what she thought of him, but again discretion won out. *Better to ignore him*, she thought.

When she finally finished decorating just before supper, she had a skeleton hanging from a hook on the porch in place of her fern, and freshly carved pumpkins with leering smiles on the bale of straw and the front steps. She had her witch costume ready, too. She'd be sitting in the old rocker on the front porch handing out candy with haunted house noises coming from the stereo inside. She loved Halloween.

Betty adjusted her long black dress as she sat down on the front porch rocker. She checked to make sure her pointed black hat was firmly in place before touching to see if the fake long rubber nose with a wart was secure. She hoped the elastic band running behind her head and holding the nose in place wasn't too obvious. Probably it wouldn't be since the only light came from a lamp inside the front window and the candles in the Jack O' Lanterns. Eerie noises of screeches and howling came from inside. She kept the volume down so it wouldn't frighten the littlest ones or upset the neighbors, especially that old sourpuss, Henry. Marybelle was too hard of hearing to be bothered especially with all her windows and doors closed.

It wasn't long before the first trick or treaters came up the walk. *What darling little children,* she thought before she said in her best witch imitation. "Hello, dearies. Are you here to scare an old woman or do you want a treat?"

The little princess sidled up closer to her mother, but Superman said boldly, "We're here for treats." He held out his bag while his mother pushed her little princess closer to Betty.

"It's just Mrs. Brunsweiger," she assured her daughter.

"Pick out your favorite candy from the dish, dearies," she cackled. "Now just one. We have to save some for other trick or treaters who come. Mustn't be selfish."

"You don't scare me, Mrs. Brunsweiger," Superman said as he took a Milky Way candy bar.

"I'm glad I don't because I like little children. They're quite delicious." She gave a slightly evil cackle and licked her lips. She'd save her really evil cackles for the older kids. It always seemed to delight them even though they screamed in pretend fear before giggling.

When the two hours of trick or treating were up and there hadn't been any more pirates, vampires, mummies, fairies or any other costumed children for at least fifteen minutes, Betty stood up, stretched and pulled off her fake nose. She was glad to be rid of that abomination. She checked the bowl. Good, there were still a few candy bars left. If she ate no more than one a day, she could make them last for at least a week or two, although she knew she shouldn't be eating that much candy. Not good for her cholesterol. As she started to blow out the candles in the Jack O' Lanterns on the steps, a figure taller than the children who'd been coming came up the walk wearing a red-lined black cape and a vampire's mask.

"Any more treats left for a poor beggar?" he asked in a low gravelly voice.

His voice sounded familiar, but she couldn't quite place it. It sounded as if he were trying to disguise it.

"Nothing for adults." She felt a mixture of fear and anger. *Who was he? What did he want?*

"I think you do. I want you to go inside quietly. I have a gun and don't want to use it if I don't have to." His voice was menacing now.

Betty swallowed hard. Her heart started racing. Following his instructions, she went inside and stopped inside the door. She jumped when he poked something into her back. "What do you want?" She started to shake.

15

He gave a snort of laughter. "I want your money."

"Okay. Okay. Let me get my purse, but it's not much, you know." Her voice quivered.

"Oh, I'll take that, too, but I want the money you have hidden in your bedroom," he said.

"I don't keep money in my bedroom or anywhere, except the little I keep in my purse."

"We'll see when we get to your bedroom." He prodded her again.

As Betty walked down the hall to her bedroom, her back felt exposed and vulnerable with the intruder following behind. *Will he just leave when he realizes I don't have any money, or will he kill me?* she wondered.

"Turn on the light," he ordered.

When she flipped on the light switch, he looked around and saw her purse. He picked it up and emptied out the contents onto the bed then checked the pockets. "You sure don't carry much in your purse," he said as he picked up a few one dollar bills plus a five and a ten. He ignored the loose change.

"I told you I don't have money in my house," she said and swallowed.

"Don't try to con me. I heard you tell Mrs. Jones you kept your treasure in your bedroom. So if it's not money, is it jewelry?" He grabbed her arm and twisted it behind her back. "Where is it? Do I have to tear your whole bedroom apart?"

Betty started to cry. "I told you I don't have any money or treasure. It was a joke when I said that to my neighbor."

"I don't believe you. I will find it, you know." The vampire released her and picking up one of the two large candlesticks on the dresser raised it and hit her on the head. "That will keep you out of the way while I search."

She fell to the floor dazed and barely conscious. *So you do see stars when you hit your head*, she thought. Just as she was losing consciousness, she heard the Vampire shout "No! No!" and then heard a thud.

She slowly woke to voices and someone shaking her a little.

"Mrs. Brunsweiger, Mrs. Brunsweiger are you okay?"

She opened her eyes and looked into Billy's anxious blue eyes. "I think so. Where's the vampire who attacked me?" She turned her head and felt a sharp stabbing pain. The vampire was lying on the floor with Josh sitting on his back holding him down although he didn't seem to be conscious. Next to both of them Jack lay grinning.

Then she saw the vampire under Josh start to move. "Better tie the guy up, Billy, and watch out for a gun," she said as she struggled to sit up. "Get the tie from my robe hanging on the closet door and there are some scarves in one my top dresser drawer, too."

Just as the boys started securing the vampire with a pink robe sash and some brightly colored scarves, two policemen walked in with guns drawn.

"So what's going on? What are you doing here, Josh?" The older policeman asked when Josh turned around and looked at them.

Josh scowled at him. "Takin' care of a crook, Dad. You gonna complain about that, too?"

Betty looked between the two of them, father and son. She could see the family resemblance. *Hmmm,* she thought. *Two strong willed macho men. Maybe this was Josh's problem and not anything worse.*

"We saw the guy sort of force Mrs. Brunsweiger into the house, at least that's what it looked like, but we were too far away to hear anything," Billy said. "Josh thought it might be a boyfriend or even her son, but I know she doesn't have any kids, and well, she's too old to have a boyfriend."

Betty smiled. *Not too old. Just not interested,* she thought.

"I just got this bad feeling, ya know?" Billy went on, "So we sneaked around outside and looked through the bedroom window, and it didn't look good. I mean a vampire standing there and her lookin' so scared and all. So I called 911 and then me and Josh went in to rescue Mrs. Brunsweiger."

"Thank you, Billy," she said with a smile. "And you, too, Josh."

"You two mind getting off the guy so we can take over now?" Josh's dad said as the vampire started to move.

17

The two boys quickly got up and stood back as Josh's dad, Sargent Tyler pulled off the mask.

Betty gasped. It was Mr. Paulson, her mailman. "Mr. Paulson, how could you do this to me? You know I'm not rich, and even if I were, why would you try to rob me?"

As soon as the younger patrolman untied the scarves and tie from the robe, he snapped handcuffs on him and Sargent Tyler read him his Miranda rights, Mr. Paulson turned to Mrs. Brunsweiger. "I didn't mean to hurt you, and I don't have a gun. I lied about that. You see, I've been desperate. I can't even sleep nights, and when I heard you tell Mrs. Jones you kept your treasure in your bedroom, I thought maybe it would help me out with my problem.

"Which is?" She narrowed her eyes as she looked at someone she'd considered a friend.

"Gambling. I'm in danger of losing the home Louise and I have had for years. I'm in really deep hock. Louise will be crushed if she finds out I've gambled away our home."

She shook her head, ignoring the shooting pain. "My treasure is my gnome, Jack, the last gift my husband gave me."

As Sargent Tyler helped Mr. Paulson up, the younger patrolman picked up Jack to stand him upright. "Whoa! This guy is heavier than he looks. Did you boys hit Paulson with this? If you did, he's lucky he's still alive."

"Not us," Billy said. "He was knocked out with the gnome lying beside him when we came in."

They all looked at Betty Brunsweiger. She smiled. "Not me. Mr. Paulson had knocked me out with that candlestick lying on the floor."

"Maybe he accidentally knocked it over," Sargent Tyler said.

"Do you want us to help clean up or anything?" Josh asked.

"No, I'll be fine. Thanks for your rescue, boys."

"I think you should go to the hospital and have your head looked at," Sargent Tyler suggested. "You've got quite a lump there."

"Have her head looked at? That's what I been saying for years," Henry said as he came shuffling down the hall. "What in

18

the hell's going on over here, Betty? What're the police doing here? These boys causing you trouble? I told you to watch out for them." Henry scowled at the boys and then Betty. "Fool woman dressing up like a witch is asking for trouble, if you ask me."

"Nobody's asking you, Henry. You're not needed so you can leave with the others," she said.

As they all turned to leave, Betty noticed Mr. Paulson turn and look back at Jack with a look of disbelief mixed with horror on his face.

She smiled at him and winked. She waited until they were outside before turning to Jack, once again standing beside her bed with his goofy missing teeth grin. "Thank you, Jack, for saving me." She bent down and kissed his orange face.

Gloria Alden taught third grade for twenty years. She loved teaching, but wanted to have more time for writing, and much of her retirement years have been spent that way. Her published short stories include "Cheating on Your Wife Can Get You Killed,*" winner of the 2011 Love is Murder contest and published in* Crimespree Magazine; *"Mincemeat is for Murder" appearing in Bethlehem Writers Roundtable,* "The Professor's Books" *in the* Fish Tales *Anthology; and* "The Lure of the Rainbow" *in* Fish Nets, *the newest Guppy Anthology.*

Her Catherine Jewell mystery novels are The Blue Rose *and* Daylilies for Emily's Garden. *She also has a middle-grade book,* The Sherlock Holmes Detective Club *based on a writing activity her students did at Hiram Elementary School. In addition to writing, she's passionate about books and they are rapidly taking over her home. She lives on a small farm in Southington, Ohio with two ponies, some cats, five hens and her collie, Maggie. She blogs on Thursdays with* Writers Who Kill *and once a month with the* Fish Tales Anthology Blog.

The Taste of Copper

by Alex Azar

Seized in an alley, the five-foot-five cocoa-colored victim doesn't seem to recognize the danger she's in. "What do you mean, 'no'? I have a knife. I'll kill you woman, don't mess with me." Her attacker thinks: what is going on when a lone woman in an alley faced with a stud like him holding a knife to her throat isn't afraid? He presses the dull side of the blade harder into her flesh to let her know he means business.

She's laughing at the would-be assailant: "Walk away now, little man, while you still can." She taunts him as if she's completely oblivious to the danger he thinks she's in. He pulls her hair to show her how serious he is.

Seething with anger at her impudence, he growls into her ear from behind: "I don't care how tough or quick you think you are, girly, you're not tougher or quicker than this knife. Got it?"

In response, she squeezes his wrist at her neck with such incredible force he's forced to drop the knife. In a flash, she pulls him in front of her and raises him off the ground by the neck with one hand. "That terror in your eyes--is that what you wanted from me?" She knows her grip on his neck isn't allowing him to breathe, let alone answer. "I warned you, I actually didn't want to harm you. Trust me, I was a predator once, albeit a much better one than you'll ever be, but I could have sympathized. However, now you've upset me, and that I can't stand."

This mystery strong-woman lowers the now-whimpering man-child and punishes him with a sickening punch to his mouth that could have shattered a brick. She can tell before even seeing his face that he's lost most, if not all, of his teeth.

While spitting blood and teeth in dangerous amounts, he musters the fortitude to call this fury of a female a word she hasn't

21

heard since the Thirties. Satisfied with the effect of his insult, he reaches for the dropped knife to make good on his earlier threats.

"You don't get it do you, meat bag? I haven't turned anyone in decades, but this will teach you respect for your elders." Once again the woman picks him up, holding him at eye level.

In a final display of utter defiance, he spits a bloody wad in her face and follows it with a toothless grin. In response, she licks what blood she could from around her mouth, and smiles in return. Where his was a hallow gesture with an equally hallow mouth, hers was sincere in all of its fanged-tooth glory. She pulls him in close. "Good night, Jack."

Jack wakes up the following night at sundown in his own apartment with no memory of what transpired. Too hungry to worry about what he just assumes is another alcohol-induced blackout, he makes his way to the fridge. Opening the door, he's practically blinded by the light, forcing him to opt for food from his cupboards. Reaching for a bag of store brand cereal, Jack can't remember ever being this hungry. The pangs aren't even coming from his stomach. It almost feels as though he's hungering from deeper within himself than he thought possible.

He grabs a handful of the fibrous O's and throws them in his mouth. The excruciating pain when he tries to chew causes him to spit them up into the kitchen sink. He sluggishly makes his way to the bathroom to see what's wrong with his mouth. Turning the light on, he's once again blinded. However, he discovers he can see perfectly fine with the lights off.

Or so he thought. As he makes his way to the mirror, he finds no reflection in the glass before him. Cautiously, Jack reaches out and touches the glass to make sure he is in fact looking into his bathroom mirror. Positive he knows what he's looking at, Jack exclaims, "I'm invisible! This is great; I can do all the things I've always wanted to do. Just gonna stroll into the movies without paying. I can spy on the hottie that lives across the street. Hell, I can rob a bank and no one will know any better."

Talking to himself, Jack realizes something's wrong with his mouth. He probes around the inside with his tongue and can't find his teeth. Parting his lips, he looks into the mirror again, "Damn it, invisible."

Feeling with his fingers, he runs his fingertips along the bumpy ridge of his gums where his teeth should be growing from. This sparks a memory last night where he recalls being savagely attacked by a female power lifter. "She knocked my teeth out for no reason, then I think she kissed me and somehow turned me invisible. I've got to find that bitch and have her fix me."

Foregoing any clothes to remain invisible, Jack runs down the stairs of his apartment building, hoping to have some invisible fun with any of a number of neighbors that have looked down on him. However he doesn't see anyone until he gets outside onto the sidewalk where he hears a cacophony of shouts apparently directed at him.

"Put some clothes on, you pervert!"

"I'd kick you out too if you came at me with that tiny thing."

"Get back in your box, you bum."

"Go play with yourself somewhere else."

Still thinking he's invisible, it takes Jack a moment to realize they're talking to him. He rushes back upstairs to his apartment. "What the hell is going on? Am I not invisible anymore?"

He returns to the mirror, and confirms he still can't see his reflection. "What the hell did that chick..." He looks around to make sure no one is around him to hear what he just said, but to be sure he corrects himself, "... that manly giant of a chick do to me?"

Now understanding that other people can in fact see him, Jack puts clothes on before leaving his apartment this time. "I've got to find what kind of spell that witch put me under." He decides to head back to the alley she attacked him in.

Shielding his eyes from any source of light, Jack stands in the alley he remembers being attacked in last night, waiting for the amazon woman to show her face. He waits for what feels like hours, but has actually only been thirty minutes. While he doesn't see her, he does hear her placing thoughts in his mind.

"You're confused aren't you? You're not invisible, you twit, you're a vampire now. Now you can heal from any wound you may suffer." Hearing this, Jack reaches into his mouth and feels where his teeth once were, but once again only feels the odd ridges of his toothless gums. The vampire woman enlightens him. "You'll heal from any wounds you suffer since I've turned you. Knowing you'll never regrow your teeth was the beginning of the lesson I want to teach you. I can reach you anytime I want, but you will never see me unless I want you to. I suggest you try living your life as a predator now that you can't feed."

And like fog in the wind, the sensation of Jack's maker in his mind vanishes, leaving him in a cloudy haze stumbling out of the alley.

Having just woken up for the night, Jack futilely looks in a mirror feeling where his teeth should be. He realizes he needs to see a dentist about getting new teeth so he can feed properly. Wasting no time, he grabs his cellphone to make an early morning appointment. He swipes to unlock his smart phone, but it won't take. "Come on, you piece of shit, what's wrong with you?" Repeatedly swiping his finger with no results, Jack can't help but wonder why his phone no longer works. Feeling his own hand against his cheek, he remembers that he's now a vampire and doesn't have a pulse, and can't work the screen of his phone.

Digging through his storage in the closet, he finds the land line that he hasn't used since he moved in. He's not even sure why he still kept it, but he's glad he did. Dialing the nearest dentist he was able to locate, Jack makes an emergency appointment first thing the following morning, while leaving out the specifics of having no teeth.

"What the hell am I going to do for the rest of the night?" With nothing better to do and no ideas how to fill the time, he decides to go to his favorite watering hole around the block.

Jack forgoes his usual high stool at the bar, and chooses a dimly lit booth in the rear. Having ordered his drink from the lone waitress in the bar, he eagerly awaits his forthcoming libation to whet his lips and temporarily soothe the growl in his body.

Unfortunately for Jack, the moment the alcohol touches his tongue, the muscles in his abdomen wrench and he vomits what little was in his stomach. Thinking him already drunk, the bartender kicks Jack out, sending him on his way home.

For the remainder of the night Jack lays in his tub weeping until his alarm goes off, letting him know it's time to go to the dentist and begin fixing his problems. What he didn't plan on was the sun and his inability to go to the dentist during work hours.

"Uh yeah, hi, I'm going to have to cancel my appointment today. Can we do it later, like after the sun goes down?"

"Mr. Hagerman, we had to bump a different appointment for this *emergency*." The receptionist says the final word with no hidden amount of doubt and disdain. "And now, you'd like to postpone your appointment until 'after the sun goes down'? I'm sorry, but we can't accommodate that request. Our doctors' hours are until 6:00 pm."

"Six! It's June, the sun doesn't go down until around eight. Do you have any late nights?" Jack asks desperately.

"Sir, 6:00 pm are our late hours." Before the receptionist can make another suggestion, the line is cut with Jack slamming his phone, a privilege he hadn't realized he missed with his smart phone.

He paces his apartment living room, perplexed at the dilemma before him. Jack knows he's not the smartest person, but there has to be a solution to this. He needs to fix his teeth so he can feed, but the dentists close before the sun goes down. He'll die of hunger if he waits until daylight savings time ends in November. With no answers before him, he begins searching for answers on the Internet, and discovers the solution: an emergency 24 hour dentist not too far from his apartment building.

Calling the provided number immediately Jack schedules an appointment for ten that night. The receptionist on the other end of the line seems confused at his request to schedule an emergency, but she does it anyway due to the urgency of his voice.

Arriving earlier than expected for his emergency appointment, Jack shocks even the seasoned nurse with his toothless grin. "I can see what the emergency is, sir. Just fill out

25

this paperwork, and the doctor will be with you in a moment. Do you have an insurance card?"

"I'll pay in cash," he says while filling out his medical information, once again surprising the nurse. Completing the paperwork in haste, he begins pacing the waiting room.

Moments later, the nurse enters the waiting room with the dentist, and points at Jack for the doctor. She whispers something in his ear before shuffling off. The two walk towards an examination room together, but halfway through the dentist asks to see Jack's mouth. He parts Jack's jaw, revealing the empty cavity.

"Jack, if I may? Is this drug related? I don't see the normal signs of heavy drug use, but damage this extensive combined with the odd request to schedule your appointment has me concerned that whatever work you want done will be for naught. You understand?"

"Yeah, yeah doc, but I don't do no heavy drugs like that. Just booze and weed for me." Jack tries to smile to show his good natured spirit, but he can tell the dentist is just examining his mouth.

Once inside the room, the dentist asks Jack what he'd like, and before he can give him options, Jack blurts out, "Vampire teeth! Doc, I'm starving and I need the vampire teeth to feed."

Doubting Jack's earlier claim to predominantly being sober, the doctor tries to reason with him. "If you'd like vampire caps atop your regular teeth, I can recommend a specialty dentist for you, but I highly suggest you allow me to implant a standard set of teeth you can later adjust."

Refusing to take the unnecessary middle steps, Jack insists on the name and number of the specialty place, which to his pleasure has night hours for his convenience.

"Right on man, so Mindy says you want a full set of vamp caps. She explained we only take cash, right?" the venerable Doctor Fang asks through his own specialty werewolf teeth. Jack nods in agreement, just wanting the process to be over so he can feed, most likely on the doctor so he can get out of having to pay him. Leaning his head back in the chair, Jack opens his mouth to show the Fang what he's working with.

26

"Whoa, man, you got no teeth!"

"I know; that's why I'm here. Now, you gonna fix me or not?" Jack asks with impatience seething through his gums.

"Buddy, I do acrylic caps, I can even file your teeth down if you want on the D.L. But I can't make you teeth." Dr. Fang scratches his head while looking around. "You do realize you're in the back of a tattoo parlor. Besides, what you're looking for will cost thousands of dollars, and while in this lifestyle I know firsthand not to judge by appearances, I have some doubts you'd be able to front that kind of cash. Know what I'm saying?"

In a rage, Jack lifts Dr. Fang in the air single-handedly, but his strength gives out. He tries gnawing at his neck hoping the ridged-ness of his gums and jaws is enough to break the skin. "I just need to feed!" he howls into the doctor's ear.

"Dude, you're getting your spit all over my neck. You mind letting go?" After Jack complies, Fang straightens outs his lab coat and says, "Listen man, whatever lifestyle you wanted to be into before, you can't without teeth. Worry about getting a normal set, then come see me. I'll even give you a discount because you're obviously dedicated to whatever it is you're into. But I've got paying customers, and you need to get the hell out of here so I can clean my neck."

Not seeing any options before him, Jack does the most desperate thing he can think of, he searches blogs and forums for a possible solution to feeding with no teeth. "Thank God I don't know any other vampires; it'd be like high school all over again. I'm a joke of a creature of the night, can't even get any blood."

He tells one group of twi-hards that last night he resorted to sucking on a raw steak hoping to get blood that way, when a thirteen year old girl with the handle edwarDelicious condescendingly informed him that the red liquid packaged in meats isn't blood. In fact, that liquid is mostly just water with myoglobin, and that's why he didn't get any sustenance from it.

He defends himself with language and insults a thirteen year old should never hear, and is promptly banned from the blog. "I can't believe I got booted just for calling that blood bag a..." Jack's attempt at an insult inspires him. He begins thinking of various movies and TV shows he's seen, confirming the validity of his next plan: "I'll break into a blood bank!"

He spends all of five minutes researching his big plan, and decides the closest option is the best one. "Looks like this Asian doctor does blood transfusions. That's perfect; she's only four blocks away. I'll break in, steal some blood, get my super strength, and settle the score with the vampire chick that did this to me."

Without warning, said "vampire chick" infiltrates his mind. "I must admit I'm disappointed you haven't learned your lesson. This torture was supposed to be a lesson in humility, not fuel for your revenge. Rest well knowing I won't allow you to succeed until you learn the error of your ways." And just as suddenly his nameless creator once again leaves him alone with his thoughts, the few that remain that is. As soon as he's alone in his head, he makes the decision to leave immediately for this doctor's office, knowing that at a quarter after one in the morning, it's surely to be vacated.

Dressed in black Jack makes his way through the streets towards the doctor's office. After three blocks a scent assaults him that literally stops him mid step. He turns his head, asking aloud "What is that amazing smell?" Craning his neck left and right to find the source of the intoxicating aroma, he tracks it to a woman exiting a convenience store across the street.

Thankfully there aren't many cars on the road, because Jack crosses without looking, fixated on the woman who senses he's approaching her. "Stay away from me. What do you want?" she nearly shouts as he steps onto the curb ten feet from her.

In a dreamlike voice, he repeats the question she had no chance of hearing earlier. "What is that amazing smell?" He lunges towards her causing her to drop her bag. He begins sniffing the air all around her. "Why do you smell so tasty?"

"Please let me go." She begs as she looks at the items she just bought spilled all over the sidewalk, she appears more embarrassed than frightened. "I don't feel well, and have to get home."

28

Jack follows her eyes to a blue box on the ground. His eyes light up, "Is that... Are you..." he stammers the half questions before blurting out, "Let me go down on you?"

In absolute horror, the woman hits Jack with her purse as hard as she could. Had he any teeth left, he surely would have lost some. Ignoring the contents of her shopping bag scattered on the ground, she runs away screaming at the top of her lungs.

Too weak and mentally preoccupied to follow, "Missed your shot, man," Jack says to himself as he picks up the woman's box of tampons.

Nearing the hematologist's office, Jack can't shake the memory of the woman's smell emanating from her nether region and doesn't notice the security guard inside the lobby until he's at the door. Just then he remembers he didn't put on his ski mask to conceal his face. "What does it matter? As soon as I get some of the blood from upstairs I'll just kill him." Still, Jack pauses outside the building contemplating how he should get to the office.

Retreating from the door with a friendly wave to the security guard, he circles around to the side of the building looking for the fire escape. Locating the metal stairwell at the rear of the building, Jack places an overturned garbage can beneath the ladder. Unfortunately, he is still unable to reach the chain to lower the stairs. He attempts to jump for the dangling chain, however his blood deprived legs barely lift him inches off the can before he crashes down with an audible ruckus.

The noise was enough to rouse the security guard from his post, where he finds Jack a jumbled mess covered in garbage and a half worn ski mask. "I don't know what you're planning pal, but I'm calling the cops." Instantly he dials 911 on the cellphone already in his hand.

Jack unsteadily rises to his feet before threatening with a finger pointed at the guard. Calm and collected, he speaks with an air of confidence, "I wouldn't do that if I was you. You have no idea who I am, and what I can do." He pauses to brush of trash from his shoulder. With his mental image shattered to reveal a broken man, he meagerly suggests, "Hang up the phone, or else..."

Shrugging off the open ended threat, the security guard speaks into the phone, with a voice that seems more annoyed than in danger. "Yeah, I'm calling from 170 William St. Got some joker tried breaking into the building through the fire escape, but he looks cracked out of his mind. Barely got his ski mask on. Was even dumb enough to wave at me as he walked around."

Jack can't hear the rest of the conversation, as he mumbles to himself, "Easier in the movies, what the hell?" His frustration mounting, he starts questioning more. "How the hell am I gonna live if I can't get no blood? Too weak to even attack anyone. I need help bad. I need that chick that turned me to come back."

No sooner had he said it, does his maker appear in the alleyway behind the security guard. She takes the phone from his hand and hangs it up before looking in his eyes. Her own eyes take on a different intensity as she says to the guard, "Thank you sir, you've done your job. I'll take him from here."

Absentmindedly, the guard responds, "Sure thing officer, just part of the job." And he turns, walking away with sunken shoulders.

"Holy shit, you Jedi'd him. That was awesome!" Jack exclaims, momentarily forgetting how famished he is.

Tossing the guard's cellphone in the trash Jack knocked over, the woman before him responds coolly, "No, what was good was hearing you ask me for help. Your lesson in humility is all but finished. It's too late to search for a suitable meal for you. We'll have to go under for the day, and tomorrow night I'll feed you all you can stomach."

They return to her house in Brooklyn with her flying them above the buildings. Jack takes in the sights, happy to know his ordeal is at an end. He remains silent throughout the short trip watching the brightening sky in the distance.

His maker leads him into the house, and through a maze of hallways meant to keep the sunlight out. "You will stay here with me as my apprentice, until I'm satisfied with your progress. You will do what I say when I say, and only feed when I tell you to. Is that understood?"

Without hesitation Jack replies, "Yeah, sure, good. Where am I sleeping?" As he continues to follow her, he thinks to himself that as soon as he has the strength he's going to kill that bitch for what she put him through.

The woman Jack is following stops abruptly, placing her hand on a doorknob indicating this is the room he will be staying in. Instead, she informs him, "Seems you've forgotten I'm in your mind and can hear all your thoughts."

Not understanding the implication of what she's said, Jack begins to walk through the door into the open courtyard in the rear of her house directly into the morning sun. The woman shoves him beyond the threshold of the door, saying, "Perhaps an eternity of non-existence will teach you a lesson. She closes the door, avoiding the rays of the sun while securing it firmly, and walks away with a smile on her face. "Jackass."

Alex Azar is an author born and raised in New Jersey. After studying two years to become an electrical engineer, he realized he took every English course the college offered. Changing schools and majors, he is now a happy struggling author. This is his tenth publication.

Indricotherium
by Rosalind Barden

It's a struggle for research projects to find funding. The Oregon Group's fondest hope was to bring back an extinct plant or two, an insect, and, maybe, if luck was with them, a bird.

Small financial grants here and there kept them afloat while they tinkered with bits of bird bone DNA, and assorted flotsam melted from ancient glaciers. Desperately, the scientists wished for the miracle of a huge grant.

The military's sudden interest granted their wish. The avalanche of military money shook them out of their world of rented trailers and second-hand equipment, and into pristine labs set in acres of Oregon's peaceful countryside, perfect for relaxing strolls after hours hunched over decayed leaf matter. It was the miracle they'd long wished for.

For about a year the military asked nothing of them. The scientists blissfully rejoiced after sprouting a long-gone member of the cabbage family. They carefully watched a chicken egg wherein grew -- hopefully! -- the extinct Carolina parakeet. An ancient butterfly looked soon to follow.

When their joy was at it zenith -- The butterfly emerged from the cocoon! The parakeet hatched! The cabbage made excellently crunchy, if bitter, coleslaw! -- a man from the military stopped by with no warning, no heads up, and frowned.

He asked what military application the cabbage, etc., had, and if the butterfly, etc., was known to be "aggressive." The scientists had no answers for the military man, and as far as aggression, neither the cabbage, the butterfly, nor the parakeet had the slightest.

Within two days, a half dozen of his associates swarmed the Oregon Group's bucolic labs, shuffling through files, and peering at the mounted specimen of the last passenger pigeon, the Group's next project. As suddenly as they came, they left.

Six months of uneasy silence followed while the Group nervously continued its work, focusing on a member of the parsley family and finding the perfect surrogate pigeon mother for the no-longer-extinct passenger pigeon hatchling.

The military broke their silence with both good news and bad. Tersely, they informed the scientists that the military could no longer grace them with its financial blessings if their work did not have a military application. However, the military, in its wisdom, determined there was yet a military application to be had. Therefore, it was increasing its financial blessing ten-fold. Included in the package was a certain quantum physicist, and the requirement that the Oregon Group do as he say.

Dr. Shombum arrived with many trucks and contractors in tow. He came with his "Critical Researcher," a woman of vague credentials who worried the scientists since they suspected she had no PhD.

As the contractors got busy erecting an airplane-sized hangar on the scientists' favorite stretch of lawn for strolling, Dr. Shombum informed them that their late night hunching over bits of insect legs and moldy feathers was a "waste of time." And speaking of time, since it didn't really exist, and on a quantum level, all time happened simultaneously, and thought had more power than reality, his "Critical Researcher" could bring back any species any time he wanted her to. He silenced any objections, by asking, "Oh, so you want your funding to disappear?"

Unhappily, the scientists stayed out of Dr. Shombum's way and continued hunching over their peeping hatchings and tasting the newly sprouted parsley.

After construction of the hangar finished, Dr. Shombum grandly invited the scientists inside for a demonstration of, "how real science works -- not that crap you guys do." The vast space was dimly lit and was empty but for a handful of computer monitors and a colossal iron cage that encompassed most of the hangar's floor space and reached nearly up to the roof. Smiling, the Critical Researcher stood with a mesh sack of what the cabbage scientist was horrified to see were the sheared off heads of his precious ancient cabbages he had been carefully prepping for his sauerkraut experiment. He put his hands to his mouth to keep from breaking out in sobs. Dr. Shombum chuckled. "See, those cabbages had a military use after all."

The woman slung the cabbage sack over her shoulder, entered the cage through a door-sized gate, then disappeared into the gloom.

About an hour later, after the scientists kept asking, "Can we go now?" to which Dr. Shombum snapped, "Hold your pants on!" the woman came charging out of the darkness, the cabbage sack bouncing on her shoulder. "Open the gate!" she screamed, though it was already open. She charged through it, slammed and latched it. Frantically, she grabbed a hook hanging from a long chain, ran it through the cabbage filled sack, and hauled it up nearly to the top edge of the cage. Then she ran away from the cage to join Dr. Shombum and the huddle of puzzled scientists.

They felt it before they saw it, a steady "pound-pound" vibration in the floor. Then slowly out of the darkness emerged a massive, towering creature. It had something of an elephantine aspect, though larger and with a long neck topped by a small head that looked about with twitching ears and baffled eyes. It had no trunk. It sort of had tusks, though were much smaller, more like long teeth. It spotted the cabbage sack, ambled toward it, then tore a cabbage out with its protruding teeth and munched happily.

Dr. Shombum broke out in the largest smile, spread his arms wide and exclaimed to the creature -- softly, so not to cause alarm -- "I love you! I love you!" To his critical researcher: "Oh, girl! You are my girl!" as she beamed.

"You, cabbage guy," Dr. Shombum ordered, his tone now all business, "you need to grow more of those. This Baby's got an appetite."

Of course, ancient cabbages cannot be rushed, so the scientists found themselves driving rented trucks to local farms to buy up as many cabbages, corn stalks, rutabagas, and whatever edibles were on hand because the thing ate and ate and ate. They had to compete with an elephant sanctuary for hay, which caused the angry elephant handler to corner the butterfly scientist at the feed store and demand, "What the hell?" The scientists were also

35

unhappily recruited ("Oh, so you want your funding to disappear?") to hose down the floor of the creature's cage once an hour. The thing produced droppings of such size to shame the largest bull elephant known to humankind. The smell, likewise, was enormous. And if they fed it too many apples or carrots, which it loved, "Oh, my God!" the cleanup was unimaginable.

The situation remained this way for nearly a year, with Dr. Shombum beaming at the creature and blowing it smacking kisses, and his Critical Researcher strutting about mocking the first flight of the fledging Carolina parakeet and insulting the ancient cabbage sauerkraut as "bourgeois."

Life changed once again with the arrival of a fleet of shiny black vehicles. Out of the finest vehicle emerged a man in a uniform heavy with medals and elaborate with braid. He was accompanied by dozens of other men and woman likewise attired in military fashion, though with lesser levels of fanciness.

Dr. Shombum fluttered about this apparent general with smiles and offers of tea and lunch, which the general indifferently waved away. They proceeded to the hangar. The creature eyed the new faces curiously as it continued chewing on cabbages.

The soldiers bustled about plugging in speakers. One of them passed out ear protectors to the assembled, including the Oregon Group scientists, who stood silently as they had long learned to do. The general manfully declined the ear protectors and stood stiffly watching the creature.

At the press of a button, the speakers blasted the sounds of shrieking rockets, gunfire, explosions at an extraordinarily high volume.

Cabbage in mouth, the creature's eyes widened in shock. It stood unmoving for a beat, then turned, and for first time that anyone had seen, it ran, its footsteps shaking the structure, until it was at the other end of the cage. Fearfully, it turned to watch the strange new people. The cabbage remained in its mouth, like a comfort to the animal.

With a wave of the general's hand, a soldier cut the sound, plunging the hangar into silence. Then he motioned to another soldier. The man, thick with body armor, unlatched the doorway gate and entered the cage. The creature's eyes opened wider, watching him. From the many pouches and pockets in his uniform, he pulled out a thumb-sized stone and an elaborate metal slingshot. He inserted the stone into the slingshot, bent down on one knee, and shot the stone at the creature.

The stone hit it somewhere in the area of its massive gut. In shock, it dropped its cabbage and made a sort of pleading groan, the first sound anyone had heard it make. It made a movement as if to follow the rolling cabbage, then realized that would take it closer to the scary man, so stopped and huddled ever closer to the far corner of its cage.

The body-armored soldier looked back toward the general. The general jerked his chin and the soldier left the cage. Angrily, the general turned toward Dr. Shombum and demanded, "How the hell is that an attack beast?"

The general and his soldiers packed up their gear and left. Within a few days, so too did Dr. Shombum and his Critical Researcher.

The Oregon Group scientists were left alone with the creature. It was too frightened to move away from the far corner of its cage. So, perched on ladders and fumbling with ropes and swearing, the scientists had to rig up a new water trough and feed bag it could reach. Even so, it was too nervous to eat, which lead to much reassuring cooing from the scientists, nose patting, and slowly reaching out one cabbage leaf at a time, with a, "Good boy! Get your strength up!"

It did not take long for a letter to be crisply hand-delivered to the Oregon Group, informing them that as of "now," all funding was terminated, the property, which was owned by the military, was to be vacated "immediately," and all "experimental life forms," cabbages, butterflies, pigeons and parakeets included, must be "put down," especially the "Main Prototype," which the scientists assumed must mean the large creature in the hangar.

More than the cabbage scientists were reduced to tears. After recovering from the initial shock, they began to plot. No more were they going to be the helpless victims of the industrial military machine. Time to be radical! Quickly, cabbage and parsley sprouts were hidden between slices of bread and stashed in plastic sandwich bags. Insects were tucked in the toes of shoes.

The birds were trickier, but careful rigging of a file cabinet did the job.

With the clock ticking and nerves frayed, now came the big question: what to do about it, the creature, the thing Dr. Shombum called "Baby."

Since Dr. Shombum and his Critical Researcher had studiously avoided sharing with the Oregon Group by what slight of quantum physics hand the thing was extracted from the dim past, they had no clue how to send it back. They had to put it somewhere, but where?

By the blessing of good fortune, the butterfly scientist recalled the angry elephant handler who ran the sanctuary for abused circus and zoo elephants. After a frantic internet search for the phone number, the parakeet scientist made the call:

"Please," out of breath, panting, "we have a special elephant. A funny looking elephant. Remember? We're the ones buying all the hay?"

"Oh, yeah, you guys," unhappy voice.

"Well, we have to find this elephant a new home."

"Bull or a cow?"

"What?"

A long pause, then, slowly as if talking to a dim child, "Is it a girl elephant or a boy elephant?"

"It's a boy."

This prompted a long dissertation on how dangerous bull elephants are, all the special -- and expensive -- extra strong fencing required, etc. etc., and would his 'girls' take to 'this cowboy . . . ?'

The parakeet scientist named the balance left in their account from the military. Being that this figure was several times a multiple of the sanctuary's annual operating budget, it prompted another long pause followed by a much more friendly, "Well, just as it happens, I've been actually setting up the fencing for a bull. Been looking for a cowboy for my gals. Gets lonesome up here in the country for them. They're still young, you know, missing a little romance and all. Now, where'd you say this bull came from?"

This caught the scientist unprepared. Being a scientist, she wasn't very good at creating fanciful stories, particularly on the spur of the moment, but she did a serviceable job with a halting, rambling story of a baby boy elephant beaten with chains, which caused it to be deformed and look funny, then auctioned to a canned hunt outfit, that the bank later foreclosed on, seizing all assets including the deformed elephant, which then sold it to the scientists for experiments, but now they didn't want it anymore. "It's really deformed, okay? It doesn't look like a normal elephant, understand?"

"You science people do crazy things to animals. I don't like you guys. That poor cowboy will have a good home with me. You just wire that money to me like you said."

And they did, like lightning, before the military thought to look at their accounts.

Now how to get the creature to the elephant sanctuary twenty miles away?

They didn't think there was a truck made that would hold it. Besides, its neck would stick out the top and people would notice and word would get back to the military. No good. They'd have to walk it through the woods.

They decided to lure it out with the carrots and apples it loved but rarely received because of the diarrhea risk. All risk was on the table now, so after a hurried run to assorted farms, they had a supply large enough to feed the army that surely would be arriving soon.

They couldn't figure out how to get the cage open wide enough for the creature to walk through, so they hooked chains on the side of the hangar where it liked to cower, hooked the other end of the chains to their largest rental truck, then, with the parakeet scientist at the wheel, floored the gas and the whole galvanized metal sheeting side of the structure pulled loose.

This alarmed the creature and it refused to move, even as the entire structure tottered. Much cooing and waving of apples and carrots barely coaxed it out in time before the roof collapsed. The crashing sound compelled it to take off at a run. More panic, sweat and carrot waving ensued until it was trotting in the correct direction.

The scientists ran a tag team, with the cabbage and butterfly scientists jogging with the creature and tossing up apples and carrots that it skillfully caught with its protruding teeth, then the parakeet scientist roaring down the two-lane rural road in the carrot-apple stocked truck, while the pigeon scientist, crazily crashing through the woods on a bicycle, made dashes from the truck to the jogging scientists to restock their carrot and apple bags.

They arrived at the elephant sanctuary near dawn, bedraggled, and collapsing with exhaustion.

"That ain't no elephant."

The elephant handler stared up at the creature with a look of horror and backed away.

"Get that cowboy outta here, away from my girls."

No, no, this couldn't be happening.

The cabbage scientist dropped to his knees. Sobbing, he begged, "Please, sir, please take this poor thing. He's never done anything to anybody. The army will shoot him dead. Please hide him up here!"

The man's look of horror intensified. "This is getting too weird for me. I ain't getting mixed up in no army monkey business. You people get that cowboy and get outta here!"

Cleverly, the butterfly scientist thought to apply Dr. Shombum's old trick: "Oh, so you want your funding to disappear?"

Now, they had the man. Operating an elephant sanctuary, even one as seat-of-the-pants as his, was no cheap matter. The girls always needed some special medicine or electric blanket for the damp mornings or the fancy vet from the city to come check their feet. And they ate. A lot.

"Lord have mercy, you just don't tell nobody I ever seen you. This cowboy just happened to wander up here, all by his-self."

The scientists promised and swore up and down absolutely. After more threats of the funds disappearing, they extracted from the man his absolute promise that, "Swear to God and Jesus His-self," he would keep the creature forever hidden from curious eyes.

40

After a tossed bag of applies and carrots, the creature placidly ambled into the extra-strong corral the man had built for a bull elephant. But this was no elephant.

The scientists left, never to be seen again. The man closed the sanctuary to tourist visitors, not that he got many way out in the woods like he was. He quickly learned to withhold the apples and carrots from the creature, since they did something crazy to its digestion and the mess was awful ("Jesus, cowboy! What the hell is this?"). He stuck with cabbages and hay.

Otherwise, it was no trouble. Whatever it was, it was old. No, elderly. Not a drop of vim or fire left in this cowboy. The thing didn't do much but eat and look around at the trees, the sky, his truck, and most of all, it liked to crane its long neck to get a good look at the girls.

The girls did not share the feeling. The matriarch elephant trumpeted warningly at it and waved her ears in a threatening manner, which its puzzled eyes appeared not to understand. The girls stayed as far away from it as they could. All the while they snorted and huddled together restlessly.

About a week into the creature's stay, the matriarch elephant strode up to the handler. She looked toward the odd creature, then stared at the handler with undisguised wrath. She pulled up a clump of grass with her trunk and flung it at his face. Then she turned her tail to him and trotted back to the rest of the girls, who proceeded to turn their backsides to him as well.

They'd never done such a thing to him before, ever.

As the phrase goes, "A happy wife, a happy home," so too it is with the lady elephants.

"Well, cowboy," the handler, head bowed, said to the creature. "I know you're old, and life out in the woods is going to be rough, but you're just causing too much grief with the girls. They're my heart, understand? I'm sorry, cowboy, but you gotta head on out."

With a sigh, he opened the gate to the bull corral. The creature stood where it was and kept chewing the cabbage in its mouth. The handler waited a couple of hours, and still it hadn't moved. So, he gathered up what was left of the scientists' apple

41

and carrot supply where he'd stashed it in the shed, and flung it as far out into the pine forest as he could.

After a sniff of the air, the creature wandered out of the corral toward the treats. The handler closed the gate and locked it.

The creature hung about the sanctuary for a couple of weeks. After much angry trumpeting and charges from the matriarch elephant, it finally got the message and disappeared into the forest.

It took a good six months for the girls to settle down enough for the handler to start showing them photos of eligible bachelors who'd come to his attention. "I promise, girls, the next cowboy will be much better."

As for the creature, he couldn't have dreamed of a finer life. He most certainly was elderly. Back where he came from, the ladies had long lost interest in him. The younger bucks had driven him far from the ideal tree munching grounds, toward the dangerous flatlands where the drooling, snarling predators lurked. It was only a matter of time before he would feel fangs tearing his neck. He was standing in lonely, hungry despair, desperately wishing for a miracle, when the odd being wandered toward him waving the sack of cabbages. He had nothing to lose, so he followed.

After his puzzling and rather stressful experience with people, and the elephants who'd hurt his feelings, all turned out to be perfect. The tall trees with their spicy pine needles or succulent leaves seemed endless, and there were no young bucks to drive him away. The predators were tiny compared to the monsters back home, and wheeled about in terror at the sight of him. He wasn't lonely anymore because an elk with a bad leg had taken to hobbling beside him, probably because the predators stayed clear.

On a misty afternoon, as he lounged in a lake to take the weight off his old joints, he realized he truly had experienced the miracle he'd wished for. His contentment was complete.

Of course, as time went on, his contentment faded to discontentment as he wondered whether he could likewise wish for a female of his kind: preferably young, sexy, and attracted to the mature gent. When wishing did not make his fantasy gal

42

materialize, he decided to wander back to where his puzzling journey began.

By this time, the military had sold the compound to a resort developer who transformed it into The Oregon Spa of Mind-Body-Soul-Spirit, featuring, along with the usual mud soaks and yoga, a resident a self-help author touting his "Visualizing the Miraculous" tomes.

The results were interesting.

The creature learned to never, ever bother people again (the rolled yoga mats, hurtled like missiles, made that clear).

Furious over the thousands of dollars of "Visualizing the Miraculous" packages the Spa had to refund, their attorney lit after the most likely suspect, the elephant handler. Under threat of "immediate seizure of all elephant assets to secure payment of damages suffered," he broke his vow of secrecy in a weeping, rambling story about mad scientists, aliens and army monkey-business. The military, when pressed, issued a dismissive denial, though the butterfly scientist was briefly detained in an off-shore facility typically reserved for "enemy combatants," which the military also denied after the butterfly scientist escaped and sold his story to Hollywood. The resulting low-budget movie, featuring a T-Rex thrashing about Paris during the French Revolution and capturing a busty Marie Antoinette, was entertaining, though wildly inaccurate.

But, that was all in the future. For now, as he soaked in the lake, all was right with Indricotherium and the world.

Rosalind Barden's short fiction has appeared in print anthologies, including CERN Zoo, *part of the award-winning* Nemonymous *series, and in webzines, such as the UK's late, great* Whispers of Wickedness. *She wrote and illustrated the children's book* TV Monster. *Her fiction has placed in numerous competitions, including the Shriekfest Film Festival. Her darkly humorous e-novel* American Witch, *now available on Amazon.com, follows the adventures of society's castoffs in a Hollywood stripped of glamour. She lives in Los Angeles, California. Discover more at RosalindBarden.com.*

County Water
by David Bernard

When the county finally decided to run public water pipes out to Sander's Grove, my Mama could have danced on the lawn. When you live this close to the Everglades, no matter how deep you drill a well, you will get water that tastes and smells like it came from that big swamp next door. If you've never visited Florida, imagine taking a drink of something that smells like sulfur and tastes like it came from a limestone quarry filled with dead fish and gator piss.

Daddy had done what he could over the years, but water softeners and electronic doodads just couldn't keep up with the water. Now, we have barrels on all the drainpipes that stored rain water for baths and cooking, but Mama thought we could do better than living like we just unpacked the Conestoga wagon. In other words, she wanted county water. And if Mama wanted something bad enough, she got it. Now that the county was running pipe into town, it was just a matter of how long Daddy could stand the constant harping on the subject.

Daddy didn't last as long as usual. I think he kind of liked the idea of clean clothes that didn't smell like something died in his dresser. He contacted the county and found out the water main was only going up Lockhaven Road and into the center of town. Since we were so far off the main road, we'd have to pay to run the pipe from the main to the house. The county water people came out and walked from the house to the main road with some sort of measuring device that looked like a bicycle wheel on a handle. They calculated how many feet of pipe and the cost of excavation. The estimate they came up with was so high that Daddy actually considered telling Mama it wasn't going to happen.

Mama knew. She always knew. So to make her point, she made dinner by boiling the spaghetti in water from the well. Once he stopped throwing up, Daddy was convinced. He decided to talk to a plumber, who happened to be his drinking buddy Ski. Mama never much cared for Ski. The more she didn't like you, the more polite she was to you. Mama was a lot of things, but subtle was never one of them. So, when she discovered Daddy brainstorming with "dear old Mr. Ronkowski," we all knew it had better be a brilliant plan or there was going to be trouble.

Daddy and Ski came up with a plan so simple that even Mama was impressed. The county people preferred to run the pipes themselves, but admitted that any licensed plumber could do the job, assuming the plan was approved by the county. Ski had a license, so Daddy called the county and said he had a plumber to run the pipe. A few permits later, Daddy had a water meter to install and Ski had managed to get his Bobcat up and running.

Now this brilliant plan involved installing the water meter down at the intersection at Lockhaven Road so the county could read it without driving all the way up to the farm. And if the meter reader didn't need to come to the house, he couldn't accidentally notice the pipe placement was absolutely nothing like the plans Daddy submitted to the county. The "Ski version" of the plans was slightly different. Instead of following along the road, they'd cut a channel through Winston Woods, making a straight line from the meter to the house, instead of doubling back along the road. It cut the amount of pipe needed down by three quarters and the county would never know the difference because it would all be underground.

Daddy started working at the house, changing the pipes over in the bathroom, kitchen and hot water heater. Ski would start at Lockhaven road and bury the pipe up to the house then connect to the pipes from the house. And on the remote chance the county sent an inspector (which never happened out here in the boondocks), Ski would run a plow along the road to make it look like a pipe had been recently installed legally.

Mama, knowing Ski, still had her doubts, right up the moment when Daddy turned on the sink and the water coming out of the faucet had no color and no smell. Mama was happy, which meant everyone was happy. In fact, she even warmed up to Ski a little bit and started calling him "Ray." Of course it couldn't last.

The trouble first started in the shower stall – whenever anyone took a shower, the cold water would cut out just about when your hair was good and soapy. It didn't matter if you washed your hair first, last or in the middle. The minute you lathered up, you got hit with a spray of scalding water. If you took a cold shower, the water would just stop. If you made the mistake of looking up at the shower head, it slammed back on, damn near knocking you down. Then it spread. Suddenly you were taking your life in your hands with the toilet. Let's just say I got a pretty good idea what an enema feels like and I am not a fan.

Mama blamed Ski for screwing up the pipes. Ski blamed Daddy for screwing up the hot water tank connection. Me? I just gave up and washed up in the sink. Of course, that didn't work for long either. The water in the sink started coming out in spurts and then stopping. There was no rhyme or reason to it except it always happened when it was the worst possible moment. The funny thing was it only happened in the bathroom – the kitchen sink was on the same water line and it was working perfectly normal.

Mama had no patience with first degree burns so Daddy, in a flash of self-preservation, called in a plumber in Lockhaven. The man from Mr. Fix-a-Pipe looked at Daddy and Mama like they were crazy when they told him what the problem was, but he said he'd take a look. Well, he may have thought they were crazy at first, but he became a believer when he took the shower head off and it turned itself on and nailed him with a face full of scalding water. He went outside to shut off the main water to the house and discovered that Daddy had forgotten to install one.

So, Mr. Fix-a-Pipe had to get into his truck, drive out to Lockhaven Road, shut the water off at the meter and drive back. As soon as he walked into the bathroom, water started pouring out the faucet of the sink in short spurts, like a water conga beat. He looked a little spooked and a little confused. Or maybe he didn't like conga. I was starting to enjoy seeing someone else get harassed by the plumbing. He decided to try and install the missing shut off valve anyway. He got a bucket to block the water and headed outside. He cut through the pipe where it came out of the ground. There was no water. He attached the valve to the pipe and turned to get a fitter to attach the new valve to the house. The second he turned his back on the pipe, the valve fell off the pipe. He looked at it with that spooked look again. He reattached the valve and as soon as he turned his head, the valve just fell off again.

Mr. Fix-a-Pipe was looking downright nervous by this point. He took a rag and wiped down the pipe. There was a blurble from inside the pipe, so he grabbed his flashlight and looked down into the pipe. He jumped straight up in the air, screamed like a baby, ran to his truck and just sped away, leaving all his tools.

Mama watched all this from the porch and she was wearing a frown she normally saved for Daddy. Daddy saw it too, and decided he'd just put the valve together with the tools the nice plumber forgot. It went together with no blurble, no problems, and no screaming. We went inside for lunch and waited for the telephone call from Mr. Fix-a-Pipe we knew was coming. Sure enough, the nice lady at the dispatch wanted to know what happened to Mel the plumber. Mel was just sitting in his truck in the dispatch parking lot, white as a ghost and refusing to unlock the truck doors or talk to anyone. Mama said she had no idea, but she'd appreciate if someone could come back and pick up Mel's tools, and maybe turn the water back on at the meter. The lady said she'd have someone out there as soon as the paramedics showed up to get Mel out of his truck.

Later that afternoon, a different Mr. Fix-a-Pipe showed up. Daddy told him he put the valve on the house. The new plumber apologized for Mel as he picked up the tools and said he'd turn the water back on and there'd be no charge. Seems poor Mel had finally snapped under the pressure. He was strapped down at the hospital, swearing that when he looked down the pipe, someone looked back.

Mama was still frowning as Mr. Fix-a-Pipe drove away. She turned to Daddy. "Go get that moron buddy of yours and walk along the pipe. I want to know exactly where that drunken halfwit buried the pipe." Daddy took off in a run. Mama didn't call people names unless there was going to be big trouble. And by big, I mean Old Testament, Wrath of God big. And Daddy had been on the receiving end often enough that he was perfectly willing to let Ski take one for the team.

An hour later, Daddy came back alone, proving Ski was smarter than I thought. Daddy walked in. "Ski and I walked the line. There are no leaks I can see."

Mama looked at him. "I know there are no leaks. But that idiot cut across the old cemetery in Winston Woods, didn't he?"

Daddy looked down at the ground. "Yes. But not much, he just cut across the corner. The rest of it just follows the tree line."

Mama came toward Daddy with a monkey wrench. He flinched but she simply handed it to him. "Go take that valve off again."

Daddy looked confused but took the wrench and headed outside. He took off the valve. Mama strode over and yelled into the pipe. "I know it's you and I'm just going to tell you once. Stop it – or else."

Mama walked back to the house. "You can put the valve back on. That should be the end of it."

When Daddy came back in, Mama was sitting at the table with a cup of tea. He looked at her with a confused look on his face. I noticed he carefully put the wrench down beyond her reach.

Mama sighed. "Think about it - the pipe cutting through the cemetery? You know very well who is buried in there."

Daddy's eyes widened but he said nothing.

Mama glanced over at the wrench, which Daddy decided to pick up and start cleaning with a napkin. She gave him a look that made the blood drain from my face, and I wasn't even the one she was glaring at. "How long did it take to get him back in the ground last time? Now we need to go and sanctify the fence line of the cemetery before he gets bored and wanders off into town again. You know we got enough trouble around here with another zombie panic."

Daddy just sat there, looking like a whipped puppy. "But why would Ted do that with the pipe?"

Mama looked at him like he was an idiot. "You know Uncle Teddy – he always loved bathroom humor."

David Bernard is a native New Englander who now lives (albeit under protest) in South Florida. His stories have most recently appeared in Rymfire Books' State of Horror: Florida, *where he destroys a railroad, the Pill Hill Press anthology* BUGS! *where he destroys a subway and the Harrow Press anthology* Mortis Operandi *where he destroys Al Capone. His next, less destructive, story will answer the burning question of what happens when* "The Little Mermaid" *is relocated to Dunwich, Massachusetts in the upcoming anthology* Once Upon an Apocalypse *from Chaosium Publishing.*

Something Plucked This Way Comes
by Leslie Carmichael

The week before Easter, during the full moon, my neighbor Eddy called me over to look at something he'd found beside his barn. Two greenish-brown oblongs were hardening on the gravel, their cracked and crusted surfaces revealing glutinous interiors dotted with chips of white. They were each about the size of my hand.

"Don't touch 'em!" Eddy warned, as I hunkered down for a closer look.

"Shit!" I gasped, scrambling back. I'd gotten used to a lot of foul smells on the farm, but this was by far the worst.

"Yep. But from what?" said Eddy, scratching his head.

I wiped my eyes on my sleeve, then shrugged. "Dunno. Cougar? Fox?"

"Naw," said Eddy. "I've seen their scat. Doesn't look anything like this." Eddy was a man who knew his shit.

He moved over to the side of the barn and pointed down. There were tracks in the dirt, from something with three long claws on the front and a shorter, bigger one on the back.

"Bird?" I asked. "Some big hawk?"

"Looks kind of lizard-ish to me," he said, scratching the back of his neck. "Somebody's pet?"

It was possible. In town, I'd once seen a tourist with an iguana on a leash. With a rhinestone collar. On both of them.

"Some lizard!" I said. "From the size of this stuff, it would have to be huge."

"Yeah," Eddy agreed. "Like one of those whatsit dragons."

"Komodo? Those things have poisonous spit," I said. "Who'd be dumb enough to keep one as a pet?"

"Well, you know the cottagers. They're not too bright, most of the time," Eddy said, with that blank-faced expression that meant he was laughing at me.

I did know. I'd been one, as a kid. The Windermere Valley is a beautiful place, just right for spending the summer in a cottage by the lake. It's a great place to raise kids, even if the 'cottages' are mostly upscale condos, these days. But the kids get bored. That usually means trouble.

"If some idiot did have a Komodo dragon for a pet, and one of those kids let it out, we could all be in danger," I said.

"Hm," said Eddy. "I wonder . . ."

"What?" I asked.

"Remember two years ago? The crop circles?"

"Oh, yeah," I said. That had caused quite a commotion. The local media had run a story on it. It had attracted reporters in droves, who treated us like rednecks. Especially when they found out about Eddy's Bigfoot obsession.

Eddy had thirty years on me and one hell of a lot more experience. He and his wife, Aileen, had gotten me and Clara out of more than a few tight spots when we had bought the little farm next to theirs. Good neighbors, they had taken a proprietary interest in our rustication. I might have 'book learning,' as Eddy called it, but of common sense, he had the larger share. As far as I was concerned, that more than made up for his one irrational belief.

In all my years of prospecting, I had never run across any hairy 'missing links' (well, there had been that one guy in Radium Hot Springs, but I'd been almost sure he was human).

Eddy, though, had a fascination for the 'wild man of the mountains,' and claimed he had even seen the creature once, climbing over the wooden fence that marked the back boundary of Eddy's land near the treeline. It left behind a hank of auburn hair which Eddy had wanted to display along with the chunk of shit he'd bought from some old con artist in the china cabinet, but Aileen had put her foot down about *that*.

Aileen told me later she'd seen a tourist in town the next day with a piece missing from her red fur coat. What the woman had been doing climbing over Eddy's fence, I did not want to know.

When the reporters had found out about Bigfoot, they made a mess of Aileen's house, interviewing Eddy and taking pictures of his prized possessions. Eddy had been proud of it until he saw the newspaper article, which had also included a bit about the crop circles and an explanation of how that particular prank was done, with boards and string and geometry. It made us all look like idiots.

"So you think this might be another prank?" I asked.

"Could be." Eddy went into his barn, then returned with an empty gallon pickle jar and a shovel. "But I'm going to keep the shit."

"What for?" I asked, as he shoveled the blobs into the jar. They oozed down the glass side.

"Thought I might take 'em to the Mounties in Invermere. See what they make of 'em. Might be a nice change from drunk drivers and boneheaded tourists, wouldn't it?" he said with a grin. There was a little bit of the prankster in Eddy, too.

He capped the jar and carried it into the barn. Something rustled in the bushes by the door. I turned to look, but I couldn't see anything, even when I cautiously parted the branches.

"Come in for a coffee," said Eddy, as he returned, sans pickle jar. "Aileen'll have the pot on."

She always did, and it was always great coffee.

"Good morning, Niall," said Aileen, as I sat at their kitchen table. She poured a cup for me and handed me a plate of sliced coffee cake. "What's Clara up to today?"

"Making goat's milk soap this morning," I said, taking a bite of Aileen's blue-ribbon baking. Clara and I had bought the farm to get away from the 'rat race,' and ended up working harder than we had in our entire lives.

"Tell her I'm making lemon meringue pies this afternoon for the church social, if she wants to come help."

Eddy and Aileen attended the little church in town, and Clara had decided we should join them. Reverend Timmins was a bit too 'fire and brimstone' for my taste, so I didn't go as often as she did.

53

"I will. But only if you promise not to tell her any more old wives' tales," I teased. Aileen liked to fill Clara's ears with advice and stories passed down from her Shuswap great-grandmother. She smiled and pretended to swat me with her dishcloth.

I leaned back in the chair and turned to Eddy. "Think the crops will be good this year?"

"Too soon to tell," said Eddy.

No farmer likes to be too optimistic. We'd just had a bad year and a hard winter. The fields looked promising, though.

After a comfortable grouse with Eddy about possible yield and how much the damned government was going to take, I went back to our farm to finish my chores.

First thing the next morning, Eddy called again, telling me to meet him at his chicken coop. More of the green-brown oblongs littered the bare ground, along with more of the tracks.

"Aileen saw this when she went to get the eggs," said Eddy.

"Did you see or hear anything last night?" I asked. The cottage kids liked to do their mischief when it was dark out.

"Nope. Went to bed early. Aileen heard Booker bark a couple of times. But she didn't see anything when she looked out the window."

"What about the chickens?" I asked. "Missing any?"

"Nope." His dozen Chantecler hens, his 'girls,' as he called them, ran around the coop, clucking and pecking at the grain Eddy had scattered. They seemed fine.

"Aileen said they're layin' good today. The eggs are bigger than usual, too," said Eddy.

"Hm," I said, looking around the coop. "Well, at least we know one thing."

Eddy grinned. "Yeah. It ain't a poultrygheist."

I groaned. "Damn."

Chuckling, Eddy went to add the shit to his pickle jar.

I returned to our barn. I was letting the goats out of their stalls when something blocked the light from the door. It was Clara.

"Hi. Want some breakfast?"

"Just let me finish this," I said, as I unlatched the last stall, letting Blossom, Clara's favorite goat, out to graze with the others.

Her arm snaked around my waist as we left the barn and she hugged me close.

"That's nice," I said.

When we got to the kitchen, I saw she'd only put out one plate. "You're not eating?"

She dimpled. "I already had a piece of Aileen's lemon meringue pie. A couple of pieces."

"If there's any left, I'll have some for dessert," I said around my poached eggs.

At supper time, the goats made their own way back, as usual--all but Blossom. She'd been known to stray before, so I went looking for her. I found her, eventually, near the back fence of our land, just up the hill from one of the abandoned mine shafts that I'd covered so none of the goats would fall in. Blossom lay on the ground beneath a pine tree, dead, her throat torn out and her belly gone, right up to her backbone.

Dried needles showered down around me. I looked up to see a grey squirrel scurrying from branch to branch, then straight up the trunk until it disappeared.

I carried Blossom to my truck, then went looking for Eddy. Dust plumed behind his old green pickup as he drove down the dirt road that divided our fields. He headed my way when he saw me waving.

"I've been looking for Booker," he said, getting out of his pickup. "She's been gone all day, Aileen said."

Booker was a blue heeler, solid and protective, but she was getting on in years and had gone a little blind and deaf.

"Did you find her?" I asked.

"Not yet."

I showed him Blossom's body.

"Damned kids!" he said.

"You think so? What should we do? Call the Mounties?" I asked. Pranks were one thing, but a dead goat and a missing dog were something else entirely.

"For a goat? Nah," he said. Then he grinned. "I got a better idea. Remember last fall, when we found those two kids in my barn?"

I grinned back. We'd caught them making out and decided to scare the bejesus out of them. I bet that boy still has hay in places he doesn't want to talk about.

"We could stake out my barn," I suggested.

Eddy nodded. "Yours has the best view."

The loft was also easy to get to. Along with a large picture window, I had installed a set of stairs against the wall by the door. I still planned to turn the loft into an office one day, when I had the time.

Eddy and I climbed the stairs, prepared for a long night. He had brought his shotgun and chuckled when he saw I had my big wood-chopping axe. Nothing like a couple of armed madmen to encourage young idiots to vacate the landscape. I had also brought my brightest, most intimidating flashlight. While I put it on the floor, Eddy propped our weapons against the wall, and unscrewed the top of a thermos. The aroma of Aileen's coffee wafted through the loft as he handed me a cup. We leaned back against the hay bales, sipping and watching the sky above the mountain across the lake.

Stars popped into existence, and the moon rose. Eddy and I talked, off and on. I think I learned more about Eddy that night than I had in the last two years. He and Aileen had been high school sweethearts and lived all their lives on the farm, raising three boys. They were grown now and didn't visit often enough for Aileen's peace of mind.

"Always thought one of them would take over the farm," said Eddy, shaking his head. "But they all went for jobs in the city."

I told him we'd been trying to start a family.

"I know. Aileen, she got it from Clara. We been hoping for you."

"We went to the doctor, but he says we're both perfectly healthy, no reason to worry. He said we should relax."

56

"It'll happen," said Eddy. "And if not, there's ways, eh? Artificial insemination and the like. I do it for my cows all the time."

"Thanks, but no thanks," I said, straight-faced. "I think we can handle it without you."

"Not what I meant," he mumbled. Then he snickered. "You got me."

"Yeah," I said, pleased to have pulled one over on him. It didn't happen often. I took a sip of cold coffee, then looked out the window and froze. Eddy followed my gaze. We grabbed our weapons and scrambled to peer out over the sill.

Something large and pale moved across the field, faint in the dim moonlight. The figure crested a hill and paused, as if testing the air. Apparently satisfied, it started down the hill, disappearing in the darkness. It was big, but not big enough to be a man. Or a kid, for that matter. A few minutes later, it limped into the yellow glow of our yard light, and we could see its shape.

"My God," said Eddy. "It's a chicken. Or . . ."

The thing moved into the shadow of the barn. Below us, the door creaked open, then shut with a bang. Erratic clicks echoed across the floor. Trying not to rustle the hay, I wriggled over to the edge of the loft and peered into the darkness.

As light flooded the barn, I yelped, covering my eyes with my hands. Eddy had turned on the flashlight.

I squinted through my fingers, trying to blink away the black spots. Eddy was peering over the edge of the loft. I edged closer. A pebble-skinned, monstrosity about the size of a Canada Goose glared up at us out of red-rimmed black eyes. Its short, featherless wings lifted, then fell. It looked like nothing so much as a small, pink dinosaur.

"Ko Chawk," Eddy whispered.

"Oh, hell," said the thing.

"It talks," said Eddy, in a strangled voice. The light wavered.

I tried to speak, but it was as if my brain had forgotten how to make words. A small, gibbering part of me wondered how the creature could talk with a beak. Then I realized. Of course.

"You got me, Eddy," I said, with a laugh as I rose. "Brilliant!"

Eddy didn't say anything, just stared at the thing, with a puzzled frown.

"That's amazingly realistic, Eddy. How'd you do it? Robotics?" I chuckled. "And the shit. Wow. You had me there. Lizard, eh?"

Eddy still didn't say anything.

"Eddy? I said you got me. You can knock it off now."

No response.

"So what did you call it? Ko Chawk?" I glanced at the creature and smiled, admiring Eddy's handiwork. "How about Elvis? Naw, too ugly."

"Hey!" it said. "I'm right here."

"Uh-huh. Who's doing the talking? Aileen, is that you?"

"Idiot," said the creature.

"Okay, I'll bite," I said, grinning at Eddy. "I've never seen a, um, chicken like you. Featherless, I mean."

"Bald. I'm bald," it said. It looked away, then back again, its skin shivering. "Gets damn cold in the winter, too."

"I'll bet. So, *are* you a chicken?"

It paused. "My mother was."

That made me laugh outright. "Good one."

"Say, bub, those your chickens in that henhouse?" the creature asked. "Cute bunch of girls. I sure enjoyed them these past nights. Lots of eggs, too, you noticed?"

"Let me guess, Eddy. You gave this thing an impressive . . . pecker?"

The creature limped closer, then scratched one clawed foot on the floor. "You got anything to eat around here?"

"I could get you some grain," I said.

It tilted its head one way, then the other, just like a bird. "Grain? I don't eat grain. How about another goat? They're delicious."

I'd forgotten about Blossom. I turned to Eddy. "You killed my goat, Eddy? That's going a bit far."

Eddy grunted, like he'd been punched in the stomach. "Wasn't me," he whispered.

58

"That dog almost stopped me," said the creature. It lifted one leg to show us a long gash in the pebbled skin. "But I got her. Stringy old thing."

"Chickens don't eat meat," I said, glancing at Eddy, who shook his head.

"Yeah, well, I evolved, man," said the creature. "The rest of my flock were seed-eaters, but they were a bunch of brainless clucks." It made a rasping sound, which I realized was supposed to be laughter.

"Were?" I asked.

It looked away again. "Okay, yeah. They're gone. Dead. I'm the only one left."

"You ate them, didn't you?" said Eddy.

The creature shifted its gaze to him. "Yeah, so? It was a hard winter. I even ate the eggs."

I sighed. "Eddy, enough. This was funny, well, except for Blossom, but it's gone far enough. You got me."

"Niall," said Eddy, "I know you think I'm crazy, because of Bigfoot."

"Of course not."

"Niall, this is no joke. It's real."

Eddy started down the stairs, watching the creature. The creature watched him, its mouth opening to show a tiny pink tongue. Eddy propped the shotgun by the door when he reached the floor, then put his hands out, palms forward.

"I'm not going to hurt you," he said softly. "I just want to look."

"Yeah, right," the creature sneered.

Before Eddy could take another step, the creature leaped. It knocked Eddy to the floor. While Eddy wrapped his hands around the creature's neck, its claws dug into the front of Eddy's flannel shirt, ripping it open. Blood poured out of Eddy's torso as those sharp claws disemboweled him, a bright red tide that washed over them both. I stood staring, mouth open.

"Help! Niall!" Eddy grunted. I ran down the stairs, axe in hand. Just as I reached them, the beast lunged and clamped its beak over Eddy's throat, crushing it. Eddy gurgled, then went limp, his hands sliding from the beast's neck.

The beast looked up at me, licking its beak.

"You . . . you can't be real," I whispered. "It's impossible."

"Tell that to your friend," it panted, eyes glittering.

I hefted my axe.

"Go ahead, make my--"

The beast dodged my swing, and the axe head stuck fast in the barn wall. I tugged at it, but it wouldn't move. The beast stalked towards me, its beady eyes unblinking.

The barn door swung open. Clara stood there in her nightgown, her hair mussed from sleep.

"Niall, is everything . . ," she began. Then she caught sight of the beast and her mouth dropped open. The beast and I stared at her as she stared back. Then it ran for her.

I wrenched the axe out of the wall, blessing the years of wood chopping that had strengthened my arms, and turned it around over my head in a wraparound swing as I ran after the beast.

Clara reached down, picked up the shotgun by the stairs, aimed, and calmly blew the creature's head off. Blood spattered the floor.

The report echoed around the barn, then faded. One of the goats bleated in the sudden silence.

Clara slowly turned to face me, as she lowered the shotgun.

"How . . . when . . . who . . .?" I sputtered.

Clara tossed her hair aside. "Aileen taught me. We don't just bake and compare recipes, you know."

"But why?"

"You're out a lot, Niall. On the property, or in town, or having coffee with Eddy . . ." She put one hand over her mouth. "How is he?"

"I don't know." Flinging the axe to the floor, I rushed to Eddy's side. His eyes were open, but he was already dead.

"Dammit," I said, tears starting in my eyes.

"Oh, Niall, poor Eddy," said Clara. "Poor *Aileen*." She trembled.

Just at that moment, Aileen rushed into the barn. "I heard a shot!" she said. She saw the beast first. Then she saw Eddy. She dropped to her knees on the floor beside her husband, and leaned over his body. Her shoulders shook.

Clara crossed to me and flung her arms around my neck. Both women were sobbing. I wiped tears from my own face.

After a few minutes, I asked in a choked voice, "What do we do now?"

"I don't know," said Clara. "Call the Mounties."

I looked at the gory floor, illuminated by the white beam of the flashlight. "No, not yet. I won't call them."

She blinked at me as she rose. "Not yet?"

I stepped around the mess on the floor. "Remember the Bigfoot debacle? And the crop circles? Remember how the media made us look like stupid bumpkins? This will be worse. Much worse. We can't let anyone know about this."

"But it's real," she began.

I sighed. "I know. And it would make for a great story. And Eddy would have loved it."

Her lips quirked up in a brief smile.

"We don't need that again." I said. I looked at the beast again. "Besides, who would believe us?"

"What do you mean?" asked Aileen.

"Look."

I moved so they could get a good look at the beast's body.

"Oh my God," said Clara.

"Ko Chawk," Aileen whispered. "The chicken-lizard. It's said it used to roam the New York Valley in the last century. It was supposed to be real. But…"

Clara shook her head. "What's it doing here?"

As we watched, the beast's body changed. Before we realized what was happening, it had mutated into something else. An ordinary red rooster.

"Oh," said Aileen.

We just stared at it, and then I shook my head. I knew we had to hurry.

I left the weapons, and Eddy's poor body, but I took the beast up the hill, running as fast as I could. I had decided to drop the body down the abandoned mine shaft. Meanwhile, Aileen had

61

cleaned Clara's prints off the shotgun and put it into Eddy's dead hands.

"Shit!" I said, snapping my fingers.

"What?" asked Clara.

I ran to Eddy's barn and retrieved the pickle jar, disposing of it deep in our garbage.

We looked around, trying to see if we'd missed anything. The blood, we left on the floor. It would have been too obvious if we'd cleaned that up. Then I called the Mounties.

Constable Iverson and Captain Singh arrived within the hour, patrol car lights flashing, not looking best pleased about having been roused from their beds.

"What happened?" asked Iverson, her notebook out. Singh knelt down beside Eddy, careful of the blood.

"Eddy and I stayed up, trying to catch a prankster that might have been bothering us," I said. "Someone killed one of my goats, and maybe Eddy's dog. But just a while ago, I went out to take a leak, and then I heard Eddy's shotgun go off. By the time I returned, he was like this. I tried to help him, but . . ."

"You didn't see the perpetrator?" asked Captain Singh, while Iverson prowled the barn.

I spread my hands and shook my head. "I saw something. I think it might have been an animal."

"There do seem to be claw marks," said Iverson. "Maybe a cougar. Awful lot of blood, though."

"He must have hit the beast," I said.

Singh rose from the body. "Are you sure of what you saw?"

"It was just a glimpse," I said, shaking my head.

"Well. I'm sorry, but we'll have to take you in for questioning."

"Me? What for?" I asked.

"It's a suspicious death, sir," said Iverson. "And you were the only one here."

"Oh. Right," I said. "Can I change first? Clean up?"

"No," said Singh. "What you're wearing is evidence. But you can bring some clean clothes."

They gathered more evidence while I grabbed some jeans, a shirt and underwear. I'm sure they were thorough, but forensics in real life is never as cut and dried as it on the TV shows, for which I was grateful.

When it was light enough, I showed them where I'd found Blossom. We also found Booker's body a little further up the hill. Then the officers went to talk to Clara and Aileen. When they returned, they were carrying one of the homemade lemon meringue pies. Clara must have thought they needed sweetening.

It was several hours before they were satisfied that I hadn't murdered my friend, Eddy. In the meantime, they'd called a doctor from Cranbrook, who served as medical examiner for the area. He sent swabs from Eddy's body to a forensics lab for testing.

We buried Eddy three days later, Rev. Timmins presiding. Eddy's three boys came for the funeral, but spent most of their time on their cell phones and laptops. We decided not to tell them what really happened. When the lab's answer eventually arrived, the DNA. test was 'inconclusive.' "Death by animal attack" was the doctor's final report.

With country practicality, the congregation turned the food intended for the church social into food for the funeral. So many people came, we almost didn't have enough. Rev. Timmins, being allergic to lemons, didn't have any of Aileen's pies.

A good man had been taken from us. We expected to mourn for weeks. But somehow, that didn't happen. Clara and I eventually got to noticing how happy folk seemed to be--at least, all those who had attended the funeral. And I've never seen such contented-looking Mounties.

Clara figured out what was giving us all such sunny dispositions. It was the eggs. They say aphrodisiacs are all in the mind, but maybe there's something to it, after all. I know Clara and I have been enjoying a much more active sex life. Rev. Timmins has been a bit suspicious of the general air of cheerfulness in his flock, but what he doesn't know won't hurt him.

With Aileen's blessing, I've been looking after Eddy's land. And with Clara's blessing, I was invited to 'look after' Aileen, too. It's astonishing what an old wife can teach you.

We kept all the eggs that the beast produced with Eddy's chickens, and had been making a fortune off them--under the table, of course. But we ran out. I did go looking for more; didn't find any. We did have a couple more minor animal 'incidents', after that, but we kept quiet about them. We still don't know where the beast came from.

A couple of weeks ago, some guy came by wanting to buy Eddy's Bigfoot collection. Aileen sold it to him for a ridiculous sum, and made him promise not to tell where he got it. Hey, it costs a lot to run a farm. Especially two of them.

Oh, and we're papering the nursery. The triplets are due at Christmas. A lot of the other Valley women have been surprised to find themselves pregnant, too.

Next month, when the crops are all in, I'm planning to take a trip up past the treeline, just to check on things.

And who knows? Maybe I'll run into Bigfoot.

Leslie Carmichael has been inside the Great Pyramid at Giza, has watched the world turn purple during a total solar eclipse, and has been an honoured guest at a Canadian-Scottish-Taiwanese wedding. She has swum in the Red Sea, picked amethysts out of the ground near Thunder Bay, watched a space shuttle land, and cooked a Medieval dinner for 200 people. She has worn a corset, a suit of armour and a Klingon outfit (but not all at the same time). Leslie also likes to work on miniature dolls and dollhouses when she's not writing.

Her publication credits include short stories, articles, comic interactive murder mystery plays and children's books, Lyranel's Song *and* The Amulet of Amon-Ra. *Her publications in the speculative genre include* "Hockey Night in Canada," The Journal of Dracula Studies; "Predators," Storyteller: Canada's Short Story Magazine; *and* "Miracles," Crossroads: a Speculative Anthology.

Leslie lives in Calgary, Alberta, with her husband, three children and two cats.

Tom & the Roadside Café
by Kimberly Colley

We stopped at the roadside café because I thought it was cute. I want to make that perfectly clear at the outset. Katie thought we -- meaning I -- needed directions. She claimed we were lost. I tried to explain to her for the fifty-seventh time that vampires, like the bats they are likened to, have a stellar sense of direction which enables them to hone in on whatever target they please. My explanation availed not.

But because the café was an old, converted Pullman coach and had been dubbed The Waggin' Train, I was captured by its quaint charm and pulled off Highway 7 into its graveled lot.

"Thank God they're still open," Katie said, unbuckling her seat belt. "It's going on 11:00."

"They're probably an all-night café," I said, switching off the ignition of Katie's hybrid car.

"Out here in the middle of nowhere? This is Ohio, Tom, not New York."

She slammed the door much harder than she needed to and preceded me up the wooden steps to the entrance. Above the door was mounted a neon sign in the shape of a dog. The only part of the sign that blinked was its tail, first a lower tail, then an upper.

"That's odd," I said. "Why in the world would they have a sign like that? People will think they serve dog food."

But Katie had already pulled open the glass door, letting out a rush of warm air redolent of marinated beef.

"The owner's probably just a dog lover," she said, and flounced in.

The interior surprised me just as much as the sign. The walls were painted indigo blue, which might be a nice color for a bedroom, but personally, I like a nice red in a dining room.

Brushed nickel lamps sat at each table and bracketed the walls between the windows facing the road. These windows themselves were empty of ornament save Roman shades custom-fitted at each, all of a thick black canvas material.

The diner was empty of customers, except for us. No waitress stood behind the counter, which looked to be made of steel.

I slipped my fingers around Katie's elbow. "I think maybe we should go."

"But we need to find Deliverance before sunrise."

My friend, Ralph, lives in Deliverance, Ohio; at least he does now. Up until last week, he'd been residing happily in Indianapolis -- I know, it seems impossible to me too -- but he'd recently been outed by a bunch of goth teenagers who'd worked out his true nature. They wanted him to be their cult master. So he beat feet out to this little farmhouse he'd fixed up as a getaway. Katie and I were on our way up to help him settle in.

"At this rate," Katie continued, "you'll be toast."

Someone stirred in the kitchen, though I couldn't see who despite the wide pass-through. A second later, a solid rectangle of a man came through the swinging door. It took me a moment to get who he reminded me of -- one of those Eurotrash male models who terrorized Bruce Willis in *Die Hard*.

He wiped his hands on an enormous black towel, but not before I could spot the blood staining his fingers.

"Can I help you?" he asked. To my surprise, he didn't have a trace of a European accent. I didn't think they grew male models in Ohio.

"You're probably closed," I said. "Sorry to intrude."

Katie jerked her arm out of my grasp. "We need directions to Deliverance. Can you help us?"

The bell over the door jingled, and I turned. A gust of snow-tinged air brought in with it another male model type, this one darker and more wiry. He had odd eyes. He trailed them over Katie hungrily.

"Alan," said the cook, though I suspected he didn't do much in the way of cooking. "You're the first to arrive."

"Are they joining us?" Alan asked, jerking his head in our direction.

One corner of the cook's lips lifted. "They're just here for directions to Deliverance. Her man can't find his way."

Oh, dear.

"Tom can find his way," Katie said, her cheeks red with indignation. She shrugged her shoulders with a little harrumph. "It's just all these crossroads. They're confusing."

Alan pursed his lips, giving Katie the once-over. "I like you," he said. "I'll give you directions."

The cook stepped out from behind the counter and took a seat on one of the stools. Facing us, he rested his elbows on the countertop and cocked his head.

"What was that you were saying earlier?" he asked Katie. "About needing to get there before sunrise?"

Alan, who had begun pulling down the blackout shades, stopped and turned to gaze at us.

"Well." She shoved her fists into her coat pockets. "It's just that we're very tired."

Bless her heart, she'd finally cottoned on to the fact that all was not kosher at The Waggin' Train.

The leather bench seat that Alan had been kneeling on squeaked as he moved toward us once more. He padded behind Katie, his nostrils flaring as he sniffed inaudibly at her hair. Satisfied, he circled back to me. One sniff was all it took.

He grinned.

"You can go, pretty girl." He touched the lapel of her coat with one fingertip. "But I think we'd like your friend to stay for dinner."

The color in her cheeks had disappeared entirely.

"No," she said, and hooked her arm through mine. "No, we're together."

"Katie, it's okay." I extricated myself from her clutches. "Go on to Deliverance. Tell your parents that I was unavoidably detained."

"My parents? Oh." She nodded. "Yes. Dad will be so disappointed," she said, her voice half an octave higher.

Not the greatest actress in the world, but I love her. I mean, you know, sort of.

Gravel crunched outside as a vehicle pulled into the parking lot.

"That'll be the others," the cook said. "Finish pulling down the shades in the front, but leave the ones on the door up." He grinned. "I think I'll enjoy a little moonlight tonight."

An ignition switched off and several car doors slammed, followed soon by the thud of heavy boots on the wooden steps leading to the door. I turned, ready to push Katie out as the first wave of werewolves en masse entered, but these new arrivals bore not the slightest resemblance to male models, European or otherwise.

"This is it, man," said the one in front, his pale face alighting in triumph, purple-black lips spreading to reveal a set of teeth covered with braces.

"Awesome!"

His cohorts crowded around him, their kohl-rimmed eyes taking in the surroundings with delight. The sole female of their band cast a disdainful glance at us.

"Who're these posers?" she asked. "They don't look like werewolves."

The cook, who had already begun to spread his arms preparatory to herding the gaggle of Goths out, stopped in his tracks. He threw a worried look at Alan, who was too busy gaping at the new arrivals to acknowledge it.

"What?" The cook made an attempt at a laugh. "Werewolves? This is just a diner, kids. And we're closed."

"It's okay, dude," said the leader of the Goth Scout troop. "We're totally cool with that. We want to join you."

The Mini-Vampira advanced on the cook, one black lace gauntleted arm outstretched, while the boys shuffled towards Alan, now backed into the corner. I took the opportunity to edge out the door, pulling Katie along behind me.

The parking lot was still empty of any vehicle other than Katie's car and the teenagers' van. The wind gusted and I glanced up. Clouds still covered the full moon, but I suspected that would not last long.

"Come on," I started to say, but Katie grabbed the keys from my hand and jumped into the driver's seat. I quickly found my place on the passenger's side.

Sometimes, it's a good thing to let the woman take the lead.

Kimberly Colley is an attorney who turned her back on the practice of law in order to pursue something approximating a real life. So far, her efforts have met with limited success. She writes chiefly to amuse herself, and occasionally others.

She is a shameless rabble-rouser.

Criticus Ex Machina
by Sarah E. Glenn

My cigarettes were in the trash. Probably the cleaning lady Nunnelly had hired. I fished them out and lit up. I needed my little rituals if I was going to finish this book on schedule.

The lights on the front of the PC winked out when I pressed the power button. I cursed and pressed the button again. I must have left it on last night. They tell me it's not good to leave computers on, but I don't know much about them. They've taken over the publishing world, though, making the process of converting manuscripts into books much simpler. At least that's what Nunnelly told me when he insisted I submit my new book in electronic form.

He said that he didn't care how popular the *Dick Haggard: Vice Squad* books were, the company couldn't afford to keep typists any more. No one else in his stable of writers got away with hard copy in this economy. It was time I joined the herd.

"I even have a computer you can start with, until you get a feel for what suits you. I'll have my intern enter what you've already got into a file, and you won't have to waste any time."

Waste time? I was doing nothing but wasting time. Once this thing booted, I'd have to jump through the proper hoops to open my story. I hadn't even really started writing, thanks to this gadget, and I only had the condo for the summer. Scanning through the last few paragraphs, I reoriented myself and began working.

I finished the scene, began another. Little wiggly red lines appeared under the words I'd misspelled – I don't limit my creativity to plots – and most of the slang and expletives. I'd fix the real errors later. Nunnelly said I could add words to the computer dictionary so they wouldn't get flagged, but I didn't have time for that. The book would be finished by now if I'd done it my usual way.

I wrote, broke for lunch, went back to work. Scrolling up, I discovered that the red lines were gone. I checked words I knew I couldn't spell, but everything looked right for a change. Maybe some function was built in to correct spelling errors. Most useful thing I'd seen so far. More red appeared as I wrote, but I decided I could put off my spell check till the next day and see if the PC worked its magic again.

Tuesday morning. I got up and crossed to the PC. I wiggled the mouse, but the screen didn't come up. It was off; I'd finally remembered. I pressed the power button, then went in search of my smokes as it cranked. In the trash again. Had the cleaning lady already been here? I looked around the condo for signs of straightening. No, the dishes were unwashed and the ashtrays were full. Maybe the cigs had gotten knocked off the bedside table. I started the coffee pot and lit up.

When I reviewed my work, I saw that the red lines were gone. Great! A convenience of computers had revealed itself at last. This day's work went by much faster.

My cigarettes were missing again. I cursed and made a morning run to the local quickie mart, getting myself a cup of brown water so I wouldn't waste more time making coffee. I was definitely speaking to Mrs. Buckner. She'd denied throwing my packs away, but they didn't have legs of their own.

When I sat down – at ten! – to start work, I made another discovery. There was a red line under one phrase – 'grizzly death' – and next to it, the words: "UNLESS A BEAR DID IT, FIX THIS!" I stared for a moment, then laughed. Whoever programmed this beast had a sense of humor! Reassured by signs of a human touch, I corrected the word.

It wasn't funny later, though, when I skimmed some earlier chapters for the name of a minor character and discovered that portions of my work had been rewritten. A scene where Dick had been sweating up the sheets with a hot witness had been changed to clasped hands and a closed door. Explicit language had been

72

reworded. Dick Haggard had been given a mother. Worse, he regularly went to her place for Sunday dinner.

I grabbed the phone and punched in Nunnelly's number. His secretary answered, and I demanded to speak to him immediately about the computer.

"It sounds like you need technical support," she said in soothing tones cultivated by years of dealing with the creative temperament. "May I have them call you?"

"No! Mr. Technology-Is-Our-Friend forced this – this electronic Sunday school teacher on me. I want to know why it edits stuff it's not supposed to!"

She put me on hold and relayed my message. His voice was all smiles when he answered. "Rich! How are you? Louise tells me you're having a problem with the PC. We have people who can help you with that, you know."

"I'm not so sure. Tell me, do word processors… edit your work for you?"

I told him about the adjustments to my hard-hitting police procedural. His response was patronizing. "It's all right, Rich. Everybody thinks computers do stuff on their own after a while. You probably just deleted some paragraphs by accident. You can rewrite them, no sweat. If you have any more trouble, Louise will be happy to get Tech Support for you."

Two rewritings and two bowdlerizations later, I contacted Louise. It was five when Ted from Tech Support replied (time spent fussing, fuming, and hunting for my latest missing pack). He wasn't any more sympathetic than Nunnelly, assuming that I had hit a wrong combination of keys. When I insisted that entire characters and scenes had been altered, I suppose I got a bit abrasive. Ted's anemic but supercilious voice on the other end suggested that perhaps I had been writing while sleep-deprived or in some "other" (pejorative tone) altered state.

"You're telling me there is no way the computer can create material on its own. Absolutely none?"

"Maybe some frustrated author is breaking in and adding their own text." The geek snickered. "A ghost writer."

"Hah, hah. Don't quit your job for stand-up just yet, kid."

Ted muttered something I could have worded better, then made his first useful suggestion. "Maybe a previous user installed something that's causing the problem. Some sort of software glitch." He suggested I ask Louise.

I had no trouble getting the information from the secretary; she'd been a fan of the previous owner. Three months ago, the PC had belonged to Elaine Dysart, another of Nunnelly's writers. The now deceased Ms. Dysart specialized in New England cozies. No cats, though – she was a severe asthmatic who spent most of her time inside, surrounded by air filters. Her career was cut short by a chain-smoking cousin and an empty inhaler. "He visited for two weeks. She begged and pleaded, but he told her it was all in her mind. Then he hid some butts under the papers in her study trashcan as a test. He found her later, sprawled dead over her keyboard. She still had the inhaler clutched in her hand."

Crap. That's all I needed: a haunted computer.

It was time to strike back. So, she didn't like cigarettes? I'd smoke her out! That evening, I went into town and made myself some new friends. I can be personable when I want to be, really. When the bar closed, I invited everyone to my place. We laughed and drank and smoked till the bottles were empty and the ashtrays were overflowing. It was around five when the last guest wavered out the door. I said something nasty to the computer and flopped on the bed.

At noon, the PC was still on. Chalk one up for the living, I thought, as I went into the bathroom to soak my aching head. When the pounding stopped, I lit a celebratory cigarette and sat down in front of the glowing screen to check my manuscript.

A box popped up and asked for my password.

Nunnelly choked back a laugh. "You're amazing! How did you password-protect a document without entering a password?"

"Just send someone to fix it," I sighed. I also requested that he go ahead and get me my own computer – brand new, and with as little extra software as possible.

He was delighted, and had Ted show up at my condo the following morning. Naturally, I had to deal with a round of muffled chuckles from the kid as he did his Open Sesame act with my story.

I watched his white-shirted back as he began assembling my new PC, crawling under my desk to plug in the part that sat on the floor. Wasn't it impractical to wear a white shirt if you were going to crawl around on the ground? I asked, and he told me it was policy. We agreed that it wasn't a very smart one.

When he finished, he pulled a cable out of his kit. "I'll move your documents over now."

I blanched as he connected the two PCs. "Just move the novel over. Nothing else!"

Ted's voice was patient. "Nothing else, sir."

"Is there anything you can do to clear the old machine?" I asked. "I think it has some leftover programming from its last owner."

"I could reformat it," the kid said. "Although I don't think that's the problem."

I knew where he figured the problem lay. "Just do it."

Goodbye, Elaine, I thought as he clicked in the commands to deep-six all Dysart programming. *And good riddance.*

When my new computer was ready for action, he made a special point of showing me how the word processing software worked, and how to avoid the mistake he was sure I'd made before. I didn't comment, just gave him a tip to go away and keep his mouth shut.

Free! I was finally free of prissy programming. No more *Dick Laggard: Nice Squad.* Let us return to those days of old, I told myself as I sat down to write. Those good old days of sex, shootings, and uncensored street talk. I was into the third page when a gray box popped up.

"Start a new paragraph with each speaker."

Elaine had loaded onto the new computer with my book.

What could I do? I didn't have much time left to write. So I forged ahead, finishing the novel despite snippy corrections, cleaned-up language, and the irrepressible Mrs. Haggard (though God knows I tried).

Nunnelly was shocked when he read the manuscript. "You've put some real surprises in here, Rich. Some strong new characters and human interest."

"It's the virtual me," I said. "The medium became the message."

Would you believe the novel won an Edgar? It sold millions of copies, mostly to women. I received love letters for the first time, and invites from women's magazines and television shows to discuss the fresh direction my writing had taken. "You've reached out to women in a new way," one interviewer commented, to clapping from her studio audience. I nodded with the appropriate level of humility.

"Is there someone special in your life, perhaps?"

"Sadly, she's deceased," I said to sympathetic coos. "But when I write, I know she is near." I ignored the itch of the nicotine patch on my arm. It needed to stay on, at least until the movie deal came through.

Sarah E. Glenn, a product of the suburbs, has a B.S. in Journalism, which is redundant if you think about it. She loves writing mystery and horror stories, often with a sidecar of humor. Several have appeared in mystery and paranormal anthologies, including G.W. Thomas' Ghostbreakers *series,* Futures Mysterious Anthology Magazine, *and* Fish Tales: The Guppy Anthology. *She belongs to Sisters in Crime, SinC Guppies, the Short Mystery Fiction Society, and the Historical Novel Society.*

Happy Anniversary
by Laura Huntley

Well, I was absolutely furious. Martin was so late, not answering his phone and there I was, squashed into the tiniest black dress which was barely bigger than a handkerchief and wearing heels so high that I could actually reach that top kitchen cupboard shelf, which I had never been able to do before. I had been to the salon, gone were those pesky stray grey hairs, I'd had a restyle, a long floppy fringe which covered one eye. It looked sexy on the model in the magazine. Now, it was getting on my nerves and I was becoming increasingly aware of how silly I appeared. I'd been waxed all over, sprayed a golden bronze shade. All for Martin, my husband, for our first wedding anniversary. The bastard.

I looked at the scattered red rose petals on the bed and my temper rocketed out of control. If he wasn't back in the next few minutes, he could forget it, I would not be doing that special thing, and he would be sleeping on the sofa. For a month. A couple of drinks with the lads, he'd said, I'll be back no later than nine, he'd said. I looked at the taunting clock which screamed half past ten. I threw off the neck-breaking heels and stomped back down the stairs.

I gingerly peered into the saucepan which had spent far too long on the hob. The Béarnaise sauce had resigned, the egg yolk had tried to escape and it was all just a disappointing mess. I was seething, no doubt Martin would berate me, if he dared. It's not hilarious living with a chef when you're culinary challenged. He fawned over recipe books, perfected his chopping techniques, grew his own herbs, and ran his restaurant, while I was quite content with comforting beans on toast and noodles in pots. Besides, I had seen how much butter and cream he added to everything, frankly it was his fault that this stupid dress was

77

causing me breathing difficulties, that and the fact that I had long forgotten where the hell the gym was.

I examined the steak. Martin preferred his meat rare, as do so many chefs I find. He liked to just about wait until the heart had stopped beating before he picked up his knife and fork. Martin would have to make do with burned to the point that it could now be used as a hockey puck. Realistically, there was no way that either of us could eat this. I liked my teeth where they belonged, still embedded in my gums. I emptied the pans into the bin and started to rummage through the fridge for something idiot-proof to cook, a quick tasty snack. Bacon, yes, bacon was always good. I was separating the rashers when I heard him stagger through the doorway.

Immediately, rage boiled my blood, I was so angry that my hands trembled and knots formed within my temples and tied themselves into bows. I heard him crash into the coat stand. I couldn't believe that he had chosen to drink himself into a stupor on our wedding anniversary. I was becoming more livid by the second. He hadn't even come crawling to me with apologies and excuses. He had switched on the television, he was actually watching the football, and I could hear the rowdy cries of the spectators and the rapid orgasmic voice of the overexcited commentator, which was just too much. We may have only have been married for one year, but everyone knows that you don't get to watch football on your anniversary, surely? I glanced at the beautiful spice rack that I'd had especially made for him, his initials carved so intricately into the dark wood. It took me all the strength I had not to go and hit him around the head with it. I guessed that there wouldn't be a thoughtful and sweet present coming my way.

I tried to ignore the grunts and moans coming from the lounge but, by that point, I was beyond incensed and ready to blow my top. I stormed through and I stood there, waiting, with my hands on my hips. He looked like shit, his clothes were filthy, his hair was in utter disarray, his eyes were vacant and expressionless, bloodshot and a peculiar yellow colour. How much had he had to drink, the entire contents of the bar? Still, he did not look at me. He offered no words, he wasn't even trying.

I turned on to my heel and returned to the bacon, spreading out the rashers on the tin foiled tray. I heard him try and get up and he stumbled around like a new-born deer learning to walk for the first time. I hoped that the neighbours hadn't seen him in this state. Next week's barbeque would be pretty embarrassing. My cheeks flushed scarlet at the notion; Shirley would never let me live that down. Out of the corner of my eye, I saw him loitering in the doorway, leaning into the wall to assist him with the art of standing up. I had seen Martin a bit tipsy, and after he'd had one too many, but I had never seen him like this, not once in our time together had he been this inebriated and useless.

"Happy anniversary, darling," I spat out the words, the sarcasm was thick in my voice.

He just mumbled and then slowly crept up behind me. His rested his chin on my head.

"You must be joking if you think you're getting any," I snapped, moving away from him.

His hands grabbed at the raw greasy bacon. He snatched a rasher and stuffed it into his mouth. I couldn't speak, I stared at him, completely baffled and most disgusted. On he went, stealing my bacon and eating it uncooked, even the rinds, in it went and he barely chewed. I wanted to stop him but I was struck dumb and rendered silent. What the hell was he doing? At once, the bacon, mushed up and somewhat gross, came back to haunt him. He retched and heaved until it all fell from his mouth and on to my new lino floor. I walked away, dazed and entirely perplexed, and stood in the middle of the lounge. He had another thing coming if he thought that I was cleaning that up. He lumbered towards me and, once again, he put his mouth to my head, messing up my new hairstyle and, generally, getting on my nerves.

"Get off," I shouted, irritated.

He wouldn't, it was ridiculous, his lips and teeth kept on nuzzling at my head. I tried to get away from him, I pushed him on to the sofa, he wriggled and struggled but he was like an insect that had fallen on to its back and couldn't get up again. The television distracted me, the football programme had been interrupted by an important news update. I wondered what was going on, the coiffured blonde presenter looked shockingly pale and there was a

79

definite sense of terror in her eyes. I grabbed the remote control and turned up the volume. I instantly knew that it was serious; they didn't even bother with the bunkum of the music and lead up.

"We interrupt the programming schedule with some breaking news. Up and down the country, we have received harrowing reports of the dead coming back to life. Corpses in funeral parlours woke up and walked out, and they are now infecting people by biting them, transforming them into the half-dead. The streets are descending into chaos as civilians run for their lives. So far, we only have one known way of killing them and saving yourself. Hit them. As hard and forcefully as you can. In the head. And avoid being bitten, at all costs."

I continued to stare at the television, waiting for someone to announce the news as a cunning hoax, an elaborate mass joke on the unsuspecting nation, I even checked the calendar to make sure that it wasn't the first day of April, despite knowing exactly what day of August it was. I started laughing, in that nervous uncertain way, half smile and half grimace. I shut up once the channel cut to some live footage. I could not believe my eyes. The true horror of the situation hit me at once. I could see a man slowly meandering down a street, grabbing a poor woman and biting down on her crown. She fell to the floor and more arrived, heaving out her insides with a fierce and unrelenting hunger. Scorching bile caught in my throat in reaction to the terrifying and sickening images. My knees felt weak and my head was spinning.

I faced Martin and I knew what he had become. He hadn't forgotten our anniversary, he hadn't gone out and got wasted, he had been transformed into a monster, into a zombie. A shiver raced down my spine and caused me to shudder as I attempted to take in and accept the hideous new reality. So many emotions crashed around my brain simultaneously. I couldn't allow myself to feel the pain and the sadness, I couldn't deal with that yet. I couldn't feel anything except for the paralysing fear. I closed my eyes and tried to think. My natural curiosity kicked in and I went over to the bay window and spied through a gap in the curtain.

I could see Shirley, out in her silky pink dressing gown and black fluffy marabou feather slippers, I wouldn't have been seen dead dressed like that, I thought. Her husband Gordon sloped down the path, she stretched out her arms to greet him and he went for her. I had to look away as I heard her shrieks and piercing screams. I glimpsed back for a second and her cries had died down. Bloody hell, he was eating her, Shirley was no more. Martin wouldn't be making his potato salad then; there definitely wouldn't be a barbeque to attend. As shocking as it had been to witness the scene, I did breathe a relieved sigh about not having to go round for Christmas Eve drinks, I'd been bored out of my brains last time and they only ever bought supermarket branded spirits, the skinflints.

I knew that I had to do something about Martin. I couldn't have him hanging around here, trying to eat my brains. But, what could I do? He was still flapping about in the chair, I looked into his eyes and it was confusing, they appeared mostly empty and devoid of emotion but I was sure that there was a flicker of something. He'd remembered where he lived and that he was a football fanatic. Perhaps he did recall more than the likes of Gordon? I had always sensed that we were far the more superior couple.

I helped pull Martin to his feet, and he veered towards my head again. I tried to keep him at arm's length as I dragged him through the kitchen and out into the back garden. I could hear the yelps of the local residents from nearby. I found the key for the shed, underneath the terracotta plant pot, and opened the door. I stuffed him inside and locked him in. He would have to stay there until I could figure this out. I returned indoors and watched some more of the news. They seemed to think that only a few managed to retain parts of their personalities. I just couldn't imagine Martin eating some brain tissue. This was the man who lectured people about locally sourced produce and refused to eat vegetables if they were unseasoned. But, there had been the bacon incident. Clearly, his diet had altered. What the hell was I supposed to do about that? I couldn't keep him in the garden shed indefinitely and I couldn't just let him starve. At the same time, it wouldn't be responsible of me to set him free for him to run amok on the streets either. To have and to hold, from this day forward. In sickness and in health. Shit. I was going to have to feed him.

I paced up and down, mulling over the disturbing facts. My husband was a zombie. He wanted to eat brains. I wished to keep him safe and secured, yet fed. I was going to have to go out there and do something horrific. I would have to kill someone. I gulped hard. The only time that I'd ever come to blows with someone physically was when I was seven years old and at primary school. Sarah Hammond had pulled my hair and scratched my face, I'd turned around and walloped her so hard that she had fallen to the tarmac of the playground floor. How did you kill someone? And, even if I did, how would I get the brain and other organs out? I felt faint and ever so much like crying. But I didn't, because I had always been somewhat of a trooper; I had to find a way. First things first, I had to get out of this dress, perhaps my breasts did look fabulous in the restrictive fabric and push-up bra, but it was no longer even faintly suitable.

On went the ancient jogging bottoms, and the whiter than white trainers that had never seen exercise. I tied up the new silly fringe and grabbed the killer shoes. I only hoped that they could live up their name--the pointy stiletto heels looked rather evil. I grabbed Martin's most precious kitchen knife, the one that I wasn't allowed to use, and the broom, because it was there. I tentatively peered through the window. I couldn't hear anything. I tiptoed to the front door and sneaked a peek. I wished that I had an actual plan. I didn't know what I would do when I actually got outside.

I started punching the air. I thought it might help motivate me and help to psyche myself up for the job in hand, but I guessed that I just looked like an idiot. I opened the door, just a little, waiting for a zombie to jump out at me like they did in the horror films, but it didn't happen and that was quite a relief. I positioned myself behind the ridiculously overgrown hedge which I was definitely going to cut back last Wednesday. I felt a bit smug, Martin had chastised me for being lazy after I had spent the afternoon reading gossipy magazines instead, but who was right now? Oh, that would be me. It was perfect, nobody would have the slightest inkling that I was there. All I had to do was wait. For ....
For what? An unsuspecting human I supposed, I began to feel

quite bilious imagining the moment when I .... When I .... Oh my god, could I ....

That's when I heard footsteps heading in my direction, too brisk to be a lumbering half-dead, I could dimly make out the sound of music, perhaps headphones, quiet and tinny in the night air. I gulped, my throat felt tight and I thought that my heart might actually explode out of my chest. I waited until I heard the steps almost at our gate and then I pounced. I say pounced, I jumped out on to the pavement with a broom in my hand, dropped the knife and shoe to the floor and stared at the man who worked at the garage where I sometimes bought my wine. He'd always been a tad judgemental, especially when I took him up on the generous offer of three bottles of Chardonnay for ten pounds. He must have thought I was either seriously pickled or a complete lunatic. I willed myself to do him over, but I didn't have it in me. This was insane, even for me. I looked crazier than the man who drank cans of lager at the bus stop in town, wearing the pink tutu, on Saturday nights.

I was about to apologise when I saw Pat from over the road. She was chewing on something which looked like a string of sausages, except that it wasn't a string of sausages and I realised that she, too, had become one of them. Garage man tried to get past me but I deliberately stood in his way, raising the broom handle into the air. Pat shuffled forward and attacked him from the back, he never saw her coming. As he fell to the ground, I stole his iPod and put the earphones in. Heavy rock music screamed into my ears and helped to muffle out some of his desperate pleas and awful gurgling noises as she opened up his skull. With my new soundtrack, I knew that it was now or never. As Pat chomped down and tugged out his brain, I aimed the broom handle at her head and, once it met flesh, I kept on pushing until it came out the other side. She instantly fell silent and still, I had done it, I had killed her. I took the spongy brain out of her hands and tried my hardest not to look at it. I rushed back into the house and locked the door behind me.

I kept the blaring music playing until I had pulled the salad bowl out of the cupboard and thrown the brain inside it. I washed my hands like I'd never washed my hands before. I could still feel it on me, warm and mushy and terrifying. I walked towards the shed, my hands trembling, causing the brain to rattle around. I put my ear to the wooden door, I could hear Martin wailing. I knocked twice, lightly and he quietened down.

"It's me, I'm coming in, just don't you try any funny business, do you hear me?"

He groaned but remained still. I unlocked the padlock and he stood there, with a confused and forlorn expression on his face. I held out the bowl with the putrid contents. He stepped forward and my stomach somersaulted.

"It's for you, your anniversary supper," I announced, thoroughly pleased with myself.

He sniffed and picked it up and rolled it around in his lumbering hands. He looked cross and then disinterested and he plonked it back in the salad bowl. I must admit, I felt pretty angry about that, after what I had gone through to get it. I hadn't anticipated such a lacklustre response. Martin, quite frankly, was skating on very thin ground. What did he want, a silver platter?

"What's wrong with it? It's fresh," I scoffed, remembering a million and one lectures about only buying fruit and vegetables from the market or, even better, growing and picking your own. His hands shot up and he made a sprinkling motion and I wanted to laugh and cry all at the same time.

"Are you seriously asking me what I think you're asking me?" I said, shocked to my core.

The sprinkling action started up again.

"You want me to put herbs on it?" I said, disbelieving what I was seeing.

He snatched the bowl from me and scrambled back into the house. I watched with bemusement and incredulity as he tried to haul down a pan. They all came toppling and crashing down on to the floor. He settled on the frying pan. For the love of god, he wanted to cook it. I had seen it all now. I switched on the hob and popped a knob of butter into it. His teeth snarled, he wanted goose fat, which was so typical of him. I sighed and fetched it for him. He opted for lemongrass, which he added liberally. I felt a pang of pity at that point. He had lost his finesse, he was clumsy and all over the place. He'd never earn his eagerly desired Michelin Star. I resolved to be more helpful. He pointed to the pan; it was cooked to his liking. Married couples just know this stuff, like when one of you is destined to shortly cut a fart. You go and brush your teeth for a second time out of politeness and the desire to not be gassed into a premature grave because, my god, they got sandwiched between the sheets and then there's no escape for either of you.

Martin nodded at the knife on the sideboard. I shook my head at him, I never cut food correctly, and it was always too thick and uneven. He nodded again. I slumped my shoulders at the notion but did as he wanted. It was an utterly gross task. The second that the sharp blade met the brain, my legs wobbled violently. I sliced it up the best I could and popped it on to a plate. He dropped a sprig of parsley on the top and I waited for him to eat it. He growled at me. I didn't have a clue what he wanted. I shrugged my shoulders. He barged past me and took out a knife and fork from the cutlery drawer. Seriously? A knife and fork, this wasn't what went down in the movies. It was so inherently Martin that I burst into a loud and uncontrollable bout of laughter. I couldn't stop once I'd started; it was the sort of laughter where you genuinely fear pee will leak down your leg. My jaw hurt, my face throbbed but I couldn't stop it until my stomach ached, then it felt too much like a keep fit workout and, finally, I calmed down.

I stifled one last giggle as he attempted to use a napkin and then he sat, at the dining table, dusted on a healthy amount of cracked black pepper and he ate it. His eyes rolled in the back of his head, he moaned and made his sex face, obviously this was what he wanted and needed and I was glad for him. I just wished that he hadn't used his sex face. Then, I had an idea. What about Martin's loyal paying customers? Would they flock to the restaurant out of habit? Would the foodies still want serving? Did they, like my husband, need brains cooked and dressed in fancy herbs? I won't lie; I saw a big giant squishy fluffy pound sign dancing in front of my eyes. It was the same as anything. You had to get in there first and bring the half-dead folk what they wanted. I leaped up and down with jollity. Martin could still work, he could keep his restaurant and continue to do what he loved, and there would be no need for his aspirations to fade away.

85

I needed to find out if this was possible, I needed to show him that it could be done. We had to pick our way through the dangerous streets and get to the restaurant. Now. We had to strike whilst the brains were hot. He looked satisfied and more at peace but I worried about how long for. When would he need his next fix? I stroked his hand and he gazed at me, I thought I spotted a flicker of tenderness buried, somewhere, in his eyes. I beckoned him with my fingers and he struggled to his feet.

"We're going to the restaurant," I stated.

I couldn't face the gruesome act of recovering the broom which still had Pat's messy head attached to it. I picked up the knife and the shoe and I lugged him along the street. I cursed the loss of the car which I expected still sat in the restaurant car park. I dashed as fast as I could, huffing and panting, the weight of my husband difficult and cumbersome, but I was determined that we would make it.

When the restaurant was in sight, I felt tremendous relief, until I heard a noise behind us. Another zombie. I rifled through Martin's pockets and found the keys and put them in my mouth. The zombie was an old man and I hoped that we would simply be faster than he was but it wasn't that easy with a zombie husband, a knife, a shoe and some keys between my teeth. Before I knew it, he was stretching out his hands and grabbing at my top, he was bloody strong for a pensioner. I flailed about, trying to wriggle free of his zealous clutches but it was no good. I let go of Martin and put the key in his hand.

"Go open up," I ordered.

He looked at me quizzically and then his face fell blank. "Martin, will you go and open the restaurant door?" I screamed at him.

He flinched at my barking tone and ambled away. I swung around to face the old zombie fellow.

"Oh no, you don't, we've got brains to cook," I yelled.

I lifted up my leg and kicked as hard as I could. I was impressed with my moves; I briefly considered taking up some kind of martial art. Maybe. Probably not. He staggered backwards, his feet off balance. The blade of the knife glinted in the darkness; it was too much of a real weapon. I glanced at my other hand and selected the silly shoe instead, and I cracked him in the head with it. He was down at once. I was getting good at this. I tried to yank the heel back out of his head and, to my intense glee, his brain was attached. I was proving to be something of a natural at this zombie slaying business.

Martin still faffed with the bunch of keys, he couldn't remember which one it was. I gave him the shoe-brain combo to hold as I frantically tried to unlock the door. I could sense more of them. I could hear their dreary moans and groans. I looked up and they were arriving in drones.

"Shit," I hissed, the panic was creeping in. I'd never be able to fight off this amount of them.

Finally, I felt the lock turn and I bundled us inside.

"Time to prep," I demanded, pointing to the kitchen.

Martin was at home there, he even brought me his chef whites.

"Seriously? We haven't got time to get changed," I snorted. Still, he held out his jacket.

I rolled my eyes and helped him into it. I dashed into the kitchen, switched on the lights and the ovens. He set to work, finding his ingredients and I, cautiously, opened the back door. It looked empty in the alley way; the zombies had been attracted by the light of the restaurant and they had all assembled around the front. I could hear them knocking on the windows. I seized a meat cleaver and took the knife again. I ran, out into the dark streets. I could see a couple of late night revelers about to meet their impending doom. I hid in the shadows and it was only seconds before they were attacked, hungry desperate hands and mouths upon them.

"I think you'll find that's mine," I said, smacking the feeding duo over the head with the meat cleaver and pulling the brains and intestines and lord only knows what the other things were, from them. My fingers delved inside and I ripped out their hearts, this was no time for squeamishness. I darted back to the restaurant and plonked the organs down on the work surface. Martin looked especially delighted by the hearts. He nodded thoughtfully and opted for red wine and sage as culinary bedfellows. He was having the time of his life.

"Locally sourced," I teased, with a wink.

It was time to open up for the late night special shift. I armed myself with the fire extinguisher and, as my hands opened the door, I could only hope that wasn't the last thing that I ever did. I whipped it open quickly and stood behind it, watching them file through. To my utter astonishment, they found tables and seated themselves on the chairs. Some picked up the napkins and folded them over their laps. Loyal customers indeed, I thought, emerging from my hiding place and beaming my best hostess smile.

"Money, please," I asked, my palm held out.

I went round them all. They merrily emptied their pockets until mine were bulging. I daydreamed about a holiday in the sun as I counted it all out and stashed it in the till. Martin appeared with plates full of delicate little zombie treats, so exquisitely presented. He had created dainty brain canapés, garnished with sprigs of mint and a little coriander. I served intestine pâté on what might have been a toasted kidney cracker. I watched them as they embellished their meals with salt and pepper and parmesan. Martin got an appreciative round of applause for the heart in herby red wine jus.

I hugged him once they had left, he had impressed me with his inventiveness and his customers had left feeling well fed and thoroughly satisfied.

"Happy anniversary, darling," I whispered into his ear, "same time tomorrow?"

Laura Huntley is a published writer of short stories, flash fiction and poetry. She has won several writing competitions with her teeny tiny kooky stories and is now attempting to write longer fiction. She is a high heel shoe addict, biased mother of three phenomenal superstar children, nosey neighbour, chatterbox and fan of all things horror. Laura is happiest when writing twisted tales of oddball characters, late into the night. She would like to be a novelist, if she ever grows up and stops being distracted by pretty much everything on the internet. That, or a vampire, she hasn't quite decided yet.

Window Watching
by Joseph Jude

"Goodnight."

Sylvia nodded to him as he walked out. The goofy student with long hair and glasses who always stayed until the last minute was leaving early tonight. That meant that, most likely, Sylvia could leave early too and catch the 8:00 train instead of waiting fifteen minutes later for the next one. There was nobody else in the Learning Resource Center. It was a good possibility that nobody else would show up.

"Maybe I'll be able to catch CSI on time."

Sylvia stepped out from behind the desk and wandered the center. Even though she could leave a few minutes early, she still had a good hour to kill. She walked around, shutting off the copy machine and printers, turning off some of the lights, essentially going through all her procedures for closing the LRC at night, a little at a time.

Running her hands through her short curly hair, Sylvia walked from the main lobby of the center, down the one hallway which led to the other hallway where the individual computer labs were, four in all. She had already closed up two of them, and was now going to lock up a third. The last she would close right before she left. She strolled into the third lab, straightening all the chairs that had been pulled away from the PC desks and left all over the room. She looked around for anything that was out of place or left behind. She started closing and locking the windows, but stopped to stare for a minute. The LRC was on the sixth floor and the view of the city homes was nice. The sun had just gone down, but the sky still had a tint of blue. The houses, stores, and buildings stretched out before her.

Intrigued enough, Sylvia trotted back to her desk and took out her binoculars from the bottom drawer. A while back, she found herself staring out all the windows of the labs for long stretches of time, and decided that a pair of high powered binoculars was in order. Now, she rushed back to the third lab, and pulled out one of the chairs to sit in. She placed the eyepieces up against the lenses of her glasses. Like always, she found it uncomfortable. When she took her glasses off to replace them with the binoculars, she cursed herself. She'd just remembered the optometrist appointment that she forgot to make, again.

She knew she should just go back to the desk and write it down on a post-it so she didn't overlook it anymore, but had just sat down to look out the window and wasn't up for running back to the desk again.

"Make sure to remember to write it down when you go back, dummy."

She held the binoculars up to her eyes, scanning the landscape. As she adjusted the lens, she thought about her eye problems a little more.

"Was it nearsighted or farsighted? You always get 'em mixed up."

She searched the buildings facing her for anything of curiosity. She was pretty familiar with the scene by now, but she always discovered something new; a church with interesting architecture, a person doing something peculiar.

"You're nearsighted. You can only see things near."

She seemed pretty sure of herself. Sometimes, for whatever reason, she imagined the two words were used to describe the opposite. Hence, nearsighted meant you couldn't see things near. She couldn't understand why she had such a problem with those terms.

"Hmmm"

She focused in on a row of old warehouses, skimming across them. Only plain buildings. Nothing to hold her attention too long. She was surprised to find one that actually was an anvil factory.

"Look out for coyotes."

90

She was hoping to see somebody up to something. More often than not she spied people necking on a street corner for extended periods of time. She'd also caught a few hookers earning their bucks. She recalled one time that she observed two guys in a fist fight, seemingly over some girl that watched from the corner. They went at it for almost an hour. Sylvia had to leave to help a student, and when she returned, they were still going at it. Finally, the less bloody of the two walked off with the girl, while the other guy stumbled away alone. That is, after a couple of minutes of searching for what she assumed were his teeth. Odd how many people conducted their romantic business out in the open for the entire world to see.

"Show offs."

She panned up past the roofs and noticed something else entirely.

"What the heck!"

It was something she'd never seen before, and it certainly wasn't romantic. In fact, it took her a couple minutes of staring to make it out clearly, or rather conclude that she was indeed seeing what she was seeing.

It was large, bigger than a man. She could tell because it had a man in its clutches on the roof with it. It was some kind of animal, although it was bipedal. It sat on the edge of the roof holding some guy tight while it dug its teeth into his neck and ripped out big meaty chunks. It was green. It looked reptilian, with a long beaklike snout that revealed large fangs. It had ears like a bat and wings folded up behind its back.

"This can't be right. I'm seeing things."

Sylvia trembled, trying to decide what to do. She could barely hold the binoculars still enough to keep it in sight.

"I should call security. I should call the cops. What do I tell them? Say a gargoyle just climbed down off some church and grabbed a guy to eat? I need a camera. I don't have a camera. If I leave, it might not be there when I get back. Maybe I should just watch it, see where it goes. Then I can call security."

It was chomping into the dead man's stomach now. It was mostly hidden in the dark. However, Sylvia was able to make out enough detail.

"I'm not seeing this. I'm watching a regular man kill someone and my mind can't handle it. That's it. I should call the cops. Tell them there's someone being killed on um, um, whatever street that is. They have to send a car or something. Let them see it for themselves."

She was just about to look away to try to find a street sign, when it did something new that made her blood freeze.

It looked right at her.

Past all the houses and buildings, over at least fifty miles, it caught wind that somebody was watching it, and stared right into her eyes. She could see the red dots glowing from the dark pits above its muzzle. Sylvia looked into it, not sure what to do, her mouth fluttering but no sounds coming out.

Suddenly it threw its dinner behind it, into the blackness, and started for her.

"Oh my-SHIT!"

Bounding from rooftop to rooftop, at a feverish, atrocious pace, it galloped on its hands and feet. Occasionally, it stretched its massive wings to assist the jumps and glides over the large gaps. Sylvia watched it as it approached, constantly adjusting the focus on her binoculars and trying to keep her eyes on it. She had to adjust her line of vision as it hopped up and down, sometimes dropping out of view altogether behind a structure, only to leap back into view a second later, now on top of the structure and ever closer.

Despite its movements, it never seemed to stop looking directly at her. The two red eyes glowed brighter, the closer it was.

"Holy Geez, it's coming for me! It's coming right for me!"

Sylvia didn't know what to do. She was glued to the sight. Soon, she recognized the buildings it was charging over as places she personally passed. That's when she realized how much time she'd wasted watching it rush towards her. She dropped the binoculars and put her glasses on, and was able to see it. It was heading right for her. It would be at that window in a matter of a few more rooftops.

"Oh no! Oh no! Oh no!"

Sylvia fell backwards in her chair. She tried moving fast, but was tripping over herself. She rushed for the door to the hallway, expecting to hear the shattering of glass any second. She ran out of the room, slamming the door behind her. She ran through the hallways to the front lobby and waited, bracing herself at the desk.

Then she heard it: an explosion of brick and metal. It was a gargantuan, ridiculous commotion from inside the third lab. She covered her head in her arms. She was too afraid to think of anything else.

The noise died down. Slowly, she lifted her head again to look at the hall, expecting that thing to roar out any second.

She watched.

Nothing came.

Then she became conscious that it wasn't the sound of glass shattering that she heard. It sounded more like a wall collapsing. Actually, much of the noise was unusually muffled for something going on in the next room.

Cautiously, Sylvia stepped away from the front desk. She took one deliberate step at a time to the end the first hallway, until the door to the third lab was in view. She couldn't make out anything through the glass window on the door.

She quietly walked to the door and then leaned her ear against it, hearing nothing.

She turned the knob and pushed the door open.

Inside was a mess. Chairs, tables and computers were shattered and spread out along the floor. Light fixtures were handing by a few wires while some were totally liberated from the ceiling. The left wall had seemingly collapsed in and was now a pile of rubble. A small hole was visible that let air in from the outside world and a few windows were indeed shattered, but not from anything coming through it.

Sylvia saw the thing, buried under the rubble of the left wall. One of its arms stood out, clearly covered in dust and dried blood. She could also see patches of skin under the broken cinderblock and plaster. Following along with her eyes, she eventually found its mouth peeking out of some debris, reddish black blood pouring out of it.

It wasn't moving. The amount of blood exiting it convinced Sylvia that it was the creature's own. If it wasn't dead, it was out.

"It missed. It missed the window."

Pretty much entirely. Sylvia lightly ran out of the lab just in case it wasn't as lifeless as it seemed. She went to the desk, and picked up the phone. She called the downstairs security desk, telling them that an intruder had broken in and that they should come up and possibly call the police.

When she hung up the phone, she continued to think about how it could've possibly missed the window. Sure it was coming fast and furious, but it seemed to have her zeroed in very accurately. At least when it was almost fifty miles away.

"Nearsighted, Farsighted."

As she waited for security, she jotted down on a post-it note a reminder to call the optometrist.

Joseph Jude is a writer, filmmaker, and painter. He has a BFA from the University of the Arts in Philadelphia, and he is a winner of the Spokane Film Festival Drama Award for his short, Lip Service. He also has had work appear in the Aphrodite Gallery, AngelCiti International Film and Music Market, and has been published in magazines and E-zines such as Death's Head Grin, Nth Degree, Wink, Aphelion, cc&d Magazine, Down in the Dirt, *and* Poetry.COM, *and in collections such as* A Time To Be Free, *and* Time After Time.

Ruby
by Jon Michael Kelley

The day Ruby went missing was occasioned appropriately with sodden skies and a dreary, almost forlorn disposition; a grayness that extended all the way downward to the gutters running fast and full along the Institute's sea-blanched facade. And so shocked was I that, when initially calling out for my assistant, only a papery gasp issued forth. Successive attempts eventually produced a hoarse but hearable plea, and Miss Petticourt appeared forthwith, wide-eyed in the doorway.

She'd stopped just short of fully crossing the threshold, reticent to venture farther until the situation was assessed, and the safety of her progression guaranteed.

"Ruby's gone," I said, fighting back tears.

Miss Petticourt fixed her attention immediately upon the room's two-hundred gallon aquarium. Her expression turned from frightened to utterly annoyed. "Escaped? Again?" she said, then shook her head. "Crafty little cuss, that one." Then – suddenly remembering the recent safeguards I'd finally employed to staunch such occurrences – she looked at me, astonished. "But, sir, *how*?"

"Not an escape, this time," I assured her, "–but a larceny!"

Miss Petticourt looked quite taken aback. "Who, pray tell, would want to abscond with your bloody, ill-tempered, octopus?"

Ruby was not, as my daft assistant alleged, "ill-tempered". She was just … patiently determined. Her name came by way of a popular American song made famous by Kenny Rogers and the First Edition. The song, if you'll indulge me one moment, is about a paralyzed war veteran and his woman, Ruby, stepping out on him, and not for the first time; "taking her love to town", if one is to believe the lyrics. Although Ruby the octopus didn't get her name because of such lasciviousness, I can't let pass without mention the very real possibility that her previous attempts at

95

freedom weren't to satisfy such desires. After all, she's only going to successfully mate once in her lifetime. Then die.

Better odds, I might add, than I give Miss Petticourt.

Was it love that inspired Ruby's determination? Despite octopuses having three hearts, I hardly think so. They're way smarter than that. Besides, what has love got to do with procreation?

But to finish explaining the reason for naming her as I did: on the second day of her captivity, that folksy album happened to be on the phonograph, and when that aforementioned song began playing, the shy octopus finally eased out from under her rocky shelter in the aquarium and attached two pairs of appendages to the facing glass, while allowing the other two pairs to buoy unconcernedly in the water, as if she were 'channeling' the music, the tempo, and swaying accordingly. Then she began blushing with the rhythm, an arterial redness pulsing across her otherwise whitish skin, and in perfect cadence with the beat. Whether she was purposefully imitating the true color of a ruby, or was passionately empathizing with the song's enraged protagonist, I can't be certain. You see, I stopped thinking of octopuses as merely clever creatures years ago, and have since come to realize them as being highly intelligent, and uniquely cunning.

There again, the pulsing redness could have simply been a deimatic display, something cephalopods do to ward off predators – though I hardly think myself or Kenny Rogers and his band threatening enough to encourage such a demonstration.

And while we're there, I should note that Ruby was quite adept at mimicry, as most octopuses are, putting to shame even the most practiced chameleon. In fact, Ruby's gift at imitation surpassed her species' customary levels and approached something I would call – *if I were so inclined to use the term* – supernatural.

Not so much that she could simulate her own disappearance, but...

So, "Ruby" it was to be. Miss Petticourt thought the name absurd, of course, but I don't pay her to think.

And how, you might ask, did I know I was dealing with a female of the species? That: how does one even know where to begin looking under such a seemingly undefined spillage of limbs?

Well, the way to find out is not quite that conventional. But trust me, sexing an octopus isn't as hard as one might think. And if all else fails, trust the animal's disposition, as it will, more times than not, lead you to realizing its true gender.

In fact, that is how I came to discover that Miss Petticourt was, for the most part, female, as she once referred to Ruby as a "tentacled Houdini", prompting me to correct that common misunderstanding by explaining that only certain cuttlefish and squid have "tentacles", or "bothria", as I insist they be called here at the Institute, thereby inciting Miss Petticourt to counter with a contemptuous expression only the female of her species can effectively produce.

Not an air so much of disdain, I should amend, but of *jealousy*.

Besides gender, Ruby and Miss Petticourt share one other characteristic: both have blue blood. Well, Ruby actually has blue blood coursing through her veins, whereas Miss Petticourt only acts like she does, but I feel it's worth mentioning.

I strode over to the aquarium, and tugged at the fastened lock for emphasis. "You see," I said, "her cage is locked, yet Ruby is gone." I shook my finger, careful to not yet point it in anyone's direction. "This can only mean that someone knew the whereabouts of the key's hiding place."

Although her expression remained firm, Miss Petticourt had begun a mild wringing of her hands; slowly, carefully, as if reallocating the sediment of an earlier applied balm or lotion.

An act of simple contemplation, I wondered, or of manifest guilt?

Then her eyes narrowed ever so slightly; her tone low, but threatening. "Careful where you're heading, Professor."

I met her scowl likewise. "There's only two people who know the whereabouts of that key, and I'm looking at the other. So, you can come clean, confess your sins, and I might take some pity on you. Employment is a hard thing to find these days," I reminded her, "as would be a letter recommending your talents, glowing or otherwise."

Indignant, chin up, Miss Petticourt became even more erect. "Very well then. She made me do it. Ruby, that ... that *sorceress*."

"Made you do ... what?"

"She imitated me. Behind the glass. At first I thought it was my own distorted reflection – but then I saw those eight arms balled up beneath her, and ... and it changed, my expression. *Her* expression, one of stark befuddlement, then onward to freeze in gaping horror! Sir, she mimicked my own death mask!"

I didn't tell the poor dear that Ruby didn't likely have to go to any extra lengths to achieve such a countenance.

"That sounds a bit preposterous," I said, though it didn't really. We were, after all, referring to Ruby's skills.

Miss Petticourt had begun trembling by then, an affliction that seemed embarrassingly incongruous to her otherwise bold persona. "A death mask, sir!" she repeated. "My own face behind the glass, staring back, appearing ... drowned!" She drew an arm to her mouth, and gasped. "It was a warning! What, what else could it have been?"

"A warning?" I asked suspiciously. "Warning you from what?"

There was more of that hand-wringing as her eyes darted to random points on the floor. "My emotions, of course," she said finally. "Ruby knew I'd taken a ... a fancy to you, sir."

This I had not seen coming. But I hid my surprise, and finally asked, "Where is she now, Miss Petticourt? Where is Ruby?"

Staring down at her feet, Miss Petticourt said, "Gone, sir, I'm afraid. I took her down to the beach, and eased her gently into a nice tide pool."

"Eased her into a tide pool," I asked, "or onto a salad fork?"

Miss Petticourt quickly looked up, aghast. "Granted, we weren't the best of friends, but I wouldn't have steamed her up!"

"All right, for argument's sake, let's say I believe you. My other question would be then: How did you manage to get such a large, slippery and most evasive creature out of her enclosure?"

"Why, it was no chore at all, sir," explained Miss Petticourt. "After I unlocked the lid, she shimmied right up the glass and into my arms."

"Now I know you're lying."

Her upper class accent had splintered now, becoming more a Cockney one. "On me mother's grave, sir, I swear it. Just plopped right into me arms, pleased as peas, and off we went, down to the beach!"

It was a feeble attempt, but I had to smile in spite of myself. Knowing now that Miss Petticourt was nurturing feelings for me had softened the blow of Ruby's abduction. But I was still determined to find the truth.

"Miss Petticourt, I should remind you that I've dealt with cephalopods for a very long time, and I can assure you that no such antics took place!"

"Oh, very well then," she sighed, shoulders sagging, the weight of it all having finally become too much. "I muscled her into a pillow case, and tossed her into the shark tank."

It took three volunteers and nearly half a day to rescue Ruby from the sharks. But she'd managed quite well to keep them at bay, and I imagine it had something to do with her impersonation of a certain assistant of mine.

But I let her go, in the end. Ruby, that is. With Miss Petticourt's help, I had finally realized that Ruby the octopus had become, to me anyway, more than just another exhibit at the Institute.

Miss Petticourt, on the other hand, is still with me, and has become well-known to the staff for her sober avoidance of all areas where cephalopods are kept.

She's quicker with the tea, as well.

Jon Michael Kelley's fiction has appeared in such magazines and anthologies as Chiral Mad, Tales of Terror and Mayhem, Evil Jester Digest II, Father Grim's Storybook, *and many others. His novel* Seraphim *was released this past summer by Evil Jester Press to a flurry of favorable reviews.*

Deadbeat
by John Lance

The intercom on James Royal's desk buzzed. "A Mr. Bernard Mattick to see you sir," Heloise announced.

"Don't be ridiculous, Heloise, Bernie died of a heart attack two weeks ago," James snapped.

"Hey, hey! Jimmy old boy!" a familiar voice yelled.

James looked up to see Bernie Mattick, or at least, someone who was the spitting image of Bernie Mattick, standing in his office. If he was an actor, he not only had Bernie's look down, but his mannerisms as well, right down to Bernie's mischievous grin. He was dressed in an expensive blue suit that looked an awful lot like the one Bernie had been buried in.

"Heloise, I told you that I was not to be disturbed this afternoon," James growled at the intercom, his anger barely held in check. He was going to need a new secretary. James Royal did not believe in second chances.

"Yes sir. I know sir. That's what I told Mr. Mattick. He must have left because he's no longer waiting."

"No, Heloise, he's here in my office."

"But, that's impossible," Heloise gasped.

"If I had a competent secretary, it would be," James snarled before switching off the intercom.

"Don't be too hard on the girl, Jimmy. She couldn't have stopped me if she had tried."

James picked up the phone. "I'm calling security. I suggest you leave before they get here."

"Oh, I don't think they'll have any more luck then your secretary did," replied Bernie. With three long strides Bernie was standing in the middle of James's desk. Not on top of it, not beside it, but literally in the middle with the desktop cutting him in half right through his ample stomach.

101

James slowly put down the phone. His hand brushed Bernie's side and a cold shiver ran up his arm.

James was a stout atheist who found the notion of a god or devil ridiculous. He had always secretly believed that there might, just might, be ghosts. So while some people would have questioned their sanity and general health at the sight of Bernie Mattick, James Royal was not one of them. Indeed, being the fast thinking cross examiner he was James did what he did best, which was immediately adapt to this new set of circumstances.

"So, you're a ghost now, Bernie?" James asked.

"Apparently," replied Bernie. "Isn't this something?" he asked pointing down at the desk. "I haven't quite figured out how it works. Like why I don't drop through the floor or why I still have to take the elevator to get up to your office. It's probably just a matter of practice."

"Bernie, what are you doing here?" asked James.

"I need a lawyer. They're trying to sue me," Bernie said.

"Someone is, was, always trying to sue you Bernie. You're going to have to be more specific than that," James replied.

"It's the Feds! They're threatening jail time as well!" Bernie exclaimed.

"That really doesn't seem like a problem given your current condition," James observed.

"I don't know, Jimmy, they're the ones that brought me back to begin with. They got some Voodoo priest to do it. What if he's also got a spell that can keep me in prison? I'm too pretty to do time."

"Well, Bernie, if you're going to bilk people out of hundreds of millions of dollars, it seems like you have to be prepared for these eventualities." James did not add that at least one of those millions had belonged to him. If Bernie hadn't had a heart attack when the Feds came to arrest him, James had little doubt that several hit men would have been hired to do the job. James might have even pursued that option himself and considered it money well spent.

Bernie laughed. "I thought you had to have morals in order to be self-righteous, Jimmy." Bernie paused and then added, "You know, the Feds haven't found all the money."

James sat very still, like a cat watching a mouse.

"There are still plenty of foreign bank accounts and other assets that someone with the right name and passwords could own," Bernie said. "But, if you don't think your firm is interested…" Bernie turned and started to walk toward the door.

"How much?" James asked.

"You know the amount they say I embezzled?" Bernie asked.

"Yes?"

"They're off by about two zeroes. And they'll never even find a fraction of it."

James broke into a smile. "Let's see what we can do for you."

When Royal Law Offices, one of the most elite law firms in New York announced that it would be representing Bernie Mattick in his upcoming trial, James' phone began ringing night and day with reporters wanting interviews. Bloggers wrote incredibly nasty things about him. The windbag pundits on the television and radio were apoplectic with gibbering, incoherent, outrage.

James loved it.

Still, just because the firm had taken on the case didn't mean that James had a plan as to how to pursue it.

He summoned his top two lieutenants to his office. This sent a shudder through the entire firm as countless peons and low level associates whispered and debated the significance of the meeting. Whenever the "unholy trinity" got together something momentous was about to occur.

"You're thinking settlement?" asked Mike Peterson. Of the two junior partners he had been with the firm the longest and dreamed of one day adding his name to the front door of what would then be Peterson and Royal Law Offices (alphabetization being the most logical approach for the ordering of the names).

James, who had no intention of adding any more names to the door, shook his head. "No. Bernie doesn't want to do any time and I don't think the Feds are in a generous mood. We're going to have to go to trial."

"It's going to be a hard sell, convincing a judge that Mr. Mattick is the wronged party here. After all, he embezzled millions for decades and was only found out because the entire world went into a recession that he helped precipitate," said Laura Zarnowski, who, while junior to Mike in years at the firm, was older and had more experience and therefore felt that Zarnowski and Royal Law Offices had a certain ring to it (reverse alphabetical order being all the rage in ordering of names).

"Oh I don't know," Mike said, "If there's one thing in the world people distrust more than greedy bankers, it's their own government. There's probably some scandal brewing down in Washington right now that'll prove our point. And if not, I'm sure we can manufacture one. What about what's-his-name on the House Budget Sub-committee. He's got a few skeletons and I hear he's being represented by Wade, Whiley, and Wicker now. We don't owe him anything."

"Let's wait on that for now," said James. Turning to Laura, he asked, "So, where do we begin our defense?"

Laura looked skeptical. "Obviously there aren't any exact precedents. I suppose we could have some of the estate planners look at it."

James nodded. "Good idea Laura. Mike, we want to get out there and start winning hearts and minds. Show this was all a large misunderstanding. Things just got out of hand. Do we know anyone on the talk show circuit?"

"Sure. How about something soft, like one of the morning shows?"

"Perfect…"

Laura, still focused on the tactical side of the defense, said, "I wonder if there would be some precedent in the extradition and rendition laws?"

"It's worth a look," said James.

"Don't forget about *habeas corpus*!" chimed in Bernie.

The three lawyers looked up at Bernie who was floating above them.

"I told you this was a private meeting," said James.

"I know Jimmy, but…"

"Please leave," said James.

"Oh, fine." Bernie melted through the ceiling.

"Is he gone?" asked Laura.

"I think so," said Mike.

"That is going to be a problem," said James.

The others nodded. Nothing was worse then a client that took an active interest in his own defense.

"Pssst, Jimmy, wake up."

James's opened his bleary eyes. Looking through Bernie's semitransparent gut to his alarm clock he could see that it was 2:22 AM. Not that it was a surprise. Bernie had been turning up in James's house at roughly 2:00 AM every morning since he had engaged the services of Royal Law Offices.

Of course, Bernie had been notorious for late night phone calls when he had been alive. It was just now he came to see James in person, which felt a hell of a lot worse for some reason.

"Bernie, it's two in the morning. Again," growled James as he turned on the light.

"So?"

"So I was sleeping."

"Oh. You know, you were a lot more fun at Harvard when we used to do coke and stay up all night. Remember those days?"

"Not really," James said with complete honesty.

"Anyway, I've been thinking about the case. I've got some more ideas for my defense."

"Bernie, you're in good hands. The strategy for your defense is all set. We just have to wait for the trial. Isn't there someplace else you could go?"

"What do you mean?"

"Well, what do other ghosts do at two in the morning?"

"I don't think there are any other ghosts. At least I haven't met any yet."

"What about visiting other people? How about going to see your wife?"

"You mean my widow? That's how Elvira is referring to herself these days, as 'the very merry widow.' She refuses to

105

acknowledge me. She says she signed on 'until death do us part' and now that it has she's planning on enjoying what remains of my fortune. Apparently that means sleeping with every young stud she can find. Do you think she was doing that when I was alive?"

James shrugged his shoulders, but that didn't mean he didn't have an opinion.

James reached back into his encyclopedic memory for the names of other spouses. Royal Law Offices had handled all of Bernie's divorces. "What about Helen? Or Jazell."

"Please, that's like me asking you about your ex-wives, what's-her-name, the blonde, and whose-er-face, the brunette. Do you still talk to them?"

"Not civilly," James conceded.

"I see you're not making any progress in that area either," James nodded toward the empty half of James's king-sized bed.

"Oh no, I am not going to discuss romance and women with you, Bernie. You are a client, and we're going to take care of you and win your case. But you have to let me sleep if I'm going to represent you effectively."

"Oh, sure, but I did have those thoughts…"

"Then you'll have to send me a memo in the morning. Good night, Bernie."

Bernie looked like he was going to argue some more, then gave up. "Fine, I'll see you in the morning Jimmy." With a sigh he turned and drifted out the window.

James watched him go. He waited five minutes to be certain the ghost had really left. Sometimes Bernie came back. When he was confident the ghost was gone, James picked up his phone and dialed.

"Hello, Judge Stone? James Royal here, yes, I do realize the time, I apologize for the lateness of the hour, but this is rather urgent. I was wondering if we can move up the Mattick trial. Uh huh. Well, how about tomorrow?"

Despite James's wheedling and (minimal) begging, the trial did not start for another two days, meaning James had to endure two more nights of visits from Bernie. Yet eventually he and Bernie found themselves in the courtroom. John Garrison, the federal prosecutor, looked smugly confident as he unloaded several impressively thick files onto his table.

"Shouldn't you have more files?" Bernie asked.

"No, we don't need files. Just remain calm," James replied.

"Easy for you to say, you're not looking at hundreds of years of jail time," Bernie fidgeted and added, "I still think we should have gone with a jury. Look at this face. Who could convict this face?" Bernie gave James what he thought was an endearing smile.

"Just about any American who has read a paper in the last three months," James replied. "Don't worry, I've got a plan."

The bailiff appeared and announced, "All rise. The honorable Judge Stone is presiding."

Judge Stone quickly mounted the stairs and took her seat behind the bench. James knew Judge Stone well. The meticulously compiled dossier that Mike had given James told him that she was a serious judge who disliked the media circus that most courtrooms had become. Still, she had allowed cameras into the courtroom for this trial because she felt the public deserved to be informed of the proceedings. Difficult as it was to swallow, James thought Judge Stone really believed that.

Mike's dossier also included at least one embarrassing secret that could wreak untold havoc on the judge's personal and professional lives if it fell into the wrong hands, hands such as Mike's. Still, James had decided to win the case legitimately. If that failed, there was always Mike's way.

Eyeing the cameras befouling her courtroom, Judge Stone tapped her gavel and said, "All right, let's get started."

James stood up and announced, "Your honor, we move that the case be dismissed outright so that we can save the taxpayers some of their hard earned money."

Garrison smirked and absentmindedly fingered one of his thick folders. He obviously felt prepared to counter any motion that James was about to make.

Still, James was pretty sure this motion had not occurred to Garrison.

"On what grounds?" asked Judge Stone. She looked less than enthusiastic about the gamesmanship that had already kicked off in her courtroom.

"On the grounds of separation of church and state, your honor," James replied.

Out of the corner of his eye James saw Garrison's smirk fall away.

Even more important, Judge Stone perked up. She was a constitutionalist at heart and James knew his argument would interest her.

James continued, "Your honor, by using Voodoo to bring Mr. Mattick, a devout Christian, back from the dead, the government has turned religion into a weapon against the citizenry. What are the limits of a government that can summon its citizens back from eternal bliss to account for unpaid parking tickets?" James's speech continued for another twenty minutes. It was filled with soaring rhetoric and nice succinct sound bites that would play well on the 6 o'clock news.

When James finished, Garrison leapt to his feet and loudly protested the motion. He argued that Bernie was unique and that the case was about justice for his victims. But James could tell from Judge Stone's eyes that he had won.

It took the judge half an hour of deliberation to return her decision and throw the case out. Garrison again protested and threatened appeal, but James wasn't worried.

James basked in the cameras and attention on the steps of the courthouse. This, he thought, was what it's all about.

"The judge's verdict was just and right," James said. "But justice has hardly been served. Mr. Mattick's civil rights have been violated and we plan to sue the government for resurrecting Mr. Mattick and interrupting his eternal rest." The cameras snapped. The reporters gabbled. James smiled and smiled.

"Psst, Jimmy."

James opened one eye. 2:06 AM.

"Will you put me on the stand? I've always wanted to take the stand. Hey, what's that smell?"

"Garlic," muttered James, eyeing the cloves he had strung around the window and headrest.

"That's odd, what's it doing in your bedroom? And when did you start wearing a cross necklace? I thought you were an atheist."

"I am. Look Bernie, I told you, you have to stop visiting me at home. You are a client, not a friend."

Bernie laughed, "Always the kidder." Then Bernie got serious. "Look Jimmy, I have no place to go and an eternity of hanging out before me. The wives don't want to talk to me. The kids don't want to see me. Hell, I can't even get laid. What else am I going to do?"

"Just one night off, Bernie, ok? I have an important case tomorrow. And no showing up at my office either, I don't want you spooking the clients again."

Bernie smiled, "Oh, all right Jimmy. But tomorrow night it's an all night party session like the old days, ok?"

"Sure thing Bernie," James said.

Bernie floated out the window.

James waited five minutes. Then he picked up his phone. "Hey Garrison. Yea, I know what time it is, sorry about that. But the good news is, I want to offer you a settlement. We'll reduce our demands from a 100 million to 10 million if you can get that Voodoo priest to send Bernie back. He's ready for a rest. When? Is tomorrow good for you? Great. Oh, one last thing, Bernie may not be there but he has authorized me to have the ceremony performed in absentia, that won't be a problem, will it? Didn't think so, see you in the morning. "

James hung up and lay back down to catch a last few hours of sleep. He dreamed of cameras, spotlights, and long nights of uninterrupted sleep.

John Lance has had stories appear in the anthologies Wolfsongs, Wolfsongs 2, All About Eve, A Taste of Armageddon, *and others. He has also written two picture books:* Priscilla Holmes, Ace Detective *and* Priscilla Holmes and the Case of the Glass Slipper, *a collection of short stories,* Bobby's Troll and

Other Stories, *and a young adult book* Charlotte Cauldron and the Prince of Nevermore. *His blog is at www.johnmlance.com.*

Jake Blossom, Pixie Detective
by Ken MacGregor

Jake pushed himself to his hands and knees and spat blood on the floor.

"Hit him again, Victor," Grady said without inflection. Victor kicked Jake in the ribs; he also kicked him in the hip, the leg and the head. Victor had big feet. Jake flew across the room, though not the way he usually did. He didn't think he'd be doing much flying anytime soon, the way his wings felt. He could even see part of the left one, bent over his shoulder. That was probably not a good sign. Jake hit the far wall and slid down, still conscious. Another hit like that was going to put him out, though.

"Once more, I think, Victor," Grady said.

"Hang on," Jake said. Even his voice sounded broken. He managed to hold up a hand. The right one. His left arm hung limp across his body. The thug looked at Grady, who shook his head once. Victor stepped back from Jake, close enough to kick him, in case Grady changed his mind.

"I'm listening."

Once more, Jake got up, mentally taking inventory of his body. He'd heal, and pretty quick, too, but this was going to hurt for days. He looked at Grady. Here was a man you had to respect, even if you hated him. Grady was polished. He radiated calm and self-assurance. This guy was a gentleman bad-ass. Jake threw a quick glance at Victor. He couldn't be less like Grady: huge, coarse, smelly and mean. It was his nature; he was a troll. Of course he, too was a bad-ass. Jake had just found that out the hard way. He looked back at Grady.

"I'm getting there," he said. "I have some leads, but I've run into a couple snags. You gotta give me some more time."

"I am not a patient man, Jake. If you don't deliver soon, I will have to do something violent."

111

"Victor isn't violent?"

"Not by comparison, no."

"I'll deliver," Jake said. "Give me a week, and I should have it all wrapped up."

"You have five days. If you don't deliver by then, I shall be very disappointed."

"I guess I have no choice."

"Very astute. Come, Victor. There are others who require your talents this day."

Victor made a noise in his throat that sounded like a sledgehammer smashing boulders. Trolls: nature's scariest bipeds.

"See ya later, Victor," Jake said. "Come on back when you want another ass-kicking."

Victor ignored him. Jake wasn't surprised. It wasn't that funny. He stood up and flexed his aching muscles. He could feel the cracked ribs scraping. His left side was already turning into one big bruise. Both his wings were broken. So was his nose. He crossed the empty lobby, where he'd been ambushed by the two professional tough guys, to the stairs.

"This is what I get for working late," he said as he climbed the steps, wincing at the effort of getting his leg up each time. The stairs were half his height. This never bothered him before, because he never used the stairs; he always just flew up.

It took Jake seven minutes to get to the third floor. His leg muscles burned. He limped to his office door and opened it with the key, thankful he'd installed the lock closer to the floor. Higher up on the door, it said in what he thought looked like a very professional font, *Jake Blossom, Private Eye*. He went in and closed the door behind him. He sat at his miniature desk, opened a nip bottle and had several medicinal swallows from it.

Jake Blossom, Private Eye was a Pixie. He was just over two feet tall, had pointed ears and wings and, under the right circumstances could grant wishes.

"I wish I had some ice," he said. No ice magically appeared. Even if he'd actually been trying, a Pixie's wish wouldn't work on himself. He lay down on the middle cushion of the human-sized couch and was asleep in seconds. In his dream, Victor was Jake's height; Victor hit him again and again while

Grady played classical music on a purple violin. Next to him, Jake's girlfriend Lynette danced to the music. Victor's blows were a nice counterpoint, coming as they did off the beat. Lynette is Celtic for "pretty"; that was an understatement. In Jake's dream, Victor punched him again and again, though Jake couldn't feel it. That's kind of nice, he thought, and then: dreams are so weird. I really need to go see her.

When he woke up, Jake was so sore he could hardly move. But, his wings and his nose were straight again, and the bruise was more yellow than purple. Pixies are small, but tough. He splashed water on his face and straightened his slept-in clothes; he still looked like Hell. He flexed his wings. Yeah. They would carry him. Good. He had less than five days. He was gonna need his wings.

Jake flew down the stairs, out the open front door and into the sunshine. The weather was lovely, people were smiling and he could hear the sounds of children laughing. Hard to believe this was the same city in which he got his ass kicked by a Troll less than ten hours ago.

"Every city has its dark underbelly," Jake muttered, "I spend way too much time there." He headed toward the park, dreading what he had to do next. He had been avoiding this for three weeks, with good reason. Victor was scary, but he had nothing on Lynette.

Lynette was at her tree, of course. She always was; it wasn't like she had a choice. She was a Dryad, and couldn't be more than ten feet from her tree without suffering horrible pain and guilt. Which made her an excellent girlfriend, because Jake always knew where to find her, and she never came around when she wasn't wanted. Of course, she never came around when she was wanted either, so it was a mixed blessing.

"Hey, gorgeous," she said, stepping out of the tree as if it were made of air.

For a moment, Jake thought maybe she was no longer mad, but then she gut-punched him.

"Oof!"

"You got a lot of damn nerve showing your face at my tree."

"Jesus, Lyn! That hurt," Jake said

"Not as much as what you did."

"She used magic! It's not like I cheated on you..."

"You most certainly did!" Lynette glared at Jake, daring him to contradict her.

"Not on purpose!"

Lynette stared at him, fuming. For once, he was smart enough to keep his mouth shut. After a while, her expression softened.

"You look like hell," she said. She was still pissed, but Jake was hurt. Lynette might not forgive him, but she still loved him.

"Thanks."

"Who'd you piss off this time?"

"Grady." Jake shrugged.

"Again?"

"Some habits are hard to break," Jake said. He smiled at her.

"One of these days, he's going to kill you. You know that, right?"

"I'm pretty hard to kill, sweetheart."

"Yeah," she said. "You are. It's part of your charm. Since you look like you can barely stand, can I assume you are here on business?"

"I'm afraid so, yeah."

"I'm tempted to forgive you," Lynette said, "but I think it may only be because I'm lonely."

"I'm lonely, too," Jake said.

"Yeah?"

"Yeah. You know I'm crazy about you, don't you?"

For a long time, Lynette just looked at Jake. Dryads were loyal by nature, and forgiving, too. This one was having a hard time letting go of her anger, but she did love him. And, it wasn't like he did it on purpose. And he was her Jake. Her Pixie in shining armor. Damn it.

"One of these days," Lynette said, "I'd like to see you ... socially." Jake grinned.

"Nice euphemism, Lyn. I'd *social* you right now if I wasn't so damn sore."

"What do you need, tough guy?"

"Grady is looking for a guy named Musky. He's human, but just barely. Musky used to run errands for Grady, mostly drugs and guns. Recently, he ran a large quantity of cash for Grady, but never made it to the drop. No one has seen him since he picked up the money. Grady hired me to track him down and bring him back, along with as much of the stolen loot as possible."

"All right. I'll see what I can do."

"Thanks, baby. You're a peach."

"Don't be crass. I'm a maple." Lynette slipped back into her tree. Jake sat down. He realized he had skipped breakfast. No help for it now. If he left to get food and missed her, she'd be pissed and wouldn't tell him anything.

Twenty-seven minutes later, Jake's stomach growled and Lynette stepped out.

"Hungry?" she said.

"For information."

"Hm. Well, here's what I've got: Musky has stayed off the streets, hiding in the woods. Which would be smart if it wasn't a Dryad trying to find you. He's just north of 23 by Warren and Nixon Roads."

"Is that Ann Arbor?"

"Barely. It's the outskirts. It's a patch of woods right by the highway, south of Warren, east of Nixon Road. I know that covers a lot of ground, so I'll have someone meet you at Nixon and Warren to let you know where he is when you get there."

"Have I told you I love you?"

"Not nearly enough," she said.

"I love you."

"I know. It's mutual. Got get him, Tiger." He kissed her; she tasted like maple syrup. He loved that. He went back for another taste.

Jake flew as fast as he could to Ann Arbor, which he always thought of as Ypsi's trendy big sister. Ann Arbor's like a popular kid - a cheerleader, maybe; Ypsi's the punk chick with a pierced smile who gives you the finger. Cute, but a little scary.

It was a nice town, filled with people who cared about it a lot. And people like Grady and the lowlifes he employed were hardly a blip on the radar. Besides, they just made it a more exciting place to live. Jake was almost there when he remembered he still hadn't eaten. He wouldn't have noticed if his belly hadn't cramped up. He dropped down to the strip mall on Plymouth Road and snagged the door to the diner as someone was coming out. They got bug-eyed when they saw him, but said nothing. Humans always seemed to forget that the Fae were real. Jake went in and stood on a stool at the counter, spreading his feet for balance. The stool spun a bit, but he stayed on.

"Help you?" the waitress said, not meeting his eyes.

"Yes, thank you. I'd like four scrambled eggs with cheddar, multi-grain toast with strawberry jam, a small glass of orange juice and coffee with cream and lots and lots of sugar."

"Must be hungry." Now she was looking at him.

"I forgot to eat. Bad habit." Two stools over, a little boy was staring at him. His mother told him it wasn't polite, but he kept right on.

"Hi, kid," Jake said.

"Are you a fairy?"

"Pixie. Common mistake."

"Cool," the boy said.

"Thanks. What are you? Nine?"

"Six."

"Ah. Common mistake." The boy smiled at him and Jake smiled back. His mother relaxed a little.

When Jake's food showed up, he devoured it. It was the best thing he'd ever tasted. He finished his coffee, handed the waitress a ten and told her to keep it.

"See you, kid," he said, flapping his wings and rising off the stool. The boy waved, agog at the small flying man.

Jake took off to find a dirtbag named Musky.

When he got to there, he was met by the ugliest dryad he'd ever seen. Most Dryads are heartbreaking in their beauty. Not this one. She was a mess. Skin falling off in strips. Missing one eye. Left arm exposed to the bone.

116

Jake knew her tree was sick or dying, but you didn't mention this sort of thing to Dryads. It was the height of bad form. So, Jake kept his expression blank, then smiled at her.

"I'm Jake Blossom. Lynette should have told you I was coming."

"She did." Her voice was faint. Hell, everything about her was faint. "I will take you to the human you seek."

"You will?" Jake forgot himself. "I mean..."

"I know what you mean. My tree is dead, and I am no longer bound. I am free to go wherever I choose." Never in his life had Jake heard someone say they were free with such profound sadness.

"I'm so sorry. I don't know what to say."

"Say nothing. Just keep up." She moved through the trees with speed and grace, feet barely tapping leaves, roots and dirt as she ran. If Jake had been on foot, he never could have kept up. She led him a quarter mile into the woods. He could hear the traffic on the highway, but not see it. The Dryad stopped several feet shy of a small clearing. Jake could make out the remains of a fire, a thermos, a saucepan and a sleeping bag with someone in it. Jake landed and turned to the Dryad.

"Thank you," he whispered. "Um..."

"Guinevere."

"That's lovely. You have been a huge help. Is there anything I can do to repay you?"

"Are you serious?"

"Yeah. Finding this guy and bringing him in will likely save my hide, so, yeah." Guinevere looked him in the eye for several seconds.

"Can you," she whispered, "fix my tree?"

"I don't know. But, I can try. This guy can wait a little longer. Take me to it."

She gave him a cautious smile and ran to the left. He flew after, hoping he wasn't about to disappoint her. This was a tall order, even for a Pixie. They got to her tree. It was a large, old, gnarled cherry with five main trunks. It had withstood lightning, termites and the better part of two centuries, but it was clearly dead now.

117

Jake landed on the ground and put his hands to the trunk. He could feel a lingering presence; trees this old take forever to die all the way, which explained why Guinevere was still kicking around. Which Jake had been counting on. Once a tree was all the way dead, just like any other living thing, you wouldn't want to bring it back. It's possible, of course, but a really bad idea. A really bad, stupid, dangerous idea. The Fae have an expression: if it's all the way dead, leave it the hell alone. It sounds prettier in Gaelic.

"I need something from you, Guinevere."

"What?"

"A kiss." She cocked her head at him, suspicious. "Look. I'm not trying to pick you up. Lyn is the only Dryad for me. It's for the wish. All wishes need to be paid. Blood works best, but you've suffered enough, so I asked for a kiss."

Guinevere knelt down so they were the same height, she put her hands on the sides of Jake's head and looked him in the eye.

"You can really do this for me?" He nodded. She closed her eyes and leaned in; she kissed him on the mouth. She tasted like cherries that were a bit past their prime. Sharp, slightly acidic, but not unpleasant. His right hand still on the tree, Jake held her with his left. He drew power from the earth, from the air, from the kiss. It filled him until he thought he would burst, and he channeled it into the tree, coaxing it back, shaking its stupor. Most things want to be alive, so this wasn't as hard as it might have been. The tree came back, tentative at first, then aggressively reclaiming its life.

The Dryad was whole again, and she kissed Jake hard, tears of joy wetting his shirt. He kissed her back, high on the power still coursing through him and on the happiness radiating from the Dryad and her tree.

After a moment, they came to their senses. Guinevere hugged him one last time and gave him a quick peck on the cheek. She slipped inside her tree, and he never saw her again. He flew back to the clearing, the taste of sweet cherries on his tongue. His wounds were all the way healed; he always forgot that side-effect of wishes. It was time to deal with Musky.

When he got back to the clearing, the sleeping bag was empty.

"Son of a bitch."

Jake searched the campsite. He found the satchel the money had been in. It was buried next to an oak tree; Jake never would have found it if that tree's Dryad hadn't poked her head out and shown him where it was. He thanked her and he could have sworn she winked at him.

"Great. Now, all the Dryads think I'm easy." He opened the satchel. Inside was a great deal of money, but Jake did a quick count. It wasn't all here. Musky must have some on him.

Jake flew up above the trees. He started in slow, ever-widening circles, looking for his prey. It was a trick he'd learned from watching hawks. On nature shows. He'd lived in the city his whole life and had never seen a real hawk. Probably just as well. He'd never been a big fan of aerial combat. Finally, Jake spotted the human.

Musky was just leaving the woods, heading across farmland toward Warren Road. Jake tucked his wings and dove. He imagined his raptor's beak and talons stretching out for the kill. Just before he hit Musky, he flipped around so he was feet first. He kicked Musky in the head, both feet, with the power of the dive behind it. Jake bent his knees to absorb the impact; even so, it jarred him hard.

Musky went face down in the rich, soft dirt. He didn't get up right away, so Jake flipped him over. He was out cold. Jake took off Musky's belt and used it to bind his hands behind his back. He pulled Musky's pants off and used them to tie his ankles together. He propped the human up on a stump and waited for him to come around. It took about fifteen minutes.

"Where the hell did you come from?" Musky spat when he saw Jake.

"Grady."

"Shit."

"Yeah. Where's the rest of the money?"

"Go to Hell," Musky said.

"I'm sure that attitude will serve you well," Jake said, "when Victor the Troll is smashing your face against the wall."

119

"You know Victor?"

"I kicked his ass."

"Wow," Musky laughed. "You gotta be the toughest two-foot fairy ever."

"Two-four. And it's Pixie. Common mistake. Now, please, Musky, before I get violent, where's the rest of the money?"

Musky shrugged.

"Spent it," he said.

"How did you spend twenty grand in three days?"

"Hookers and dope, mostly. And it was two days. I slept most of the third. Hookers and dope wore me out." He grinned, remembering.

"Well," Jake said, getting to his feet. "I'll guess I'll just have to take you and the rest of the money to Grady. I'm sure he can find some way to make up for what you spent. He's very creative."

"Yeah, right, Pixie. How you gonna get me there? Carry me?"

"That's what I love about humans," Jake said. "You always underestimate us."

With that, he flipped Musky onto his stomach again, grabbed the back of his shirt and lifted him off the ground. All the way back to Ypsi, Musky complained and whimpered, afraid Jake was going to drop him. Jake flew higher than was strictly necessary. He came down in Depot Town, the nice historic district where Grady had his office. The office that ran his legitimate businesses anyway. Jake had no idea where the other stuff took place and didn't want to know.

He dragged Musky into the lobby, startling some tourists who were looking at the plans for a new museum.

"Pickpocket," he told them. "I'm making a citizen's arrest." Even though this was not the police station, this seemed to satisfy them. People prefer comfortable explanations. Jake dragged his burden through the big door, kicking it closed behind him. Grady was here. Good.

Jake tossed the satchel to him, then slid Musky across the floor so he banged lightly into Grady's desk.

"He says he spent the rest on hookers and dope, but most of it is still there."

"While I do not appreciate you bringing this garbage to my office, I am happy to have my property returned. And in only one day, too. You continue to impress me, Mr. Blossom. I wish you'd reconsider the offer to come to my employ."

"I've worked for other people in the past. It doesn't agree with me."

"Ah well. It is for the best, I am sure. Here is your fee, plus a small bonus for being expeditious."

Grady tossed an envelope across the room. Jake had to fly up six feet to get it. He noted that it was sealed. Grady had known he'd deliver early. Interesting.

"Thanks. What happens to pretty boy here?"

"I don't believe that is any of your concern, Mr. Blossom. Have a lovely afternoon." It was a dismissal. So, Jake left. He went around the corner to the bar and ordered Glenmorangie single malt on the rocks. It was his standard treat after a case. He sipped it for a long time, ignoring the stares of the few humans who still weren't used to his kind. When his drink was gone, he left a $20 on the bar and walked out.

Jake flew to the park, the one by the river, the one with the tree where Lynette lived. She was glad to see him, and he made it a social visit. Very social.

Ken MacGregor's short stories have appeared in several speculative fiction anthologies, including A Quick Bite of Flesh, The Dead Sea, For All Eternity, At Year's End, What's That Scuttling Down My Chimney, Horrific History, Slaughter House: The Serial Killer Edition, vol. 3 *and* Oomph! A Little Super Goes a Long Way; *his work has also appeared in magazines and podcasts. Ken is a member in good standing of The Great Lakes Association of Horror Writers. Ken will sometimes reread a piece he wrote and shudder in revulsion and/or glee. He lives in Ypsilanti, Michigan with his wife Liz and their children Gabriel and Maggie. He can be found on Facebook (Ken MacGregor - Author), Amazon and Goodreads.*

A Proper Job for a Lady
by Gwen Mayo

Fear hung heavy in the room, unspoken worry drowning in a sea of trivial chatter. Nobody spoke above a whisper about the deadly evil responsible for every maiden in town seeking refuge in Wilde-Woods Inn. That wouldn't have been so bad if this were just a visit home to see the family. It was not. Atalanta Wilde was call home to deal with the current crisis.

Atalanta didn't like crowds. Their emotions pummeled her senses with hammer-like blows. With as much resolve as she could muster after the long journey, she left her bag by the door and took possession of one of the leather wing-chairs nearest the hearth. She signaled her traveling companion, Theodora Lee, to take the other. A maid appeared with a tray, but hurried away without speaking. Not that it mattered. Her face revealed more about the mood at the inn than any conversation could have ferreted out.

The wing-chairs were a well-chosen location. They not only provided warmth and comfort after an arduous journey, they also gave her a full view of the assembly while keeping her half-turned away from their company. She sat for a moment content to breathe in the mingled scents of old leather, hickory smoke, fresh baked bread, and warm spice tea. After a while, one or two of the youngsters attempted to engage the battle-weary huntress in conversation, but she remained silent, spine erect, eyes half closed, one graceful hand resting on the silver dragons-head knob of her walking stick. The girls assumed that she was half asleep and left her alone.

It was annoying to have so many young women crowded into the room. On the train Atalanta had read and reread Constance's letter, but in her cousin's usual fashion, the correspondence had been long on dramatics and painfully short on details. She had hoped a private chat with Constance would enlighten her on the true nature of the threat hanging over Bridgeport. Instead, Constance Woods was playing hostess to a room full of frightened young women and Atalanta was obliged to pluck fragments of truth from the backwash of girlish gossip.

Behind hooded eyes, Atalanta watched and listened. An hour passed, then another. She sorted through the conversational debris. Bit by bit, her agile mind pieced together a picture of the evil preying on women. Half a dozen likely monsters were ruled out by talk of a dark mist. Her first inclination was vampire, but that was before she overheard talk of the ground shaking. She didn't want to form a fixed conclusion as to what manner of monster was stealing women from the township, but she had to know if the old evil had returned.

Her fears were confirmed when one of the girls whispered, "I swear, the mountains moved."

Her eyes shot open and she clutched her walking stick tighter.

"Come, Theodora," she said. "I've heard enough."

Conversation stopped. Every eye in the room turned to watch as the huntress moved catlike through the assemblage.

"You can't go out unescorted," Constance insisted. "Let me call Peter to take you to your cottage. Better yet, forget the cottage and stay here in the inn."

"My dear cousin," Atalanta said. "I've come to Bridgeport to hunt the monster, not be protected from it."

"Yes, yes," Constance replied, "but surely that can wait until dawn. You need rest."

"Is your monster likely to wait for the light of day to strike?"

Constance's face flushed.

"Tell Peter to saddle horses and pack provisions for a few days travel. Theodora and I will ride for the mountains as soon as we change."

Constance stood silent, her eyes forming a question too horrifying for her lips to speak.

"It has returned," Atalanta said. "Have you reinforced the wards around the Inn?" We've two days until the new moon brings the beast to the height of his powers."

124

"That's just an old story, told around the hearth on stormy nights. You can't believe such a creature exists."

Atalanta picked up her bag and turned toward the door. She had nothing to say to the willfully ignorant. There was no turning away from the heritage of Wilde-Woods, but Constance had chosen to learn only the most basic protections. She could believe or not, fight or remain inside the relative safety of the inn; either way, the new moon would bring darkness to their doorstep.

"Good-night, cousin," Atalanta said. "See to the wards."

"What are you planning to do?" Theodora asked when they were safely out of earshot.

"I am going to change into something more suitable for the task."

"Really, Atalanta? Just like that, you are going to change your gown and the monster will bend to your will?"

"Theodora, many of my male acquaintances are of the opinion that all I have to do is appear in town, gaze wistfully into the distance, and the local monster will be naturally drawn to me." She sighed. "If only it were that simple."

"There was that vampire in West Madison," Theodora said. She grinned at the memory.

"He practically fell at your feet declaring his love. And what did you do?"

Theodora's voice held a note of reproach as she answered her own question.

"For his trouble, you drove a stake through his heart and cut off his head."

"Theodora it is much easier to stake a vampire while he is prostrated at your feet than it is after you reject his proposal."

"But he was such a handsome devil," Theodora said.

"Honestly Theodora, if you don't stop romanticizing what we do, you are going to end up becoming a creature of the darkness. Monster hunting is equally dangerous for ladies as it is for the most adventuresome gentleman. We must be as well armed for resisting the seductive charms of evil as we are in fighting attacks."

"You think we are in danger of seduction?"

The tone of her voice told Atalanta that Theodora was

125

hoping for a flirtation with one or more attractive villains.

Atalanta thought about the streaks of silver running through her dark hair and the way the lines around her eyes had deepened. She couldn't remember if it had been seven or eight years since a werewolf or vampire had last tried seducing her. She wasn't quite past the age of childbearing. Still, the kind of danger Theodora wanted was becoming more unlikely for Atalanta with each passing season. Not that it mattered today. Neither vampire nor werewolf would be behind the disappearances in Bridgeport. They were facing a more primitive form of evil.

Her eyes traveled west to the mountains as she considered the tales those young women whispered.

"I swear, the mountain moved," Atalanta repeated, into a cold wind that tugged at her cloak.

"What did you say?" Theodora asked, as she stepped closer to her friend and turned to examine the distant mountain range that held Atalanta's attention.

"The girl near the window said she saw the mountain move," Atalanta said.

She held her walking stick firmly in her right hand and spread her arms into the wind.

In response to her gesture the wind picked up, swirling leaves around them and blowing her cloak with such force that Atalanta had to lean forward to keep from being knocked off her feet.

"It was a trick of the mind," Theodora replied. "The way the forest sways in the wind makes everything appear to move. Nothing short of an earthquake would move those mountains."

"You can't trust mountains, Theodora. They are old, tricky, and have seen much more than you or I."

Theodora's eyes filled with disbelief.

"Are you saying the mountains are taking those girls? That's crazy talk, Atalanta."

"You said much the same thing about the sand demon."

"That was hardly the same," Theodora insisted. "The sand was moving because the monster lived underground. Even if a sand demon could lift thousands of tons of rock, trees would be uprooted. There'd be slides and quakes. Evidence would be

126

everywhere."

"Perhaps," Atalanta said, "but humor me in this. We've three more days until the new moon, and I will need your help to complete my work."

"What work is that?" Theodora asked.

"We ride toward the mountains," Atalanta said. "Out there, beyond the most remote farmsteads we must find and reinforce the old wards."

"This has happened before?"

Atalanta gave her friend a wry smile.

"This is the reason Wilde-Woods Inn was built, and why the Wildes have always hunted monsters."

She turned to face Theodora.

"Perhaps I shouldn't have brought you with me, Theodora, but I cannot win this fight alone. Constance should be beside me now, but I have little faith in my cousin's ability to stand against the monster. It has been more than a hundred years since our great-great-grandparents drove the darkness out of Bridgeport. Constance knows what she must do, but doesn't truly believe the legends. That makes her a dangerous ally. One must be resolute in fighting evil. Her doubts will weaken her ability to ward the inn."

"What is this creature, some sort of vampire?" Theodora asked. "Did they drive it into torpor?"

"An entire clan of vampires couldn't create the black mist those girls described. Nor do the undead have the power to make the mountains rise up. Bridgeport sits in the shadow of a nameless beast, older than the caverns where he slumbers, and rising only once every century."

"How do we fight such a monster?"

"First, we dress for the occasion," Atalanta said. "Come Theodora, I've just the thing for you at the cottage."

"Really Atalanta, you go on as if being fashionable is some essential part of battle."

"My dear, being fashionable is always essential to a lady. In our line of work, it is particularly true. One simply cannot go about being careless in their dress without facing dire consequences in the field. Take vampires, for instance, since they are one of your personal favorite creatures of darkness."

Theodora scowled. It was true that she preferred matching wits with a handsome vampire to facing a room full of decaying zombies, but Atalanta didn't have to make such a fuss about it.

"Would you really want to face a vampire without a high collar, reinforced with silver?"

"Of course not," Theodora replied.

"Exactly. Not unless you wanted to risk an embarrassing biting incident," she warmed to her subject. "Now if you were in the East, you might consider white, their traditional mourning color, instead of our Western preference for black, but the silver is an essential for all vampires. If you possess a true belief in divine providence, you might also want to include a necklace with the appropriate symbol of your faith, in purest silver, of course. I personally choose an elegant design over one of large size, but that is a matter of taste. The latter always appears gaudy to me, and is of no greater value in repelling monsters. It is the possession of the truest faith that matters."

While she rambled on about the proper dress for vampire hunting, the two women made their way to the closed cottage where Atalanta had spent her childhood. Once inside, Atalanta didn't bother lighting a lamp. So familiar were the surroundings that she moved with ease through the dark receiving room and entered the parlor beyond. Practiced fingers explored the wainscoting on the west wall until a concealed latch clicked, revealing a door so carefully constructed it was undetectable to the eye a moment before.

She paused in the doorway and struck a match, and the darkness gave way to the warm glow of lamplight. Atalanta removed a sheet from an overstuffed chair, sending up a cloud of dust that made her friend cough.

"I'm sorry," she said. "I haven't been home in a while. I'll have Peter send a maid to air the old place out while we are in the field."

She dropped the dust cover to the floor.

"Please have a seat. I'll just be a moment."

With that, she turned and disappeared into the hidden room, returning a moment later carrying a large bundle.

"These were made for my mother," Atalanta said, as she

128

pulled a blade from the pocket of her gown and sliced through the bindings. She never had occasion to use them. I think you are of a similar size."

"I should think you would want to have your mother's gown for yourself," Theodora said.

"Nonsense. Mother was four inches shorter and similar to you in both coloring and build. I'd look simply dreadful in her clothing."

Theodora hid her laughter in a fit of sneezing.

"Really dear, you must do something about those allergies. It would be most inopportune to have an attack in the middle of a fight with a pack of werewolves," Atalanta said.

Their ride into the foothills to the better part of a day before reaching the river road. In the twilight the old stone bridge was foreboding, its great black pillars rising from the riverbed. Where silver spirals should be glowing, she could see only black stone. How could Constance let the wards fall into disrepair? As much as Atalanta wished they could get right to work, it was necessary to rest. She found a suitable campsite and placed small wards to conceal the two of them from the rising beast. They were a day's ride from the peaks where he lived, but she could feel his breath on her skin.

She shuddered. Protections only went so far. Cries from deep within the earth echoed in her dreams. Atalanta could feel the monster calling out to her, drawing her to the blackness with all the primal power of his being. She awoke shivering, her blanket knotted in her fists. Sleep would not return. Atalanta left her friend to finish her rest and went to care for the horses. Unlike most people, the animals could sense the danger. She took the time to sooth them as well as provide food and water, before turning her attention to the bridge.

By the time Theodora called for her, Atalanta had poured fresh layers of molten silver into the deep spiral wards protecting the old stone bridge. Silver hardened quickly in cold stone, concealing the layer of her own blood she painted into the spiral. She could feel them now, the wards pulsed with her heart and her heart with the Wilde-Woods. The first wards were restored.

"Over here," Atalanta said, in answer to her friend.

"I would have helped."

"There was no need to wake you, Theodora, but now that you are up, you can help me with this."

Atalanta held out her arm, revealing the cut at her wrist.

Theodora's brows furrowed as she examined the wound. Her eyes traveled from the wound to the knife at Atalanta's waist, and then to the wards glowing in the morning sun. She closed her eyes and let the matter rest as gently as her friend's arm rested in her hands. Warm energy flowed from the palms of Theodora's hands taking away the pain and healing the wound. When she had done all that she could, Theodora let the arm fall and turned back to camp.

"Breakfast will be ready soon," she said. "You need to eat."

"Do I have time to bathe?"

Theodora's mouth gaped open. "Bathe? Really Atalanta, out here?"

"Theodora, a lady should always look like a lady. Being on the trail is no reason to slack off on personal hygiene."

She tried to keep her voice cheerful, but Theodora knew her too well to believe that Atalanta was unconcerned about the future. Worry was in the tilt of her chin and the way her nostrils flared at each change of the wind. Atalanta was on the hunt and the watchful gaze that followed any movement on the horizon. There was a glint of steel behind those catlike eyes.

Trouble came sooner than expected. Atalanta spotted a slight movement of the mountains just as the last rays of sunlight disappeared. Little by little the blackness spread blocking out the stars.

"Theodora, take the horses to the other side of the river and secure them there. We'll make our stand here."

"Do you think Constance is coming? We need a triad."

"Be resolute," Atalanta said. "With or without my cousin's help, we will drive him back."

"What is he?"

Atalanta looked at her dearest friend. Like Constance, Theodora was a gentle soul, a natural healer. There, the similarity ended. Theodora would stand firm in the face of darkness. It was true that she romanticized a few handsome creatures. Still, when the moment of decision had come, Theodora had driven her stake through the heart of a vampire and cut off his beautiful head. Together they had faced a thousand threats. Each stood ready to die for the other.

She turned and stared into the unknown darkness. No, she couldn't tell her friend that today she had to stand alone. This beast was not like others. He was coming for the last Wilde. She could taste the blend of coal and sulfur in the air. Low rumbling thunder told her it was time. The mountain was moving, spreading a cloud would bring suffocating dust.

"See to the horses, Theodora. We can't afford to lose them."

Theodora's mouth opened but her protest was muffled by a thunderclap unlike any she had ever heard. She could see the horses straining to break free. Atalanta was right; they could not afford to be left afoot in such a storm.

Once her friend was safely across the river, Atalanta took a stick from the fire and touched it to the great spiral she had carved into the road.

Flames rose.

The cloud stopped, drew together, and took the form of a giant.

Horses' hooves pounded on the bridge.

Atalanta dared not look. Her mind had to remain focused on the dark shape towering forty feet above her.

She lifted her staff and summoned the winds.

Behind her she heard Constance's voice, shouting above the wind. Her words were swallowed whole by the roar of the wind.

Atalanta held her staff with both hands. Circling slowly she drew the winds together into a spiraling tornado.

Constance and Theodora ran to her. "Water," they screamed. "Not fire, water."

Understanding reached her seconds before the tornado reached her flaming spiral. Constance and Theodora lifted their staffs and together the three women struggled to draw the tornado back to the river.

The giant lifted his fists and thunder rolled followed by flashes of lightning. A shower of pebbles rained down on them from the belly of the beast.

They ignored the cuts and bruises throwing all their energy into the cyclone as they released it toward the beast.

Wind and water circled the beast, turning black.

It seemed an eternity passed before the lightning subsided. Then the rains came, black and heavy.

"Hold fast," Atalanta shouted. "He's still in there."

Voices screamed from the eye of the cyclone. Women's voices cried out for help.

Atalanta could feel Constance wavering.

"They are dead, cousin. The only help is to release their souls to the afterlife."

Constance nodded, but her chin quivered with each plea.

There was a final roar of rumbling thunder as an earthquake split the ground between them. The face of the beast crumbled into the eye of the cyclone.

Souls of the dead, some long imprisoned within the beast, flew free.

The triad of women stood watching the dead depart as the storm dissipated.

Atalanta looked down at her ruined gown. "I need another bath," she said, "and a good night's sleep."

"I think you need a new line of work, cousin," Constance said. "Have you considered taking your place at Wilde-Woods Inn?"

Atalanta took out her lace edged handkerchief and wiped a handful of black mud from her face.

"Honestly, Constance, me--inn-keeping? Cooking and tidying up, or worse, the drudgery of daily accounts? My dear, I have an image to uphold. That's just not a proper job for a lady."

Gwen Mayo is passionate about blending the colorful history her love for fiction. She currently lives and writes in Tarpon Springs, Florida, but grew up in a large Irish family in the hills of Eastern Kentucky. Her stories have appeared in anthologies, at online short fiction sites, and in micro-fiction collections.

Circle of Dishonor, *her first novel, is set during the turbulent political upheaval of post-Civil War Kentucky at a time when murder was more common in Kentucky than it was in anywhere else in the United States. Her second novel is currently under consideration.*

Tommy and the Trolls
by James McCormick

"Mom," little Tommy called out as he positioned himself carefully inside the chalked pentagram on his bedroom floor, "come in here!" He put a hand to his mouth, stifling the snigger unless it turned into a full- blown laugh. But there was no response. He waited … and waited.

"Mom," he yelled again, this time at the top of his voice, "I need you a minute… *Mooommmmmmm!*" The oversized warlock robes he'd made from his silk bedclothes were starting to feel uncomfortable on his tiny frame. He'd not really done a good job of stitching and designing them he had to admit. But it wasn't his fault, he's been forced to work at night, his foam filled python draft excluder blocking out the light from under his door. His mother had told him he was too young to be playing with needles and scissors and dangerous things like that. Well, he'd show her. A psychometric test at school had revealed him to have an IQ of over 160. He might only be eight but he was also a genius, and you don't mess with geniuses. When she opened the door and broke the seal of the banishing spell he'd written on a strip of paper, she'd get it. It was a shame he'd never get to see her expression though when she realised what had happened. Still, you couldn't have everything.

He'd initially thought about using a summoning spell, bringing forth a demon to tear the flesh from her bones. But he'd relented. She wasn't that bad, after all, but she had done monstrous things that had to be atoned for. He had a little dark blue note book crammed with such grievances; of wrongs she'd done him. The last, pencilled in no less than yesterday was not letting him have that third helping of toffee and chocolate ice cream at the restaurant. There were many more: insisting he went to bed before ten at night, not letting him watch the horror channel and worst of

135

all, making him go to school when he expressly told her that he didn't want to. What good was a mother if she made you do things you didn't want to do? Well, no longer. Today her power over him ended. With her banished to realm of the Azathoth, he would do just what the hell he wanted. Amazing what books on magic taught you if you knew which ones to read. And the Necronomicon, written by the mad Arab, Abdul Alhazred, told him everything he needed.

The corner of his eye twitched and his chubby cheeks coloured. He was beginning to get really irritated now. He was on the point of letting out another scream when he heard the footsteps on the stairs. At last he thought. He hated it when the old battleaxe (he'd heard that word on TV somewhere and quite liked it) kept him waiting. Like the other day when he told her he wanted a pizza delivered instead of the muck she'd set down in front of him for dinner. It had taken an hour of haranguing before she'd relented and ordered him one.

"Yes honey?" a soft voice called out, "What is it? I'm a little busy."

"Get in here," Tommy yelled, "Now." The footsteps halted and the door creaked open. Little Tommy watched the paper stretch then begin to tear. His small frame shivered with excitement, any moment now, any moment now. He squeezed the strip of paper in hand, the spell of protection that would keep him safe inside the pentagram.

"What's wrong sweetheart?" his mother asked as the paper finally tore. Tommy stared at the petite blond figure of his mother for the briefest of moments before the world exploded in blue and red fire. He saw the shocked, terrified look on her face, then her desperate arm stretching forward. She screamed his name and started to race towards him. But before she had taken more than a couple of steps, the bright lights swallowed her completely.

"Yes!" Tommy cried, punching his fist into the air. The dance of multi-coloured prismatic lights faded and all was still. As his eyes adjusted to the dim lighting he very quickly realised something was wrong. The doorway where his mother had stood was gone. Instead he was staring at an irregular archway carved from slime-covered rock. Whatever was on the other side was hidden in shadows. He looked down. The pentagram was gone. And instead of the polished, oak wood panelling of his bedroom floor he was standing on moss covered soil. Something albino white wriggled near his foot. He gasped, recoiling from it just in time to avoid the snapping mandibles it directed towards his bare toes.

He turned frightened eyes on his new surroundings. Wherever he was it, the chamber looked as if it had been mined out of rock. But someone did live here. A rude assemblage of logs, strapped together in the shape of a huge bed and covered in a woven straw mat, occupied a far corner of the chamber. Two luminous red eyes stared at him from underneath it.

Tommy screamed and raced for the doorway. He found himself in a long, narrow tunnel. He sprinted along it for some moments then half fell, half stumbled down a flight of stone steps that led downwards in a sharp spiral. The sound of sharp claws scratching stone echoed close behind him.

Finally he made it to the bottom of the stairwell. His little legs still pounding away, he tripped and fell as he reached ground level. He was on his feet again in moments.

Just ahead was a large rusted metal door. He raced towards it, grabbing hold of the grotesque copper face that was the handle. He pulled on it with all the might his immature, undeveloped muscles could muster. The scuttling noise on from the stairwell grew louder, whatever it was, was almost on him now. Stiff hinges whined in protest but he eventually succeeded in opening the door, just enough to squeeze through.

He tried to close it again but he had no strength left. He collapsed back against it, eyes screwed shut and panting for breath. It was some moments before he sensed he wasn't alone. He opened his eyes again and found two deep- set, onyx black ones staring at him. They belonged to a huge troll, dressed in a flower covered piny. By the way she was crouched by the huge bubbling cauldron over the fire she had been in the middle of stirring a broth of some kind. But now her full attention was on him. She withdrew the ladle from the liquid and waved it at Tommy,

"Who are you?" she demanded, her voice something akin to thunder. "And where's that snivelling little Kolkus?" A dozen troll children, all gathered around the same large table, empty bowls in front of them, looked at Tommy. No-one spoke. The silence continued for a moment until a spider like creature, midnight black and possessing a series of twisted and crooked limbs jumped onto the table. One of the troll children took it into her arms, staring into its luminous red eyes,

"There, there Starala," the troll girl said, "it's okay."
Another little troll waved his spoon in Tommy's direction,

"It's a human!" he squealed, "a dirty human." The others gasped. The mother troll wiped her slab like hands on her piny and came forwards, inspecting the intruder up close. A look of distaste passed over her granite like features.

"It is," she said, "by my boulders it is, but how did it...?" She looked him over, inspecting his strange garb and pointed hat. Her already hard features hardened even further.

"So, we've got ourselves a little warlock, have we?"

"Mummy," one of the children said, "where's Kolkus? He needs to serve us dinner. He should have finished making our bed and sweeping the chamber by now." He whacked his spoon on the table, "he knows what he gets if he's slow." The others grinned and banged their spoons down also. The Troll mother looked little Tommy up and down. Her eyes fell on the slip of paper in his hand.

"What's this?" she said snatching it from him. She read it over, muttering as she tried to make sense of the strange, forbidden language passed down by Great Cthulhu.

"I don't think your wretched little half-brother is coming," she said after some moments, "This human has used magic on him." She shook her head, "Well, well. The warlocks banished us to this infernal realm eons ago and now one of them has ended up in his own prison." Her eyes narrowed as she continued to decipher the spell,

"By using a dual displacement spell of all things. He probably though he was using a banishment spell, they do look similar as I recall." She gave a low grunt of surly satisfaction. 'It seems the humans aren't as adept at their magic as they once were.' Her granite lip curled into a sneer, 'and they've shrunk too.' She turned to her brood,

"Well, children, it looks like Kolkus is gone. This human's taken his place."

"We don't want it," the girl troll holding the spider pet said. "Kolkus has chores to do. I need my boots fixing. Kajina needs her dress stitching."

The mother shook her head. "Impossible," she said, "the spell only works once. We're stuck with him."

"Kill it," one of the trolls suggested. Murmurs of agreement accompanied the proposal.

"No," the mother said, grabbing Tommy by the arm and lifting him into the air. "Like you said, there are chores need doing."

She locked eyes with Tommy's. "You hear me, human? You want to stay underground, and you do, because outside these caves are things you can't even imagine in your world; you're going to do everything I tell you. One word from you, one complaint, one sigh, you don't do everything I tell you as quickly as you can, then I'll let the Chthonian have you." The troll children gasped.

"W-what's a Chthonian?" Tommy managed to stutter.

"Trust me," the mother said, "you don't want to find out." She let him go. Tommy dropped back to his feet.

"Now get stirring that broth," she said. "After you've served dinner, washed up and cleaned the kitchen then maybe I might let you have what's left of it." She pushed him towards the fire where the mixture bubbled and boiled. She was so strong the boy's feet hardly touched the floor as he moved towards it.

He took the ladle and started stirring. The stew smelled awful. He looked down and saw eyeballs and ears floating in it. He put a hand to his mouth, trying to stifle the retch that was rising up in his throat.

The good people of Arkham never really had the courage to ask what had happened to little Tommy. Some type of accident some said, a disfiguring disease was another popular belief. But the odd thing was, ever since whatever it was that had happened to her son, Sara Curtis had seemed brighter, happier. Many people had noted before on her greying hair, stooped posture and premature wrinkles as if she worried too much, but they had suddenly gone.

She and Tommy didn't go out that much, but neighbours often saw them playing in the back yard, laughing and having fun together. The boy was always covered up, usually by a hooded jacket of some sort and often with a scarf around his face. But on one or two occasions the odd nosy neighbour had caught a quick glimpse of the boy.

"No hair," was one comment. "Grey, mottled skin," was another. But the boy seemed healthy and was big and strong for an eight year old.

"Such a shame!" many said. Yet, as old widow Mayne, the wisest and un-appointed head of the town's silver haired gossips remarked, "They did seem happy."

James McCormick is a college lecturer from England and has been writing for over twenty five years, mostly science fiction, fantasy and horror. His published short stories include: "End of the Day" *(Ethereal Tales) Issue 12 (2011) and* "If You Can't Beat Them ..." (Jupiter SF, *issue 14, April 2009). He also has a horror novella,* Sundown *(Deathgrip 3: It Came From the Cinema, Hellbound Books Publishing, 2004).*

One Scareful Owner
by Catriona McPherson

You'd think a person would know a haunted house when they saw one. If, for instance, they read its details on the multiple listings. Or at least, they'd recognise it when they pulled up and got out of the car to take photos on their phone. What idiot would make an appointment with the realtor? What flavour of moron wouldn't wonder why the price was so low and the fliers so faded? How big a doofus would you have to be to feel lucky when you tested the water with a low offer, and they bit your hand off at the elbow and paid closing costs?

Hear me out. If it had been on a hill, leaning forward over the road and glowering down, or had even one turret, or if bats had fled in a whispering cloud from every broken window as the key turned in the squeaky lock and the door creaked open. If some kindly neighbour had stopped me at the gate, clamped a horny hand on my wrist and told me no one had spent a night in the old Crutchley place since that Christmas Eve the family died…

I mean, I'm not a fool. Blood dripping down the walls, slime coming out of the taps, the pitter-pat of little dead feet on the dust of the nursery floor, I'd have run a mile and signed a lease on a condo.

But 666 13th Street, Lucifer, CA rang no alarm bells at all.

It's a 1970s ranch, for crying out loud. Sunken lounge, wet bar, fake stone fireplace the size of the Albert Memorial, gold-on-gold pampas-grass wallpaper, and a sea of brown shag-pile carpet that starts at the front door and goes all the way to the back of the master bathroom, where it washes up the side of the Jacuzzi tub. (Also brown.) A haunted house should be gray, with lavender touches, and the yellow-white of old bleached bones. Whoever heard of slime dripping out of onyx taps or blood dripping down gold-on-gold pampas-grass walls?

And it didn't *feel* haunted when the realtor showed me round that day. She opened the lock box, pulled the screen door, pushed the door, and stood back to let me step in.

"Smells a wee bit foosty," I said.

"A what bit whatty?" she said. She was still on the doorstep and her grip on the screen-door handle was making her knuckles crack.

"A little bit stale," I said. "There might be a…" I sniffed, "…mouse or two."

She let go of the handle, stretched out her hand like a starfish to get the blood back in her fingers and let her shoulders drop down from inside her hairdo.

"Are you okay?" I asked. How could you be a realtor if you were scared of empty houses?

"I," she said, putting her head inside and looking from side to side, then beaming at me with every one of her hundred and eighty teeth, "am absolutely great." She stepped in and let the door shut behind her, stood listening for a minute, then beamed some more. "I'm great," she said again. "Now let me show you all the delights of this unique home."

Unique was one word for it. Surprisingly affordable were another two. It was a hundred thousand dollars for three beds and two baths in a town where three grand was the norm. It had an eat-in kitchen (a rough mark on the orange and yellow daisy-print wall showed where a table used to be), a laundry room with a sink, a garage bigger than my first flat in Glasgow, and five trees in the yard. All that plus the sunken lounge, wet bar and fireplacarama.

Looking at the fireplace was the first sign of trouble, actually. I stood on the brown shag carpet and stared.

"Wow." I said. "That is… big."

"Original feature," said the realtor. "This house has had only one owner. She bought it from the builder and owned it until she died."

"How easy would it be to rip something that size ou- Whoa!"

I put my hands out to steady myself as the ground shook underneath me.

"Was that an earthquake?" I said. "My God, was that an actual California earthquake?"

"Ye-es?" said the realtor.

"Wow!" I said again. I was still at the stage where anything about my new country could excite me. Four-way stops, gas station coffee, lemonade stands. An earthquake was glamour undreamed of. I looked at the fireplace again.

"Well, if those fake boulders have survived thirty-five years without dropping off, I reckon they should stay."

"Come and see the master suite," said the realtor. "The bathroom is another unique original feature. Very vintage, very retro, very . . ."

"Brown," I finished, standing at the bathroom door.

"And orange," said the realtor, sweeping her arm wide to show off the walls, as if I could miss them.

"That bath's a bit of a joke," I said. There was a slight shiver underfoot again. "But not even a hairline crack in the tile work. Maybe it can stay."

Buying a house in America goes quite quickly. When you don't need a mortgage because you got a lump sum in the divorce and your granny left you a wedge and the exchange rate has cleared every tourist out of London it does anyway. I didn't understand a word of the forms – indemnities, disclosures, waivers – no clue what any of it meant, so I just signed them all and moved in, with a blow-up camping mattress and a lawn chair.

The neighbours were nice. A firefighter and an ER nurse on one side, which might come in handy, and Mrs. Guzman on the other, who brought a ginger cake and a bunch of irises the day I got the keys.

"Come in, come in," I said.

"I won't," said Mrs. Guzman. She took a step back to show me she meant it too. "I'm only saying welcome to the neighbourhood."

"Well, thank you." I smiled and wondered if I was imagining the hawk-eyed stare she gave me.

"What brings you here?" she asked.

"Microbiology," I answered.

"Ah, you're at the biotech plant?" Then she frowned. "I thought perhaps you were a – That is, I wondered if maybe- Someone said you were- Oh, I don't know what it's called these days. I wouldn't want to offend you."

I stared at her. She thought I was a what? Offend me how?

"Sex worker?" I guessed.

Mrs. Guzman rattled off a string of warbly little noises like a hen who'd been surprised.

"A Wiccan!" she said, when she'd recovered. "A shaman. I don't know what they're called anymore."

"No, no. Sorry to disappoint you." I smiled. "I'm a boring old gene jockey like everyone else who moves here. International recruitment drive, you know?"

She nodded, told me there were no nuts in the cake and left. I watched her safely down the steps and out of the gate. If she was as far gone as that in her head, she might be wobbly on her old legs too. I put it out of my mind and went back to my dust mop and my daydreaming.

I quite like vintage, really. The day I first came to see the place I was sporting a sixties handbag I'd bought at the Goodwill – one like the queen carries, solid as a rock with a clasp on top – and a polyester tunic with pom-poms round the hem. It's a dress, but I'm tall so I pair it with jeans. My ex-husband hated it, so I get a lot of pleasure out of wearing it now and turning heads, if I'm lucky. And I've washed my hair. And the light's behind me. It's been seven years since I actually went on a date, though.

Anyway, vintage, yeah. Big fan. But there are limits. And this house couldn't see them in its rear view mirror with a telescope. Starting with the wet bar which, as far as I could tell, was a sink. In the living room. In an open-plan house where the sink in the kitchen was ten paces away (two of them up the steps that made it sunken). So all in all, the wet bar had to go. I opened the doors of the cupboardy bit underneath to see how firmly it was attached to the wall. Then I sat back on my heels and drank in what was facing me.

Mirror-backed shelves with holders for wine glasses and a tray that rolled out with dimples for bottles and an ice-bucket in its own wee ice-bucket dent. With some highball glasses and champagne saucers, some still-in-packaging cocktail napkins off eBay, this wet bar could be the grooviest thing since Austin Powers.

All of a sudden a wave of warmth flooded over me, leaving me tingling and euphoric, like nothing I'd ever felt before. I closed the cabinet doors and went to fire up my lap-top to start shopping. The plans to rip out the shag-pile could wait for another day.

At first, it was just little things. I bought some Ikea dishes and they fell off the shelf in the night and smashed to splinters. I swept up the shards and went to a yard sale, where someone was selling an old person's stuff who'd died. The dishes were pretty bad – rough stoneware in beige and black with Spirograph patterns on, but there was a full-set – coffee-pot and everything – and they were cheap so I took them. I checked the shelf and pushed the china right to the back. It looked god-awful in the avocado cabinets with the burnt-orange counter-tops but it survived the night. And the next night, and even when I dropped a cup it just bounced. Not so much as a chip in the rim. Lucky.

Steve from work wasn't a little thing, mind you. Steve was massive, even before the trouble began. He was a date. I knew it would happen. Biotech's a young industry, lots of singles, more men than women and I was new. And I'd told myself I'd get back on the first horse that asked me. So when Steve stopped by my cube and mentioned lunch, I kicked my sandwich box out of sight and said I'd love to.

Lunch went well. No spinach in the teeth of either and he didn't check his texts or ask me my star sign. We re-upped to dinner on Friday. And dinner on Friday was fine. So when he saw me home, I asked him in for coffee. In he came. Coffee was made. I set it down on the kitchen table and was reaching for the milk jug when the phone rang. The landline. Which never rings after the cold callers have knocked it off for the day.

"I'll let the machine pick up," I said.

"Hey, honey," said the voice, after the message and bleep. "Hope you're not lonely. Fort Lauderdale is enormous! We should come back together one day. Don't forget it's Jamie's birthday on Tuesday. D'you want me to pick up a Florida sport shirt from the airport? I know how busy you are."

145

I stood holding the milk jug as if I'd been turned to stone.

"Who was that?" said Steve, when the voice was done.

"I have no idea," I told him. "A wrong number. I should let that guy know so he can phone his real wife, eh?"

"What was that accent?" said Steve.

"Yeah, true, Glasgow, like me," I said. "What were the chances of that?"

"And who's Jamie?"

"My nephew," I said. "I'll see you at work on Monday."

But he was already gone. And when I hit redial, the robot said there were no available numbers. I poured the coffee away, but I might as well have drunk it. I lay awake all night anyway.

Then there was the drama of the laundry room. I had to wash the slip covers that had come on the couch from the Sally Annie. They were good quality, professionally made and fit like a glove, but they were filthy. So my inaugural load in my brand-new, silver, Bosch washer and dryer was high stakes. I consulted the manual, lowered the temperature to be on the safe side and chose an extra-gentle program with fabric-care finish. When I turned my back though, I heard something I shouldn't have. The dials were spinning. TEMP went round to 60, WASH to heavy soil, SPIN SPEED to nuclear. I started punching buttons, pulling and pushing and trying to stop whatever Armageddon was raining down on my covers in there. I'd spent all my money on this damn machine; I couldn't afford upholstered furniture too. But the dials wouldn't move. The hot water was sloshing in and the drum was hammering round. Desperate, I pulled the plug out of the wall.

And the hot water sloshed in and the drum hammered round. And I ran.

Out the front door, down the path, over the fence, up Mrs. Guzman's path and across her porch. She answered my knock with a baseball bat in her hand and I could hardly blame her.

"Tellmeaboutthe-" I said. Then I took a breath and started again. "Hi, Mrs. Guzman. Thanks for the cake. Say, did you know the lady who lived in my house before? I'd love to hear a bit about her."

It was an hour later when I stumbled down her path and up my own again.

Olivia Turnbull had a hard life, if not an unusual one. When her husband died in 1972, it was all she could not to dance a jig on his grave. Oh, she mourned; she wasn't heartless. But she recovered before the wreaths had wilted. She cashed in his insurance, sold his dry-cleaning business and bought her dream-home at 666 13th Street. She had the best of everything, Mrs. Guzman told me. The fanciest schmanciest height of fashion, chosen by flipping through magazines as thick as the phone book. It was perfect. As perfect a medley of orange and brown and gold and bronze as 1973 could muster. With a sunken Jacuzzi and onyx taps. But the day before she was due to move in, Olivia Turnbull woke up in her old bed in her old house with packing cases all around her, uttered a single cry, and died.

Every realtor in town tried to find a buyer. Then there were the auction years. Then, in the eighties, my realtor bought it herself and started the remodel. She cleared the furniture out during the worst thunder and lightning storm Lucifer had ever known, then sent a contractor to take out the avocado cabinets with the burnt-orange counter. He left a message on her phone telling her no charge and don't call again.

"And it's been empty all these years?" I had asked Mrs. Guzman. "Since the seventies?"

"Sometimes people come from the university," she told me. "And once from the TV."

"And then me."

We stared at one another.

"And then you."

On my own porch again, I paused. I almost knocked. But in the end I pushed the door open and tiptoed in.

"Olivia?" I said. "Are you here?"

There was no sound except the slow wheeze of a washing machine finishing its final spin. I edged round the laundry-room door just as the latch released and the drum sprang open.

Well, they were gorgeous. I thought they were beige when I bought the couch, with a subtle pattern of blobs and squiggles in tan and taupe. But after Olivia's hot wash, they'd burst into colour: yellow and purple and fuchsia and coral and all on a background, of course, of the brownest brown. They were vibrant edging into migraine and I loved them.

I didn't love the fact that my posh Bosch washer was a one-hit-wonder, mind you: it shrank my clothes when I ran them through on cool and gentle (they'd been stored for months and I only wanted to freshen them); it turned my white towels gray and ate the black sock that must have been in there. Must have been. But I never found it. Finally, it took a pair of cotton kitchen curtains – Pottery Barn, well-made, washable, said it right there on the label – and shredded them to ribbons. So I called the repairman.

"And what's the address?" he said. I told him. "Nuh-uh, lady," he shot back. "Not me, not again, no way." Same with the next guy. And the next guy too.

I went into the laundry-room and stood there with my hands on my hips.

"Olivia?" I said. Then I stopped. *Look*, I said inside my head. Then stopped again. Which was worse: talking out loud in an empty room or thinking she could read my mind?

"Look, Olivia. I can't afford another one and if no one will come to fix this one, well we're stuffed aren't, we? I, and your house, will very soon start to smell."

She had no answer for that. Unless you'd count the fact that at the estate sale on Sunday morning where I bought the yellow towels with the appliquéd back-brushes and rubber ducks along the hems (still in the wrapper, never been used) and scooped the treasure trove of clothes from some poor dead lady's closet, (she was just my size and she loved a polyester pant-suit) I also saw a behemoth of a top-loader. It was twice my age, twice my weight, and had a walnut-veneer backboard that would do a tail-fin Caddy proud in low lighting. I paid twenty dollars and lugged it home along with the sewing machine I'd learn to use to make the curtains I couldn't afford to buy.

"Or should I say *replace*?" I said to the living room while I set it up and tried to thread it. "Those Pottery Barn" – rumble – "don't shake the foundations at me, old woman! Those Pottery Barn curtains were described in the catalogue as "window treatments" which means bloody expensive in case you didn't

148

know. So here I am, trying to get this- Lift the- Gently slide the foot- Turning the spindle at a steady- Bugger it!"

I went to bed in a huff and a brushed nylon shortie nightie with matching hen's bum knickers from the estate sale, never worn. And slept eight hours straight like a baby.

In the morning, back-combing my hair in front of the mirror – If you're going to wear a pink polyester pop-art pant-suit there's no point holding back, right? – it struck me that I was twenty years too old for an imaginary friend and forty years too young to be waking up alone. So the next guy that stopped at my cube with a twinkle in his eye and tickets to a ball game got lucky.

It did not go well. It would have needed a hop-skip-jump and a leg up before you could even say it went badly. The game was fun. I hadn't a clue what was going on so I cheered a half-beat behind the rest of the crowd and checked my texts a bit in the last innings but beer and hotdogs always help and the cocktails on the way home were served in iced glasses – ice that melted where his fingers touched and turned into little droplets of water that ran down the glass until he caught them with the tip of his tongue.

Shoot me, I asked him in. I showed him into the living room, made him a Martini with two olives from the wet bar, and excused myself, to go and floss out the hotdog and hide my laundry.

"Whath are you may-hing?" he said when I got back again. He was standing by the sewing machine. I didn't think the Martini had been strong enough to make him slur.

"Curtains," I said.

"Thumb huller," he said.

What did he mean "some colour?" I thought. Basic white thread to sew basic white cotton- *Huh*? It was orange. It was perfectly threaded, both bits, ready to go. But it was bright, day-glo, fluorescent orange. I turned to look at my date. He was bright day-glo fluorescent orange too. Like how you'd get if a massive purple rash spread over your whole face on top of a tan. And his tongue was hanging out of his mouth like a five dollar hotdog on a three buck bun.

"Do you have any food allergies?" I asked.

"Anshovieth," he said.

149

I checked the olives to see what they were stuffed with. It had been pimento when I bought them, but it was sure as hell anchovies now.

Our date ended in the ER. I stuck with him as long as I could but when the nurse came with the needle and asked him to loosen his pants and rest his hands on the gurney, it was time to say goodbye.

"Thanks a bunch, Olivia," I said, when I got home again. "I was going to try to fix that tap, you know, but you've had it now, lady."

Did I mention the bath? Did I happen to mention Olivia's very firm views about the sunken brown Jacuzzi with the gold and onyx taps? Well, it wasn't working. When I turned it on it made a noise like a garbage disposal and no water appeared. (No slime either, which was a bonus, it's true.) So first I used it for storage, but the sweaters got moths and the moths had babies until my bedroom was like a big brown butterfly farm and one night I ate one and that was the end of that.

Next I filled it with water from the garden hose and bought some goldfish, some gravel, some plastic weed and a bridge. One of those bridges you get for goldfish. Like a fish needs a bridge. They looked pretty cool swimming round under the sunken ceiling lights at bedtime.

They looked bloody awful floating upside down in the harsh morning light the next day.

"I was going to look up faucets on YouTube and try to get it working, Olivia," I said now. "You scratch my back and I scratch yours, you know? Or you swell my date's face and I dump dirt in your tub. Your choice, old woman. Nothing to do with me."

Five bags of potting soil, two bags of decorative mulch, eighty-five dollars' worth of indoor orchids. What is *wrong* with me? Like a woman who'd kill a fish wouldn't kill a flower?

"This is not cool," I told her as I shoveled the dirt back out again and barrowed it away. "You don't know me very well if you think I'll get tired of this before you do."

I spent the rest of the day sewing up the lengths of fabulous sunburst fabric I'd been so lucky to find, making it into curtains to match the lucky find of the hearthrug, which looked pretty good with the lucky find of the lampshade. But I did it very briskly to show her she was still in trouble and going to stay that way.

And although I went out with another of my colleagues that very Saturday night, it's true that I only said yes to stop him bugging me and I kind of half-hoped that if she was going to play nice she wouldn't start with this guy.

She didn't. We had an early dinner – Mexican: I reckoned no one would eat all those black beans and chilies if they had allergies, so we were good on that score. Then I unhooked the phone when we got back to my place, in case my fake husband was on the road again. So far, so good.

We were on the couch together – side by side but entwined – when he started getting frisky. Wriggly. Twitchy. Antsy.

"Waarrgghhh," he yelled and leapt to his feet, ripping at his clothes, pulling his shirt off, sending the buttons flying. If this was a move, it was a new one.

"Ah, ah, ah, ah!" he whimpered, kicking off his shoes and shucking off his jeans so quickly I couldn't even pretend to stop him. I looked with interest at what the strip had revealed.

"Waarrgghhh," I yelled. "Ah, ah, ah, ah." I leapt to my feet and started picking them off, whatever they were, stamping them dead, leaving him to rub the red weals they'd left behind.

"Where the hell did you get that couch?" he screamed at me.

"Um," I said. "Goodwill?"

He gathered his shirt, shoes and jeans and with as much hauteur as any man in powder-blue boxers and beastie-bites can muster he left me.

I drank three Martinis sitting in the little bit of potting soil left in my Jacuzzi, looking at my sunburst curtains (oh, there's been plenty fabric left for in here too) and listening to my walnut-dashboard top-loader dealing tenderly with another load of dry-clean only, vintage fashion finds.

"Okay," I said. "Here's an offer for you. Let's us try to make a deal."

There was silence then: a careful, attentive silence.

"I will fix the bath," I began. "I will get rid of the fridge and buy one you like. Because don't think for a minute I missed that, old woman! I know milk should last longer than three days. I know there weren't all those grubs on the broccoli when I brought it home. Also, I will continue to use my cell phone only when I'm out. Since there's no reception anyway. And I will bring any future dates to the front porch and wait for a sign that you approve. You choose the sign. I'm sure I'll understand. I mean, you're not exactly subtle, Olivia, are you?"

Learning to mend a Jacuzzi from a YouTube vid was a pipe-dream. That much was clear straightaway. And there wasn't a contractor in the town (or towns adjoining) who didn't bang the phone down on me.

But then one day at the farmers' market, reading the bulletin board while I waited and waited for my coffee (stoner baristas are sweet but they do not hustle) I saw an interesting sign. SAPPHO SEPTIC, it said. I pushed aside the drummer needed and room for rent fliers and read more. Read it, wrote down the number and sang a quiet hallelujah. For California and farmers' markets and for lesbian plumbers most of all. I called the number. Rosie was sick with a cold, Martha told me, but she herself would be out to size up the job tomorrow. The estimates were binding, the website had their testimonials and they sold a line of bath products too.

I was in the powder room when the doorbell rang, as it happened. That's a lie. I was hiding in the powder room *until* the doorbell rang. If Olivia was a homophobe and brought the house down I wanted to be in the safest place, which is the smallest room with the least wall space between the corners.

"It's open," I sang out. "Just come in! I'll be right there!"

I listened. There were no rumbles, no creaks, and the floor beneath my feet was flat and still.

"Thank you," I whispered.

"Whoa!" said a voice from the living room. "This place is amazing!" It was a deep voice. A very deep voice. Not a butch voice so much as a male voice. I was pretty sure the person in my house was a...

"Man!" I yelped to my reflection in the powder-room mirror. I burst out, took the foyer corner like NASCAR and dashed into the living room to drag him out of there before disaster could strike.

He was standing in the middle of the floor, turning round slowly, gazing at the fireplace, the lampshade, the wet bar, the couch covers and the sunburst curtains. A man. A man with aviator frames on his yellow-lensed glasses, and a Frank Zappa moustache and – how could these even exist? – flared overalls! Donkey brown overalls with yellow stitching and flares that covered his work boots.

"Hi," he said. "I'm-" he pointed to the orange and yellow embroidery on his hanky pocket. *Oliver.* "I'm Martha's brother. She caught Rosie's cold so I'm helping. I'm not a plumber, but I can size up the job and book you in, okay?"

"Oh-kay," I said, still kind of waiting.

"This place is amazing," he said again. "Love your pant-suit too. Say, do you mind if I go back out to the truck and get my camera? Take some shots? I write for this little style magazine and…"

"Oh," I said. "You're a design journalist?"

"Yeah," he said. He was halfway back out the door. "A plumber and a designer! Mom and Dad are so proud and confused."

"Right," I said. "Of course, I see." The disappointment must have been dripping off every syllable, because he heard it and turned back to me.

"I'm straight, though," he said. Then he blushed, which looked really terrible with the yellow lenses, and I blushed, which looked just as bad with the cerise pant-suit, and he ducked outside and I went to splash my face.

By the time he left we had a plan: brunch in the morning and then a tour of the yard sales I had such a knack of finding. I waved him off at the gate and came back in, looking round to see it through his eyes.

It was cold inside. Quiet and kind of empty.

"Olivia?" I said, but she was gone.

Catriona McPherson was born in in Scotland in 1965. Formerly an academic, she has now been a full-time fiction writer

153

for ten years. Until 2010, Catriona lived on a farm in a beautiful valley in Galloway. She now lives on a farm in a beautiful valley in northern California with her scientist husband and two black cats. She is the author of Dandy Gilver and the Proper Treatment Of Bloodstains *as well as* Dandy Gilver and an Unsuitable Day for a Murder, *which was awarded the Agatha for best historical novel.*

What Were You Drinking?
by David Perlmutter

I.

Jefferson Ball was drunk.

She was also, for good measure, scotched, tipsy, pickled, loaded, smashed, lit, hammered, jonesed, stoned, tippled, bashed, pixilated, looped, high as a Georgia pine, gassed, Harvey-wallbangered, flipped, up-*set*, just drinkin', salted, hard-boiled, fried and [insert your own term for inebriation here. There are many to choose from.]

The most obvious evidence was that she, the most powerful human-shaped female dog in a universe chock full of them, was lying face down on the floor of the bar she was in- one of many ignominiously-styled establishments in her home town of Hugopolis. Clad only in her trademark monogrammed black bikini and black boots, she seemed much more like a typical skid row derelict barfly, someone who had long ago abandoned herself to the winds of fate, chance and alcohol, than the larger than life heroic- or, as her enemies saw her, *anti*-heroic figure she truly was.

Jefferson Ball possessed many virtues, chiefly of the physical variety, that she was wont to exploit in her favour, manipulative creature that she was. Fortunately for herself and the universe around her, she used most of them in the service of her kind. Centuries of breeding and body conditioning among her ancestors, coupled with some shady DNA and genetic manipulation at one point, had created, in Jefferson, a creature possessed of astonishing physical abilities, among them the ability to run a four minute mile in less than two, and powerful physical strength, enough to balance hundreds of thousands of pounds on her fingertip *alone*. Not surprisingly, these abilities, plus a deadly accuracy with the whip she always kept at hand, made her a very

155

formidable opponent of the forces of evil, particularly all aliens, robots, and other supernatural beings who thought they could outfox her in the speed and muscle department, and especially those who employed those beings in a futile attempt to destroy her.

But, like most heroic types, she had an Achilles heel. Two, in fact- both of which she bore the scars of, though less than you might think given her remarkable resiliency.

The first of these was the more obvious and the more hurtful to her reputation. Boys of her race- and the males of any alien race she encountered- and plenty of them! In both the actual evidence known, and her own personal Munchausian exaggeration of her abilities, she was, indeed, a formidable lover. Mata Hari and Mae West had *nothing* on *her*! But, rather than experienced lovers, she preferred to initiate virgins- especially *fine* young things- into the ways of the world. It was common for her, during her adventures, to regularly slip out of a young male's boudoir, having blown his genitals to smithereens (metaphorically) with her own, more powerful ones, and to leave him permanently longing for her touch- and/or cursing her to the heavens for tricking him into giving up his cherry for good.

As powerful and influential she was as a hero or lover, however, Jefferson had an equally colorful reputation as a drinker- or, more accurately, a lush. When boys were not available, she drank, and, even when they were, she drank. Socially and professionally, she drank as well, and this damaged her social status as much as her being a lover of renown. For this reason, most beings of her gender, despite her heroism, were reluctant to establish lasting friendships with her on two counts. She would, it was said, either steal your "man" from you with her charms, good looks, and muscular, pneumatic physique, or she would do so in a duplicitous way- by drinking you under the table!

It was at this point, almost on cue, that Jefferson's sole female friend- indeed, the only friend of either gender she truly had in the whole universe- entered the bar-room, spotted Jefferson sprawled on the floor, put her paws on her hips, and exclaimed:

"So there you are!"

Hamilton Pomeranian (Major, Star Soldiers- Ret.) was far more sober and responsible than her friend, though this was a facade she could easily drop if she was in the mood for it. They seemed an unlikely pair, as many such friendships seem to be on the surface, but, as with those friends, it hid the long period in which they had developed and cultivated their relationship. Having met while training for the Star Soldiers- Hamilton went on to further glory there while Jefferson was expelled for insubordination, leading her to her own independent heroic career path- they had found in each other a relationship that transcended their personality and physical differences. (Hamilton, it must be said, was smaller than her companion and less attractive physically, but only when compared to Jefferson- and not by *that* much.) This relationship, much to their surprise, had survived their joint adventures across the cosmos, as well as several disastrous joint business ventures, which had liquidated Hamilton's finances more than once, to her everlasting regret.

Still, when they were on the same page, there were no two finer pals alive, for Hamilton, despite a limp and a lost eye gained in combat, could be Jefferson's equal in speed and strength (when driven chiefly by fear-motivated repressed energy) as well as in boozing and tail-chasing. The latter traits, however, as noted above, were only when she felt like it, which, because of the military discipline with which she regulated her life, were extremely rare occasions, to Jefferson's disappointment.

It was the sober Hamilton who now confronted her drunken friend, not the playful one Jefferson hoped, in her drunken state, would appear.

"Get up!" Hamilton ordered, and Jefferson righted herself with a quickness that would have surprised anyone else. But not Hamilton. She knew her friend. *Too* well.

"Aren't you *ashamed* of yourself?" Hamilton intoned, speaking as the non-drinking temperance advocate she was most of the time. "Think of how your reputation will suffer because of this!"

"My 'reputation' is in the toilet!" Jefferson drawled drunkenly. "Nothing could make it go lower than this!"

"Then think about what you're doing to your health- and your pocketbook..."

"You just can't take it like I can, or else you'd..."

"Not to mention my health and my pocketbook! Not to mention my reputation!"

"How is this about you? I thought it was about me..."

"It is about you, you lousy tippling *skank*!"

"Shut up!" Jefferson held a well-muscled arm up to her head, covered, as was her whole body, in attractive brown fur. "I got a headache!"

"And well you should!"

"What is that supposed to mean, Hamilton?"

"It means, Jefferson Ball, that I am very disappointed in you!"

"When are you not?"

"Good point," Hamilton remembered. "But don't change the subject, Jefferson. I..."

The bartender interrupted Hamilton by telling her to order a drink or leave his establishment forthwith. As he had already cut Jefferson off, the two took leave of the tap room, Jefferson leaning on Hamilton for support. The interim allowed Hamilton to regain her patience with Jefferson, and allowed her to address her friend in a calmer and less lecturing tone.

"Look," she said. "The only reason I talk to like that is because I want to help you..."

"...join AA and sober up and become a tet....tat....non-drinker!" Jefferson cut her off. "Nothing doing!"

"I'm not saying you should give up drinking," Hamilton said, trying her best to ignore the interruption. "Or sex, either. These things are important to you, for some perverse reason only *you* know about. And far be it from me to stand in your way..."

"...because you know what I do to creatures who do that to me. Even you, Hamilton!"

"Yeah, Jeff. I know. I'm just saying, maybe you should cut back."

"*What?*"

"Yeah. You know, maybe like having only one bottle of beer at a sitting..."

"*One* bottle?"

"...or making love to only one boy a night..."

"*One* boy?"

"Relax, Jeff! Those are just suggestions!"

"Well, I'm suggesting something now! That you *put up your dukes*!"

"Jeff, please! You're not in any condition to..."

"I can take you, or anybody else, sober or drunk! So come on- put 'em up!"

Jefferson separated herself from Hamilton and threw a punch, but the target moved, and Jefferson instead drove her fist harmlessly (mostly) through a telephone pole, retracting it only when the pain became too much for her.

"Aah!" Jefferson screamed. "Look what you made me do!"

"You did it to yourself!" Hamilton answered. "You always do it to yourself. And you'll keep doing it to yourself until you either die or figure it out- whichever comes first!"

With those exasperated words, Hamilton angrily left her friend alone to find her way home. Which wasn't far, as their apartments were in the same building- which was now only steps away.

III.

After Hamilton strode away from Jefferson with disgust, the latter, through limited but forceful exertion of her inebriated body, made it into the elevator of her building, barely missing catching the cage only because the operator, all too familiar with her and her antics, held the door long enough for her to enter. For the same reason, he ignored Jefferson's flirtatious banter with him as he punched the co-ordinates for her floor. That being done, and the floor doors opened with a "ding", he promptly "dinged" Jefferson onto the floor by putting his foot on her posterior and kicking her onto the floor. She, in her state, barely noticed. Failing to find her keys, she simply ripped the door off its hinges and then re-assembled it once she entered, hoping to avoid future confrontations with the landlord over tearing off the door as she had done in the past. Still staggering, she managed to find her bedroom and then her bed, and, finally, fell fast asleep.

Now, it must be said here, in spite of the obvious nature of the statement, that Jefferson, someone who took particular pride in her status as a lover, would go to extreme lengths to maintain an exceptional physique in order to gain as many "catches" as she possibly could. This did not extend to her wardrobe- she wore copies of the exact same outfit every day so people would always know what to expect of her- but certainly did to her physical appearance. In particular, she was proud of her fur, especially the luxurious upper portion of her pelt, which entirely covered her erect ears and gave her a dead ringer appearance to a human female of the long-ago time with short, light brown hair. This, she was convinced, was the secret to everything in life she had succeeded in, especially her success with boys, and she went to exacting lengths to make sure that her "'do" always remained intact, especially when she was expecting and willing to make love to a new squire--which was *always*.

However, the morning when she arose from the previously noted drunken debauch was not to be normal- even for a life as abnormal as Jefferson Ball's was.

Waking as she normally did, with the first rays of the sun that got into her tired eyes, she arose masterfully, having entirely recovered from the hangover that had debilitated her the previous evening. Heading to the bathroom to give her fur its customary styling before launching whatever business she had in mind for the following day, Jefferson began as normal, giving it a good "fluff" with her powerful paws before proceeding to the next step: brushing.

However, that process was interrupted almost as soon as it began. As Jefferson began to stroke the fur with the brush, a horrendously loud "ripping" sound was heard. Jefferson, upon hearing this, withdrew the brush...

...and promptly saw that a goodly portion of the luxurious upper portion of her pelt was now residing in the brush, instead of on her head!

160

It is safe to say that the anguished scream Jefferson uttered at that point woke up every resident of her building not yet risen, as well as everyone in all of the houses, apartments, condominiums, and tenements in all five of the counties that then composed the greater metropolitan area of Hugopolis.

IV.

"Hamilton! Ham-il-ton! Open your door, now! I'm being real serious here! *Hamilton!*"

Jefferson was not one to wait a moment when a crisis involving herself was in the process of manifesting itself. Nor was she one to politely request an audience with her best friend on the telephone prior to showing herself at said person's residence. Hence, having vaulted upstairs to Hamilton's residence in a sprint that even Usain Bolt would have envied had he seen it, Jefferson was now pounding on Hamilton's door as if her life depended on it.

She was still pounding a few minutes later, when a bath-robed Hamilton finally opened the door, and then, not knowing when to stop, she accidentally hit her friend in the nose, nearly crumpling it in the process.

"Damn it, Jefferson!" Hamilton bellowed. "I know we've had our differences, but did I really deserve that particular haymaker?"

"Sorry," Jefferson said, with unusual meekness in her voice. Then, switching back to her normal tones, she announced why she had come:

"We have an emergency here, Hamilton! You have to help me- you're my only friend! And we only have a short time to act before the full effect of it comes in. My God! I've already lost some of the top of my pelt, and you don't want to know what'll happen if I lose the rest of it! It's horrible..."

Jefferson continued to speak more incoherently, as her emotions ran the gamut from sadness and incredulity to a cold-blooded desire for murderous vengeance. Hamilton endured as much of this as she could, but even she had her limits. Eventually, she reached them, and showed them to Jefferson by punching her in the face, just as she had been punched moments earlier.

"Snap out of it!" Hamilton ordered, with a forcefulness that drove Jefferson back towards the door. "How the hell can I help you with whatever your problem is *today* if you don't let me even get a word in edgewise? And how in the hell do I know this isn't another one of those fairy tales you usually come up with when you *drink*?"

"I'm sober, Hamilton! I didn't have a single drink after I got done last night. And I only just got up a few minutes ago!"

"You-and me- and everyone else around here! Do you want us to get evicted, or what?"

"Cram it, Pomeranian!"

"Oh, real mature, Jefferson! Anybody says anything you don't like about you..."

"I said *shut up!*"

Jefferson threw her hairbrush at Hamilton like a baseball pitcher, and the latter caught it like an outfielder make a desperate grab for the ball at the far end of the field. Once it was caught, Hamilton noticed the pelt-strewn base of the brush.

"Is this what you're yammering about?" Hamilton asked.

"Yes, Ms. Genius!" Jefferson shot back. "Nice to see you finally figured that out!"

"We get fur stuck in brushes all the time, Jefferson! It's nothing to worry about..."

"Says *you*! You don't have as much fur as I do, and you don't need to worry about what happens to *you* when you *lose* it. *I*, on the other hand, *do*."

"Why?"

"Because..." Jefferson said hesitantly, not wanting to tell the truth. But Hamilton pressed her.

"Why, Jefferson?"

"All right! But don't you dare *laugh!*"

"I wouldn't dare, given the gravity you seem to want to apply to the situation, even though it might not warrant it. So what is it?"

"Okay. Along with our fabulous inherent abilities, my family has a history of....premature mange."

162

"There, now!" Hamilton said jocularly. "That wasn't so hard to confess, was it?"

"You don't understand, Hamilton!"

"Fine! What don't I understand?"

"If I lose all of my fur, either in one fell swoop or gradually, like with the brush, I lose all of my powers and abilities. Just like my uncle Firemans Ball did before that incident with the vacuum cleaner that killed him..."

"But, Jefferson, losing your fur isn't the end of the world. *Lots* of dogs can survive without having any..."

"You still don't *understand*!"

"Fine! What else?"

"If I lose my fur, my skin will start melting off of me. Then my skeleton will collapse beneath me, beginning with...my pelvis. And then my internal organs will..."

"All right! I get it! If you lose all your fur, you'll start to *die*! And *you* think it has something to do with that rotgut they called "beer" you were swizzling all night last night. And you want me to help you find out who was responsible and get your revenge before you blow up like a bomb on account of the loss of your precious fur! Is *that* it?"

"Exactly. But how did you...?"

"Jefferson, I've known you for ten years. Ten years that sometimes seems like a lifetime! Do you really think I don't know anything about you? I know everything about you- and you about me. We can't hide anything from each other."

"So you'll help me?"

"'Course I will! You may be a major league pain in the ass, but you and I also have the one thing remotely resembling a *friendship* in my life..."

"Now, that's not true..."

"Don't argue with me! It *is*!"

"Okay. Sorry."

"Fine. Only thing is, I can't go out like this," – indicating her bathrobe. "Maybe you can get away with showing that Muscle Beach body of yours all the time, but I sure as hell can't with this old leaky dam. Let me change!"

163

"Sure," Jefferson said, not knowing whether to be pleased or insulted by her friend's last comment.

V.

Soon afterward, Hamilton had outfitted herself in one of the many pairs of camouflage pants that were as much a part of her wardrobe as Jefferson's clothes were of hers, along with a number of white T shirts that showed off an upper torso that could, at times, be as powerful as Jefferson's was. That being done, the duo retraced their steps back to the bar where Jefferson had done her cellar rat act the previous evening. Seeing them coming, the bartender insisted he had just closed, even though it was quite clear that he had just opened for the day's business.

"Don't give me that!" Hamilton insisted, in a voice hardened by years of military experience.

"Fine," he admitted. "But me no let her in again,"- meaning Jefferson and pointing at her. "She bankrup' me!"

"Drop dead!" Jefferson shot back.

Before anything else could be done or said, Hamilton resumed her stentorian, police detective manner, completely ignoring Jefferson's interruption.

"Do you happen to know what brand of beer my friend consumed last night?" Hamilton asked the bartender. "Or brands, if she did switch during the night."

"Why?" the bartender demanded. "She gonna drink all the rest of me stock now?"- indicating Jefferson. "Or you?"-now indicating Hamilton herself.

"You little shithead!" snapped Jefferson. "If you don't want to be knocked into the Earth, you'd better..."

She would have continued in this line, but Hamilton growled sharply to silence her.

"Behave yourself!" Hamilton ordered her friend. "You want to get to the bottom of your little "hair" problem, don't you?"

"Yeah, but..."

"Then *shut up* and let me deal with this guy!"

"All right. But if you *can't*...or...*don't...*"

"I can and I will! So choke on yourself while I do it!"

164

Turning back to the bartender, Hamilton resumed her line of inquiry.

"She is *not* going to drink the rest of your stock- and neither, for that matter, am *I*. What we want from you is simply some information."

"Tell me and I see what I can do," replied the bartender, somewhat reassured.

"Okay. Did my friend drink only one brand of beer last night, or several different ones?" Hamilton asked.

"Oh, it was all one brand," said the bartender, mentioning the brand by name. "Whole entire case."

"And how many are there in a case?"

"Twelve."

"And she had them in succession?"

"No. Two at a time, wit' bot' han's. After six these, she get drunk and fall on floor, and I cut her off."

Upon hearing these details, Hamilton glared at her friend wordlessly, making it clear to Jefferson the size and the breadth of how she disapproved of this behavior. But Jefferson didn't take it lying down.

"You weren't there, girl!" Jefferson said. "I got stood up by a stupid boy who was too much of a *coward* to go out with me, and I just had to..."

"I don't need to know that!" Hamilton said. "Shut *up*!" Turning back to the bartender, she said: "You have another case of that stuff?"

"Yeah. But I no give it to you..."

"We'll pay you for it. The exact sum you yourself paid for it in the first place, if that's what it'll take."

"You pay for two of them, 'cause I need to restock after she bankrup' me!"

Jefferson, in response to this parting salvo, immaturely made funny faces at the bartender while Hamilton counted out the price he named in hundred bone credits.

VI.

"No!"

165

"But, Ham, come on...._"_

"I said no and I meant no!"

"I need a _drink_, Hamilton!"

"You "need" to sit down and let me handle this! And leave the damn case alone! For the amount of money we- or should I say _I_- paid for it, it damn well better have the solution to what's ailing you. But we won't find out if you drink the entire case!"

"I was only going to drink _one!_"

"That's how it starts! Soon you'll be drinking two...and three...and four..."

"Hamilton!"

"We can have one after. But just let me look at first- and _shut up_ while you do it!"

The two of them had placed the case of the offending beer on Hamilton's dining room table, and Hamilton, using the forensic skills she had gained as a soldier, was preparing to identify the source of Jefferson's hair loss from within it. That is, after she had expelled Jefferson from the dining room to the living room, with Jefferson doing an unflattering mimetic impersonation of her friend as she left. As she sat down, Jefferson soon came to squirm uncomfortably as Hamilton opened one bottle of beer and then another until she had opened all of the bottles- _without_ drinking any of the contents. After enduring endless rounds of the precious liquid being analyzed and poured and re-poured and spread on microscopic slides and God knows what else, Jefferson, never patient, found whatever patience she had melting away, and she marched back into the dining room.

"Hamilton, what the hell are you....?"

At this point, she uttered a scream nearly as loud as the one she had uttered on first discovering her hair loss.

Hamilton, it seemed, had been using herself as a guinea pig to help her friend. And it seemed that, in doing so, she had been forced to make a major sacrifice. Having already doffed her clothes, she was lying prone and semi-conscious on the floor-with her yellow-and-white pelt, separated from her body, strewn across the floor like hay in a barn!

"Hamilton!" Jefferson bellowed sorrowfully. "What have you _done_ to yourself?"

166

"I haven't done anything, Jefferson!" Hamilton said, sounding slightly inebriated on account of the after-effects of her "experiment" with the beer. "The beer did it- it did it all!"

"You're sounding like me now. And you had the nerve to drink that beer *without* me, you backstabbing asshole...."

"Is that all you can think about?" the now-naked Hamilton said as she got on her feet and walked over to Jefferson. "I'm naked, and all *you* can think about is your precious beer..."

"Sorry, Ham. Reflex action. I don't like seeing a good pint wasted, even if it *is* in such a good cause. How many of those...things did you *have*, for it to cause that much loss?"

"I took about an ounce of the liquid from each of the bottles," Hamilton said. "Then I poured them together and sipped them. It only took a minute before I started belly-flopping around like you did last night..."

"Wait a minute!" Jefferson interrupted. "I drank *twelve full bottles* of that crap last night, so why haven't I lost all of my...oh, my God! *No!*"

Having not looked at herself for nearly all of the preceding day, and therefore not aware of the true extent of her hair loss, Jefferson rushed to the bathroom. In the floor-length mirror, she touched the top of her pelt....causing every single strand of fur on her body not covered by clothing (which was not much) to drop precipitously from her frame!

For only the third time that day, the heavens around the Hugopolis metropolitan area were pierced by a Jefferson Ball scream.

VII.

"Hey, Jefferson! How ya like me *now*?"

Jefferson turned around- and saw that she was now face-to-face with a tall, white-furred male dog in a red speedo, boots and flowing cape. He was Remus XXIII, alien king of a planet in a far away solar system, and he was Jefferson Ball's most fearsome archenemy- as well as one of the few males in the universe she *hadn't* slept with at one point or another. The fact that he hated her intensely- and she him likewise- probably had something to do with it.

"Remus!" Jefferson bellowed viciously. "This is all *your* fault!"

"No shit, Sherlock!" answered the monarch, in the most un-imperial voice imaginable. "You should have figured that out a long time ago!"

"What the hell do you mean by *that*?"

"Oh, for....Didn't you even look at those beer bottles before you chugged them? That big 'R' on the label should have tipped you off right away!"

"You mean...that was...?"

"Riiiight! My personal brand- brewed *only* at my personal brewery by my hand-picked brewmeisters. *And* shipped specially to that little alehouse you were tippling at last night specifically 'cause I knew you were coming in there!"

"But what about the loss of my fur? And Hamilton's, also?"

"So others have gone commando, too, huh? Never thought I'd see the day..."

"Stop bullshitting me, Remus! Did you plan this whole thing?"

"Actually, I didn't. That whole hair loss thing was a symptom of a bad batch that we had to recall before it caused any damage- to *my* people. Earth I don't care a flying fig about, as you well know."

"Uh-huh."

"But, as you also know, I am aware of the genetic...deficiencies in your family, Jefferson. When you hate somebody, you really go to big lengths to destroy them! You know that, too, *don't you?*" Remus pointed out a scar under his eye that Jefferson had caused in a previous encounter. "Consequently, when I discovered this anomaly in the beer, I made certain that you would drink it and become powerless without your fur, and I would come here to Earth to reap the rewards of my actions!"

"You rotten son of a bitch! Do you even *know* what my pelt means to me?"

"I do, or I wouldn't have done it!"

168

Jefferson, forgetting herself as well as her declined abilities, screamed viciously and launched herself at her enemy. Remus simply stood and watched her come, unafraid. Once she was in his reach, he grabbed both of her arms and held her tight in a painful, calcifying grip- not unlike the one she herself had at full power.

"Tut-tut, Jefferson!" Remus mocked the now-powerless heroine. "You forget that *I'm* the one with the edge here- for once!"

So saying, he punched her solidly in the face, and she flew through the closed bathroom door, landing with a loud crash in the center of the living room. She offered no resistance, unusually for her, but she could do nothing without her powers. Remus delighted himself in gaining revenge on her for past indignities, bashing her head with a vase, tearing her clothes off and beating her with her boots, and, finally, smashing her head on a coffee table and rubbing it sadistically in her own shed blood.

Having reduced the most powerful female dog in the universe to a bloody pulp, Remus XXIII now prepared to complete his degradation of his opponent, ironically enough, by raping her, an act of vengeance, he said to her, for all the virginal, innocent boys in his army she had be-spoiled and rendered insane and unfit for battle. However, he never got that far. For Hamilton Pomeranian, furless as her friend but still with her strength intact, was pointing a rifle at the interplanetary ruler.

"You get away from her," Hamilton ordered him, "or I'll drill you! She may be a jerk, and a lush...and..many other bad things, but she's still *my best friend*, and even she doesn't deserve what you just did to her...or were going to do to her!"

"You dare to order me?" Remus snapped. "Do you not know who I *am*?"

"Oh, I know, all right! Jefferson's told me all about what a pompous royal dickhead you are! And, even though I can't believe her on everything she says, I will on this one!"

"You diminutive demon..."

Remus lunged for her, but Hamilton was ready. One shot grazed him in the arm, another in the leg, and, finally, one landed right in his genitals. As he fell to the ground and clutched his crotch in pain, he melted into a pile of mist and disappeared, vowing vengeance not just on Jefferson, but Hamilton (who he had never encountered before) as well.

Hamilton then gripped Jefferson's body, and slowly took her friend downstairs to her room and bed so she could recover.

VIII.

"You shot him in the *balls!*"

It was sometime after the incident, several weeks, in fact. Hamilton had waited that long to allow her and Jefferson's pelts to grow back, making sure they were well secluded in the process. Now, Hamilton had surprised her friend by suggesting they go out together. They had both had a few by the time Jefferson made that remark, and the effects were starting to show.

"I kicked him there a few times," Jefferson continued shouting, "but you actually shot him there!"

"Not too hard to do!" answered Hamilton. "His stuff is so small that I could find it under his briefs easy*!"*

"Oh, boy!" Jefferson said. "I should have you around any time I have a sketchy date! Keep the fellow in line with a dead-eye blast!"

"Only if I get one myself alongside him!" Hamilton leered. "Woo-woo!"

The racket they were making had aroused the ire of the maitre-d', who drew the attention of the bouncer to them. Soon afterward, predictably, they were rolled out the door of the restaurant.

"Why, th'se b'ms!" Hamilton slurred. "They c'n do th't to *us!*"

"S'all right!" Jefferson slurred in response.

"How come?"

"B'fr' th't g-rilla grabb'd us, I had th' good f'rtune of stealin' us an'udder bottl'!"

Jefferson then produced this object.

"Wher'd y'...Wher'd y' *hide* it?"

"Y'don't wanna know! Really! Y'dont wanna *know!*"

Happy, content and drunk, the two best friends stumbled down the street that starry night, continuing to slurp from the stolen bottle of wine as they did.

David Perlmutter is a freelance writer living in Winnipeg, Manitoba, Canada, where he has lived his whole life. His passions are American television animation (the subject of his MA thesis and a projected historical monograph), literature (especially science fiction and fantasy) and music (rhythm& blues, soul, funk and jazz.) This explains why much of his writing is as nonconventional and defiant as it is. He is challenged with Asperger's Syndrome, but considers it an asset more than a disability.

No More Blue Pills
by Suzanne Robb

Doctor Roberta Jones, Bobbi to her friends, drove home with a wicked smile. In her briefcase the fruits of her labor to combat the little blue pill men took in order to solve their erectile dysfunction.

Hailed as a miracle drug, women once again needed to claim headaches as boyfriends and husbands approached them morning, noon, and night with Mr. Happy.

As a result, men used other outlets which led to divorces and a rise in the "insanity defense" when women caught their cheating man, and took matters into their own hands. The rate of incarcerated or institutionalized women grew exponentially.

When Bobbi's own sister, Vicki, fell victim to the damned blue pills and took out her husband with a golf club after she caught him with the nanny and the maid, Bobbi knew something needed to be done.

For the last six years, she and Rose Myers worked on the red pill. When they first wrote out the funding proposal, they were denied. Looking back, perhaps their mission statement of wanting to "End all the sex" could have been worded better.

Six months later, they wrote up a new proposal and an altered mission statement "To create a pill men would only have to take once and never again suffer from sexual performance issues." Within a week of mailing it out, a man called them to ask where the money should be transferred, and if they needed anything else to let him know.

Bobbi shook her head, men were so easy. Over the years, they bilked their backers of millions of dollars and created the red pill. Of course, this pill did something entirely different than indicated. She knew they would need a biologist of some kind to help with the tests they were supposed to run, so she made one up.

Seven years, 348 imaginary impotent apes, monkeys, mice, and rabbits later, they were ready to mass produce the red pill. Bobbi falsified the final reports and sent in statistics on human trials which indicated a ninety-nine percent success rate.

Every man who took the red pill had the ability to "perform" at any given time. Side effects listed: weight loss, sound sleep, higher muscle tone, and mood improvement. A week later, the company wanted the red pill on the market within the month. Twenty-seven days later, the first shipment went out.

A honk roused her from her musings of a husband who no longer wanted to have sex, who would rather do the dishes or yard work. Of course, she planned to leave Henry, he'd been patient zero.

Last week, she offered one of the red pills to him. Since then, he hadn't shown the least bit of interest in sex. There were some weird side effects, like his love of red meat and declining verbal skills.

Traffic was at a dead stop, so she turned on the radio. She'd been so busy hiding money in offshore accounts, making withdrawals, and slipping samples of the pills into co-workers lunches, she'd lost touch with reality.

"More reports of cannibalistic attacks are rolling in. All over North America and Europe, men seem to have been infected with some sort of virus causing them to turn into mindless zombies bent on getting brains."

A car honked its horn, and Bobbi looked around to see what the commotion was. Up ahead was a mob. Police ushered people backwards with flares.

She put the car in reverse, last thing she needed was the cops finding a briefcase full of pills and cash. Bobbi hit the gas without thinking and backed into one of those pretentious luxury sedans. She swore to herself and got out to see how bad the damage was. A tall man with dark hair and a slightly disheveled appearance made his way out.

She watched as he slowly progressed towards her. Saliva dripped down his chin. His face was blank, eyes void of color.

Sirens went off as screams from up ahead echoed down the road. Bobbi glanced around. Strong arms grabbed her from behind.

174

She stomped her foot down on her attackers. Other than a slight moan, he didn't respond. Bobbi repeated the process until she wiggled free from his grip. When she turned to rip the guy a new one for being such a pervert, she shrieked.

The man bled from his eyes and nose, blood came out of his mouth, and the rancid smell of decomposition caused her to wretch. She stepped back opening her car door. One look around at the chaos and she knew there was no way could she drive out of there. The road was packed full of people panicking or trying to eat the others.

Bobbi grabbed the briefcase and ran. She kicked off her heels and jumped the guard rail. Thirty minutes later, she crossed the row of hedges separating her subdivision from the road beside it. She stood still at the sight in front of her. The gardeners, pool cleaners, and home owners meandered around, moaning.

The mailman, or at least what was left of him, lay in the middle of the Carl Edward's driveway. The package he intended to drop off was splattered with blood. The label caught her eye, a shipment of red pills from her company.

A trail of intestines led to Charlotte William's house. Bobbi always thought the woman was a bit off.

A closer look revealed an empty skull lolling around in a sticky pool of grey matter. Bobbi could see her house; Henry was watering the driveway.

Jake Hawkins approached her, sniffing the air wildly. He let out a guttural moan, and all the others turned towards Bobbi. Why did she wear *Irresistible* today? She picked up an abandoned pair of hedge clippers making sure to keep the brief case within easy reach. When Jake was close enough to take a bite, she drove the shears into his stomach.

To her amazement he kept coming at her. She pulled out her makeshift weapon and gagged at the piece of bowel caught on the end. Jake had corn for dinner. She opened them up and, with a quick scissoring motion, lopped off his head.

Others approach. She tossed the gardening tool to the ground and snatched the briefcase. The roar of a motorcycle caught her off guard. Bobbi watched as the rider tore down the street. One hand steered while the other chopped a zombie's head off with an axe.

The biker skidded to a halt and jumped off, brandishing a machete pulled out of a hilt strapped to his leg. Bobbi took in the sight of the Prince of Carnage as he hacked and slashed his way towards her.

A low moan to her side caused her to look down. Lisa Tomkins, or at least the upper portion of her, grabbed at Bobbi's ankle. She kicked the nasty woman in the face then picked up a pair of electric hedge trimmers. Bobbi brought them down on her former neighbor's head.

"That's for your stupid tuna casserole that gave me the runs for a week."

Smiling she turned to her next attacker. Jim Folley. He liked to pinch her backside when no one was looking. With glee, she raised the trimmers above her head and introduced them to the center of his face.

As the blades stuttered their way through his skull cap, she cackled. His head split in two like a peeled banana. The body twitched, then fell to the side taking her weapon with it.

She looked around frantic as three zombies made their way towards her. Out of weapons and unwilling to fight them off with her hands, she froze.

Harold Grimly stood three feet from her. No way could she grab the briefcase and make a run for it. Harold's eyes widened a bit, then she saw the tip of a machete appear as his right eye popped and squirted a milky like substance all over her. The body shook as if being electrocuted then crumpled.

The biker nodded. Then with his right hand he drove the axe into the throat of one zombie and hacked the arm of the one on his left off as it grabbed for Bobbi. Smart enough to get out of the way and let her leather clad knight in shining armor do his thing, Bobbi moved back a few steps.

He tore the axe out of the neck, and Bobbi took a step back as the carotid artery sprayed darkish colored blood all over the place. The smell made her nauseous. The biker spun around and lodged the axe into the face of the one armed zombie. An audible crack could be heard as the nasal cavity split open, and a slimy substance seeped out.

Bobbi could see he had a hard time getting the axe out and left it there, resorting to the razor sharp machete. The zombie spurting blood still headed towards Bobbi even though she could see him deflating from rapid fluid loss. When he stood less than a foot away, the machete appeared out of nowhere severing the head from the body.

The biker turned and placed a large boot clad foot on its face, lifting the handle of the axe up and down, he managed to release it. Bobbi watched in fascination as he wiped the weapons clean on the nearest corpse.

She waved to get his attention and motioned towards her house. The biker shook his head and nodded towards the bike.

"I need to go to my house. There are some important things I need to get."

The biker shrugged, and Bobbi interpreted it as okay for her to go. The biker poked corpses making sure they were dead. Bobbi stood entranced at the way he moved, the subtleness of his hips, the narrow waist. She almost swooned when Henry went down like a wet rag doll, his head rolling into the middle of the street.

Bobbi tore herself away and entered the house ready for anything. The first thing she did was slip on sneakers. She ran to the study, popped open the safe, grabbed two duffel bags, and the nine millimetre she bought on E-bay a few years ago in case the people she embezzled from came after her.

She exited her house and ran to the bike. Bobbi looped the bag handles around her arms and shoved the gun in the waist band of her skirt. Thinking back she should have changed, but this skirt fit her butt like a glove.

The revving of the motor and the rumble of the beast beneath her made her wonder why she never experimented with bikers. As she wrapped her arms around the small waist, she imagined strong arms holding her. Content and happy, the carnage and bloody chaos they passed through did nothing to ruin her mood. In fact, she liked the change of pace.

177

When her saviour took a turn off for a gas station, she sighed in relief. Getting off the vibrating hulk would prevent her dying from dehydration, she thought with a mental laugh.

She lifted an achy leg over and stood on limbs which still trembled. Bobbi watched with bated breath as her biker took off his helmet. Long black silky hair fell free blowing in the wind. Fair skin revealed itself as did sky blue eyes and high cheek bones. When Bobbi got over the shock, she blurted. "You're a woman."

"Yeah. Problem?" said a husky voice.

Laney Davis gave her most intimidating look to the chick with the nice butt. She'd planned to ignore her and cut a bloody swath through the rising army of undead, but fell for the whole damsel in distress thing.

As she looked at the woman, she debated whether or not she'd made a mistake. She held two large duffel bags and a briefcase. This chick thought the middle of a zombie apocalypse an appropriate time to pack her favourite outfits. As she looked her up and down with a critical eye, she noticed the gun.

Interesting, maybe she wouldn't be dead weight after all. Laney glanced around and didn't see any signs of movement or hear any strange noises. She took a few steps forward then pulled a large bowie knife out of her boot. The woman behind her let out some sort of moan as she bent over, and Laney turned to make sure she hadn't turned into a zombie.

"You okay?" Laney asked.

"Fine, sorry, something in my throat."

Was she blushing? Laney wondered.

Bobbi could not explain the feelings in finding out her hero was a woman. Beggars can't be choosers and all that, she thought. The weird sensation she felt when the biker bent over confused her more, but not unpleasantly.

"Hey, no daydreaming at a time like this, and what's your name?" The biker asked in an annoyed tone.

"Bobbi, and you?" she stuttered like a teenager.

"Laney."

Bobbi nodded as Laney turned and cautiously approached the gas pump. She took one of the nozzles and filled the tank. Bobbi wanted the other woman to talk more; she enjoyed the velvety sound.

As she watched the other woman hitch up her leg to rest on the curb, Bobbi let her eyes roam across the woman's backside. She filled out those leather pants nicely.

It didn't mean anything. She could appreciate the form of a woman, the sound of her voice. Imagine the feeling of her hands on her. Bobbi shook her head and remembered their situation. Zombies were everywhere, vigilance.

"You really need all those bags?"

"Yes."

"Fine, but I ain't carrying them. We need to stock up on supplies. Let's go. Hope you know how to use that fancy gun of yours."

Bobbi dropped the bags next to the bike making sure no living soul was in sight. She pulled out the gun and followed.

Laney held up a fist and crouched down. Bobbi, unsure what the hell was going on, hit the deck assuming they were under attack. She cocked her gun and fired a shot in the air.

Laney turned with a look of death on her face. "What the hell are you doing? Now any undead bastard within miles of here is coming to get some lunch."

Bobbi worked her mouth, but no words came out. "Sorry, got scared."

"Great, a premature shooter, just what I need," Laney said.

Bobbi followed behind as they entered the small store. Laney reached behind the counter and grabbed several plastic bags, shoving some into Bobbi's hands. The leather clad vixen moved around the store collecting jerky and bottled water.

She went over a few aisles and grabbed some expired crackers, cheese in a can, and several bottles of five dollar wine, and some beer.

Bobbi reached for a chocolate bar when a hand appeared in front of her. She opened her mouth to scream, but the thing clamped her mouth shut before any noise came out. She pushed them back into a postcard rack.

Out of the corner of her eye, she saw Laney checking out some bottles of motor oil. Bobbi clawed at the hands holding her pulling away strips of decomposing skin, and pulled her head forward to avoid the snapping teeth.

"Try and keep it down. If I'd known you were this noisy, I would've left you behind."

Bobbi made a face and spared a second for a less than kind gesture with her finger. With one more powerful shove, she pushed the thing back so the counter stopped it. The glossy postcards on the ground caused both of them to lose their footing. They fell together in a heap of flesh, Bobbi finally able to let out a scream. Laney turned with widened eyes. She looked between the bottle of oil and Bobbi. With a sigh she ran over, grabbed Bobbi and pulled her away then used her foot to kick in the rotten head of the zombie.

Bobbi rubbed her throat as she watched the woman go to town beating the crap out of the monster. Laney stomped until nothing but a syrupy mess of bone and brain matter remained. The body twitched, and Bobbi heard the rattling of a bottle of pills. A moment later it fell out of the man's pocket. Laney picked it up, shook her head and tossed it to Bobbi. She read the label and felt a stone settle in her stomach. *Hardware*, written where the drug name went. He took a whole bottle?

She had no idea what taking several of them would do to a person. Then again, she had no clue what taking one would really do, other than cause impotence.

Bobbi watched as Laney picked up the discarded oil, then approached the front door with a serene expression. Killing zombies improved Laney's mood, something to keep in mind Bobbi thought.

"Let's go. I don't want to stay in one place for too long. The end of the world might be here, but it doesn't mean Laney Davis is going down without a fight."

Bobbi followed her out of the store. Laney opened two large black bags strapped on each side of her bike. She tossed in her bag of supplies then reached a hand out for Bobbi's.

She handed them over looking away as she did so. Bobbi heard the woman grab the nozzle and screw top back on the gas tank. Bobbi bent down and looped the bags through her arms once again.

"You sure you need those?"

"Positive."

"You do understand zombies are taking over the world as we speak. The apocalypse is here, and it's arrived in the guise of the undead."

Bobbi nodded. "I don't know if I really believe in all this apocalypse stuff."

Eight seconds after the words came out of her mouth, a shadow passed over them. They both watched as a large mass moved in front of the sun turning day into night.

"You were saying." Laney said.

Bobbi eyed the woman admiring her smile. Some sort of astrological phenomenon did not an apocalypse make. As for the zombies, she had some suspicions as to what was going on. However, she didn't want to argue with her only hope of survival. So what if the woman was a little eccentric.

"Let's get going," Bobbi said exasperated.

Laney kept an eye out for any zombies as they rode on the shoulder of the road. Abandoned cars, wrecks, and bodies littered the main highway. She felt Bobbi squeeze her and knew she had to pull over so the woman could pee -- again. Did the woman have a bladder the size of a hamster?

As the motorcycle rolled to a stop, Laney kicked out the stand. She took off her helmet and waited for Bobbi to get off, tote all those stupid bags to the side of the road, and squat behind a car.

"You know there are zombies everywhere. Hiding because you're shy might not be the best idea."

After a few moments of silence, she placed the helmet on the bike and slid off. She reached into one of the saddle bags and grabbed a small hand axe.

"Everything okay?" Laney asked as loud as she dared.

She walked quietly, and as she turned to corner, she saw a zombie straddling Bobbi. Laney hefted the axe high and brought it down in the center of the corpses head. She kicked the zombie with her boot then screamed when a hand grabbed her ankle. She raised the axe again and brought it down into thing's chest.

"It's me, you idiot," Bobbi said through gore covered lips.

Laney glanced at Bobbi, annoyed she was alive. She pulled the axe out of the zombie's chest, enjoying the sucking noise it made. The irritating woman stood, and Laney looked her over for any sign of a bite, hoping. Sadly, she found nothing to indicate the woman was infected, but did smile at her obvious annoyance in being covered in zombie gore.

"Why didn't you call out?" Laney stared at Bobbi wondering if she had a death wish.

First, she finds her in the middle of some sort of zombie version of suburban hell. Then she gets attacked in the store and doesn't ask for help, and now another situation in which she didn't indicate trouble.

Bobbi straightened her skirt. She picked up the bags and looped her arms through the handles.

"I couldn't scream, I had a cracker in my mouth and when I got into position, he startled me, and I started choking on it."

Laney nodded. The woman was a lunatic and would likely get them both killed. She would have left her behind, but if they were the only two survivors, she wanted someone to talk to. As she watched the woman round the corner, she reconsidered her need to converse. She could always talk to inanimate objects or animals. Hell, people had pet rocks.

Bobbi held tight to Laney, she seemed to be going faster than before and taking corners tighter than necessary. No way would she be gotten rid of so easily. After two more hours of riding and no zombie sightings, they stopped.

Laney pulled off the shoulder and rode down an old dirt road for a few miles. Bobbi assumed if they were attacked this gave them ample room to move, and multiple directions to run away.

Laney paced the field, perfect it they were ambushed. The bag obsessed woman could fend for herself, and she could hop on

182

her bike and take off in any direction. She smiled with self-satisfaction.

Bobbi put down the duffels and picked out some of the food they'd collected earlier. Laney came over and sat next to her, a strange look on her face. She watched as the woman pulled a small radio out of one of the black bags and fidgeted with the knobs.

"This is...an....iller...today...ecember...enty-first...thousand twelve...arks the eginning...the end...ombies...are everywh....eems to be...men who are...ostly affected....scientists are...linking the outbreak to...ardware a new medication...nvented by Roberta...no cure...seems that...doo...sday is here....ay your...rayers."

"I knew it, you didn't believe me, 'I don't buy all that end of the world crap' you told me. Now look, a zombie apocalypse of our own making. Man, would I like to get my hands on whoever invented that medication."

Bobbi sat still. This was one of those moments that defined a person. She could either speak up and admit what she did, or keep her mouth shut. Three seconds of deep thought later Bobbi made her decision.

"I know, whoever invented those pills really needs to be shot."

Laney glanced at her with an incredulous expression. "Are you kidding? I want to shake their hand. I've been waiting for this day as long as I can remember. The thought of an apocalypse, it's a dream come true." Laney sounded downright whimsical.

Bobbi set out some of the spray cheese with crackers and unscrewed the top on one of the bottles of wine she'd grabbed. Perhaps this Laney chick wasn't so bad after all.

"So, you'd thank them?"

Laney snatched a cheese covered cracker then took a swig from the bottle before answering.

"I'd sure as heck praise them for getting rid of all the men. It's a lesbian utopia now."

Bobbi's cracker got stuck in her throat causing her to choke--again. Laney reached out slapping her on the back.

183

"What are you talking about?" Bobbi managed.

"All the infected are men who took that 'Hardware' pill. The only women who were turned were ones that were attacked," Laney explained as if talking to a child.

Bobbi watched Laney tore into a package of jerky nibbling on the end of it in a rather seductive manner. She tossed another cracker in her mouth wondering what a world where women ruled would be like. Shoes would always be on sale. Matching purses and belts would be mandatory upon punishment of death. She could learn to love this apocalypse thing.

"How are so many men affected? I'm sure the target demographic was married men who cheated."

"Are you serious, or are you really that dumb?"

Bobbi wanted to point out she'd developed this apocalypse and designed the pill in the first place, but held that information back for fear of death.

"I'm serious."

"What man in his right mind would turn down a pill which will let him perform at all times? Not to mention the side effects listed were all bonuses. People probably smuggled them out of the factories and flooded the black market. College guys, married, divorced, single, gay, and any other kind of man you can think of gobbled them up like candy."

Bobbi thought for a moment. It made sense, and she kicked herself for not trying to tap into the under the table sales. Then reality dawned on her. There were no more men.

"What about sex?" she almost yelled.

Laney looked at her with a serious expression. "Bobbi this is an apocalypse, the end. There is no future, there's only surviving. As for sex, we'll just have to come up with a solution." Bobbi swore she saw the woman wink at her.

Laney chuckled and Bobbi felt left out. She wanted to laugh too, but the realization she'd caused an apocalypse made her think. She'd caused an ancient prediction to come true. She'd created a historical event, something which would be remembered for generations to come, or at least for this generation. She was a tool of God.

Laney watched Bobbi run off to the side of their makeshift encampment. When she was out of sight, she went straight for the duffel bags. What stared back at her caused two reactions: what the hell was this woman doing with this much cash? And where did she get all the cash?

A card to the side caught her eye. She looked at it, and realization dawned on her. The sound of her friend's return caught her attention and she went back to her spot with a wad of cash.

"What are you doing?" Bobbi asked her.

"Why do you have all that money?" Laney shot back.

Bobbi approached with caution. "I emptied my bank account in case we became a cash only economy after the apocalypse."

"You don't believe in the apocalypse. Where did you get it from?"

Bobbi stood in front of her, a strange smile on her face. Was she puffing out her chest?

"I embezzled it. Me and you can run off together and live like queens," Bobbi said.

Was this chick serious? Run off during the end of the world.

"If you want to live, you need to start thinking about survival – Roberta."

Bobbi's eye's widened. "How do you know?"

Laney held up a library card. She wanted to kill her, but being annoying wasn't a crime…yet. However, a woman who could bring about an apocalypse was something special.

Screaming interrupted Laney's moment with the Apocalypse maker. She turned her head and watched as a horde of zombies appeared. With a feral smile, Laney tossed the library card into the wind and unsheathed her axe and machete. Time for her to do what she'd be born for.

Bobbi watched in horror as Laney whipped out her weapons. She thought for sure she would kill her. The axe hefted high, Bobbi closed her eyes. A whoosh noise, seconds later a sickening crunch as it impacted with bone.

The sound of something rupturing and a spray of warm fluid on the side of her neck let her know Laney had just saved her life -- again.

Bobbi turned to look at the damage. The body fell on top of her duffels, oozing blood all over them.

She tore the hem of her skirt so she had more range of motion then grabbed the nine millimetre from her waistband. With a vicious smile only someone happy to have brought around the apocalypse would dare sport, she pulled the trigger.

A zombie approached her as she knelt to grab some extra magazines out of her bag, progress hampered by the dead body on top. Bobbi was enveloped in decomposing arms. She did her job, brought about the apocalypse. But, she didn't deserve to go out like this, she thought as a mouth full of rotten teeth and bits of skin snapped at her. A second before the mouth clamped down, she heard Laney yell.

"Am I always going to be saving you?"

The woman lifted the zombie off of her while disemboweling it with her machete. As all the insides became outsides, Bobbi watched in annoyance as her duffels filled with guts. Laney let the body drop then squashed its head with her foot. A move Bobbi realized was becoming Laney's trademark.

Bobbi wondered what the future held. Would it always be like this?

"Hey, so I know this isn't the best time, but are you into chicks at all?" Laney asked in a casual voice considering the situation.

Bobbi raised an eyebrow. "Well, there was this one time in college..."

Laney smiled. "Figured, we got time."

Bobbi watched as the biker woman ran off hacking at limbs with both hands, the axe and machete extensions of her being.

Bobbi loaded the gun and aimed. If this was to be the future, so be it. She wondered if she should feel guilty about ending the world, but took solace in the fact she really just got rid of the men. This was an apocalypse she could learn to love.

Suzanne Robb is the author of Z-Boat, Were-wolves, Apocalypses, and Genetic Mutation, Oh my! *and* Contaminated. *She is a contributing editor at Hidden Thoughts Press, and co-edited* Read The End First *with Adrian Chamberlin. In her free time she reads, watches movies, plays with her dog, and enjoys chocolate and LEGO's.* *http://suzannerobb.blogspot.com/*

The Homunculus Caper
by Joette Rozanski

"I'm serious, Charles," Emmie said. "Don't mess with my magic."

Charles didn't take his eyes away from the game.

"What makes you think I wanna mess with your magic?"

Emmie stood in front of the television set. "You might get bored and I won't be here to bail you out. The Board of Alchemists won't be kind after your last accident."

Charles sighed and tried to peek around Emmie's jeans-clad legs.

"Don't worry about me, Emmie. Go see your mom. Have a good time in Jersey."

Emmie shook her head, making her dark curly hair bounce. "Behave, Charles. For your own sake, please behave."

Two days later, Charles looked around at the living room. Pizza boxes under the sofa, crusty dishes on the coffee table, dirty clothes in the corners. At this rate, he'd be featured on his own reality show by the end of the week.

Charles hated housework. Loathed it. He did enough to keep Emmie happy; not that she bugged him about it, but he didn't want to look like a total slug. Magicians of the Alchemy Class were notoriously neat and precise, a reputation he was never able to live up to. Sometimes he wondered if his talents lay elsewhere, like Spiritual Exorcism. Nobody ever complained about the messes involved in that.

Charles needed someone to keep things in order, but neither he nor Emmie liked strangers in their home.

After rambling around the house, he stopped by the his-and-her labs and snapped his fingers. The Homunculus Project!

189

Charles walked toward Emmie's lab and paused in the doorway, taking in the retorts, test tubes, dusty tomes and mysterious boxes. A large boy doll, dressed in a yellow t-shirt and red shorts, sat in the middle of a narrow table.

He'll do, Charles thought as he searched for the quicken dust.

Both Charles and Emmie belonged to families who were Alchemists, clans who plied their magical trade in secret through the centuries. Many had died during persecutions and inquisitions by the Mundanes, so they kept their discoveries to themselves. They solved the problem of transmutation two centuries ago and now experimented with homunculi, or non-living, human-like, servants.

Mundys and robots, Alchemists and Homunculi, each human family had their solution to boring chores.

A notebook lay next to the doll. On the first page Emmie had written: Roger. Good companion. Great around the house.

Exactly what he wanted!

On the second page she had written, "...the homunculus is a prism, projecting an array of character traits from its owner. To see it in action..."

Blah, blah, blah. He knew how to see it in action.

Charles wasn't a very good Alchemist, but he figured a single dose of quicken dust would make Roger his servant for a week. Emmie would return in ten more days so the timing was right.

"There it is," he muttered, grabbing a tube from beside Emmie's spell book. He shook the shimmering dust over the boy doll and mumbled a few words of power.

Roger opened his big blue eyes and said, "I wuv oo."

Charles stepped back. "Blech! No. I'm not Emmie. No mushy talk."

Roger looked puzzled. "You must be Chuck. I only come out when you're gone, but I've seen pictures. Big guy, shaved head, beard, wears black, and according to Emmie, a slob."

"My name is Charles," Charles said coldly. "Skip the review. I need your help with housework."

Roger's glass eyes narrowed and he flexed his plastic fingers.

"We'll see about that, Chuck."

Roger jumped off the table and ran into the living room.

"Wow, this place is a disaster."

Charles followed him. "Do you know what to do?"

"Yeah. I started helping Emmie a couple of weeks ago when you were at the races."

Charles wasn't sure how he felt about Emmie keeping Roger a secret, but maybe she wanted to surprise him for his birthday. Charles liked that thought. He wasn't doing anything wrong by using something meant for him, right?

Charles walked into the living room, grabbed the television remote and flopped down on the couch.

"So what're you waiting for? Get to work."

Roger was, indeed, great around the house. He washed dishes and windows, scrubbed floors, did laundry, and even cooked gourmet meals. When not needed, he returned to Emmie's lab.

Five days after the quickening, Roger cleaned the living room as Charles watched a football game. Late morning faded into early afternoon and Charles drifted in and out of sleep. Suddenly, he became aware of the silence and sat up. Something wasn't right.

A large purple rabbit popped up from behind the couch and looked back at him.

"Aaaack!" Charles cried.

Roger poked his head up beside the bunny's and grinned, his plastic pink lips stretching like rubber bands. "I guess you know Flopsy, right? She was Emmie's favorite girlhood toy but lives in the spare room now. Meet the rest of the gang."

Charles looked around the pristine living room and saw ten more stuffed animals. All of them, whether patchwork dog or calico cat or fuzzy giraffe, gazed at him with baleful button eyes.

"What the hell is going on?" Charles asked.

"You ain't the only one who knows how to use quicken dust," Roger snarled. He raised his right hand and pointed a revolver at Charles' head.

191

"We're goin' for a ride."

"Where…where did you get that?"

"The spare room. Flopsy knew where you hid it under the bed."

Charles slowly got to his feet.

"But I brought you to life. You're supposed to obey me."

Roger chuckled evilly. "Guess you didn't use the right words of power, buddy. Anyway, I lost that cleanin' feelin' I used to have with Emmie. Come on, get movin'."

Charles walked to the front door. "Where are we going?"

"To First Bank on Western. We're gonna rob it."

"What! You can't rob a bank!"

"Oh, yes, I can. I been thinkin' about it while I vacuumed, Chuck. Hoovering does strange things to a doll's mind. Now shut up and get in the car."

Charles and the stuffed animal gang got into his Civic. Roger hopped onto the seat beside him.

"No sudden moves, Chuck. Got it?"

Charles' mouth felt dry. "Yeah."

He backed out of the driveway. Flopsy's big purple head filled the rear view mirror. She yawned and he saw long sharp teeth protruding from fabric lips.

"Roger, what are you going to do after you rob the bank?"

"You're my hostage, Chuck. The cops will think we're little people in disguise. I wanna go to Disneyland where everybody can see real toys come to life. The heist will start getting eyeballs turned our way."

Charles gasped. The Family secrets would be exposed to Mundys!

No matter how he looked at it, Charles didn't see an easy out for himself. Either the cops, Roger, or the Families would kill him. If only he'd listened to Emmie!

But Emmie would probably want to kill him too.

"Robbing this bank will be a good thing for you and Emmie," Roger said.

"How do you figure that, Roger?" Charles asked.

192

The doll looked at him.

"Money is tight for you and Emmie, Chuck, mostly because you're a bum. Do you really think Emmie planned on visiting her mom for a month? She actually wanted to carve oosik into staves of power with her girlfriends in Iceland but didn't have the money to go there."

"Oosik? What the hell is that?"

"Phallic bone from a walrus. They make great wands but walrus wee-wee don't come cheap. You don't pay much attention to your wife, do you?"

Roger's harsh words brought tears to Charles' eyes. "I...I try, but..."

"No, you don't, Chuck," Roger snarled. "You want easy money so you can lie around all day or hang out with your Mundy buddies." Roger snorted. "Well, Chuck, I'm gonna help you out. Pull over."

"Roger, I'll change! I swear! Let's not do this."

The doll's blue eyes regarded him with profound sadness. "Too late, Chuck, too late."

At the bank Roger yelled and waved his gun, customers hit the floor, the stuffed animals put money into canvas bags, Charles stood and looked guilty for the cameras.

Cop cars, lights blazing, came screeching to the front of the bank. A loud voice told them to give up.

"Okay!" Roger said, prodding Charles in the back of his thighs. "Move!"

Charles placed his hands on top of his head and, with the plush toys flopping behind him, pushed past the bank doors and into the street.

"Don't shoot!" he cried. "I'm a hostage!"

"What the hell are those things behind you?" a cop yelled.

"Little people!" Charles yelped. "If you don't do what they say, they'll kill me."

"We got demands!" Roger shouted. "First, we want a helicopter..."

"All the little guy can do is shoot him in the ass," a cop muttered to his captain.

"I guess we can take that chance," the captain said.

Something cracked loudly and Roger went down. A cop pulled Charles away as more bullets riddled the toy animals near the doors. Stuffing and plastic and bits of fabric flew everywhere.

A button eye rolled toward Charles and bumped against the toe of his shoe; the eye stared at him accusingly.

Charles screamed and passed out.

Three days later, Charles appeared before the Alchemists Board. Emmie stood beside him and held his hand. A long table and several chairs stood beneath a golden star that glinted in the dim light.

"I told you not to mess with my things," Emmie whispered.

"I didn't know Roger was a devil doll."

"He wasn't. A homunculus takes on the character of the one who animates him. Since when did you want to rob banks?"

"I didn't! I must've screwed up the words of power." Charles squeezed his wife's hand. "Emmie?"

"Yes, Charles?"

"I'm a changed man, Emmie. No matter what happens, I'm going to try to be a better husband to you. First thing will be the honeymoon we never had. Does Iceland sound good to you?"

Before Emmie could reply, the black-robed Elders shuffled into the room and sat down at the table.

"You've caused a great deal of trouble," Wizard Anthony, he of the silver hair and severe face, told him. "We paid hundreds of thousands of dollars to the right people as hush money, which included a truckload of It Was All a Dream powder and a crop-duster with which to sprinkle it over the city. We are not pleased, Charles."

Charles hung his head.

"You are suspended from practicing Alchemy for two years," Wizard Anthony said, banging his ebony wand upon the table.

Charles raised his head. That wasn't so bad. He didn't like working at the craft anyway.

Wizard Belinda squinted at him from behind her thick spectacles.

"But because it was your laziness that precipitated this unfortunate event, we require further punishment."

Charles trembled.

"We sentence you to clean offices and homes with Maid Men and Chimneygents, beginning tonight in this very building. May you learn a lesson in diligence."

Charles closed his eyes. He'd be all right. He was now a man of sobriety and serious intent.

"Meet your cleaning crew," Wizard Belinda said.

Charles opened his eyes. Roger, followed by Flopsy and the rest of the stuffed animal gang with their brooms and pails, stood before him.

Roger blinked his big blue eyes. "I wuv oo."

"Isn't he cute?" Emmie squealed. She turned to the Alchemists Board and asked, "You re-animated all of them for me?"

Wizard Belinda smiled. "Yes. It wasn't your fault that your beloved toys were shot to pieces. Of course, they must learn their lesson now that they've become true homunculi. The words of power your husband intoned are not easily taken back."

Charles smiled at Roger. After all, the doll was instrumental in his renewed commitment to honest work.

"You know something, Chuck?" Roger asked, a puzzled expression on his face. "I got an urge to scrub a toilet. That sound right to you?"

Charles regarded the homunculus with a smile. "Yeah, Roger, that sounds just right."

Joette Rozanski is a native of Toledo, Ohio and works as a desktop publisher for a non-profit organization. She creates video and audio projects. Her hobbies are photography, walking the trails of the local metroparks and, of course, writing. Her favorite genres are science fiction, fantasy, and horror. She also enjoys the humorous tales of P.G. Wodehouse and Donald Westlake.

Aunt Bessie and the 'It'
by Norman A. Rubin

Through bygone years, Number Five Beale Street was considered the most feared place in the town by folks near and far. But that was before a new owner took possession of the property. Our dear Aunt Bessie moved in and somehow changed the atmosphere of the place. Today, the house with the address of Five Beale Street is just an ordinary two-story dwelling of five rooms and conveniences. There is nothing unusual or terrifying about the place, except when the shaggy watch dog of mixed breed feels like barking; it was more or less annoying to hear as his bark sounds like a thirsty barfly roaring and burping. But the past history is still in the back of the town folk's thoughts.

Strangely, none of the good people of the town really knew how the tales of the horror of Five Beale Street began. The good people really did not know what the shape of horror was. They all figured it must be something really horrible, since no one could spend a night alone in one of the upstairs bedrooms and remain alive - or not driven crazy from the sight.

It was evident in the morning that people who had been in those rooms had either died of fright, or gone mad and raged in the street. Except for the nervous sheriff and one of his equally nervous deputies; they had the unpleasant duty to attend to the aftereffects. They dared not talk of what they had seen.

Stories abounded of the horrors which encircled the dwelling at Five Beale Street. A maid who slept in one of the upstairs bedroom had gone completely mad. When she was found, she yelled, "Don't let 'it' touch me!" A tramp that sought shelter in the empty house screamed when he was pushed down the flight of steps: he had broken his neck and his face was frozen in terror. Additional stories of horror continued to be told through the years.

197

The house remained empty for many years because of tales that related scenes of terror and madness the house remained empty for many years. Residents of numbers Three and Seven Beale Street built high fences of stout timber to hide the sight of the house. But the continued screams of terror from foolish tenants of the neighboring structure forced them to bolt their own homes and flee with their sticks of furniture. Nobody walked past number Five Beale Street for fear of the encroaching terror. When they neared the house the crossed the street and made a sign of protection or fingered beads.

To Aunt Bessie, the dwelling at five Beale Street was a blessing as the asking price was rather low and so was her bank account. It seemed that her former dwelling was zoned for a highway and the law demanded the immediate vacating of her property. Aunt Bessie just put her mark on the contract for the dwelling, ghosts or no ghosts, after her nearsightedness didn't allow her to read the fine print. She then used part of the pittance she received for her old residence as a down payment with an easy-to-pay mortgage for the rest of the amount.

Aunt Bessie was a no-nonsense woman nearing her sixtieth year, but she was a lonely creature who did not have the love of a man nor caring children. She was a sprightly bird-like creature hopping about the town in her daily errands and her good work in Christian charity. All the folks about the town knew the cheerful smile and laughing blue eyes of Aunt Bessie, as she was always there when needed.

Aunt Bessie within a short time hired a contractor from out of town to spruce up the house with a bit of carpentry, electricity, plumbing and painting: No living creature in the town dared employment which demanded entrance into a so-called house of horror. Well, Aunt Bessie took with a 'never you mind' as the out-of-towners quoted a lower price for the work.

Within time the antique furniture of Aunt Bessie was in place, curtains decorated the windows, and a new letterbox at the entrance gate was ready to receive mail. Only one thing bothered her, and that was a reddish-brown splattered smear on a wall in one of the upstairs rooms that defied removal. The contractor put it down to a weathering stain and coated it with a bit of fresh paint.

But the contractor was astonished when the stains reappeared and damp to touch.

Everything was tried by the workmen to remove it from sanding and scrubbing to oiling and waxing, but to no avail. So, being a clever woman, Aunt Bessie said to the contractor 'never you mind' and tacked a circular hearth rug on it, but she couldn't understand how, after she banged in the points, that the following day the carpet was crumbled on the floor. She said 'never you mind' again as she covered the spot with storage boxes and old bric-a-brac and furniture in the converted storage room... and locked the door.

Aunt Bessie settled down in her new home, quite comfortable and cozy. Lights burned brightly in the downstairs living room as she read the daily passage from the Scriptures through a large magnifying glass. Saintly music screeched and crackled loudly from the radio apparatus encased in a large polished wooden cover. The sound of the music was rather loud, as Aunt Bessie was deaf in the right ear. There were no complaints as numbers three and seven Beale Streets were empty. All was content and peaceful in Aunt Bessie's life until the night 'It' showed up.

Aunt Bessie was at her usual occupation in reading the words when she thought she heard a loud harsh coughing sound. She peered through her thick spectacles and only saw a shadowy form in front of her, which she took as a person in need of her charity. The door to her home always opened to those in need. "Poor dear, she is suffering from a nasty cold," she muttered in sympathy.

Aunt Bessie grabbed the shadow before it was able to utter a 'boo' in protest and forced it into the bathroom. With a swift movement Aunt Bessie took a bottle from the medicine cabinet and stuffed two heaping spoonfuls of bitter cough medicine down its throat. With frightening screams to the right side of Aunt Bessie, the 'It' vanished.

A few nights later, Aunt Bessie was disturbed in her sleep in the upstairs bedroom by a creaking sound on the floorboards and the rattling of a door handle. The good woman, thinking about an unlocked door squealing and banging, left the warmth of her bed to investigate and correct. When she opened the door to her room, she saw the 'It' who was there trying to enter the locked storage room. Without her specs, Aunt Bessie put the sight down to sleepy eyes.

Then the 'It' turned and saw in the dim light from a reading lamp a horrible specter. There in front of its eyes was a terrible white-faced minikin covered from head to toe in ghostly cloth of white. The teeth of the 'It' chattered and its knees shook together loudly in sound to the right side of Aunt Bessie and with a scream of terror fled from the sight.

In due time the 'It' made its spooky appearance in the silence of its oiled rusty chains in all ghostly forms. After all, this was the habitat of 'It' that in all its horror removed the tenants from living in its walls; those who survived the night; it rendered mad. Now this infernal creature came and interfered in its nights of haunt.

The 'It' tried desperately to put in a scary sight to Aunt Bessie, but to no avail. Frightful horrid noises were tried, but the 'It' had the hard luck of screeching on the right, deaf side of the good woman. Then 'It' enlarged its shadowy form to terrible proportions on the day that Aunt Bessie mislaid her specs. Every night, and even in the daytime, the 'It' tried some form of scary pose, but the futility of its desperate efforts were seen in its frustrated movements that showed dejection and indignity.

When the 'It' tried to stretch out its arms from its shadowy form that lengthened in frightful proportions, Aunt Bessie simply called out, "You are such a dear!" and put a skein of knitting wool on the arms. The poor woman was getting so dotty in her elder years that she imagined that a friend had popped in for a chat. But the 'It' was humiliated as it sat on its haunches patiently while Aunt Bessie unrolled the wool from its arms into a ball.

According to the folks hereabouts, the scary haunt of five Beale Street was a thing of the past. The owners of numbers three and seven moved back into their homes with their sticks of furniture. Nobody made the sign or read the beads as they walked past the house, now spruced with a delightful garden.

As for Aunt Bessie, she had found a new companion to fill her lonely life with gay companionship. She and the 'It' read the daily passage of the Scriptures together, had genial chats over cups of tea and biscuits, and together helped each other in the daily chores. The 'It' was quite useful, as it was able to stretch his arms and clean hard-to-reach places. Together, they lived harmonious life, and there was a never a 'boo' or anger between them.

Of course the 'It' never made its appearance on the outside, which Aunt Bessie discerned to shyness. So with a 'never you mind' she attended to the outside errands and the charity work. The chained shaggy dog was unleashed to watch the interior of the house, and it took its watchful stance stretched out on the living room carpet.

And 'It', in her absence, watched scary movies on the newly bought black and white television set. 'It' squealed in joyful terror when Frankenstein or Dracula appeared on the fourteen-inch black and white screen.

Norman A. Rubin, of Afula, Israel is a former correspondent (Israel) for the Continental News Service, USA. and has become a free-lance writer, composing articles on subjects that include Near East culture and crafts, archaeology, history and politics; religious history and rites, etc.

His articles have been featured in publications worldwide: the Jerusalem Post, *Israel;* Coin News, Minerva, Oriental Arts, *etc.,* England; Ararat, Letter Arts Review, Archaeology, *etc. USA;* Spotlight, *Japan;* International B, *Hong Kong.*

Now retired, he writes informative articles and short stories, which have appeared in WritersHood.com, storymania.com, Good All Days *magazine, etc.*

If You Can't Trust a Rhyming Demon, Can You Trust a Demon Not to Rhyme?

by David Seigler

"Holy crap! Mrs. Agnaught was right?"

Barry could hear his Sunday school teacher shrieking: "Playing those games is walking the path to damnation! They're spells and witchcraft, the very same as congress with demons!"

Mrs. Agnaught also believed little men lived in her TV set, so Barry chalked her warnings up to elderly dementia. And yet, what else could this be standing before him with such a wicked smile? It not only had horns and reeked of brimstone, it looked just like the illustration on page one hundred sixty four of the *Handbook to Conjuring Demons for Wicked Intent*.

When he found the book at Crazy Dale's Game Emporium, he knew it would be the perfect source material for the campaign he was running for his after school gaming group. Familiarity with the material is important for any good game master, and Barry was certainly not going to be accused of skimping on the ambient details. So he grabbed every candle he could find in the house, turned to page one hundred sixty two, and set about memorizing the proper incantations.

Now, Barry might have been clueless about hygiene. He might have lacked a bit in the social skills department. But he was still an intelligent guy with the algebra grades to prove it. Barry Docus knew the things in his fantasy games were just that: fantasy. But, somehow, here he was, face to face with a demon.

> *"To deal soul for a boon,*
> *Hast thou summoned me true.*
> *I'm here by your asking,*

So I'll soon have my due."

"Wow," was all Barry could think to say. "You look a lot taller in the book."

Indeed, the demon standing before him was less than four feet from the tip of his horns to the end of his pointed hooves. It had deep red skin, of which there was quite a lot, for this demon wore not a stitch of clothing. Thick tufts of shiny black curls covered its head as well as parts of a more immodest nature.

"Speak not of my stature,
Lest ye injure my pride.
Now your boon you must name,
For no patience have I."

"Oh, hey, total mistake here! I was just practicing for a Crypts and Creatures game, you know, looking for a level eight creature for my party to take out. Who'd have thought you'd turn out to be real? Anyway, false alarm, dude! You can go back to the depths of heck, or wherever you're from."

"Your intent matters not,
be it jest or in fun.
You have summoned me now,
the deed can't be undone."

"What? Oh, no. I can't barter my soul away. Mom would ground me for a month!"

"If a boon you shan't name,
Then our business is done.
I will just have your soul
And away I shall run."

Barry had no experience with real demons, the only reasonable facsimile being Mrs. Finklestein, his World History teacher. So he did what any thirteenth level game master would do and grabbed his players guide book. He scanned the glossary, searching for anything that could help him, while the demon tapped one hoof on the floor impatiently. Finally he was certain he had found the information he needed.

"Upon further contemplation, demon, I have decided instead to challenge you by right of wager."

"I tire of this prattle,
This foolishness you spout.
You have summoned me fair,
And for that there's no out."

"Dude, don't you even read these books?" Barry said. "By right of wager, if I beat you in a game, then I keep my soul. It's all right here in chapter fourteen"

The demon stomped over and yanked the book from Barry's hands. His lips moved slightly as he read, his thin moustache alternately curling and straightening. Finally he slammed the book shut and glared at Barry.

"Very well, reckless child,
These rules force me to play.
But know when we're finished,
I'll brook no more delay."

Barry had read enough stories to know the demon would undoubtedly best him in most games. But there was one game in which Barry was virtually unbeatable. He went to his nightstand, pulled out a genuine imitation leather case and carefully opened it. As he pulled out the deck of cards within he said, "The game I choose is Sorcery: The Collection! I've got an extra deck you can use…"

"Ay, a fair choice it is,
this game I know quite well.
I have got my own deck,
And we play it in Hell."

And with that a deck of worn cards appeared in the demon's hand.

"Aw, dude," Barry said, "you're naked. I really don't wanna know where you were keeping those cards."

It was the first time Barry had played a collectible card game using his soul as the ante. It was, admittedly, a remarkably mundane setting for such a titanic clash. Barry sat on his bed facing this rather short demon, who sat slouched on the only chair. Barry knew the demon's disinterested posture was merely a ruse to hide his cheating. Luckily, Barry was cheating as well. Besides, his deck had never been beaten. He even gave serious consideration to entering the big regional tournament next month, but only if he wasn't condemned to eternal damnation by then.

The game grew long and it wasn't going well for Barry. His health points were almost gone and only a few cards remained in his stack.

"Ere your turn has ended,
This last card I shall play.
With it your fate be sealed,
Your soul now mine to take."

With a smile that sent chills down Barry's spine, the demon played a life sucking card. There was nothing he could do. The game was over. Then it occurred to him…

"Wait a minute! You've already played one of those!"

"Yes, another played I
What matters it to you?
Though quite rare this card be
In my deck I have two."

"But it's not legal! That card is restricted! You can only have one in your deck."

"I have followed the rules,
And my deck beat you fair.
Now prattle no longer

206

You've lost your silly dare."

"No, really! They just put it on the restricted list last week. Here, let me show you." Barry immediately went to his computer and accessed the Official Sorcery Card Game Rules Web Page. He pulled up "Recent rule changes" and pointed at the list. The demon reluctantly looked at the computer and scowled. His eyes turned red and his black hair drew into tight curls. His fingers gripped the keyboard tightly until it smoked, finally melting into slag. He tossed the keyboard aside, and then swiped at the monitor, smashing it with his fist. Teeth bared, he turned and grabbed the back of the chair, ripping the covering into shreds and then picked the chair up and repeatedly smashed in to the floor. Barry backed against the wall, terrified at the demon's rampage. Still breathing heavily, the demon stopped and spoke through tightly gnashed teeth.

"Very well, brazen cur!
Of recourse I have none.
It appears I have erred.
So my service you've won."

"Whoa, let me get this straight. Now you have to do my bidding, and I don't have to give you my soul?" Ideas suddenly raced through Barry's mind.

"Though it is clumsily put
It is none the less true
Your bidding I'll answer
Until I'm released by you."

"Awesome! But your rhymes are terrible. That stuff's gotta' go."

The demon looked at Barry with one arched eyebrow raised high.

"I command you to, um, cease the poetry. Um, herewith."

The demon sighed heavily before speaking in a contemptuous tone.

"If that's your command
I've no choice but to follow.
And lament lost style."

The first period bell pierced the formidable noise of students milling around in the halls, casually making their way towards class. It was a day like any other at Omar F. Kennedy High School, but with one distinct difference. The teachers noticed nothing out of the ordinary. The jocks were oblivious. In fact, in the entirety of the school, only a circle of Barry's friends seemed to notice anything unusual as two cheerleaders walked down the hallway.

"Dude, am I going crazy?" Pete leaned against the wall, his mouth open in disbelief. "Tell me you see what I see."

"I've died and gone to heaven." Kenny's eyes followed the girls, a small patch of drool gathering at one corner of his mouth.

"I just saw Mandy and Lisa down the hall. It's the whole cheerleading squad. Every one of them is completely naked." Harold spoke softly, his voice breaking.

"Maybe it's a prank." Pete said.

"Then why isn't anyone else noticing?" Kenny said as Barry walked up.

"Greetings fellow programs! It's a great, great day, huh?" Barry said with a grin.

"The cheerleaders are naked," Pete said without looking at Barry.

"That they are, that they are! Just the start, my friends. Today is going to be a stellar day!" Barry opened his locker and grabbed two books.

"Lancy really has a tattoo on her butt." Kenny finally wiped the drool from his mouth. "I thought that was just a legend."

"A butterfly. How original. Well, boys, time for some schooling." Barry slammed his locker door shut, saluted his friends and headed to his Chemistry class.

Barry sat at his desk and smiled. No one else noticed as Julie Kettleman, the head of the cheerleading squad, entered the room, her breasts slightly bobbing from side to side. She sat at her assigned spot, directly in front of Barry.

"Hi Julie," he said, leaning forward. "It's kinda' chilly today, don't you think?"

Even though he couldn't see her face, he knew that she was rolling her eyes. It wasn't often that Barry mustered the courage to talk to her, but she always rolled her eyes when he did.

"Troll!" was all she said.

"All right everyone, time to settle down!" Mrs. Nessmeyer clapped her hands twice and then walked out from behind the desk as the room slowly became quiet.

"I have your midterm test results and I must say I am shocked at the scores." She began passing them out to the various students, each one groaning as they looked at the paper. "I'm afraid that each one of you got an 'F'. Everyone that is…" she smiled as she approached Barry "…except for Barry Docus, who got an 'A+'!"

Julie turned in her seat to look at Barry's grade, providing him with a view that was worth more than any 'A'. He leaned back and grinned. This was going to be a stellar day for sure.

"So let me get this straight…" Kenny stuffed yet another French fry into his mouth. "You accidentally summoned a demon and then beat him playing Sorcery: The Collection and now he does whatever you say?"

"Yep, that's right." Barry said.

His friends burst into simultaneous laughter.

"Dude, you're on crack!" Pete said, showing the entire table his partially eaten sandwich.

"Hey, have you guys heard? Bloody Holiday's playing here!" Harold was out of breath, as usual.

"Here? In town?" Kenny almost spit a French fry out.

"No, here at school. In the cafeteria! I just saw the poster!"

"No way! You can barely fit 200 people in here. Bloody Holiday can't possibly play here." Pete said.

"But they are. There are posters up everywhere! Hey, Barry, isn't Bloody Holiday your favorite band?"

Barry just smiled.

"Barry says he's got a genie that makes his wishes come true," Kenny smirked.

"Demon," Barry said. "There's no such thing as genies."

"There was a rhyming demon in this comic I used to read," Pete said. "Don't think it granted wishes, though."

"You can believe it or you can not believe it," Barry said. "Doesn't matter to me."

Kenny was about to speak when Julie approached, still obliviously nude.

"Say, Barry," she said, bending over the table, "any chance I could get you to help me with my Algebra homework?"

"Well, yeah, I might be able to work it in," Barry said casually.

"You're a doll! I'll call you, ok?" Julie actually winked at Barry before turning and bouncing away.

The entire table sat mute for several long moments before Harold broke the silence.

"Say, Barry...this demon of yours? Any chance he could hook me up with Ellen Nessman?"

After a quick knock on the door, Barry's father entered his room. He never waited for Barry to answer; he just knocked and then came right in. That would have to change, Barry thought.

"Barry, do you know anything about..." he said before trailing off.

"What's wrong, Dad?"

"I'm not sure. Your room just seems...a lot bigger, somehow," his father said.

"You're getting old, dad. Spatial memory's the first thing to go. Now, what were you going to ask me?"

"Oh, um... we just got the bank statement on your savings account. I think they've made a mistake. A really big one." He handed the paper to Barry, who looked at it quickly before handing it back.

"No. That looks about right."

"It is? Are you sure? This is..." His father seemed dazed. "This is a lot of money."

"Oh yeah, positive. If that's all you needed, I've got some studying to do."

"Ok, yeah. That's all I guess…" he paused again, bewildered. "Uh, Barry? When did you get a big screen TV?"

Barry sighed and rolled his eyes.

"I've had it for a long time, Dad. Practically forever."

"Oh. Okay. Well…I guess I'd better go, then." His father almost bumped into the doorway before leaving.

Barry thought it interesting that his father didn't even notice the demon sitting at the computer, intently staring at the screen. In fact, anytime Barry wanted something, he had to drag the demon away from the computer.

"Dude, all you do is hang on the Internet. They don't have the Internet in Hell?"

"Yes, of course we do.
But our connection is slow.
You see, it's dial up."

Barry spit his soda all over his bed.
"You're kidding! I bet that really is eternal torture!"

"Only the low realms.
The big guy's got the best speed
You can imagine."

"Satan? Satan uses the Internet?"
The demon was indignant.

"It's his invention.
In fact the best tool around
For recruiting souls."

"Makes sense, I guess. I've decided what I want next."

"How I yearn to know.
What could it possibly be?
Unlimited porn?"

211

"Better," Barry said.

"Well then, what, pray tell?
A one billion gig iPod?
More pizza perhaps?"

"Way better. I want you to hook me up with Julie Kettleman."

The demon smiled somewhat sadly and shook his head.

"This I expected.
Man is ever so foolish.
Be sure what you ask."

"I've wanted her since the sixth grade." Barry eyes glazed. "Just arrange it."

"Very well, it's done.
Though you know not what you ask
I've granted your boon," the demon said, his wicked smile returning.

"Really? What do I do now?" Barry was already excited.
"Just follow the scent.
Your fate is no longer yours.
Stronger wills shall rule," the demon said, as the phone on Barry's nightstand rang.

Barry wanted Julie like no boy had ever wanted a girl before. He once spent an entire first period Chemistry class memorizing the exact curve of her shoulder. But Julie was out of Barry's league and he knew it. She was head cheerleader. She was pretty. She was popular. Her blond hair fell in perfect arrangement around carefully sculptured features. She even had an incredibly cute birthmark in a place that only the very, very lucky would ever see.

212

Tonight Barry was feeling very, very lucky. Before he could ring the doorbell, the door opened and there she stood. Her shirt was tight. Her skirt was short. Her hair fell casually around her face. Suddenly Barry's chest felt tight and he wasn't sure if he could walk.

"Hi, Barry, thanks for coming so quickly," she cooed.

"I always do," he said before he could stop himself.

"So…are you coming in?"

"Yeah, sure. Right now. I'm coming in," he stammered.

The house was dimly lit, with only a single lamp illuminating a couch.

"So, where are your parents?" he asked, circling the couch.

"I don't know, really," she said, somewhat confused. "They're gone. And…I think I need help with my algebra."

"No problem. Algebra's my specialty."

Barry sat on the couch and grabbed her book from the coffee table. She sat beside him, softly biting her lower lip. He opened the book and started nervously thumbing through the pages.

"Algebra's really boring," she whispered in his ear.

"Oh, no. Not when you begin to understand it," Barry said, his voice cracking. "You can do anything with numbers when you know how."

"I can think of some things you can't do with numbers," she said, her fingers slowly tracing a line along the back of his neck.

He swallowed hard and squeaked, "Yeah, I…I guess."

She slowly leaned back on the couch, gently pulling him down with her.

"What is it about you that's so different?" she purred.

"Nothing," he said

"Nothing?" She pushed him away and started to scoot to the edge of the couch.

"Well, Okay, um, it's this demon. I have a demon that does anything I want."

"A demon. You're teasing me." She moved closer and ran her fingertips across his back.

213

"No, for real. I beat it in a game and now it does whatever I want," he said, his lips inches away from hers.

"That's so exciting." She closed her eyes.

"You have no idea," he said, his fingers moving clumsily to the buttons of her shirt.

"I'd like to." Her hand softly blocked Barry's hand at the second button.

"Yeah, me too." His breathing was heavy and he trembled as he tried again to undo her button. Her lips parted, glistening in the dim light. He leaned closer, attempting to kiss her.

"No, I mean, your demon. I'd like to know what *that* felt like," she said, just avoiding his lips.

"What? What what felt like?" he said quickly.

"To have that kind of power. You know, like your demon." She pulled him closer and gazed into his eyes.

"Okay," he said and the second button came loose.

"Really," she said.

"Oh yeah, really," he said tugging desperately at the third button.

"You promise?"

"Yes, yes, anything you want," he said frantically.

"Ok, done!" she said as she pushed him off.

"Done? Oh no, we can't be done. I think I'd know 'done'."

"Your little demon, silly. I can't wait to meet him," she said.

"What? I never said you could actually…"

"A promise you made,
'Twas a deal consummated.
Her purpose was clear."

The demon now stood behind the couch. Julie jumped up and clasped her hands together in delight.

"Oh he's cute!"

"Hold on! I didn't mean you could have him," Barry protested.

"'Anything', you said

214

That can not be disputed.
Her claim is quite fair."

"And he speaks in Haiku!" Julie was giddy.

"Wait a minute! You were speaking Haiku?" Barry counted with his fingertips. "Hey, that's not fair. I ordered you to stop the poetry. You cheated!"

"Why are you surprised?
Could there be an act more rash
Than trusting my word?"

"Hey, look, Julie, what I said… I was just… we were gonna…"

"With you? Ew! Don't be silly Barry! But thanks for coming so quickly." She brushed her hand across his cheek and then nodded at the demon.

"Foul, Demons may be.
But beware the fairer sex.
They're smarter than you."

Suddenly Barry was back in his room, his 19 inch TV providing the only illumination. He sat on the bed and wondered just how everything had happened so quickly. Perhaps none of it really happened and everything was just a really great dream. If that was the case, he wanted to get back to it. He brushed the potato chip crumbs from his bed and jumped in, nervously pulling the covers to his chin.

Already the Bloody Holiday posters had been ripped from the walls and new ones placed in their stead.

"Robbie Tenderloin?" Barry said to himself. "I hate Robbie Tenderloin!"

Dejected, he walked slowly to class, ignoring the snickers that came from some of the girls in the hall. He smiled at Julie as he passed her desk, but she just curled her lip in a sneer and muttered "freak!"

The girls in the class stifled giggles as he sat down. Everything seemed normal, but he couldn't shake the feeling that something was different.

Mrs. Nessmeyer came into the room and stopped, her eyes wide with disbelief. Barry just shivered and tried to shrink in his chair.

And with sudden clarity he realized, he was very, very cold.

David Seigler grew up on the dusty plains of West Texas, dodging rattlesnakes and reading science fiction. He recorded Mexican Tejano bands at the local recording studio for a few years before setting out for California to sell electronics and attend jazz concerts. After being injured during the end of an eight hour hostage standoff at his workplace, he decided California just wasn't working out and moved back to Texas to sell comic books during the day and write science fiction and fantasy stories at night. His work has appeared in Neo-opsis, Triangulation Anthologies *and* All Possible Worlds.

Turtle
by A.P. Sessler

Dedicated to the Skahl brothers

It was a hard January snow. To ring in the New Year and erase the joys and sorrows past, the heavens took its broad brush and laid a thick coat of white wash over December's icy blue. Everything on Ocean Street from the motionless cars and bare-naked trees, to the frozen birdbaths and vacant doghouses, were all blanketed in foot-deep snow.

It nestled in every nook outside the Neal's two-story home. It clung to the yellow wood-paneled siding, the dark brown shutters and white trim window sills--dreading the light of sun that was lost somewhere in the blizzard of white sky.

The Neal boys, Kurt the elder and Calvin the younger, shared a room on the second story. Though each had his own bed, during the harsh winters they often shared the older brother's bed beside the wall-mounted radiator, alternating nightly whose turn it was to sleep next to it. Though Calvin considered the space by the radiator the prized position, being on the outside next to Kurt was certainly warmer than his own bed by the drafty window.

They had to be careful, however--the temptation to lie on the metal radiator occasionally led to a scorched a pajama leg or scalded a bare one, either which earned the trespasser a serious scolding.

When Mr. Neal reached the top of the stairs he continued herding the boys down the hall to their bedroom to turn in for the evening. The burning wood stove on the bottom floor heated the entire downstairs, but its reach didn't extend beyond the landing at the top.

Mr. Neal already felt the cold setting in. "Keep moving,"

he said with a puff of frozen breath as he rubbed his arms with both hands. He was anxious to turn in and get a little warm companionship himself. "All right, boys. Go ahead and put away your toys then go right to bed."

"Yes, sir," said Kurt. He turned and stood on his tip-toes to hug his father.

"Good night, Son," said Mr. Neal as he stooped down and kissed Kurt on the forehead.

Kurt walked quickly past his room on the right to his parents' door with both arms around himself in a warm embrace. He shoved the door open with his right shoulder just wide enough to peek inside.

"Thanks for making tacos tonight, Mom," he said.

"You're welcome," she said, placing her book in her lap momentarily. Just like Kurt, her toasty side of the bed was right next to a wall-mounted radiator. "Now get to bed before you catch cold."

"Yes ma'am," he said. "Good night. Love you."

"Love you," she echoed.

Calvin ran ahead of his father to catch up with Kurt.

"Hey!" said Mr. Neal as he reached out and lifted Calvin off the floor. "Aren't you forgetting something?"

Calvin glanced through his open bedroom door. The space on Kurt's bed by the radiator was all he could comprehend.

"Aren't you going to tell me good night?" asked Mr. Neal as he held Calvin at eye level.

"Love you," said Calvin with his eyes still on the bed.

"You know, I'm cold, too."

"Okay."

With a disappointed smirk Mr. Neal placed Calvin back on the floor then tousled his hair with a firm rub. "Good night, Son," he said.

"Night," said Calvin as he ran into his room.

Mr. Neal peeked in to find Calvin quickly picking up the floor full of week-old Christmas toys while Kurt changed into his two-piece, full-length pajamas, about to climb into bed.

Calvin didn't have to change into his pajamas--he always did so the moment he stepped in the front door from school, church or play. He wore his one-piece, full-length footies so much there were holes in the soles.

"Son, are you going to let your brother put all those toys away by himself?" asked Mr. Neal.

"Those are all Calvin's toys," explained Kurt.

"And you didn't play with any of them?"

Kurt frowned as he laid the handful of blankets back on the bed. He hurried to the shrinking pile of toys and helped Calvin put the rest into the large trunk inside their closet.

Calvin pushed the closet door shut in vain. Something about the door wasn't quite right. Mr. Neal tried on two occasions to fix it--first by sanding the edges then by replacing the lockless door set--but the thing never would shut.

He looked at the rebellious door with disdain when it creaked back open, then gave the floor a final once-over to make sure the boys had finished their job. Only one item remained.

"Don't forget your baseball mitt," said Mr. Neal. "You don't want to trip over that in the middle of the night, do you?"

"No, sir," droned Kurt. "I'll get it."

"Good boy," praised Mr. Neal as he walked past their room to his own.

Kurt picked up the mitt then walked mechanically to his dresser with both legs close together. With a shivering hand he pushed aside several dresser-top items to make room for the mitt. As soon as he made a spot he placed the mitt there and returned to his bed. Before he could get in, Calvin reminded him of their nightly ritual.

"Hey, you can't get in bed until we race," said Calvin.

"You only want to race so you don't have to turn out the light," murmured Kurt as he walked to the far side of the room by the light switch in his rigid, robot gait.

The white, plastic light switch plate featured a relief of Jesus with a heart surrounded by thorns and a cross, all radiating outward. The artwork of Catholic origin (circa 1960s) was clearly inspired by Jeffrey Hunter's portrayal of the Messiah in the film King of Kings, right down to his devilish anchor beard and hypnotic Svengalian gaze in an apparent state of divine trance.

"Okay," Kurt sighed. "Get ready."

The boys hunched their backs and positioned their feet into a running stance.

"Get set," continued Kurt as he glanced over at Calvin. "Go!"

As usual, before the word escaped his lips, Kurt was already halfway across the room. By time Calvin reached the same spot, Kurt pounced into bed.

"No fair," mumbled Calvin as he slumped his shoulders in defeat. He walked back to the light switch. "You always cheat."

"Do not."

"Do too."

"Just turn off the light and run to bed. It's too cold to be scared of the dark," said Kurt.

Calvin stood between the bedroom door to his left and the closet door on his right. He calculated how many leaps it would take to make it to the place of refuge once he hit the light switch.

"Hurry up!" teased Kurt. "If you wait too long, the Boogeyman will come out of the closet and turn the light off himself."

"Don't say that!" said Calvin.

"You have until the count of three to turn the light off."

"No, don't!"

"One," Kurt started.

Calvin looked at the closet door. "Come on, Kurt."

"Two."

Calvin could have sworn the crack in the door was growing wider. "Stop it, Kurt."

"Three!"

Calvin hit the switch and leaped for the bed. In his imagination his feet never touched the floor. He could hear Kurt's taunting laughter in the dark.

Calvin landed on the bed. The metal springs squeaked loudly as they buckled beneath his weight, then squeaked again as they rebounded to support his body.

"Keep it down in there!" came their father's muffled voice through the thin wall.

Kurt was still laughing at Calvin.

"You got me in trouble," whined Calvin as he got under the

blankets.

"No, I didn't," said Kurt.

"Yes, you did."

"If you were in trouble, you'd be getting a whipping right now."

Calvin couldn't argue with that.

"You ready, now?" asked Kurt.

"Yep."

Kurt pulled the blankets over their heads. The cold of the room disappeared in seconds as their warm breath filled the confined space.

"We're gonna say our prayers now," said Kurt.

"Okay," Calvin agreed.

Kurt started then Calvin joined in.

"Now I lay me down to sleep. I pray the Lord my soul to keep. If I should die before I wake, I pray the Lord my soul to take. Amen."

"Good night," said Kurt with a yawn.

Calvin giggled.

"What you laughing at?" Kurt asked.

"Let's play Turtle."

"No way."

"Please?"

"Don't you remember what happened last time?"

"Mom and Dad said you're not allowed to tease me about that," reminded Calvin timidly.

"That's why we can't play. You might do it again."

"I won't, I promise."

"No. Besides, I'm ready to go to bed."

"We're already in bed."

"You know what I mean. I don't want to play."

"Aw come on, Kurt."

"When we got caught last time I had to sleep in Mom and Dad's bed for a month."

"Mom and Dad said it was just two weeks."

"So. You weren't the one who had to sleep with them even though it was *your* fault."

"But you made me play."

221

"No one's making you play now--and you're sure not gonna make me play."

"Please, Kurt?"

"Just go to sleep."

"I'm not tired," said Calvin.

"That's 'cause you won't shut up," said Kurt. "I'm going to sleep now, so stop talking."

He rolled to his right side, toward the unseen radiator. Its heat passed through the blanket.

Calvin farted. A few seconds later Kurt smelled the foul scent.

"You stink," said Kurt.

Calvin let out two rapid-fire farts, then laughed out loud.

With his back still turned to Calvin, Kurt waved the odor away with a constricted hand. "I told you I don't wanna play!"

Calvin's face tightened and his eyes squinted as he let out a long fart.

Kurt had enough. "All right, you're on!" he accepted. He let out an equally long, but much stronger, fart.

"Ew, that smells like tacos!" said Calvin in a nasal voice as he pinched his nose shut.

Kurt rolled over.

"No cheating. Just 'cause you didn't go up for air doesn't mean you can hold your nose," he clarified.

Calvin unplugged his nose but he couldn't stand it. He let out a short fart hoping to force Kurt up, but it backfired. He pulled the blankets down to go up for air.

Kurt laughed. "I've never seen someone lose Turtle 'cause of their own fart!"

While Calvin remained above surface to recuperate, he saw a shadow move from the open closet to the walls, then across the floor to the foot of the bed.

He quickly got back under the blankets.

"Kurt: 1, Calvin: 0," said Kurt. "You ready for Round Two?"

"There's something out there," whispered Calvin.

"Yeah. The loser who can't stay inside his shell," said Kurt then let out another foul fart.

"Stop!"

"What's a matter? Afraid of losing?" Kurt taunted, then farted again.

Calvin held his nose. "There's something in the room," he said in his nasal pitch.

"I told you, no cheating. If you hold your nose again you automatically lose the whole game."

"I don't wanna play anymore."

"See. That's what happens every time we play something. As soon as you start losing you don't wanna play. Then you go and tell Mom and Dad I was cheating."

After a moment his own farts got to him. "Man, I stink!" said Kurt as he pulled the blankets down.

"Don't!" begged Calvin as he tried to pull the blankets back over their heads.

"Too late to play now," said Kurt. "You forfeited so I win."

When Calvin couldn't pull the blankets from his big brother's stronger grip, he inched his way down the bed so that no part of his body was left exposed to the clutch of the creeping shadow.

"Is it still there?" asked Calvin.

"Is what still there?" asked Kurt.

"The thing I saw."

"There ain't nothing out here. You probably saw some car lights through the window."

"It came out of the closet," said Calvin.

Kurt could see the closet door was wide open. He looked into the tall, endlessly black rectangle.

"W-what did you s-see?" he stuttered.

"First it went across the wall then it went under the bed," Calvin recounted.

Kurt's eyes followed the invisible path from the closet to the foot of the bed. He reluctantly peeked over the edge closest to him then quickly withdrew. He scanned the perimeter of the floor surrounding the bed until his view was blocked by the large lump beneath the blankets.

"Sit down, Calv," he said. "I can't see over your big butt."

Calvin didn't comply.

"I said, 'sit down'!'" repeated Kurt as he swatted the large lump.

A cold, hairy hand gripped his left leg. Long fingers squeezed Kurt's calf so hard it felt like a charley horse. Before Kurt could say a word he was pulled forcefully beneath the blankets.

The large-headed thing lying next to Kurt stared at him angrily. Its head was almost entirely nose. The corners of its mouth curved upward to form the alae of its nasal face. Immediately above the alae were its large, black eyes, and in the middle of its nose a small horn.

It had hairy ears like a rhinoceros, and under its lower jaw was a large, white, translucent sac like that of a bullfrog, only on the humanoid thing it looked more like a fat person's double chin.

Compared to its head, the thing's body was disproportionately small--about the size of either boy's body.

"It's not nice to hit," said the thing in the silliest voice such a monstrosity could possess.

Kurt's chest swelled as he inhaled to scream, but as soon as his vocal chords vibrated the thing inhaled deeply through his nose and sucked the sound from Kurt's mouth.

Kurt clutched his throat in fevered panic. The fear he had stopped breathing relented once he inhaled again. He went to shout. "Help," he barely whispered.

"You'll have to try harder than that," encouraged the thing.

"Help," screamed Kurt in a soft voice.

"No one can hear you," the thing teased.

"Help!" yelled Kurt, but again the thing took a deep breath and inhaled it.

The thing giggled. "You can keep screaming if you want to, but I'll just suck it up."

"W-w-what are you?"

"Just a thing."

"W-where's my brother?"

The thing inhaled deeply again before speaking. "He's over here."

The thing laid his large head back into the pillows and rolled its eyes for Kurt to follow. Calvin lay on the opposite side of the thing staring straight up--oblivious to his brother's presence.

"He keeps screaming, too," the thing explained.

Calvin screamed again, but the thing inhaled it.

"Calv, stop screaming," said Kurt. "No one can hear you."

Calvin turned his trembling head to look at Kurt past the thing between them.

"I'm right here," comforted Kurt.

"Can you hear me, Kurt?" Calvin whispered.

"Yeah. So can he," answered Kurt as he nodded toward the thing. "Right?" he asked the thing.

"Yep," the thing answered. "But I'm the only one who can," he snickered. "Every time I breathe, I suck up your noise."

"Can anyone hear *you*?" asked Calvin.

"Nope," the thing giggled. "Not unless I want them to."

"Why do you want *us* to?" asked Kurt.

"Your little brother was afraid. I smelled his fear from inside the closet, then I followed it here," the thing answered.

"W-what do you want with us?" stuttered Calvin.

"I heard you two playing a game. I like games. What were you playing?" the thing asked.

"T-t-turtle," Calvin answered.

"How do you play T-t-turtle?" the thing repeated.

"He means Turtle," corrected Kurt. "You have to keep your head under the blanket while the other person farts. Whoever sticks his head up for air first loses."

"That sounds fun," the thing said with a smile. "I'll play, too. If you win, I'll leave you alone. If I win, you have to do whatever I want."

"Mom told us to never to make a deal with the devil," said Kurt.

The thing laughed. "I'm not the devil."

"Then you're a d-demon!" said Calvin.

"Am not."

"Are too!"

"Am not."

"Then what are you?" asked Kurt.

"I told you. I'm a thing."

"What's that?" asked Calvin.

"You wouldn't understand," the thing said.

"Just 'cause we're kids doesn't mean we're stupid," disagreed Kurt.

"Even grownups don't understand. Why should you?" the thing said frustrated.

"Just tell us," pleaded Calvin, somewhat comforted the thing wasn't a demonic minion or the devil himself.

"All you need to know, is some of us are benevolent."

"What does that mean?"

"That's a big word for good."

"And what are the others?" asked Kurt.

"They're malevolent," answered the thing.

"Does that mean bad?" Calvin asked.

The thing nodded his head.

Kurt dared to ask. "Which kind are you?"

The thing chuckled. "Guess."

"Good?" asked Calvin.

The thing chuckled again then shook his head. "Uhn uh."

"If we lose, what do we have to do?" asked Kurt.

"You have to feed me," the thing answered.

"What do you like to eat?" asked Calvin.

"Oh, stuff like a Rolo--" the thing said.

"Candy?" interrupted Calvin.

"--Estevez," the thing finished his sentence. "And a Heath Barrr-ton," he said, intentionally slurring the word.

"That's not their names!" said Calvin. "There's no candy bar called Heath Barton."

Kurt swallowed hard. "I don't think he's talking about candy, Calvin."

The thing snickered. "Nope."

"What is he talking about?" asked Calvin.

As the answer rose from Kurt's mind to his lips, his body trembled violently. The rattling box spring rippled with churning waves beneath the three contestants.

"He's talking about people," whispered Kurt.

Calvin also began to tremble. "You mean--"

"Yep. But not just *any* people--" the thing snickered again. His widely spaced eyes rolled opposite each other as he looked at both boys concurrently then back forward. Every time he moved or blinked his eyes it sounded like someone walking in wet shoes. His stomach quivered as he closed his eyes tight and gritted his teeth to trap the laughter inside. He glanced back at the boys again and sheepishly finished his confession, "Children!"

The boys screamed again, but their voices were immediately sucked into the thing's giant proboscis as he inhaled deeply.

"W-we don't know any ch-children," stuttered Calvin.

"Sure you do. You and you," the thing said with a smile as he poked Calvin then Kurt in the belly with a bony finger. "If I beat you, I eat you."

Calvin squirmed to escape the bed but the thing reached over and caged him in. Poor Kurt couldn't move an inch either. It was the cold, hungry thing on one side or the searing metal radiator on the other.

The thing's body shook the bed as he laughed loud and long. His giant jaws clapped open and shut again and again until he hurt himself.

"Ow! My tooth!" he groaned. "Please! Pull it out!"

The boys didn't move a muscle.

"There's something in my tooth and I can't reach it," the thing whined.

When the boys didn't assist he threatened them. "One of you better pull it out of my tooth or I'm gonna eat somebody!"

Images of Aesop's Lion and the Mouse flashed in the dark before Kurt. He saw the vulnerable mouse pulling the thorn from the injured lion's paw, and the lion's indebted gratitude that followed.

"I'll do it," volunteered Kurt. "You promise not to bite me?"

"Yes," the thing answered. "Just do it quick, will ya?"

"Okay. Just point to where it is."

The thing opened up his mouth and pointed to the rear of his jaws. Putrid odors poured from his mouth as he spoke with his finger between his teeth. "I hink i's o'er here."

Kurt cautiously placed his hand into the thing's mouth. His large, wet tongue saturated Kurt's hand and pajama sleeve with its

227

sulfuric saliva.

"Don't bite me," Kurt reminded the thing.

"Urry up," the thing said as a tear ran down one cheek.

Kurt took a hold of the wet piece of gristle and gave it a yank. In his grip he held a severed adult hand by its mangled wrist bones. He screamed a silent scream as he pulled down the blankets and threw the hand onto the floor.

"What was it, Kurt?" Calvin asked.

"Nothing," lied Kurt.

"That was Mr. Estevez," said the thing as he pulled the blankets back over their heads. "He tried to stop me from eating tasty little Rolo."

A crack of light shone into the room as the bedroom door opened. Through the prison bar mesh of blankets the boys could make out the fuzzy outline of their father.

"Boys?" called Mr. Neal as he stood half-awake in the doorway. "You still up?" he asked. He stared with his half-open eyes at the blurry, dark shape on the floor. "I thought I told him to pick up that mitt. O, to be young without a care in the world," he yawned then closed the door.

All the while their feeble attempts to get their father's attention were sucked into the vacuum of the thing's nose. When their throats were raw from screaming and they heard the door to their parents' room shut they finally ceased.

"How long can you suck up sounds?" asked Kurt.

"As long as you can make them," the thing answered.

He pulled the blankets down to find where the hand had landed, then shot out his frog-like tongue. It extended several feet, wrapped around the severed hand and pulled it back, all in a single movement. He chewed the bloody morsel. The soft, decaying flesh slid off the hand, down the thing's throat, leaving the bare bones. When he ground the skeletal remains between his large molars it produced the unnerving sound of knuckles literally popping.

"Okay," said the thing as he pulled the blankets over their heads. "I'm ready to play. You go first."

Their stomachs were in knots. They tried to fart but were so tense only faint spurts and sputters came out.

The thing was disappointed. "Is that it?" he asked. When

the boys didn't answer he smiled. "This is going to be easy."

The thing let out a rancid fart that smelled like rotting meat. The boys coughed until their ribs hurt. They held their sides with one hand and their mouths with the other to keep from throwing up. The thing laughed at their plight.

"That was nothing," he boasted. "I'm just getting warmed up. You wait 'til next turn--you'll see."

Kurt tried to relax. He thought of greasy tacos and refried beans dripping with hot sauce, but all he got was a case of constipation con queso. His stomach ached from straining so hard.

"I'm on empty," Kurt confessed. "Calvin, what you got?"

The smell of the thing's fart had turned Calvin's stomach sour. He let out a slippery, wet fart.

"Mmm," taunted the thing. "That smells good. What was that?"

"That was dinner. We had tacos," Calvin answered.

"What are tacos made out of?"

"Meat."

The thing laughed. "That's not meat. This is meat," he said, then winked his eye before letting out a fart that literally rumbled the bed.

Their noses burned from the hot stench. They held their breath as long as they could then gasped for air, only to inhale the lingering stink into their tiny lungs. They kicked their feet and rubbed their burning chests to alleviate the pressure of the noxious fumes trapped inside but it didn't help. They exhaled again and coughed on the thick, humid air.

"Your turn," said the thing.

Kurt was still too tense to compete. "Calvin, remember what happened last time we played?" he asked.

"What happened last time you played?" the thing asked.

"I told you Mom and Dad said you couldn't tease me," Calvin reminded Kurt.

"I'm not teasing, Calv," said Kurt. "Remember what happened?"

"What happened last time?" the thing asked again.

"I don't want to talk about it," mumbled Calvin.

"We have to," insisted Kurt.

"Why?"

"It's the only way to win the game."

"Hey," said the thing suspiciously. "You two didn't tell me you had a secret weapon."

"Secret weapon?" Calvin asked, confused.

"Yeah, Calvin--our secret weapon," said Kurt. "Don't you remember?"

"I can't. I'll get in trouble."

"Calvin, if you don't do it we'll be dead!"

His stomach still sick from the foul fumes, Calvin strained every muscle in his bowels. He felt a long, curving bubble moving around his insides. It was stuck on his left. He rolled to his side and strained until the bubble worked its way down and out with a grunt and a wet, gurgling squirt.

When the thing smelled the stench of soiled pajamas he shook his head in agony and fought to remain under the blankets.

"That's it, Calvin! Keep going!" cheered Kurt.

Calvin strained again, and with one more, long squirt he forced the thing to yank the blankets down. The thing lifted his large, nasal head straight up and inhaled the refreshing odors of laundry detergent on soft blankets, cedar dresser drawers and moth balls; the sweaty leather of cleats, tennis shoes, baseballs and mitts; but alas, the foul smell of defeat.

"No more!" the thing yelled. "You win!"

The boys sat up as the thing stumbled out of bed and scurried across the floor toward the wide-open closet door. Before he reached the closet he had become no more than a shadow in the moonlight coming through the open windows.

The exhausted boys lay back in their bed and reluctantly closed their weary eyes. A second later the loud slam of a door jarred them from their momentary rest. They quickly sat up to see the closet door on the far end of the room that would never close now shut tight.

They slowly lay back down and stared at the moving shadows on the ceiling, cast by car lights outside their windows, until they fell asleep.

"Do you see this?" asked Mr. Neal, infuriated, as he held

the soiled pajamas in front of Kurt. "What did I tell you about making your brother play that game?"

Kurt wore a fake frown on his face to appease his father's wrath. Mr. Neal threw the pajamas into the washing machine where the soiled sheets had already been placed and cranked the temperature dial to HOT.

The bathroom door next to the washer and dryer creaked open as Calvin came out to see what was happening. He wore a clean pair of underwear and stood shivering as the droplets of water ran down his wet hair onto the floor.

"It's all right," said Mrs. Neal as she stepped from the bathroom with a large towel and knelt in front of Calvin. "Your father is just scolding Kurt for making you play that game again. Now hold still so I can finish drying you," she said as she used both hands to run the towel over his hair.

"You thought two weeks was a long time, mister?" said Mr. Neal as he held up two fingers then shook one pointed at Kurt. "You'll be sleeping in our bed for a whole month!"

Mr. Neal turned his back to Kurt and slammed the washer lid shut. When Kurt saw his mother turn to throw the wet towel in the clothes hamper, he quickly smiled at his little brother. Calvin smiled back with a toothy grin.

The boys resumed their repentant facades as soon as their parents faced them for their second sermonette on the evils of such foolish games.

From time to time in the years that followed, Kurt and Calvin challenged each other to a game of Turtle, just to make sure they still had what it took in case another hungry thing crawled into their bed on some unsuspecting night. Though it was crude and childish, the boys never regretted playing the malodorous game that had saved their lives. Ah, the sweet smell of victory.

A resident of North Carolina's Outer Banks, Sessler searches for that unique element that twists the everyday commonplace into the weird. His first published story, The Perfect Size, *was included in* Zippered Flesh 2: More Tales of Body Enhancements Gone Bad!

We Bring Them Back. For You!
by George S. Walker

In 1719, the English pirate Peter Roberts was hanged in St. Augustine, in the Spanish colony of Florida. Though he tried to bribe his captors with claims of a buried treasure worth over ten thousand pounds sterling, the secret of its location died on the gallows.

"No, Mrs. Giovanni. You can't order Viagra for someone else. Even Canadian pharmacies require a prescription."

Matt's doorbell rang, and he peeked through an opening between the curtains. A half-dozen people stood outside. They didn't look like bill collectors: two held a banner.

"I have to call you back."

Matt opened the door of his apartment and blinked in the Florida sunshine.

"Mr. Roberts?" said the man on his doorstep, face beaming.

"Yeah?" Matt noticed a van from a local TV station. A cameraman was filming him.

"Congratulations, Mr. Roberts! You're our Grand Prize Winner! I'm Ed Jackson of 'We Bring Them Back. For You!'"

The man shook his hand vigorously. Matt saw that the people holding the banner had moved to get into the camera shot. It read, "We Bring Them Back. For You! (TM)"

"Uh, thanks."

"Who will you be bringing back?" asked a blonde woman holding a microphone.

"An ancestor. The contest rules said all I need is a DNA sample. I have a lock of his hair."

"Wonderful! A beloved relative," said Ed Jackson. "That's what we exist for, bringing back loved ones. Dear parents and

233

siblings. Anyone who's passed on. We feel your pain, and we bring them back. For you!"

"Have you won anything before?" asked the blonde.

"A few bucks from lottery tickets."

"And this relative, he's your... grandfather?"

"Farther back. He was a sea captain."

"Wonderful!" said Ed Jackson. "The stories he'll be able to tell! Because our process brings back the real person, with all the memories, all the love!"

"So how long will it take? Before I meet him."

"Less than six weeks!" said Ed Jackson. "We know the pain of loss. No one wants to delay that blessed reunion."

"And I don't have to pay anything, right? Because I can't afford..."

"Not a penny. You're our Grand Prize Winner!"

The blonde from the TV station checked her iPhone. "We need to wrap this to get it on News at Noon."

Ed Jackson nodded. "Mr. Roberts, my associate will have you sign the necessary forms."

The blonde was already walking away. Ed Jackson hurried after her.

A young man with a goatee, carrying a clipboard and a large manila envelope, joined Matt.

"I'm Carlos," he said. "Here's your kit: two specimen vials, instructions, and prepaid envelope. You need to sign here." He held out the clipboard. "What do you do for a living?"

Matt signed. "Pharmaceutical courier."

"A drug dealer?"

Matt flushed. "No. International discount drugs."

"Florida must be a gold mine."

"Don't I wish. Most of these people don't have any more money than I do."

Matt watched as he and the others left.

His phone chirped. It was a text from Sam: "r u up yt?"

He called her. "You're not going to believe what just happened..."

The last week of September, Matt's doorbell rang.

He recognized Carlos. Beside him stood a short, older man with a black beard. His small deep-set eyes regarded Matt warily. Matt recognized the man from the painting in the museum. The man on the gallows.

"I thought you'd call first." Matt looked at the street. "No TV crew?"

"If we call the media every time, we wear out our welcome. Mr. Roberts, meet Mr. Roberts."

Matt stuck out his hand. The older man looked down at it, looked up at Matt, then slowly extended his hand. They shook. Peter Roberts had a strong grip, and for this warm day, a very cold hand.

"Ye be my great-great grandson," he said. His voice was deep and gravelly.

"More greats than that, I think," said Matt.

"Aye." He looked into Matt's eyes. "And the Roberts blood has thinned."

Carlos held out his clipboard. "If you'll sign, please."

Matt signed. "Will I do publicity appearances?"

"The company mostly does that for reunited lovers," said Carlos. "That's not you two, right?"

Roberts' eyes narrowed.

"No," said Matt.

"I'm sure you have lots to talk about." Carlos turned and walked to his car.

Matt and the captain looked at each other.

"This be your abode?" Roberts' gaze took in the strip of low-rent apartments.

"Not the whole building. Come in. Want a drink?"

"Have ye any rum?"

"Sorry. How about a beer?"

"Ale? 'Twill do."

Matt got a can from the fridge, realized Roberts didn't know what a pop-top was, and poured it into a glass. He poured another for himself.

"You're probably wondering what you're doing here."

"Ye know about me treasure," said the captain.

"What treasure?"

"Ye don't lie well for a Roberts, lad."

"Well, I heard stories. What's the last thing you remember?"

"A noose about me neck." He rubbed it with both hands.

Matt choked on his beer, then raised his glass. "To new adventures."

"Aye, starting with getting me treasure back. Our treasure, we being family."

"How can they get memories from hair?" asked Sam, sitting across from him in Starbucks. "That's like, not even part of his brain!"

"Geez, Sam, I don't know. But it's not like they could hire actors for all these people."

"I'll believe it when I see the treasure."

"And if not, how many times have I taken you for an Atlantic cruise?"

"*Nunca*, babe. Do I have to dress like a pirate?"

"Dress any way you want."

"I can't believe that lady's loaning you her boat for free."

"Well, not exactly free. Mrs. Giovanni has a boyfriend, even older than she is. She wanted some special prescriptions."

"Prescriptions for... sex?"

"Um, yeah."

"OMG. This is that stuff from China that –"

He shushed her, and she put her hand over her mouth.

"It's a really nice boat, Sam."

An old man dressed in black waited by Matt's apartment. "*Señor, por favor...*"

"Sorry, no soliciting." Matt brushed past into his apartment and shut the door. The air conditioning felt colder than normal.

The captain sat at the kitchen table, carving a piece of wood.

"Where'd you get that?"

Roberts held the largest of Matt's kitchen knives. "Me dirk? Found it." He stood and slid the knife into a scabbard at his waist. The scabbard was a braid of black cables. Matt looked at his home theater system and saw the hacked-off stubs of HDMI cables.

The captain followed his gaze. "That be the devil's own rope to cut, lad."

Matt gritted his teeth. "I bought a map down at the marina." He spread it out on the table. "Does this refresh your memory?"

The captain furrowed his brow, tracing a finger around the harbor of St. Augustine. His finger shook at one point. "That be the fort. Best we steer clear of her cannons."

"Do you recognize where you buried..."

The captain scratched his beard. "It will call to me when I sail close."

"Are you sure? It's been a long time."

Roberts gave him a dark look. "Ye be doubting your captain, lad?"

"No... sir."

"That be good, for it be a small crew, we two, and I make short work of mutiny."

"Three."

"Eh?"

"Three of us. Sam's coming."

Roberts scowled. "There be no share for Sam."

"Half my share. You keep yours."

Roberts considered this for a moment. "Best we shake on it, then."

He reached out his hand, and Matt shook. The hand was like ice.

Matt sat with Sam outside the marina. The air smelled of decaying bait and French fries. Sam's mirrored sunglasses reflected the boats.

"He creeps me out," said Matt. "Like last night, I woke to a noise in the living room. The lights are out. The captain's sitting on the floor, holding a candle and running a knife through the flame. And whispering."

"Are you saying I shouldn't come along?"

"No, no. It'll be an adventure."

237

"Did he say where the treasure is?"

"No. Up north, I know that much."

"When you said you had a boat, I was thinking a twenty-footer. But the boat you showed me, I could *live* on that."

Matt's phone chirped. A text. He looked at it and frowned.

"What's the matter?" asked Sam.

"It's the second one of these I've gotten." He showed her the phone.

"It's gibberish," she said. "And what's with the weird rune font? Who's it from?"

"Area code is 666. Somebody's idea of a joke. There's no such area code."

"One of your customers?"

"Sam, my customers don't know what a text is."

Matt closed the car door for Roberts, then got in. When he started the car, it dinged: the captain's seatbelt. Matt ignored it. He wasn't going to belt in a guy with a knife.

Roberts gazed at all the cars. "Every man be a prince with carriage."

"Yeah. And some of us are behind on our carriage payments."

A rap on the glass startled him. He turned to see the old man in black. "Damn repo man." He accelerated away from the curb.

"Now I'm no prince, Captain. But the lady who loaned me the boat, she's like... an old princess. We've got to be careful with her boat, and have it back Sunday evening."

"Ye and Sam been at sea before?"

"I worked a trawler one summer."

"Ye know these waters be treacherous, then. That be how the Spaniards caught me in the shoals."

"That was before GPS. We're not running aground."

"That be what I told me crew."

Matt parked at the marina. They walked out on the dock toward Mrs. Giovanni's boat, the *Lusty Lady*.

Sam was already aboard, sunning herself in a bikini.

"There be a naked wench on board," said the captain.

"Hi, Sam," Matt called.

"*That* be Sam?"

"Sam I am. Samantha." She held out her hand. "Pleased to meet you."

The captain bowed and kissed the back of her hand.

"How sweet," she said.

"I think you should wear more clothes," Matt whispered.

She frowned. "You said I could wear what I wanted."

"Dress as ye please, m'lady," said Roberts.

Matt stowed his duffel bag in the master stateroom and took the helm. The twin engines started with a rumble. He eased the boat out into the "No wake" channel.

"Thanks for buying groceries, Sam."

"How many weeks provisions have ye stowed?" asked the captain.

Sam laughed. "One party weekend. Longer if I ration my Diet Cokes. Go check out the galley."

Roberts went below, and Matt put his arm around Sam. "What do you think?"

"The cold hands, not so much. But he seems O.K., in a crazy uncle sort of way."

"A rich crazy uncle."

"Did Mrs. Giovanni get what she wanted?"

"She acted like a kid in a candy store when I explained the contents."

"Any more prank texts?"

"Now the jerk has my address. I got a black envelope with red runes and a sulfur smell."

Roberts returned from the galley.

"Only one bottle of rum," he growled. "As your captain, I be in charge of rationing it."

By afternoon, they were past Jacksonville, cruising along the coast. Matt stood on deck with Roberts while Sam took a turn at the wheel.

The captain inhaled deeply. "I can smell it."

Matt sniffed. "What's it smell like?"

"Spanish gold, lad." He gave Matt a hearty clap on the back. "I remember the day I buried it. Just me and a lad like yourself. Dark weather as we rowed to the island."

"Do you think he might have gone back later, after you – um – died? And dug it up himself?"

"Well, there be a sad tale. Ye see, no more than a day after we buried the treasure, there be a bad storm, and the poor lad, he be swept overboard. He was no swimmer." He turned to Matt. "Can ye swim, lad?"

Matt nodded. "Sam and I, we're both good swimmers."

"That be good to know," said Roberts.

Matt backed off the throttle. "This is the island? You're sure?"

"Aye. The very same."

The spit of sand held a couple storm-weathered cottages on stilts. The *Lusty Lady* cruised along the mainland side, toward a battered boat dock.

"Looks deserted," said Matt.

"Good," said Sam. "If it was like those islands we passed with mansions, can you imagine them letting us dig?"

It had been sunny in the morning, but now, mid-afternoon, clouds were gathering. Matt slowed near the dock. He eased the boat against a pair of old tires roped to the side of it. Sam and the captain leapt out to tie up. When Matt shut down the diesels, the only sounds were surf and seagulls. He stepped onto the unsteady dock.

"Best we split up to search," said the captain.

"But you're the one who knows where it is," said Matt.

"I have to smell it, and best without the distracting scent of a lady, eh?"

"I'm not sure if I'm insulted or flattered," said Sam.

"I be taking the north end o' the island. Ye best take the east and west shores."

"I think we should stay together," said Matt.

Roberts' eyes narrowed. "Who be the captain here? We split up." He stomped off down the deck.

240

Matt snorted. "The shovels are stowed in a locker, and I've got the keys, so he's not digging without us."

He watched Roberts climb over the dune above the beach line. "There's no point in us searching anyway. It's *buried*. I hereby order the crew to gather in the master stateroom for a round of rum and Diet Cokes."

"Aye, aye," said Sam.

"What's that?" asked Sam, snuggled against him on the bed.

Matt handed her the form he'd started to fill out.

"Customer Satisfaction Survey?" she read. "You're the first guy I've slept with who felt he needed to fill out one of those."

"Not for you. It came in the mail yesterday, along with the letter from Sulfur Boy. But this one's from 'We Bring Them Back. For You!' Want to help with the answers?"

"Sure."

"Question 1. Does the physical appearance of he or she match the appearance before passing on? Scale of 1 to 5. I'd say 5, just like the painting."

"I guess. You showed me a long time ago."

"Question 2. Is his or her personality the same as before passing on?"

"Well, the Spaniards hung him. I guess I'd agree with them on that."

"Yeah. 5 it is. Question 3. If you called our Technical Support hotline, were you satisfied with the response?"

"N/A," said Sam.

"Yeah. I wonder if I can return him when this is over?" Matt skimmed the rest of the form. "The rest are marketing questions, like 'What's your annual income?' Yada-yada."

"What *are* you going to do with him when this is over?"

"Well, he's rich. Or going to be. Rich white dudes usually do whatever they want, don't they?"

Sam and Matt huddled inland of the dune, in a hollow sheltered from the blowing sand. When they finally spotted Roberts returning, it was late afternoon.

"Ahoy!" Sam called. "Did you find it?"

"Mayhap. And your search?"

"We didn't know what to look for," said Matt. "You never told us."

The captain scowled. "Where be the shovels?"

"I trust me nose more than a witch's dowsing rod," said the captain, eyeing the metal detector.

Matt turned it off. "I'm telling you there's nothing buried where you stand. The only metal nearby is right here. Centuries have passed. The shoreline changed."

"Who be the one that buried me treasure? Ye or me?"

"Sam and I are digging here. You dig where you want."

"Your captain don't dig alone. I be happy to watch ye make fools of yourselves." He sat.

"Luddite," Matt muttered.

Matt did most of the digging. There was only room for one in the pit. Whenever he rested, Sam dug a little.

"Should've. Rented. A backhoe," he gasped.

"Would it be buried this deep?" asked Sam. "How deep is the metal detector rated for?"

"Four. Meters. Ideal. Conditions." Matt tossed one more shovelful of wet sand. "Your turn."

She took the shovel from him, and he collapsed on the sand.

"Tide's coming in," he observed.

"Uh-huh," she grunted.

Gradually the waves reached higher up the beach. Even though piles of sand ringed the pit, water was seeping in from below.

"If we don't hit something soon, we'll have to start all over again tomorrow."

Sam groaned. "Don't say that."

"We got here at low tide. Another twelve hours till the next one. Then one Sunday afternoon, but the boat's due back Sunday evening."

Sam's shovel clunked against something hard.

"Metal!" She rapped it a couple more times with her shovel.

"We're rich!" said Matt.

~~The captain got to his feet as Matt jumped into the pit with~~ Sam.

"Let me have the shovel!" said Matt.

She climbed out as he began digging. Finally he abandoned the shovel, clawing with his hands below the pooling water. It wasn't a chest or trunk, but something much smaller, and his hopes ebbed. Finally he lugged it out.

"A cannonball," he said.

Beside Sam, the captain chortled. "A fine treasure that be."

"Maybe it's like, a warning," said Sam, "and the real treasure's buried deeper."

"Yeah." He tossed the cannonball. "Hand me the metal detector."

But when he turned it on, there was nothing, only the hiss of the induction field. The display showed nothing below the bottom of the pit.

"Dammit!"

"It be too late to dig for me treasure," said Roberts. "We wait the next tide."

Lightning flashed over the strait, followed by a clap of thunder. "It was supposed to be sunny all weekend," said Matt. "Where'd this freak storm come from?"

"Can I keep the cannonball?" asked Sam.

"Yeah. Don't say I never gave you anything."

It was pouring by the time they reached the boat. Sam bundled herself in beach towels. They sat in the main salon, drinking coffee as rain streaked down the windows. The tires between the boat and the dock creaked with the waves.

"It's getting worse," she said.

"I'll check the forecast."

But there was something wrong with the radio. When Matt turned it on, an eerie chanting came from the speakers. The band selector didn't seem to work.

"What *is* that?" he said. "It's not Spanish."

"Turn it off," said Sam. "It's creepy."

They sat in silence, with only the sounds of the rain and waves and the creaking tires.

"Can we go home?" she mumbled, eyes on her coffee cup.

"Sam, it's only one more day. We'll try again at dawn, with the low tide."

"Your lad be a rich man on the morrow," said the captain. "Enough to keep a wench like a queen."

"You're not helping," said Matt.

His phone chirped, and he looked at the caller ID. "666," he muttered.

"I am *so* not spending a night on this boat," said Sam.

"Do you want to stay on the island? Like, see if we can break into one of the houses?"

"No!"

"Just give her a slap, lad."

Sam shot Matt a hard look.

"Geez, *I* didn't say anything," he said.

"Maybe you should have," she said.

"O.K., O.K. I'll take you back."

"The wench be your captain?"

Sam looked daggers at both of them.

"This isn't your boat," Matt said to him.

"Aye, ye told me. It be some princess'."

The dock was in a little cove. Back in the strait, the boat had to fight the waves.

"A long way to St. Augustine in this weather," said Matt at the wheel.

"How about Jacksonville?" Sam asked.

"Good idea." He turned his head. "Where's the captain?"

"Gone below. Matt, he never intended to show us the treasure. If it exists."

"There's a treasure," Matt insisted. "We just need to find where to dig."

From the galley, the captain roared, "Ye been at me rum!"

"I thought you were going to stay, too!" said Sam. They were in the lobby of an inn by the Jacksonville marina.

"I never said that."

"You let me think it! All the way from the island!"

"You thought what you wanted to. I always intended to go back. Low tide is at dawn."

"Jesus, Matt! It's not safe. There's no treasure. Stay here!"

"I'm sorry, Sam. This is something I've got to do. I'll pick you up tomorrow morning. Noon at the latest."

"Matt, stay with me!"

"I'll call."

By the time the boat was refueled, it was night. The storm quickly swallowed the lights of the harbor as they headed out. Matt steered by the map of the GPS navigator.

"Now your share be one quarter," said the captain.

"What? I still have half. Sam's was part of my share. We shook on it."

"I be the captain and ye be crew. Now the crew be half what it was. I know me ciphers."

"What happened to honor among thieves?"

"Who be a thief? It be me treasure, lad."

"And I brought you back to help reclaim it!"

"Disputing with me," said the captain, putting a hand on the hilt of his knife, "be mutiny."

Matt froze. "I'm not arguing."

"Best not be."

Jagged bolts of lightning flashed from all directions, followed by booming thunder. Rain hissed in sheets against the boat's windshield.

"A sweet storm," said the captain. He inhaled deeply. "This calls for more rum."

After Roberts went below, Matt's phone chirped.

"Sam?" he answered eagerly.

"Join us." It was a deep, ancient voice, accompanied by labored breathing. Then a second voice, slightly higher: "Join us."

Matt checked caller ID. "Mrs. Giovanni?"

He listened for a minute, then said, "No, don't send photos! Yeah, I can get you more of those pills. And it's a great boat, Mrs. Giovanni, *fabuloso*. We're taking good care of it." It lurched as a wave sent spray high into the air and the engines labored. "Bye!"

Matt was seasick by the time they finally reached the island. He locked himself in the stateroom for the night. It was too late to talk to Sam, but he sent her a text message: "Drk & strmy nyt. I do nt lyk it, Sam I am."

He hadn't slept well, and when the captain pounded on his door at dawn, Matt had a headache.

"Time to dig, lad."

The storm had died, but the sky was still gloomy. The captain carried the shovel, and Matt the metal detector. It was low tide and the beach was covered with shells. He wished Sam had stayed.

"Here be the spot."

It wasn't the same location as yesterday. When Matt used the metal detector, there was a strange reading. Something, but what?

"The captain digs first." Roberts plunged the shovel into the damp sand, scooping and tossing heavy shovelfuls toward the surf.

As they took turns digging, the sky gradually brightened. The captain took his shirt off and Matt saw lash-like scars covering his back.

"The tide be rising."

Roberts was a stronger digger. By now the pit was over six feet deep, with sloping sides. Sandy muck filled the bottom.

It was Matt's turn again. Sore muscles made him pause after every shovelful. Water pooled in the pit, sucking at his sand-filled Nikes.

His shovel hit something, and he reached down, feeling in the muck. He pulled up a thin, bone-white piece of driftwood and tossed it toward the surf.

"Dig, lad!"

Another shovelful. Again he felt something below. It felt like a cage of roots, brittle with age.

A wave broke closer. Suddenly water forced a channel into the pit. Matt lost his balance and fell to his knees in the rising water.

The captain cursed. "Give me the shovel!"

Matt handed it up to him and tried to clamber out of the pit, but another wave poured in, washing him back to the bottom. He was completely drenched. His feet sank into the muck, wedged in the cage of roots.

"Get out," ordered the captain. "I dig."

"I'm stuck. Reach down the shovel."

"I be doing the digging now."

"No! I mean pull me out!"

"I be saving me strength to dig. Climb yourself."

Another wave poured in. Water was up to Matt's chest. He kicked, breaking free of the roots, and lunged at the opposite side of the pit. He managed to cling there through the next wave, panting, then crawled out onto the beach.

The captain leaned on the shovel and growled, "Ye be too slow, and the tide too high for digging now."

Matt rolled over and sat up. He felt the phone in his pocket and pulled it out. He shook off the muck and pressed a button. It didn't light up.

"You told me so, Sam."

He headed the boat back toward Jacksonville.

Roberts fumed. "The sooner we dig me treasure, the safer it be."

"I have to get Sam by noon."

The captain stomped out on deck in disgust.

Matt tried the radio again. All channels were filled with the same eerie chanting. As he kept tuning, the radio went dead. The readout said "No signal." He fiddled with it without success.

It wasn't till a few minutes later, looking back, that he noticed the captain dancing on the deck at the stern. Not exactly dancing. Fencing with a long metal foil in his hand: the radio antenna from the *Lusty Lady*.

"Goddammit!" said Matt.

He left the wheel and stormed out on deck.

"What the hell are you doing! This is Mrs. Giovanni's boat you're tearing apart."

The captain looked at the foil in his hand.

"It not be a true mast. There be no sails on this boat."

"Give me that!" He grabbed the end of the antenna.

"If this be a sword, lad, that be the wrong end to hold."

They were engaged in a tug of war when the boat, with no one at the wheel, took a large wave broadside. The captain slipped and fell against the gunwale and went over backwards. His momentum and hold on the antenna slammed Matt chest-first against the gunwale.

Over the side, Matt saw the captain clinging to the other end of the antenna, legs dragging in the water.

"Pull your captain in, lad."

Matt let the antenna slip through his fingers.

The captain dropped into the *Lusty Lady*'s wake. Roberts vanished, but came up a few moments later, sputtering. He jabbed the antenna at Matt, then submerged again. It was clear he couldn't swim. The boat was still under power, leaving him behind.

Matt's giddy relief turned to panic. He tossed out a life jacket, then ran back to the wheel and turned the boat around. But by the time he returned to where the life jacket was, there was no trace of the captain.

"Oh, shit. I killed a man." He began to shake.

Matt spent the next hour searching with binoculars for some trace of the captain. Nothing. In his mind, he began rehearsing what to tell the Coast Guard.

The first thing Matt did after tying up at the marina was to jog to the inn. It was past noon, the checkout time.

The clerk handed him a message from Samantha.

You didn't call. You didn't show. Taking the bus.

Matt walked to the Coast Guard station by the marina.

"I need to file a missing person report," he said.

"O.K. You have to fill out forms for the Coast Guard, the state of Florida, the Jacksonville PD and Duval County. We need full ID, a recent color photograph, and –"

A hand clapped Matt hard on the back.

"There ye be, lad."

Matt turned and went white. "You're alive," he squeaked. He cleared his throat. "Great! Great! I was afraid you couldn't swim."

"When a man no can swim, he learns to hold his breath. Though it be a long walk to shore. A man with a carriage brought me south. What of yourself?"

"I searched. Searched and searched." Matt was at a loss for words.

He turned to the clerk and gave back the forms, hand shaking. "I won't need these."

On the boat ride back to St. Augustine, Matt was a nervous wreck. He almost got in an accident on the drive to his apartment.

He let the captain in and poured himself a stiff drink.

There was a knock at the door.

"Sam?" he called.

He opened the door. It wasn't Sam. It was the old man in black, the one he figured was a repo man.

"*Señor –*"

"For the love of God!" said Matt. He pushed him away.

The man fell sprawling in the grass. His briefcase burst open, scattering its contents.

Matt saw crosses, wooden stakes, an old leather-bound Bible. A handful of silver bullets spilled out. Only now did Matt notice the priest's collar at his neck.

"*Sí, por el amor de Dios.*"

"I'm sorry, *Padre,*" Matt stammered. "I thought..."

He noticed a hand-lettered business card on the sidewalk: "*Yo devuelvo. ¡Garantía!*"

"You send them back?" said Matt. "Guaranteed?"

In addition to Strangely Funny, George S. Walker has sold stories to Ideomancer, Stupefying Stories, Perihelion SF,

Steampunk Tales, Bards and Sages Quarterly, and elsewhere. Paperback anthologies containing his stories include Bibliotheca Fantastica, Mirror Shards, Gears and Levers, and Heir Apparent. More about George can be found at:
  http://sites.google.com/site/georgeswalker/

I Must Be Your First
by Paul Wartenberg

The house alarm goes off while I'm in the kitchen for an early liquid lunch. I have a good idea which part of the house to worry about because I hear a woman's voice cursing loudly down the hallway to the foyer.

I'm not dressed properly for greeting visitors, even unwanted ones, but curiosity and defensive reflex compels me to rush around the doorway and towards the front of my home. I consider making a quick stop at the closet under the stairwell to check for weapons, but I'm only hearing the one woman at the moment as her footsteps creak upon the wooden floor. I can handle one woman.

No, I'm not being sexist. Fine, let me rephrase: I can handle one mortal. I can handle several. Last time I checked, seven was tricky but doable. Five is easy for me. Hope that clarifies.

I get to where the woman is at the alarm box, fiddling with the buttons like her turning it off now reclaims any hope of a surprise. I see her before she notices I'm here, and I get a good three seconds to appraise her threat level. I really only get three types of unwanted guests: the genuine burglars not knowing who or what I am, the fangirl wannabes, and the slayer wannabes. I'm still not sure which of the wannabes are more annoying though: at least the burglars are forgivable. I know she's not a burglar: it's still daylight out and they tend to use the back door where there's more cover from unwanted witnesses.

She's blond, with a long ponytail sticking out of the backside of her cap. High collar jacket. Half a head shorter than me, putting her about five-four. Sneakers, no heels, so her height's about right. Strapped to one pants thigh is a sheathed knife. An empty scabbard draped across her back where a sword would be.

Great. A slayer wannabe.

I see the sword the second she realizes I'm in the room and five feet from her. Raising it up as she turns to face me. Polished steel. Not silver. If she's done her homework that's probably the knife still strapped to her leg, saving that for last.

The woman's young, guessing college age. I get a clean look at her face, its dark scowling and burning amber eyes. I don't know who she is, so it's not personal for me I know that. I don't think I can ask her at the moment.

She swings the blade right at me. Opening attack. She's not good at it, more like she's trying to get me to step back from her. I dodge it without moving backward, sidestepping at her speed and sliding my body to where I can knock the sword away. She's off balance and I'm not: a quick blow with one hand on her right arm weakens her grip and I slap at the wrist. The sword flies into the living room, rattling against the wooden floor and rolling onto the rug.

She uses her lack of balance to keep moving into another attack. She knows how to work with her momentum at least. I'm too close to move any faster when her low kick slams into my left knee, letting her push off against me. She doesn't flip so much as slide away from me, planting both feet down and adjusting her stance.

There's not much pain from my knee. I can tell she kicked as hard as she could. The knee is a sensitive spot, even for me, but that's just how I roll when it comes to handling the physical abuse. At least we're back to having some floor space between us. I take the moment to raise one hand. Pausing gesture, a universal signal for Can-We-Talk. "Can I just get a little idea of why you're here?"

She takes the moment to appraise her situation and to appraise her target. She gets a good look at me now, wearing casual just-woke-up clothing of a rumpled tee, unbuckled short pants, bare feet. It's a late morning for me. And yeah, I'm usually up most mornings. I'm not at my most seductive, I'll grant. Probably need to comb my hair. Haven't even brushed my teeth yet.

Yes, I cast a reflection when I'm in the bathroom. Every physical thing does. It's not why I and my brethren hate mirrors, okay. I also take pictures too. Just no flash. Use a flash and I'll kill you. Serious.

Her evaluation of me gets to my face and for a moment we lock eyes. Her amber glance is still fierce but for a second there's fear and she looks away. It's not the cobalt color of my own irises though. I've been told my eyes are more emo than deadly for the ladies. Byronesque, which is appropriate.

"Vampire," she finally hisses. "Blood demon. You'll not seduce me this day."

That confirms it, she's avoiding eye contact because she thinks that how I seduce my prey. How ill-informed. She's better off not breathing through her nose to keep my scent from doing its work. Also, who talks like that anymore? I haven't heard that kind of dialogue since, oh, 1904.

She jumps at me, trying for a few swift – for her – blows with her hands but following up with a high kick that has to be a powerful striking blow. So she's got that going for her, some martial art skill. Savate with any luck.

She's not fast enough for me. The punches don't even make me flinch. I can see her hips turning before she even starts on her kick, so I'm ducking and rolling into the living room before she's even halfway through the high arc.

I take a moment during my roll to reach for the sword. Can't have that lying about. Someone could get hurt.

She follows me into the living room. She stops when she sees me holding the sword. I get a good grip on the handle and half-bow as I salute with the blade turned to the body. "If I can get your attention now, if we can..."

I'm not even finishing my attempt at a parley as she fishes out a foot-long sharpened wood stake from inside her coat lining. I'd facepalm but not with the sword in my facepalming hand. Look, sharp wooden stakes are handy if you want to give a guy like me splinters. They're real handy keeping a corpse walker pinned into a coffin while you do the real work of finishing off a pure Revenant. But for weaponry...?

She flips the stake about in her hand. She's clearly thinking about throwing it. After three twirls she grips it, coming to her senses and playing it smart. Holding the point downward, icepick grip. Good. The woman's had some stick fighting mixed in with her savate. Most of the time your amateur fighters go with holding a knife or stabbing weapon like that for the simplicity of downward stabbing attacks. But it also works well for those with defensive training and deception attacks. And I've already seen her use some martial art.

She charges. I like to think it's her youthful enthusiasm. If she's doing this in a blind rage of revenge I doubt I'll talk her down, and I don't want to be doing this all day. Not like she could. She'll tire before I do. But even if she tires she's gonna want to keep fighting.

The woman does a good job of mixing her attacks. A fist blow aimed at the shoulder. A series of mid-kicks to the gut. A slice of the stake-hand at my face, trying for a distracting painful cut. A low kick to the knee again, a high piston kick with the other leg to my chin, boot-toe up.

I dodge each one. I'm not even trying to move faster than she's seen. One of the advantages of agility and speed working in combination. I can pace myself.

"Damn you," she gasps as she pauses after getting both feet back to the ground to steady herself. She's not tired yet, just catching her breath. I doubt my aroma's working on her yet. Her anger has her mindset focused the wrong way.

I take the moment to ask. "Did I do something to anger you up like this? Because, honestly, I don't think we've met."

The woman stands herself upright. Shoulders back, defiant or proud, however she wants to see herself. "It is not that we've met. One does not have to know you to destroy you."

So it's a generalized hate for the *Homo strigoi* class. "At least you ought to be knowing the name of the person whose house you broke into."

"I know your name," the woman snarls, which is a huge giveaway. I'm totally expecting her high kick, this time a whip kick and a decent one at that, toe first aiming for the chin again.

I block it with my hand and toss her foot back downward, shifting her balance off. She pauses and re-balances. "Your name is Blood Drinker."

She aims a high punch, a cross to the face again with the back of her stake-clenching hand. "It's Day Shunner."

Her voice is slurred as she speaks and her blow moves slowly. My perceptions speed up with my reflexes as I finally decide to do more than just stand there. If I let her reach in like that all she has to do is stab downward with that stake. Too obvious a move. So I leap out of her reach.

I don't even need to bend at the knees to do it. Pushing off with my toes, the floor creaking from the pressure. I fly upward, her punch grazing my stomach instead of my cheek. I clear her head and flip over her, twisting my body around mid-flight. My toes scrape the ceiling even as I bend my knees to my gut to complete the jump, stucco flaking off from contact. I can't see her reaction to seeing me move so fast – the blur is all she'll get – but I can tell she's stunned because she keeps her fist hanging out there with nothing to hit far longer than it takes for me to land behind her.

Perception slides back to normal speed as I rise up from my landing crouch. Her ponytail is too tempting to avoid so I take it, literally, with one hand. I pull her into my grasp, my other arm wrapping around her upper chest. I don't press my arms against her breasts – she's slim but curvy – mostly to just get her to stand still and stop fighting. She's cute but she's not my type.

The young woman gasps in shock. There's a hint of fear in that gasp as well, and I can smell the immediate change in her. The adrenaline in her not from fighting but from the terror. I know the feeling, especially when I get tricked into getting onto rollercoaster rides at the beachside theme park up the road. It's my friends, some of them are faster than me and before I know it I'm getting bolted into a seat before the cars roll up the ramp. I know too many sadists.

She's struggling against me, hard. The floor is creaking but then again so is the whole house. I'm getting a better picture of what I'm up against now that I've reduced the distractions to just her and the noises. And best of all I'm able to speak to her without getting interrupted with body blows.

I decide to go with an observation. Part taunt, part truth. "I must be your first."

The woman tries to glance over her shoulder. Maybe to get a decent spit lob in. "I assure you I will be your last!"

You know, I take back what I thought earlier. I think I heard somebody talk like this way more recent than 1904. Yeah, it was that neo-gothic hippie guy from 1971. The one who came back from a weekend long Hammer Horror marathon at college and decided he was the next Van Helsing. He was a bit more prepared than this young lady, just not as athletic or skilled. He was vastly disappointed by how he ended his night. That shock of truly understanding what he was up against haunted me... until I got a good night's sleep. Gods, I hadn't even thought about him until now.

The house is still creaking. The woman's doing her best to wriggle out of my grasp. I continue my observations about her. "It's just there's so much you're getting wrong if you're going about being a vampire hunter. I mean, wearing a neck-high collar is a good idea here, but it's cloth. I can bite through that."

"Oh you would, wouldn't you?" she hisses.

"Have you noticed I haven't?"

She stops her struggling. The creaking floorboards and walls continue for a moment then stop. There's silence except for her breathing and the tapping of a curtain against an open upstairs window. I'm impressed with how silent it's gotten in here. The alarm's long been finished with what it needed to do. Have it on a timer. The loud beeping gets my attention but gets annoying right quick.

I continue. "You've got wooden stakes, but wood's only good for so much. It's not lethal and it's not toxic, not for me. That knife you've still got, at least that's silver, right?"

She hisses again, close enough to saying, "Yes."

"Other problems? You're wearing long hair. Even tied up in a tail it's too easy to get snagged or caught. You've got some fighting skill, true, but hand-to-hand combat is not how you kill us."

"There are other ways of killing you, that I know," the woman whispers. I don't like the way the tone of her voice is. She's gone from too fearful to too confident.

She drives her hand down hard. The stake in her grip slams into my thigh. Shattering against the skin. I can feel the puncture, but it's the pieces digging into weakened skin, the splinters. All the damage she could really do.

It hurts. It's what she wants, so I give it to her. And I let her slide out of my grip, waiting to see what she does next.

The woman bolts to the far side of the living room. Not too hard to do when all the furniture I've got is a sofa and a pair of end tables in the far corners. Vampire bachelors are still bachelors: no sense of interior decorating.

She turns to face me, one hand gripping a curtain at the wide patio window. I see the stake's splintering didn't do her any favors. Blood smearing on the curtain's white trim. "I know enough about vampires to know what kills you!" She's practically singing in triumph. "Vampires abhor sunlight! None of that silly fangirl crap about sparkling! Look upon the day, and despair!" I wonder for a moment how often she practices her delivery.

And then she pulls the curtain wide open.

A curtain that was already gauzy and nowhere near being a solid sun-blocking material.

A curtain to a window overlooking a wide patio with long outsized roofing providing decent shading even at sunrise, thanks to the high trees surrounding the property.

"I don't know if you've noticed," I tell her as I take a few steps towards the now-opened view to a sunlit yet shaded day. "But here I am walking about my own home during daylight hours, in a house with windows everywhere and curtains that let sunlight through." I don't know if she can tell if I'm squinting a bit more than usual. "And you're thinking sunlight's gonna burn me to death?"

The woman's triumphant smile is clearly gone. She's too far away for me to smell it but I'm sure the fear adrenaline is pumping into her body again.

The house is creaking but it's not from my footsteps. I let it pass for the moment. "It's not sunlight that kills. It annoys. It hurts the vision. Much like noise hurts the ears, or the smell of spices and garlic affects the nose." I'm giving away trade secrets, but it doesn't bother me. I like the idea of educating the ignorant.

"Vampires have heightened senses. All of them. Made us better hunters back in the day, but not now. Not anymore."

"Shut up!" She pats at her thigh with her bloodied hand. Grasping at the knife. She's got to unbuckle it first. "You admit it. You're a hunter! You're a killer of innocents!"

"You don't know, do you." I say it not as a question. "Hasn't been a need to hunt since refrigeration techniques for blood storage improved since the Fifties. Last person I fed off was in... 1953. Some middle-aged homeless woman."

She's got the hilt unbuckled and pulls out the knife. Yup. Silver. She aims it at me, point first. She's been serious but now she's deadly serious. I stop walking towards her.

But I keep talking. "I know there's no statute of limitations on murder, but I know you're not here for that. Or any of the other kills I've had to do to survive over the centuries. You're just here to prove yourself a slayer. I can tell."

"Shut up!"

"Look at you. You think you know what you're doing but you don't. First off, breaking and entering someone's home? That is against the law no matter what right you think you've got. Now, past that about vampire hunting. You didn't even know your Dracula myths. He walked about in daylight just fine. Most do. Only pure-breeds can't handle sunlight at all. What you think of as vampires are really half-breeds."

She opens her mouth to threaten me again, but stops mid-thought. Calling myself a half-breed got her attention.

"Real vampires are like modern-day zombies. True name for them is Revenant. Mindless attackers from the grave. Usually don't last very long because they give themselves away too quick. The few that do regain some sense and memory and last a bit longer. Long enough to breed with victims. Well, rape their victims, I won't lie."

I take a few steps back. Partly to calm her down a bit and partly towards the creaking noise from the hallway. "We're really the Dhampyrs you might read about. Except for the boneless stuff, I think someone was drunk when they tricked their biographers about that. Long-lived. We don't spread vampire infestation through biting. Seriously, if we could, humanity would have been wiped out centuries ago. Ever watch the Hammer Horror movies? I'm a bit of a fan, even if they get half of it wrong."

She keeps the knife aimed at me. I think for the throat. Clever girl. "It doesn't care what I watch." She's doing her best to snarl, poor thing.

"The only movie they got right was Captain Kronos, about how different types of vampires there are, certain ways to kill us." I liked the movie for being clever like that, but I really didn't enjoy it. They killed off so many cute actresses during the film, ruined the mood for me. I'm a lover, not a biter.

"You're trying to stall."

"No, I'm trying to explain myself and letting you know what you're getting wrong." I drop my hands to my side. Getting ready for my next moves. "Staking through the heart is tougher than you think, unless you've got the upper body strength to pull it off. Holy water doesn't work. Neither do crucifixes." I'd tell her the only ones who feared those things were Revenants, only because back in the dark ages priests were the only vampire hunters working. And Revenants aren't too bright.

The woman steps toward me, knife still aimed for my throat. "You're being so helpful, what does work, may I ask?"

"Oh, well, obviously. Working in teams."

I turn and move, perception speeding up as time slows. The arrow is already halfway into the room, the crossbow having already fired just a heartbeat before. It only takes me four steps in a half-gallop to where I can watch up close as it slices through the air. Grabbing it in mid-flight is easy at this speed. I wrap a hand around the bolt, making the hand and arm move a little faster than the arrow's normal rate, using my momentum to drag the arrow out of its own.

I spin, taking the arrow with me, swerving into the hallway and towards the stairs, swift and focused. I slam the arrowhead into the wooden post right next to the kneeling teammate slayer wannabe.

Whenever I move that fast, the wake follows up pretty quick as I slow down. The wind whooshes hard against my back and onto the stairwell, forcing the second woman to slump against the wall. She loses her balance and slides down to the first floor.

Slides, not tumbles, so nothing in her gets broken or bruised much. Just her ego, most likely.

One of the great advantages of living in a wooden frame house with a slight elevated foundation: I can hear the footsteps of anyone anywhere in the abode, even if they're sneaking into a window on the upper floors. The first slayer wannabe's effort to bait my attention was a clever move, I'll give them that.

I take a moment to let my eyes adjust. It was a little too bright in the living room compared to the sedate hallway. The second woman pushes herself against the wall to force herself to stand, grappling behind her for her quiver. It broke off just a second earlier, dangling off the edge of the third stair step. Her crossbow's useless for the moment, and she's terrified. I can hear the heartbeat.

My eyes finally get used to the adjusted lighting and I see her. This one I like. Brunette short hair angling along her chin. Reminds me of the hairstyle from the Twenties. Soft face and wide eyes. I'm thinking Bohemian. She's got on a high-collar vest as well but I can tell from the part in her jacket how curvaceous she is compared to her partner.

Oh shush. I've got my fetishes, I'm allowed that much. I won't bite her. Much. And I'll be nice about it too if she gets to be nice about me. It's her call. Just wondering if she's into steampunk Victorian dress. Some women can really pull off a decent corset look.

She's looking right into my eyes, still terrified. I try not to do anything to spook her. Although I'm pretty sure my pheromones are kicking into high gear with a pretty woman like her in range. She'll settle in a minute once she inhales the scent.

"Can I ask you something?" I make it as polite and simple as possible.

The brunette's breathing hard, heartbeat still racing. She's realized she's got no shot and she's acting like she's lacking back-up weapons. She shakes her head but doesn't say anything.

"Can I ask whose idea this was? Yours or hers?"

Her breathing slows a little, she's breathing deeper now. The scent's getting to her. And she's locking eyes with me, bright amber compared to her teammate's darker fiery gaze. It takes her a few seconds to whisper. "Hers."

The blond slayer wannabe is already charging at me when the brunette answers. I don't turn, which is a mistake because she leaps up and wraps herself completely around my upper body. Legs pinning one arm to my side, I get my other arm raised in time. She gets one arm snaked around my chest and she flashes the silver blade before my eyes. "I know enough, vampire, about what really kills you," she snarls, half-shouting into my ear as she angles that knife edge to my throat.

It's my own fault, letting my guard down like that. She doesn't even have to fully decapitate me, not with silver. Wood hurts but silver wounds, and a serious cut throat that won't heal fast enough is certain to ruin the rest of my life.

Time dilates down to almost nothing at all. My senses are at the point where I can perceive whatever light is in the hallway as both a wave and a particle. Well, not really, but the image is trippy. The knife's held by a statue draped over my shoulder as I reach up with my free hand to knock it away. At that speed I know I'm hurting the poor girl, but enough is enough.

Still moving at that ungodly speed, I shrug my shoulders, knocking her still form an inch off of me, more than enough space to swirl about and face her. Her expression is just beginning to change into one of surprise. The pain from her broken wrist hasn't even registered yet. I can't knock her legs away, not without serious damage, so I slide under her as she stays slow in my sped-up reality. By the time I stand up again to face her she's got a pained look on her face. As gently as I can I push against her before I've slowed down enough to reduce the effect of my momentum.

At that speed, even the weakest movement is powered up. I can't reduce the amount of strength or pressure I'm applying even if I tried. I hope it's not enough to knock her through the living room wall on the far side of us.

It's enough to blow her full across the room, but angled well into the sofa, cushioning her impact. Her rate of speed is still enough to bowl over both her and the sofa.

I wince. "Eh. I gotta work on that."

It takes another ten minutes for the first cop car to show in response to the alarm. During that time I'm coping with bandaging up a wounded wannabe slayer. Placing a splint on that wrist after resetting the break. The blond is stunned, almost concussed, so there's definitely a need to get the cops to call in an EMT truck.

The brunette's in better shape. Obviously. And more talkative once she realizes I'm not a "bad vamp". Naughty vampire, sure, but not bad, I tell her that much. That gets her to laugh and gets her to tell me her name's Sophia. I can tell my pheromones have dialed it back a little but she's well into a comfort zone with me now. Turns out she's not Bohemian or Central Euro. Spanish-Irish. Good Catholic girl too from that cross necklace she's got on and eager to show me. No, not that she's trying to see if it works on me, but because she's undone most of the buttons on her neck-shield vest and showing me her pale neck and cleavage as well.

More cops show and the ambulance gets into my dirt driveway off the main road a few minutes later. By now the cops have gotten all the information from Sophia and her friend Hannah, especially the fact that the two broke into my house and are going to be facing charges of home invasion and assault.

Hannah's fully conscious when the lead cop tells her as she's getting strapped into the medic trolley. "What?" She's clearly not thrilled. "He's the blood-sucker! He's the monster here!"

"Weren't you listening?" I tell her, leaning in close to her face. She's strapped in and feeling helpless and she slinks into the trolley padding as much as she can. "Not since they developed refrigeration techniques back in the Fifties! Thank God for modern marvels! I don't have to hunt anymore. None of us do. All I have to do is go to the blood bank for withdrawals anymore."

Hannah's not buying it from her facial expression. "What?"

"Why do you think there's always a shortage and Red Cross calling for more blood drive donations? Duh. Vampires!"

The woman's expression doesn't change. "You're still a monster," she whispers.

262

I lean back and shake my head. "And does that make me any different from you fellow humans? Compare me to the next spree shooter if you want."

She starts struggling against her bonds as the medics cart her to their van. "You're all cops! He's a monster! Shoot him! Shoot him...!"

One of the older cops at the doorway answers her. "And break the Treaty of '57? I'm working on a pension here, kid. Don't expect any crazy crap out of me."

Hannah's screaming all the way out the driveway into the EMT van. Sophia's still in the hallway, not in handcuffs but pretty much aware she's in trouble. "So what happens to me?" she asks the lead cop when he approaches.

The cop looks back to me. "You serious about pressing charges?"

I give an expression of thinking it over, but I kinda figured what to do already. "As long as they pay for repairs to any damages here and for inconveniencing you guys. I won't press charges."

Sophia can't suppress the happy grin.

"And also if I get your phone number to ask you out to a dinner and movie, perhaps?"

Sophia blushes and giggles, and looks down. She probably realized at that moment she was showing most of the cops – all guys – a pretty good view. It snaps her out of the fangirl daze I've put her in and she buttons up her vest with reflexes fast enough to impress me. Halfway, though. She gives me a stern, Not-Happening glare. I figure I can give her a few return visits to clean up the place before I charm her the good-old-fashioned way of witty repartee. I can wait. I'm getting close to 350 years old. And I'm always keen on seeing what the next day brings.

She stays long enough for most of the cops to depart with the ambulance and with the lead cop finishing up paperwork out on the porch. "Why are you being so nice? I mean, we came to kill you and everything."

"Well, it's the risk of being a vampire, when it all breaks down." I shake my head at her. "Every so often I get some moron

263

through here – sorry about your friend by the way – who thinks he or she is the next Van Helsing."

Sophia smiles at that. Charm has its advantages. "So you're cool about it."

"Hey, I met the real Van Helsing so I'm cool with it. Well, Peter Cushing actually." I grin when she gapes at me name-dropping. "No, really. True story. Back in the Big War, I made the mistake of hanging around Prague during the wrong year and I get captured by the Nazis. So I'm getting experimented on while in this creepy abandoned Italian monastery, no really, when right about 1942 this team of British agents raid the facility."

"Peter Cushing was a British spy during the war?"

"No, better, it was this team that had Christopher Lee on it. True... absolutely true. He was working on a special unit run by his cousin Ian Fleming. I am not making this up. Stop looking at me like that." She's giggling and I'm giggling while I'm telling her this. "So yeah I work with his squad of Ungentlemanly Behavior, yeah that's their designation, and then years later I see him on the screen playing a vampire and I'm the only one laughing my ass off during the movie."

Sophia's laughing now. It's a deep solid laugh, she's having too much fun hearing all this.

"So then I get myself to England, and there's the casting party I sneak into for a Sherlock Holmes movie and Lee's there, and oh man, first thing he does is apologize for all the crappy vampire movies he's done to that point, and I'm trying to calm him down and tell him it's cool, I'd seen worse, and then he invites his friend Peter over and after a few minutes of explaining Peter's all deadpan and riffing off which one's the real vampire and which one's fake and even Chris is laughing it up..."

Sophia gives me her number at this point. Thanks Christopher. Hope you didn't mind me name-dropping you and Peter like that. I have to admit, Sophia's the first I've tempted into a date by telling old funny war stories.

This story has been brought to you by the Red Cross Association and the Society Advocating Legal Vampiric Equality, who would like to remind you to help uphold the 1957 Treaty of

Salzburg codifying acceptable behavior between humans and dhampyrs (proper classification) by donating often with your local blood drives. Keep the Peace and Give Blood.

Paul Wartenberg, long-term Florida resident, which already makes him a bit more off-kilter than most. Earned a bachelor's degree in Journalism at the University of Florida and a masters in Library Information Science at the University of South Florida. He's published a short-story anthology titled Last of the Grapefruit Wars *(2003), and has published e-stories "Welcome to Florida" (via BN.com) and "The Hero Cleanup Protocol" (via Smashwords.com) available in most ereader formats. He's currently stuck finishing up any novel to be his first, because his cat Tehya is insisting he gets something finished for once.*

Down for the Count
by Ted Wenskus

"And I am now a full-blown solicitor! I began to rub my eyes and pinch myself to see if I were awake. It all seemed like a horrible nightmare to me..."

Jonathan Harker's Journal, 5 May

Dracula

Ferd trudged up to the immense, wooden doors of the decaying castle, pounded loudly, and waited for a response. The journey to his new client's abode had not gone well. The throng of superstitious natives who forced religious paraphernalia, garlands of garlic, and wooden stakes into his possession, he could handle. Foreign people were like that; some gave you necklaces of flowers, others gave you wooden mallets with the words "Vampire Killer" carved on them. No problem there. The series of hairpin turns that his driver put him through could have been a more pleasurable experience, but he'd ridden through London at rush hour before, so he took that in stride as well. But for him and his luggage to be booted out of the carriage in the pouring rain a good hundred yards from the castle's main doors was the last straw.

If that driver has a license, I want it revoked, Ferd stewed, thrusting his hands into his pockets and jumping up and down for warmth. *Surely this Count guy has more than one serf to replace him.* Ferd shivered and jumped some more. *And more than one doorman, for gods' sake.* He pounded on the dark, wet wood much harder.

The sound of a bolt being thrown answered Ferd's persistence. With an age-worn creak, the door slowly opened and Ferd quickly stepped inside.

"It's about bloody time—" he started, but upon realizing that there was no one present to berate, he simply snorted to himself.

Ferd shook the chill from his limbs and inspected his surroundings. Thick layers of dust and cobwebs covered the hall's expansive stone floor. Large, torn tapestries, some green with mildew, shrouded numerous pieces of furniture around the chamber. A dank, moldering odor prevailed in the stale air, accented only by the faint, oily tinge of black smoke, rising from scattered clusters of lit candelabra.

Ferd shook his head. You just couldn't find a good peasant for upkeep these days.

A slow, graceful movement caught Ferd's attention and he turned to find a regal-looking gentleman regarding him with wide lupine eyes.

"Good evenink," the aristocratic figure intoned. "I am ... the Count." The man arched his thick eyebrows in time with his announcement. "Velcome and enter of your own free vill."

As if the alternative had any appeal, Ferd thought as he outstretched his hand and shook the Count's. "Ferd Liftpick, lawyer extraordinaire, at your service Mr. Count."

"Ah," the Count returned. "Mr. Renfield's colleague. I am so sorry to see that he could not make this final journey. I trust he is vell?"

"Actually, he's turned into a drooling, raving psychotic with an appetite for bugs, your Countness. I'd told him to watch out for the local cuisine on his last trip, but ... well, that's why he was only a junior associate."

"That is ... unfortunate."

"That's one way of putting it, I suppose," Ferd said, breathing on his hands and rubbing them together. "Regardless, I think we can finalize your real estate purchases today. And may I add on a personal note that we, the solicitors of Smith, Corgi, and Liftpick, truly appreciate your fine taste in architecture and antiquity. I sincerely believe that, in lieu of your current housing, you will feel quite at home at every charnel house—er, I mean abandoned manor that you have chosen."

A serpentine grin slithered onto the Count's face. "I find great comfort in your assurances, Mr. Liftpick. I vill sign now any papers that are needed."

Ferd hefted his shoulder bag onto a nearby table and began riffling through its contents. "Just out of curiosity," he said after a moment, "what do you plan to do with these properties? Is this part of an investment scheme by some chance?"

"I intend to renovate the properties and sell them at a future date for profit," the Count said, without hesitation. "Your esteemed country has many amenities that my land lacks."

"The child labor itself makes it worth the move," Ferd nodded. "But, if you're really keen on fine property," Ferd glanced briefly from side to side before continuing in a hushed voice, "I've got a bridge you might be interested in."

"Thank you, no. That is quite all right."

"How about some swamp land then? Comes complete with a wide variety of bogs, a lifetime supply of peat moss, and a large spectral dog that runs around on the occasional rampage. It's very *en vogue*. And the people of Devonshire would just love a new face in the area."

"No, I am quite pleased vith my own choices."

"All right, I've got one, last, special item that you can't possibly refuse."

The Count sighed. "And vhat might that be?"

"Canterbury Cathedral."

The Count drew back and hissed.

"Oh, come on, it's not that bad. Admittedly it's not easy to heat, and they're running out of flagstones to bury archbishops under, but other than that..."

The Count smoothed his flowing black cape as he regained his composure. "I apologize," he said, his voice like quicksilver. "Religion and I do not ... agree."

"I have the same problem with curry, so I know exactly how you feel. Oh, speaking of food," Ferd produced a small bulbous vegetable from his coat pocket. "You wouldn't happen to like garlic by any chance, would you?"

The Count retreated and covered his mouth and nose with a pale hand. "Put it avay!" his muffled voice commanded.

269

Ferd looked perplexedly at the vegetable and then at the Count. "No religion, no garlic ... say, you wouldn't happen to be a—" Ferd paused. "No, never mind. Just thought I'd offer you some since I'm starved." He bit into the white clove and munched contentedly.

The Count's skin took a faint green tinge.

"So what's the deal? You have some sort of allergy to garlic or something?"

"My sense of smell is rather sensitive," the Count explained. "I vas, uh, how you say ... gassed in the var."

Ferd blinked. "What, with garlic?"

The Count fidgeted. "The enemy vas still vorking on the mustard derivative at the time."

"And just what war was this?"

"It vas the ... uh, Crimean Var, of course."

"I see," Ferd said calmly. *Yup, that confirms it. Another insane aristocrat.* He ran his hand through his beard. *Better step up the pace a bit.*

Without ceremony, Ferd emptied the contents of his shoulder bag onto the table and squared the predominantly white, pink, and yellow stack with his hands. "Well, here are the papers you need to sign, your Countship. If you have any questions, I'll be staying at the local Food and Fool tavern for a couple more days, after which you can reach me at my London office."

The Count looked up from the legal forms just as a peal of thunder shook the castle walls.

"Surely you cannot be thinkink of departure so soon after your arrival," the Count purred.

"Oh, I assure you I can," Ferd said. "The legal world, as they say, waits for no mortal."

"How very interestink," the Count considered with another raised eyebrow. "Especially since you vill have to delay your return. This storm—" the Count gestured a hand toward a small window, which immediately displayed a lightning-flecked tempest, "—I fear has vashed out the bridge."

"Oh," Ferd said. "Well, I suppose taking the back road will make the trip a bit longer, but no matter, I guess."

"Ah, surely, you are mistaken," the Count said, shuffling a bit. "There is only von vay to and from my humble abode."

"No, I saw one from the coach on the way up. Leads right to the back of the castle, I'm sure," Fred said. "You know, the one lined with the skulls?"

"Oh, ah, that road." The Count slapped his forehead with the palm of his hand. "Of course. It is not safe." The Count shook his head. "Nope. Not safe at all. Uh-uh."

"Not safe?"

"Horribly, dreadfully unsafe. It is very prone to ... sudden rockslides. In fact—" the Count closed his eyes tightly for a second, placed a cupped hand to his vaguely pointed ear, and smiled when he heard a deep rumbling through the torrents of rain. "—I think I hear von now that is undoubtedly blocking any means down."

Ferd tapped his foot for a moment. "And this bridge of yours is washed out."

"Yes."

"And you're sure you wouldn't like to buy a new one?"

"No," the Count snapped.

"No, you're not sure, or, no, you don't want one?"

The Count's face tightened. "I vill attend to both matters myself, Mr. Liftpick."

"I see. So you're going to go out and build one." Ferd nonchalantly pawed through some of his forms. "Did you know that I handle insurance coverage as well?"

The Count bit his lip in a manner that should have drawn blood. "Vhy don't you try to get some rest? You have had a long journey."

Ferd exhaled wearily. "Probably not a bad idea. I'm not much of a night person myself. But that shouldn't matter. You'll most likely be signing forms till sunrise anyway, so I can see you then."

The Count shifted uneasily, but then produced a quill from the recesses of his dark cape. "You are velcome to stay in any of the rooms on the vest side of castle. Be sure that vhen I am finished, I shall attend to you immediately, Mr. Liftpick."

271

"You are too kind, your Countasity," Ferd replied, picking up his shoulder bag. "Hope my stay here won't prove to be too much of an inconvenience."

"Believe me," the Count darkly intoned, "it von't."

Ferd tenaciously tested yet another door on the east side of the castle. As with the other dozen or so he'd tried, this one also seemed to be bolted from the inside.

Leave it to the peons to bungle something as simple as closing a door, Ferd mentally muttered. *Probably their own quarters anyway. That's it. Must be why this section looks like it hasn't been cleaned in the past few centuries.*

Not that the west side of the castle had been any better. Nearly every room he had opened sent various specimens of the animal kingdom fleeing from his scrutiny; all, save the rats, which merely twitched their whiskers at him and then resumed gnawing on the banisters. The remaining rooms were filled with fallen masonry, which, although picturesque in a gothic sense, still looked none too comfortable to sleep on. Acceptable quarters, Ferd reasoned, were definitely to be found elsewhere.

Ferd yanked at another door and felt it shift slightly. After glancing from side to side, he grabbed the large iron handle with both hands and pulled hard. With a grinding of stressed metal, the handle popped off and sent Ferd stumbling backward.

He regained his balance, leaned against the wall, and stared at the still-closed door. It was going to take all night. He knew it. He was going to have to conclude a major real estate deal without any sleep. Just great. Ferd kicked the loose handle in frustration.

The handle skittered across the hallway and ricocheted off the door, which, as if on its own volition, glided open, shedding darkness into the already dimly lit corridor.

Ferd was still frowning over the logistics behind this luminary feat when a gentle caress teased the end of his beard.

He blinked and moved a hand to his beard, expecting to find a bat or a similar rodent caught in it. As he did so, he felt an icy finger trace its way down the back of his neck.

Ferd turned. "Hello?"

The wall in front of him refused comment.

Ferd scanned the wall in search of any stray, icy fingers that just might happen to be hanging around when he felt a distinctly palm-shaped pat on his posterior.

Ferd spun sharply. "We're skirting awfully close to a harassment case here," he warned.

An icy-looking finger appeared in the darkened doorway and coquettishly beckoned Ferd.

"Persistent, aren't you?" Ferd said as he advanced toward the digit.

The finger had already vanished when Ferd entered the room.

The dim chamber looked as if it had, at one time, been the quarters of a lady of nobility. A shattered mirror hung over a carved bureau, its shards now intermingled with dusty perfume bottles on the bureau's surface. A large, canopied bed was positioned squarely in the middle of the room with a number of deteriorated gowns spread across it.

Ferd scanned for the elusive finger and, failing to find it, sauntered around the room. Unlike all the other chambers he'd examined, this one bore absolutely no sign of life. Even the spiders hung dead in their webs. He had expected to at least see footprints in the dust from whomever had taken interest in him, but the floor remained undisturbed. He wandered over to the bed and casually brushed some grit off one of the gowns.

As if in response, a pale, feminine hand materialized within the gown's sleeve and stroked the length of Ferd's forearm.

"Oh, my," said Ferd, as he watched the rest of the woman appear. "Did they always make corsets that tight?"

The woman stretched languidly, smiled, and ran her hands through her long, raven-black hair. "I like men with beards," she cooed.

"So do I," said Ferd, nodding quickly. "That's why I'm one of them. Lucky me, huh?"

"You have no idea," the woman replied, tapping experimentally at the soft venous bulges on each side of Ferd's throat.

Ferd swallowed. "Can I ask you something?"

"Mmmmm?" the woman returned.

"Was it me, or did you just ... appear out of thin air?"

"Trick of the light, honey beard," she said, playfully petting his sideburns.

Ferd nodded. "Thought so."

As he sat on the bed, Ferd felt a set of hands begin to slowly rub his shoulders. He turned his head and found a buxom, blonde-haired woman gazing down at him with brown, liquid eyes.

"Hello," said Ferd. "Are you two together?"

"You're just too cute," the blonde woman responded.

"Could you tilt your head just a bit to the left?" the first woman asked. "Yes, just like that."

Ferd felt his knotted muscles unwind from the massage. It was probably a full minute or so before he noticed that one of his boots had been removed and that a brown-haired woman was kneading his foot.

"Oh, three is just too many," he said.

"Shush," said the foot-rubber, winking. "We don't want your blood pressure *too* high."

Ferd anxiously drummed his fingers on his chest. "Anything I can do to help?"

"Oh, no," the first woman purred, now snuggling closer. Ferd could now distinctly feel the impression of each corset string against his chest and the soft touch of her hair against his neck.

Ferd looked into the woman's face. "Can you breathe at all in that thing?" he asked, nodding to the gown. "You know, it's so tight, I can't even feel you inhale."

The woman opened her mouth to respond, but suddenly she spun her head away. "What," she gasped, "have you been eating?"

Ferd wilted. "I had some garlic a little while ago..."

The women scurried off the bed, the first one clutching her mouth and stomach. "I've never been so repulsed in all my lives!"

"You've spoiled everything," said the foot-rubber, a pout on her lip. "Now what'll we do?"

"I guess it'll be more Gypsies tonight," the blonde woman sighed. She then turned to Ferd. "Do you mind? You're stinking up the room."

"I was just ... um, that is," Ferd managed. "I can drink some peppermint extract or something if my breath's that bad."

"Beat it, fuzz face," the first woman snapped and Ferd suddenly felt himself being propelled into the hallway. He slapped into the wall at the same time the door slammed shut. Only the briefest of moments passed before the door opened again and ejected his boot in a similar trajectory.

Ferd massaged the hand that had absorbed his impact and stared, once more, at the closed door. "And people wonder why I'm cranky," he muttered.

Ferd heard the wailing cry just as he returned to the west side of the castle, having abandoned his quest for decent sleeping quarters in the east wing. He angled toward a small, stone window and peered out. An older woman, dressed in the multi-colored attire representative of the indigenous Gypsies, stood alone in the courtyard.

"Monster!" the woman cried, wiping strands of wet hair from her face. "What have you done with them?"

"Hello," Ferd called down. "Can I help you?"

"Why are you still robbing our village?" the Gypsy woman wailed. "Have we not done all that you ask?"

Ferd paused. "You wouldn't happen to be part of the cleaning staff, would you?"

"We cleared the mountain road for you, and you reward us by taking our menfolk!"

"Well, if you did as good of a job out there as you did in here, I could see why," Ferd returned.

"Please," the woman pleaded. "Let them return safely!"

"Well, I'll pass your message on to the Count, but it's going to be his call," Ferd called back. "If these men of yours are actual janitorial staff, I'd say chances are that they're going to be gone for quite some time."

"You are not the Count?" The woman outstretched her hands. "Who are you? Are you one of his prisoners?"

"I'm his lawyer, actually," Ferd said, somewhat proud.

The woman put her hands to her head, screamed, and ran into the night. "The Evil has redoubled!"

275

Ferd drummed his fingers on the windowsill. *I hate people.*

He found the Count still hunched over the table. The papers in front of him were now stacked in a variety of smaller piles instead of one larger one.

"Ah, Mr. Liftpick," the Count lilted, looking up. "You are still avake?"

"Your Countship, I— wait. Don't fill that one out in ink." Ferd fumbled around in his shoulder bag and tossed an off-yellow pencil onto the table.

The Count picked it up and began slowly rolling it between his fingers. "You vere sayink?"

"I was saying, Sir Count, that avalanche, washed-out bridge or not, I wish to return to the village tonight."

The Count's eyebrows knitted together. "My humble abode is not to your likink?"

A crash of thunder shook the castle, cascading a cloud of dust and loose masonry into the hall. Ferd waved through the cloud until he could see the Count again, who had lifted the paper he'd been filling out and brushed a pile of grit from it.

"Just for the sake of argument," Ferd said, "let's say no."

The Count tapped his chin. "This vouldn't happen to have anythink to do with three vomen on the east side of the castle, vould it?"

"Nope," Ferd said.

"So, you did not see them this eveninck, yes?"

"Yes. Uh, that is, no. See who again?"

"My vives," the Count answered plainly, gesturing with an envelope containing the England-bound steamer tickets that Ferd had purchased prior to his visit. "They do not know that I am leavink."

"Ah," said Ferd. "Did you know that I handle domestic cases as well?"

"Leaving where?" asked a female voice.

Both Ferd and the Count spun and regarded the three women who now leaned against one of the less dusty pillars of the hall.

"I see the human garlic press has made his way down here," the black-haired woman noted.

"Oh, *those* three women," Ferd said.

The Count's face grew dark. "You do me a dishonor vith your untruth," he said to Ferd.

"Speaking of which," the Count's blonde wife interjected, "you still haven't answered us about this 'leavink' of yours."

"It is of no concern," the Count said, turning. "A small matter."

"What, with that much paperwork?"

"You vould be surprised," the Count said, regarding Ferd again.

"Hey," Ferd said. "If you want fix-em-up West European properties, you have to go through the proper channels—including, in this case, the English one. Ha-ha-ha-ha— er. Um." Ferd tapered into a cough and then into nothing.

"England?" the women said in unison.

The Count bent his head and covered his eyes. "Yes."

"You're not buying new property in a new country and having it still look like this ruin, are you?" This, from the Count's brown-haired wife.

"Ve need our solitude," the Count said curtly.

"So, we have to live in cemeteries or abandoned abbeys in order to get that?" Brown-Haired Wife shifted. "What's wrong with Hampstead?"

"Oh, I can help you there," Ferd chimed in.

"Silence!" the Count roared. "You," he pointed at his wives, "are not comink, and *you*," he pointed at Ferd, "dispense vith this needless paperverk at once!"

Ferd opened his mouth to say something, but promptly closed it upon seeing the bale in the Count's countenance. He shuffled over to the piles of paperwork and started flipping through them. "This may take a minute or two."

"What do you mean, we're not coming?" Blonde-Haired Wife demanded.

"I forbid it," the Count intoned.

"Forbid *this*," the Count's black-haired wife gestured. "We've been stuck in this place for centuries, without so much as

277

an evening out in Bucharest. And now you're moving to an upscale country and leaving us here to tend the rubble?"

"I vill send for you later," the Count said, unconvincingly.

Centuries? Ferd pulled a single form from a medium-sized stack, grabbed the pencil from the table, and held both out to the Count. "You absolutely have to fill this one out."

The Count covered the distance to Ferd in a blink. "You are the solicitor. You fill it out!"

"Well, I'll have to ask you some questions..." Ferd started.

"And now you're just trying to change the subject," Blonde-Haired Wife accused the Count.

The Count flashed over to her. "You vill not speak to me in that tone!"

"Could I have your social security number?" Ferd asked.

"I do not have von!" the Count barked, and then to his wife, "You vill do vell to remember your place here."

"What do you mean you don't have one?" Ferd said.

"I mean vhat I say!" To his wife: "I should have left you ages ago!" He gestured to his other two wives. "All of you!"

"Now that would be a welcome change," Brown-Haired Wife challenged.

"Everybody's got a social security number," Ferd maintained. "Do you have something official like a tax return that I could look at?"

"No, I do not!" the Count thundered, then pivoted again. "I have lost all patience vith you," he said, pointing at the three women. "You shall be driven from this land, never to return!"

"Oh, scare me," quipped his black-haired wife.

"I know!" said Ferd, pointing the pencil at the Count. "How about a marriage license?"

Ferd almost didn't even see the Count move this time, so impossibly fast he was. Suddenly, he was just there. In front of him. With the pencil that Ferd had pointed with planted firmly in his chest.

"Oh," Ferd said. "Now, see what happens when you rush the legal process?"

The Count's face twisted into a silent scream as he crumpled to the floor. As Ferd watched, the Count's skin

278

tightened, eroded, and flaked onto the gray flagstones. In seconds, all that remained was a body-shaped pile of dust with a half-buried pencil in what used to be the Count's chest area.

A moment passed before Ferd spoke. "Oh. I get it. He was a vampire, right?"

The three women blinked.

Ferd raised a finger. "That wouldn't happen to make you ... by any chance, that is..."

The women looked to one another and then to Ferd, each with a surprised look much like that of a cat that had been suddenly, unexpectedly, caught tormenting a small animal. And, at Ferd's direct address, they each covered their noses and mouths.

Ferd paused again and picked up the reservations for the England-bound cargo ship. He looked at the Count's widows and then, much like a cat himself, a smile crept onto his face.

The man held the front of his coat closed with one hand and waved wisps of fog away with the other. Across the street, a single gas-lamp lit the narrow London alley.

"This had better be good," the man said.

"The best," Ferd replied.

The man scowled but then lifted the sheet and his eyes roved for a moment before he spoke. "I'll give you three hundred for them."

"That's a little low, Doctor," Ferd said. "I defy you to find even a mark on them."

The man continued to peer. "Five hundred."

"For all three bodies?"

"All right, six. But no more, I tell you." The man dropped the sheet.

Ferd considered. "Agreed."

The man grimaced as he counted out the bank notes into Ferd's hand. "Good specimens are hard to come by," the man said, begrudging. "Especially female ones."

"As well I know." The wad of money disappeared into Ferd's overcoat. "It was no mean feat coming up with these on such short notice. Demand has been high."

279

The man grunted. "I would have taken Dr. Chutney's if the three he had hadn't disappeared after the inquest." He smirked. "It wasn't as if he was going to need them, six feet under Highgate sod."

"Indeed," said Ferd.

The man peeked under the sheet once more and stared at the pale faces of the three women. "Still, it will be good to have an ample supply of material for my work. My assistant is rather clumsy."

"Yes, Master," a short, hunched figure agreed. "Very clumsy."

The man patted the short figure placidly on the head. "Get the horses ready, Humpfrey."

As the little man lurched toward the front of the wagon, Ferd ambled to the man's side and nonchalantly brushed some dust from the corner of the cadaver sheet. "I hope everything will be to your satisfaction," he said.

The man dropped the sheet and latched the wagon door. "This meeting never happened. And for God's sake do something about your breath."

Ferd nodded and watched the man clamber into the open-aired wagon seat. Once situated, the man took the reins offered by his companion and glanced dismissively down at Ferd. "I think that will be all," he said.

"You took the words right out of my mouth," said Ferd as he watched the three bodies under the sheet slowly shift and rise as the wagon clattered forward, disappearing into the London fog.

Ted Wenskus is a freelance writer and lives in Rochester, NY. His work has appeared in a number of anthologies including Rom Zom Com, Zombie Zoology, *and the forthcoming alternate-history collection* Rochester Rewritten. *His first novel,* The Mostly Weird Chronicles of Steffan McFessel, *co-authored with Marcos Donnelly, was released in 2011. Ted has also written numerous short plays which have been produced in England as well as throughout New York State. He is currently working on numerous fiction and theater projects, including his first full-length play. On his rare days off, he enjoys long walks, which to date has included climbing Kilimanjaro and trekking across Iceland from coast to coast.*

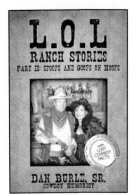

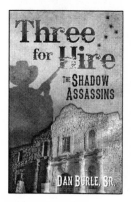

FRONTIER JUSTICE

Dan Burle, Sr.
2016

DAN BURLE, SR.

Wasteland Press

www.wastelandpress.net
Shelbyville, KY USA

Frontier Justice
by Dan Burle, Sr.

First Printing – March 2015
ISBN: 978-1-68111-012-7
Library of Congress Control Number: 2015931454

Printed in the U.S.A.

0   1   2   3   4   5   6   7   8   9   10

Dedication

This book is dedicated to my three beautiful granddaughters:
Maddie
Karina
and
Felicity
and all future grandchildren.

Disclaimer

This book is a work of fiction. Names, characters, places, and incidents either are the products of the author's imagination or are used fictitiously, and resemblance to actual persons, living or dead, businesses, companies, events, places, or locales, is entirely coincidental.

Author's Foreword

Stories of the Wild West have been handed down from generation to generation through oral communications and through documentations found in original newspaper articles from that time period which have been discovered in the mildewed basements of old courthouses and in the musty attics of long-standing rural abodes.

Dime novels and word of mouth stories seemed to always glamorize what was not so glamorous and stretch the truth for the sake of romanticizing a tale.

It is surely certain that the Old West had its share of every type of character imaginable: gold seekers, adventurers, pioneers, ranchers, cowboys, men of the cloth, entrepreneurs, lawmen, soiled doves, vigilantes, and gunslingers who tried to make a fast buck at the expense of others and many times at their own peril.

Cow towns sprung up all around the state of Kansas following the advancement of the railroad after the horrid years of the Civil War. Vice, corruption, lawlessness, gunfights, and death ensued. Ellsworth and Hays City, Kansas both were considered amongst some of the most vicious cow towns of their day.

Many times it was the culprits and the initiators of the violence who found themselves on the receiving end of a fatal .45 slug. These hardened criminals were not welcome in the burial grounds of the faithful and righteous so they found their final resting place in a location that was aptly named "Boot Hill".

Hays City was the first town in the Old West with a "Boot Hill". The lawbreakers making their eternal residence in the graveyard of the wicked were not born of violent character. However, somewhere in the path of their lives, they were influenced by evil and lost their ability to judge the differences between right and wrong. Subsequently, they went awry during their all too frequent short life spans, and paid an exorbitant price, their last dying breath.

Oh not all the residents of Boot Hill were criminal sorts. Some were just innocent bystanders and victims of passing violence who died inauspiciously, with their "boots on".

Here is an actual article that ran in the Saline County Journal, out of Salina, Kansas, on March 29, 1877. It appeared on page 2 of

4 in columns 2 and 3. It's an article that the Journal copied from the Hays City Star. It tells the story about how the residents of that time in history, from the very location I spoke of, felt about the infamous cemetery in the Old West known as "Boot Hill".

"Boot Hill" – Where Lie Thirty-seven Men Who Died "With their Boots on"

On the northern limits of our city rises a prairie mound, and capping its summit may be seen a few stone and wooden crosses, marking the last disappearing, before civilization, law and order.

The eminence referred to, is pointed out to a stranger, as a relic of the ancient regime of Hays, and bears the euphonious and characteristic title of "Boot Hill". On the eminence and its slopes, lie thirty-seven victims of the pistol and the knife – men whose delight and animus were to carry terrorism in their presence and spread it on their approach, and who, like all such desperadoes, at last died, to use a border phrase, "With their Boots on." In other words, their summons to Eternity came to them as unexpected and sudden as lightning's flash-came, perhaps, as they had meted death to others, and without mercy or shrift hurled them suddenly into the "vale of shadows."

"Boot Hill" encompasseth these victims of a mistaken life as a mother enfolds her little ones, hiding as it were from curious eyes in sorrow, the off springs that disgraced the fullness of her love. It is, but earth returned to earth, but these men will long live in the memories their lives created, and the God of Nature may not register their lives a wreck-existence a loss? "Boot Hill" has its victims; may it not too have its romance.

There, side by side, quietly sleeping the last long sleep, that knows no waking but in eternity lie these victims of a wild career. For all, they were men – not cowards; they were not all "bad." And there was something in the very quality of the daring courage that led them into a wild revelry, where life for life, was gave – that under other circumstances, would have led them into scenes where leaders of a storming party or a forlorn hope, laurel wreaths would have been their tribute. As it is, they lie unhonored and unsung.

No, they were not always bad.

Who knows of their childhood, and from what tender influences they may have strayed? Who of us all, dare question the innocence of their childhood? Mothers have watched over their baby foot-steps, joyed in their joy and grieved with their grief. Mothers may have, in the long ago, parted from them, and in prayer and tears sent them forth into the world's tempest of temptation, pure in thought, pure in purpose, holding high and noble aspirations, alas! only to fail.

No mother's tears have fallen o'er their last resting place, but the great mother of all has gathered them to herself – and Earth hides from sight her erring children.

There is one more, a little child, sleeping on "Boot Hill", a victim to the lawless society in which it existed. Innocent of any crime and fleeing for safety from a drunken street brawl – the little one had but scarce crossed the threshold to the building on the corner of Main and Ft streets, where it fell, shot through the brain, by a stray bullet from a pistol in the hands of one of the "roughs" fighting on the street. We give it as one, and the most pitiful, of the hundred bloody scenes that marked the early history of this locality in which some of the most noted desperadoes of the Western border engaged.

But all this is past and gone, and like the thirty-seven and the little one who lies beside them, they and their deeds live only in memory. – Hays City Star.

Just how evil the town of Hays City was perceived during the first few years after its founding in 1867 is seen in another article that appeared on the front page in the third column of the Saline County Journal, April 18, 1878. It is an article on Hays City, Kansas and is said to be the Editor's Journal. Here is an excerpt from that article.

From Hays City. Hays City, Kansas Editors Journal: *- This is my first visit to Hays City, except in passing through on the line, and is indeed a surprise. This place had a pretty hard name some years ago, but is now a quiet and enterprising town. The story was told some years ago of a passenger taking a train somewhere east of here who was somewhat intoxicated and boisterous. The conductor, in collecting his fare, asked him where he was going. He replied: "Going to Hell." The conductor reckoned up his fare to Hays, and told him to get off there, thereby signifying he would find "hell" at Hays.*

By 1881, it seemed like the violence in Hays City was put to rest and was figuratively buried in the infamous unhallowed grounds of "Boot Hill" along with the perpetrators of the evil doings. However, in my book, *Frontier Justice*, the gates of hell will reopen one last time in Hays City and then crime will spread ever so rapidly throughout the Plains like an uncontrollable brushfire destroying everything good in its path. However, hell's fury will eventually come face to face with righteousness and the two extremes will battle to the end in which time and place has become known as the Wild West.

Hang onto your saddle horns my friends with one hand, grip your reins tightly with the other, keep your boots in your stirrups, and prepare yourselves once again for another wild ride through the Old West.

Dan Burle, Sr.,
"Keeping the spirit of the Wild West alive" with this Historical Fiction.

Fictional Characters

Marshal Rick Tanner
Deputies Bradley and Bardsley
Dead-eye Derrick (a.k.a. Montana Mike) and his gang
Lillian Langtree (a.k.a. Diamond Lil)
Tommy Schaefer
Frank George (a.k.a. The Colorado Kid)
Rusty Blake
Leroy Harris
Connelly's boy
Judge Cole Parker, Judge Jed Parker, Judge Robert Parker
Cherie
Reverend Walker
Eight slain church members and their families
Hangman Gil Brown
Dakota Wilson and Pecos Fransisco
Mr. Jerod Brinkman, Kathleen Brinkman
Billy Greer (a.k.a. the Kansas Kid), Cole Fletcher, Arizona Palmer
Charlie Todd
Johnny Dane, Bobby and Kenny Burkley, Lawrence
Joseph
Doctor Eddie Hawkens
Jeff Porter
Old Man Jessie
Marshal Richards
Chan the cook
O'Malley
Pinkerton's men: Billy Horton, Bob Brennen, Jake Nichols (a.k.a. Frank Lackey)
In Pinkerton's binder: Glen Merrit, Cole Dempsey
Molly Nichols
The dance hall girls: Ruby Star, Krystal Belle, Amber Dawn, Molly Fae, Flossy Mae, Maggie May, Sadie Jane, Emi Lou, Josie Lee, Ginger, and Becky Jean
Mr. Bonner and Billy Crane
Don Hawkens
Jacob Scott, President of the Virginia City Bank
Mr. Wippley, President of the Northfield Bank

Table of Contents

PROLOGUE 1

CHAPTER ONE: *The Day of Reckoning* 3

CHAPTER TWO: *The Kangaroo Court* 35

CHAPTER THREE: *It Begins* 55

CHAPTER FOUR: *Rocking "The Walls"* 89

CHAPTER FIVE: *Governors' Call for Action* 101

CHAPTER SIX: *Pinkerton's Theory* 111

CHAPTER SEVEN: *The Anamosa Setup* 119

CHAPTER EIGHT: *Vigilante Revenge* 149

CHAPTER NINE: *The Northfield Surprise* 163

CHAPTER TEN: *Midnight in Nevada* 183

CHAPTER ELEVEN: *Torture on Wheels* 213

CHAPTER TWELVE: *Back to Hays City* 225

EPILOGUE 239

BONUS SECTION: *Actual Article on the Death of Jesse James Published April 6, 1882* 241

Bibliography 246

PROLOGUE

"Oh if that River could talk."

There's a river that flows through the heart of the central Plains of Kansas and stretches out over 500 miles to the frigid snowcapped mountains of Colorado. For thousands of years it bore witness to events that left a mark on the annals of history: written and unwritten, spoken and unspoken. The name of that river is the Smoky Hill River.

The magnificent buffalos of the Great Plains, numbering in the millions, traveled their trodden paths from the northernmost tips of the grassy Plains to the southernmost point of the lush green grasslands. They crossed the swift currents of the Smoky Hill River and its tributaries numerous times to get to their destinations seeking forage and drink to prolong their own existence and the existence of their species. One frontiersman recollects seeing over 700 buffalos drown trying to cross the Smoky Hill River during high waters resulting from a springtime monsoon-type downpour.

The Smoky Hill River has been a source of survival for many Native American tribes throughout history before the migration of European whites to the new frontier. It was the favored ground of the Plains Indians: rich soil for growing crops and an abundance of wildlife for food and clothing.

In 1867 the Comanche and Kiowa, and in 1868, the Sioux and the Arapaho signed treaties with the U.S. Government removing their opposition to the construction of a railroad along the Smoky Hill River thus opening the floodgates of progress and growth.

But "Oh if that Smoky Hill River could talk." It would tell tales that resulted in a range of "events" and "emotions" through the pioneer years on the banks of the river and through the wide open prairies and flatlands of Kansas.

An article ran on page 2 in the Saline County Journal on March 16, 1871 reporting the migration of thousands of European immigrants into the fertile valleys of the Smoky Hill River. They were anxious and elated to start a new life in their own "Promised Land".

On January 25, 1872 in the Saline County Journal on page 2, Harry James ran an ad announcing the sale of his 1,120 acre ranch

1

along the Smoky Hill River. He boasted it as the "Finest stock ranch in Kansas" with fertile soil for lush green grasses.

On July 11, 1872, the Saline County Journal reported on page 2 that farmers were announcing a good wheat crop, better than expected on the farm land along the Smoky Hill River yielding twenty or more bushels per acre. Their prayers were answered.

"Ring the Ton Jong! Strike the Lyre! Rejoice!" was the headline on page 3 in the Saline County Journal on June 8, 1876. It was the announcement of the first steam yacht placed on the Smoky Hill River. Its name was The Belle of Salina.

On September 16, 1881, the Iola Register, Iola, Allen County, Kansas, on page 2, reported that Richard E. Clark, age 23, a printer in the office of the Junction City Union for the past year, drowned while swimming alone in the Smoky Hill River; he was too young to die.

During the same year that Richard Clark met his fate in the Smoky Hill River, two separate outlaw gangs were out to create their own brand of havoc in the West. They were made up of notorious gunslingers, thieves, and cold-blooded murdering scumbags, living near the banks of the Smoky Hill River in different locations. Both bands of outlaws were scheming to raid towns and banks and make a name for themselves that would transcend even decades after their destiny with eternity.

The question that civilized townspeople wanted to know was, "Who had the grit to stop these ruthless marauders and bring them to justice?"

CHAPTER ONE:

The Day of Reckoning

"The LORD is my shepherd; I shall not want. He maketh me to lie down in green pastures: he leadeth me beside the still waters. He restoreth my soul: he leadeth me in the paths of righteousness for his name's sake."

As the tall, slim and aged preacher, dressed in black and wearing white preacher tabs, read his favorite psalm while trying to disguise his fear, perspiration profusely rolled down his forehead and off his brows and onto his open Bible, staining the pages of the 23rd Psalm, the Psalm of David. This small Christian church in Hays City, Kansas just north of the Smoky Hill River was always overcrowded on Sunday mornings; but today, more so than ever before.

"Yea, though I walk through the valley of the shadow of death, I will fear no evil: for thou art with me; thy rod and thy staff they comfort me."

The mothers were holding and clutching their children closely. Fear was written all over the prematurely weathered faces of these hard working farm and ranch women. The small children were oblivious to the perils that were about to befall on their small town peaceful community.

"Thou preparest a table before me in the presence of mine enemies: thou anointest my head with oil; my cup runneth over."

The elderly lady, who was playing the church's new Mason & Hamlin pump organ which was positioned next to the baptismal font, was depressing all the wrong keys because her small fragile hands were shaking so badly from overwhelming fright.

"Surely goodness and mercy shall follow me all the days of my life:"

The men in the church were twirling the cylinders of their six-shooters one last time to be sure every single chamber was loaded. But they knew all too well that they were not pistol toting gunslingers; they were just farmers, ranchers, and townspeople who were peaceful, law abiding citizens.

"and I will dwell in the house of the LORD for ever."

Then they heard the dreaded sound of countless hooves pounding the hard dirt road directly outside, followed by the tromping of the murderous outlaw riders walking up the wooden steps toward the front door. The white painted steeple with a cross at the very top seemed to reach for those golden gates in the sky.

4

But on this day; none other than the gates of hell were about to be opened.

ON THE OTHER SIDE OF TOWN

The town's marshal, Rick Tanner, and his two deputies, Bradley and Bardsley, along with many townspeople, some toting 10 gauge double barrel shotguns and others carrying breech-loading lever action Winchesters were positioned and hidden inside buildings up and down Main Street.

On this chilly, misty Sunday morning in early March, they too were awaiting the arrival of the notorious murdering and thieving bandits known in the cow towns of Kansas, the Great Plains of Nebraska, and the mountainous regions of Colorado as the Outlaws of Smoky Hill River. And on their minds was this; justice was about to be administered right in the middle of the cattle trodden dirt streets of Hays City, Kansas. They called it *Frontier Justice.*

At precisely 9:15 a.m. on Sunday, March 13, 1881, this gang of nine mangy looking gunslingers came boldly riding into town, armed to the hilt. Four outlaws rode up to the town's church which was already well into their service, while the other five trotted down Main Street to the Mercantile Bank, riding tall and bold in their saddles.

Mayhem, the likes this town had never seen before, was about to erupt like an unexpected methane gas explosion in a West Virginia coal mine. Many lives would be lost today in what would be a fierce gun battle reminiscent of the James-Younger Gang's raid in Northfield, Minnesota on September 7, 1876. Only this gun battle would be more deadly, for both sides.

EIGHT DAYS BEFORE - ELLSWORTH, KANSAS

It has been said that Abilene was the first cow town, Dodge City was the last, but Ellsworth was the wickedest of all. And indeed it was.

Ellsworth, incorporated in 1867, sits virtually smack center in the heart of Kansas; Abilene is due east of Ellsworth, Hays City is due west, and both cities are situated about 65 miles from Ellsworth by the way the crow flies. Dodge City is 124 miles southwest of Ellsworth.

Ellsworth's cow town boom years were between 1872 and 1875; but this often-time lawless town was in the cattle business in a period which stretched out from the late 1860's into the mid 1880's. The noisy and smelly Texas, tick infested, longhorn bovines polluted the already unsanitary dirt streets of Ellsworth during the hot and humid fly plagued summer months of June, July, and August.

During those years, Ellsworth played the infamous role of the cowboys' playground at the end of the cattle drive trail by sporting numerous saloons, brothels and gambling halls. The town crawled with prostitutes like keen-eyed vultures, preying on the trail worn cowboys and picking their pockets clean of their hard earned wages; the swags never came so easy to the greedy residents of the brothels.

Ellsworth was the scene of numerous shoot-outs and killings by drunken cowboys who wallowed in whiskey at Diamond Lil's Saloon and Dance Hall. The town was consumed with violence everywhere you turned. If you were a lawman in Ellsworth, you would likely have a short life span. Marshal Will Semans was shot and killed in Diamond Lil's Dance Hall on September 26, 1869 in an attempt to disarm a rowdy cowboy.

After Semans' death, two small time outlaws whose names were Craig and Johnson, took advantage of Semans' demise. They began bullying people and committing armed robberies without fear of reprisal. That is, until *Frontier Justice* kicked in and a vigilante group overwhelmed the two low-life scumbags and hung them high from a branch of a tall cottonwood tree next to the Smoky Hill River.

"Oh if that Smoky Hill River could talk."

It would tell tales of the struggles of Native Americans, surviving during the harsh winters along the eastward flowing river and waiting out the long hot mosquito infested humid summers that sometimes seemed to never end.

It would recount stories of the gold seekers and prospectors who took a chance, traveled and camped along the Smoky Hill Trail on their way to the Rocky Mountains of the western Kansas Territory to participate in the Pike's Peak Gold Rush of July, 1858 through February, 1861.

It would also describe the vigilante *Frontier Justice* that ran rampant during those lawless days in the cattle boom towns, which bordered the river and its tributaries. When citizens in those small new communities became disillusioned and fed up with the lack of law and order in their hometowns, they decided to take the law into their own hands.

The Smoky Hill River is a 575-mile long river that runs through the states of Colorado and Kansas. It originates in what is known as the High Plains of eastern Colorado and moves eastward. It gets its name from the Smoky Hill region of north-central Kansas through which its currents flow.

One can find the earliest reference to this river on a 1732 map by French cartographer D'Anville who labeled the river, the River of the Padoucas. The source of the river was located in an area that was occupied for ages by the Comanche Indians or as they were first known as, the Padoucas.

Later it was noted that an American explorer by the name of Zebulon Pike referenced the river as Smoky Hill during his 1806 expedition to visit the Pawnee.

There are several stories on how the Smoky Hill River received its name. James R. Mead (May 3, 1836 – March 31, 1910, lived to age 74), a Kansas pioneer and one of the founders of Wichita, Kansas arrived in the Kansas Territory in 1859 when the land was still the ancestral home of many great North American Native tribes: the Osage, Kansas, Kiowa, Comanche and more. During that time period you could still bear witness to herds of buffalo in the tens of millions roaming from their northern range in Canada all the way down to the southernmost plains of South Texas.

It was a hunter's paradise. Buffalo, deer, elk, antelope and smaller game were plentiful for the Plains Indians' hunting parties.

James Mead suggested the following as the origin of the river's name. "The Smoky Hill River takes its name from the isolated buttes within the great bend, landmarks widely known, to be seen from a great distance through an atmosphere frequently hazy from smoke." The smoke was thought to be generated by the many tribes who camped along the river, built their campfires for warmth and also to smoke their copious amounts of wild game meats which they harvested for tepee food for the long upcoming winters.

George Bird Grinnell (September 20, 1849 – April 11, 1938, lived to age 88), an American anthropologist, historian, naturalist, and writer had an alternative theory on how the river acquired its name. He said that a large grove of cottonwoods about twenty-five miles west of old Fort Wallace, which served as an old camping ground and burial place of the Indians along the river, was a landmark in that locality and could be seen for miles. At a distance those trees appeared like a cloud of smoke to the Indians in the area. Thus was the origin of the name Smoky Hill.

This story sounds similar to the way the Black Hills in the Dakota Territory was named. From a distance, the dark pines made the hills look black. So the Sioux named the mountainous region, the Black Hills. Ironically, Grinnell, as a graduate student and naturalist, accompanied Lieutenant Colonel George Armstrong Custer on his 1874 Black Hills expedition.

As cattle towns began springing up in eastern Kansas, the Native American tribes in the area signed treaties in 1867 and 1868 withdrawing their opposition to the railroad along the Smoky Hill River.

As a result, what was called the Smoky Hill Trail, which ran parallel to the river and used by prospectors heading west to the gold mines in Colorado, was soon replaced by the Kansas Pacific Railway. The railroad was completed in 1870, rendering the Smoky Hill Trail obsolete.

The year was 1881. The infamous gang, known throughout the central Great Plains as the Outlaws of Smoky Hill River, made its base in the unruly town of Ellsworth.

The leader of the gang, a notorious outlaw, gunslinger, cattle rustler, and murderer who was known by his gang members as Dead-eye Derrick (a.k.a. Montana Mike) had a relationship going with Lillian Langtree, owner of Diamond Lil's.

Lil was as much of a desperado as her boyfriend ole Dead-eye. People who knew of Lil's reputation were cautious to never get on her bad side because, at the drop of a shot glass, she could become as mean as a rabid South Texas badger and twice as ornery as a cornered rattler.

At the top of her boot was a special holster always covered by one of her long colorful ballroom gowns. In that holster she toted a deadly derringer known as a pepper-box that was a small four-barrel rim-fire repeating pistol. Cross Miss Langtree and you'd be looking cross-eyed down the four barrels of her mighty little, but deadly .32. And as her reputation was verified by past actions, she was not hesitant to engage her itchy trigger finger if the situation warranted such.

Besides being as mean as a snake when she had to be, she was a clever businesswoman who always liked the finer things in life. Diamonds, she loved to wear diamonds: diamond necklaces, earrings and bracelets. Ole Dead-eye gifted Miss Langtree with jewelry boxes full of diamond jewelry which were worth well into the tens of thousands of dollars. She knew that the diamonds were compliments of blood-money but that didn't trouble Diamond Lil one bit.

Some of the old codgers in town would say, "She's so classy, she wears a polish like a brand new spankin' $20 gold piece fresh out of the San Francisco Mint". Diamond Lil, of Irish descent, was stunning and gorgeous, a natural beauty. She was tall, about five foot nine, slender, and always wore her reddish hair swept up in an elaborate coiffure. She had the appearance of European royalty and made sure that she presented herself as such every day, no matter what time of day it was.

Ellsworth was just a stopping off place for Diamond Lil. She had bigger and better plans. Her manager, Tommy Schaefer, convinced her that a lady of her beauty, stature, initiative, entrepreneurial spirit, risk taking exploits, and desire for wealth needed to head west to the town that never sleeps and where possibilities were endless. That town was San Francisco. There she could make a real name for herself.

The Bay City was booming. Entrepreneurs from around the country sought to capitalize on the wealth generated by the California Gold Rush. The banking industry was raking in millions. With the new ports and the cross-country rail system, San Francisco became a center for trade. The population was growing by leaps and bounds and the entertainment industry was living high on the hog.

But for now, Diamond Lil lived in Ellsworth and harbored one of the most cold-blooded outlaw gangs west of the Mississippi River.

Dead-eye's gang consisted of nine murderous gunslingers, which included Dead-eye himself, plus one just hired professional locksmith whose specialty was quite unique. He could crack any lock on any bank's safe or spring any padlock on any strongbox within a few minutes. That's why the gang never had to rob a bank when it was open for business anymore. In fact, it was safer for the longevity of the gang to rob banks when they were closed. So their mode of operation became to hit banks on Sunday mornings while half the townspeople were in church. And of course, it seemed reasonable to ole Dead-eye to clean the pockets of the churchgoers before the collection basket was passed around.

Unlike the James-Younger Gang who shot their guns into the air to scatter the crowd after their bank robberies, the Outlaws of Smoky Hill River preferred to be quick, silent and ride out of Dodge faster than a pack of hungry wolves chasing down a nice plump bison yearling that got separated from its mother during a stampede on the prairie. However, if they had to, they weren't hesitant to unload their revolvers in the chests of any townspeople who were naive enough to try to stop the gang from completing their unlawful mission.

The gang's meeting place in Ellsworth was practically in plain sight. It was in an upstairs room at Diamond Lil's. They would use the steps at the back of the building to enter the room. This is where they would meet to divvy-up loot from robbing towns along the Smoky Hill River and where they would make plans for their next raid. The stolen money was divided into 11 shares because Diamond Lil received an equal share for the use of her parlor.

It was about 10:30 p.m. on Saturday, March 5th, when members of the gang began showing up one-by-one. The safecracker, who went by the name of Rusty, was the first one to enter the upstairs room, followed by the gunslingers.

Diamond Lil was pouring everyone a drink as they arrived. Oh it was quite a celebration because Dead-eye was about to arrive on the scene with the loot from the last bank robbery that took place in Salina. This was one of their riskier jobs but it went off without a hitch. The loot was huge, $250,000. The timing for this heist was perfect. In the earlier years of Salina, the take would have been much less.

Salina, founded in 1858 by journalist, Civil War soldier, and U.S. Representative from Kansas, William A. Phillips (January 14, 1824 – November 30, 1893, lived to age 69), initially was the westernmost town on the Smoky Hill Trail when the trail was in use.

The town eventually established itself as a trading post for the likes of Indian tribes in the area, prospectors who were headed to the Pike's Peak Gold Rush, and westbound immigrants seeking out adventure and a new way of life. However, the town's growth ceased at the outbreak of the Civil War and the men in the area were called to arms.

During the first two years of the War, the town suffered from Indian raids and was assaulted by bushwhackers after easy booty. Luckily for the town the "Salina Stockade" was built in May and June of 1864 to protect the town against further Indian raids, and looters who called themselves Confederate soldiers. The Salina Stockade was first nothing more than wagons in a circle. It was then immediately built with logs in an upright position resembling a military frontier fort. Troops were maintained there until the War came to an end.

After the War, Salina began to expand rapidly especially with the arrival of the Kansas Pacific Railway in 1867. In 1870, Salina was incorporated as a city and in 1872 it became a cow town. However, the cow town atmosphere, which transformed the place into a virtual sin-city like most cow towns became, was short-lived because the residents got fed up with the vice, the loud train whistles and the never-ending bawling of those filthy Texas longhorns.

Wheat and alfalfa were grown by farmers in the area throughout the 70's. However, by 1880, Salina became an industrial center. The bank safe was overflowing with cash, because of the successful mills, a carriage and wagon factory, and a farm implement works.

It was a prime target for the notorious Outlaws of Smoky Hill River. And the outlaws hit the bull's-eye, with one of the biggest bank robberies in the history of Kansas. Ole Rusty, the infamous safecracker, had no problem opening up the doors to the man-made gold mine. He would later tell his gang that it was as easy as taking a lid off of a candy jar at T. Kiefer's General Store across the street from Diamond Lil's.

Everyone had arrived now except for Dead-eye. Whiskey was flowing fast and freely as they waited to get their share of this huge loot and hear where and when the next raid would be. One hour went by and the men were getting fairly sauced-up and began to grow impatient.

A trigger-happy and ex-Quantrill guerrilla fighter, raider and bushwhacker by the name of Frank George (a.k.a. the Colorado

Kid) started shooting off his mouth. He was one of the grubbiest of the lot: never shaved, never bathed, about six foot tall and skinny as a rail. He always had the smell of whiskey on his breath when he talked. But rest assured, the odor of the rotgut never masked the smell of the body odor coming off his foul smelling attire.

"Where da hell is dat dang Dead-eye?" Frank shouted, halfway slurring every word that came out of his mouth while he clutched a bottle of rye in his left hand.

"Take it easy Frank and slow up on that rotgut before you pass out on us. Dead-eye will be here shortly," Diamond Lil insisted.

Just then, Dead-eye walked through the door with a sack of gold coins, a sack of silver coins and a sack of gold certificates in $100 and $1,000 denominations. The higher percentage of the loot was in gold certificates. There were some greenbacks mixed in with the gold certificates but their worth was insignificant.

There was a large round table in the middle of the room. Ole Dead-eye walked up to it and tossed the three sacks on the table trying to avoid knocking over the whiskey bottles and glasses. Everyone was all smiles as they gathered around the table to grab their share of the loot. However, Dead-eye had a change in plans regarding the divvying-up of the wealth that night.

"Come on Dead-eye, open up those sacks and dish out our shares," Frank insisted.

The others agreed with Frank's demand and all slurred the same.

"There's been a change in plans, men."

"What kind of change, Dead-eye?" Rusty asked.

"I'm not divvying-up the money tonight. It's going in Lil's safe up here."

"Why?" Frank yelled before Dead-eye could explain his reasoning. They all turned their heads to hear Dead-eye's explanation.

"If you shut your trap and hobble your lips for two minutes Frank, I'll tell you why. A week from Sunday we're hitting our final town for a while. It's Hays City. I heard that the bank there is busting at the seams with gold certificates. The town has some right qualified lawmen there and I need each and every one of you participating to be able to pull this job off. To ensure you're with me, we'll divvy-up this loot and the Hays City loot when we get back to Ellsworth. In other words, nobody gets their share until after the Hays City job. When we split up the money, we'll lay low for about six months and then meet back here again if you guys want to continue to grow your wealth; any objections?"

"You bet there are!" Frank shouted. "How do we know that our money will be here waiting for us when we get back from Hays? I want my share right now." Frank demanded.

The room began to get very tense. You could see the anger building on Frank's face and hear it in his voice.

"Well you'll have to wait like the others," Dead-eye said with authority.

Frank refused to wait. He started backing away from the table with his gun hand just inches away from his .44-.40 single-action Merwin & Hulbert's open top Army revolver. The others could sense that Frank was not taking no for an answer so they began backing away as well, knowing that there was no way to talk Frank out of this potentially fatal gunplay decision.

"Now boys, there's no need for this," Diamond Lil pleaded.

Dead-eye stood his ground and with his sober eyes never leaving Frank's eyes, told Diamond Lil to back away.

"Your play," Dead-eye said to Frank.

Frank just stared at Dead-eye as sweat began rolling down his forehead. He knew that this could be a fatal indiscretion but his Quantrill-type pride kept him from backing off.

He stared and stared into Dead-eye Derrick's eyes. The room was as silent as an abandoned adobe Spanish mission church in southern New Mexico. Then Frank's eye gave an involuntary nervous twitch and he drew his pistol.

Only one shot rang out in Diamond Lil's parlor on that night. That lead ball sunk deep into Frank's chest and penetrated his heart killing him instantly. Dead-eye was just too quick on the draw for that no good cuss.

Frank fell backwards, over a chair and then his lifeless body slammed to the floor. Dead-eye held his gun in position and moved it around pointing it at everyone in the room and asking the question,

"Is there anyone else who wants their share tonight?"

No one spoke.

"I'll take that as a no. Now, Lil, grab these sacks and put them in your safe. Let's all meet back here tomorrow night at 9:00 and we'll talk about our Hays City raid. A couple of you guys grab Frank's body and dump it in the river."

"Oh if that Smoky Hill River could talk."

The drunks hanging around in the noisy saloon down below never paid mind to the gunshot. It wasn't the first time they heard the sound of gunshots coming from upstairs and they figured it wouldn't be the last.

Diamond Lil grabbed the three sacks of money and carried them over to the safe while everyone with the exception of Dead-eye exited the building from the back. The unusually large safe was loaded with stash: Lil's diamond jewelry, her cash shares of past robberies, profits from her business and now the $250,000 from the Salina raid. All-in-all there must have been close to a half a million dollars in that safe. Miss Langtree didn't trust banks for obvious reasons so she kept her wealth underneath her roof.

Dead-eye hung around upstairs for a while with Diamond Lil, behind closed doors. He was always spellbound by the alluring fragrance of Diamond Lil's Perfume De La France. He left the building at about midnight.

When the next night rolled around which was Sunday, March 6th, everyone showed up on time right at about 9:00 p.m. Dead-eye and Diamond Lil were both waiting for them. There was no liquor being served this time since Dead-eye wanted everyone to be of keen mind and clear-headedness. This was actually standard procedure for every meeting when discussing a future raid. Sober minds meant a better chance for success. It's the same way ole Jesse James operated back in Missouri and Dead-eye and Jesse both learned the importance of sobriety when they rode with Bloody Bill Anderson (1839 – October 26, 1864, lived to age 24 /25) back before 1864 during the Civil War.

Dead-eye unfolded a map and laid it out on the table. It was a map of Hays City. He had been there many times in the past so he knew the town like he knew every inch of his single-action Smith & Wesson No. 3 American Model .44 caliber revolver.

Dead-eye began,

"Alright everyone listen up and pay close attention. This is a map of Hays City. We'll ride in from the east side right here. This building I drew here is the church. It's about 50 yards from the outskirts of town and on Main Street. You can't miss it. You all know what a church looks like, at least from the outside. Doubt any of you know what one looks like from the inside.

It's a white building with a steeple and there are a few steps leading up to the front door. Their church service starts at 9:00 every Sunday morning. We'll ride into town at about 9:10 to 9:15 after the service has started.

~~Main Street dead ends into the Mercantile Bank about 150~~ 200 yards west of the church. So the Mercantile Bank sits on Mule Skinner Street right here facing the middle of Main Street. Mule Skinner Street is perpendicular to Main Street and runs north and south."

Most of the clueless gunslingers had no idea what perpendicular meant but they knew how to read Dead-eye's map and understood it, especially when Dead-eye pointed as he talked.

"Now, there are buildings up and down Main Street and also up and down Mule Skinner Street."

"Where's the marshal's office?" Rusty asked.

"I was just about to get to that, Rusty. It sits right here in the south corner of Main and Mule Skinner. Hays City has one marshal and two deputies. Generally there is just one deputy on duty on Sunday mornings and most of the businesses in town are closed until noon. Are there any questions at this point?"

No one said a word so Dead-eye continued.

"OK, then here's the plan. All nine of us will ride into town from the east. Billy, Jim, Tommy, and Bob, you four will hit the church. Billy, you stand at the entrance door and keep an eye on us while the other three hold the churchgoers hostage until we finish with the bank. Clean their pockets in the meantime. We'll signal you when we're done. That will be your sign to ride east back to Ellsworth.

Rusty and I, along with you other three, will ride down to the bank. I'll take out the deputy and you other three will break into the bank so Rusty can go in and crack the safe. Rusty, we're after those gold certificates only so sack them all up and head out of there as quickly as you can. When we've got the loot, I'll signal Billy. Billy, like I said, you guys ride to the east to Ellsworth with your loot from the church and we'll ride directly south down Mule Skinner Street. We'll continue to ride south out of town, cross the Smoky Hill River, and then head east to Ellsworth. I'll bring the gold certificates here, directly to Lil's place. We'll all plan on meeting here the Wednesday night after the raid at ten sharp. Billy, bring the church's money then too. At that time we'll divvy-up everything we have and go our own ways for several months. You can blow your money on whiskey and women or any way you see fit. Any questions?"

"When will you fellas be leaving for Hays City, Dead-eye?"

"Good question, Lil. We'll meet west of town by that old abandoned sod house. You guys know the one I'm talkin' about. It's about three miles outside of Ellsworth. Be there on Friday morning, March 11th at about 10:00. We'll make camp Friday night about halfway to Hays City and then camp out Saturday night about five miles just east of town.

Everyone needs to pack your own food as you always do. I'll bring the Arbuckle's. Is there anything else ya need to know?"

No one responded.

"Well then if there aren't any more questions, let's make ourselves scarce for now and keep a low profile and stay out of trouble this week. I'll be dang if I'm gonna give anyone an equal share of the loot if he gets into trouble between now and the time we leave for Hays City."

With all of that said, everybody saddled up and left, even Dead-eye. It was then that Diamond Lil began putting her creative criminal mind to work. On Monday morning, March 7th, she met with a shady businessman in town named Leroy Harris who was always interested in buying her out. She made a deal that morning to sell Diamond Lil's to him. She said she would knock $10,000 off the asking price if he kept the deal a secret until a week from today, Monday, when he would take ownership of the saloon. If word got out that she was selling, the deal was off and she would sell Diamond Lil's to Harris's competitor. She put that stipulation right in the contract.

Harris promised to keep the deal quiet, papers were signed and the money was exchanged two hours later with the provision that Leroy Harris did not have ownership until Monday, March 14th.

Later that afternoon, Lil secretly met with her manager Tommy Schaefer who had a romantic passion for her but never made it to first base with Lil. Lil decided to take advantage of his infatuation. She called for Tommy to come upstairs to her room.

Diamond Lil's wasn't very busy yet. Business didn't start picking up until about 4:30 in the afternoon on weekdays. When Tommy arrived at Lil's room, he knocked on the door.

"Come on in."

Tommy opened the door and walked into the parlor.

"Close the door behind you Tommy."

This was a strange request because Lil always insisted that the door remain open anytime a man other than Dead-eye would enter her room. Tommy closed the door and wondered what was cookin'.

"Can I pour you a glass of brandy, Tommy?"

"I'm not allowed to drink on the job, remember? That's one of your rules."

"Normally that's true Tommy, but today's different."

Lil went over to the table where she kept the liquor and poured Tommy a snifter of brandy. She turned and handed it to him and then immediately went back to the table and poured one for herself. Lil then turned toward Tommy and held the snifter up, and with a seductive smile on her overly painted face said,

"Let's toast, my darling."

"To what?" Tommy asked.

"To you and me secretly running off together to San Francisco."

Tommy looked as surprised as a horse having a second bucket of grain dumped into his feed trough.

Lil put her drink down and then wrapped her arms around Tommy and said,

"My darling, I know how you feel about me and I have come to realize that I feel the same way about you. In fact, truth be known, I have felt that way all along but I was always worried that if Dead-eye would ever find out about you and me, why he would kill you sure as he can shoot the wing off a June bug at 20 paces."

"Well, obviously you have something in mind. What is it?"

"Do you trust me Tommy?"

"Of course I do, Lil."

"I mean, do you trust me with your life, Tommy?"

"Yes, Lil, I do. Let me prove it to you. Let's hear what you're thinkin'."

"Tommy, there's about $500,000 in that safe that can be all ours. I already put my plan into motion. I have secretly sold

Diamond Lil's for 50 grand. No one is to know about this. But you have to do your share so that Dead-eye and his gang don't come lookin' for us."

"What do you want me to do? Just name it Lil."

"You need to pack up your belongings into a wagon now and leave town for Hays City. Take only your clothing. That's what I'm doin'. We'll have enough money to buy whatever we want when we get to San Francisco. Dead-eye and the gang are leaving here this coming Friday and plan to raid Hays City Sunday morning."

"Yeah, so?"

"I want you to visit with the marshal in Hays City and tell him you have firsthand knowledge that the notorious Outlaws of Smoky Hill River are gonna hit their town reminiscent of Quantrill's Raid on Lawrence, Kansas, on August 21, 1863. I remember that date well because my parents were killed in Lawrence on that day."

Ole Diamond Lil was a pathological liar. Her parents were never killed in Lawrence. They were still alive and well and living in New Orleans. She was just looking for sympathy to aid in the success of her adventurous and daring scheme.

"Tell the marshal that the gang plans on hitting the town Sunday morning at about 9:15. They're gonna disrupt the church service, rob the poor souls there and then break into the bank and rob it as well. Then they're gonna kill anyone they see on the streets while setting fire to the entire town. Tell the marshal it's the gang's last hurrah and they're planning to make history by destroying the entire town of Hays City.

If you can convince the marshal that this story is true, he should be able to rally the townspeople to kill every gang member, including that old flea bitten weasel, Dead-eye Derrick."

Tommy was taken aback at Lil's ruthless scheme, but he was crazy about her and he had no problem going to extremes if it meant that he could live the rest of his life with the infamous, and beautiful, Diamond Lil whom he always had a secret lust for.

"After you leave Hays City, don't come back here. Head south and cross the Smoky Hill River and then head east. I'll meet you east of Ellsworth by that bridge on the Smoky Hill River that overlooks the old Montgomery ranch. Do you know where that is?"

"I know exactly where it is. It's about four miles east of Ellsworth and it's nice and secluded."

"Exactly. Plan to be there around noon on Saturday. We'll take my buggy and then head to Salina where we'll catch a train to San Francisco. Now give me some sugar, honey, and be on your way."

They hugged and kissed each other on the cheek and Tommy left Lil's room with a sense of urgency and a newfound love. He went directly to his rented room at the famous Drover's Cottage which was a hotel initially built in Abilene at the end of the Chisholm Trail to house Texas drovers. In the early 1870's it was dismantled and moved to Ellsworth when Abilene residents shut down the cattle trade in their town.

Tommy packed all of his clothes and miscellaneous belongings that could fit in two traveling bags. Then he walked over to the livery stable to buy a wagon and a horse. After the horse was hitched to the wagon, he drove it back to the hotel to pick up his bags. While he was loading his luggage, Dead-eye spotted him and rode over on his stallion and started up a conversation with Tommy. Tommy did not expect to see Dead-eye and he became somewhat fearful hoping he wouldn't blow his cover.

"Where you goin' in such a hurry?" Dead-eye asked.

Tommy had to think quickly on his feet and luckily for him, he did.

"I just got word that my mother took seriously ill. She lives just outside of Dodge City, so I'm headed that-a-way to be with her."

"When you comin' back?"

"Don't rightly know yet. I just told Lil I needed time off and she agreed to let me go."

"Well, see ya when you get back, pard."

Dead-eye paid it no mind and rode over to the barbershop for a two-bit shave and a haircut.

Ole Tommy climbed up into his wagon and headed out of town faster than a big ole bullfrog could snatch up an unsuspecting dragonfly on the banks of a crooked creek.

He drove the wagon hard and fast for two days and arrived in Hays City early Wednesday, a couple of hours before high noon. It was cool but bright and sunny on this morning in early March. His horse was worn out after the ride; but even with that, Tommy had no desire to hang around town after telling Diamond Lil's lie. No sir, his plan was to skedaddle as soon as he spewed the fabrication.

He waited a few minutes to get his story straight and to conjure up some nerve before visiting with the marshal. After sitting in his wagon for about five minutes, he finally got up enough courage to walk into the marshal's office, only to find one bearded 80 year old toothless codger sitting behind the marshal's desk who was wearing a dirty old cowboy hat with the rim pinned up in the front.

"Are you the marshal?" Tommy asked.

"Was, about twenty-years ago sonny, over in Sedalia. Actually, I weren't the marshal. I joined the posse, whenever marshal needed a good gun. Yes sir sonny, in my day I could shoot the beak off a rooster at a hundred yards and render it go toothless like me the rest of its life, hee, hee."

Tommy sort of laughed half-heartedly right along with the old man and then asked,

"Is the marshal around? I need to talk to him."

"No sonny, he and his two deputies are chasing after two outlaws who robbed the saloon across the street. Don't know when they'll be back."

"When did they leave?"

"Bout two days ago."

"Dagnabbit."

"What's wrong sonny, you gotta problem?"

"Sort of, I guess I'll get a room in the hotel for the night and hope they return tomorrow."

"Suit yourself stranger."

Tommy began sweating bullets. He had no idea what to do if the marshal and his deputies didn't return soon. He began thinking this whole thing was crazy and had second thoughts about carrying through with this deadly lie. Was Diamond Lil really worth all of this, he wondered?

He climbed into his wagon and turned the horse around to go across the street to the hotel where he signed in. Before taking his traveling bags from his wagon and up to his room, he visited the attached saloon and had a few drinks, sitting at a small table toward the front and just staring outside through the large plate glass window.

After about five minutes, he saw a group of trail worn riders trotting down the street. He jumped up from the table and stood by the window to see where they were headed and wondered if it was the marshal. Sure enough, it appeared it was him, his deputies, and a posse because he kept an eye on them for a while and watched them dismount from their horses, clover hitch their reins to a rail, and then walk into the marshal's office. Maybe, just maybe, his luck was beginning to change. Those fellas looked beaten, dusty, and worn down.

Was this a good time to approach them? Maybe so, maybe not. He couldn't make up his mind. Then he sat down at his table, took a couple more swigs from his glass of rotgut and thought it was best to get this thing over with, right now, and get out of town as quickly as possible.

With the attitude of a frightened coyote with his tail tucked between its back legs, he went down to the marshal's office. As he was walking in, four posse were walking out. The marshal was already sitting behind his desk while one deputy was putting on a fresh pot of coffee and the other was sitting at a small table on the far side of the room, cleaning his rifle.

Tommy timidly walked up to the marshal and asked,

"Are you the marshal, sir?"

"That's right, I'm Marshal Tanner. Those two guys over there are my deputies, Bradley and Bardsley," he said as he nodded toward each identifying the two. The trail worn deputies just looked over at Tommy as they were introduced. They didn't speak a lick or even nod their heads.

"Who are you?"

Tommy paused a second wondering if he should divulge his real name or give an alias.

"You forgot your name fella?" The marshal asked while thinking that this guy was acting mighty peculiar.

"No sir, my name is Tommy Schaefer from Ellsworth and I have some horrifying news for you and your town."

With that surprising revelation, the marshal looked up with a little anxiety in his face and the two deputies stopped what they were doing and walked over to the marshal's desk.

"What's your news, stranger?" The marshal asked.

"Your town is in grave danger, marshal. Have you ever heard of the gang called the Outlaws of Smoky Hill River?"

"Sure I have. So has everyone in Kansas, Colorado and Nebraska. Whatever you're trying to say, spit it out boy."

"I have firsthand information that the Outlaws of Smoky Hill River will be raiding your town this Sunday at about 9:15 in the morning. Their plans are to ride into town, hit the churchgoers during service, rob the bank, kill anyone on the streets they see and then torch the town."

"That's ridiculous. Where did you get that information from?"

"From the gang leader's girlfriend."

"Why would she give you information like that if she's the gang leader's girlfriend?"

"Because she didn't want a dead town on her conscience. Her parents were killed in Quantrill's Raid on Lawrence and she wasn't about to sit by and watch another town get destroyed. I'm the same way. Knowing this information, I just couldn't stand by and do nothing."

"Why would they want to destroy Hays City?" Deputy Bradley asked.

Tommy looked at Bradley and said,

"It's their last hurrah before they split up. Some of the gunslingers, when they were in their early twenties, participated in that Lawrence, Kansas Raid and they still have that bloodthirsty desire to destroy whatever gets in their path. It's just the way they are."

"Well boys, it looks like we have a lot of preparation to do before Sunday," the marshal said to his deputies. "We'll show them how we administer justice out here on the frontier, eh boys?"

"You bet we will," Deputy Bardsley said.

"You gonna stick around Schaefer and watch the fireworks?" The marshal asked Tommy.

"No sir, I'm leaving town right now and headed east to Salina."

Tommy left the marshal's office, and rode his wagon south on Mule Skinner Street thinking that he probably just sent nine men to Boot Hill. His self-justification was that they were no-good outlaws and bloodthirsty murderers anyway.

The marshal and the townspeople of Hays City now had a lot of planning and preparation to do before Sunday so that they could successfully foil the plans of the Outlaws of Smoky Hill River.

Hays City, Kansas was once a lawless town, completely out of control. But now things were different; law and order prevailed.

Shortly after the War Between the States came to an end in 1865, a migration began westward into central and western Kansas with increasing intensity. The influx of settlers and railroad workers provoked the indigenous inhabitants of the area, the local Native Americans. Fort Hays was established to provide protection in 1867 followed by the founding of Hays City the same year.

In those early years, Hays City was as dangerous and violent as any frontier town in the American Old West. It was filled with saloons, dance halls and brothels. Several notable characters like Wild Bill Hickok (May 27, 1837 – August 2, 1876, lived to age 39) (served as sheriff for a few months in 1869), George Armstrong Custer (December 5, 1839 – June 25, 1876, lived to age 36), his wife Elizabeth Custer (April 8, 1842 – April 4, 1933, lived to age 90), "Buffalo Bill" Cody (February 26, 1846 – January 10, 1917, lived to age 70), and Calamity Jane (May 1, 1852 – August 1, 1903, lived to age 51) lived in Hays City in the early years. Elizabeth Custer, Libby as she was known by many, once said of Hays City, "There was enough desperate history in that little town in one summer to make a whole library of dime novels." Oh that town was violent alright. Why between August of 1867 and December of 1873 there were 30 killings in and around Hays City.

Many people believed that the original Boot Hill cemetery was located in Dodge City, not true. It actually was located in Hays City. It is well documented that when Dodge City was founded in 1872, the Hays City Boot Hill was well populated. Libby Custer noted in her own personal diary in the summer of 1869 that there were already thirty-six graves in the cemetery known as "Boot Hill".

Boot Hill was the name given to many cemeteries in the American Old West. Back in those days it was a common name for the burial grounds of gunfighters, cowboys, and criminals who "died with their boots on". The implication was that they died violently as in gunfights or hangings and not of natural causes; therefore, they died with their boots on.

Many famous towns of the Old West had Boot Hill cemeteries, towns like: Hays City, Dodge City, Tombstone, and Deadwood.

Marshal Tanner had every intention to expand Boot Hill with the bodies of the Outlaws of Smoky Hill River. He sent his deputies out to gather up the City Council members in order to apprise them of the precarious situation about to befall on their community. When they arrived at his office, he didn't hold back. He stood up behind his desk while everyone gathered around.

"Gentlemen, we have a serious crisis on our hands. If we don't act with courage and fortitude, we will lose our town, and many of our innocent townspeople will be slaughtered like dogs in the street."

"What in God's name do you know, marshal?" One of the councilmen asked.

"I received word just an hour ago from a credible source that the Outlaws of Smoky Hill River are planning a raid on our town on Sunday morning at about 9:15. They plan on robbing everyone in church and cleaning out our bank. If that weren't enough, they plan on gunning down anyone they see on the streets and then burning down our town to the ground. I found out that most of these gang members belonged to Quantrill's Raiders during the War and they plan on making this their final brutal campaign."

"My word marshal, we're no match for those gunslingers," a councilman declared. "We're gonna have to send for help."

"With that type of attitude councilman, we have already lost. We don't have time to send for help. You are men aren't you? You own guns don't you? All the farmers and ranchers outside of town own guns. They use them to shoot coyotes, varmints, and such, don't they? This time they'll have to use them on human varmints. There's no other alternative if we intend to keep our town."

"We can do this thing," Deputy Bradley insisted. "What's your plan marshal?"

"The gang is coming into town thinking that they will have the element of surprise on their side. They won't, but we will. That's how we'll defeat those saddle bums."

Now, many things were going on simultaneously: the town was making plans for an ambush of the bushwhackers, Tommy Schaeffer was scurrying back east to meet up with Diamond Lil west of Salina, Dead-eye and his ruthless gang members were making last minute plans for their raid on Hays City, and Diamond Lil was secretly getting her business in order and her things together for her quick and surreptitious exit from Ellsworth.

Marshal Tanner told the councilmen to inform all of the townspeople, ranchers and farmers of an emergency town meeting to be held at the Silver Spur Saloon and Dance Hall on Friday morning at 9:30. This would give him all day Thursday to work up an effective strategy with his two deputies. He also made the councilmen swear that they would not give out specifics of the reason for the meeting. Marshal Tanner did not want panic running rampant in the streets of Hays City. He also didn't want businessmen boarding up their windows on Main Street. That would be a sure give away to the outlaws that they were expected. These were the types of things he would talk about in the town's meeting on Friday.

The councilmen informed everyone in and around town of the meeting and stressed the importance and urgency of everyone attending.

It was now 9:00 Friday morning; people were arriving at the Silver Spur like it was a presidential election. The town was packed. Businesses along Main Street had no plans to open their stores until after the meeting. The anticipation was great. The councilmen did what the marshal asked; they told no one the reason why their presence on this day was so important.

As the Silver Spur began filling up with townspeople, ranchers and farmers, the noise level became almost unbearable. At 9:20 a.m. the marshal and his two deputies walked in and stepped up onto the small stage at the east end of the dance hall. At that point the noise level abated and people began turning their attention toward the marshal and his deputies to hear what they had to say. The marshal then raised his hands and asked for complete silence. When his request was honored, he began.

"OK folks, thanks for attending today's urgent meeting. We've got a problem. Our town is about to be besieged by one of the most ruthless gangs west of the Mississippi. It's all going down on Sunday morning at 9:15. The gang I am talkin' about is the Outlaws of Smoky Hill River. The word I received is that they intend to rob the churchgoers during service, hit our bank, torch our town and kill anyone they see on the streets like some of them did during the Lawrence, Kansas Raid by Quantrill's Raiders. These guys are dangerous and bloodthirsty.

However, what we have going for us is the element of surprise. Now you all need to listen up. Here's my plan…"

Marshal Tanner spent about 45 minutes outlining his plan and the importance of everyone keeping a cool head now and at the time of the raid. He also stressed that they make sure that their firearms were in good working order and that they had plenty of ammunition. In fact, he told them to go to the gun shop right after the meeting and fill up their saddlebags. Another very important point was to be in position at least forty-five minutes before the gang was due to arrive in town. That meant everyone needed to be at his assigned post by 8:30 a.m. and all of the ranchers' horses were to be hitched and hidden behind the buildings west of Mule Skinner Street.

Before he adjourned the meeting, he made one last comment that really rallied the crowd. He said,

"Folks, we'll show those outlaws how justice is administered out here on the frontier. Since they intend to take our town, we'll fight them their way. We'll shoot first and ask questions later. We'll pick off those varmints one by one. I don't have plans to take any prisoners but just in case we do, we'll give 'em a fair trial, find 'em guilty, and then hang their sorry hides from a large cottonwood on the banks of the Smoky Hill River. Are you with me?" The marshal shouted.

A deafening cheer rose up from the crowd. The town was now fired up and ready to take on the Outlaws of Smoky Hill River.

While Marshal Tanner was holding his meeting in Hays City, Dead-eye and his gang had just met west of Ellsworth and began their two day journey to Hays City completely oblivious to the fact that they were walking right into an ambush. The question was, "Did the townspeople have enough grit and courage to hold the line and fight bravely during the raid?"

In the meantime, Tommy Schaefer was still traveling by wagon to rendezvous with Diamond Lil at the old abandoned Montgomery ranch east of Ellsworth.

It was now Saturday morning, March 12th, just twenty-four hours before the day of reckoning. Dead-eye and his gang had just broke camp and began riding east toward Hays City. Their plan today was to ride all day and then camp just a few miles outside of town that night.

As the morning wore on, ole Tommy drove hard and fast with great enthusiasm and came closer and closer to the rendezvous point with Diamond Lil. It wasn't long now that the two lovebirds would be riding together to Salina and then eventually onward to San Francisco.

Lil was already packed with her lavish clothing, diamond jewelry and the stolen loot and riding east to meet Tommy. She arrived first and parked her buggy underneath an oak tree on the old abandoned Montgomery ranch near the Smoky Hill River. It was chilly and windy that day so she was bundled up fairly warm, but she was still dressed to kill.

After Lil anxiously waited there for about thirty minutes, Tommy finally came into sight. He spotted Lil and pulled up next to her. They were both grinning from ear to ear.

"Throw your bags into my buggy," Lil said, "and let's get the hell out of here."

Tommy hopped out of his wagon, tossed his luggage, climbed into Lil's buggy and they hugged and kissed each other.

"Did everything go OK in Hays City?" Lil asked.

"Perfectly," Tommy said. "We won't have to worry about Dead-eye and his gang anymore. After tomorrow morning, they'll be buried in pine boxes on Boot Hill.

Although, I must tell you Lil, I feel sort of guilty about what I did knowing that I'm gonna be the cause of a lot of men gettin' killed tomorrow."

Then Lil said,

"Before you break out in a rash of righteousness, you need to calm down. In fact darling, I'm gonna make it so you don't have to worry about it anymore."

"How you gonna do that Lil?"

"Like this dear."

Lil reached down, pulled up her long flowing dress and faster than a snake slithering into a rat hole, pulled out her derringer and shot Tommy squarely between the eyes, killing him instantly.

"You poor sap. You didn't really think I was gonna share this money with you, did you now Tommy?"

She then drove her buggy onto the old wooden bridge and pushed Tommy's body out into the Smoky Hill River and tossed his luggage out too. Then she slapped the leather reins on the hindquarters of her Morgan and galloped off to Salina sending up a cloud of dust that could rival an Oklahoma dust storm.

"Oh, if that Smoky Hill River could talk."

In the meantime, Dead-eye and the Outlaws of Smoky Hill River were riding toward Hays City and into a sure ambush; that is, if the townspeople could maintain their courage and stand their ground.

On Saturday evening at about 6:30, with the sun already over the horizon, Dead-eye and his gang stopped their advance toward Hays City and made camp just a few miles outside of town. A couple of the raiders gathered wood for a fire while two more tied a picket line to tether the horses to and then they grained them. Each gang member brought his own food. Some had to prepare their meals while others just chewed on jerky. Rusty put on a pot of coffee for everyone.

Dead-eye did not allow anyone to drink whiskey when going on a raid so he was upset when one of the younger gang members went to his saddlebag and pulled out a pint and started sipping rye. Dead-eye caught a glimpse of it out of the corner of his eye and went over and slapped the bottle right out of the youngster's hand. The bottle hit a rock, shattered, and briefly spooked the horses sending a couple rearing up in the air before they all calmed back down. Dead-eye told the young thug if he ever caught him doing that again, he'd drill him and leave his body dry up in the sun for vultures to fatten up on.

Then Dead-eye walked over to Rusty who was sitting by himself against a tree chewing on some venison jerky. Rusty was never real talkative unless he had something important on his mind. He'd rather just sit quietly by himself while he let his mind wander.

"Rusty, you have the most important job tomorrow. I don't know what kind of lock they have on that bank vault but I have confidence that you can crack it. We'll give you plenty of cover but to be safe, you need to bust that vault open in under five minutes so we can take the loot and high-tail it out of their before anyone is the wiser."

"You don't have to worry about me boss. I can crack any safe in this country. Just give me four minutes and then get ready to ride."

Dead-eye smiled, patted Rusty on the shoulder and then walked over to the campfire and threw another log on the fire before pouring himself a cup of coffee. The night was becoming cold with the typical bone-chilling March winds picking up steam across the open plains. Everyone began leaning toward the campfire to stay warm.

They went over their plans one last time while cleaning their firearms and checking to make sure they were fully loaded. They were totally confident that tomorrow was "gonna be quick and easy" and they were convinced that no blood was gonna be spilled, this time around. However, Dead-eye and his gang had no problem filling someone with lead if conditions necessitated such.

In and around town there was a totally different mood, a more somber one, especially on Saturday evening. The townspeople, farmers and ranchers were spending precious time with their families not really knowing the extent of what tomorrow would bring.

The marshal told everyone that the element of surprise would be the key to surviving the raid Sunday morning. The churchgoers were told to go to service as they always did but pack their loaded pistols and be ready to use them when the time was right.

Each farmer and rancher was instructed where they would be positioned around town. They were told to bring their rifles with them in addition to their pistols. They would be positioned on rooftops, by second story windows, and scattered about at ground level inside buildings up and down Main Street.

The clash between law abiding citizens fighting to save their town, and the murderous Outlaws of Smoky Hill River looking for an easy take, was just hours away from reality. The question was, "who would be the victors?"

For the Outlaws of Smoky Hill River, the night dragged on, but for the townspeople of Hays City, morning came by way too quickly. And when first light on Sunday did arrive, it was a gloomy looking morning, apropos for what was about to befall on this peaceful railroad town carved out of the flat lush grasslands of Kansas.

It was cloudy, misty and cold. Some of the gang members put on their slickers while others just wore their trail worn woolen coats. At 8:30 a.m., they took down the long picket line, checked their firearms one last time, saddled up their horses and began their short ride toward Hays City, each one sitting tall in their saddles, ready and equipped for action.

By now, the men of Hays City were in their positions on the west side of town and the churchgoers were arriving in their buggies dressed in their Sunday go-to-meeting attire on the other side of town. Normally they came to praise and worship on Sunday mornings. Today they would come to pray for their well-being. Many of them felt that they would be safe in the house of God, many others, not so much.

It was now 9:00 a.m. Remarkably, every man in town was standing his ground, so far. Oh they were nervous, sweating and fearful alright; a state of mind which no one could fault them for. But they were drawing from the untouched inner power of their very souls which had never been tested to this degree before. This was their town. This is where they planned to raise their children, watch their grandchildren grow up, and live out their lives in peace and harmony; they were determined to not let anyone take that away from them.

Nervous anticipation was now widespread throughout Hays City as the minutes continued to tick away, one-by-one. And then, right at 9:15 a.m. sharp, just as predicted, the churchgoers heard the sound of pounding hooves outside and they knew that this was it, the time had come.

When the gang arrived in front of the church, the outlaws split up into two groups. Four stopped at the church and dismounted. The other five rode down to the bank watching from side to side as they cautiously trotted down Main Street. Their keen awareness had the appearance of both predator and prey. They were looking for anything that seemed out of place.

The marshal and his deputies thought it best not to be in their office which was located across the street from the bank. This was a wise decision because Dead-eye had plans to gun down any lawmen present, right at the start. So Marshal Tanner and Deputy Bradley hid in the bank while Deputy Bardsley was stationed in a building close by with some of the local ranchers. Marshal Tanner was toting his 10 gauge shotgun that he affectionately called "Old Nellie". It was loaded with buckshot and he had no problem spreading the lead to protect himself and his town.

The four outlaws at the church, who were Billy, Jim, Tommy, and Bob, waited to make their move until the other five reached the bank down the street. Once those five reined in their horses at the end of the street, that's when Jim, Tommy, and Bob stormed into the church while Billy stayed outside as planned.

The church crowd knew right away who they were and some of the ladies began to scream. Tommy shouted,

"Shut your mouths, we just want your money. If you cooperate, no one will get hurt." At this point the townsmen, who were armed, did nothing.

While this was going on, Dead-eye discovered that there was no one in the marshal's office so he ran across the street and yelled to his men,

"Hurry, hurry, break the door down, something doesn't seem right!"

So they did and Rusty went to work cracking the lock by putting his ear to the door of the safe while listening for tumblers to click as he meticulously turned the combination dial slowly to the right, then to the left and once again to the right.

Two outlaws were inside with Rusty, while Dead-eye and another one were standing outside. Out of nowhere and totally unexpectedly, Dead-eye looked at the other gang member and said,

"After Rusty opens the safe, I want you to go inside and kill him."

"Kill Rusty? Why?"

"I have my reasons. I'll tell you later. Just do it."

"OK boss," he said as he looked inside the bank to see if Rusty heard the order.

In the meantime, as the minutes passed, Dead-eye was becoming more and more uncomfortable because the town seemed too quiet. He broke out in a nervous sweat which he never experienced before, even during some of his most dangerous criminal deeds.

"It's open!" Rusty shouted.

Just then, mayhem broke out. The marshal yelled to the three inside to drop their guns but two of the outlaws quickly pivoted around to shoot. The marshal wasted no time and in the blink of an eye, unloaded both barrels in one of them while Deputy Bradley aimed perfectly and put three slugs into the other.

Rusty fell flat on the floor shouting, "Don't shoot, don't shoot!"

As Dead-eye and the other outlaw ran for their horses, a fusillade of bullets rang out from every which direction on Main Street peppering the bodies of Dead-eye and the other gunslinger with lead. They didn't have a chance, not even a chance to return fire.

However, down by the church, it was a different story. Once the gunshots were heard coming from the bank, that was the cue for the townspeople to open up on the gang inside the church. And open up they did. Bullets were flying everywhere. With the courage of infantrymen on the front line, the townspeople, with pistols in hand, bravely stood up and fired on the outlaws; but the outlaws fired back. Women and children were screaming and ducking under the pews. The noise level from the pistols became earsplitting while clouds of black powder gunsmoke filled the air. Billy came running into the church to help his fellow gang members but was gunned down instantly.

When the shooting was over and the smoke cleared, the four outlaws lay dead. But they weren't the only ones. Six men and two women were shot and killed as well; one child was wounded in the leg. A haunting quiet came over the church for an instant and then you could hear the moaning coming from behind the podium. It was the minister. He was shot and it didn't sound good.

Then reality set in and the wailing began when spouses and children discovered that their loved ones were shot and killed. The church was like a war zone. It was good against evil. Good triumphed, but the price was high.

The doctor was one of the men in the church and he immediately went to work, checking to see who was mortally wounded and who was still alive. He was having no luck finding any of the wounded still breathing except for the child and the minister; but the minister was in bad shape. Doc immediately asked several men to carry the minister down to his office. The parents of the wounded child picked him up and rushed him to the doctor's office as well after applying a makeshift tourniquet to his leg to stop the bleeding from the gunshot wound.

All the outlaws down by the bank were killed except for Rusty. Deputy Bradley pointed his pistol at Rusty, pulled back the hammer, and was ready to pull the trigger when Marshal Tanner shouted,

"No, don't shoot him. Let's hang him after his trial. We'll show this varmint how we administer justice out here on the frontier. There's a nice hanging tree down on the banks of the

Smoky Hill River. That big old cottonwood has this outlaw's name written all over it."

Bradley held his gun on Rusty. The marshal frisked him while he was still lying on the floor. Rusty was carrying a small pistol in his pocket. It was a Colt M1877 double action revolver which began production in 1877. Colt produced three versions of the pistol which came in different calibers. The "Lightning" was chambered in a .38 Long Colt, the "Thunderer" in a .41 Colt; and the "Rainmaker" which was chambered for a .32 Colt. All three revolvers were available in barrel lengths from 2.5" to 7.5". The shorter barrel versions were marketed as a "shopkeeper's special".

The notorious outlaw John Wesley Hardin (May 26, 1853 – August 19, 1895, lived to age 42) frequently used both the "Lightning" and "Thunderer" versions of the Colt M1877 revolver. The "Thunderer" version was the preferred weapon of Billy the Kid (November 23, 1859 – July 14, 1881, lived to age 21) and was his weapon of choice when he was gunned down by Pat Garrett (June 5 – February 29, 1908, lived to age 57).

Rusty was toting the "Rainmaker" model with a 2.5" barrel. Rusty wasn't a gunslinger. He was just a safecracker. He toted the small pistol for his own protection, but he never used it to kill a man.

Marshal Tanner handed his shotgun to Deputy Bradley. He then pulled Rusty up by the shirt collar and led him to the jailhouse. Rusty looked around and saw all of his gang members lying dead in pools of their own blood. On the way over to the jailhouse, they were surrounded by townspeople with rifles and pistols shouting, "String him up!"

The marshal immediately yelled back,

"He gets a fair trial first. Then we'll string him up and bury him on Boot Hill with the rest of his gang."

CHAPTER TWO:

The Kangaroo Court

After Rusty was thrown behind bars, the marshal's job was far from over. He called one of the townspeople over to his office and told him to go fetch the undertaker and tell him to take the dead bodies of the gang off the street and prepare a place for them on Boot Hill. Then he gave orders to his deputies.

"Bardsley, you stay here and find out who this guy is we just jailed. Bradley and I are gonna ride down to the church and see what's goin' on down there."

So Marshal Tanner and Deputy Bradley went out the back door, mounted their horses and trotted down Main Street. By the time they arrived at the church, the minister and child were already carried to the doctor's office. Most of the churchgoers were standing outside, some crying, while others were just quiet and in a temporary but understandable state of shock. They had not seen anything like this for years in Hays City.

When the marshal and his deputy dismounted and tied up their horses to the hitching rail, the marshal asked one of the town's elders,

"How bad is it?"

"It's real bad marshal. Oh we killed the four outlaws alright, but we paid a high price too."

As Tanner, Bradley and the town's elder were walking up the steps to the church the old man said,

"Too much carnage marshal: six of our men and two of our women are dead, and the preacher and a little boy were wounded."

"How bad is the preacher?"

"He may not make it. Looks to me like he's pert near gone."

"Whose youngen was shot, and how bad is he?"

"It's Connelly's boy. He was shot in the leg. Oh it was bleeding pretty bad but it was mostly just a flesh wound from what I saw. The poor kid was scared to death, but he'll be alright, I reckon."

When the marshal entered the church and saw the dead bodies of his townspeople stretched out on the floor, he was sickened at the carnage he was witnessing. He had no idea that his plan would result in so many innocent lives being lost.

He walked by each, stared down at the lifeless bodies with their Sunday go-to-meeting clothes all stained with blood, and just shook his head. He knew every single one of the victims by name. Then the last one he came upon really stunned him.

"Not the judge too?" The marshal said in disgust and anger.

The judge took a slug in the neck and it did him in almost instantly. The marshal looked at Bradley and said,

"I'll have to send for a judge from Dodge City, if we're gonna give that guy we captured a trial."

"Let's not give him a trial, marshal," Bradley insisted. "Let's administer our own justice down by the river."

"No, he'll get a trial alright. I know the judge personally in Dodge City. He's fair in matters like these. But he's even more fair when he gets paid off. With him as the judge, and twelve jurors who were in church at the time of this slaughter, we'll have no problem finding that sidewinder guilty. You can bet your farm, Bradley, that there's gonna be a hanging in Hays City alright."

The undertaker and his helper came over to the church after collecting the dead bodies at the bank and taking them to his mortuary. They each brought a wagon to load up the victims and the dead gang members.

In the meantime, on the other side of town, Deputy Bardsley began questioning the prisoner. With a piece of paper and pencil in hand he began the inquiry.

"What's your name fella?"

Rusty was sitting on the bed in his cell with his face in his hands and was looking quite peaked. He looked up and said,

"My name is Rusty Blake."

"How long you been with that gang, boy?"

"Only about three months."

"That's so?"

"Yeah, that's so."

"Well boy, I don't know what happened down at the church, but if any townspeople were killed, you're gonna have a noose around your neck and be pushing up daisies on Boot Hill with your dead friends before you know it."

"I don't think so," Rusty said with confidence in his voice and manner.

"Why you arrogant little weasel. I'll be lookin' forward to stringing up your sorry hide this week," Bardsley sharply remarked.

Thirty minutes later, after the marshal talked to the eye witnesses about the church shootings, he and his deputy rode back to the jailhouse. When the marshal entered, he could not contain his anger when he laid his eyes once again on Rusty. He slammed the door behind him, walked over to the cell and with the temper and look of an angry cougar, said to Rusty,

"You and your cowardly gang killed eight of my townspeople today including the judge. You're gonna pay for that."

"I didn't kill anyone," Rusty insisted.

"The hell you didn't boy!" The marshal shouted. "We have two eye witnesses right here who saw you do it, Deputies Bradley and Bardsley. They'll swear to it in court, won't you boys?"

"You bet we will," Bardsley acknowledged.

"Yep, we saw it all. You killed one of our citizens in cold blood," Bradley said as he lied convincingly just as he planned on doing in court if it came to that.

This was beginning to sound more and more like Rusty's worst nightmare. He had heard about these types of bogus trials carried out in shameless frontier towns all around the untamed West, and he feared that he was about to experience one firsthand.

They were known as kangaroo courts. The origin of the term is in dispute. Some suggest that the term was popularized during the California Gold Rush in 1848 "as a description of the hastily carried-out proceedings used to deal with the issue of claim jumping miners". Others say that the term originates from the "notion of justice proceeding 'by leaps', like a kangaroo". Yet another explanation is that it "could refer to the pouch of a kangaroo, meaning the court is in someone's pocket".

A kangaroo court is held by a community to give the appearance of a fair and just trial. However, it's nothing more than a sham because the verdict, for all practical purposes, had already been decided before the trial even began. One can surely conclude that a kangaroo court is a mock court that unashamedly disrespects recognized standards of law and justice.

A kangaroo court was exactly what Marshal Tanner and his deputies had in mind. With the town being wound up like a two dollar Swiss watch about the killings, they felt like the jury would have no problem finding Rusty guilty, even before they deliberated.

Since it was Sunday, the telegraph office was closed so the marshal had to wait until Monday to send a wire to his friend Judge Cole Parker in Dodge City. Cole Parker had two brothers who were also judges. One was a judge in Missouri named Jed and the other one who was Robert Parker, was a judge in eastern Kansas. All three judges were suspicioned to be a bit on the shady side but no confirmation of unlawful activity, on or off the bench, was ever verified.

These three brothers were cousins to the famous judge who resided in Fort Smith, Arkansas. His name was Isaac Charles Parker (October 15, 1838 – November 17, 1896, lived to age 58), better known as the "Hanging Judge". On March 18, 1875, President Grant nominated Isaac Parker, at Parker's request, for the position of judge of the federal district court for the Western District of Arkansas. He indeed was confirmed and Parker arrived in Fort Smith, Arkansas on May 4, 1875 and held his first trial on May 10th of the same year.

Isaac Parker resided on the federal bench for 21 years trying 13,490 cases of which 344 were capital offenses. He was a tough judge but he was respected. Of the accused who went to trial in his court, 9,454 pleaded guilty or were convicted; 160 of them were sentenced to death by hanging. They were 156 men and 4 women. However, only 79 of them (still a large number by anyone's standard) were actually hanged. The rest died in prison, were appealed, or were pardoned.

When Monday morning rolled around, yesterday's nightmare was still on everyone's mind. At 9:00 sharp, when the telegraph office opened up for business, Marshal Tanner was the first in line. He composed a telegram to Judge Cole Parker:

Judge Cole Parker
Dodge City, Kansas

We had an attempted robbery by the Outlaws of Smoky Hill River here in Hays City yesterday. They killed eight of our citizens. One of the persons slain was our judge whom you knew very well. All of the outlaws are dead except for one. We captured the killer and need you to serve as the judge for his trial. We will pay you well. We know that he will be found guilty and sentenced to hang as we have two credible witnesses who saw him gun down and kill one of our townspeople in cold blood. Please inform me if you are interested in the case and when you could arrive in Hays City.

Marshal Tanner
Hays City, Kansas

Within two hours, the judge responded to Tanner's telegram. The telegraph operator ran the wire over to the marshal as soon as he received it.

"Marshal, here's your response from the judge in Dodge City."

"Let me see that," the marshal said as he grabbed the telegram.

Rusty stood up and walked to the bars to hear what the judge from Dodge City had to say. Then the marshal read the response out loud so everyone could hear:

Marshal Tanner
Hays City, Kansas

I will arrive in Hays City on Thursday March 17th and will plan to hold the trial at eleven o'clock Friday morning, March 18th. If what you say is true about the facts, the trial shouldn't last longer than one hour. I will leave it up to you to find twelve jurors you can trust. I expect to be paid immediately after sentencing.

Judge Cole Parker
Dodge City, Kansas

"Well boy, you better start saying your prayers. You're gonna meet your maker soon," Deputy Bardsley said as he laughed right in Rusty's face.

Rusty didn't say a word. He just turned around and sat down on his bed again. It was about noon now and the marshal's girlfriend, who was a French cook at the local café, brought a special lunch over to the jailhouse.

"What's in the Dutch oven today, Cherie?" The marshal inquired.

"Fricassee, I made you fricassee. I even have enough for your jailbird."

"What in the world is fricassee?" Deputy Bradley asked.

"It's a dish from the old country. It comes from the French words frire meaning to fry, and casser meaning to break into pieces," Cherie said with a smile as pretty as a Rocky Mountain sunset.

"It's just a method of cooking I learned from my mother in our native country. It's meat that is cut up, sautéed, and braised, and served with a white sauce and a few vegetables. This is chicken fricassee. It's like a French stew."

"It sure smells good ma'am," Deputy Bardsley said.

Well they all sat down and ate lunch. They even shared some with Rusty. Rusty told Cherie that he was much obliged. After lunch, Tanner and Bradley went over to the doc's office to check on the minister and the young boy. The young boy was already bandaged up and taken home. The minister was still fighting for his life.

Then the two visited with the undertaker to get the latest on the burials. The undertaker hired carpenters to construct pine boxes for all of the deceased. The plan was to bury the dead gang members on Tuesday in Boot Hill with no ceremony. The townspeople would be buried on Wednesday in the town's cemetery after a special group church service which would be conducted by a visiting preacher from Salina.

On Tuesday, several of the townspeople dug the graves on Boot Hill and tossed the boxes of the gang members into the shallow holes showing no respect for the outlaws. A couple of the men even spit on the pine boxes before they shoveled dirt to fill in the graves.

Wednesday was a different story though. Several wagons carried the caskets from the mortuary to the church where the preacher from Salina held a solemn funeral service for all the townspeople who were killed on Sunday. The wailing and crying echoed throughout the church as all of the caskets enclosing the eight murdered innocent townspeople were carried into the house of worship while everyone stood. Two were placed between the platform where the minister's podium was located and the first pews, one on either side of the middle aisle. The other six were lined up down the aisle. Each casket was placed on a small wooden structure so that they were respectfully two feet off the floor.

The minister then began:

"My dear friends in Christ, let us begin on page eleven in your songbooks by singing, Amazing Grace, verses 1, 3, and 7. The first six verses of this song were written by the English poet and clergyman John Newton and published in 1779. The seventh verse was added much later. The message of this beautiful Christian song my friends is that forgiveness and redemption are possible regardless of sins committed and that the soul can be delivered from despair through the mercy of God."

The organist played the last 4 bars of the song as an intro and then the congregation began to sing:

Amazing grace, how sweet the sound,
That sav'd a wretch like me
I once was lost, but now am found,
Was blind, but now I see.

Thro' many dangers, toils, and snares,
I have already come;
'Tis grace hath brought me safe thus far,
And grace will lead me home.

When we've been there ten thousand years,
Bright shining as the sun,
We've no less days to sing God's praise,
Than when we first begun.

"My dear friends in the Christian faith, my name is Reverend Walker. I have come from Salina to minister over our departed family in Christ and pray with you that these poor souls may be received with open arms by our Savior. I don't come to you with answers on why this tragedy happened. This heartbreak is tough on the whole community. We're stunned, we're hurting inside, we don't understand. 'Why me? Why did you take my loved ones?' We ask the Lord. Some of you are even angry.

Most of you are searching for answers this morning. I want you to know that it's OK to ask those questions. It's natural to wonder why this had to happen.

Each one of us must face the realities of life every day. Today, however, in a special way, we face the reality of death. Death is truly a strong power. It can separate us from loved ones. It can bring moments of loneliness for those who survive. It can make us call into question all we believe. Today we are faced with the deaths of the ones we loved.

Mrs. Sarah Johnson, wife of Ted Johnson and mother of 3 daughters

Miss Amanda Baker, 21 years old, and daughter of Mr. and Mrs. Frank Baker

Mr. Jesse Chandler, husband of Sarah Chandler and father of 1 son

Mr. Mark Blain, husband of Martha Blain and father of 2 daughters

Judge Ben Wilson, husband of Anna Wilson

Mr. Matthew Reed, widower and father of 2 daughters

Young Tommy Williams, the 19 year old son of Mr. and Mrs. Tom Williams

Mr. Patrick Kelly, husband of Molly Kelly and father of 3 daughters and 2 sons

I know that many of you have already thought ahead to the many moments of loneliness you will face. But death is not the end of the story. If it were, there would be no reason for us to be here together. We are here because we realize: death, with all of its power, can be overcome; our Lord and Savior, Jesus Christ, overcame the grave that we might have life, and whoever calls upon His name might live.

We should take comfort from the King James Bible version of John 11:21-27 and demonstrate the faith shown by Martha.

I am the Resurrection and the life.

Then said Martha unto Jesus, 'Lord, if thou hadst been here, my brother had not died.

But I know, that even now, whatsoever thou wilt ask of God, God will give it thee.'

Jesus saith unto her, 'Thy brother shall rise again.'

Martha saith unto him, 'I know that he shall rise again in the resurrection at the last day.'

Jesus said unto her, 'I am the resurrection, and the life: he that believeth in me, though he were dead, yet shall he live:

And whosoever liveth and believeth in me shall never die. Believest thou this?'

She saith unto him, 'Yea, Lord: I believe that thou art the Christ, the Son of God, which should come into the world.'

In Romans 8:18 we read:

For I reckon that the sufferings of this present time are not worthy to be compared with the glory which shall be revealed in us.

In John 14:1-6 we read:

Jesus said, 'Let not your heart be troubled: ye believe in God, believe also in me. In my Father's house are many mansions: if it were not so, I would have told you. I go to prepare a place for you. And if I go and prepare a place for you, I will come again, and receive you unto myself; that where I am, there may ye be also. And whither I go ye know, and the way ye know.' Thomas saith unto him. 'Lord, we know not whither thou goest; and how can we know the way'. Jesus saith unto him, 'I am the way, the truth, and the life: no man cometh unto the Father, but by me.'

And so I pray: Our Father in heaven, we thank you today for these blessed words of joy and comfort from your heart to ours as we grieve the loss of our dear friends and family here today. Bless us as we now come to honor their lives and remember their love and loyalty to us all, Amen.

And so dear friends in Christ, this is a time for us to remember. Secondly, it's a time for us to say good-bye to Sarah, Amanda, Jesse, Mark, Ben, Matthew, Tommy and Patrick. And thirdly, it's a time for all of us here today to search our own souls and take a look at our own lives. And as in 2 Timothy, Chapter 1 verse 18, let us ask the Lord that when we stand before the Lord on that great day, may the Lord grant mercy on these departed souls and our own souls when our time comes. Amen.

And now my dear friends, as the pallbearers pick up the caskets for the long walk to the Hays City Memorial Cemetery, let us sing 'Shall We Gather at the River.'

The song's lyrics, my friends, refer to the Christian concept of the anticipation of restoration and reward, and reference the motifs found at Revelation 22:1-2 - a crystal clear river with water of life, issuing from the throne of heaven, all presented by an angel of God. We will sing verses 1, 4 and 5 with the refrain after each verse. Organist, please begin."

> Refrain:
> Yes, we'll gather at the river,
> The beautiful, the beautiful river;
> Gather with the saints at the river
> That flows by the throne of God.

And so the congregation sang while the pallbearers picked up the caskets and processioned out of the church followed by

Reverend Walker and then the congregation. It was a somber setting beyond belief.

The town declared a "Day of Mourning" so most businesses were closed on that day to respect the deceased.

The funeral procession slowly walked west down Main Street and made a left turn down Mule Skinner Street and traveled south to the Hays City Memorial Cemetery which was just outside of town. Rusty glanced out of his cell window as the procession went by the jailhouse. He was emotionally taken aback at the sorrowful sight while watching the caskets of the innocent slain townspeople go by, followed by men, women and children openly weeping for their departed loved ones.

It was a sight too heartbreaking to bear, unless of course you were an evil criminal who lacked a conscience. Rusty did not seem to be one of those types. However, that didn't matter to the marshal and his deputies because somebody was going to pay the price with their life for these killings, and Rusty was the only one left alive to wreak revenge upon.

Judge Cole Parker was due to arrive in town on Thursday. However, preceding his expected arrival was another funeral. This one had the appearance of a death of an important dignitary. When the funeral procession went by the jailhouse, Rusty was standing up and looking out the cell window again. The procession was over a city block long. The casket was a fancy brown wooden one. It was in a black enclosed mortuary wagon with windows and you could see that the casket was smothered with wreaths and flowers. The two horses pulling the wagon wore long black plumes attached to their headstalls. There were four drummer boys leading the procession playing a solemn drumbeat march, banging the drums to the rhythm of the slow walk. Main Street was lined with onlookers as the procession traveled the same route as the one the day before.

Marshal Tanner and Deputy Bardsley were in the procession while Deputy Bradley stood in the open doorway of the jailhouse with his hat in hand watching the funeral cortege slowly parade by.

When the procession was moving out of sight, Rusty asked Deputy Bradley who the funeral was for.

"It was for the town's preacher. He died on Tuesday from a gunshot wound on Sunday when your gang raided our town."

"What was his name?"

The deputy responded directly with no signs of emotion in his voice.

Rusty looked at the deputy, then outside again toward the left trying to grab a last glance. Then he looked down showing distress on his face. His white knuckles, from clenching the window cell bars tightly, tacitly spoke his piece without uttering a word.

"Did you know him?" the deputy asked.

Rusty did not reply. He just turned around, sat on his bed, sunk his face in the palms of his hands and for unknown reasons, appeared to be very saddened by the revelation. Bradley saw no need to push the issue any further.

Judge Cole Parker rode into town that afternoon at about two o'clock and stopped by the marshal's office before signing into the hotel. The marshal and his two deputies were present when Judge Parker entered the jailhouse. He greeted the marshal and then Tanner introduced him to his two deputies. The judge then looked over at the wood burning stove with his eyes almost burning a hole through the coffee pot.

"Bradley, pour the judge a cup of coffee," the marshal said.

"Thanks, I can use a hot cup; it was a long cold ride up from Dodge City."

Rusty was looking on with anxiety and was paying attention to every word being spoken.

The judge then looked over toward the cell and straight at Rusty and asked Tanner,

"Is that the murderer who you wired me about?"

"I'm no murderer!" Rusty shouted.

"Fessen up is good for the soul, son," the judge responded.

The four laughed and turned their backs toward Rusty.

"That's him," Marshal Tanner said. "We're looking forward to his hanging."

"Well, he'll get a fair trial first. I'm going over to the hotel and sign in now. What do you say we have dinner together tonight Tanner. I'm buying. How does six o'clock sound?"

"Perfect," Tanner replied.

The trial was set for eleven o'clock Friday morning and was to be held at the Silver Spur Saloon and Dance Hall. It was the largest building in town and would be a perfect place to hold a trial and accommodate a large group of people. And afterwards of course, the bar would open and the town could celebrate the first hanging verdict in years assuming the kangaroo court jury would bring back a guilty verdict. Actually, no one thought otherwise and there were no wagers on the contrary.

On Thursday, Tanner's deputies selected a jury of twelve for the trial: three were town drunks, one was the barkeep of the Silver Spur, five were ranchers that lived just outside of town, one was the president of the bank and two were business owners in town. It just so happened that eleven of them were frequent visitors of the Silver Spur and loved to drink, gamble and watch the dance hall floozies strut their stuff up on stage. The twelfth juror worked in the joint.

At 10:45 Friday morning, Tanner walked over to the cell, grabbed the ring of keys hanging on the wall and unlocked Rusty's cell door with his right hand while holding his pistol on Rusty with his left hand.

"Let's go son, the judge and jury are waiting for ya," Tanner said.

Rusty was lying on the bed staring at the ceiling. He got up, looked at Tanner and the two deputies who were standing behind Tanner with their pistols drawn as well, walked out of his cell and said what sounded like a sure threat,

"If I'm found guilty and hung, you poor excuses for lawmen are gonna pay the price."

The three lawmen laughed. Bardsley shoved Rusty forward from the back as they were walking toward the front door and boasted,

"I've yet to see a criminal climb out of his hole in Boot Hill."

The four then walked over to the Silver Spur. Horses and buckboards lined the dirt street. The saloon was buzzing like it was the 4th of July. It was packed with townspeople, farmers, and ranchers; there was standing room only. Curious out of town cowboys and saddle bums found places to sit on the steps going upstairs and people were lined up on the second floor by the railing looking down onto the dance floor turned courtroom.

Yep, the hall was set up like a courtroom the best they could. The judge was sitting at a square table on the small stage at the end of the hall where the upright piano was located. Next to him was a witness chair; but as a mockery, they used the swivel piano stool. Chairs were lined up in rows with an aisle down the middle. In front of the row of chairs were two tables, one on either side of the aisle: one for the defendant and his assigned lawyer and one for the prosecuting attorney. The twelve jurors were sitting on the right side of the room. The only ones who were properly dressed for the trial were the two lawyers and the judge.

When the marshal and his deputies walked into the room with Rusty, everyone stood up and the shouting began. "Hang the murderer! String him up!" Several ranchers pulled out their pistols and began shooting them into the air. Rusty ducked at the sound of the gunshots. The noise level from the yelling and shooting was almost unbearable.

The judge was already sitting at his place and began beating his gavel on the table.

"Order in the court! Order in the court! Put those guns away or I'll throw you out of my courtroom. Silence I say, silence! I want complete order in my court or you will be asked to leave!" The judge yelled. The place finally quieted down.

Everyone sat down and the lawyers took their places. The marshal and his deputies sat in the first row of seats. The prosecuting attorney sat at the table on the right and Rusty and his court assigned defense attorney sat at the table on the left. The judge then spoke.

"My name is Judge Cole Parker. I reside in Dodge City, Kansas. Marshal Tanner asked me to judge this case since your judge was murdered by the very gang the accused belonged to."

"The kangaroo court begins," Rusty thought after that somewhat incriminating statement by the judge.

Then the judge continued,

"We are here to seek justice. The accused is innocent until proven guilty, at least that's what it says in the book," the judge said as he smiled.

The courtroom burst into a loud laughter while many stood up and shouted, "String him up! String him up!"

The judge banged his gavel again on the table and ordered everyone to quiet down. Then he asked the prosecuting attorney to read the charges.

"Your honor and the jury, Rusty Blake is accused of an attempted bank robbery, assault, robbing innocent folks in church, and murder. We will prove beyond a shadow of a doubt that he is guilty as charged and deserves to hang from the tall cottonwood tree down by the Smoky Hill River."

Yet again the crowd in the courtroom stood up whooping and hollering and once again the judge pounded his gavel to quiet them down.

Then the judge asked the defendant to stand up.

"How do you plead to the charges, son?" The judge asked.

"Not guilty," Rusty replied.

The defense lawyer surprisingly waived his opening statement and the judge asked the prosecutor to call his first witness.

"I call Marshal Tanner."

Tanner walked up to the stage, stood up near the stool, raised his right hand and swore to tell the truth, the whole truth and nothing but the truth. Then he sat down.

"Marshal Tanner, can you explain to the court the circumstances by which you and your town were prepared for the raid by the Outlaws of Smoky Hill River?"

Rusty's ears perked up because this was the first time he was hearing of this.

"Yes sir I can. A few days before the raid, a person by the name of Tommy Schaefer came riding into town and told us that the gang was planning to raid our town, steal our money, kill everybody who got in their way and then they were gonna burn the town down."

"That's a lie," Rusty shouted.

"Quiet," the judge said, "or I'll hold you in contempt. Continue counselor."

"How did this Tommy Schaeffer know about the raid, marshal?"

"He said he heard it from the gang leader's girlfriend."

Well that didn't make one bit of sense to Rusty. "Why would Diamond Lil send Schaefer to squeal on Dead-eye?" He wondered.

Then the marshal added, "We got word this morning that Schaefer's body was found floating in the Smoky Hill River. He was shot in the head by a small caliber pistol."

After hearing that testimony, Rusty put two and two together: he figured that there would be only one person who would benefit from Dead-eye and his gang's demise, he knew that Schaefer was sweet on Lil and would do anything for her, and that Lil was capable of stealing the loot and even committing outright murder. He also had a feeling where she would be heading with the gang's stash because he heard her talk about her ambitions quite a few times. However, Rusty did not spill the beans on Diamond Lil at this time. He had his reasons for remaining quiet on the subject.

The prosecuting attorney continued,

"Tell the judge and the jury what happened when the gang rode into town on Sunday morning."

"Well, we were prepared for them. We knew their exact plans and what time they were supposed to arrive in town. We had men stationed in the church, men stationed up and down Main Street, and Deputy Bradley and I were hiding in the bank. After Rusty opened the safe…"

"Stop there," the prosecuting attorney demanded. "This Rusty you speak of, the one who cracked the safe open, is he in this courtroom right now and can you point him out even in this crowd?"

"Yes I can, it's him right there," the marshal said as he pointed to Rusty.

That piece of courtroom drama was not necessary. It was meant to draw a reaction from the crowd and that's exactly what it did as the crowd stood up and yelled yet again, "Hang him, hang him!"

"Quiet!" The judge shouted as he once again pounded his gavel, over and over again, on the wood table.

Then the judge, throwing all legitimate courtroom procedures aside, asked Rusty,

"How did you know how to open that safe, son?"

"I'm a locksmith and that's my specialty," Rusty said.

"Interesting," the judge responded. "Continue with your questioning counselor."

"Now marshal, what happened after Rusty opened the safe?"

This is where the marshal told a bold-faced lie.

"Rusty ran out of the bank and pulled out his pistol and shot one of the townspeople who was standing across the street. Shot him in cold-blood. Then all of the shooting began. Rusty ran back inside of the bank while the other outlaws stood outside and exchanged gunfire with the townspeople. Our brave citizens mowed them down in the street like the polecats they were. Deputy Bradley and I arrested Rusty when he came cowardly running back into the bank."

"That's another lie!" Rusty shouted out.

"One more outburst like that and you'll be asked to leave your own trial," the judge said. "Deputy Bradley you were there, is Marshal Tanner's testimony accurate?"

"Yes your honor, it happened just as he said," Deputy Bradley confirmed.

"Well that's good enough for me," Judge Parker said.

Rusty knew that he had just been railroaded. He put his head down and shook it in despair. He had mentally given up and knew that his chances of getting out of this mess were slim to none. This was the kangaroo court to beat all.

The judge asked Rusty's defense lawyer if he wanted to cross-examine the witness. The defense lawyer said, "By all means, your honor."

Then he stood up, slowly walked over to the witness, put his hands in his pockets, lowered his head to look over his reading glasses at the marshal and asked,

"Marshal Tanner, are you sure you saw what you saw?"

"Yes sir, I'm real sure."

The defense lawyer turned to the judge and said, "No more questions, your honor."

The courtroom burst into loud laughter at the ridiculous question then once again, some pulled out their pistols and shot them into the air putting several more holes in the already perforated ceiling.

Rusty continued to keep his head down knowing it was all over for him.

The judge then spoke,

"Well it's getting close to lunch time and we heard all the testimony we need to hear. Did you have anything to say Rusty?"

"Yes I do judge. This trial is a disgrace and…"

"Sit down," the judge ordered as he pounded his gavel. "I will not have any kind of back talk from a murderer like you."

Then Judge Parker looked at the jurors and said,

"You twelve jurors have a big decision to make. You heard the accurate testimony. This Rusty character came to town with his gang, the Outlaws of Smoky Hill River, with the intention to murder, and they did, and to rob you of your hard earned money, and then burn down your town. My recommendation is that you find this no good criminal guilty and then let's get on with our lives. The sooner you find him guilty, the quicker the bar opens. Now go and deliberate."

The jurors stayed in place and talked amongst each other for no more than two minutes. Then the lead juror, the town drunk said,

"Judge, we have a verdict. We find the accused guilty of first degree murder."

The courtroom exploded with shouting while the judge pounded his gavel over and over again. Then everyone quieted down to hear the sentence by the judge.

"Would the defendant rise and approach the bench."

Rusty stood up and, with his head down and shoulders slumped, walked in front of the judge.

"Rusty Blake, you have been found guilty of murder in the first degree. I order you to be hung by the neck until dead, a week from today on Friday, March 25th. That will give the town plenty of time to build the gallows in the middle of Main Street. Now deputies, take this lowlife scumbag back to his cell. Barkeep, open up your bar and set 'em up. That's an order. The drinks are on the house."

Yelling and laughter rose to a noise level that could be heard across the Kansas Plains and over the snowcapped majestic mountains of the central Rockies as the crowd rushed to the bar for their free drinks. The piano player tickled the ivory keys and the two glamorous sisters, Molly Fae and Flossy Mae, ran up to the stage and began their flashy little song and dance.

Deputy Bradley handcuffed Rusty and pushed him out onto the street as both deputies led Rusty back to the jailhouse.

"This is a sham and a disgrace," Rusty said. "All I was guilty of was cracking open a safe and you guys know it."

"That's your story," Deputy Bradley said as he continued to push Rusty toward the jailhouse.

Marshal Tanner hung out with Judge Parker for a while in the Silver Spur. They sat at a table by themselves and broke open a new bottle of Tennessee whiskey. The barkeep always saved the best for the marshal.

"Thanks for coming to Hays City judge. That dirtbag is gonna get what he has comin' to him. Do you know who I can hire to hang him proper like?"

"Yes I do. When we're done drinking here, I'll send him a telegram. I need to go over to send a wire to someone else anyway; might as well kill two polecats with one slug. The hangman's name is Gil Brown. He works in Dodge City. He ties a good noose that snaps the neck without snapping off the head."

"You don't have to be so graphic," the marshal said as he laughed and then took another swig of Tennessee's finest.

"Say Tanner, that Rusty is pretty skillful when it comes to opening safes, isn't he? It's hard to believe that someone can just put his ear to a safe and crack a combination lock. I guess that's the type of lock that was on the safe, wasn't it?"

"That's what it was alright. My deputy and I saw him do it ourselves. I was quite amused at his skill too. It's too bad his talent will end up buried with him on Boot Hill. He'll have no use for that illegitimate gift in hell, that's for sure," the marshal said as he took one last swig from his tall whiskey glass. "I better get back to work now and lay off the rotgut. Don't think it would look too good for the marshal to be walking down the street half sauced. Thanks again for coming up Parker."

"Anytime my friend. I'm headed over to the telegraph office and then traveling back to Dodge City. Incidentally, Ole Gil Brown's gonna charge you $200 to hang Blake. My cost was $500 for the trial plus $500 for getting the verdict you wanted. I'll collect it from you before I leave town."

"It'll be waiting for ya at the jailhouse, Parker."

Like most hangmen, Gil Brown prided himself on making a hangman's knot which would break a neck and make for lights out at a snap of a finger, or more appropriately stated, at a snap of a neck.

The hangman's knot is not designed to be a slipknot. One coil would make the knot equivalent to a slipknot. The more coils that are added, the more friction created. Even back in the eighteen hundreds, the number thirteen was thought to be unlucky; unlucky for the convicted criminals like Rusty who were going to get their necks stretched. Consequently, hangmen like Gil Brown used thirteen coils in a hangman's knot. This became standard in the Old West and guys with warped callous consciences like Gil Brown took personal pride in their hangman's noose.

When Marshal Tanner arrived back at the jailhouse, he sent Deputy Bardsley out to fetch a councilman. The councilman arrived within fifteen minutes and Tanner gave him explicit instructions.

"I want you to hire a carpenter and have him begin building the gallows for the hanging. I don't want him to build it on Main Street. I want you to have him build it on Mule Skinner Street so that our jailed varmint, Rusty Blake, can see and hear every single nail being pounded into his own personal death trap."

"You're wicked marshal."

"So they say."

And so it happened as ordered. On Saturday, the wood was thrown from a buckboard wagon onto the street and the beating of the two-pound carpenter's hammer echoed up and down Mule Skinner and Main Street and bounced off the walls of Rusty's cell block. The constant hammering and pounding almost drove Rusty insane as it continued for several days.

On Wednesday, two days before the hanging, the gallows was completed. Rusty thought he knew something no one else did. On Wednesday night at about nine o'clock, Rusty asked Deputy Bardsley, the deputy on duty, to pour him a cup of coffee. Bardsley obliged and when he handed the cup of coffee through the cell bars to him, Rusty brazenly said,

"I'm not convinced that this town is gonna see me swinging Friday, Mr. Deputy."

"No? What's you gonna do, lose some weight and shimmy through the bars?" Bardsley responded as he laughed and went over to the stove and poured himself a cup of Arbuckle's.

This was the week for Bardsley to work late. The deputy that worked the night shift had a specific duty before locking himself in the jailhouse. He would make a final walk around town at 10:00 p.m. to make sure everything was in order. Then he would go back to the jailhouse, lock the door, and hit the sack, lying on a small bed which was situated by the wood burning stove. The late night deputy always slept with a loaded double barrel 10 gauge shotgun at his side. This was standard procedure.

On this night, Rusty just stared at the ceiling while lying in bed wondering if he had only one more day left on this earth. So he did something most criminals didn't know how to do.

He prayed.

CHAPTER THREE:

It Begins

It was now Thursday morning, March 24th. While spring was bringing new life to the countryside, Rusty was staring at death just outside of his window. Gil Brown, the hangman from Dodge City arrived in town Wednesday night and checked out the gallows first thing Thursday morning. It was Gil Brown opening and closing the trapdoor that woke Rusty up from a short night but a sound sleep.

Marshal Tanner arrived at the jailhouse at about 8:00 a.m. and was greeted by a full pot of hot Arbuckle's on the potbelly stove which Deputy Bardsley had put on thirty minutes before. Oh it was strong alright. If it had legs it could walk across the room. But as Tanner would always say, "There's nothing like the aroma of fresh made coffee on a chilly morning no matter how strong it is."

Just when Tanner was pouring himself a steaming hot tin cup of morning Joe, Deputy Bradley walked in. Both Tanner and Bradley already ate breakfast before they arrived, so Bardsley put on his gun belt and walked over to the café for some hot flapjacks, fried sliced peppered up potatoes, chuck wagon style biscuits dipped into red-eye gravy, and a couple of fresh eggs, sunny-side-up. The town was quiet. There wasn't much activity on the streets yet.

Tanner and Bradley shot the breeze for a while and then Tanner walked over to the cell to talk to Rusty.

"Whelp fella, how does it feel to know you'll be worm food tomorrow afternoon?"

"You're sick marshal," Rusty said.

"Maybe so, but I'll still be breathing tomorrow. After you fall through the trapdoor and your neck snaps, Hays City will be able to get back to normal. We're expecting a huge crowd for your hanging boy. It's gonna be quite a party. We'll even let you hang around for a while so the town can celebrate your demise," the marshal said as both he and Bradley laughed at Rusty's expense.

Rusty wasn't giving up hope, even though time was running out. He just knew his other buddies weren't going to let him down. However, if they didn't arrive in time, he would have to inform the marshal of something that he originally had no intention of doing.

The day went by fast for Rusty but dragged on for the townspeople and the lawmen who were eagerly awaiting the hanging party. Ole Gil Brown was even anxious to get the party started. That afternoon, he came over to the jailhouse to meet the outlaw he was going to put his pride noose around.

Gil Brown was a tall, thin, gray looking fella, with a long drawn weathered face. He was all decked out in black and wearing a straight-rim black hat with a rounded crown. He looked like the grim-reaper himself. When he walked into the jailhouse, he was holding his rope with the hangman's knot already made. He fancied carrying it with him everywhere he went. He was mental in that regards.

He walked over to Rusty and didn't say anything except for, "How tall are you mister?"

Rusty, who was stretched out on the bed, looked over at Brown, stood up and said, "There, does this help?"

"Looks like you're about 5'8" with your boots on. That's perfect. See you tomorrow at your hangin'. By the way, I tie the best hangman's knot in the country. After the trapdoor opens, and when you experience that sudden stop, your neck will snap quickly and you won't feel a thing. So they say."

"Get the hell out of my sight you morbid creature."

When nightfall came, the town lit up. The word got out around central Kansas that the last member of the infamous Smoky Hill River Gang was going to be hung Friday. So people came in from all over Kansas to witness the final demise of the infamous gang which terrorized, murdered and looted every town along the Smoky Hill River and beyond.

The Silver Spur was rocking with piano and banjo music and whiskey was flowing as fast and wildly as the Colorado River rapids. Women of the night were hopping from table-to-table and lap-to-lap, looking for free drinks and some profitable action. Oh they were all there alright: Maggie May, Sadie Jane, Emi Lou, Josie Lee, and Becky Jean.

At 10:00 p.m. Deputy Bardsley, began making the rounds, walking up and down Main Street checking on things with a keen eye and with every chamber in his pistol loaded. The street was virtually empty because everyone was in the saloons and the Silver Spur. Marshal Tanner and Deputy Bradley had gone home and had no plans to join the out of control nightlife. They had a big day ahead of 'em tomorrow.

After Deputy Bardsley made his rounds, he walked back to the jailhouse and stooped over some to put his key in the lock to open the door. Just then he felt the steel barrel of a .45 pressed into his back and saw a hand reach down and pull his pistol out of his holster.

"Open the door and get in there quickly," the voice said as someone pushed him forward through the door opening. "Don't say a word, or we'll plug you right where you stand."

Rusty looked across the room, stood up and walked over to the cell bars. There were two gunslingers in the jailhouse, both wearing bandannas covering their faces, with their guns drawn pointing at the deputy.

"Where's the key to that cell?" One of the gunslingers asked in a demanding tone with a Mexican accent.

"On the wall, right there," Bardsley said as he pointed to the keys showing very little emotion on the outside but he was shaking in his boots on the inside.

One of the gunslingers hurriedly walked over to get the keys and then he unlocked Rusty's cell door. Rusty quickly ran out of the cell and went over to the marshal's desk and started frantically opening drawers looking for his Colt M1877 "Rainmaker" revolver. He found it in the bottom drawer.

In the meantime, while the Mexican bandit turned and held his gun on the deputy, the other gunslinger pushed Bardsley into the cell, hog-tied and gagged him. When he was finished, the Mexican locked the cell, and then threw the keys on the floor in the corner of the room behind the potbelly stove.

"Our horses are out back, Rusty," one of the outlaws said.

The Mexican gunslinger peeked out the door, to the left and then to the right, to see if the coast was clear. It was, so they ran out of the jailhouse, closing the door behind them and sprinted to the back where three saddled horses were waiting. Simultaneously, they put their boots in a stirrup, grabbed a hand full of mane, pulled themselves into their saddles and galloped, as fast as lightning, south down Mule Skinner Street until they came upon the banks of the Smoky Hill River. They then headed eastward with their eventual destination being a revitalized cow town, Abilene, Kansas.

Abilene was about 120 miles, by way the Sand Hill crane flies, directly east of Hays City. It lies on the north side of the Smoky Hill River in the Flint Hills region of the Great Plains. Mud Creek, a tributary of the Smoky Hill River, flows south through the city. Abilene was a four day ride from Hays City, three days if they rode hard and switched out horses in the middle of the night with some remote ranches along the way. In fact, that was their plan.

They rode by the light of a rustler's moon, a quarter moon giving just enough light for them to find their way in the dark. Rustlers on the Plains used this moon to steal cattle from drovers and ranchers. It gave them just enough light to pull off their lawless deeds without being spotted.

After about twenty miles of hard riding, they stopped along the bank of the river to give their horses a rest and a drink. Rusty had not spoken to the two gunslingers as of yet since they were riding like the wind to stay clear of any posse which by chance, might be trailing them. There was no posse though. It was a clean getaway.

When the three dismounted their horses, one of the hired guns walked over to Rusty and took his small revolver away from him. The other one asked Rusty,

"Were you surprised we busted you out of jail, pardner?"

"I was expecting to get out of that hell hole but not by you guys. Who are you anyway?"

"We'll let you know in good time."

"Where are we headed and the obvious question is, why did you bust me out of jail?"

"Our boss has a proposition for ya. You can take it or leave it, but we highly suggest you take it if you know what's good for ya."

"Say, what's going on here?"

"You'll find out soon enough pard. We're on our way to Abilene. I guess it won't hurt if I told you our names. We'll probably be working together anyway. My name is Dakota Wilson and this is Pecos Fransisco."

"Pecos Fransisco of the Laredo territory? The so-called fastest gun south of the Red River?"

"Si senor, one and the same, amigo."

"Well if that don't take the slack out of your reins. What are you doin' this far north?"

"Dineros mi amigo, mucho dineros. You'll have that chance too, my friend."

"I heard of you too Dakota. They say you're the fastest gun north of the Red River."

"So they say, pardner," Dakota acknowledged.

"Your wanted posters are in every post office west of the Mississippi River. How is it that I got busted out by two of the most wanted notorious desperados on the Plains?"

"Enough questions," Dakota sharply demanded, "Let's ride to Abilene."

"No wait Dakota, one last question. How do you guys know me?" Rusty asked.

"Let's say we had an inside track. Now, for the last time, mount up and let's ride."

So they did. They rode by night and slept by day. It was three days later when they rode up to a remote two story cabin surrounded by cottonwoods, just about two miles west of Abilene, and about 100 yards north of the river. It appeared to be a hideout. There was a good size barn about 100 feet from the cabin where they walked their horses to, removed the saddles, stalled and fed them. It seemed to be a fairly new structure that could stall up to a dozen horses or so.

Then they strolled over to the cabin. When they walked in, Rusty was quite amazed at what he saw. It was a cabin like no other he had ever seen before. He thought it was pretty darn fancy for an out-of-the-way lodge. It had a large kitchen that was well stocked with canned goods of all sorts.

Just off the kitchen was a large dining room with an impressive candle chandelier which hung over a long beautiful oak wood dining room table. The table was large enough to seat fourteen people, six on either side, and one on each end. Adjacent to the dining room appeared to be a large get together room that was set up like an office or one of those fancy library rooms from out East. There was a large desk near the stone fireplace, a huge round table in the center of the room, fancy leather furniture scattered throughout and a small bar along the wall. The floor was even carpeted.

Hanging on the wall was a huge map of all of the northern and southern states and territories west of the Mississippi River with circles drawn in what appeared to be strategic locations. Some circles were drawn in black while others were drawn in red.

Dakota was showing Rusty around. When Rusty saw the map on the wall, he walked over to it and stared at it, trying to figure out its significance.

"Impressive, ehh Rusty?" Dakota asked.

"Yeah, what's all these colored circles mean?"

"Have no idea. You'll find out soon enough when we do. Let's go upstairs; that's where all the bedrooms are. I'll show you where your room's located. Around here you're gonna get three hots and a cot. We have one hell of a cook and actually, you'll be sleeping in something better than a cot. It's a feather bed. By the way, the privy is out behind the barn. We'll come back to the meeting room after I show you where you're bunking. Then we'll have a drink and wait for the boss to show up."

"The boss? Whose boss?"

"Our boss," Pecos said as he tagged along. "He's the guy who's gonna make us rich, amigo. He looks to be pretty successful himself, wouldn't you say, my friend. He had this place built just for us. We are his 'specialists'. Welcome to the club, amigo."

Ole Rusty was at first quite confused but the more he heard and the more he saw of this place, he began piecing the puzzle together. After he got a two bit tour of the place, all three of them went down to the meeting room for brandy. If you were one of the few chosen for whatever it was, your liquor was upgraded from cheap rotgut rye which was made in the backroom of a saloon from unknown ingredients and aged one hour, to high priced brandy, aged in European oak casks for 12 years and imported from Spain.

While the three were sipping brandy from their snifters, a horse-drawn wagon drove up to the lodge. Rusty looked out of the window and asked,

"Is that the boss coming?"

Dakota looked outside and then laughed.

"No, that's the cook. He's Chinese. His name is Chan something or another. We just call him Chan. He might be Chinese but that little guy can cook."

Chan walked into the kitchen toting boxes of groceries. He was a little skinny guy with a typical Chinese pigtail. He looked at Dakota and said in very broken English,

"Boss ask me to prepare meal for five. Dinner will be at six bells. Now stay out of my kitchen."

Dakota and the other two looking on smirked, and then went back into the meeting room.

At about 5:30 p.m., two riders approached the lodge. This time it was the boss. He was with what looked to be another gunslinger toting a Colt .45 like Dakota's and Pecos's. He also had a Winchester in a scabbard attached to his saddle. This tough looking hombre appeared to be the boss's bodyguard.

They both walked in and went right to the meeting room. The gunslinger walked straight to the bar and poured Brinkman a brandy and then poured one for himself. Rusty was trying to assume a nonchalant appearance but in reality, his knees were close to knocking out the tune, "I Wish I Was in Dixie".

The boss was about 6' 4" tall, medium built, clean shaven, wearing an expensive custom made suit and looking all business-like. He never cracked a smile.

He looked at Rusty, then walked over to his desk, opened up a cigar box, lit up a Cuban, turned around and said,

"Welcome Rusty, I'm Jerod Brinkman. You can call me Mr. Brinkman until we get better acquainted and I tell you that you can do otherwise. This fella here is Billy Greer, you may have seen his wanted posters around. He's also known as the Kansas Kid. He hangs around out of sight."

"I've heard of him," Rusty said as he looked at Greer. Then he looked back at Mr. Brinkman and continued, "It's a pleasure to meet you, sir. I guess you're the one I should thank for breaking me out of jail and saving me from the hangman's noose."

"Yes, you could say that."

"Well, the obvious question is why did you spring me, and the next question is, what am I doing here?"

"Your reputation precedes you son. See that safe over there?"

Brinkman pointed to a large combination lock safe that was five foot tall and about three foot wide. It stood behind a large oak desk.

"Walk over there. If you can open it, you can stay. If you can't open it, we'll have no use for you."

Rusty knew he didn't have a choice because he wasn't toting a pistol to defend himself. He correctly interpreted Brinkman's request as both a challenge and a threat. Immediately, he began to perspire because he knew that if he could not open the safe, his body would most likely be drilled full of lead and dumped into the Smoky Hill River.

So Rusty walked over to the large safe while wiping his wet palms on his pants, knelt down, placed his ear to the door, and then put his thumb, forefinger and middle finger on the Yale brand rotary combination lock. He first turned it slowly to the left holding his breath and listening for a soft click, while the others looked on as if they were in a trance. He stopped when he thought he heard a slight click. He paused, blew his fingers dry, took a deep breath and then he turned the combination wheel slowly to the right. There it was, the second click. Now came the defining moment. He meticulously turned the dial to the left again and there it was, the third click. Rusty smiled with a sense of relief and accomplishment, grabbed the handle, turned it downward, and pulled the large safe door wide open. He then stood up proudly and turned around and grinned from ear to ear.

"Excellent," Brinkman said.

The other three looked at each other, all astonished at Rusty's unusual talent.

"That's why I broke you out of jail, young man. I have a proposition for you which will make you a rich man. But first, look into the bottom of the safe." Rusty turned around and peered in.

"Go ahead, take one out and put it on. It's yours."

Rusty reached into the safe and pulled out a holster with a brand new, nickel plated, pearl handled Colt .45, known around the Wild West as the "peacemaker". It was a beaut. It was just like the ones the other three were wearing. Rusty slid the revolver out of the holster and looked it over.

"Go ahead, Rusty, put it on," Brinkman insisted.

Rusty did. He buckled the holster belt around his waist and his smile became bigger and bigger.

"Fits you like a custom made leather boot, Rusty. Now look in the safe one more time. See that door at the top. Open it up."

Rusty turned around again, opened the door and saw about twelve envelopes.

"Take one out Rusty, it's yours. See what's inside."

Rusty grabbed an envelope, opened it up and immediately said, "Well roast a rooster on a spit, wow!"

"Count it Rusty," Brinkman insisted.

Rusty began counting the bills that were in the envelope. There were thirty $100 bills, $3,000 in all. Rusty was taken aback.

"Now Rusty, the question is, do you want to join up with my gang and be one of my 'specialists'? I can promise you ten times more in the next two years than what you're holding in your hands right now. Are you interested?"

"You bet I am," Rusty said.

"Well good then."

On that cue, Chan walked into the meeting room, bowed and said,

"Dinner is served, gentlemen."

Oh and it was a fine dinner alright: a large beef roast with seasoned boiled potatoes, creamed carrots, and fresh steamed greens. Chan even baked cornbread from a southern recipe which he stole from a café where he worked in Little Rock just three years before. He too was on the run because he sliced up his assistant cook with a meat cleaver back there in Arkansas because his helper called him a Chink. Ole Chan had no tolerance for this vulgar term of hostility and contempt, especially if it was directed toward him.

Every place setting was absolutely perfect, set with the finest china and silverware. The chandelier with nine twelve-inch white lit candles which hung above the middle of the long dinner table gave the appearance of a dining room set for European royalty. That's exactly how Brinkman wanted it.

There was also a glass of the finest French wine from Bordeaux at every setting. The gunslingers had no idea where the wine came from or its reputation for being of great quality. However, Mr. Brinkman did. He knew that Bordeaux was a port city on the Garonne River in the Gironde department in southwestern France and that Bordeaux wine had been produced in that region since the 1st century. Mr. Brinkman had the money to enjoy the best of everything and he accepted no other life but the good life.

After that fine dinner, they all went back into the meeting room. Brinkman lit up another cigar and then asked the group to gather around the large map on the wall.

"Just so you know Rusty, I'm the only one who knows what these circles on this map represent. All of you will find out in due time. When the time is right, you will also be told the reason for our exclusive club. For now though, we'll just keep building our team.

Pecos and Dakota, your next job will be in Huntsville, Texas. There's an outlaw in the Texas State Penitentiary at Huntsville who's serving life in prison. His name is Johnny Dane. He's from El Paso, Texas. His expertise is explosives: dynamite and nitro.

He and two others, one being his brother, robbed a Wells Fargo stagecoach which was carrying a gold shipment from California to St. Louis. They hit it at a narrow corridor in Apache Pass in Arizona by creating a landslide with nitro and blocking the passageway. They got away with one hundred thousand dollars in gold coins and bullion. Dane was convicted of robbery, but that's not why he's serving life. It's for murdering one of his partners.

You see, after they robbed the stagecoach, a posse was hot on their trail, I mean, really hot on their trail. They were headed back to Texas but then they stopped and buried the gold just outside of Las Cruces, New Mexico. The three decided to split up and agreed to meet in one month back at Las Cruces where they hid the gold, after things would settle down. That's when they would divvy-up the loot and go their own separate ways.

Well, things didn't quite work out the way they planned. After a month went by, Johnny Dane went back to Las Cruces on the exact date and time when they said they would all meet. When Johnny arrived at the location, no one else showed up. He waited for about an hour. Then he began digging at the exact spot where the gold was buried. Ole Johnny had a morbid surprise though when he dug down about two feet deep. Instead of finding the gold, he found his brother's body decomposing and being eaten by little critters. Obviously, the gold was gone. It appeared that Johnny's two other partners had similar ideas, to get there a little earlier than planned and take the gold for themselves. The only problem was, those two swindlers showed up at the same time, I reckon, and his brother got the short end of the stick, or to put it another way, got the sharp end of a knife.

Johnny had a suspicion that the one who killed his brother headed north to Santa Fe. He was correct in his assumption. To make a long story short, he saw his partner, his brother's murderer, in a cantina through a glass window, walked in, skinned his smoke wagon, and shot his partner in the back of his head; just like ole Wild Bill got it up in Deadwood back in '76. Unfortunately, as luck would have it, the sheriff of the county was in the same cantina at the time and arrested Dane on the spot. He went to trial, was convicted, and sent to Huntsville. They didn't hang him because he had a good lawyer who said Dane went out of his mind finding the sliced up corpse of his brother buried where the gold was supposed to be."

"How do you know all of this stuff?" Rusty asked.

"I have my ways son," Mr. Brinkman replied. "You'll find out when the time is right. Let's just say, I have a boss too and he knows how to keep his finger on the pulse, especially if he knows it can make him healthy and wealthy."

Well, that was a revelation Rusty didn't expect to hear. It sounded to him that there was definitely someone higher up in this criminal organization running the show and calling the shots; someone with more brain power and more authority than Mr. Brinkman.

Dakota and Pecos were ready to take on their new assignment but had a few questions first. They needed to know how to get to Huntsville. Brinkman had that all figured out. He gave them both railroad tickets to Austin, Texas. There they would buy their horses and ride east to Huntsville. He also gave them a satchel case with fifteen sticks of dynamite. The plan was to sneak a few sticks and matches to Dane and he would use them to blow his way out while Dakota and Pecos would give him cover with a fusillade of bullets.

However, it was a very risky strategy. Pecos and Dakota would have to visit with Dane first, tell Dane the scheme and if Dane agreed to participate in the breakout, then they would go on with the plan. There was no doubt that breaking Dane out of the Texas State Penitentiary was going to take more planning and skill than the breakout in Hays City. On the flip side of a $20 gold piece, if Dane refused to go with the two, he could blow their cover. But the chances of that scenario coming to fruition, that is, Dane refusing the offer, was as low as the chances of a three legged mule outrunning a Colorado catamount.

The Texas State Penitentiary dates all the way back to October 1, 1849. That's when the first inmates arrived. Originally, the unit was only for white Texans. During those years before 1865, the only penalties available to black Texans were whippings and hangings. During the Civil War, the prisoners at the penitentiary were put to good use for the Confederacy. They produced tents and uniforms for the Confederate forces.

John Wesley Hardin, a notorious outlaw and gunfighter, served in the Huntsville Penitentiary from September 28, 1878 to March 16, 1894. He became good friends with Dane but there was no plan to break him out with Dane. The bosses knew that Hardin was too independent and too high strung and unpredictable for Brinkman's special gang.

Brinkman handed Pecos and Dakota their expense money and said,

"Catch the train tomorrow and I expect to see you both back here in about a month with Johnny Dane."

~~"No problem, Dakota said. Consider it done."~~

"Do you want me to go with them Mr. Brinkman?" Rusty asked.

"No, you're staying right here with me. You're gonna start work tomorrow at my place of business in town."

"What type of business is that sir?"

"The banking business. I'm the President of the Abilene, Kansas Bank," Brinkman said as he beamed with a devious grin.

The others began laughing.

"For real?" Rusty asked.

"For real, son. When you come to town about 8:30 tomorrow morning, I want you to first go to the tailor and pick up a couple of suits. Use the money in your envelope there. Then come over to the bank and I'll put you to work as a teller."

Mr. Brinkman then walked up to Rusty, got face to face with him, looked him squarely in the eyes and said with a stern voice,

"Now listen up real good, Rusty. I have a daughter about your age who comes to visit me every day. She has no idea about my business on the side, nor does she know about this place. I want it kept that way. I also want you to stay away from her. Oh, she'll talk with you at the bank, but that is the only place I want to see you two talking together. Do you understand?"

"Yes sir, I do," Rusty confirmed.

Well the next day, Pecos and Dakota were on their way to Austin and Rusty was suited-up for legitimate action at the bank. At about 11:30 in the morning, Brinkman's daughter came walking into the bank with a hot lunch for her father. She worked at the town's newspaper office but she would go to the café across the street, three days a week, and bring her father the special for the day. When she walked in this morning, she looked at Rusty and said with the sweetest voice you could ever imagine,

"Good morning, you're new here."

"Yes ma'am, I'm Rusty Blake. You must be Mr. Brinkman's daughter."

"Why yes I am."

Her name was Kathleen, Kathleen Brinkman. She was about 5' 2" tall, a brunette, and one of the prettiest young single ladies this side of the Mississippi. At least that's what Rusty thought when he laid eyes on her for the first time.

While they were talking, Mr. Brinkman came out of his office to greet his daughter. Brinkman looked at Rusty with a look in his eyes which Rusty interpreted just perfectly. Rusty, remembering what Brinkman had told him the night before, put his head down and immediately went back to work, doing what the other teller taught him to do. However, he did sneak another peek at Kathleen.

When Kathleen and her father went into Brinkman's office and closed the door, Rusty did some clever questioning of the other teller named Joseph. Rusty looked over with his head still tilted downward so as not to be too obvious and whispered,

"I can't believe a pretty gal like that is still single."

"She isn't, well she is in a way," Joseph said, which sounded very confusing to Rusty.

"What do you mean?" Rusty inquired.

"What I mean is that she was married to a bum. Her husband had a habit of beating her. When Mr. Brinkman found out about it, he pistol-whipped the guy within an inch of his life. Brinkman was arrested for attempted murder but got off scot-free. I think he knew the judge."

"Who was the judge?"

"I can't recollect but I think he was from one of those cow towns farther west.

Rusty looked up at Joseph quickly.

"Do you think you know him?" Joseph asked.

"Might. What happened to Kathleen's husband?"

"As soon as he was able, he saddled-up and high-tailed it out of town never to be seen or heard from again. In fact, we don't know if he's dead or alive. Since then, Brinkman has become extremely protective of his daughter. There's one last thing."

"What's that?"

"Well the rumor is that Kathleen is not Mr. Brinkman's biological daughter. They say he adopted her when she was about eight years old, long before he moved to Abilene from Virginia. Don't know more than that."

Rusty wanted to know just one more thing from Joseph. So he asked one final question.

"How much do you know about Mr. Brinkman?"

"I keep my nose clean mister. That's all you need to know."

Rusty caught the meaning of that real quick. This guy knew certain things but preferred to mind his own business.

As the days went by, Rusty and Kathleen became friendlier. Truth be known, Kathleen was just as attracted to Rusty as Rusty was to her. The problem was that this could develop into an unhealthy situation for Rusty, and he knew it.

In the meantime, Pecos and Dakota had made it to Huntsville. They signed into a room when they reached town so that they would have a place to stay for a couple of days to plan the escape and to hide the dynamite they were carrying with them. They left their guns and the dynamite in their rooms when they went to the penitentiary for the first time.

The whole scheme would be a brazen move on their part since they were both wanted up in the northern territories and Pecos also in the south for a sundry of different criminal activities. That's why they thought it would be wise to use aliases when they identified themselves at the penitentiary gate. Pecos would use Juan Diego and Dakota would go by the name of Tom Smith, not a very creative choice by anyone's standards.

Ole Pecos was a little bit shaky. Oh he was fast, fast on the draw alright, but it wasn't every day that he entered a penitentiary to visit someone he didn't know, and whom he intended to help break out of a state prison with armed guards lurking around every corner. Dakota's hands were far from being steady as well. So they decided to hit the Hitching Post Saloon and gulp down a few swigs of rye to build up some grit and cowboy courage before visiting Johnny Dane.

Things did not improve however, regarding the calming of nerves when they walked into the Hitching Post Saloon, because of the shiny stars they spotted on those two rugged looking fellers playing poker at the card table in the corner. They were the marshal and his deputy. Dakota and Pecos spotted them right at the get-go. Their eyes were trained to spot such things immediately just as a coyote in an instant could spot a lame buffalo calf in a herd. Survival was the name of the game, on both counts.

Pecos (a.k.a. Juan Diego) and Dakota (a.k.a. Tom Smith) walked up to the bar and made sure they kept their backs to the lawmen. They ordered a couple stiff drinks from the barkeep as Dakota flipped 2 bits to the bartender. With the large mirror on the wall behind the bar, Dakota could keep an eye on the marshal and his deputy while they each "bottoms up" on a shot glass of courage and listened to the piano player softly play the slow melodic ballad, Sweet Genevieve. After they gulped two down the hatch, they walked out of that saloon faster than a bullfrog could snatch up a dragonfly in a sodbuster's farm pond.

After they unhitched their horses and pulled themselves up into their saddles, they rode south to the prison. When they saw the prison walls at a distance, ole Pecos said,

"Dakota, mi amigo, dis gives ole Pecos chills like being cornered by a ten-foot rattler."

"Calm down Pecos, I mean Juan. We're only visiting today, remember? And don't call me by my real name while we're in Huntsville. I'm Tom Smith, comprendo?"

"Si, I'll remember."

When they rode up to the prison, they were confronted by a guard at the entrance.

"State your business, fellas," the guard ordered with a disrespectful tone.

"We're here to visit Johnny Dane," Dakota said.

"Do you have any firearms or knives on your persons?"

"No sir," Dakota answered.

The guard then led them to a courtyard and told them to sit and wait until he went to fetch Dane. Dakota was surprised that the guard did not frisk them for weapons. That seemed unprofessional or maybe more like lackadaisical or careless. Either way, that lack of routine would be beneficial when sneaking in the dynamite.

It took about ten minutes but the guard finally came out to the courtyard with Dane. Dane showed no emotion on his face because he didn't want to give anything away, not knowing what those two strangers were up to.

"Here's Dane. You can sit at any of those tables over there. You have no more than fifteen minutes to visit so you better get to it," the guard said.

When they sat down Dane immediately inquired,

"Who are you guys and what are you up to?"

Dakota did all the talking, keeping his voice low so the guard couldn't hear.

"How would you like to break out of this joint?"

"Are you crazy? Did you look around here? This place is swarming with guns.

Say, who are you anyway and why would you wanna break me out?"

"We need your talents. We know how good you are with explosives. Our boss is willing to pay you dearly if you join up with us."

"Yeah, well exactly what does dearly mean in real dollars?"

"Three thousand up front then equal shares on our takes. Does that interest you?"

"I'd be lying if I said no. Break me out of here and we'll discuss it further."

"No deal. You commit to us now, and then we'll break you out," Dakota said.

"That's right gringo. If you later try to finagle on the deal, we'll hunt you down like a dog and leave your pickin's for the hungry buzzards. Can't be any more blunt than that, amigo," Pecos added with a wicked grin on his face.

"OK, just how the hell do you expect to get me out of this place?"

"You're gonna blow your way out of here tomorrow."

"Explain."

"Before we come tomorrow evening, we'll cut the telegraph wires going out of town. Evening is the best time to do the breakout because in most prisons, the guard force on duty is the lightest. Plus with the sun goin' down, it'll make our getaway a lot easier.

When we come to visit, we're gonna sneak three sticks of dynamite and some matches to you. As soon as we exit this place, we'll light up several sticks ourselves outside. We'll blow the guard tower first and then set up a diversion by blowing up the east wooden wall with more dynamite. The opening will allow us to send a barrage of bullets into the prison. The guards will be ducking for cover and running away from the explosions and the gunfire. You run toward the front and use your dynamite to blow the front gate wide open. We'll have a horse waiting for you there.

Then we'll ride north to Fort Worth and pick up a train there to Kansas. That's our final destination. Now, one last time, are you in?"

"Deal me in pardners. You're playing my type of poker. This scheme is just crazy enough to work."

This was truly a risky game these three outlaws would be playing. But when the chips were down, Pecos and Dakota were the best there were. So when six o'clock rolled around the next evening, the two gutsy outlaws were ready to roll.

Visiting hours were over at 7:00 p.m. so they had to move fast. The first thing they did was to ride outside of town and cut the telegraph wires. Then Pecos put three sticks of dynamite inside his shirt and matches in his pocket before they reached the prison.

The guard that let them in the day before was on duty this night. He went to fetch Dane and the three sat at the table to discuss the plans once more. There were other prisoners meandering in the courtyard at the time. Pecos secretly passed Johnny the dynamite and the matches and Dakota told Johnny to tuck them quickly into his shirt. He then told him to wait for the tower to blow, then the east walls to cave in from the explosions. "That's when you make your move and blow your way out the front gate. We'll be right outside with your horse. Then we'll ride hard toward the north. Are you ready?"

"I'm ready."

"Well then Pecos, let's go light off some fireworks," Dakota said.

And so it began.

As soon as they left the prison courtyard, they both mounted their steeds and Pecos lit the first stick and quickly tossed it into the guard tower setting off an earsplitting explosion. The tower collapsed and the guard in the tower fell to his death. The explosion blew a gap in the wall enabling Pecos to shoot right into the courtyard. Dakota rode over to the east wall and began throwing lit sticks of dynamite from his horse toward that wall. One blast after another shook the ground like an earthquake and the blasts sounded like a barrage of cannon fire pounding the wooden walls. Large and small chunks of the wall flew everywhere. Pandemonium broke out inside the prison courtyard. Everyone began to run and scatter for cover.

The two continued firing wildly into the courtyard. Seconds later, Dane lit his sticks and threw one toward the gate. Then he spun around and hurled the other two at the guards rushing up behind him.

When the gate was wide open, Dane ran out, jumped on the horse that Dakota was holding for him and they whipped their horses to a wide open gallop sending up a cloud of dust that would rival a South Texas Plains dust storm. Dakota and Pecos continued to fire their pistols behind them as they rode northwest toward the open country.

At this point the guards were busy rounding up the prisoners who were in the courtyard and dashing for the openings in the gate and the east wall. Several inmates were shot in the back and killed while trying to escape. There was no cover for those hardened criminals so their escape efforts were futile and many met their maker that night.

On the other hand, Pecos, Dakota, and Johnny Dane got a clean getaway and were riding hard as the sun disappeared from the western sky and darkness prevailed. Their destination was about 195 miles north to Fort Worth.

One of the prison guards tried to send a telegram about the breakout but all of the lines were down and the word of the prison break was foiled as planned.

The three rode by night and rested by day. Pecos was from Texas so he knew the area like he knew the senoritas at the La Rosita Saloon south of the Rio Grande. This was the time of a Comanche moon so they had plenty of light to see their way to Fort Worth. They could travel 30 to 40 miles per night by horseback so they made it in about six days.

They broke into a few trading posts and general stores along the way to pilferage food for their long journey to keep their energy levels up. When they arrived in Fort Worth, they were able to board a train to Kansas at about 8:00 in the evening when it was dark. All they took with them were their saddles and firearms.

And so the new gang of men with special talents was about to increase by one more, this time by an explosives expert, if of course everything went well back at the lodge.

After a long train trip back to Kansas, Pecos, Dakota and Dane finally reached Abilene. There they purchased three horses and rode over to Mr. Brinkman's bank. Dakota walked into the bank to get Rusty's attention and then he walked right back out.

Joseph, the other teller, pretended to pay it no consideration. Although, he looked over at Rusty as he was counting out bills for a customer. He had his suspicions that something nefarious was taking place, but he wisely kept his nose out of it. Rusty immediately went into Mr. Brinkman's office and informed him that Pecos and Dakota were back in town.

"Did they have Johnny Dane with them?" Brinkman asked.

"I think so. I saw another guy through the window sitting on a horse next to Pecos when Dakota came into the bank. Dakota nodded at me and then they all three took off to the lodge I presume."

It was about three in the afternoon and that's exactly what Dakota and the other two did. They rode out to the lodge. The plan was to show Dane around the place, inform Chan that there would be six for dinner, and then Mr. Brinkman would introduce Dane to the operation, only the bare minimum of course.

Brinkman went through the same routine with Dane as he did with Rusty, giving him the new Colt .45, an envelope with $3,000 in cash, and welcoming him to the club.

This whole operation was right up Johnny Dane's alley. He saw this as an easy way to get rich quick and to him, it sounded like a well thought out operation with a boss who had the brains, contacts and know-how to make them all wealthy.

Brinkman gathered the gang around the large map on the wall. This time he pointed to the red circle around Little Rock and said, "Pecos and Dakota, your next assignment is right here, in Little Rock, Arkansas. It's the Arkansas State Penitentiary. You're taking Johnny on his very first assignment."

"Who are we breaking out this time?" Dakota asked.

"You're breaking out Doctor Eddie Hawkens. He's an excellent, or should I say, was an excellent doctor and surgeon but he got himself in a little trouble when he robbed a train. Oh he had a bandanna on to cover his face alright but unfortunately, one of the clerks in the payroll car was a patient of his and identified him in court. He was after a gold chest on its way from Little Rock to Dallas, Texas. He practiced in Little Rock and that's where he boarded the train. His plan was to jump off as soon as he had the chest. That point was about a mile outside of Little Rock. That's where his accomplice was waiting for him with a horse.

He and his accomplice thought they made a clean getaway until the marshal showed up at his office a week later and they found the chest and most of the gold stashed in a closet. His partner got away but Doc received ten years for armed robbery.

We need this guy in our gang. Let's face it, in the course of conducting our business, someone's going to get shot and we'll need a doctor to patch up the wounds, somebody we can trust. So it makes good sense to have a doctor on our payroll."

"I have one question for you Mr. Brinkman. Why would a doctor rob a train?" Dakota asked. "I thought doctors made a decent living."

"They do and that's probably why he became a doctor, to live the good life. However, the trouble with Doc Hawkens was that he had a sickness called gambling fever. He gambled at poker and finally lost every dollar to his name. It almost drove him insane. That's why he robbed the train. He was desperate. He needed money to live and to feed his gambling frenzies."

"How do you know this stuff?" Dane asked.

"He has some great contacts," Rusty answered.

"Anyway men, he has a thirst for money and we can quench that thirst for him. Rest about two days Dakota, before you, Pecos, and Dane travel to Little Rock. Here are your train tickets and $500 each for food, horses and tack. I'm giving you guys one-way tickets because I want you to travel back to Abilene on horseback. I'm under the opinion that it will be safer to do that to evade the law. Unfortunately, you'll be riding back through the Indian Territory and through terrain unfit for scavengers. But that's just how it is. So tough it up boys and get back here safely."

While the group was talking, there was a knock on the door. Chan didn't think twice as he opened the door and asked the gentleman to come in. It was Jeff Porter the owner of the newspaper in Abilene. Jeff walked into the meeting room and to his surprise he saw Mr. Brinkman, the bank president, surrounded by three well documented criminals whom he recognized: Pecos, Dakota and the Kansas Kid. Brinkman had a deadpan look on his face when he turned around and saw Porter. Porter looked around the room and realized that he was smack dab in the middle of a rattlesnake den. He knew he stumbled upon something that was not for his eyes.

"Why hello Porter, what brings you to my humble lodge out here in the wilderness?" Brinkman asked.

"Oh I was just riding by and saw several horses out front. I didn't know who lived here so I thought I would stop and introduce myself."

"Well Porter, let me do the introductions for you. This gentleman here is Rusty. He's a safecracker. You would be amazed at his skills. I broke him out of the Hays City jail."

Porter began perspiring from his forehead knowing that he was in serious trouble.

"This is the Kansas Kid. He's wanted for murder in Missouri."

Now Porter took the handkerchief out of his pocket and began wiping his palms and then removed his spectacles and patted his forehead.

"Meet Dakota and Pecos. Dakota's wanted up north and Pecos is wanted in the south. And lastly, meet Johnny Dane. He's an explosives expert and we just broke him out of the Texas Penitentiary.

This is my team of fugitives from justice with exceptional special skills. They're gonna create havoc all over the West. You'll probably want to publish that in your newspaper, won't you?"

"No sir, I promise you, I have no desire to publish any of this. Your secret is good with me Mr. Brinkman."

"No Porter, I don't think it is. Kansas, take Mr. Porter out back and show our guest what the Smoky Hill River looks like this time of night."

"Oh no Mr. Brinkman, please, I promise I'll keep all of this to myself, please, I'm begging you."

"Get this weasel out of my sight, Kansas," Brinkman ordered.

"Kansas drew his .45, poked it in Porter's ribs and pushed him out back toward the river. The gang on the inside of the lodge heard three gunshots and it was over. Porter was dumped into the swift flowing Smoky Hill River.

This unexpected slaying demonstrated to the others that Brinkman had no conscience when it came to murder and that his business was more important to him than anyone's life. Brinkman's appetite for killing was fed by his greed. This incident was a lesson learned by the others in the lodge that night; don't get in the way of Brinkman's goals, no matter who you are, or you'll find yourself full of holes, floating face down in the currents of the Smoky Hill River. That's just the way it was.

"Oh if that Smoky Hill River could talk." It surely would have many tales of woe to tell.

At 9:00 the next morning, Kathleen went to her work place only to find that the door to the newspaper office was still locked. This was not normal as Mr. Porter opened the door at least 15 minutes early every day. On this day though she thought he either overslept or was sick. She unlocked the door herself with her key and went upstairs to Porter's bedroom and knocked on his door to wake him up. After receiving no response, she opened the door and was surprised to find that Porter never even slept in his room last night. The bed was still made.

The first thing she did was to quickly run over to the marshal's office. But on the way over, a flatbed wagon cut her off in her tracks and drove by her with a body on it covered with a blanket. The wagon stopped and the driver said,

"Miss Kathleen, I have some bad news. We pulled Mr. Porter's body out of the river this morning east of town. It looks like he was shot several times and then dumped into the river."

"Oh my Lord, who would have done such a horrible deed?"

"Had to be Satan himself ma'am cause Mr. Porter was a real fine man who had no enemies; nope, not a one, ma'am."

Kathleen immediately ran over to the bank to tell her father about the killing never knowing that her father was the one who gave the order that caused Porter's demise.

When he saw Kathleen walk into the bank at a fast pace and tears running down her cheeks, Rusty knew that Kathleen received the bad news. He wasn't feeling so good about the whole situation himself.

"Father, father, Mr. Porter's been killed," she shouted as she opened up the door to Brinkman's office.

"What did you say, dear?"

"They found Mr. Porter's body in the river this morning. He was shot and killed. Who could have done such a thing?"

"I don't know dear. Does the marshal know about it yet?"

"I presume he does now. Old man Jessie was taking the body over there. Jessie's the one who found him."

"I'll go over and talk to the marshal as soon as I tie up one loose end here. You go over to the newspaper office and do what you have to do over there."

When Kathleen left, Brinkman called Rusty into his office and closed the door.

"I'm sure I don't have to warn you to keep your mouth shut about all of this, do I?"

"No sir, you don't."

"I didn't think so. I'm going over to the marshal's office to talk to him. I'll be back in about twenty minutes. There's still a lot you don't know about our organization and it will stay that way for a while until I know I can trust you fully."

"That's fine but you can trust me sir," Rusty responded.

When Brinkman arrived at the marshal's office, the marshal told his deputy to go over to the telegraph office and see if a wire arrived that he was waiting for. The deputy greeted Mr. Brinkman and began walking out. Then he thought of something and turned around and asked the marshal,

"Oh by the way marshal, is it OK if I take an hour off? I'm getting married in a few months and my fiancé wants to tell me about some of her plans."

"Sure son, go right ahead, take all the time you need," the marshal said.

When the deputy walked out of the jailhouse, the marshal looked at Brinkman and said,

"He's a fine young man, and mature for his age too. He's only 22 years old you know."

Now the marshal got down to the business at hand.

"Old man Jessie just brought in the body of Jeff Porter," Marshal Richards said. "You wouldn't happen to know anything about that would you Brinkman or is that why you're here?"

"He found our hideout last night with the gang present. We had no choice. I'm counting on you to keep the investigation away from our organization. Do you foresee any problems with that marshal?"

"Don't I always handle your problems, Brinkman?"

"Yes you do and you get paid handsomely for it too. Your other challenge is to keep everything from my daughter as well. She'll be searching for information to write an article about the incident. I don't want her to get within a hundred feet of the first piece of evidence."

"You're covered. But you and I both know someone has to hang for this crime."

"I know and I'll give you a person when the time is right."

"Alright, but the sooner the better. Now get out of here before someone gets suspicious and starts asking questions."

"Relax marshal, you worry too much."

As Mr. Brinkman was walking out of the jailhouse, the deputy was walking back in.

"There was no telegram for ya sir," the deputy said to the marshal. "So I'll see ya in about an hour."

Of course there wasn't, the marshal sent his deputy on a wild goose chase to get rid of him while Brinkman was there.

The next day Kathleen and her assistant at the newspaper published an article with the headline, "Mr. Jeff Porter, Newspaper Editor, Found Slain. No Leads Yet." The subtitle read, "Mr. Porter's Bullet Ridden Body Pulled from the Smoky Hill River".

On that same afternoon, Rusty snuck over to the newspaper building on his lunch hour to talk to Kathleen. He could see that she was really taking it hard. Her eyes were red and swollen from crying.

He greeted her and said, "I'm truly sorry for your loss Kathleen. I'm sure they will eventually find out who's responsible, and justice will be served."

"That's kind of you to come over here and say that Rusty. Say, how would you like me to cook you dinner tonight?"

"I would love that if it's just the two of us. I understand your father is pretty protective of you."

"That he is Rusty, but he doesn't need to know."

"Can I be at your house around eight o'clock?"

"That's perfect," Kathleen said. "I'll make us some fricassee. Have you had that before?"

"Just once, when someone put me up in their small one bedroom home in Hays City."

"Oh, how quaint."

During dinner that evening, Kathleen talked freely about her foster father.

"He's a perfectionist in everything he does. It's almost like it's a disease with him. If something doesn't go quite right, or not the way he wants, he loses his temper and I'm afraid he's capable of anything."

"Joseph told me about your husband," Rusty said.

"Yes," Kathleen replied as she sort of looked away into space as in a trance and then softly said,

"I saw the devil in father's eyes that day. He was like a madman."

Then Kathleen came out of her temporary daze and commented,

"But I'm sure that was a onetime occurrence. I'm sure of it."

Rusty looked at her and wondered if she really was as sure as she made out to be. Or did she know more about her foster father's personality and capability than she was leading on to know.

Kathleen also told Rusty that her father was a very intelligent man and seemed to always be one step ahead of everything and everybody.

Well that night after dinner, those two lovebirds became pretty good friends and afterwards, Rusty went back to the lodge very late and snuck in through the back door. The other guys felt ole Rusty was out socializing with a lady friend as they did on occasion themselves and thought it was none of their business to ask who his female companion was.

The next morning Pecos, Dakota and Dane caught a train to Little Rock. This time Dane carried the dynamite since he was the explosives expert. Pecos and Dakota had no problemo with that for sure, except they still had to sit close to the explosives on the train.

Little Rock, Arkansas was founded in 1821 and incorporated in 1831. It is located in the middle of the state. Historical Native American tribes which inhabited that and the surrounding areas were the Caddo, Quapaw, Osage, Choctaw, and the Cherokee.

Little Rock was named for a stone outcropping, a small rock formation, on the south bank of the Arkansas River. It was used as a landmark by early travelers of the river and became a well-known river crossing. Little Rock (La Petite Roche, in French) was named in 1721 by the French explorer and trader Jean-Baptiste Benard de la Harpe (February 4, 1683 – September 26, 1765, lived to age 82). This area marked the geographical transition from the flat Mississippi Delta region to the foothills of the mountain range in west central Arkansas and southeastern Oklahoma called Ouachita

Mountain. The area was continually referred to as "The Little Rock" and so the name held.

Jean-Baptiste was also the first known French explorer to set foot in what would become known as the Indian Territory and then Oklahoma which was taken from a combination of the Choctaw words ukla (person) and huma (red). The word was used by the Choctaw to describe Native Americans, "red persons".

The history of the Arkansas State Penitentiary which Pecos, Dakota, and Dane were traveling to goes all the way back to 1838 when the Democratic Governor of Arkansas James Sevier Conway (December 9, 1798 – March 3, 1855, lived to age 56) signed legislation that allowed the building of the state's first penitentiary.

During 1839, the State of Arkansas purchased a 92.41-acre tract in Little Rock where the prison was built. From 1849 to 1893 the State of Arkansas leased its convicted felons to private individuals. When Dakota found out about this, he thought that they might have an easier job breaking Ole Doc Hawkens out of the penitentiary; but not so. Doc was not allowed to go beyond the prison walls. This pleased Johnny Dane because he had a desire to blow things up anyway. He couldn't wait to blast the walls down and create a prison break with a bang.

Yep, he'd rather do that and skip watching his ma pour flapjack batter onto a hot griddle in a small cafe in El Paso where he grew up. She made the fluffiest flapjacks in Texas and Dane's favorite thing was to eat those fluffy flapjacks smothered in maple syrup on Saturday mornings. Then again, that was his favorite thing until he learned how to blow up things. After that, eating his ma's flapjacks became his second favorite thing.

During the first visit to the penitentiary, unlike Dane and Dakota, Pecos stayed about 50 yards away on horseback. He combed the place on the outside to become familiar with it and to look for the best escape route. Before riding to the prison though with the other two, Pecos' first assignment was to find where telegraph wires entered the town from the north and the west. His job would be to cut those lines.

Dane and Dakota approached the front gate and asked permission to visit with Doc Hawkens. It was about nine o'clock in the morning and other visitors were arriving to meet with incarcerated family members as well. Visiting hours in this prison were from 9:00 a.m. to 11:00 a.m. and 2:00 p.m. to 4:00 p.m.

As expected, the guard asked Dane and Dakota if they were carrying any weapons. They were not. So the guard asked them to state their business.

"We would like to visit with Doctor Eddie Hawkens. We need to tell him something about one of his family members."

Dakota thought that this type of introduction would ensure that Doc Hawkens would agree to visit with them for sure. The problem was that ole Doc had no surviving family members that he knew of. His parents had died years ago and he hadn't heard from his estranged brother in over ten years. Since he thought that something was up, his curiosity got the better of him and he agreed to visit with the two.

When the guard walked Hawkens out, he pointed to Dakota and Dane. Hawkens walked over to a faraway table in the courtyard while Dakota and Dane followed. They all sat down and Hawkens looked at Dakota and asked,

"What's this all about? You and I both know that you don't have any information about my family."

"That's right we don't," Dakota admitted. "But we do know more about you than you could ever imagine."

"Yeah, so?"

"Well we figure you don't want to spend the rest of your life in this dump so we have a lucrative proposition for ya."

"Talk to me."

Dakota looked around to make sure no guards were listening or paying attention. Then he looked Doc Hawkens squarely in his eyes and said as he kept his voice plenty low,

"We have a group of talented men dedicated to becoming rich beyond anything you could fancy and we need a doctor in our organization."

"For what?"

"To take care of potential gunshot wounds."

"Gunshot wounds? What kind of an organization is this anyway?"

"Let me put it to you this way. The law will be the predator and we'll be the prey. But this prey will be meaner than a pack of mountain lions and twice as cunning. That's all we can tell you for now except for one more thing. You're gonna become wealthier than you could ever imagine and you'll be able to go back to gambling again not worrying about losing your stake because you'll be able to buy your own gambling house, saloon, and dance hall. Does that interest you, Doctor Hawkens?"

"I'd be lying if I said no. How did you find me, anyway?"

"We have our ways. That's what makes us so special. That's about all we can tell you for now. Are you interested in joining up with us?"

"If it means gettin' out of this rat hole soon, count me in."

"Good, we'll break you out of here tomorrow then we'll head north. We'll let you know where we're traveling to when we hit the trail," Dakota said.

"OK you have my curiosity up. You make it all sound so easy. Just how do you intend to break me out of this joint?"

"We're gonna blast you out," Dane said. "Here's the plan..."

Dane and Dakota laid out the strategy. The only difference between this breakout and the one in Huntsville would be that Doc Hawkens would not be using dynamite himself. Dane would be throwing the sticks from the outside. All Doc had to do was to be in the courtyard at 3:45 tomorrow afternoon and, when he saw the front gate being blown off its hinges, run to the horse Pecos was ponying for him.

Pecos' first job tomorrow afternoon at about 2:00, just two hours before the gutsy jailbreak, was to cut telegraph wires going into town. They had it all figured out. He would cut several sections so that the wires couldn't be spliced together quick enough to send out word that afternoon of the escape.

When it came time for the breakout the next day, Doc was standing in the courtyard right on time; but so were five armed guards. There was also a guard with a repeating rifle stationed in the tower near the gate. The walls around the courtyard were made of bricks, about three deep making for a solid fortress.

The best plan was for Dane to create a diversion on the east wall with dynamite, then for Dakota to blast the eight-foot wide wood gate open going into the prison, and finally for Pecos to take out the guard in the tower with his Winchester.

And that's just what they did. Explosions rocked the fortress, blew open the gate, and the guard fell from the tower with a .44 slug to his head compliments of Pecos.

Then Pecos and Dakota jumped off their horses and gave Doc Hawkens cover at the gate shooting wildly into the courtyard with their pistols while Hawkens ran out of the prison and jumped on one of the horses. Explosions were blowing the bricks into the air and gunfire was being exchanged back and forth sounding like the Battle of Bull Run.

Pecos mounted up while Dakota threw more sticks of dynamite into the prison to scatter the guards who were running forward; one loud explosion after another shook the grounds of the courtyard. Then Dane rode around to meet the guys in front, Dakota jumped on his horse, and they all high-tailed it out of there faster than you could spit a chunk of tobackie in a spittoon. But not before Dakota took a .44 slug in the leg which ripped off about two inches of flesh.

He grabbed his upper leg and yelled out,

"I've been hit!"

Pecos looked back and saw Dakota grimacing in pain and bleeding profusely from the open wound. Pecos shouted to Doc and Dane,

"Dakota's been hit, Dakota's been hit!"

Dane looked back and saw that Dakota was conscious and still on his horse so he shouted back to everyone,

"Keep riding. Let's get out of here!"

And they did, for about five more miles until they came to a wooded area with a lot of high brush. Doc Hawkens told everyone to stop so he could apply a tourniquet to Dakota's leg to stop the bleeding.

Everyone hurriedly dismounted and tied their reins to small saplings except for Dakota. He was slumped forward in his saddle and nearly unconscious. His pants leg was soaked and dripping with blood and he was in a state of shock. Dane and Pecos helped him off his horse and sat him up against a large black oak tree. They were in trouble. They knew that there was a posse on their trail but they also knew that if they didn't take care of Dakota right away, he would surely die and with no time to give him a proper burial, he'd be an easy meal for the coyotes and buzzards in the area.

Doc immediately took charge. He told Pecos to build a small fire and heat up the blade of his 12" Arkansas toothpick.

"Does anyone have another knife?" Doc yelled.

"Here you go Doc," Dane said as he handed Doc his small six inch blade.

Doc grabbed the knife and ripped Dakota's pants leg to about six inches above the wound; the wound was right above the knee and it was deep. He threw the knife down beside him and then untied Dakota's bandanna, picked up a stick and made a tourniquet to stop the bleeding. At this point, Dakota was in a semiconscious state. By now he had lost a lot of blood, maybe too much. But Doc wasn't giving up.

"Is your blade hot yet?" Doc asked.

"Not yet Doc," Pecos shouted back.

"What are you gonna do with that knife Doc, cut off his leg?" Dane asked.

Doc sort of laughed and said,

"No, I'm going to cauterize the wound to keep it from exsanguination."

"Dangit Doc, speak English."

"OK, I'm gonna apply the hot knife blade to the wound to seal it off and stop the bleeding so he doesn't bleed to death. It will also keep an infection from setting in. This technique was used during the Civil War on bad gunshot wounds and on amputations also. Now if any of you have any whiskey in your saddlebags, get it now, quickly."

Pecos ran to his horse, opened up his saddlebag, reached in and grabbed a bottle of whiskey and then ran it over to Doc Hawkens. Doc opened the bottle, and poured some on the wound to disinfect it. Dakota yelled out in pain. Doc then told Dakota to take a few swigs, then a few more. Then Doc took a swig himself and handed the bottle to Dane. Dane took a swig and then handed the bottle to Pecos. Pecos gratefully drank what was left.

Doc then took a stick, held it up to Dakota's mouth and told him to bite down on it as hard as he could.

"Pecos, hurry up and give me that hot knife!" Doc shouted as he extended his arm for it.

Pecos ran over to the campfire, carefully picked up the knife by the handle and ran it back to Doc as Johnny Dane looked over Doc's shoulder.

"Are you ready, Dakota?" the Doc asked.

Dakota nodded his head yes. Wasting no time, Doc Hawkens pressed the red hot blade against Dakota's wound like he was branding a longhorn steer. It sizzled and smoked against Dakota's leg as he screamed to high heaven clenching his teeth to the stick.

Within seconds, his eyes rolled back into his head and he passed out as he smelled the burning of his own flesh.

"Is he dead?" Pecos asked.

"No, he just fainted from the intense pain. He should be ready to ride in about an hour when he comes to. I'm gonna remove the tourniquet now and wrap the wound. In the meantime, throw some dirt on the fire and keep an eye out for the posse."

While Dane and Pecos stood guard, Doc sat down next to Dakota and rested. He was plum tuckered out. After about an hour, Dakota did wake up but he was in a lot of pain. The three helped him onto his horse and then everyone mounted up as well. Dakota, who was always as tough as nails, was the one who shouted,

"Let's ride!"

And so they did. They galloped hard to the west and then to the north. They rode by the light of the quarter moon heading north through the Indian Territory. They rode by night and rested by day. Oh they had a posse on their tail alright, but ole Pecos knew all the tricks on how to cover their tracks and lose the posse. Once again, it was a clean getaway.

However, in their wake, they left six prison guards dead, three guards wounded, and the prison blown to smithereens. This brazen prison break eventually made headlines all over the country as did the Huntsville breakout.

It was a long and tiring ride back to Kansas through the Indian Territory. Not only did they have to worry about a posse but they also had to worry about renegades who may have left the reservation. After a while, they decided to rest by night and ride by day. But the weather was hot and windy, the dust was choking, and the sun could scorch your eyeballs in this barren country.

About halfway through the Indian Territory near the Choctaw reservation and as the sun began to set, they spotted a small herd of reservation cattle alongside of a small but swift flowing creek. There was only one Choctaw brave on horseback watching over the herd. He was a peaceful Indian but these four outlaws were hungry and as thirsty as a herd of wild mustangs in a desert valley located in Eastern California's Mojave Desert which is the lowest, driest and hottest area in North America. They call that place, Death Valley.

They trotted up to the Indian and asked if they could buy one steer for meat. The Indian said no. So they roughed him up a bit, shot a steer, and cut out the backstrap for dinner. Then they rode off five miles up the creek to make camp for the night. The Choctaws were able to salvage the remainder of the steer for food.

When they stopped up the trail a piece, they gathered up some dry wood and brush and built a campfire. Dakota always found a way to carry a small coffee pot and cups in his saddlebags while Pecos toted the ground coffee beans in his, along with an iron skillet and a slab of bacon and some jerky. After the coffee was hot and ready to be sipped, Pecos fried up the beef steaks. It was a pretty good meal for a bunch of saddle bums trailing across the Indian Territory.

After they ate and drank, they rested around the campfire, and got better acquainted. Dakota was still in pain but was happy that the vultures weren't picking the meat off his bones.

"Say, I don't know anything about you guys but I do know what side of the law you're on," Doc said. "I know what got me in trouble. It was my gambling habit. I was really poor at it. That's why I lost so much money. But the more I lost, the more I gambled. I'm a doctor but I still couldn't heal my sickness. How crazy is that?"

"We all have our demons, mi amigo," Pecos said. "Mi padre was killed by a lawman in Laredo when I was only ocho, eight. He stole a neighbor's steer to feed our familia. We had nothing, nada. I had three brothers and three sisters. We lived in a one room casa. We were starving. A lawman came to take back the steer. Mi padre was desperate. He raised his long gun to keep the steer. The lawman drew his pistol and shot mi padre dead where he stood, in front of mi whole familia. Then his deputy roped the steer and took it away. I never forgot that day. Later I had to steal to help feed mi madre, hermanos y hermanas. So I had no padre growing up, we were poor, and I had to steal to help mi familia survive. I now have no conscience, I'm not sorry for my sins, and I made a promise to myself, I will never be poor again. That's how it is with me."

"How about you Dakota? How did you get on the wrong side of the law?" Doc asked.

"Adventure, I love the adventure. I have no education. Maybe that has something to do with it. I grew up in the Dakota Territory.

It was me, my ma and pa and my brother. We lived in the wilderness. The land was our enemy and so were the Sioux. It seemed like every week we were fighting off small bands of savages. For some reason I wasn't scared. I guess I got that from my pa. I actually enjoyed shooting those redskins off their horses. It was a thrill for me and I was good at it too. Then I went…"

At this point, Dakota moaned in pain and said,

"Hey, let's kill this conversation and hit the sack. We have some hard riding ahead of us the next few days. Although, I will tell you this. Right now I'm looking forward to the future when I can live in my own two story ranch house and not worry about tomorrow. Mr. Brinkman's gonna get us all wealthy; I'm banking on it."

After many days and nights on the trail, they finally approached Abilene. When they arrived at the hideout, they all four dismounted and Dakota, taking charge again as if nothing had happened to him, ordered Pecos to tie the four horses to the hitching rail. Then he went inside and told Chan to go into town and get the boss,

"and by the way Chan, there'll be seven for supper tonight."

After Pecos and Dakota showed Doc Hawkens around, they then went outside and took the horses to the barn, took off their bridles and saddles, curried the horses since they were sweating so badly, and hayed and grained them.

Being a medical doctor and well educated, Doc was looking forward to meeting the brains of this operation.

CHAPTER FOUR:

Rocking "The Walls"

Chan was instructed by Mr. Brinkman to plan a late dinner "Say 7:30," so that he, the Kansas Kid, and Rusty could spend some time with their new gang member, Doc Hawkens. Introductions were made by Dakota when Brinkman and the other two arrived at the lodge at around 5:30 p.m. Dakota informed Brinkman how Doc saved his life.

Brinkman was impressed but a bit surprised at how young Doctor Hawkens appeared. He looked to be in his late twenties. In a way, this was a good thing because Doc knew all the latest surgical techniques and procedures, plus he would have plenty of stamina to ride the trails with the other outlaws.

After the introductions, Mr. Brinkman tested Doc with a few questions to be sure Doc was in fact committed to the lawless cause of his desperados. Doc definitely proved to Brinkman that indeed their causes were one and the same, and that the gang could count on him to be a loyal comrade.

After verifying what needed to be substantiated, Brinkman gave Doc his envelope with $3,000 and his pearl handled peacemaker. Ole Doc was as elated as a wild Mustang stud discovering a box canyon full of five year old mares.

Nobody in the gang knew of any actual robbery plans. However, they all speculated that Brinkman and his boss were conniving to pull off something big, real big. This had to be true because of both the quality and the variety of expertise that the outlaws possessed who were busted out of the state penitentiaries with such great audacity.

After another exquisite dinner which you would expect to find in a fancy Eastern uptown restaurant, they all assembled in the meeting room. Brinkman asked the gang to gather around the huge map on the wall.

"By now most of you know what these red circles in various locations on the map represent. These are prison sites that are housing criminals with special talents like all of you and who would potentially qualify as members for our team.

My boss supplied me with a list of names of prisons, the inmates and their qualifications. The list is hidden in a safe place and it's for my eyes only. I have more names than what I really need. He's leaving it up to me to select who I want for our team. I'm still developing my final list.

However, I have selected our next two members. They are brothers and were professional snipers for the Union Army in the Civil War. Their names are Kenny and Bobby Burkley. They terrorized the Iowa-Missouri border during the mid and late 1870's, robbing trains and banks until none other than their own cousin Lawrence gave them up. Lawrence's righteousness though cost him his life. The story as I know it goes like this.

Bobby and Kenny were visiting their family farm in northern Missouri for a few days and boasting about all the banks they robbed and the people they picked off with their Winchesters as they rode out of those towns. That talk didn't sit well with Lawrence who was staying at the family farm helping Bobby and Kenny's ma. When Lawrence rode into town one day, he stopped at the marshal's office and ratted the two out.

The very next morning, the Burkley boys found their small Missouri farm house surrounded by the marshal, his posse of twenty strong and a vigilante group known as the Missouri Do-Righters. The marshal gave the Burkley boys both a demand and a warning,

'You in the house, Bobby and Kenny Burkley, throw out your guns and come out with your hands up or we'll burn your place down with you and your ma in it.'

Kenny and Bobby grabbed their Winchesters, broke the glass out of the windows with the butts of their rifles and began picking off the posse, one-by-one with pinpoint accuracy. They had no intention of going down without a fight. I admire that kind of fighting spirit. But there were just too many gunmen outside hidden behind trees, fence posts, the water trough and everything that provided them cover.

Kenny asked Bobby how the hell those guys knew that they were at their homestead.

Bobby said that there was only one guy who left their house to go to town the last three days.

They both turned around and looked at Lawrence. Lawrence said, 'It's time to stop the killing.'

Kenny cocked his rifle and pointed it at Lawrence and said, 'not quite yet.' Then he and Bobby both put two slugs each right into Lawrence's gut. While his blood and guts were spilling out on the floor, a barrage of bullets poured into the Burkley house."

"Wait a minute. You mean they shot their own cousin?" Pecos asked in disbelief.

"That's right Pecos," Brinkman confirmed. "I would have done the same myself. Keep that in mind."

"What happened then?" Dakota asked.

"Well, after about three hours in a complete standoff, the marshal ordered the men to torch the house. They weren't showing any mercy. From what I gather, it was actually the vigilantes that lit the fires. Beings that the boys had their ma inside, the boys decided to come out with their hands up and surrender. Although it wasn't until the heavy wood beams were falling from the ceiling in flames that they exited the old farm house. Those guys had grit.

They had the book thrown at 'em during the trial for everything you can imagine. They are due to be hung in two months. We can't let that happen men. We need their sniper skills. You'll understand why later."

"What prison are they in?" Dakota asked.

"They're both in the Missouri State Penitentiary in Jefferson City. Dakota, if you are up to it, you, Pecos and Dane are going to break the two out; or should I say, blow them out."

"I'm up to it," Dakota replied

"Good, you'll be taking twenty sticks of dynamite this time. I have them packed in a travel case over there on the floor. Here are your train tickets to Jefferson City. They're one-way tickets. You'll have to travel back to Abilene on horseback to elude the posse. So here's $500 each to buy horses and saddles when you get there. The extra money is for food and lodging, and of course, horses for the Burkley boys. Are there any questions?"

"Just one, sir, when do we leave?" Dane asked.

"In two days," Brinkman said. "That gives you one day to rest."

"How do you know all this stuff, Mr. Brinkman?" Doc asked.

"From his boss," Rusty offered.

"Who's his boss?" Doc asked as he looked at Rusty.

"We don't know."

Brinkman just looked on with an arrogant smirk as he took a drag from his Cuban cigar.

The Missouri State Penitentiary, also known as "the Walls" was constructed in the early 1800's directly after Missouri became the 24th state in the Union on August 10, 1821. It was constructed in Jefferson City which was the capital of Missouri. The prison opened in March of 1836, the same month and year that the Alamo in San Antonio fell to Santa Anna's Mexican Army. Before it closed decades later, it was the oldest penitentiary west of the Mississippi River.

The reason it was nicknamed "the Walls" is because of the stone wall built around the prison house. The walls were first made of wood but as they started filling up the prison with hardened criminals, the prisoners themselves constructed the stone walls. The walls were made from limestone quarried in Jefferson City. Ironically, the Alamo was also built of limestone as well. The walls were built so that no one could escape, theoretically that is. They stood twenty-three-foot high, three feet thick at the bottom and two feet thick at the top.

The distance from Abilene to Jefferson City was about 307 miles. By train it took about 12 hours with a couple of stops in between; that is, if the James boys didn't barricade the tracks with hickory trees and hold it up at gunpoint. The return trip was a different story though. By horseback it would take much longer, about twelve days of hard riding in the saddle, dodging lawmen and posse at every turn.

When Dane, Pecos, and Dakota reached Jefferson City, they immediately signed into a hotel, under aliases of course. Then they strolled over to the livery stable and purchased good, sound broke horses along with tack, for themselves and the Burkley boys.

Since they arrived in town at about eleven in the morning, they decided to chow down after they squared the basics and before they rode over to check out the prison, the telegraph wires, and possible escape routes.

At lunch, they decided to wait until the next day to visit with the Burkley boys. But they still did their scouting around to look things over. That evening they spent a few hours in the Bent Elbow Saloon on Osage Street, quietly discussing their breakout plans and sipping on some of that strong Tennessee firewater.

Dane proposed the first toast when he held up his glass, and said,

"As a famous man once said, 'Giving up drinking is the easiest thing in the world. I know because I did it thousands of times.' Bottoms up my friends." To that they downed the hatch.

"Who said that?" Pecos asked as he chuckled.

"I don't know. I think it was some author guy named Mark Twang or Tang or somethen like that," Dane said. "Who the hell cares who said it, drink up my Mexican friend."

Then Dakota put on a serious face.

"You know pardners, this job looks to be a right bigger challenge than some of the other jobs."

"Why do you say that, amigo?" Pecos inquired.

"Did you see the walls around that place? Looks like Fort Sumter. Saw Sumter after the rebels secured it back in '61," Dakota said.

"Whachya guys gettin' all worked up about for?" Dane asked. "Don't ya remember what I brought with me? I have enough dynamite to blow that prison across the border into Iowa."

"Don't think ya do Dane," Dakota remarked.

"Yeah, actually I think you're right. I don't think I do either. But after seeing those walls, I've been thinking about another possibility. It'll just require us to be in town a couple of days longer."

"What's your plan Senor Dane?" Pecos inquired.

"I'm gonna get a job," Dane said.

"Have you lost your mind?" Dakota asked.

"On the contrary boys, I'm using my head. Did you see that limestone quarry when we came into town on the train? Well those boys use explosives to mine that rock. I think our situation calls for a little upgrading, like nitro for instance. Oh I know it's been outlawed, but my experience tells me that there's some in this town somewhere. I just have to find it. And just to make you think some, if this stuff isn't handled properly and explodes with us around it, there wouldn't be any meat left on our bones for the buzzards to pick on. A cheerful thought, eh?"

After killing two bottles of rye, discussing how they were gonna meet the Burkley boys, and becoming a little rotgut cockeyed in the process, they decided to head back to their hotel rooms and get some shut-eye.

They met for breakfast the next morning at the Buck Horn Café and it was there that they made a wise decision to purchase two used Henry rifles and a couple of boxes of ammunition for the Burkley boys. It was Dane's idea as he said,

"Thought it would come in handy fighting off posse on the way back to Abilene. Those boys can help us get back to Kansas in a vertical position instead of a pine box."

On this day, they wisely decided to skip on meeting with the Burkley boys until after Dane got things lined up with the nitro. But Dane did tell Pecos and Dakota to go ahead and purchase the rifles and ammunition plus a derringer with two barrels and a few rounds of ammunition for it. Then he told them to go back to the livery stable and purchase two Missouri mules and saddlebags for each.

"They don't have to be prime stock, but buy the youngest ones you can find," Dane said.

At this point he did not let the cat out of the bag on how he intended to use the mules.

Johnny Dane visited the limestone company around mid-morning and offered his services as an explosives expert who knew how to use both dynamite and nitro. In his conversations he was able to find out where the supplier for explosives was located in town. He was asked to report to work the next day at 8:00 a.m. sharp.

It was now Wednesday evening. All three met in Dakota's room at the hotel. It was time to make hay now. Everything was in place and ready to go: firearms, horses, tack and mules were all purchased. Dane sort of took charge of the meeting from here.

"I'm gonna have to show up for work tomorrow at the limestone quarry. You two need to visit with the Burkley brothers tomorrow morning and offer them the deal. If they say yes, then come by the limestone quarry and let me know. I'll get the nitro tomorrow afternoon. By the way, go by the back of the saloon and steal me twelve empty whiskey bottles. I'll need them to mix the nitro. Here's what I want you to tell the Burkley boys about how and when we're gonna break them out. The plan is this ..."

Dane went over the plans in great detail and both Dakota and Pecos were enamored with Dane's conniving expertise.

"I have never heard of anything like this before," Dakota said. "It's just crazy enough to work."

"I think you are loco, Dane, maybe even el diablo himself," Pecos said as he laughed. "But I think it will work too, mi amigo."

The plan was to do the breakout on Friday morning which meant that the telegraph wires had to be cut at least two hours before the getaway.

On Thursday morning, everybody did what they were supposed to do. The Burkley brothers agreed with the offer while meeting with Dakota and Pecos and they supported the breakout plans. While inside the walls, Dakota and Pecos cased the place real good to get an idea where everything was: the guard tower, gates, location of guards and the like.

Then they left the prison, galloping over to inform Dane that it was a "go". Dane rode over to the crooked supplier to purchase the two ingredients (concentrated sulfuric acid and concentrated nitric acid) which was used to make the nitro. He carried a fake purchase order with him that appeared to be signed by the foreman of the quarry.

He hid the nitro ingredients in the woods after the purchase. Then at midnight, with Pecos standing guard with a rifle, a good distance away from the walls of the penitentiary, Dane went to work with Dakota assisting him. Luckily, it was cloudy making for a very dark night which aided in Dane getting his job done without being spotted.

Dakota's job was to carve out a hole in the limestone wall about three feet off the ground, insert a wooden peg in it and attach a two foot long string to the peg. Dane mixed the two ingredients into an empty whiskey bottle to create the nitro and then cautiously tied the string around the bottleneck so that it dangled one foot off of the ground. Dane then covered the bottle with dry brush to conceal it while Dakota repeated his project down the wall. Just after the first bottle was in place, and Dane was tying-up the second bottle of nitro, a slight breeze began to develop with a cold front coming in out of the northwest. When Dakota saw Dane perspiring profusely, Dakota was about to have a coronary on the spot.

Nevertheless, Dane continued to push on even with Dakota's disenchantment. They installed five bottles of nitro on both sides of the front gate, twenty feet apart from each other, starting about thirty feet from the gate on each side. Dynamite was the explosive of choice around the main gate since it was more manageable to handle. They finished at about 3:00 in the morning and then went back to their hotel room for some shut-eye, all the while hoping that a strong breeze would not materialize and set off the nitro prematurely.

When the brilliant orange colored sun appeared over the eastern horizon the next morning, and you could hear a rooster crowing from the farm just down the road, the three desperados were ready for action. Pecos had problems sleeping; so he saddled up early and cut down telegraph wires just outside of town before anyone was stirring.

When he came back, the three loaded their pistols and rifles, packed up the gear they brought with them and saddled up their horses and two more for the Burkley boys. Dakota installed scabbards on both escape horses and inserted the loaded rifles.

Dane attached the saddlebags to the mules and put an empty whiskey bottle in each. He carried the two ingredients for nitro in his own saddlebags as they rode through the woods toward the penitentiary and pulled up their horses near some cedars about 100 yards from the prison walls.

The morning went by fast. It was now 7:45 a.m. and visiting hours were only fifteen minutes away. The guard rotation already took place at 7:00 a.m. and fortunately, no one had spotted the hanging bottles of nitro along the outside walls.

Dane meticulously poured the concentrated sulfuric acid into the whiskey bottles and then slowly and carefully added the concentrated nitric acid. The nitro was ready to go. Now he held his breath as he cautiously placed the bottles back into the mules' saddlebags. At this point any sudden movement could be catastrophic.

Pecos' job was to stay outside with the horses and take out the guard in the tower when he heard the sound of an explosion coming from the inside. Then he was to immediately take aim and fire at the first nitro bottle on the right side of the gate and quickly shoot the one on the left side of the gate.

It was now time, do or die. At 8:00 sharp, Dakota, with a few sticks of dynamite hidden in his shirt, cautiously lit up a cigar while standing first in line at the gate. Dane was right behind him leading two mules. They pretended that they were not together.

The guard at the main gate first asked Dakota to state his business.

"I'm here to visit with Bobby and Kenny Burkley."

"O'Malley, fetch the Burkley boys for this gentleman," the guard ordered.

The guard then allowed Dakota to enter.

"Now what do you want?" The guard asked Dane.

"I have the two mules here that the warden asked me to bring by this morning."

"I don't know anything about any mules," the guard said.

"You don't? That's strange. He said they were a gift for one of the guards in the prison. He paid top dollar for these long ears. Look, here's the warden's bill of sale."

"OK, well bring them in."

"I'll have to check to see what's in the saddlebags."

"Oh you wouldn't want to do that sir, that's part of the surprise too. The warden would really be disappointed if someone spoiled his surprise."

"OK, then come on in and I'll go get the warden."

While Dane was walking the two mules into the middle of the courtyard, the other guard walked the Burkley boys out of the prison building. Dane asked the same guard to hold onto the warden's mules because the warden was coming right out to check 'em over.

Now Dakota, the Burkley brothers and Dane slowly backed up and began moving toward the center of the courtyard. Dane decided to wait until the guard returned with the warden. He waited, and waited and then finally the two came through the front door and Dane could hear the warden say, "What's the meaning of this?" as he approached the mules.

Then it began.

Dane quickly took off his hat, removed the derringer, and rapidly fired two shots right between the back legs of each mule. They frantically jumped up and mule kicked their back hooves setting off two huge deafening nitro explosions, killing the mules, the warden and two guards. Dane laughed like a crazy man.

Pecos immediately blasted the guard in the tower. Dakota, while running to the front, lit the wicks of two sticks of dynamite with the red hot end of his cigar and tossed them toward the gates, blowing them wide open. Chunks of wood flew in every which direction, some shooting as high as 100-feet into the sky. A cloud of black powder smoke filled the air making it virtually impossible to see ten feet in front of them.

Dane then ran to the front door of the prison building and tossed in several sticks of dynamite. The resulting explosion partially filled the doorway with bricks and mortar and sent up a cloud of dust almost as high as the three story prison itself. He then turned around and ran as fast as he could toward the gate.

Now the fireworks really began. Pecos put a bullet in the first bottle of nitro on the right and that blast shook the walls and set off a chain of nitro explosions down the wall with smoke and limestone dust filling the air like a volcano eruption. By now Dane, Dakota, and the Burkley brothers were sprinting out of the main gate and jumping on their horses. Pecos then aimed at the first nitro bottle on the left, pulled the trigger and with a dead-on shot, set off another chain of explosions the likes that hadn't been seen nor heard since the Battle of Gettysburg. The smoke in the prison courtyard was so thick it could cure a green ham.

The remaining guards, who cleared the way and ran out of the prison building with their rifles to their shoulders, scattered like frightened prairie dogs at the sight of a chicken hawk, as the walls violently exploded all around them. They thought they were being bombarded by cannon fire.

The Burkley boys while on horseback pulled out their rifles and sent a wild barrage of bullets into the courtyard. Then they all turned their horses around whooping and hollering, took off hell bent for leather, and galloped west to Abilene never to be seen or heard from again by the local marshal or posse.

On that day, "The Walls" came tumbling down amid the smoky bloody chaos.

When the five finally reached Abilene and arrived at the gang's hideout, introductions were made and the Burkley boys were welcomed into the club with an envelope of $3,000 each just like the rest of the gang members. However, unlike the others, Kenny and Bobby were given brand new repeating rifles with the most current rifle scopes on the market for long-range sniper shooting.

The rifles were the Winchester Model 1876, also known as the Centennial Model. This model had a heavier frame than the 1866 and 1873 models and was the first to be chambered for a center fire rifle cartridge. This is the same rifle that Geronimo was carrying when he surrendered in '86 to First Lieutenant Charles Bare Gatewood (April 5, 1853 – May 20, 1896 lived to age 43) in the Sierra Madre (Spanish for "Mother Mountain Range").

While Kenny was holding up the rifle and looking through the scope, Bobby was looking over his new rifle like he did when he checked out a cute little redhead named Ginger in the Cattlemen's Saloon and Dance Hall in Sedalia. He smiled and slowly rubbed the beautiful walnut stock with his right hand and then ran his left hand up the barrel and touched every part of the rifle.

Pecos looked and Bobby and said,

"Senor, you treat your rifle like I treat my women."

CHAPTER FIVE:

Governors' Call for Action

Much farther east, in Washington, D.C., President Garfield (November 19, 1831 – September 19, 1881, lived to age 49) and his staff were preparing to host the Governors' Ball which was scheduled to be held on Saturday evening, June 25th, at seven o'clock. In attendance would be the governors and their spouses from all the states and territories in the Union.

The governors of the western states and territories were able to witness the stark contrasts between the firetrap wooden-constructed town buildings, dusty and sometimes muddy manure-filled streets and the gun toting cowboys of the Wild West versus the brick and Victorian homes, paved and brick streets, and the civilized nature of the men and women of the East.

It was like two different worlds but belonging to the same Union, under the same flag, and theoretically governed by the same laws of one Great Nation. Yet the new West brought challenges that the East had not known for generations and, at times, it administered its own *Frontier Justice* not found in any law books sanctioned by the civil laws of the United States.

The Governors' Ball was an extravaganza affair. The Vienna Philharmonic Orchestra, perhaps the greatest classical ensemble in the world, was touring the Northeastern United States at that time. The Governors' Ball at the White House was on their scheduled agenda.

The Vienna Philharmonic Orchestra which was booked to perform at the White House gala consisted of 10 violins, 4 violas, 6 cellos, 4 bass fiddles and 4 French horns. The orchestra was to be conducted by the Hungarian born conductor, Hans Richter (April 4, 1843 – December 5, 1916, lived to age 73). Their musical program for that evening called for waltzes and polkas by the ever so famous and brilliant Austrian composer, Johann Strauss II (October 25, 1825 – June 3, 1899, lived to age 73).

Some of the waltzes Conductor Richter planned to perform were:

Wiener Bonbons, Op. 307, Viennese Sweets (1866)

Feenmärchen, Op. 312, Fairytales (1866)

An der schönen blauen Donau, Op. 314, The Blue Danube (1867)

Wein, Weib und Gesang, Op. 333, Wine, Women and Song (1869) and

G'schichten aus dem Wienerwald, Op. 325, Tales from the Vienna Woods (1868)

A few of the famous polkas he planned to perform were:

Im Sturmschritt, Op. 348, At the Double! (date unknown)

Vom Donaustrande, Op. 358, By the Danube's Shores (date unknown)

Auf der Jagd, Op. 373, On the Hunt! (1875)

Licht und Schatten, Op. 374, Light and Shadow (1875)

Banditen-Galopp, Op. 378, Bandits' Galop (1877)

Unfortunately, President Garfield's wife, Lucretia Rudolph Garfield (April 19, 1832 – March 14, 1918, lived to age 85) would not be able to attend. Lucretia became very ill in May when she contracted malaria and possibly spinal meningitis. Her doctor suggested an environment with salty air. So on June 18th, President Garfield took his wife to a seaside resort in Elberon, New Jersey where she stayed until the President was shot in an assassination attempt on July 2, 1881. Garfield later died from his two gunshot wounds on September 19, 1881.

Vice President Chester Alan Arthur (October 5, 1829 – November 18, 1886, lived to age 57) would be at the reception line with President Garfield. Arthur's wife had a more tragic ending with her sickness than Garfield's wife. Ellen Lewis Herndon Arthur (August 30, 1837 – January 12, 1880, lived to age 42) came down with a cold in January of 1880. The cold quickly led to pneumonia and she died two days later. The poor soul was only 42 years old. The Arthurs were married from 1859 to 1880.

Since Arthur was all alone, his sister Mary Arthur McElroy (July 5, 1841 – January 8, 1917, lived to age 75) would serve as unofficial Second Lady and eventually unofficial First Lady and would hostess at social events during Arthur's vice presidency and presidency. So during the night of the Governors' Ball, President Garfield, Vice President Arthur and Mary Arthur McElroy received the governors and their guests as they were announced when they entered the White House.

Oh it was quite a fancy ordeal. The elaborate black covered carriages each pulled by a single tall majestic Standardbred gelding rode up in front of the White House carrying a governor and his spouse or guest. The men were in formal tails and top hats and the women wore beautiful evening gowns with narrow skirts which were extravagantly trimmed in contrast fabrics. Curly hair was in vogue and the ladies wore their hair fashionably piled loosely on top of their heads. High society, the likes you would expect to find at a gala in Vienna, Austria at the opening of a Beethoven Concert Festival, found its way to the White House on that very special evening.

And of course, as the guests entered, they were greeted by the musicality of the beautiful Strauss waltzes performed by the renowned Vienna Philharmonic Orchestra. Around the room, there were tables filled with punch bowls, luscious fruit centered pastries, trays of cheese, and chocolates of all sorts. Butlers wearing white gloves walked around with sterling silver trays offering flutes full of the finest European champagne.

There were three governors at the Ball who were anxious to meet each other on this festive night. These were the governors who had something uniquely in common. They all had their state penitentiaries blown to smithereens and had escapees at large who looked to be on the run for quite a while. It was the governor of Missouri who suggested that they talk at the Governors' Ball and endeavor to get an audience with President Garfield Monday afternoon after the scheduled governors' meeting with the President.

Those governors were:

Texas Governor Oran M. Roberts (Democrat) (July 9 1815 – May 19, 1898, lived to age 82), he escorted his wife Frances Wycliffe Edwards Roberts (March 4 1819 – November 27, 1883, lived to age 64); Arkansas Governor Thomas James Churchill (Democrat) (March 10, 1824 – May 14, 1905, lived to age 81), he escorted his wife Ann Sevier Churchill (March 12, 1830 – February 20, 1917, lived to age 86); and Missouri Governor Thomas Theodore Crittenden (Democrat) (January 1, 1832 – May 29, 1909, lived to age 77), he escorted his wife Caroline Wheeler "Carrie" Jackson Crittenden (August 1, 1839 – January 27, 1917 lived to age 77).

The three caught up with one another about thirty minutes into the Ball. They introduced themselves to each other and their wives. Then they asked their wives to excuse them for just a few minutes while they discussed their plans for a special meeting with the President.

Governor Thomas Crittenden of Missouri took charge of the conversation from the start.

"Gentlemen, I know we are all after federal funds to rebuild and repair the damages inflicted on our penitentiaries by the escapees' accomplices but I think we also should ask for federal help to aid in tracking down the criminals."

"I agree," Governor Roberts said, "how do you feel about it Governor Churchill?"

"Count me in, gentlemen. In fact, let's see if we can corner the President for a few minutes and set up a Monday afternoon meeting with him to discuss our concerns."

So they waited until they saw President Garfield momentarily by himself and then they approached him with great respect and requested a short meeting on Monday afternoon. They briefly informed Garfield about the subject matter. This President was a man of action and decisiveness so there was no hesitation. Garfield immediately consented to their wish. He set the meeting for two o'clock Monday afternoon in his office. The three governors were elated and went back to join their wives and paired-up on the dance floor for the beautiful Strauss waltz, Tales from the Vienna Woods, which the Vienna Philharmonic Orchestra had just begun to play. The crowd waltzed and danced the polka until midnight and a good time was had by all.

After church services and then breakfast on Sunday morning, the three governors met for about thirty minutes to organize their thoughts and develop a strategy that they would employ when they had their audience with President Garfield. During the rest of the day, they toured Washington, D.C. together with their wives and became better acquainted. It was a beautiful summer day in the capital with temperatures in the high 70's and with a clear blue sky up above. One could easily forget his troubles that he left behind out West.

However, sooner than one would like, the Sunday feeling of utopia turned into the harsh reality of the day when Monday afternoon made its presence and likewise did a summer thunderstorm with flash flood rains beating down on the streets of D.C. The ugly day mirrored the unpleasant subject that was about to be discussed in the President's office.

The three governors waited in the hallway of the White House to meet with the President. At 2:00 sharp, President Garfield summoned his aide and requested that he escort the three governors to his office. When the governors arrived, the President greeted them and asked them to sit down on the chairs which he placed in front of his desk. The President began the conversation.

"Well gentlemen, I'm happy that we could get together and meet today. I'll do everything I can to help with your situation but I don't know what that is until you inform me of your request. So why don't you begin."

The governor of Missouri was the spokesperson for the group.

"Mr. President, as you know, we represent the states of Missouri, Arkansas and Texas. We each have state penitentiaries that have been compromised this year. An unknown criminal element has systematically and with great professional precision, I might add, destroyed our prisons, killed guards and broke out selected criminals. The mode of operation was similar on all counts: explosives were used to create havoc and tear down walls and gates, and prison guards were gunned down with great accuracy.

In every instance, the perpetrators made a clean getaway with their men because of their swiftness and their techniques. One of the important methods was that they cut telegraph wires coming into town so that the word of the prison breaks could not get out. That aided in their escapes.

We have no idea who these highly proficient criminals were and why they broke out who they did. We are also unaware of their final destinations. Everything about these breakouts is a complete mystery to us."

"I was not aware of all of those facts. That's quite disturbing. What do you need from me?"

"Well sir, we are requesting two things. Number one, we are asking for federal funds to repair the damage done by these breakouts. We can give you estimates of our monetary needs right now if you so wish."

"What are they?" The President asked as he reached for a pencil and a piece of paper.

The governor of Missouri continued,

"Sir, these are the numbers. Governor Roberts is requesting $20,000, Governor Churchill is requesting $28,000, and I am requesting $32,000."

Garfield wrote down the numbers and then added them up. The total was $80,000. He paused and stared at the total for a few seconds while the governors looked on wondering what they would hear next.

"Gentlemen, the numbers seem a little high to me but I think the federal government can accommodate your wishes."

The three governors were relieved, smiled, and were appreciative of Garfield's favorable response.

"Now you said there were two things. What's the second?"

This time Governor Oran Roberts from Texas jumped in because he was more familiar with the subject matter about to be thrown on the proverbial table.

"Mr. President, again we are going to require federal help to track down these professional criminals and bring them to justice. I am very familiar with the three people both President Hayes and you have employed for special cases. I believe you call them the *Three for Hire*. We would like for you to put them on this case and go to work immediately to apprehend the outlaws."

President Garfield smiled and said, "Yes, the *Three for Hire*: Jesse Caldwell, Thomas O'Brien, and Scott Johnson. Jesse and Scott are Texans and Thomas is a Kentuckian. Yes, I can see why you want them on this case. The only problem is that they are on a case right now for the governors of two territories out west because of a disturbance with the Mescalero Apache. I'm afraid that their services are not available at this time."

"I'm sorry to hear that. We figured that they could bust this case wide open. Do you have any other suggestions?" Governor Roberts asked.

"Yes I do. I suggest you three catch a train to Chicago and meet with Allan Pinkerton of the Pinkerton Detective Agency. Allan Pinkerton suffered a stroke back in '69 and I believe his sons have basically taken over the business but Allan is still sharp and has stayed involved. I would lay odds that he will jump right in the middle of this interesting project.

Oh the Pinkertons have had some bad experiences at times, especially with the James – Younger Gang, but overall, they are best equipped with personnel, investigative techniques, and the expertise to get the job done. I believe they are the ones who you need to hire to track down this criminal element."

"Well then that's just what we'll do," the governor of Missouri confirmed as the other two governors nodded in the affirmative.

The Pinkerton Detective Agency was created in 1850 by Allan Pinkerton (August 15, 1819 – July 1, 1884, lived to age 64). He was born in Scotland to William Pinkerton and his wife, Isabel McQueen. Allan was a cooper by trade which is a person who makes wooden staved vessels bound together by hoops. Some examples of a cooper's work are barrels, buckets, tubs, and butter churns. Some were made for liquids like water, wine or whiskey; others were made for dry products like cereal, flour or gunpowder.

Allan Pinkerton married Joan Carfrae (December, 1822 – January 22, 1887, lived to age 64) in Glasgow on March 13, 1842. She was a singer by trade. They both immigrated to the United States in 1842. They made their way to Chicago initially. Then Allan built a cabin in Dundee, Illinois which was fifty miles northwest of Chicago on the Fox River. There he started a cooperage.

Pinkerton did not believe in slavery. As early as 1844 he associated with Chicago abolitionist leaders. His Dundee home was even a stop for the Underground Railroad. In other words, it was a safe house for slaves of African descent in the United States to escape to free states and Canada.

During his years as a cooper, he accidentally stumbled onto the hideout of a gang of counterfeiters and had them arrested. He was praised for his actions and his celebrity led to his appointment as a deputy sheriff and then special agent for the U.S. Post Office. He amazed people with his ability to catch criminals.

It was in 1849 when Allan Pinkerton was appointed as the first detective in Chicago. In the 1850's, Pinkerton met a Chicago attorney in a local Masonic Hall. His name was Edward Rucker. Together they formed the North-Western Police Agency, which would later become the Pinkerton Detective Agency. Their motto was "We never sleep". They created an unblinking eye as their symbol. This is where the term "Private eye" originated from used by independent detectives.

During the startup of their new detective agency, they also created what was known as the Pinkerton Code which was: accept no bribes, never compromise with criminals, partner with local law enforcement agencies, refuse divorce cases or cases that initiate scandals, turn down reward money, never raise fees without the client's pre-knowledge, and keep clients apprised on an on-going basis.

Before the startup of the Civil War, the Pinkerton Detective Agency was hired to solve a series of train robberies. That is where Allan Pinkerton first came in contact with George McClellan, Vice President of the Illinois Central Railroad and the railroad company's lawyer, Abraham Lincoln. Pinkerton would eventually offer his services to the Union Army.

Prior to the Civil War, Pinkerton came up with two new and revolutionary detective techniques. One was called "shadowing". This was a secret surveillance of a suspect. The other technique he called, "assuming the role". This was coined, "undercover work". This technique would be considered as an option in helping the three governors get their men. However, these techniques used during the Civil War and after often ended up in the death of good detective agents.

Case in point: In the Leavenworth Weekly Times, March 26, 1874, on page 2, in the seventh column, there is an article entitled, "The Younger Tragedy". It appears the article was copied from the Kansas City Times which was written on March 18, 1874, the day after two Youngers had a shootout with a sheriff and two Pinkerton detectives.

The article describes the killing of John Younger (1851 – March 17, 1874, lived to age 22 / 23). But also killed on that day by the two Youngers were Deputy Sheriff Daniels and a Pinkerton agent by the last name of Allen out of Chicago. Another detective cowardly deserted and rode away. The two detectives were "shadowing" and posing as Virginia land buyers according to the newspaper article with the intent of searching out the Youngers. They got into a gun battle with John and his brother Jim Younger (January 15, 1848 – October 19, 1902, lived to age 54) on a rural Missouri road while on horseback. That was where John Younger was shot and killed and Detective Allen and Deputy Sheriff Daniels were also fatally wounded. This event took place about eight miles outside of Osceola, Missouri.

Just prior to and during the Civil War, Pinkerton served the North as head of the Union Intelligence (1861 – 1862). He was able to foil an alleged assassination plot on President Lincoln in Baltimore, Maryland while guarding the President on his way to his inauguration.

Pinkerton and his agents often worked undercover as Confederate soldiers and sympathizers to the South in order to gather valuable war time intelligence for the North. His intelligence service was the forerunner to the Secret Service.

After the War, the Pinkerton Detective Agency turned their efforts toward pursuing train and bank robbers and notorious gangs like the Reno Gang and the James-Younger Gang.

There is an interesting story in a newspaper called The State Journal, Jefferson City, Mo., Friday, February 5, 1875. It is on page 1 of 8 in column 2. The article is entitled "The James Boys". It gives an account of the botched attempt by the Pinkerton agents to capture Frank James (January 10, 1843 – February 18, 1915, lived to age 72) and Jesse James (September 5, 1847 – April 3, 1882, lived to age 34) at the James' family farmhouse.

It appears as though the Pinkertons made an inaccurate assumption thinking the James boys were home. Others thought that maybe they were, but somehow escaped. Jesse and Frank's mother later said that in fact, they were not at home.

The date that the article referenced was January 25, 1875. The Pinkerton Detective Agency staged a raid on the James' homestead. One of the agents threw an incendiary device (some say a bomb) through a window into the house. They were hoping to flush out Jesse and Frank. Instead the bomb killed their half-brother Archie and blew off the arm of Zerelda Samuel, Frank and Jesse's mother. Later it was discovered that Pinkerton's plan was to burn the James' home down to the ground.

Realizing the blunder, the Pinkerton agents skedaddled out of there faster than you could say "scared jackrabbits" and took a train back to whence they came. This event backfired for the Pinkertons and created more sympathy around those parts for the James boys. Eventually Pinkerton gave up the chase for Frank and Jesse. Many consider this failure Pinkerton's biggest defeat. Allan Pinkerton conceded the same as well.

CHAPTER SIX:

Pinkerton's Theory

After the meeting with President Garfield on Monday afternoon, the three governors sent a telegram to Allan Pinkerton in Chicago to see if he was available to meet with them either on Wednesday afternoon or anytime Thursday of that week. The telegram read:

Allan Pinkerton
Pinkerton Detective Agency
Chicago, Illinois

We request a meeting with you at your earliest convenience regarding the employment of your agency by the governors of Texas, Arkansas, and Missouri to track down both the criminals who perpetrated the prison breaks at our state penitentiaries, and the prisoners who escaped during the breakouts. During the escapes, there were guards killed and extensive damage done to the properties. We are in Washington, D.C. and will be heading home soon. Please respond today if our meeting is possible as requested since we could procure train tickets today for arrival in Chicago early Wednesday morning.

> *Sincerely,*
> *Oran Roberts, Governor of Texas*
> *Thomas Churchill, Governor of Arkansas*
> *Thomas Crittenden, Governor of Missouri*

On receipt of the telegram, Allan Pinkerton wasted no time in responding back to the governors. This was a case in which he had great interest. The governors were not aware that Pinkerton had collected newspaper articles on the prison breaks and that he was also gathering pertinent information about the escapees. He had been hoping that someone would hire his agency to break this case wide open so that he could demonstrate that his agency was still relevant even after the failures over the years to capture Frank and Jesse James. So he sent the following wire back to D.C.:

Oran Roberts, Governor of Texas
Thomas Churchill, Governor of Arkansas
Thomas Crittenden, Governor of Missouri

I am in receipt of your request and have great interest in this case. Please plan to meet with me in my office this Thursday morning at nine o'clock. My address is 1400 Freeman Street, Chicago, Illinois, suite 200. My office is on the second floor. Safe trip.

Allan Pinkerton
Pinkerton Detective Agency

Immediately after receiving confirmation of the meeting, the three governors traveled to the Baltimore & Potomac Railroad Station in Washington, D.C. to purchase their tickets for the Chicago trip. Little did they know that just a few days later, on July 2, 1881, President Garfield would be shot twice at that very location by Charles Guiteau (September 8, 1841 – June 30, 1882, lived to age 40). The President would die from his two gunshot wounds on September 19, 1881 at age 49.

When the governors arrived in Chicago on Wednesday morning, they signed into their hotel and then the three toured the "Windy City" with their wives taking in all the sights and sounds of Chicago. The women even convinced the governors to take them on a shopping spree to look at all the new dresses and hats shipped in from Paris, France. The three governors demonstrated about as much enthusiasm for this event as a criminal walking up the steps of Judge Isaac Parker's gallows in Fort Smith, Arkansas.

They all walked so much that day, traipsing in and out of fancy clothing shops, that Governor Roberts made the comment that he thought he lost ten pounds from all the exercise. Governor Churchill responded with, "Our wallets are much lighter now too than they were at the start of this shopping spree." The other two governors laughed and concurred with the accurate assertion.

The hotel they stayed in was the Grand Pacific Hotel which was opened in 1873. It was located on the block bounded by Clark, LaSalle, Quincy and Jackson Streets. The Grand Pacific was one of the first two prominent hotels built in Chicago, Illinois after the Great Chicago Fire which started on October 8, 1871 and continued to October 10, 1871. According to reports, the fire killed up to 300 people. Much of the city's central business district was destroyed. About 3.3 square miles of buildings burnt to the ground and left 100,000 residents homeless. But Chicago picked up the pieces and went to work rebuilding the city. By 1881, the city was growing population-wise as well as economically.

The gubernatorial first ladies slept in Thursday morning. Conversely, the three governors were "up and at 'em" at the crack of dawn and met for an early breakfast to discuss last minute strategies relating to the employment of the Pinkerton Detective Agency.

The Grand Pacific Hotel was about four blocks away from Pinkerton's office so it was well within walking distance; although, after Wednesday, they required no additional exercise for a few days.

They arrived at their destination at 8:50 a.m. and Allan Pinkerton asked them to come in and sit down in front of his large oak desk. His office was a corner office with a bank of windows along the west and south walls. Each window had a pull down shade to prevent the bright afternoon sun from shining in. The wood paneling on the walls was walnut in color which gave the room a dark, gloomy closed in appearance, especially with no direct morning sunlight.

There were folders and papers stacked up everywhere: on his desk, scattered around on the floor, and piled up on a large round conference table in the center of his office. The files contained open and closed cases, and solved and unsolved cases.

Hanging on the wall was a huge 6' wide by 4' high map of the states and territories. It was framed with 3" wide ornate dark stained wood. The map was a great showpiece but also had practical implications for planning and strategizing.

If one could close his eyes and picture in his mind what a detective's office would look like, this would surely fill the bill.

Allan Pinkerton began the conversation,

"It's a pleasure to meet you and I am pleased that you came to Chicago to seek my services. I did some research on the breakouts in your penitentiaries before you even contacted me and I have some theories about why specific individuals were busted out of your prisons. There are many things that I can't explain yet but I may have a plan that could get us the valuable information which we need to solve these cases.

Would you gentlemen like a cup of coffee before we get into the heart of the matter?"

"Sure," the governor of Missouri confirmed. The other two also nodded in the affirmative. Pinkerton walked out of his office into the waiting room where there was a pot of coffee cooking on a wood burning stove. The three governors followed him out. It was late in June and just too hot to be burning wood in a potbelly stove in his office. In fact, he had all eighteen windows in his office wide open to take advantage of the nice breeze blowing out of the west this morning.

After he poured each a cup of coffee and then one for himself, they all four walked back into Pinkerton's office, sat down again, and continued with business. The governors, one by one, began relating their stories while Pinkerton wrote down the particulars in a notebook.

When the stories were laid out, Pinkerton pulled out three folders from his top drawer. He had a folder on Johnny Dane, Doctor Eddie Hawkens and the Burkley brothers, Bobby and Kenny. Then he proceeded to demonstrate how efficient his agency was by reading the information he had in the folders for each escapee. He also had the newspaper articles of their original captures. The governors were impressed with Pinkerton's legwork on the criminals and the background knowledge he had on each of them as well. Pinkerton had something to prove and so far this morning, he was doing it well.

Then Pinkerton introduced some important consistent facts regarding the three prison breaks by walking over to a large chalkboard attached to the north wall of his office and jotting down a few things. He wrote the words, "What we know". Under that he listed: explosives, telegraph wires cut, killings, property destroyed, clean getaways. Then he wrote the words, "What we don't know". Under that he listed: no knowledge of their destination, no knowledge of who broke them out, and no answers as to why specifically these four were broken out.

"However, let's look at what we know about the escapees from your penitentiaries:

Johnny Dane, an explosives expert,

Eddie Hawkens, a medical doctor turned thief,

Bobby and Kenny Burkley, both killers, robbers, marksmen and snipers.

Plus you may not know this. There was also a breakout from a jail in Hays City. A guy by the name of Rusty Blake was due to be hung for murder. He was busted out of jail the day before his hanging."

"What relevance does that have to all of this?" The governor of Missouri asked.

"He's an expert safecracker, which incidentally I find very strange," Pinkerton said as he sort of dazed off looking out the window. The three governors looked on in bewilderment at Pinkerton's pause but said nothing as Pinkerton shook it off and continued.

"Well, I don't see that these five criminals have anything in common," the governor of Texas concluded.

"Oh, that's where you're wrong," Pinkerton shot back. "What they all have in common is that they are experts at what they do. The other thing we haven't mentioned yet is the sharpshooters and operatives who broke them out of jail. We know that the description of two of those guys who broke the four criminals out of your penitentiaries are identical. The two guys who broke Rusty Blake out were wearing bandannas to cover their faces. However, one was a Mexican and so was the one who did the damage at your prisons.

Gentlemen, I think that there's something big in the works here. My theory is that someone is building a criminal organization of skilled outlaws who possess specific talents…"

"For what purpose?" The governor of Texas asked as he rudely cut off Pinkerton's thought.

"Well if you allow me to finish governor, I'll tell you," Pinkerton shot back in an impatient tone.

"It appears to me that someone is building an organization to pull off something big. What that might be, I just don't know yet. Maybe it's an assassination of the president or a governor or a prominent politician. Maybe it's to rob a series of banks around the country. Who knows what it might be?"

At this point, Pinkerton stood up and walked over to the bank of windows on the west wall and looked out on the hustle and bustle of the streets in the Chicago business district in frustration and said, "Hell, I have no idea what they are up to." Then he turned around quickly and looked at the governors, and stated with confidence,

"But I'll tell you this much gentlemen, I'm going to find out; that I will guarantee you."

Pinkerton had a plan but he had no desire to tell the governors about it. He was afraid that his plan would leak out and not only destroy the mission, but get one of his detectives killed as well. Over the years, due to their covers being blown, the Pinkerton Detective Agency lost many good men to gunslingers and notorious outlaw gangs. Pinkerton was still aggressive with his bold tactics but exercised much more prudence regarding strategies as the years went by, in order to protect the lives of his detectives. But even with that, his overriding drive was to "get his man".

Pinkerton had one more unanswered question that was annoying him. Instead of voicing what it was, he wanted to see if the governors were on the same track or had any other ideas of the motive for these criminal events.

"Gentlemen, is there anything else that stands out to you about this case?"

The governors looked at each other and then back at Pinkerton. They all agreed that they couldn't think of anything else.

"Well gentlemen that surprises me. There's something that stands out to me like a twenty-foot column cactus in the Arizona desert. Don't you wonder who and how someone knew about each of the escapees, their talents and what penitentiaries they were incarcerated in?"

As astute as the three governors were, that question at no time entered into their minds because they never saw the whole picture as well as Pinkerton.

"So now we know certain important things and we still have critical things to discover. At this point, leave everything up to me. I will keep you informed of my progress as I see fit but don't expect consistent periodic updates; the fewer people who are aware of my plan and movements, the higher the probability of success."

At this point, Pinkerton called his bookkeeper into his office to go over the tedious task of estimating the cost of this project to the governors. When that was completed, the meeting was over. They shook hands and Pinkerton smiled and said,

"As me Scottish mother would say, "Lang may yer lum reek!" which means, "May you live long and stay well". With that, the governors walked back to their hotel and made plans to head back to their home states.

Pinkerton spent the next several hours in his office reviewing all of his notes and pondering his next move. He thought he knew where to go from here but first he wanted to run it by a few of his most trusted agents. His idea was a very risky proposition which might not even work at all or, if it did, it had the potential of getting one of his agents killed.

CHAPTER SEVEN:

The Anamosa Setup

After the meeting with the three governors, Allan Pinkerton took a few days to organize his thoughts and go over his notes, newspaper articles, and history of the criminals who were busted out of the state penitentiaries in Texas, Arkansas, and Missouri. On one of those days he took a horse and carriage ride up to Lake Michigan and sat on a bench along the edge of the lake just enjoying the scenery of the seagulls walking along the banks and flocking out in the waters around schools of small bait fish.

He loved to listen to the high-pitched wailing and squawking calls of those beautiful large white feathered seabirds. He considered it nature at its best. To other people, maybe not so much; more like noisy disconcerting screeching chatter and definitely not music to the ears.

It was a peaceful place for him to collect his thoughts. Pinkerton couldn't get around very well because of the debilitating stroke he experienced several years prior. But that did not keep him from getting out in a horse buggy and enjoying the sights of this growing metropolis and one of the most beautiful Great Lakes in the northern hemisphere. He never gave up horseback riding either fearing that backing off physical activity would accelerate his aging and lack of mobility.

Sitting on the banks of Lake Michigan was a great place for him to clear his mind and to better see things with greater clarity. What he often thought about was how there seemed to be two distinct worlds, two diverse cultures within the United States. It was no longer the North versus the South. That War ended back in '65 yet everyone knew that there still existed animosity amongst some. Rather it was the civilized nature of its citizens and the prosperous economies east of the Mississippi contrasting with the lawlessness, unrest, and backward civilizations west of the Mississippi.

After a few days passed and he had time to map out a strategy in his mind, he summoned by telegram two of his best detectives to his second story office in Chicago. The two gentlemen were from out of town. He also invited a local agent to attend his meeting as well.

It was Wednesday morning now, approximately one week after Pinkerton met with the governors. A cold front had rolled through during the night bringing with it some severe summer thunderstorms in the early morning hours. However, by the time his meeting began at nine o' clock, the storms were over and clearing skies allowed the bright morning sun to make its way through the parting clouds. He opened up most of the windows in his office to take advantage of the cool breeze blowing off of Lake Michigan.

The three gentlemen who came to meet with Pinkerton were: Billy Horton, Bob Brennen, and Jake Nichols. Billy Horton had been with the Pinkerton Agency since 1875. He was currently managing Pinkerton's Ohio office. Bob Brennen had run the Tennessee office and had been a Pinkerton detective since 1872. He was now stationed at the main office in Chicago. Jake Nichols was the oldest of the group with the most seniority; he ran the St. Louis office. Nichols' association with Allan Pinkerton dated all the way back to the Civil War when he successfully became a double agent at age 19 for the Union Army while working for Pinkerton. His claim to fame was the intelligence he gathered which enabled the Union Army to defeat the Confederates at the Battle of Fredericktown in Missouri which was fought from October 17 to October 21, 1861.

On October 31, 1861, Wyatt Earp's older brother James (June 28, 1841 – January 25, 1926, lived to age 84), who fought at the Battle of Fredericktown on the Union side, was wounded in the shoulder not far from the site of the original battle and lost the use of his left arm. He was discharged in March of 1863. He later became deputy marshal with Wyatt in Dodge City. Jake Nichols had become good friends with James Earp after Earp was wounded in the field of battle.

After pouring a cup of coffee for the three and himself, Pinkerton began the meeting.

"Gentlemen, I called this meeting to inform you that our agency has just been hired by the governors of Texas, Arkansas, and Missouri. Let me put it this way. There's a hornet's nest in the making out West that's going to harbor some vicious varmints which are planning to sting the life out of its victims. We have to bring their swarming to an end. First we need to hunt down the tree they're building their nest in, and then we'll smoke them out and destroy their colony. Hornets attack hard and fast and their sting can give you a big hurt. There's one difference here men. These hornets that we'll be dealing with are killers, so prudence with an aggressive offense will be our strategy.

It's difficult for me to acknowledge it but our agency was far from being effective in the 1870's. Oh we had our share of successes alright but we had embarrassing failures as well. Those Missouri James brothers pert near ruined our reputation."

Pinkerton then pounded on his desk once with his fist and said with authority and vigor,

"So now by golly we are going to prove that the Pinkerton Detective Agency will indeed be relevant in the 1880's and beyond. When I was a young lad in Scotland, my father would always say, "Gie it laldy", which meant 'Do something with gusto'. Well that's exactly what we are going to do with this case. We are going to give it everything we've got.

Here's what we have men. There have been three major penitentiary breakouts and one breakout from a Kansas jailhouse."

Pinkerton then walked over to the large map on the wall, and asked the men to follow him. The three curious men lined up side-by-side behind him and faced the map anxiously waiting to hear what Pinkerton was about to reveal.

Pinkerton pointed to specific locations on the large map as he systematically identified the prison breaks one-by-one.

"Gentlemen, the jailhouse breakout was here in Hays City, Kansas. A professional safecracker and convicted killer by the name of Rusty Blake was broken out of jail by two unidentified gunslingers the day before he was to swing from the gallows.

The second breakout was here in Huntsville, Texas. An explosives expert, a two-bit thief, and killer by the name of Johnny Dane made a clean getaway with the help of two gunslingers as well. Dynamite was used in his escape.

The third breakout was right here in Little Rock, Arkansas. This time there were three men who busted the jailbird out. They broke out Doctor Eddie Hawkens. He's not a killer but he's a no good thief.

Lastly, two snipers, thieves and killers by the names of Bobby and Kenny Burkley, who are sheer evil to the bone, were broken out of the Missouri Penitentiary right here in Jefferson City, Missouri. They call that place "The Walls". It was supposed to be escape proof. But nitro and dynamite blew the walls to smithereens and those felons got a clean getaway."

"Nitro, isn't nitro illegal to possess nowadays? And how do you know nitro was used?" Billy Horton asked.

"Of course it's illegal. But it can be found on the streets just like anything else that's illegal. How do we know it was nitro? They found the pieces of glass from the bottles of nitro scattered throughout the crumbled walls and mixed in with the pieces of mule parts. That's right, I said mule parts. It looks like they hid nitro in the saddlebags of two mules. When the mules kicked up, so did the nitro.

There were several eye witnesses in most of the breakouts. The descriptions they gave of the ones busting the prisoners out could match four wanted posters that I have in my book of criminals."

Pinkerton walked back over to his desk, moved his chair away, placed his left hand on the top of his desk, leaned over and opened up the top drawer with his right hand and then removed a binder of sorts. The binder had wanted posters pasted to each page. Pinkerton was the first one to ever create a mug shot book and it was thanks to the widespread use of photography during that time period.

While still standing, he flipped through his binder to Glen Merrit, Cole Dempsey, Dakota Wilson, and Pecos Fransisco. He was certain Pecos was his man but he wasn't sure who the other one was of the three remaining possibilities. He also figured that Johnny Dane was present at a couple of the prison breaks because of the dynamite and nitro that were used. Dane was well known around the country for his criminal explosive exploits and some said he was a little bit crazy too.

Pinkerton was a shrewd detective and had a keen mind for solving criminal cases. He had a premonition that someone was creating a group of professional criminals to carry out an elaborate scheme. However, he had no real evidence to support his theory. Rather, it was just intuition and conjecture on his part.

Then he made this comment to the three detectives,

"What has me perplexed is this; who and how did someone know about which criminals to choose for their operation and what penitentiaries and jails to find them in? And of course, the next question is, where is the next prison breakout going to be? Lots of questions that need answers, gentlemen."

"I'm sure you have an idea of where to start, sir," Bob Brennen commented.

"You bet I do, Brennen. I've been thinking about this for several days. We need to infiltrate their gang."

"Might be easier said than done sir," Horton offered.

"That it might lad, but then I have a hunch. I have an idea that they are still searching for experts in different fields to fill the voids in their gang. Think about this, in every prison break, they took down telegraph wires. They are obsessed with it. It's a means of escape. It could also be a means of sending false messages to send the posse on a wild goose chase.

A criminal who is a telegraph operator may be appealing to them. Now, I think that this guy needs other talents too. Maybe they need another sharpshooter or a fast draw, or even a gunsmith. If we can make this guy interesting enough for those guys to take the bait, well we just might be able to get an agent into their gang. If we can do that, just think of the possibilities. Our insider could warn us by telegram where the gang plans to make their hit and we could ambush them and take them out like the Hays City citizens did to the Outlaws of Smoky Hill River back in March."

"Keep talking Mr. Pinkerton. Knowing your creativeness, I'm betting you have something else up your sleeve," Nichols said. "What is it?"

"Well, walk back over to this wall map with me. Look at where all the breakouts have occurred: Texas, Arkansas, Missouri and Kansas. You can draw a circle around those four states with the center being the Indian Territory. Now I know they can't be operating out of the Indian Territory. However, with the first breakout being in Kansas, I would lay odds that their base of operations is stationed somewhere in that state.

The other thing I know is that the next closest nonmilitary prison is in Iowa, right above Missouri. If they were going to break another person out of a penitentiary, I would wager that it would be in a nearby geographical area and obviously different from the prisons they already breached. That Iowa penitentiary could be very useful to us.

"Which prison is that, sir?" Horton asked.

"It's the Anamosa State Penitentiary, right here in east central Iowa," Pinkerton said as he pointed to the exact location on the map. "Men, that's where we need for them to target their next breakout. Oh, there's another penitentiary in Fort Madison which is in southeast Iowa which would probably be easier to break in and out of. However, these criminals seem to like challenges, so let's give 'em one."

The town that was then called Anamosa was originally founded as the settlement of Buffalo Forks in 1838. It was incorporated in 1856 as Lexington which was a popular name for towns during that time period. In fact, it was so popular that it caused mail delivery confusion. So when Lexington became incorporated as a city, the name was changed to Anamosa.

The story about how that town became known as Anamosa centers around a local Native American girl whose name was Anamosa, which means "White fawn". A deaf gentleman by the name of Edmond Booth (August 24, 1810 – March 29, 1905, lived to age 94) was the one who suggested the town be called, Anamosa. Booth was an incredible man himself. He was deafened and totally blind in one eye by meningitis when he was four years old. By trade he was a journalist who published, managed, wrote for, and edited the local newspaper, The Eureka. He helped to establish the National Association of the Deaf and chaired its National Executive Committee advocating for deaf rights even until the day he died.

The origin of the town's final name has a somewhat romantic flair to it. This is according to legend handed down over the generations. In the year 1842, a Native American family was passing through town. The family stayed at what was known as the Ford House. The town grew to love the sweet little Native American girl named Anamosa and she in turn loved them. When the family departed and moved on, the townspeople agreed to name their city, Anamosa.

Anamosa is the home of the Anamosa State Penitentiary. It was built in 1875 in the architectural style of Gothic Revival which is a style that began in England in the late 1740's. The building was constructed from limestone quarried in Anamosa and its shape resembles a castle which inspired its nickname, "The White Palace of the West".

Pinkerton continued with his plan,

"There's only one man in this room with the experience of being a spy, is good with a gun and knows how to send telegram messages," Pinkerton said as his eyes turned toward Jake Nichols.

"If you are considering me for the mission Mr. Pinkerton, count me in," Nichols said with noticeable enthusiasm in his voice and posture as he sat up straight in his chair and leaned forward.

"I knew you would jump at the chance Nichols, but how is your wife going to feel about it?" Pinkerton asked.

"She's going to hate the idea, no doubt, and so will my two daughters. But they'll understand when I tell them the importance of this mission."

"You think so?" Pinkerton questioned.

"No I don't," Nichols said as he gave out a somewhat nervous chuckle. He knew his wife and children were going to hate the idea, plain and simple, and that they would not comprehend the reason why he would put the government's needs over his family's. But Nichols accepted the job anyway.

"OK then, the first thing we have to do is give you an alias."

"Let's make it simple," Nichols said. "Let's use the same one I used during the Civil War. It was Frank Lackey."

"Sounds good, now we have to determine a crime that will land you in the state penitentiary for about ten years," Pinkerton said.

Billy Horton quickly offered an idea.

"Bank robbery would be a good one. But what I think is most important is that you make it in a remote town in maybe Wyoming or the Dakota Territory where no one will be able to check up on the story. I also suggest that you don't have a real trial. I would just have a judge, whom you know of course and can trust, sign a statement that there was a trial and that Nichols, I mean Frank Lackey, was found guilty and was sentenced to ten years in the Anamosa State Penitentiary. You can have Pinkerton agents escort Nichols, sorry again, I mean Lackey, to Anamosa."

"Great idea Billy," Pinkerton said. "I know just the judge who will do that for us. The other thing we'll need to do is to get every newspaper in Kansas, Arkansas, Missouri, Nebraska, Iowa and Texas to print the article. I'll get the story out on the wire and make it a couple of paragraphs long and then let the local newspapers embellish it from there. I'll do the legwork on that."

"I guess I'll be able to spend a little time with my family before we do this thing, right?" Nichols inquired.

"We'll give you a week to get everything in order at home in St. Louis. You must not tell your family anything about this mission. Just inform them that you are going on an assignment for a few weeks and will be back as soon as the assignment is completed. Before you go home to St. Louis, I'll write you a draft for $500 for your wife and children so they have plenty of money for the necessities while you're gone.

While you're in St. Louis, I'll order a special train to transport me and several agents along with our horses. We'll be able to roll at a moment's notice wherever the action takes us.

If this plan works the way I think it will, and you become a member of their gang, somehow you will have to get to a telegraph office and send us a wire when and where they decide to do whatever criminal act it is they intend to carry out. When we get your telegram here at the office, we'll head west by rail and be on those outlaws like flies on a buffalo's dung pile."

Pinkerton and his agents went over a few more details and then decided on a time and place to pick up Nichols to head to Anamosa. When they broke up the meeting, the two visiting agents made arrangements for their train rides back home.

Pinkerton had several things to take care of now: notify a judge to send a letter to the Anamosa prison regarding the arrival of Nichols (a.k.a. Frank Lackey), call in several agents for field work, order a special train, and write the article of Frank Lackey's arrest and sentence. He performed these tasks with a sense of urgency.

This is the message he sent out to newspapers around the country and of course to Jake Nichols.

July 14, 1881

Ace marksman and telegraph operator Frank Lackey of Wyoming Territory was arrested and tried for bank robbery, pistol-whipping a teller, and attempted murder. He was sentenced on July 11, 1881 to ten years at the Anamosa Penitentiary in Iowa. Lackey was a skilled telegraph operator for twelve years. He was one of three gang members who called themselves, Lackey's Raiders. His other two gang members were shot and killed during the robbery attempt. Lackey escaped but the posse caught up with him when his horse went lame about two miles outside of town. He held his own in a gunfight until he ran out of ammunition. He surrendered with the loot of $25,000 in gold certificates and greenbacks. The marshal made a comment that "Lackey would have escaped with the town's money if it wasn't for that horse folding up on him".

While Pinkerton was performing his responsibilities in great detail, Jake Nichols was trying to figure out how to break the news to his family. His wife, Molly, never did like the fact that Jake was a Pinkerton agent. But there was nothing she could do about it. She fell madly in love with him while he was a field agent and finally married him. She was elated when he was put in charge of the St. Louis Division and basically had a safe office job which enabled him to come home for dinner every night. They just celebrated their 15th wedding anniversary and their lovely daughters were thirteen and eleven years of age.

After being home for two days, Jake finally gathered up enough nerve to inform his family about his assignment. After supper on Saturday evening, Jake asked his family to gather in the parlor. Molly had sensed that something was going on because Jake was not his jovial self since he came back from Chicago; but she was afraid to say anything because she was hoping that it was just her imagination and things would soon get back to normal. But "back to normal" might never come to fruition for this family again. Only time would tell.

They all sat in the parlor. Molly and the girls all had worried looks on their faces because Jake was not smiling and had a concerned look on his face as well.

"Molly, I will be going on a special assignment for the Pinkerton Detective Agency in about five days. I won't pull any punches, it's a dangerous mission. I was asked to be the one to assume this mission because I am the most qualified for it."

"You mean you accepted a dangerous mission without discussing it with me first?" Molly asked in a somewhat angered tone.

"I knew you would be upset, Molly but…"

"But nothing!" Molly shouted as she interrupted and then stood up. "You have a wife and two daughters to support. You know the Pinkerton's history out West with the likes of the James' Gang and others. How many agents were killed going after those outlaws, five, ten, what was it? You promised me that your field work was over; you said there would be no more dangerous missions."

The two daughters saw their mother arguing with their father for the first time ever and one began to weep while the other began to sob. They were sensing that something real bad was going on that they fully did not comprehend.

"Calm down Molly, you're upsetting the girls."

"You two girls go upstairs to your room and wait there until I tell you when to come back down," Molly ordered.

They scurried up the steps, crying loudly.

"What kind of mission are you going on?" Molly asked as she sat down at the small table placing her left elbow on the tabletop and resting her head on her closed fist. She had that sunken feeling look all over her body like you do when you are about to say good-bye to your best friend not knowing when or if you will ever see him again.

"Molly, please trust me on this. I can't tell you what the mission is about. It's a secret one. In order to protect you and the girls, I'm going under an alias. For the first few weeks, I probably won't be able to communicate with you. But after that, I'll be able to send you telegrams periodically and I'll sign them with the initials F. L."

"What are we going to live on when you're gone? You have never told me how much money we have to our name."

"We're in good shape financially but Mr. Pinkerton was kind enough to give you five hundred dollars for food and such while I'm gone," Jake said as he stood up, reached into his pocket and pulled out five one hundred dollar bills. Molly didn't reach for the money so he placed it on the table next to her. At this stage, she really wasn't worried about the money as much as she was about Jake's safety and well-being. She felt like the money was just a cheap way of paying her off as a trade for her husband's life.

"So he's taking you away from me and the girls and paying me a measly five hundred dollars? What's he going to do if you get yourself killed, pay for your funeral too?" Molly asked as she began to cry. The girls were upstairs kneeling on the floor and peeking around through the banister watching and listening to every word their mother and father were speaking.

Jake then grabbed a chair, sat down beside Molly and with his arm around her said,

"Honey, I have been through these types of missions before, way before we even met. In fact, all the way back to the Civil War. I know how to handle myself very well. I'm the best at what I do and that's why I'm the only one for this job. This mission will probably come to a conclusion in about five to six weeks, then I promise you, it will be my last."

Jake had no idea that Molly would be so distraught with his decision to agree to go on this mission. If he knew it was going to upset her so, he may not have been so eager to accept it. But the wheels were in motion and there was no turning back now.

Several days passed and the time for Jake's departure was drawing near. In the meantime, Pinkerton worked with the Union Pacific Railroad to secure a special train for him and his agents. The Union Pacific was more than happy to comply with Pinkerton because they themselves had been victims over the years at the hands of so many notorious outlaw gangs. When the president of the Union Pacific was told that there was potentially a new and deadly gang being formed, he wasted no time accommodating Pinkerton's request.

Besides the obvious two, the engine and the fuel car, the train consisted of a plush meeting coach, one sleep car for long trips, a passenger car, a boxcar for their horses, grain and hay, a prisoner holding car, a caboose and an empty freight car which Pinkerton had plans to use to get criminals to squeal like stuck pigs. He didn't tell anyone how he planned to use this car, but he sure knew himself. He also was well aware that his methods would be as illegal as sending a prisoner to the gallows without a fair trial. The Union Pacific Railroad positioned this special train on a spur at the Chicago Train Depot, and it would immediately be made available to go, at Pinkerton's request.

Pinkerton also had one of his friends, who was a judge up in the Wyoming Territory, send a fake notice to the Anamosa Penitentiary announcing the forthcoming arrival of the not so notorious outlaw, Frank Lackey.

With the passing of three more days, it was now time for three assigned Pinkerton agents to rendezvous with Jake northwest of St. Louis at an agreed upon location. Jake said his final good-byes to his wife and his two daughters. There wasn't a dry eye in that house except for Jake's who was anxious to get on the road and begin his journey.

After Jake met the three agents in St. Charles, Missouri, they rode in a four seat buckboard wagon to Sedalia, Missouri, caught a train to Kansas City and then to Des Moines, Iowa which was west of Anamosa. This made it appear that they were coming in from the Wyoming Territory.

On arrival at the Anamosa State Penitentiary, Jake (a.k.a. Frank Lackey) was treated very poorly; just as the prison guards treated all hardened criminals. He was given ragged prisoner clothes and used sandals to wear, escorted to his 6' x 10' cell, pushed into it and told to listen and obey lest he discover the horrors of solitary confinement in a windowless 5'x5'x6' wooden box located outside in the elements. Ole Jake had every intention of being a model prisoner especially envisioning what it would be like sitting in a dark wooden box out in the courtyard in the scorching hot days of late summer or the frigid cold days of the dreary winter months in the upper Midwest.

Now it was a waiting game. Day after day went by, week after week and still no contact. Jake was happy to get three squares a day alright but the food, or as what some inmates called it, slop, was more appropriate for a bunch of feral hogs than for human consumption.

Showers were as scarce as hens' teeth and on many nights you would find the rats snacking on the venison jerky that you snuck into your cell after supper.

Each week an undercover agent would come by to visit with Jake to see if anyone had made contact. Two months went by and still nothing. No one appeared to be taking the bait even though newspapers all around the West and Midwest picked up the story of Lackey's capture, imprisonment, and the demise of Lackey's Raiders.

Pinkerton was now getting restless. "Was this another failed idea on his part?" He wondered. But as bad as Pinkerton felt back in his cozy office in Chicago, Jake was the one who was really suffering. After all, he was the one imprisoned in that morbid dark dungeon he had no intention of calling home. Jake was becoming depressed and was almost to the point of calling off this undercover operation.

However, through the visiting agents, Pinkerton asked Jake to stay strong, at least for two more months.

Meanwhile, back at the lodge.

Brinkman called for a special meeting of his notorious outlaw gang members. It was a beautiful September Sunday afternoon just outside of Abilene and they were all there: Dakota, Pecos, Rusty,

Dane, Doc Hawkens, Bobby and Kenny Burkley, and the Kansas Kid.

Also in attendance were three new gun hands who the Kansas Kid himself hired as per Mr. Brinkman's request. Brinkman had put his trust in the Kansas Kid to find three quick-draw sharpshooters who were interested in getting rich quick, the lawless way, and not afraid to dodge bullets.

He found them alright. They were gunslingers from Deadwood who had criminal records as long as the Santa Fe Trail. Their names were Cole Fletcher, Arizona Palmer, and Charlie Todd. The Kansas Kid rode with these three gunmen before, and he told them as much as he knew about Brinkman and his gang. All three were interested in joining up.

Cole wasn't real sharp at ducking lead projectiles since he had been shot seven times in the last three years. But one thing for sure, he had grit and always stood his ground.

Arizona was unscathed and had the courage of a grizzly. It seemed like lady luck was always by his side keeping slugs whizzing by instead of whizzing through.

Charlie Todd was daring, and fearless as well, but made unwise decisions and took chances that got previous gang members killed or himself shot up several times. If Brinkman would have known of Charlie Todd's sloppy ways, he would have sent Charlie floating down the Smoky Hill River after the introductions.

Brinkman gave the three their money envelopes but did not give them new pistols. Professional gunmen were always particular about the sidearms they used and some even superstitious. Brinkman knew this and left well enough alone.

After Brinkman introduced the three newcomers to the group, he told everyone to sit down and get comfortable. However, he didn't offer anyone a drink at this point. While everyone sat in plush leather chairs around the room, Brinkman stood behind his large oak desk. The few things that were on top of his desk were neatly placed.

In his hand he held a large brown envelope but did not open it yet. In fact he placed it down on the desk in front of him. Then he looked around the room and showed a sense of satisfaction and pride in his face as he realized that he had done something no one else had ever accomplished. He had successfully assembled one of the most skillful outlaw gangs of notorious criminals west of the Mississippi River.

Everyone anxiously waited for Mr. Brinkman to speak his piece. Well he did after he picked up a Cuban cigar from an open wooden box on his desktop, meticulously clipped about ½ inch off the end, struck a match, lit the cigar and took several puffs showing extreme satisfaction on his face as he blew the smoke into the air.

He then sat down and said this as he looked each and everyone in the eyes,

"Gentlemen, we are almost there. Our gang is almost complete. But there is something I want to discuss with you first. All of you are experts in your fields and that's why you are here. Many of you have a sense of independence running through your veins. That was fine up to now, but it isn't any more."

Now Brinkman stood up again behind his desk as a show of unquestionable authority while everyone else remained seated.

"Let me lay something out for you with great clarity, gentlemen. Everyone will accept my orders as I give them. There will not be any insubordination in the ranks and I do not expect anyone to challenge my decisions and orders. If you do, I promise you that there will be dire consequences. My intention is to make all of us rich beyond our wildest dreams and that's what will happen if you follow my commands. Do I make myself clear on this matter?"

Some nodded their heads "yes"; others replied "yes sir" as if they were in the U.S. Army which seemed an appropriate response to Brinkman's commanding officer's type dialog.

Dakota and Pecos looked at each other and both noticed the same thing and at the same time. There was something different about Mr. Brinkman. He was more intense, almost military like. No one really knew his background and never inquired about it. But today, it was on display. What they were not aware of was that Brinkman was Brigadier General Jerod Brinkman in the Confederate Army. He made one mistake while commanding his troops at the First Battle of Chattanooga, Tennessee, June 7–8, 1862. It cost him the battle and the lives of 65 men and he never got over it. But one thing it did do, it made him a perfectionist, the type who has a guilty soul. Underneath all that perfection which he exhibited was the product of guilt and shame from the results of the First Battle at Chattanooga. It's called *maladaptive perfectionism* -

"a drive to perfection that generally has social roots, and a feeling of pressure to succeed that derives from external, rather than internal, sources. It is highly correlated with depression, anxiety, shame, and guilt.

Sure Brinkman wanted to be rich. That's why he put together an overly qualified team. But most importantly, he wanted to succeed in his gutsy venture, which he had not exposed to his gang as of yet. That inner need to succeed was the reason why he became such a demanding perfectionist. He also had another secret and personal ambition which he would not reveal until later.

After everyone agreed with Brinkman's demands, he continued,

"Before we test our efficiency and skills though, we have one more individual to add to our team."

Brinkman picked up the large brown envelope that was sent to him by his boss, opened it and removed a newspaper clipping of an article in the Saline County Journal which ran the week beginning Monday, August 1st.

"Gentlemen, my boss sent me an article about a person named Frank Lackey out of Wyoming. Have any of you heard of him?"

No one did.

"The article states here that he was arrested and convicted of bank robbery, pistol-whipping a teller, and attempted murder. Supposedly he's an ace marksman. He had two other members in his small gang but they were both killed during the robbery. The only reason he got caught was because his horse went lame on him outside of town."

With the article still in his hand, Brinkman walked to the front of his desk and sat down on top of it being a bit more casual and said,

"Now what interests me the most about this Lackey fella is not only is he good with a gun but he was also a telegraph operator at one time. I can see where this guy could be a tremendous asset to our organization by sending false information out on us after jobs and sending posse on a wild goose chase."

Brinkman did not inform his group that his boss could not locate any background information on Lackey. Brinkman thought it would be better to keep that tidbit of information to himself so that the rest of the gang would concentrate on their jobs and not

Lackey. Brinkman knew in his own mind though that Lackey had to earn his trust.

"What prison is he in Mr. Brinkman?" Dakota asked.

"He's in the Anamosa Penitentiary in Iowa and we're going to break him out. I'm sending four of you to do the job and I'm mixing it up this time. Dakota, Johnny Dane, Kenny Burkley, and Cole Fletcher are heading to Iowa. Dakota and Dane, I want you two to get better acquainted with Kenny and Cole. Show them the ropes and how we all work together."

"Yes sir," Dakota responded.

"Let's look at the map on the wall and I'll lay out the plan and strategy for you guys. You four guys gather around close. I want you other guys to pay attention too."

Dakota, Dane, Kenny and Cole moved in close as they were directed so that they could hear and see what Brinkman had to say and to make sure that they didn't miss any of the instructions. The others gathered behind them. Brinkman pointed to the various locations as he spoke.

"OK men, here's the plan. The Anamosa prison is right here in east central Iowa. It's about 500 miles from Abilene. You'll be taking a train about 95% of the way to Anamosa using this route. Now listen up good. From Abilene you'll go directly to Kansas City. Then you'll transfer trains and head from Kansas City to Des Moines, Iowa. When you reach Des Moines, you'll transfer trains one more time to Cedar Rapids, right here. Now Cedar Rapids is about 25 miles southwest of Anamosa, give or take a couple of miles. There is no rail service between Cedar Rapids and Anamosa so you'll be traveling to Anamosa on horseback."

"Will we be buying our horses in Cedar Rapids?" Dakota asked.

"Good question. The answer is no, I don't want to take any chances on you not being able to find good horses up in Cedar Rapids so you'll be taking your own horses and tack on the train with you. It's somewhat inconvenient but it's the safest way to go. Of course you'll be buying a horse for Lackey up in Anamosa.

Now, the Anamosa Penitentiary is north of the Wapsie River. There's a wooden bridge going over the river right about here that you'll have to cross to get to the prison. That will be your escape route too. After you break Lackey out of prison, you'll cross the bridge again and then Dane, I want you to dynamite it. Blow it all to hell! That'll slow up the posse and the guards from the prison who will want to gun you down as opposed to bringing you back alive.

Before I talk about the route to take home after you bust Lackey out, here's some information about the Anamosa prison as I know it. The prisoners are building a limestone wall around it like the penitentiary in Jefferson City, Missouri, but they still have a ways to go. Part of the wall is still made of wood. That's the wall you can dynamite. No nitro is needed this time Dane. Cole, you'll be in charge of cutting the telegraph wires. Dakota can get you up to speed on that.

When you guys get to Anamosa, ride into town in twos about three hours apart to take away any suspicions. Of course, shack up at the same hotel. Take all the time you need to case out the prison like you always do and then, get it done. Dane, you're gonna need to take 20 sticks of dynamite with you. I already have them in a carry case for you. All of you need to make sure you take plenty of ammunition. Kenny, leave your new rifle and scope here and take one of those repeating Winchesters leaning up against the wall over there."

Brinkman then continued to point to the map as he gave his final instructions.

"Your escape route should be this. After you blow the bridge over the Wapsie River, head directly east across Iowa. Cross the Missouri River right here at Omaha, Nebraska, follow the river south to Kansas and then head southwest to Abilene. It's about a 500 mile trip and it'll take you 20 or more days to get back here. You'll have to probably trade out horses several times along the way depending on how hard you ride them. Don't ride them into the ground though so you don't get stranded in no man's land.

When you arrive in Abilene, make sure you weren't followed before you travel back here to the lodge. Here's an envelope for each of you with $500 for your expenses," Brinkman said as he passed them to Dane, Dakota, Cole, and Kenny. "Spend it wisely. Are there any questions?"

There were no questions asked so Brinkman told Rusty to fetch Chan. When Rusty came back with Chan, Brinkman asked,

"When will dinner be ready, Chan?"

"How many for dinner, sir?"

"Let's see there's…"

Dakota didn't give Brinkman time to count. He already knew the answer.

"There's twelve sir, an even dozen."

"Thanks Dakota, now Chan, what time do we eat?"

"Dinner ready in one hour, Mr. Brinkman."

"Fine then, let's have some brandy while we wait."

And so they did. Dinner was served right on time and they sat at the table for a couple of hours eating a meal fit for kings and imbibing Italian wines and some of the finest European champagnes.

Later that night, everyone bunked down in the lodge, everyone except for Brinkman. He went back to his ranch.

On Monday morning, Brinkman sent Rusty to the train depot to buy train tickets for the four traveling to Anamosa. On Tuesday morning Dakota, Dane, Kenny, and Cole loaded up their horses and saddles and boarded the train to begin their long journey to Cedar Rapids, Iowa. It was about a 475 mile trip by rail because there was no straight route by way the crow flies. It took about 24 hours to get there with all the stops in between.

They arrived in Cedar Rapids on Wednesday in the mid-morning and then Dakota and Kenny entered Anamosa on horseback at two o'clock that afternoon. Cole and Dane rode into town three hours later following Brinkman's instructions to the "T". They all stayed at the Wapsie Hotel about a quarter of a mile south of the river and less than a mile from the penitentiary. They each signed in using aliases, took their gear to their rooms, and afterwards walked their horses over to the livery stable.

Dakota contacted the other three to make arrangements to eat dinner at the same time in the hotel's quaint little restaurant but keeping in groups of two and at different tables pretending they were strangers to each other. Thick cuts of fried porterhouse steaks and potatoes were the specialty of the house. They were quite costly but not to worry, these guys had loaded pockets compliments of Brinkman.

After dinner they all met in Dakota's room upstairs to discuss their plans for the next day. It was a little chilly this time of year in east central Iowa and the insulation in this hotel left a whole bunch to be desired. So Dakota fired up the potbelly stove with a few oak logs which were stacked neatly along the wall. It was a small room but the four made do. Dakota and Cole sat on Dakota's bed facing

Dane and Kenny who pulled up chairs near the potbelly stove which was about three feet from the bed on the headboard side. Their chairs were facing Dakota and Cole. All four were trying to stay warm as they began discussing their plans to break out Lackey. Dakota took the lead.

"This is the way I see things. We're gonna split up again tomorrow. Kenny and I will go and meet with Lackey. While we're there, we'll case the joint and get a good look at everything. Dane, you and Cole check out the telegraph lines to cut. Then ride over to the prison and take a good look at the outside. We'll make plans and compare notes when we get back here tomorrow afternoon after everyone completes their mission."

"Am I gonna be the one to cut the lines?" Cole questioned.

"That's right, you heard Mr. Brinkman tell you that didn't you? You have a problem with that?" Dakota asked.

"Not at all. You gonna supply me with a ladder or do I jump 15 feet in the air and cut the wire while I'm holding on to it?"

Everyone laughed and the humor was welcomed.

"As long as you can climb about five feet up the pole, there'll be metal pegs you can grab onto and eventually step up on to get you to the wires. Hey if that little Mexican Pecos can do it, so can you."

"No problem, consider it done."

"Dane, I don't have to tell you what to look for. Check the place out tomorrow. And look over that bridge that you have to blow up. You can give us your recommendations tomorrow when we meet. Now, I have a bottle in my saddlebags here if anyone is interested."

"Pull the cork, Dakota. We'll drink out of these glasses here," Dane said as he picked up three glasses that were on a small table next to a pitcher of water and a washbowl. "You can have the bottle."

Dakota only had enough for one round of drinks, so it was gone in a matter of minutes.

"Do you guys want to catch some breakfast tomorrow morning before we go our ways?" Dakota asked.

They all agreed that it would be a good idea and a good start to another long day. Dakota suggested that they continue to do everything in twos. In other words, Kenny and he would eat at one table and Dane and Cole would eat at another. Then they would split up and go about their duties.

Well when that was settled, everyone went back to their rooms and hit the sack and got some shut-eye. It was a long day for those saddle bums, so they were all pretty much tuckered out.

The next morning came by all too soon to suit the four outlaws. They met for breakfast in twos. Cole and Kenny, who sat at different tables, just had coffee, and biscuits and gravy. Their nerves got the best of them.

However, this was old hat for Dane and Dakota. Dane filled up his plate with a stack of flapjacks smothered in maple syrup and Dakota loaded his with scrambled eggs, biscuits and gravy, grits, bacon, and a couple of pork sausage patties. They only sat there for about twenty-five minutes before they headed over to the livery stable, again in twos, to saddle up and ride.

While Dane and Cole searched out the telegraph lines, Dakota and Kenny rode over to the penitentiary and were shocked at what they saw. Oh Mr. Brinkman was correct about the half stone and half wood wall around the courtyard alright. However, he didn't tell them what the prison itself looked like, it was doubtful Mr. Brinkman knew himself.

They pulled up their reins and stopped their horses about 50 yards in front of the penitentiary.

"My word," Kenny said "that place looks like a medieval castle."

"More like a dungeon," Dakota responded.

"How are we gonna break into that place?" Kenny asked.

"We're not, we're gonna blow those wooden walls over there wide open when Lackey is in the courtyard. That'll be our escape hatch."

"How are we gonna get Lackey into the courtyard?"

"Leave it up to me," Dakota said. "When we go into the courtyard, here's what I want you to do. Without being real obvious, look around and try to figure out where the guards are stationed."

They both rode up to the gate, dismounted, hitched their horses to one of the six hitching rails in front of the prison, and then walked over to the gate. The gate, which was wide enough for a wagon to go through, was wide open now. However, it would close when the prisoners were allowed in the courtyard during visiting hours and recreational times. There was a sign out front listing the visiting hours. They were 9:00 a.m. to 11:00 a.m. and 2:00 p.m. to 4:00 p.m.

The prison guard, armed with a repeating rifle, who was standing at the open gate, asked the two to state their business. A guard in the tower to the right of the gate was looking down at the two. He was holding what appeared to be a Henry rifle. Dakota recognized it by the gold plate at the breech which reflected the morning sun. That meant he most likely had sixteen bullets in the barrel length magazine.

There was something precariously different about this entrance though. Unlike the other penitentiaries they had dealings with in the past, this prison had a guard tower on both sides of the gate. Dakota looked up at the second tower on the left and saw that the guard was standing next to a Gatling gun. He saw the barrel of the rapid-fire gun protruding out about one foot from the wall of the tower. Dakota almost had an immediate coronary on the spot.

"We are here to see your prisoner Frank Lackey," Dakota said.

When the guard asked their names, Dakota gave him their aliases. Since it was 8:55 and only five minutes from visiting hours, the guard allowed them to enter and then two other guards leaned their rifles up against the limestone wall and closed the double wooden gate. Dakota was very observant on the number of guards he saw inside and around the gate area.

The guard led them to a visiting area in the courtyard and told them to "sit down on those benches over there," as he pointed to the left side of the courtyard. So they did while they waited for another guard to bring Lackey out. Even though it was cold outside, Kenny was sweating profusely and turning white as a ghost.

"Being in here gives me the creeps," Kenny said.

"Relax, we're just here visiting. Now clear your mind so you don't screw things up for us."

A guard brought Lackey out with two other prisoners who also had visitors. Lackey waited a few seconds. Once he saw who the other two prisoners were walking to, he knew who came to see him. He walked over to Dakota and Kenny and asked,

"Are you the ones who wanted to see me?"

"That's right," Dakota said as he introduced Kenny and himself.

"What do you want with me?"

"How would you like to be broken out of this medieval looking dungeon and earn yourself about $100,000, and get $3,000 just for joining up with us?"

"Say, what kind of sham is this?"

"It's no sham," Dakota said convincingly. "Are you interested or not?"

"Tell me more," Lackey insisted.

"I can't tell you much more unless you agree to be broken out and the breakout is successful. All I can tell you is that my boss likes your qualifications and wants you on our team."

"How am I gonna earn the $100,000 you talked about?"

"Can't tell you that either except that it's sort of like under the table if you catch my drift."

Lackey stood up, turned his back toward Dakota and Kenny and appeared to be thinking about an answer. Dakota and Kenny looked at each other, both wondering if Lackey was going to accept their offer. What they didn't know was that Lackey was just being melodramatic. In reality, this was the moment he was waiting for, to be broken out of prison and join up with this mysterious gang.

This was right up Lackey's alley. He loved the acting and the adventure. He was a spy during the Civil War for the Union and helped to facilitate several victories for Lincoln's Army. Getting brought into the gang was like the high he got from breaking wild mustangs when he was a teenager on his grandparents' ranch in Montana.

Lackey turned around, sat down and looked at Dakota and said, "I'm gonna trust you guys; count me in. But I'm interested to know how you're gonna break me out of here without getting all of us killed. I guess you saw that Gatling gun in that tower over there," Lackey said as he motioned with his head toward the tower on the left side of the gate.

"We saw it," Dakota said. "We'll handle it, alright."

"Well, when are you gonna break me out of here?"

"We'll be back here tomorrow and give you the plans. The breakout will probably be the day after tomorrow," Dakota said.

When Dakota and Kenny left the prison, and began riding out across the large field in front, Dane and Cole were crossing the field heading toward the direction of the prison at the same time. They just nodded at each other and rode on. Dane and Cole had already checked the telegraph wires which Cole had to cut plus they looked over the bridge Dane had to blow.

Now Dane wanted to see where the wooden walls were that he would dynamite to create an escape opening. Dane too was shocked to see a Gatling gun in one of the towers. He wondered if the Gatling gun was placed there to prevent escapes the likes they participated in. If so, was this prison more prepared when it came to preventing breakouts?

In the meantime, Dakota and Kenny searched out possible escape routes they could take after they crossed the bridge.

Later that afternoon, all four visited the saloon for a beer, Dane and Cole bellying up to the bar shooting the breeze with the barkeep, and Kenny and Dakota sitting at a table in the corner. Afterwards they walked over to the hotel and met in Dakota's room and compared notes. They all discussed what they observed in and outside of the prison and made their plans being as detailed as they felt was necessary to perform the breakout without getting themselves killed, and ensuring a clean getaway.

On the next day, Dakota and Kenny went back to the penitentiary and informed Lackey of the breakout strategy. Lackey was impressed with the length these guys went through to put together what appeared to be a workable plan.

Lackey, whose real name was Jake Nichols, had no way of communicating with Pinkerton at this point. He assumed that Pinkerton would read about the breakout in the newspapers a few days after it happened.

Dakota and Kenny had one more thing to do before the next day. They needed a covered wagon and two long ears to pull it. Plus they purchased a horse, saddle, and bridle for Lackey.

Now it was the day of the attempted breakout. They all got up early and met for breakfast around eight o'clock. Cole was told to go out and cut the telegraph wires at first light before anyone else was stirring. Dakota brought a wire cutter with him from Abilene. He carried it in his saddlebag; it belonged to Pecos.

Kenny and Dakota hitched up the mule team to the covered wagon and saddled up three horses. Dane went over to the livery stable to saddle his as well. They walked the horses and wagon over to the front of the café.

They all completed their early morning chores before eight and then met at the café for breakfast, still sitting in twos at different tables.

Unexpectedly, the town marshal and his deputy came into the café for breakfast. Kenny was the first to see them and elbowed Dakota and nodded over to the two lawmen for Dakota to see. The marshal and Dakota's eyes met and then Dakota looked down quickly and trying to be inconspicuous pulled his hat down a bit to cover his face. The marshal then whispered something to his deputy, stood up and walked out of the café. No one thought much of it until the marshal walked back in about five minutes later with a wanted poster in his hand. At this point, Dakota thought he might have been recognized. Kenny saw the poster too. Dakota whispered to him to stay calm.

The marshal then walked toward the back of the café behind Dakota. Dakota kept watch on the marshal out of the corner of his eye until he could no longer see him. He wasn't about to turn his head around. That would be too obvious. So he waited.

He didn't have to wait long though because he heard the hammer of a peacemaker click near his ear and he felt the cold steel barrel of a pistol pressed up against his head.

"Just stay where you're sitting boys and keep your hands above the table," the marshal said as he directed the order to both Dakota and Kenny. The deputy walked over and took the pistol out of Dakota's holster and picked up Kenny's rifle which was leaning up against the table.

While all of this was going down, Cole, sitting at another table with Dane, reached for his pistol but Dane wisely put his left hand on Cole's right hand to keep him from drawing.

The marshal then tossed the wanted poster in front of Dakota and said, "You are under arrest Dakota Wilson. You and your buddy here stand up and let's take a walk."

They stood up and walked out of the café, crossed the street and walked into the jailhouse. The marshal then ordered both of them into the same cell. He closed and locked the cell door and threw the ring of keys on top of his desk. While the marshal was doing that, the deputy was going through all of their wanted posters looking for one on Kenny.

In the meantime, Cole asked Dane,

"What do we do now?"

"We bust them out after I finish my breakfast, that's what."

It was still early morning and hardly no one was stirring on the street yet. After ten minutes went by, Cole and Dane calmly walked over to the marshal's office. Cole was nervous and sweating like a lost city fella in the Yuma desert, while Dane was as cool as a cucumber. When they reached the door of the jailhouse, they stormed in with their pistols drawn and caught the marshal and deputy off guard.

"What in tarnation took you so long?" Dakota asked jokingly.

"I had to finish my breakfast," Dane responded as he held his pistol on the marshal and deputy.

Cole saw the keys on the marshal's desk, grabbed them, and opened the cell door. Dakota and Kenny immediately went for their firearms.

"What do we do with these guys?" Dane asked Dakota.

"We have to move quickly. Here's the plan..."

Within ten minutes, the group of outlaws was crossing the wooden bridge over the Wapsie River and heading north toward the prison. Kenny was driving the covered wagon pulling two saddled horses, one for him and one for Lackey. The other three guys were riding behind him.

Just before they could see the prison, they stopped.

"Check your ammunition boys," Dakota said.

They removed their pistols from their holsters and twirled the cylinders to make sure every chamber was loaded. Kenny, who was toting his Winchester in his wagon and not wearing a sidearm, made sure his repeating rifle was fully loaded as well. Then Kenny jumped down from the covered wagon and ran in back, untied one of the saddled horses and handed the reins to Dane to pony. This horse was for Lackey.

Dane, Dakota and Cole were each carrying sticks of dynamite in their saddlebags and matches and cigars in their pockets. There were also three sticks in Kenny's saddlebag.

At this point, they lit up their cigars. It wasn't all about enjoying a smoke, it was about a quick and easy way of lighting a wick. Then they all reached back and took out several sticks of dynamite and meticulously stuffed them into their shirts.

Now they moved on. Dane rode to the right to approach the prison from the weakest wall, the wooden wall which was made of eight inch diameter tree trunks standing in an upright position.

Kenny came in from the left, driving the wagon parallel to the front wall about 100 yards out. Dakota and Cole rode straight up to the gate acting as if they were visitors.

When Kenny was straight out from the gate, still 100 yards away, he stopped the covered wagon, jumped to the ground and pretended like he had a dry axle causing wheel problems. As he stooped down behind the wagon on one knee to check the inside of the wheel and axle, he briefly looked up at the tower on the left and saw the Gatling gun pointed right at him. He began sweating like a dog about to be skinned alive by an Apache warrior for a band of hungry Chiricahuas at supper time.

He removed the spare wheel attached to the side of the wagon and laid it on the ground to make it appear that he needed to change wheels. Then he walked around to the other side of the wagon, opposite the prison, so that the guard in the tower couldn't see him any longer. He lifted up the canvas in the middle of the covered wagon and climbed in, sat down, picked up his rifle, cocked it, and waited for a signal. He knew who to pick off first.

As Dakota and Cole dismounted in front of the prison, they were greeted at the gate by a prison guard. Dakota knew the procedures; so he removed his gun belt and hung it from his saddle horn. Cole did the same.

Dakota told the guard that they were there to see Lackey. The guard shouted to the two guards on the inside to open the two large wooden swinging gates to let them in. When they were inside, another guard walked up to them and asked who they were there to see.

"We're here to see Frank Lackey."

"OK, I'll bring him out to the courtyard. Go wait over there by those benches and tables."

Within about five minutes, Lackey was escorted out of the penitentiary building and the guard pointed to Dakota and Cole. They all sat down at a table and Dakota introduced Lackey to Cole.

"Are you still in?" Dakota asked.

"You bet I am. What's your plan and what do you want me to do?"

"You don't have to do anything except when you see that wooden wall explode, run through the opening as fast as you can. There'll be a guy named Dane on the other side with your horse. He'll tell you what to do from there. If you're ready, so are we."

Lackey took a deep breath, paused momentarily and then said, "Let's do it."

Dakota looked around to get a fix on where each guard was located. He was going to be the one to give the first signal. He knew there was a guard out front on the other side of the gate, two on the inside and one in each tower. Dane was ready on the outside with three sticks of dynamite tied together ready to blow down the wooden wall and Kenny was in his wagon waiting for the signal too.

Dakota said once more to Lackey, "Remember, run to that wall only after it blows. Stay put till then."

Dakota and Cole then stood up. Dakota walked toward the two guards and Cole strolled toward the front door of the prison building. They were both smoking their cigars puffing hard to get a red hot ash on the tip.

"Hey guys, look at what I have under my hat," Dakota said as he got closer to the guards. The two guards walked up to him as Dakota removed his hat and pulled out Dane's double barrel derringer and shot both guards in the chest. That was the signal. Now mayhem broke out everywhere in the courtyard. It was all happening simultaneously. Kenny stood on the seat of the covered wagon, took aim, and shot the guard in the tower with the Gatling gun. Then he took out the guard standing in front of the prison. After Dakota shot the two guards by the gate, he lit a stick of dynamite and threw it up into the tower where the other guard was located. That guard didn't have a chance to even get off one shot. In the meantime, Cole lit his sticks of dynamite and threw them into the front door of the prison. The explosion brought down bricks and mortar sealing the doorway shut. Then the wooden wall exploded into hundreds of bits and pieces and created an escape hatch. That was Lackey's cue to start running toward the opening and that's exactly what he did, skirting around the tumbling tower on the right and dodging the falling debris in front of him.

After Kenny took out the guard in front of the prison, he jumped out of the wagon, untied his horse, and rode over to Dane. In the meantime Dakota and Cole ran to the front gate, opened it up, jumped on their horses and rode over to Dane as well. Lackey mounted the extra horse while Dane threw two more sticks of dynamite into the courtyard. Bullets were heard coming from the rifle of a guard who was shooting from a window on the second floor of the prison. But he was shooting at ghosts because the five were already mounted and riding hard and fast toward the bridge.

When they crossed the bridge, Dane jumped off of his horse and threw three sticks of dynamite, one right after the other onto the bridge rendering it useless.

"That's enough!" Dakota shouted. "Let's get out of here."

Dane jumped on his horse not even needing his stirrups since his adrenaline was on overload. They galloped south and then west until their horses were all lathered up.

In the meantime, six guards in the building worked their way out through the fallen stones which were blocking the front doorway and saddled up and rode to the bridge only to find it was blown up and not crossable.

The warden and his assistant walked into the courtyard and were distraught at what they witnessed: dead bodies lying around and the prison wall and one guard tower demolished.

"Go inside and send a wire to the marshal and tell him that there was a prison breakout here and tell him to round up a posse quickly," the warden said.

Standing in the courtyard, the warden looked through the open gate and saw the covered wagon out in front. He became curious and asked two guards who just came out of the building to follow him. When they arrived at the wagon, he looked inside, then reached in and pulled back a canvas and said, "Damn!"

Just then, the assistant warden came running up to him and said,

"Sir, the wires are dead."

"Yeah, and so are the marshal and his deputy in the wagon."

CHAPTER EIGHT:

Vigilante Revenge

It appeared once again that the outlaws got another clean getaway. The town of Anamosa was in a state of shock with their marshal and deputy being murdered and their maximum security penitentiary being breached in such an easy but horrid fashion.

Dakota and his gang followed the escape route suggested by Brinkman. They rode west across the state of Iowa, took a ferry across the Missouri River at Omaha and followed the river south to Kansas and then over to Abilene. Oh it was a long trip back to the lodge alright, roughly about 500 miles. Most of the guys were used to riding horseback for long distances but for ole Lackey, well the backache and saddle sores started kicking in around Omaha. However, he didn't dare let on about the pain lest he be taken for a greenhorn of sorts.

On the way back, they swapped out horses during the night with ranches in remote locations, plus they broke into several small town general stores for food and clothing. It was every bit of 500 miles traveling back to Abilene. They made it in about 20 days.

Within that time period they surmised that the word of the breakout was all over the country by now. They were right. It was published in all the newspapers and it was making top headlines. When Pinkerton read about it in the Chicago Tribune, the first thing that came to his mind was, "They took the bait." What were his feelings about the dead guards? Well that was a warranted sacrifice for a just cause. If he felt that way, then the question was, did Pinkerton believe the end justified the means? Later, some people would believe he did. Pinkerton denied it.

Brinkman took the bait alright. But it wasn't the hook, line, and sinker. Brinkman and his boss could not find any background information on Lackey. Not taking any chances, Brinkman talked to a few friendly sidewinders on his crooked payroll, outside his immediate gang. He told them to keep an eye out for any unusual activity Lackey might be involved in. He did this before the gang ever arrived back at the lodge. Brinkman learned about the successful breakout just like everyone else, through the newspapers.

It was right after dinner and dark outside when the five gang members rode up to the lodge. Rusty looked out the window to see who the night riders were.

"They're back," Rusty yelled out to everyone. Every night, for the last six days, they had anxiously waited for the four to return with their new gang member.

Pecos walked out of the lodge to greet Dakota and said, "Welcome home mi amigo. Good to see ya."

"Good to see ya too pardner."

Brinkman walked out, didn't say anything except for, "Take your horses to the barn, unsaddle them and give them some hay and grain. When you're done with that, come on in and we'll talk."

They all grabbed the reins of their horses and moseyed on over to the barn. Truth be known, they were all pretty stiff and sore.

"I take it that was Mr. Brinkman who you told me about. Is he always that friendly?" Lackey asked.

"He's always very businesslike," Dakota said. "You'll learn that about him soon enough. He also keeps a cool head. But like I told you out on the trail, cross him and he'll nail ya as fast as you can gulp down a shot glass of Tennessee rye."

After the men had unsaddled and fed their horses in the barn, Chan stopped them just before they entered the house. He told them to dust themselves off and scrape off their boots first as per instructions from Mr. Brinkman. Dakota looked at Lackey and just smiled.

Now it was time for Lackey to meet everyone in the gang. They were all standing in a circle in the main meeting room. Dakota Wilson first introduced Lackey to Mr. Brinkman. The boss then turned around, poured a brandy, passed it to Lackey and said,

"It's a pleasure to meet you. Now, I'm assuming there is no doubt in your mind that you want to join up with us, is there?"

"No sir, there is not," Lackey replied.

"I don't seem to know much about your background before you were thrown into prison in Anamosa. Oh I'm aware why you were placed behind bars, and I know all about your skills. But that's all I know."

"Yes sir that's right. I keep a low profile. It's safer that way in my business."

"Fair enough," Brinkman said. "Now, let me introduce you to everyone in the room. Meet,

Rusty Blake, he's an expert safecracker

Pecos Fransisco, he's the fastest draw south of the Red River

Bobby Burkley, professional sniper and Kenny's brother

Doctor Eddie Hawkens, professional medical doctor and loves to gamble

Charlie Todd, he's a professional gunslinger

Arizona Palmer, professional gunslinger

The Kansas Kid, another professional gunslinger

And you met the rest but I'll introduce them and their qualifications in case they didn't tell you about themselves:

This is,
Dakota Wilson, fastest gun this side of the Red River

Johnny Dane, explosives expert specializing in dynamite and nitro

Kenny Burkley, professional sniper and Bobby's brother

Cole Fletcher, professional gunslinger and

I'm Mr. Brinkman, brains of this outfit and president of the bank in town."

"You don't say," Lackey said without thinking.

"Yes, I do say. And men, this gentleman is Frank Lackey, gunslinger, bank robber, and telegraph operator," Brinkman said as he addressed all of the men in the room.

"And you gentlemen are my gang of eleven who I intend to make rich beyond your wildest dreams. Rusty, give Lackey his envelope and his new pistol."

Rusty walked over to the unlocked safe, opened the door and took out an envelope and a holstered nickel plated, pearl handled .45 Colt peacemaker. Then he turned around and walked them over to Lackey. Lackey began smiling as did everyone else in the room. Lackey gave the envelope to Dakota to hold for a moment while he strapped on his gun belt. Then he drew a couple of times, pretty fast mind you, and got some oohs and aahs from the gang as they all smiled and laughed. He then reached for his envelope and looked inside and counted the bills. It was $3,000 just like Dakota promised.

When they were finished with all of the introductions and small talk, Dakota showed Lackey where he would bunk and then Chan warmed up some food for the riders.

Brinkman's orders to the group were to hang around the lodge. They could only go to town to visit the general store for necessities but they were to stay out of the saloon. If they wanted to gamble and drink, they could do it right there in their hideout.

Rusty was still working at the bank and secretly visiting Kathleen during his lunch breaks and immediately after work. They were really getting sweet on each other. In fact, romance was in the air. The only problem was that if Brinkman found out about it, Rusty's life would be in peril; and he knew it.

After about six days, Mr. Brinkman called the group together not one day too soon before these guys were getting irritable and restless just sitting around playing cards and drinking all day.

It was Saturday afternoon, October 15th. The bank in Abilene closed at noon on Saturdays so Brinkman held his group meeting at two o'clock. Everyone was in the meeting room either sitting on chairs and couches or standing up. They were all facing Brinkman who was sitting on the top of the front side of his desk.

"Gentlemen, the time has come. Your expertise is about to be put to good use. My plans are to hit three locations. You will hear about one today. I will let you know about the other two when the time is right.

Our first target is the Mercantile Bank in Sedalia, Missouri. My plan will be to hit that bank on Monday morning, October 31st when the bank opens at nine o'clock. That bank safe is bulging with old money from the cattle days. It's loaded with several hundred thousand dollars in gold certificates and greenbacks."

Brinkman spent two hours mapping out the strategy with his gang. He went into great detail. Lackey was impressed with all the legwork Brinkman did on this project. He paid close attention to every single detail because he was the one who had to somehow get an accurate message to Allan Pinkerton to ambush this gang in Sedalia.

"That's the plan gentlemen. You'll be leaving here on two separate trains to Sedalia on October 26th and 27th. You'll be taking your horses with you. I'll meet you at the train station with your tickets when the time comes. In the meantime, you can go to town but stay out of trouble and always come the long way back to the lodge and for everyone's sake, make sure you aren't followed."

Lackey had the entire plan now and somehow he needed to get to the telegraph office between now and October 25th to send a wire to Pinkerton. But the opportunities came and went so many times. He just couldn't find the right time to sneak into the telegraph office without being spotted. As the days seemed to fly by, time was running out.

But then, on October 21st, he caught a break. He was the only one going to town that morning. Four of the guys were re-shoeing their horses while the others were waiting until after lunch to hit the saloon that afternoon.

Lackey quickly saddled up his horse and galloped into town. He hitched his horse about three buildings down and then walked at a fast clip to the telegraph office. When he entered he told the telegraph operator that he had a private message that he wanted to send himself. The telegraph operator said, "Be my guest fella," as he got up from his desk and moved aside. So Lackey sat down and started clicking away in Morse code. While Lackey was sending a message to Pinkerton about the robbery in Sedalia, the telegraph operator sat down at another desk nearby making some notes. Lackey looked over at him a couple of times but the operator had his head down just writing away.

There, he was finished. What a relief. Lackey smiled and was proud of himself for getting the job done.

"What do I owe you?" Lackey asked.

"From what I could hear, about two bits."

Lackey paid his bill then slowly walked out onto the boardwalk. He stopped, looked down the street to the left and then to the right. The coast was clear. He felt an enormous sense of accomplishment when he walked to his horse and rode back to the lodge. A big weight was lifted from his shoulders.

Within an hour, Allan Pinkerton received the message. Catching these infamous outlaws in the act was his goal because he knew that a jury would surely find them guilty and a judge would send all of these hardened criminals up the proverbial river for the rest of their lives. And as for Pinkerton, well he would be basking in his own fame and glory.

Pinkerton had his aide summon the agents who he ordered to stay in Chicago for this very purpose. In a matter of two hours, he had fifteen agents in his office. He read them the telegram and he spelled out his plans.

The aide had also sent for a railroad executive. He was sitting in Pinkerton's reception room waiting for Pinkerton to finish his meeting with his agents. When the meeting was concluded, Pinkerton asked the railroad executive to come in while all the other agents were leaving. The railroad man walked in and began sitting down.

"You don't need to sit down. This will only take a second," Pinkerton said.

"OK, what's up?"

"It's time. Have my train ready to go to Sedalia, Missouri on October 23rd at 9:00 in the morning."

"No problem, it will be ready for you sir."

And it was. Pinkerton's plan was to get in town a few days before he figured the gang would arrive, and check the place out. On the morning of the 23rd, Pinkerton and his fifteen agents, with their firearms and ammunition, loaded their saddled horses into two railroad cars and then boarded the special train for Sedalia.

On October 26th the first group of Brinkman's outlaws arrived at the Abilene station. Dakota was in this first group as was Rusty. Brinkman met them there that morning as he promised. Only he shocked everyone when he pulled Dakota aside and talked to him in private for several minutes before Brinkman turned and left for his bank without saying a word to anyone else.

"What's up?" Rusty asked.

"We're going back to the lodge," Dakota said, "and no one can leave the hideout for any reason until next Monday afternoon."

Well this didn't sit well with the gang. They had already experienced being cooped up for days and didn't want any more of it. However, they followed Brinkman's orders because they knew the consequences if they did not.

When they all rode back to the lodge, Dakota gathered the rest of the gang together and gave them Brinkman's message. Nobody was happy with the revelation. Lackey was worried about it more than anyone else. This piece of news had him sweating bullets. He wondered if the plan was changed because somehow Brinkman found out about the telegram he sent to Pinkerton. This could be the worst predicament he had ever been in. Only time would tell.

As the days went by, Lackey became more confident that he was not the reason for cancelling the heist in Sedalia. Otherwise, Brinkman would have surely done something before now.

Brinkman never came out to the lodge during the waiting game. One of the things Brinkman told Dakota at the train depot was to come out to his ranch on Sunday for instructions. He did and Brinkman told him to have everyone in the meeting room at 8:00 sharp on Monday morning.

The suspense was agonizing. No one knew what was going on, not even Dakota. He was just the messenger.

Brinkman arrived at the lodge at 7:55 Monday morning and everyone was already in the room anxiously waiting to hear what Brinkman had to say. Brinkman walked behind his desk, opened up his top drawer but did not remove anything from it. Then he said,

"Gentlemen, right at this moment, Allan Pinkerton and his agents are in Sedalia, Missouri, hiding on rooftops, behind wagons, near windows and who knows where else with the intention of gunning all of you down in cold blood as you walk out of the bank with the loot. Luckily, you're dodging those bullets today."

Well the mumbling began and Dakota asked, "How in the hell did he find out about it?"

Now Nichols knew for sure he had been made and his palms were sweating so bad he began wiping them on his pants legs. He began thinking about his beautiful wife and two lovely daughters and began getting weak in his knees.

Brinkman reached inside his shirt pocket underneath his suit coat and pulled out a piece of paper. Nichols now knew the telegraph operator was as crooked as all the rest.

"Let me read a telegram that was sent to none other than Allan Pinkerton in Chicago."

The gang began looking at one another and no one could figure out what was going on. Although Rusty noticed that Lackey was acting quite peculiar.

"Alan Pinkerton
Chicago, Illinois
Bring at least 15 agents to Sedalia, Missouri. Gang of professional outlaws
will hit bank on Monday morning at 9:00 on October 31.
Jake Nichols."

"Who is this Jake Nichols?" Dakota asked.

Brinkman reached into the open drawer, pulled out a pistol and pointed it at the traitor and said, "Do you want to tell them or do you want me to do the honors Frank Lackey, or should I say Agent Jake Nichols?"

The charade was over for Nichols. Everyone was shocked at the disclosure and just stood there in disbelief.

Dakota grabbed Nichols' arms from behind and had him in an armlock.

"You set us up and could have gotten us killed!" Dane shouted as he raised and pulled back his fist to punch Nichols in his face. Brinkman reached over and stopped the punch and said, "Back off." Then Brinkman walked in front of Nichols and pistol-whipped him right across the face leaving a large gash in Nichols' cheek. The force of the blow knocked both him and Dakota back about two feet. Nichols tried to take it like a man but he could taste his blood in his mouth.

"Do you want me to take him out back down by the river?" The Kansas Kid asked.

"No, I have a better idea. I'm taking him into the marshal's office," Brinkman said.

"What, are you crazy?" Dane asked.

"Dane, didn't I tell you to never question my decisions?"

"Yes sir. I just don't understand."

"When I leave, Dakota will explain it to all of you."

Pecos tied Nichols' hands behind his back, walked him outside and then helped Nichols up on his horse after the Kansas Kid saddled up three horses: one for Brinkman, one for Nichols and one for himself. Nichols thought that something sinister was up. After all, why would a criminal boss take a Pinkerton agent to a town marshal?

After Dakota and the gang watched the three ride off, Dakota explained to the remaining gang members that the marshal was on Brinkman's payroll but the deputy was not. Somehow this didn't surprise anyone.

When the three arrived in town, Brinkman ordered the Kid to stay outside with Nichols until he told him to come in. Brinkman wasn't sure if the deputy was with the marshal or not. If he was, there might be a problem. If he wasn't, then things would be OK. Brinkman dismounted, tied the reins to the hitching rail and then walked into the jailhouse. The Kid and Nichols were still astride their horses.

Unfortunately, the deputy was with the marshal. Brinkman had to think fast on his feet. But he was good at that.

"Marshal, I have good news for you. One of my ranch hands tracked down Jeff Porter's killer. His name is Jake Nichols. We have two witnesses that saw him do it. I have him outside being guarded by my ranch foreman."

Obviously, the marshal knew that this story was as false as someone swearing that he witnessed the defeat of the Mexicans by the Texans at the Alamo. However, the deputy believed every bit of it.

"By gosh, that's great," the deputy acknowledged.

"Well bring that murderer in," the marshal demanded.

Brinkman went back outside and helped Nichols off his horse and told the Kid to stay put. Brinkman shoved Nichols through the open doorway and said, "Here he is marshal."

"So you're the scum who killed Mr. Porter," the deputy said.

"What, are you crazy? I didn't kill anyone. I'm a Pinkerton agent."

The marshal told the deputy to put him in a cell. While the deputy was doing that, the marshal looked at Brinkman to tacitly ascertain if this guy was telling the truth about being an agent. Brinkman nodded his head yes. The marshal sighed with disappointment knowing now that he had a bigger problem on his hands.

When the deputy slammed the cell door and locked it, Nichols yelled at the marshal,

"Marshal, I'm a Pinkerton agent, I tell you. I'm a plant. Brinkman and his gang are the criminals. He's got you and this whole town buffaloed."

Well now the deputy was really confused. Brinkman could see it on his face.

"He's lying," Brinkman said, "can't you see that?"

The deputy started walking toward the door.

"Where are you going?" The marshal asked.

The deputy turned around and said, "I know how to settle this real quick. I'm going over to the telegraph office and send Mr. Pinkerton a telegram and ask him if Nichols' story is true."

Just then the marshal drew his pistol, pointed it at the deputy and said, "I can't let you do that son." The deputy couldn't believe his ears.

Brinkman walked over to the deputy and took the pistol out of his holster. The deputy was dumbfounded to find out that Brinkman and the marshal were both no good and in cahoots. At that point too, Nichols knew as well that both the marshal and Brinkman were working together and that his own life was probably not worth a plugged nickel.

"What do we do now?" The marshal asked Brinkman.

"Keep your gun on the deputy till I get back."

Brinkman went outside and talked to the Kansas Kid and gave him orders. He was out there at least five minutes giving more instructions than just for the immediate problem at hand. Then he went back inside and tied the deputy's hands behind him and escorted him to the back door where the Kid was waiting for him with a horse. Brinkman helped the deputy onto his horse. The deputy knew what was going on as did Nichols.

"You're not going to get away with this," the deputy said to Brinkman.

"I just did," Brinkman replied. "By the way deputy, don't fret none. We'll tell your fiancé you got cold feet and left town. She'll understand. Now get him out of here Kid."

Brinkman then went back into the jailhouse and told the marshal to spread the word around town that Porter's killer had been captured. "Get them stirred up real good," Brinkman said. Before he left the jailhouse, Brinkman gave the marshal one final set of instructions. Nichols could not make out what Brinkman was telling the marshal but he was sure Brinkman was up to no good and he surmised that he was probably the focal point of the discussion.

After the Kansas Kid took care of business and disposed of the deputy, he rode back and gathered the gang together and told them about the incident at the jailhouse. Then he informed them that he, Charlie Todd, Arizona Palmer, Cole Fletcher, and Bobby Burkley had one more thing to take care of. He mentioned that what they needed for their next job was in an old wooden grain bin in the loft of the barn.

In the meantime when Kathleen heard the good news about her boss's killer being caught, she ran over to the bank to inform Rusty and her father.

"Rusty, did you hear the good news? They caught Mr. Porter's killer."

Rusty looked up as if he was in another world and said with absolutely no enthusiasm in his voice, "Uhh, what? Oh yeah, I heard. That's good news."

"Well I thought you would have showed a little more emotion than that," Kathleen said.

"I'm sorry Kathleen; my mind was in another place. That is good news."

Kathleen then went into her father's office and informed him. He told her that he already knew about it.

Later that day after sundown, and well into the late evening hours, the marshal went over to the cell and said, "Well Mr. Pinkerton agent, I'm going home now. It's been a long day. You'll be here by yourself tonight. Normally the deputy stays with the prisoners overnight, but for some reason he left town and I don't know if he's ever coming back."

The marshal walked over to behind his desk, opened the top drawer with his left hand, reached into it with his right hand, took out the ring of cell keys and tossed them on his desk. As he went toward the door, he turned back around and said, "You have a good night sleep now, ya hear?"

When the marshal exited the jailhouse, he did something peculiar. He left the door cracked slightly ajar.

About an hour later, here they came, five hooded vigilantes, four on horseback carrying torches and one driving a one horse buckboard. They stopped in front of the jailhouse and waited while one of the hooded vigilantes ran over to the saloon, went through the swinging doors and yelled, "Come on boys, we're hanging Porter's killer down by the river." The crowd of about fifteen townspeople and saddle bums who were all liquored up, hooted and hollered and followed the vigilante to the jailhouse.

Three of the vigilantes handed off their torches, stormed the jailhouse, opened the cell door and knocked Nichols to the floor. Nichols struggled for dear life, swinging his arms wildly and kicking his feet but to no avail. They pinned him to the floor, hog-tied him, and gagged him with one of the vigilante's filthy bandannas.

They then picked Nichols up off the floor, carried him outside, and threw him into the back of the buckboard. The lynch mob then got on their horses and they all rode down to the Smoky Hill River. When they reached the hanging tree on the banks of the river, the hooded vigilante driving the wagon, positioned it so that the buckboard was placed right underneath a thick branch. Three of the hooded vigilantes stayed on their horses with their torches. They were surrounded by the rest of the mob. One of the vigilantes then handed off his torch, jumped off his horse and then climbed into the back of the wagon and threw a rope with a hangman's knot over the branch. Then another mob member tied the other end around the tree trunk. Now a couple more of the men climbed into the back of the wagon while the vigilante took out a knife and cut the rope that ran from Nichols' hands to his feet so that they could stand him up and put the noose around his neck. It all happened so quickly. Within seconds, the wagon pulled away and Nichols was swinging from the cottonwood tree.

The crowd became very quiet as Nichols expired. Then the mob all rode back to town except for the vigilantes. The Kansas Kid removed his hood, took out his knife, cut the rope, and Nichols' lifeless body fell and hit the ground hard. The Kansas Kid removed the noose and he and Charlie Todd threw the dead body into the swift flowing Smoky Hill River.

"Oh if that Smoky Hill River could talk."

CHAPTER NINE:

The Northfield Surprise

A week went by, and then two weeks. Allan Pinkerton held out hope that he would be contacted again by agent Nichols, but he wasn't. He waited for some type of newspaper article announcing the discovery of an unidentified body. But that never came either.

Kathleen Brinkman, as did the entire town, found out about the vigilante lynching the very next day but her father, Mr. Brinkman, convinced her not to run an article in the newspaper. He told her that it would give the town a black mark. She agreed.

Now Pinkerton feared the worst. Hope turned into despair and then despair turned into anger. He figured that something went horribly wrong and that he lost another agent. He was now back at square one. The heart wrenching part of it all though was that he had to once again inform someone that her husband was lost in the line of duty.

Brinkman still had a plan which included three jobs. He now called his gang "Brinkman's Professionals" playing off the telegram that Nichols sent to Pinkerton.

Roughly three days after the hanging of Nichols, Brinkman gathered his gang together once more in the meeting room of the lodge to go over the details of their next hit. He wasted no time because the next heist was on a strict timetable.

Everyone was stunned when he mentioned that the next job would be the bank in Northfield, Minnesota. They knew all too well of the history of the James-Younger Gang and their failed attempt to rob the Northfield Bank on Thursday afternoon, September 7, 1876. They also knew that the Youngers were now all incarcerated in the Minnesota State Penitentiary at Stillwater, Minnesota and that Jesse and Frank were on the run.

Brinkman's Professionals had figured that they were up to any task, but so did the James-Younger Gang. Dakota was the only one who had the guts to question Mr. Brinkman's discretion in regards to his choice of banks.

"Sir, if Frank and Jesse couldn't successfully rob the Northfield Bank, how are we gonna do it?"

"I said once before that I did not want anyone questioning my decisions. However, because of the previous circumstances that occurred in Northfield, I can understand your concern.

The James-Younger Gang was good but they got too complacent because of all their previous successes. It was their sloppy mode of operation on that day that caused their demise.

The gang never did take care of the telegraph lines. That's why the word got out so quickly about the robbery. Subsequently, one of the several posses summoned to help were able to track down the Youngers. The James boys were lucky. They got away.

Another mistake they made was that they tried to rob the bank in broad daylight; one o'clock in the afternoon when the streets were buzzing with people. It wasn't their stupidity that got them into trouble. It was their arrogance.

Then after they robbed the bank, they shot their guns into the air like they always did at every holdup scene; they shot to scatter the crowd but the residents of Northfield shot to kill; and that's exactly what they did to two of the gang members. Everyone else in the gang was wounded except for Jesse."

"Mr. Brinkman, can I ask a question?"

"Go ahead Doc, what is it?"

"I believe everyone knows that they have a time lock on that safe up there. I know it wasn't on at the time of that robbery but the James boys thought it was. Is that something... well, I mean, I know you considered that sir."

"Tell them Rusty," Brinkman said.

"Not to worry boys, I know how to open a time lock safe. I helped build time locks when I worked for the Yale Lock Manufacturing Company."

Everyone looked at each other and sort of grinned. Yep, ole Rusty was one heck of an asset to this gang.

At this point Brinkman walked over to the bar and poured himself a short glass of brandy but did not allow his gang to do the same. Then he walked over to the large map on the wall and began laying out the plans like a general in the army mapping out his strategy for a surprise attack on their enemies.

"Gather around gentlemen and listen up. If everyone does what I say, the bank and town of Northfield won't know what hit them. So here's the deal. Our target is the Northfield Bank. Our take will be huge and worth the risk.

We will hit the bank on Friday, November 25th, the day after Thanksgiving. This will be a perfect day because nobody will be stirring in town that early after a national holiday. In case you men aren't aware of it, in '63 during the Civil War, President Lincoln is the one who declared Thanksgiving a national holiday to be celebrated on the last Thursday in November every year. So we can thank Mr. Lincoln for giving us a perfect day to pull off a huge bank heist," Brinkman said in disrespect to the President.

"Beings that it's going to be a holiday week, the hotel will be filling up fast. That's why I made reservations for everyone in advance by telegram. I gave the hotel alias last names for each of you but I used your real first names."

At this point, Brinkman gave everyone their aliases and warned them that if anyone forgot it while signing into the hotel, it could jeopardize the whole mission by creating suspicion.

"You will arrive in town by train in specific groups on different days. The first group will be made up of Kenny, Bobby, Dakota and Cole. You four will arrive in Northfield on Monday, November 22nd. Here are your train tickets," Brinkman said as he handed each one an envelope.

"Group two will be made up of Pecos, Charlie, Rusty, and Johnny Dane. You four will arrive in town on Tuesday, November 23rd." Brinkman then handed group two their tickets.

"Lastly, group three will be made up of the Kid, Arizona, and Doc. You three will arrive in town on Wednesday, November 24th. Here are your tickets."

At this point Brinkman gave them time to open up their envelopes to see when they would be catching the train at the Abilene station.

"By the way gentlemen, while you're looking at your tickets, I'll remind you that you'll be taking your horses on the train. If you're interested in the route, look at the map here."

Brinkman pointed at the map as he told them the route the train would travel. "The train will take you from Abilene to Kansas City. This is the only place where you will have to transfer trains. From Kansas City, you'll go right up through the center of Iowa. There'll be a stop in Des Moines, right here. You'll stay aboard. They'll be picking up passengers traveling to Minnesota. There's a few other quick passenger stops in smaller towns along the way as well before you reach Northfield which is right here. Are there any questions at this point?"

No one had any questions. So Brinkman asked the men to follow him to his desk where he had laid out a highly detailed map of the town of Northfield. It covered his entire desktop. He talked about the important areas as he pointed to specific locations.

"Gentlemen, this is the layout of Northfield. The bank is located right at the corner of Division and 4th Streets. The hotel that you'll be staying at is directly across the street from the bank, right here. The marshal's office is on the other side of town, down here. The rest of Division Street is filled with various shops.

Dane, the bridge you'll be blowing up is this one west of town. It's on the main road leaving Northfield. It crosses the Cannon River which runs north to south right here. Blow that bridge and no one will be able to follow you out of town. It goes without saying; don't blow it until everyone is across.

OK, here are the timetables and everyone's responsibilities.

Cole, you will be cutting the telegraph wires after dark on Thanksgiving Day. Nobody will notice them being down until Friday at nine o'clock in the morning when the telegraph office opens. Pecos, you go with him.

Everyone needs to have their horses saddled-up by seven o'clock Friday morning. The hotel has stables in back of their building for the guests so that won't be a problem.

Kenny and Bobby, you two will be looking out the windows of your second story rooms toward the bank starting at 7:45 Friday morning. Don't let anyone see you. Have your rifles loaded and ready for action. But don't use them unless something goes wrong and one of our men's life is in danger. If so, then shoot to kill.

The president of the bank is always the first one to arrive each morning. It's like clockwork. He opens the front door at 8:00 then locks it behind him. His office manager arrives at 8:50 and his tellers at 8:55. The bank opens at 9:00.

Now, here's the most critical part. Seven of you will ride to the back of the bank, two groups of twos and one group of three. The first group will be the Kid and Cole. You two are going to be the guards in back and hold the horses for everyone. I want you two to arrive at 7:15. The second group will be the group of three: Rusty, Dakota and Pecos. You three will arrive at 7:30. Rusty, you need to pick the lock on the back door, then you three go inside. The last group will be Charlie and Arizona. You two will arrive at 7:45 and go directly inside the bank as well.

When you are all inside the bank, hide behind the tellers' counter and put on your bandannas to keep your faces hidden and pull down your hats too. I don't want anyone to be identified.

When the president arrives and locks himself in, I want Charlie and Arizona to grab him and tie him up in a chair and gag him. If anyone harms him, you will pay the price. Make sure the chair is positioned so he can see Rusty open the lock. I wish I could see the look on his face when the safe door pops open.

When Rusty pulls the vault door open, Dakota will give you the orders. Follow them closely and I warn you, do not second guess him.

Once you get back on your horses, ride down the street and cross the bridge. Kenny and Bobby, as soon as you see the men riding out, leave the hotel and get on your horses. Dane, blow that bridge all to hell once everyone crosses."

"I haven't heard my name mentioned yet, Mr. Brinkman. Where do you want me to be?" Doc asked.

"I want you to hang out with Dane on the west side of the bridge. Are there any other questions? If you have any, ask them now."

"What's the plan after everyone crosses the bridge?" Rusty asked.

"You are going to split up and head back to Abilene in the original groups you were in when you went to Northfield."

"It's a long ride back to Abilene on horseback sir," the Kid commented.

"That's right, about 550 miles. That's why I want all of you to follow these instructions. Let's walk back over to the map again and I'll show you your routes back to Abilene."

The men followed Brinkman back over to the wall map and Brinkman gave them their routes as he pointed out their paths.

"Pecos, Charlie, Rusty, and Dane, I want you four to ride southwest to Sioux Falls and catch a train there to Abilene. Sioux Falls is right here just inside the Dakota Territory.

Kenny, Bobby, Dakota, and Cole, you men ride hard to Omaha right here: pick up your train there.

Kid, Arizona, and Doc, you catch your train in Des Moines.

All of you will be buying your tickets at those depots so take extra money along. Now, that's all I have unless there are any more questions."

"I have one sir."

"What is it Charlie?"

"Who's toting the money back?"

"Dakota will let you know about that when the time is right," Mr. Brinkman responded. "Now, I'm going back into town. I have some business to take care of. Dakota, make sure everybody understands their role in the raid. Go over all the parts several times men until you know them in your sleep. I'll leave the Northfield map on my desk in case anyone wants to review it. Remember, plan on taking plenty of money and ammunition with you."

As the days flew by and Thanksgiving was just a week away, Kathleen met her father for lunch in the Cattlemen's Café which was down the street from the bank but right across the street from the newspaper building. They sat at a small square table near the large plate glass window. After they placed their order and were both drinking their coffee, Kathleen asked Brinkman,

"What time are you coming over to my house for Thanksgiving dinner, father?"

"What time do you want me there?"

"Let's eat at five o'clock. So why don't you come over at four."

"I'll be there right on time. You have a strange look on your face, Kathleen. Is there something else you have on your mind that you want to ask me?"

"Well yes there is father. I know how protective you've been of me since you ran my husband out of town but I think I need to tell you that I may have found someone special. And I would like to invite him to our Thanksgiving dinner as well."

"Really, what's his name?"

"Actually father, you already know him. In fact, he works for you. His name is Rusty Blake."

Brinkman was in the middle of sipping coffee when Kathleen surprised him with that little tidbit. In fact he almost choked on his Arbuckle's. Brinkman stared out the window a piece. He remembered explicitly that he told Rusty in no uncertain terms to stay away from his daughter but unbeknownst to him, Rusty was going around his back.

"Well father, is it OK?"

"Uh, I guess so dear. Why sure it is; he'll be a great dinner guest. He's a very nice young man," Brinkman said as he lied straight up. Inside, his blood was boiling like the belly of a steam engine because Rusty did not listen to his command or warning.

"I have a meeting with him right after lunch so you can ask him later this afternoon."

Kathleen's eyes lit up like a Christmas tree. She couldn't wait to ask Rusty to her Thanksgiving dinner. Across the very same table, Mr. Brinkman was thinking that he couldn't wait to get his hands on Rusty.

After lunch, they both went back to their offices. Kathleen had a new bounce in her step as she walked across the street to the newspaper building. When Mr. Brinkman reached his place of business, he stormed into the bank, and said,

"Rusty, I want to see you in my office right now."

Rusty had no idea what was upsetting Mr. Brinkman so. There was no way Brinkman knew about him and Kathleen. At least that's what he thought before he entered the lion's den. Brinkman's 6'4" body towered over Rusty's 5'8" thin frame. Rusty walked into Brinkman's office and then closed the door behind him. Brinkman cooled himself off some before he spoke and then he said,

"You disappoint me son. I thought you were the one person in my gang I could trust. Didn't I warn you about getting close to Kathleen?"

"Yes sir you did. Does that mean you're gonna have the Kid take me behind the lodge and dump me in the river?"

"That's what I ought to do. But I won't. I like you Rusty. I almost like you like you were my own son. You're a good kid but you're a criminal just like the rest of us and I was hoping for someone better for Kathleen."

Brinkman then sat down at his rolltop desk and removed a cigar from his top drawer, struck a match, lit it and puffed until he had a good red hot ash on the tip. He then stood up, looked at Rusty and asked,

"Do you have feelings for Kathleen?"

"Yes sir I do and I believe she has taken a fancy to me too."

"Yes, I saw that today at lunch."

"You did? What did she say, Mr. Brinkman?"

"She's going to ask you to be a guest at our Thanksgiving dinner next week. Obviously, you will have to turn her down because you'll be in Northfield. When she offers you the invitation, I want you to tell her you are visiting your family in Des Moines. If she starts quizzing you about your family, make up some harebrained story.

Look, after the Northfield deal, there will be only two more hits. But those next two will be where the big money is. If you love Kathleen, take her away from here, maybe to say, San Francisco. Tell her you inherited the money, but you must never tell her about me, do you understand?"

"Yes sir, I do, and thank you sir. Can I go back to work now?"

"Go ahead, get out of here," Brinkman said as he waved him off with his cigar in hand.

Later that afternoon, Kathleen was disappointed when Rusty told her he had other plans for the Thanksgiving holiday, but he was looking forward to being with her when he returned.

The week before the raid on Northfield went by fairly fast for the gang. Even though they were considered by some as the fastest guns and meanest hombres in the West, they couldn't help but to think that the James-Younger Gang was thought of in the same way. They even talked about it amongst themselves when a few of them chanced their luck playing a few hands of five card draw. They also talked about how the townspeople all pitched in and filled the Youngers full of holes. Oh the Youngers survived alright but they were now caged up like animals behind steel bars in a Minnesota prison, doing time for their failed crime.

Kenny, Bobby, Dakota, and Cole were the first group to pack their things for the trip up north. They shook hands with everyone, and then headed to the Abilene Train Depot with saddlebags full of extra ammunition, and toting small traveling bags for extra clothing. The train left the depot right on time, at one o'clock Sunday afternoon, November 21st. The brothers, Kenny and Bobby, sat together on one side of the aisle and Cole and Dakota sat directly across the aisle. The weather outside was bone-chilling and cloudy. The inside of the passenger car was dark and cold as well.

For the first several miles, Bobby just stared out the window. Then he turned and asked Kenny,

"How do you feel about this job?"

"What do you mean?"

"I mean do you think we have a chance of pulling this thing off?"

"Let me put it this way brother Bobby, if it was anybody else other than Brinkman putting together the strategy, I don't think we would. This guy really knows how to put together a plan. I've never seen so much detail."

"Yeah, I know." Bobby then offered up this question, "But doesn't it make you wonder? I mean, where do you think he gets all of his information from?"

"You know Bobby, I was wondering that myself. I'm beginning to think Brinkman belongs to a bigger crime organization than what we know."

Bobby looked back out the window at the countryside whizzing by, thought about it and said to Kenny, "Look, as long as we do our job and get our share of the loot, I don't really care how many associates or bosses we have in this organization or even how big it is. When you think about it, it's not so bad having someone else being the brains and doing all the legwork for us. After all, we get to do what we do best, be snipers and we even get paid for it."

The brothers looked at each other and laughed.

On the other side of the aisle Cole and Dakota were getting better acquainted. Dakota asked Cole how he met up with the Kansas Kid.

"Before we met I understand that the Kid was wanted for knocking over a stagecoach south of Deadwood. He was captured by a deputy outside of town. He escaped but the deputy never made it back to town if you know what I mean.

It all started about six years ago. Arizona, Charlie, and I grew up in the same town together and it seems like we were always in trouble. We sort of thrived on it. The Kansas Kid was passing through our town and heard about us. He asked if we wanted to get into the backside of the cattle business. We could use the money so we said yes. To make a long story short, we got together for a little, let's say, rebranding up in Laramie.

A rancher and three of his hands caught us in the act and the shooting began. We all jumped on our horses, all of us except Charlie. Sometimes he gets a little crazy."

"Yeah, like how?" Dakota asked.

"Well, he stood his ground like he was General Custer at the Little Bighorn and shot three of those ranchers off their horses while they were charging him and their bullets were whizzing by his body. He was just standing there laughing like a maniac daring that ranch owner to ride his way too.

Well he did. He came charging in with his pistol blazing and shot Charlie in the right shoulder. Charlie twirled around and fell to the ground. He then rode up to Charlie and aimed his pistol right at him, cocked it, and was about to finish him off with a slug to the head, when the Kid came back riding hard and fast and picked off that guy with his rifle before he had a chance to pull the trigger on Charlie. The rancher fell backwards off his horse and he was dead when his body slammed to the ground.

With four ranchers blown away and lying in the grass, we skedaddled out of their faster than a stampede of cattle spooked by a lightning strike."

"No lollygagging around ehh?" Dakota said.

"That's right. That's when we decided to split up. The Kid went one way and Charlie, Arizona and I went another way. A few years later the Kid sent a telegram to Deadwood and here we are."

"Can I ask you a question, Cole?"

"Sure, what is it?"

"Can we trust Charlie?"

"Of course we can. He just gets a little high-strung at times. But he's a good man. We're like brothers. That goes for Arizona too. We're all three like brothers and loyal to the bone."

With that, the conversation ceased for a while as everyone just stared out the window at the scenery as the train advanced northward to Minnesota.

The first train arrived in Northfield at 5:00 p.m. on Monday, November 22nd. The train depot was on the west side of the Cannon River so when they unloaded their horses from the boxcar and saddled up, they slowly rode across the very bridge Dane was instructed to blow. The clopping noise of the hooves of the four horses against the wooden floor of the old bridge was eerie. It reminded Dakota how it must have sounded when the James – Younger Gang crossed that exact same bridge just five years earlier back in '76.

The passenger cars were full so there were many more travelers heading to the hotel as well. Because of that, it was not necessary for the four to ride separately; they were just part of the crowd.

After they signed in and took care of their baggage and horses, they walked to the 4th Street Steak House Restaurant in twos. But not before both Bobby and Kenny checked out their sniper views from their second story windows. They both were looking right down on the famous Northfield Bank across the street just as Mr. Brinkman said.

At the time the four arrived, the second group consisting of Pecos, Charlie, Rusty and Dane were in transit. The train ran on the same schedule every day. The four boarded the train in Abilene at one o'clock on Monday afternoon. They arrived at 5:00 p.m. on Tuesday, November 23rd.

After dinner, Rusty, Dakota, and Pecos met in Dakota's room for a nightcap. These three were the closest of the lot. Dakota went over to the Stumble Inn Saloon that afternoon and picked up a couple bottles of his favorite "mash squeezens" as he would call it. He saw himself as somewhat of a connoisseur of fine whiskeys. His favorite brand was Old Crow. He was as elated as an Alaskan griz finding a stream full of silver salmons when he stumbled upon it in the Stumble Inn Saloon.

When he poured himself and the other two a half glass of the Kentucky bourbon to wet their parched throats, he held up his for a toast.

"We toasting to the bank robbery, mi amigo?"

"Nope, we're toasting to the only good thing that came out of the South," Dakota said jokingly. "We're toasting to Old Crow whiskey. Here's to the finest bourbon in the country. Bottoms up gentlemen." They all took their swigs and then Dakota added,

"I must tell you the story of Old Crow whiskey. There was this Scottish immigrant named Dr. James C. Crow who began distilling in the 1830's. This guy knew what he was doing. He made good whiskey for various important businessmen and sold it as "Crow". But when it aged, he called it "Old Crow". He died in 1856. The company that took over sort of changed the recipe a bit from what I gathered but there was still an overabundance of the original and that my friends is what became legendary.

Now, here's an apocryphal story I wanna tell ya about."

"A hippopotamus story?"

"No Pecos, I said an apocryphal story, you know, a mythical story. It's about Ulysses S. Grant. They say Old Crow was the drink of choice for the general. He sauced himself just about every night in his tent on the battlefield. After Shiloh, a lot of his critics went to President Lincoln and complained and charged Grant with being a drunk. Supposedly Lincoln replied, 'Gentlemen, can either of you tell me where General Grant procures his whiskey? Because, if I can find out, I will send every general in the field a barrel of it!' Here, have another swig," Dakota said as he poured the other two and himself another glass full. Dakota then got serious and said,

"I looked over the town a bit today. It's laid out just like Brinkman described. The marshal's office is down the street and I found out that he has two deputies. This morning I made it my business to be outside at eight o'clock to see if the bank president actually does arrive at that time like clockwork."

"Does he?" Rusty immediately asked.

"As sure as Dane likes to play with nitro," Dakota said. "He's an old codger, probably in his sixties. He's got that little weasel look about him like most bank presidents. Rusty, I want you to meander inside that bank tomorrow when you see it filling up with people and take a peek at that lock on the safe to make sure it's one which you're familiar with. Pecos, since you're helping Cole cut the telegraph lines, ride around the town to see where they're located. You need to get 'em all, in every direction they're goin' in.

Now before we call it a night, I just have one question for Rusty. It's a little personal. Rumor has it that you're sweet on that purty little filly, Kathleen. You do know that Brinkman says it's hands off don't you? If he found out you two are messing around, he's gonna send you down the Smoky Hill River, face down. I like you Rusty and I don't wanna see that happening to you."

"He already knows."

"And your still kickin'?" Pecos asked.

"Yep, he found out about it alright, chewed me out too, at first. But we mended fences and we're good. I just need to lay low for a while."

"Interesting," Dakota added.

"OK men, I'll see ya sometime tomorrow. Before I hit the sack, I'm goin' over to Bobby's room to make sure everything is good over there."

Pecos and Rusty went back to their rooms while Dakota went knocking on Bobby's door.

"Come in," Bobby yelled out.

"Bobby and Kenny were both sipping on some rye. Dakota nodded and walked over to the window, moved the curtain aside and looked down onto the street to make sure Bobby had a good view of the bank. He did. Dakota saw Bobby's sniper rifle leaning up against the wall by the window. He liked that. Then he asked Kenny,

"Are you right next door?"

"Yep, right where I'm supposed to be."

"Good, well stay out of trouble. I'll see ya guys tomorrow."

It was now Wednesday, November 24th, and the final train carrying the last of Brinkman's Professionals arrived right on time, 5:00 p.m. The Kansas Kid, Arizona and Doc were on that train. Dakota was hanging out in the lobby of the hotel to make sure they were all on board. They were. He pulled the Kid aside and told them to eat dinner over at the 4th Street Steak House Restaurant and then for the three to come up to his room afterwards, room 206.

At 7:30 the three came knocking on Dakota's door. Dakota opened the door and let them in. Then he looked outside of his room, down the hallway to the left and then to the right to make sure no one saw them entering his room. He told the three what he had told everyone else that the 4th Street Steak House Restaurant would be open for Thanksgiving dinner between 2:00 and 5:00. He had instructed everyone to go over there by themselves whenever they wanted to tomorrow. But the most important thing was that he was holding a meeting in his room at 10:00 p.m. Thanksgiving night to go over the plans one last time.

When the time came for the meeting, everyone walked into Dakota's room one by one making sure no guests were in the hallway at the time. While they were there and still waiting for Charlie Todd, Dakota asked Pecos,

"Did you and Cole cut down the lines?"

"Yes mi amigo, they're all down," Pecos confirmed.

"We even made sure the telegraph office was closed before we started cutting wires. That way nobody's gonna know about it until we're long gone tomorrow morning," Cole added.

It was now 10:10 and Charlie still did not show up for the meeting. Dakota was becoming quite irritated at this point. When he told everyone to be in his room at 10:00 sharp, he meant it and expected it from his professionals.

"What room is Charlie in? Does anyone know?" Dakota asked as he looked around the room at everyone and curled his top lip and showed his teeth like an angry timber wolf. No one had ever seen Dakota show his anger quite like this before.

"He's in 212," Cole said.

Dakota stormed out of the room and down the hall to room 212 and opened the door. Charlie was there alright, with a cute little brunette. They were just about to get comfortable when Dakota walked over to her, grabbed her by the arm and threw her into the hallway. Then he walked over to Charlie and was about to backhand him across the face but stopped just short of it.

"I've got a mind to beat some sense into you boy. Put on your shirt and come to the meeting room right now." Dakota walked out of the room and angrily slammed the door behind him. When he walked back into his room, the group did not say a word except for Pecos.

"Did you find him?"

"Yeah, he'll be right here."

Charlie showed up minutes later. When he entered the room, everyone looked at him as if he was a loose screw. Dakota looked at Cole as if to say, "This is the guy you said we could trust?" Cole read Dakota's look perfectly and was embarrassed as was the Kid.

Dakota thought that the best way to review the plans was to have everyone tell the group what their individual responsibilities were and the timetable they were on. Dakota's point was that if the timing wasn't perfect, they could find themselves in a pack of trouble. To Dakota's gratification, everyone had their tasks down flawlessly.

"Great, let's get this thing done on time tomorrow and get the hell out of town without a scratch on any of us. Now, leave here one at a time every two minutes and sleep well men, if you can."

And so they did. One by one they opened the door, peered down both sides of the hallway and walked quickly back to their rooms.

And then it was Friday morning, November 26th. Mr. Brinkman was staring at his pocket watch, sitting at his desk at home on his ranch and picturing in his mind the events in the present as they were supposed to unfold. He was a control artist but there was nothing he could do about the situation now. He had laid out the plans in perfect detail and now it was left up to his professionals to carry them out.

Everyone had their horses saddled up right on time at 7:00 a.m. behind the hotel. Just as Mr. Brinkman predicted, the streets were empty on this Friday after the Thanksgiving holiday, at least for now. The Kid and Cole mounted their horses and rode down 4th Street and turned left into the alley behind the bank and waited out of sight. They arrived at 7:15, right on time.

Rusty, Dakota, and Pecos then grabbed a hand full of mane, put their left boots in their stirrups, grabbed onto the right swells of their saddles and pulled themselves up on their horses. Inconspicuously they too rode down 4th Street and looked both up and down the street before they turned into the alley behind the bank. They arrived at 7:30, right on time as well.

They all dismounted and Rusty began picking the lock on the back door while the other four stood there and watched. Cole and the Kid were holding the reins of all the horses. The lock was quite rudimentary. Rusty inserted a thin metal rod into the keyhole and fiddled with it for about two minutes and then it clicked and he turned the knob and pushed the door open. He looked up at Dakota and smiled but didn't say a word. Dakota, Pecos and Rusty walked into the bank.

At exactly 7:45, Charlie and Arizona rode to the back of the bank and dismounted. They handed their reins to the Kid and Cole and then walked into the bank and closed the door behind them.

Now they all took positions behind the counter and pulled up their bandannas to cover their faces. It was now a waiting game. Bobby and Kenny were watching out their opened windows with their rifles fully loaded and in hand and ready to aim if necessary. At 8:00 everyone expected the president of the bank to walk in, but he didn't. Still no president at 8:05.

Dakota began perspiring and wondering what was happening. They started looking at each other as the minutes began ticking away, 8:06, 8:07, 8:08, what to do? 8:09 and then at 8:10, there, the sound of a key was heard being inserted into the lock, the door knob turned, the door opened and the president of the bank walked in. He closed the door behind him and locked it. Immediately, Arizona and Charlie jumped up with their guns drawn, startled the guy out of his wits, and told the president to put his hands up and not to say a word. Charlie grabbed a chair, placed it near the safe, and he and Arizona gagged and tied the old man to it so that he could see Rusty standing there at work. The banker's eyes were as big as hen eggs while he had two pistols pointing at his head and watching Rusty go to work on the Yale combination lock.

"Come on man, come on, we're running out of time," Dakota said anxiously to Rusty. Rusty didn't say a word but stayed focused on his job with his ear to the door and meticulously turning the wheel to the right, to the left, and back and forth several times, trying to disable the timer and then the lock itself.

Then, there, everyone heard a loud click. Rusty looked at Dakota and Pecos, smiled, grabbed the safe's handle, pulled it downward, and heaved the heavy safe door wide open. The banker couldn't believe what he just witnessed. His eyes were now as big as goose eggs.

"Now what?" Pecos asked looking at Dakota for directions.

"Close it back up," Dakota said as he looked at Rusty. Rusty looked back at Dakota in disbelief.

"What?" Charlie shouted as he looked at Dakota.

"You heard me, close it up right now."

"Wait a minute," Charlie said as he cocked and pointed his pistol at Dakota whose six-shooter was still holstered. Pecos began edging away from Dakota. "What the hell is this all about? We're not leaving here without that money!" Charlie shouted.

The tension in the room became worrisome, especially to Rusty. A shot would wake up the entire town and put this whole mission and their lives in jeopardy.

"Arizona, go in there and get those gold certificates," Charlie ordered.

The tension continued to mount. There was a stalemate as the time was ticking away and Arizona did not follow Charlie's demand. Charlie then pointed his gun at Arizona but as fast as you could say, "the jig is up", Pecos whipped out his Arkansas toothpick and hurled it through the air at the speed of light. It slammed right into Charlie's chest. Charlie dropped his pistol and suddenly collapsed, bleeding out on the wood floor with a puddle of blood inching away from his lifeless body. The banker was befuddled as he witnessed all of this going down. They all watched as Pecos walked over to Charlie and yanked out his knife and then unremorsefully, wiped the blood from his twelve inch blade on Charlie's shirt and said,

"Sorry mi amigo, but you were as wild as a crazy prairie chicken and full of frijoles."

"Now close that safe and let's get out of here," Dakota ordered.

Rusty closed the vault and they all ran out the back door and mounted their horses. The Kid looked at everyone and then asked, "Who has the money? Where's Charlie?"

"No one has the money and Charlie's not coming with us. I'll explain after we cross the bridge," Dakota said. "Now, stay calm and let's ride toward the river in the order we came. Go ahead Kid and Cole, you first. And so by two, then three, then Arizona by himself, they rode to 4th Street and trotted down the road to the bridge. Kenny and Bobby saw the guys riding out so they grabbed their rifles and gear and calmly walked down the steps and out the back door to the stable. Their horses were already saddled.

One by one, everyone crossed the bridge. Dane was ready to blow it but Dakota told him to hold up a minute while everyone was gathered together. Dakota looked back to see if they made a clean getaway and then said to the group,

"You need to know that there's no money. The boss was testing our loyalty, professionalism, and how we operated as a team. Charlie proved that he was not a loyal member of our team. That's why he's lying dead in the bank. The boss needed to know how good and loyal we were because the next job is one of the big ones, worth millions. This one was not worth getting into trouble over. The boss is gonna be proud of all of you. Now Dane, blow that bridge to kingdom come and let's get the hell out of here."

"You got it!" Dane yelled as he held three sticks of long wick dynamite in his left hand and struck a match with his right. He lit each wick, and then threw them, one by one, onto the bridge, laughing like a maniac. He and Doc jumped on their horses and they all galloped out of there as fast as they could. The dynamite exploded with a deafening roar, echoing through the streets of Northfield, shaking the windows of the stores on Division Street, and sending up a plume of smoke and wooden bridge slats over one hundred feet into the air as the rest of the bridge collapsed and fell into the Cannon River.

The desperados rode hard and fast to their respective destinations. No one in town knew what happened. People began running out onto the street looking for anything unusual. Many people had heard the violent explosion and seen the cloud of black smoke over by the river and surmised that the bridge was blown up. No one knew why until at 8:55 when the bank office manager walked into the bank and saw his boss gagged and tied to a chair.

He left the door open and ran over to him, almost tripping over Charlie's dead body. He removed the gag and then while untying the bank president asked, "What happened here?"

"We were robbed! Well, no we weren't, I mean, I don't know what I mean. I never seen anything like it," the president said as he stood up and reached into his pocket, pulled out a handkerchief, removed his glasses and patted the perspiration from his forehead. He gingerly stepped over the body and said, "I need some fresh air," as he walked toward the open door.

The marshal was riding by heading to the bridge but pulled up his reins when he saw the bank president standing in the bank's doorway in a disoriented state. He hurriedly dismounted and quickly walked up to the president.

"What happened here, have you been robbed?"

"Yes and no."

"Talk sense man."

"When I walked into the bank, there were outlaws already in here. I guess they broke through the back door. Don't think it was Jesse and Frank this time but they all had their faces covered. They tied me up and made me watch while one of them opened the safe. We have a time lock on it. I don't know how he did it."

"How much did they get?"

"Nothing, when they opened the door, one of the outlaws told the safecracker to close it back up. Another outlaw got all upset because he wanted the money, so they killed him."

"You mean there's a dead body in your bank?" The marshal asked.

"Yes sir marshal, right over by the safe."

The marshal walked into the bank and over to the lifeless body lying on the floor. He stood there looking at Charlie and said, "Well this is a surprise."

"What's a surprise marshal?" The bank president asked.

"I can't believe my eyes. I know this guy. He was once married to my sister. He's Charlie Todd. He's as mean as a timber rattler. Even my sister told me, after he left her, that he was so mean that he would throw a drowning man both ends of a rope. He's wanted all over the west with a reward on his head for $2,000. Looks like you have an early Christmas present coming to you, Mr. Wippley."

CHAPTER TEN:

Midnight in Nevada

With about a thirty minute head start, the telegraph wires cut, and the bridge blown, Brinkman's Professionals got a clean getaway. The fact that no money was stolen was the main reason for not putting together a posse. Besides that, the bank president was not able to identify any of the outlaws because their bandannas and pulled down hats concealed their faces. By all counts it was a hopeless cause, at least that's how the marshal saw it.

The townspeople went to work splicing back together all the downed telegraph wires and the local editor of the newspaper visited with the bank president to get a story. Within days the news of the break-in and the strange incident at the Northfield Bank was all over the country.

The Northfield Gazette's headline read, "Outlaws Crack Safe, Leave Money and Dead Outlaw". When the story hit the streets of Chicago, the outlaws were not quite back to Abilene yet. When Pinkerton bought a morning newspaper and took it up to his office, he read it and then pondered upon it. He walked down the long hallway to Agent Brennen's office, sat down in front of his desk and said to Brennen as he threw the newspaper down in front of his agent,

"Read this article. It doesn't make sense. Why would a gang of outlaws break into a bank, skillfully crack a time lock safe open, close the safe and leave the money, kill one of their own, destroy the bridge, and then leave town. Everything they did was unpredictable but perfect, mind you. They were professionals no doubt."

Then it was like a dinner bell went off in his head.

"Professionals, dynamite, skilled safecracker, and the dead outlaw was a notorious gunslinger. I wonder if this has any relationship to the penitentiary breakouts," Pinkerton rhetorically asked his agent. "Maybe we'll have our first clue with this dead outlaw, Charlie Todd who is mentioned in this article. You and I are going on a trip to Northfield, Minnesota and have a talk with this Mr. Wippley."

Back at the lodge just outside of Abilene, Kansas, Brinkman's Professionals were beginning to arrive at their hideout. The first group to make it back was the group of Pecos, Rusty, and Dane. Charlie was supposed to be in this group but his over the top greed and lack of loyalty got him wasted back at the bank.

One day later, Kenny, Bobby, Dakota, and Cole arrived early in the morning. They greeted Rusty and Pecos with handshakes and laughter and were excited to see each other. Then the final group of the Kansas Kid, Arizona, and Doc Hawkens returned later that afternoon. It was almost like a party atmosphere.

Arizona and Cole were feeling bad about Charlie but they knew he had it coming for challenging Dakota. The poor sap never could take orders from anyone. Pecos, who had to think fast to keep them all from possibly getting killed, was not sorry for what he did. He felt like a soldier doing his duty for his fellow troops.

The gang hung out in the meeting room, talking and having a few drinks while waiting for Mr. Brinkman to arrive. It was Saturday evening, December 3rd, and quite frosty outside. Chan had only three jobs at the lodge: cut firewood, keep the fireplace roaring, and prepare the meals. He had the fire blazing in the fireplace in the meeting room and the dinner was ready to be served whenever Mr. Brinkman made his entrance and said it was time to eat.

At about 5:30 p.m., Brinkman pulled up to the lodge in a wagon. Dakota looked outside through the window and saw Brinkman walking toward the back of his buckboard and needed a hand with a couple of boxes so he immediately went outside to help the boss. Brinkman and Dakota shook hands and Brinkman said,

"Welcome back Dakota, I read about your success; although you must tell me about Charlie after dinner. But for now, I have a surprise for the boys. Grab a box and I'll take these two. I want the boys to have a good time tonight. They deserve it."

"Yes sir, they sure do."

When Brinkman and Dakota walked into the meeting room carrying a few boxes, the gang got quiet to see what Brinkman had to say. Brinkman set his boxes on top of his desk: one was a large box and the other was a cigar box. Dakota followed Brinkman's lead and did the same with his box. Brinkman then took off his coat, walked over to the corner of the room and hung it on a freestanding coat rack. At this point he still did not speak a word or greet the gang.

Then he walked back over to his desk, opened up one of the large boxes, reached in with both hands to grab something, turned around, held up two bottles of Grande Cuvee Charles VII

185

Champagne from the champagne house of Canard-Duchene out of Ludes in northeastern France, known to be of the highest quality, and said,

"Let's celebrate!"

A loud roar went up in the room like their horses just won the cross country race during the town's 4th of July celebration. It was the first time they actually saw Brinkman smile and show signs of elation; a rare moment indeed.

"Pecos and Rusty, pass around the champagne flutes, I'm pouring," Brinkman said.

Pecos and Rusty did and then Brinkman himself walked around the room filling everyone's flute. When he was finished, he stood in the middle of the room with the men standing in front of him and said as he held his flute of champagne high in the air,

"Gentlemen, today I toast you, the Brinkman Professionals. Because of your success in Northfield and your loyalty to the cause, we now move on to bigger and better things so that we all can become filthy rich. So drink up men and enjoy the evening."

"Here, here," Dakota said.

After about the third round of drinks Chan came into the room, bowed in the tradition of a Chinese cook and said,

"Dinner is served."

Later that evening, while the men were just sitting around in the large meeting room chewing the fat, Brinkman told Dakota to follow him into another small room, Brinkman's personal office. This is where Brinkman would go to develop his plans. When they entered his office, Brinkman told Dakota to sit down in the chair in front of his desk. Brinkman then sat down at his desk and said,

"I read about Northfield. I'm assuming it really was as successful as the papers reported. Tell me about it and why you had to kill Todd."

"Sir, we followed your plans perfectly. Everything was just as you said it would be. We had a little anxiety when the bank president didn't show up until 8:10, but when he did, we tied him up and Rusty went right to work. He had that safe opened in a matter of minutes. When I told Rusty to close it up, that's when Charlie lost it. He cocked and pointed his pistol at me, then he told Arizona to go in and get the money."

"What did Arizona do?"

"He refused to do it. That's when Pecos felt that Charlie might blast somebody and wake up the entire town causing us to be in a pack of trouble. So Pecos hurled his knife at Charlie and killed him on the spot. There was no other choice. He did the right thing. That's how everyone saw it. When we crossed the bridge, I told them exactly what you told me to tell them."

"Any negative responses from anyone?"

"No sir, not a one."

"Good, because what I am about to show you right now is our next project. There will be two of them, but this is the first. Loyalty, speed, and precision will be necessary to pull them off without a hitch. This is for your eyes only. I don't want you to tell anyone else about it. I have about two or three more weeks of loose ends to tie up before I show this to the gang."

Brinkman unrolled two drawings: a large illustration of a floor plan, and the architectural rendering of a large building. The name of the building was written on the bottom of each drawing. Brinkman looked at Dakota and smiled. Dakota looked at one of the illustrations and then back at Brinkman and just had two words to say,

"My word."

"Like I said, keep it to yourself. Now go tell Rusty I want to see him."

"Yes sir."

Brinkman rolled up the drawings and placed them inside the credenza behind him and locked the sliding door with a key. Within minutes, Rusty came into the office and Brinkman asked him to close the door and sit down. So he did. Brinkman leaned back in his fancy leather chair behind his desk and then lit up an expensive cigar while Rusty just sat there and watched wondering where this conversation was heading.

"Congratulations on your success up in Northfield, Rusty."

"Thank you, sir."

"Dakota told me about the incident with Charlie. I'm blaming the Kid for his poor judgment of men. He should have known that Charlie couldn't be trusted. I'll talk to him about that later. My question to you is, did you have any problems opening that time lock?"

"No sir I didn't. I was very familiar with that mechanism. I helped build them for Yale. It took me less than five minutes to crack it, that's all. Although I must tell you that I was as surprised as the rest when Dakota told me to close it right back up."

Brinkman grinned and said, "Yes, I guess you were. But the fact is I needed to know who I could trust, if everyone could follow orders, and how you all worked together as a team. I did not want the posse on our tails either for a meager $100,000. You see Rusty, here's the deal. Our next two projects are what we are really preparing for. I'm still working on a few issues, but this next one alone will net us over 50 times more than what was in that Northfield vault."

"Fifty times more? That must be quite a job."

"It is and Rusty, you're going to be the key player. That's all I can tell you at this point. Now, let's talk about the other reason why I wanted to see you. It's about you and Kathleen."

Rusty began squirming in his chair some not quite knowing where this particular conversation was going. Mr. Brinkman was always intimidating to Rusty since he was a very tall, well-built man and Rusty was a slight fella standing at only 5'8" with his boots on.

"Look Rusty, you need to make a decision. If you intend to keep seeing Kathleen, you can't stay here because sooner or later she's going to want to see where you live. The way I see it, you have to pick one of two choices: you can continue to stay here at the lodge and not get too serious with Kathleen for the time being or you can stay at my ranch and continue to see my daughter. I have plenty of room at my ranch house and you're more than welcome to stay there. It's one or the other Rusty, which one will it be?"

Rusty paused for a few seconds and looked down not knowing which way to turn. Then he said, "Sir, you said there are only two more jobs, right?"

"That's right Rusty. After those two, you can take Kathleen away from Kansas and move to somewhere like California or Oregon and be free and self-sufficient to buy land and raise a family. I think Kathleen would like that."

"Yes sir, I think she would. Can you tell me when we will be going on these next two jobs?"

"Yes I can. The first one will be in about 5 weeks and the next one will be in about 8 weeks. That means in two months, you can head west with Kathleen. Based on that information, can you make your decision now?"

"Yes sir, I can. I would like to remain here with the gang. I enjoy the comradery and the way it sounds sir, Kathleen and I will be together soon enough. But if you allow me sir, I have two other questions I would like to ask you, if you please forgive my curiosity."

"OK Rusty, what are they?"

"The first one is, I heard that you adopted Kathleen when she was eight years old or thereabouts. Is that true?"

"Yes it is. Her father and I lived on neighboring plantations back in Virginia. I knew Kathleen from the day she was brought into this world. Her mother died right after Kathleen was born. It was all birth related, so the doctor said. My wife took care of Kathleen while we were off to war.

Kathleen's father was part of my regiment. During the First Battle of Chattanooga, he caught a Yankee slug in the gut. I held him in my arms while he lie there dying. His last request was for me to promise to take care of his daughter Kathleen. Just as I said I would, he took his last breath and expired. Those damn Yankees killed my best friend.

I wired my wife about the circumstances. But tragedy struck my family too. Directly after the War, my wife died of typhoid fever. That's when Kathleen and I pulled up our roots and moved westward. And here we are. And now you know."

Rusty looked down and didn't know what to say.

"You said you had two questions Rusty. What's the other one?"

"The second is this. You are already a wealthy man, yet you continue to want more. I sense there is something bigger you're after, something of great significance. Something more than what meets the eye."

"That is a very astute observation Rusty. Yes there is. You see, someday son, I plan to own Abilene. But that's just the beginning. My main objective is to reside in the governor's mansion in Topeka, Kansas. Our present governor, John St. John (February 25, 1833 – August 31, 1916, lived to age 83) is going to ruin this state. He's putting ridiculous restrictions on liquor and other things. Can you imagine prohibiting the sale of good wine and champagne? Besides, he was a Union lieutenant colonel during the War. He was fighting on the wrong side and wants to clog up Kansas law books with Yankee laws.

Have you ever seen this man, Rusty?"

"No sir, can't say that I have."

"Well, he never combs his hair, he never trims his mustache, it's too bushy and long, and he never wears pressed clothes. A man like that should never be governor."

Well, Rusty unsuccessfully tried to keep from looking like he thought Brinkman was five cards short of a full deck.

At this point Brinkman, seeing the look on Rusty's face, came to his senses and thought he better hobble his lips and said,

"Now make sure that you keep our conversation, on all the matters we discussed to yourself. When you go out to the meeting room, send in the Kid."

"Yes sir I will, and thank you sir."

They both shook hands and Rusty walked out the door and into the large meeting room to fetch the Kid for the boss.

Mr. Brinkman had a good long talk with the Kid about his choice of men to add to his team and wanted to know if there was any way that Charlie could be traced back to his gang.

Allan Pinkerton wanted to know the same thing and that's why he took a trip to Northfield with Agent Brennen. He had sent a telegram to the marshal and told him that he would like to meet with him and the bank president when he and his agent arrived in Northfield. Both the marshal and the bank president, Mr. Wippley, had no problem with that.

The detectives arrived Wednesday afternoon at 1:30 on December 7th. The marshal met Pinkerton and Brennen at the train depot and welcomed them to Northfield. They had to cross the Cannon River on a temporary makeshift ferry while the town toiled long and hard to reconstruct the blown bridge. The marshal pointed out the destruction to the agents as they crossed the river upstream.

When they reached the bank of the river, the marshal had a two horse, 4-seater buggy waiting for them to take the agents down the street to the bank. It was less than five minutes away.

Mr. Wippley met the three at the front door. Introductions were made and Pinkerton said,

"Let's get right to it, shall we? How did they get into your bank?"

"Let's walk back to the alley and I'll show you. The way I figured it is that they all rode back here between 7:00 and 8:00 in the morning. No one saw them. It was clever of them to pick out the Friday after Thanksgiving because there was no one stirring in town that early in the morning after a holiday."

When they reached the back door of the bank, Wippley pointed out that the door was intact so somebody must have picked the lock clean. They concluded that the same guy who picked the time lock was probably one and the same. That was a pretty safe assumption.

Then they all walked into the bank.

"Those outlaws hid behind these counters until I came through the front door. After I locked the door behind me, they jumped me and tied me to this chair after they moved it close to the vault so I could watch them open the safe. Mr. Pinkerton, he had it open in less than five minutes. How did he do that? It's on a time lock. He had to disarm the time lock and then figure out the combination. I ask you again, how did he do that?"

"What did this safecracker look like?" Pinkerton asked.

"Well he wore a bandanna and had his hat pulled down like the other outlaws so I did not get a good look at his face. But I can tell you that he was shorter than the rest of the men, except for one other, and he had a small frame. He was probably 5'7" to 5'8" tall. Does that help?"

"It might. Did you see anything else unusual, like did anyone have a scar or walk with a limp? Did anyone say a name? I'm looking for anything."

"No one said a name, but one spoke like he was a Mexican. He was wearing a black sombrero and was no taller than me, about 5' 8" tall. He was the one who threw the knife at the other outlaw and killed him right there, right in front of me. It's because one of the outlaws, I guess the boss, told the safecracker to close the vault door and leave the money be. Have you ever heard of anything like that before?"

"No I haven't. What happened after their boss told the safecracker to close the door?"

"That's when that one outlaw, you know, the dead one, went crazy and said they weren't leaving here without the money. He even pulled a gun on their boss and ordered another outlaw to go fetch the money. The other one didn't. That's when it became very tense and that's when the Mexican hurled the knife into that guy's chest."

"There's something I have to tell you Mr. Pinkerton."

"Yeah, what's that marshal?"

"I know that guy who got killed. He was married to my sister for two years. His name was Charlie Todd."

"Really... now we're getting somewhere. None of that was in the papers that I read."

"I know. The newspaper was trying to protect my reputation."

"What else can you tell me about him?" Pinkerton asked.

"Only that he was from Dakota or around thereabouts. My sister said he hung out with two other shady characters."

"Really? Do you know their names?"

"No, that's all I know, nothing more, except that Todd left my sister and their little daughter on their homestead by themselves, a little less than a year ago. She said the guy was crazy and she was glad he rode off."

Pinkerton then looked at Brennen and said, "You're taking a trip to the Dakota Territory and talk to the marshal's sister to see what else you can get on this Todd guy."

"Don't waste your time Mr. Pinkerton. My sister and her daughter were killed by a Sioux raiding party last month," the marshal said with a somber tone in his voice as he looked down for a second and stared at the floor.

"Sorry to hear that marshal," Pinkerton said.

"Thank you Mr. Pinkerton. I know you don't have much to go on, but did any of this information help you?"

"Maybe, and then again, maybe not. The fact that no money was taken makes me believe that this was probably a test run for something else. How much money did you have in that safe at the time, Mr. Wippley?"

"Over $100,000. But what's the point? They weren't interested in the money."

"I know; that's perplexing."

Pinkerton paused and then said, "Well gentlemen, you've been very helpful. I have my theory about what's going on here and now I have to figure out what their next move will be."

With that, the agents headed to the depot to catch a train back to Chicago. Pinkerton added more facts to his theories and concluded that this bogus robbery was most likely pulled off by what he was now calling, a group of professional criminals. Their remarkable attention to detail and everything about this break-in verified in Pinkerton's mind that they were not dealing with amateurs but highly sophisticated outlaws, whose organization, size-wise, may transcend everyone's imagination. He thought that he might have a crime syndicate on his hands.

Meanwhile back in Abilene, Brinkman met with Dakota, Kenny and Bobby at the lodge and told the brothers to start target shooting their sniper rifles at 200 to 300 paces. He told them to ride out to his ranch every day for about two weeks and do the shooting out there. He did not want to draw any attention to the lodge. He told them that they needed to be accurate and consistent at that long distance. For example, be able to hit within a 6 inch diameter circle at least 25 straight times.

Brinkman excused the Burkley brothers and then told Dakota that he was taking a trip out west but wouldn't say exactly where and was not forthcoming on the why. He told him that he was meeting with a family member on a little business and would be back in about two weeks.

"Could the business have something to do with our next project?" Dakota asked.

"It might, it might at that," Brinkman remarked. "The most important thing is that you keep everyone in line while I'm gone. Let the men go to town anytime they please but tell them to stay out of trouble. And above all, don't be seen in groups larger than two. Is that clear?"

"Yes sir it is."

"When I return from out west, I'll be able to lay out the plans for the men. See you in two weeks."

Brinkman headed for the train depot with his bags packed and carrying a long tube with important drawings encased. He did not tell Dakota the specifics of his trip but he was meeting in Virginia City, Nevada with two people who were key players in his audacious and unprecedented plot. Brinkman was getting ever so close to tying up his loose ends. With him, everything had to be sound and absolutely perfect without flaw before he would attempt such a major undertaking.

During those two weeks he was gone, the Burkley boys were sharpening up their sniper skills. But it didn't take much practicing to get them to Brinkman's desired high level of accuracy. They were already skilled marksmen of the highest caliber.

Rusty kept his relationship with Kathleen on a cordial basis for now, only meeting with her three times for lunch in those two weeks while Brinkman was gone. Kathleen questioned Rusty why he seemed so distant. Rusty would only say that he wanted to take things a little slower now for personal reasons. Kathleen said she understood but in reality, she did not.

The rest of the men hung out in town and at the lodge, doing a little bit of drinking and a copious amount of gambling. Ole Pecos almost went fisticuffs with a stranger in the town's saloon but thought the wiser of it even though the saddle tramp called him a greaser.

On occasions everyone would join the Burkley brothers target shooting out at Brinkman's ranch. But the fact was, they were all becoming restless.

Dakota had told them to remain patient because when Brinkman returned from out west, that's when they would find out what they were really hired to do and the payoff would be beyond their wildest dreams. But that was all he was allowed to tell the edgy group.

On Thursday, December 15th, Dakota received a telegram from Brinkman with two orders: pick him up at the train depot with his buggy on Saturday, December 17th, and secondly tell the gang that there would be a meeting at one o'clock on Sunday, December 18th, at the lodge.

Dakota did both. He was waiting at the depot Saturday morning with Mr. Brinkman's carriage. The train arrived at 10:20 and Dakota greeted Brinkman when he stepped off the passenger car.

"Welcome back Mr. Brinkman. I trust that everything went your way."

"Yes it did Dakota, and then some. Has everyone been informed about tomorrow's meeting?"

"Yes sir, everyone will be there."

"I see you have your horse tethered to the back of my carriage. That's good. I'm visiting the bank to check on things then I'm going out to my ranch. Tell the group and Chan that I won't be there for dinner tonight. I'm having dinner with Kathleen. I'll see everyone tomorrow."

Well tomorrow finally came. It was Sunday and everyone was anxious to hear about Brinkman's big announcement. Which bank would it be? Which one had a vault overflowing with gold? How far would they have to travel this time? Would there be more risk than what they experienced at the Northfield quasi-bank robbery? The answers would come after the big lunch that Chan prepared for the group. It was like a party atmosphere. The anticipation was great.

Finally after lunch, the group gathered in the large meeting room. Chan had stoked up the fire in the fireplace and added more logs while everyone was eating. So the room was nice and toasty on the inside while it was cold and miserable on the outside.

The men were anxiously waiting as Brinkman walked over to stand in front of the large map on the wall to first say a few words.

"Men you were assembled as a skillful team for this moment. Each of you are specialists in your unique field and that's what will make this team of professionals potentially the most feared gang in the West, and rightfully so. With your skill level and diversification, we can take on any task knowing that there will be a high degree of success; and gentlemen, I'm talking about projects no other gang would dare to attempt.

The Northfield project was a test of your skills, teamwork and loyalty. Most important of all though, it was a test of your ability and willingness to follow orders. You proved yourselves and now it's time to put your skills to work."

Brinkman turned around and pointed to a spot on the map, "Here's where we are, Abilene, Kansas. And here's where we are headed, 1,400 miles due west to western Nevada," Brinkman said as he ran his finger straight across the map from Abilene to his planned final destination.

"I reckon there's a pretty big bank out there, eh Mr. Brinkman?" Johnny Dane asked.

"No Johnny, it's not a bank that's our mark. Our target is right here on the map in Carson City, Nevada. It's none other than the Carson City Mint. Gentlemen, you are destined for greatness," Brinkman said as he smiled and then took a cigar out of his shirt pocket, struck a match and lit the Cuban, puffing with a grin on his face like he just won the mineral rights to a gold mine on Pike's Peak in a game of five card stud.

The men valued the "destined for greatness" statement but were somewhat stunned at Brinkman's revelation. Holding up a bank was one thing but busting into a United States Mint, well it could be like taking on a pack of timber wolves with the pointed end of a wild turkey feather; seemed like an extremely risky, stupid, and most likely deadly proposition. Nobody said it quite that way but it was written all over their faces alright, sure as you could get sauced up on cheap whiskey at the Rickety Hinge Saloon in Abilene.

Carson City was named after the famous American trailblazer, Indian fighter, mountain man, trapper and scout, Christopher Houston Carson, better known as Kit Carson (December 24, 1809 – May 23, 1868, lived to 58 years old). The way it came about was that the first European Americans who set foot in that area known as Eagle Valley in January of 1843 were led by John C. Fremont (January 21, 1813 – July 13, 1890, lived to age 77). They came across a river there and Fremont named the river after his scout and called it the Carson River.

In 1851, what was known as the Eagle Station Ranch, adjacent to the Carson River, served as a trading post and stopover for travelers heading westward to California. In 1858, Abraham Curry (February 19, 1815 – October 19, 1873, lived to age 58), head of a vigilante group, bought Eagle Station and subsequently named the area Carson City.

Just a few months before in 1850, gold was discovered in Gold Canyon about twelve miles northeast of Carson City. During this time in history, all of this area was part of the Utah Territory before it became the Nevada Territory and then the state of Nevada.

What made this area populate so rapidly was the unearthing of what has become known as the Comstock Lode, the first major discovery of silver ore in the United States. The discovery was made public in 1859.

Mining camps sprung up overnight like wild mushrooms in a dense forest. Prospectors came from hundreds and thousands of miles away to stake their claims. Some even crossed the deep blue waters of the Pacific. Many pickaxes were swung and tin trays were panned in the mountains and streams of the Nevada Territory. From Carson City northeast to Virginia City and everywhere in between, immense wealth grew faster than Japanese Kudzu vines on a hillside in the Deep South.

The Carson City Mint, a branch of the United States Mint, was constructed for the sake of accessibility. It was established to mint silver coins from the silver mined in the Comstock Lode just like the San Francisco Mint was built to facilitate the minting of gold coins during the California Gold Rush. The Carson City Mint was created in 1863 and went into operation seven years later in 1870, minting both silver and gold coins.

During that time period, 1864 to be exact, a year before the Civil War ended, Carson City was confirmed as Nevada's permanent capital. Nevada turned from a territory to statehood on October 31, 1864. It was the second of two states added to the Union during the Civil War. The first was West Virginia which was made a state on June 20, 1863.

It is said that Nevada's creation as a "territory" on March 2, 1861 ensured that the mineral rights would help the Union, not the Confederacy. This was probably more true than not. Back then many speculated that congress and President Lincoln made Nevada a "state" to ultimately ensure that the precious metals would help finance the Union cause during the War. It seemed likely to some. However, what seems to be more credible is that Nevada was made a state for "political reasons" and not "financial" ones.

The events of the time may substantiate the latter stated theory. After Sherman's march through Atlanta, Lincoln and his generals envisioned the War to be coming to an end soon. That sort of negates the "financial" reason for Nevada becoming a state. Lincoln appointed a Republican governor for Nevada hoping to acquire the electoral votes to help him win his second term. It would also aid President Lincoln in getting the 13th Amendment passed which would abolish slavery.

Brinkman shared some of this information with his gang. He was well educated about such matters and enjoyed showing off his knowledge. However, most of the gang members could care less about the history of Carson City and Nevada. Brinkman could see it in their eyes. So he decided to bring their minds back into focus with this attention-grabbing tidbit of information.

"Gentlemen, there are millions of dollars in Yankee gold bullion, silver ingots, and $20 gold pieces in the Carson City Mint. We're loading up four wagons full of gold. We'll leave the silver for the government."

"Senor Brinkman, aren't Mints guarded by U.S. Army gringos? It sounds like suicide to me."

"Yes they are Pecos; and yes it does sound like suicide, on the surface at least," Brinkman admitted.

The other members felt the same way as Pecos, but did not speak up. Reason being that Brinkman was like no other man they had ever met. He seemed to be part of a widespread criminal network that had inside information from both high and low places throughout the West. His plans were always meticulous and tight and seemed to be well thought out and fail-safe. That's why Brinkman's men would ultimately trust his discretion and agree to participate in this project.

Besides, with the cat out of the bag, it was too late to back out now lest they become fish food behind the lodge like old man Jeff Porter. One thing for certain though, every one of these gang members had one driving force in common, greed. Their greed took priority over everything. It was their hunger for wealth that made them loyal to the cause and Brinkman knew it.

He asked everyone to move around his desk where he rolled out two drawings, one of the exterior of the building and its surroundings, and one of the floor plan of the Mint. He now began to lay out the strategy to overtake the Carson City Mint in a cadence like a general laying out combat tactics to his officers before a great battle.

"Gentlemen, pay close attention now to every detail I'm about to give you. We can't afford to make any mistakes. If one person fails, we will all fail.

We will hit the Mint on New Year's Eve at midnight. Why at midnight? It's because our gunfire will be masked by the gunshots of all the drunks celebrating the New Year in town at the Golden Nugget Saloon. I'm told they throw quite a party there on New Year's Eve.

New Year's Eve falls on a Saturday this year and New Year's Day is on a Sunday. This calendar was made for us. There will be a skeleton crew working that evening and on New Year's Day.

The Mint is a two story building that sits right smack in the middle of a five acre field that's surrounded by woods with an access road from the front side only. Look here, this is an illustration of the exterior of the building," Brinkman said as he placed it on top of the floor plan drawing.

"There will be two armed sentries in front of the building, one on each side of the front door, here and here. Normally there are four guards but like I told you before, they have a skeleton crew scheduled for the holiday. Bobby and Kenny, you're taking them out, but we'll get back to that later.

Now, let's look at this illustration," Brinkman said as he placed the floor plan drawing on top of the architectural rendering. "This is the floor plan of the inside of the building. You saw where this is a two story building. They also have a basement area as well, but pay that no mind. Again, normally they have armed guards on both floors but on Saturday night and on Sunday, there will only be guards on the first floor. Look at it this way.

The hallway system on the first floor is shaped like a square slingshot. When you walk into the building, you walk down a 20-foot hallway; we'll call that hallway (A). There is one large office on each side. The entrance hallway dead ends into a perpendicular hallway; we'll call that hallway (B). If you walk 15 feet to the right in hallway (B), that hallway makes a 90 degree turn to the left; call that hallway (C). If you would walk 15 feet to the left in hallway (B), that hallway makes a 90 degree turn to the right; call that hallway (D).

Now, here's where the vaults are. There are two on the right of hallway (C) and two to the left in hallway (D). Rusty, your job will be to open all four starting with the ones in hallway (C). All the vaults have Yale combination locks. There are no time locks. As soon as you get one open, move to the next one. If you run into a problem opening any of the vaults, Dane will be your backup with dynamite."

"Sir, do you know how many guards will be on the inside?" Dakota asked

"I was just getting to that. There will only be four on the inside; one stationed in each hallway."

"How are we gonna take them out sir?" The Kid asked.

"We have an insider working with us. But you're getting slightly ahead of me. Now that everyone knows the layout of the Mint, let's talk about particulars and your individual tasks. At 11:45 p.m., we will all ride as a group to the main access road that leads to the Mint but stop short about 150 yards from the open field. There will be a road that leads to the left where we will stop. We'll go down that road a piece until we come upon four buckboards with horses ready to go.

Those are the wagons we'll be loading the gold into. Kenny and Bobby, you'll dismount and walk up to the edge of the woods. You'll be able to take out the two guards in front from there with your long rifles. There are gas lampposts out in front so you'll be able to see your targets using your scopes. We'll all set our pocket watches so we all have the exact same time. You'll shoot to kill at precisely midnight.

Once Kenny and Bobby dispatch the guards to their maker, the Kid, Arizona, and Cole will ride up to the building. The guard in hallway (A) will open the front door for you. His name is Billy Crane. He's our insider."

"How does he fit in? I mean, how did we get him on our side?" Rusty asked.

"Good question," Brinkman acknowledged as he grinned. "He's the cousin of my boss. He's one of the men I met with on my trip out West. I'll tell you who the other one is shortly. Now listen up. Once the door is open, Crane will move out of the way. You three, I'm talking about the Kid, Arizona, and Cole, go down hallway (A), locate the other three guards and cut them down. We aren't taking any prisoners. Is that clear?"

The three responded in the affirmative.

"Once the three guards are down, Kid, come out to a lamppost so we can see you and wave us in. Cole and Arizona, you two go to the back of the building and open both doors. There's one on the far left and one on the far right.

Bobby, Kenny, Doc, and Pecos, you four will drive the wagons in. Tether your horses to the back of your wagons. Each wagon will be loaded with empty crates. There will be a canvas covering the crates. Bobby and Kenny, you two drive your wagons to the back left door. Doc and Pecos, you two drive your wagons to the other door.

Rusty, Dane, Dakota and I will ride to the back of the building. I want you, Rusty, to immediately go in and start opening the safes. While you're doing that, the rest of us will start hauling the crates in from the wagons. As soon as Rusty gets one vault open, we'll start filling the crates with gold only, no silver. That's not worth our time. If there are any problems with opening the safes, then that's when Dane comes into play. So Dane, you'll be carrying 12 sticks of dynamite with you.

Are there any questions up to now?"

"This Crane guy, how is he going to explain that he was the only one left alive?" Dakota asked.

"Good question Dakota, he's agreed to let me rough him up some before we leave. I intend to do a pretty good job of that. He tells me he has good pain tolerance and I should give it my best shot. I told him not to fret. I'm pretty good at pistol-whipping. We'll also loosely tie him up so he can break free. He plans on going to town at about 6:00 a.m. the next morning to inform the marshal of the robbery. The next shift doesn't come in until 8:00 a.m. By the time the marshal is notified, we'll be long gone. Are there any other questions?"

"Yes sir, I have two questions," Rusty said. "Where are we taking the gold to afterwards and how are we going to trade stolen gold for greenbacks? I don't think any of us are able to handle the weight of large amounts of gold. It's just not practical."

"I was wondering about that myself," Doc admitted.

"Good questions. After we fill up the wagons and cover the crates with canvas, we are riding to a bank in Virginia City, Nevada. It's about 17 miles northeast of here. My half-brother is the president of that bank. His name is Jacob Scott. We are loading the gold into his vault and in exchange for the gold, he is giving us gold certificates and greenbacks. He's getting his share of the loot for his help as is Billy Crane.

Now some of you may not like what I'm about to tell you. It's this. You won't be receiving your total share until the job after this one which will be much easier but with the same type of monetary rewards. I'm going to be square with you. The reason for holding back your shares after the Carson City raid is that I need the expertise of all of you to make the second big hit a successful one as well. If you don't like this arrangement, then speak up now."

Everyone looked at each other but no one spoke up. Brinkman also made it a point to look at every single person for discontent; but he saw no obvious signs of displeasure in the eyes or written on the faces of his gang members.

Then Pecos asked one final question, "Senor Brinkman, do you want me to cut down the telegraph wires?"

"Good question Pecos. No, I already took care of that issue. They will be cut at ten o'clock New Year's Eve night by the same people supplying us with the getaway buckboards.

Now, here's how we'll get there and back, and our timetable." Brinkman laid out the rest of the plans that afternoon. He gave everyone their round trip train tickets. Instead of making it a round trip back to Abilene though, he gave them tickets to ride back to Wichita and then they would ride on horseback to Abilene which was about 92 miles due north. Brinkman thought that would be the safest way to go to keep their hideout a secret and throw a posse or Pinkerton agents off the track. Of course, everyone would be taking their horse on the train both ways.

Now it was a waiting game. Everything sounded pretty good to the gang. Brinkman seemed to have his act together as always and his men were very impressed with the networking of his organization. But what they were more elated about was the amount of money they would be receiving on payday even though they were unsure when that day would come.

On the morning of December 26, 1881, the gang boarded the train to Reno, Nevada. Brinkman told Kathleen that Rusty and he had to go on an important business trip so she saw them off at the train station. She saw other men load up their horses and board the train as well but had no idea who they were; as far as she knew, they were just strangers leaving town after the Christmas holiday.

It was just a little less than a three day train trip from Abilene, Kansas to Reno, Nevada. The Central Pacific Railroad which met the Union Pacific Railroad at Promontory Summit, Utah to form the First Transcontinental Railroad traveled through Reno, Nevada. Reno came into being on May 9, 1868 and was named after Major General Jesse Lee Reno (April 20, 1823 – September 14, 1862, lived to 39) a Union officer killed in the American Civil War at the Battle of South Mountain. He was known as a "soldier's soldier" because he fought alongside of his men.

The gang arrived in Reno the morning of December 29, 1881 and immediately unloaded and saddled up their horses and rode twenty-six miles southeast to Virginia City, Nevada.

Folklore has it that Virginia City got its name from a man who was credited with discovering the Comstock Lode. They called him James Finney or "Old Virginny". His real name was James Fennimore and they say he fled his home state of Virginia after killing a man. According to the folklore, Old Virginny Finney christened the town when he tripped and broke a bottle of whiskey at a saloon entrance in the northern section of Gold Hill. It soon became known as Virginia City.

A famous writer by the name of Samuel Clemens lived in Virginia City and it was in February of 1863 when he first used his pen name, Mark Twain. At that time he was a reporter for the local Territorial Enterprise Newspaper. He wrote for the newspaper from late fall of 1862 until May of 1864.

The members of the gang stayed on an old abandoned cattle ranch belonging to Brinkman's half-brother. The ranch was no longer in operation so it made for a great hideout during their short stay. It was supplied with food and drink for the gang.

On Friday morning, December 30th, Brinkman had one last meeting with his men, going over all of the specifics of the raid. It was clear to him that everyone understood their responsibilities and that it appeared that they were ready to pull off one of the most daring capers in outlaw history in the Wild West.

Jacob Scott, Brinkman's half-brother came to visit the gang only once during their stay. That was during the afternoon of December 30th. Scott actually lived in a small house in town. His visit was short and sweet. It was basically to confirm to the gang that he would be ready to accept the gold and trade it for gold certificates and greenbacks.

On the morning of December 31, 1881, each member of the gang spent time cleaning their firearms and making sure they were fully loaded. There wasn't much talk, mostly thinking. Dakota put on a pot of coffee and Pecos warmed up some frijoles and fried up some bacon. After breakfast they all went over their responsibilities in their own minds. Brinkman even went around talking to everyone individually to make sure that each was mentally prepared for this unprecedented incursion.

When he got to Rusty who was sitting in a chair next to the fire that was blazing and crackling away in the old stone fireplace, he put his hand on Rusty's shoulder and said, "How are you feeling son? You've been quiet the last couple of days. I know you probably have Kathleen on your mind but I need for you to clear your mind of her and get focused on the work at hand. You have the most important job in this gang. If you can't crack those safes, it decreases our chances of stealing this loot by 50% or more. But I have complete confidence in you if you can keep your concentration where it belongs. This whole gang is depending on you."

Well that didn't help in calming ole Rusty's nerves down any. In fact that little speech reminded him of the pep talk that Dead-eye gave him the night before the Outlaws of Smoky Hill River unsuccessfully raided Hays City. Rusty was certainly hoping the outcome on this foray would be quite different.

The distance between Virginia City and Carson City was about 15 miles through hills, woods and rocky terrain. The journey would be slow and dangerous in the dark. Brinkman figured it to be a four to five hour trek by horseback; but he wasn't taking any chances this late in the game. He was going to allow six hours in case they ran into any unforeseen misfortune traveling off the beaten path.

So at 5:00 p.m. sharp the gang mounted up with guns loaded, rifles in their scabbards, and dynamite in some saddlebags as they began their long journey south to Carson City. They were led by one of Jacob Scott's men who took the point the whole distance but would disappear into the shadows when they reached their mark.

The wind was quiet, the sky was dark blue, and millions of flickering stars could be seen in the western sky after the sun slowly vanished and daylight succumbed to darkness. A rustler's moon aided the night travel throwing out just enough light for the outlaws to see directly in front of their horses while it created ghostly shadows of the tall pines all around them.

The only sounds heard that night besides the haunting high-pitched yells of the howling hungry coyotes in the wilderness were the clopping of the horses' hooves on the uninhabited rocky Nevada terrain. Oh it was chilly that night alright, even down right cold some would say. But their adrenaline was rushing like the Colorado River through the Rockies, warming them as if they had an extra layer of wool apparel blanketing their bodies.

The gang reached their destination at precisely 11:05 p.m. Brinkman directed everyone to check their pocket watches to be sure they had the exact same time. They all had brand new pocket watches from Brinkman. He called it their Christmas present from the boss. He sent Dakota down the side road to make sure that the buckboards were in place. They were. Brinkman then ordered everyone to take their positions.

Kenny and Bobby snuck quietly through the woods walking their horses behind them until they could see the bright light from the lampposts through the brush and trees. They then tethered the reins to a branch, removed their rifles with scopes from the scabbards and took their sniper positions at the edge of the woods behind two trees. They now had a clear view of their targets. It was now 11:20 p.m.

Doc and Pecos trotted down the side road to the wagons, hitched their horses to the back of the buckboards and then climbed up into their seats waiting for the signal to move out which was Kenny's and Bobby's rifle shots. As soon as they heard the two shots, they would move their wagons in position to be able to see the next cue which was the Kid waving them in after the three gunslingers took out the guards on the inside. It was now 11:30 p.m.

The rest of the gang was on the right side of the road hidden in the woods but still able to see the front of the building through the trees and brush. Ready to ride near the edge of woods but concealed in the shadows were, the Kid, Arizona, and Cole. A little further back was the next wave of outlaws: Rusty, Dane, Dakota and Brinkman. It was now 11:45 p.m.

The wait was a killer. The tension was building. Yet to many, this was no different than the excitement they experienced busting their fellow gang members out of the penitentiaries. At 11:55 p.m. gunshots could be heard coming from town. The first gunshots made everyone jump and look around since they were a bit edgy but they soon came to realize that the New Year's Eve celebration was beginning in Carson City. Everyone now nervously held their pocket watches in their hands watching the minutes tick away, except for the Kid, Arizona, and Cole. They were ready to ride hard and fast when they heard two gunshots and saw the sentries out front fall to the ground.

It was now 11:59 p.m. Kenny and Bobby closed the lids on their watches and stuck them back into their pockets, cocked their rifles, and took aim. Kenny pointed the barrel of his sniper rifle at the sentry on the left and Bobby at the one on the right. Bobby whispered to Kenny, "On the count of three...one...two... three..." Then two gunshots cracked through the cold midnight air and the two innocent sentries fell dead to the ground not knowing what hit them. They didn't have a chance.

When the two rifle shots rang out, the Kid, Arizona, and Cole rode across the field in full gallop toward the Mint. While they were riding hard and fast, they could hear all the gunshots coming from the celebration in town. That was a welcome sound to all because they felt it would mask their gunshots. As they were charging toward the building, Bobby and Kenny made their way back to the wagons. Once they reached the wagons and tied up their horses, all four wagons moved down the main road getting ready to cross the field when the next signal came.

At the sound of the two rifle shots, the guard in hallway (C) ran over to hallway (A) and asked Billy Crane if he heard those two gunshots. Billy said that it was just people celebrating the New Year, "Now go back to your post. If it makes you feel any better, I'll check it out."

Crane walked to the front door, opened it up, went outside and waved the three outlaws in and then stepped aside. The three who rode up to the building, slid their horses to a stop, jumped off, tied their reins to a rail, drew their pistols and then stormed the building running down hallway (A) shoulder to shoulder. The first guard they came upon looked on in shock and threw his rifle down and his hands up but the Kid drilled him anyway.

When the other two guards came running from their positions and ran around the corners into hallway B with their rifles to their shoulders, Arizona and Cole were in the hallway waiting for them. Arizona put three slugs into the one on the right. However, a slug hit him from behind fired by the guard on the left and it penetrated his upper right shoulder and slammed him forward to the floor. Cole gunned down that guard who put a bullet in Arizona's back but obviously not quick enough. The action was fast and violent and only lasted a matter of seconds. They all quickly reloaded except for Arizona who lay on the floor moaning and bleeding.

Cole ran over to Arizona while the Kid ran out the door, nodded to Crane, and then ran down in front of a lamppost and waved the rest of the gang to come in. Crane went back in and checked the three guards to see if any of them were still breathing, none were. The rest of the outlaws on horseback and in the wagons now came riding hard across the field and rode to their positions.

The Kid ran back into the building and over to Cole and Arizona. "Get the Doctor!" Cole shouted to the Kid. When everyone pulled their wagons around the back, the Kid told Doc to get inside and take care of Arizona. Doc grabbed his medical bag and ran through the hallway to Arizona. The first order of business was to plug the hole and stop the bleeding. Luckily the bullet went all the way through and did not hit any vital organs. However, a hole through the shoulder blade is a mighty painful thing. The Doc gave him some laudanum for the pain and propped him up against the wall until the wagons were loaded. Brinkman told the guys to place him in the back of a wagon when they got ready to leave.

In the meantime in Carson City, the New Year's Eve celebration was in full swing at the Golden Nugget Saloon and Dance Hall. The musicians were playing upbeat music while Ruby Star was singing and dancing on stage and flanked by two floozies, Krystal Belle and Amber Dawn. The Nugget was filled with cigar smoke, drunkards, and gamblers, and the noise level was loud enough to be heard all the way to Reno, so they say. Even the town marshal and one of his deputies were in a high stakes poker game just in front of the stage and sipping quite heavily on Kentucky whiskey while smoking some big ole stogies.

At about 12:05 an old prospector, who was celebrating outside at midnight, came back into the Nugget. He was half-crocked like the rest but trying to act sober and serious. He staggered over to the table where the marshal was playing cards and said,

"Marshal, I heard gunshots coming from the Mint."

"Speak up old timer; I can't hear you over all this noise."

The old timer stooped down toward the marshal's face. He was so close that the marshal could smell the whiskey on the old codger's breath.

"I said I heard gunshots coming from the Mint!" The old man yelled.

"Is that right? Well I reckon it's New Year's Eve over there too. I'll see your $50 and raise you $50," the marshal said as he threw five $20 gold pieces into the pot. The whole table laughed off the old timer and continued with their poker game.

Meanwhile, everyone was at their positions at the Mint. The crates were being unloaded while Rusty was working on the first safe. Dane was standing behind Rusty with a couple of sticks of dynamite just in case. Brinkman now walked over behind Rusty as well. The pressure was on.

"There," Rusty said as he heard the last click. He turned the handle on the door downward and then pulled it open. Brinkman hurriedly looked inside and then said, "Damn, it's all silver. Go to the next one Rusty."

Rusty did and within minutes he had the next safe open. This time they hit a golden bonanza. This safe was loaded with gold bullion.

"Load up the crates and hurry," Brinkman ordered his men.

The next safe was another disappointment. It was stocked with silver coins. However, the last safe was loaded with $20 gold pieces. It took about an hour and a half but the job was done and the wagons were loaded just short of being too heavy which could crack an axle or bust a wheel. It was now when Doc helped the groggy Arizona up and on his feet. The laudanum was really taking effect.

Now they only had one more job left to do, which was to rough up Billy Crane. Brinkman ordered the Kid to do the honors.

"Are you ready Crane?" The Kid asked.

"Do your best work," Crane responded.

The Kid socked Crane in the belly first. Crane doubled over in pain and then slowly looked up. The Kid then punched Crane with a left to the jaw and followed with a right to the face which broke Crane's nose. Crane fell backwards and then got up sluggishly.

"Are you done now?" Crane asked as he spit blood and wiped his mouth with his shirt cuff.

"Not yet," the Kid said as he removed his Colt from his holster and pistol-whipped Crane across the face. Crane fell to the ground and was almost unconscious from the wallop.

Brinkman walked up to the Kid and said, "That's enough. I didn't tell you to kill him. Now tie him up loosely and let's get the hell out of here."

At 2:00 a.m. the outlaws were on their way back to Virginia City. With the wagons weighted down heavily with gold, traveling was quite slow. However, since they took the main road back, the return trip was shorter and therefore quicker. Jacob Scott was waiting at the bank and told them to drive the wagons to the back and unload from there. This bank had a huge vault which was built back during the silver rush from the Comstock Lode. Everyone pitched in unloading the gold. Scott estimated the amount of money the gold would convert to and came up with a sum. He told

Brinkman that he would recount later that day while the bank was closed and double check his numbers. He would settle with them later if need be.

The estimate was a whopping $4,000,000. Scott filled up saddlebags with gold certificates and greenbacks that equaled the huge amount and then the men mounted their horses and headed back to Scott's abandoned ranch for a little shut-eye before they rode up to Reno to catch their train to Wichita. Like all the other towns around the West, this town was hung-over from the night before so no one was stirring.

There wasn't a lot of celebration amongst the outlaws yet because they were plum tuckered out from a long stressful night and they would feel a lot safer when they arrived back at the lodge in Abilene. That would be the time to celebrate.

It was now 6:30 a.m... Back in Carson City it was time for Crane to make his move. He was all beat up and looking mighty pale when he rode up to the marshal's home and knocked on the door. No one answered for the first several minutes. The marshal was hung-over like everyone else. Crane kept pounding and pounding on the door. Finally he heard,

"I'm coming, I'm coming."

The marshal opened the door, looked at Crane and said, "What the hell happened to you?"

"The Mint's been robbed, marshal. All the guards are dead. I'm the only one left alive."

"When did this happen?"

"Midnight last night. They beat me and tied me up. The other guards put up a gunfight but they were all killed."

"Damn, that old coot told me he heard gunshots over your way but I thought you were all celebrating like the rest of us. Go wake up my deputy and tell him to saddle up and meet me at the jailhouse right now. You say all the guards are dead?"

"That's right marshal."

"Well then rouse up the undertaker and tell him to take a wagon over to the Mint and pick up the bodies. Then wake up the doctor and get yourself fixed up. Looks like you need to get your cheek sewed up. You've got a pretty big gash their ole buddy."

"Yeah, they pistol-whipped me pretty bad. Think they broke my nose too."

When the marshal got dressed, he saddled up and went over to the telegraph operator's house and woke him up. He told the operator to quickly get over to his office and send a message to the U.S. Army Fort in Genoa which was about 16 miles south of Carson City and tell them that the Mint was robbed and the guards were dead.

In the meantime, the marshal met his deputy at the jailhouse and then they rode over to the Mint together toting shotguns. They found two dead bodies on the outside and three on the inside. Four vault doors were wide open. While they were on the inside looking things over, the undertaker arrived with a wagon. A little later the telegraph operator came riding up hard and ran into the building to tell the marshal that the telegraph lines were cut.

"Well find out where and get a crew out there to splice them together. By the way, go wake up the manager of this place. What's his name?"

"It's Mr. Bonner."

"Yeah, that's it. Go get him out of bed and tell him to get down here right away."

Around 7:45 a.m. the morning shift of guards and the administrative team began to show up and was horrified at what they saw. Their friends were slain during the night and the vaults were wide open. Mr. Bonner had one of the accountants begin taking inventory.

By now the bodies were loaded into the wagon and taken to the undertaker's mortuary. One of the undertaker's assistants went around town notifying the next of kin of all the murdered guards.

By midmorning, everyone had a job to do. Unfortunately, the telegraph wires were not fixed yet because of the severe damage done to the lines. In fact it took until four o'clock that afternoon before they were able to get the word out by telegraph to Fort Genoa and then to the U.S. Government in Washington, D.C. about the robbery and killings. However, by that time, Brinkman's gang was already on a train east bound to Wichita, Kansas toting saddlebags loaded with millions.

But at 4:30 p.m. there was a surprising discovery. The undertaker was going through the pockets of the dead guards' clothing to sort out their belongings for their kin when he discovered an envelope on one of the guards. He opened the envelope and found a handwritten letter inside. He read it and was shocked by its content.

He stuck it into his pocket and immediately ran over to the jailhouse. When he arrived, he directly showed the letter to the marshal. The marshal read it and was flabbergasted and then asked the undertaker if he told anyone else about the letter. The undertaker said no.

"This is between you and me," the marshal insisted. "Do you understand?"

"Yes sir, I do."

"I'm not even telling my deputy. I'm taking a ride to Fort Genoa and send a telegram from there for the sake of secrecy."

The marshal summoned his deputy and told him to watch over things. He told him that something unexpected came up and he had to take a quick trip down to Fort Genoa to handle it. He said he would explain things when he got back.

The marshal wasted no time, jumped on his horse, and rode hard to Fort Genoa carrying the envelope with him.

When he reached the fort, he asked to see the commanding officer and then he explained the whole situation to him. The fort's telegraph machine was in the same building as the commanding officer's office so they both went over to the operator. The commanding officer gave the letter to the telegraph operator and said, "This is top secret. Send it right now."

On the east side of the Mississippi, in the windy city of Chicago, a telegraph operator in the building ran into a private office and said in an urgent tone, "Mr. Pinkerton, you need to read this right now."

Pinkerton grabbed the telegram, read it and said, "Well, it's about bloody time."

CHAPTER ELEVEN:

Torture on Wheels

Brinkman's gang was on the Union Pacific Railroad heading due east to Kansas with a sense of tremendous accomplishment that they had just pulled off the most daring and richest heist in the history of the country. Their saddlebags were bursting with millions and everyone's share of the take was well over a quarter of a million dollars.

On the way back, Rusty asked Dakota what he was going to do with his share. Dakota looked at Rusty and said, "It's a lot of money that we earned; maybe too much for one man. Maybe I'll do something good with it."

Pecos overheard Dakota and responded, "Maybe we buy a ranch together in New Mexico or Arizona and become cattle barons, eh Dakota, mi amigo?"

"Maybe so Pecos."

Brinkman heard the guys talking and got up from his seat, walked over to them and told his gang to keep their mouths shut until they reached the lodge. He didn't want anyone overhearing their conversation.

Farther east in Chicago, anticipation was hitting a high point on the expectation scale. Pinkerton called five agents into his office. They were all there that day working on another case together that was close to being solved. But that case did not have the priority as this one.

"Gentlemen, I just received a telegram from a marshal in Nevada. He says that the Carson City Mint was robbed and that five guards were killed. He also said that they found a letter in one of the dead guard's pockets that read,

To Mr. Allan Pinkerton.

Guard Billy Crane was the insider. Knows the leaders of the gang and their hideout. Suggest you question him immediately.

L.B.

I sent a telegram back to the marshal and told him not to act on anything until we arrive."

"Who is this L.B.?" One of the agents asked.

"I'm not sure, could be anybody. However, truth be known though, he's probably somebody who worked at the Mint and found out about the plot and stuck a note in the dead man's pocket because he doesn't want to personally get involved fearing for his life. Anyway, here's my plan. We have to act fast. We're leaving tonight on our private train to Nevada. Each of you contact one more agent and bring him along. I'll contact two more agents myself. That will make twelve agents plus me. If these are the professional outlaws we've been talking about, we are in for one heck of a showdown. Let's meet at the train station at ten o'clock tonight and be sure to bring plenty of fire power with you."

He then told one of his agents who had laying hens to bring two of his older chickens with him in a small cage. The agent looked at Pinkerton like he was crazy.

"Don't worry agent, we aren't going to eat your chickens. I have other plans for them."

The agents all arrived on time at the station with their gear: extra clothes, guns, and ammunition. They loaded up their horses on the freight car and then they all went into the special meeting car to talk. It was a cold night on this New Year's Day. One of the agents built a fire in the potbelly stove to take the chill out of the air and warm up the plush car.

The trip from Chicago to Reno was just over 1,900 miles. It was a long journey, due west. However, the Union Pacific Railroad gave Pinkerton one of the newest locomotives on the market which could travel just over 45 miles per hour. Since the only stops were for fuel for the firebox and water for steam, Pinkerton's special train could make it to their destination in an amazing 48 hours. This was good because time was of the essence. His order to the two engineers was to "Ride this iron horse full throttle to Reno".

And boy did they. Black smoke belched out of the stack the entire trip across the continental U.S. like a Pennsylvania coal mine fire. The steel wheels never got a chance to cool down.

The plan was to ride the rails to Reno and then travel hard and fast on horseback to Carson City. Pinkerton had it all mapped out in his mind and discussed it with his agents during the trip. He told them that the first thing they would do when they rode into Carson City was to meet with the town's marshal.

Then he laid out the rest of his strategy and tactics. Some of the agents were quite surprised with the procedure which their boss intended to employ regarding the interrogation. But they knew Pinkerton's determination to right their reputation as the best detective agency in the country. Pinkerton's justification for his potential use of shady interrogation tactics was his desire for personal redemption from the fiascoes of the '70's with the James-

Younger Gang in Missouri. Pinkerton never could brush that burr from under his saddle.

The train arrived at Reno, Nevada in the late hours on January 3, 1882 and pulled onto a spur. They decided to sleep on the train that night and then saddle up and ride to Carson City at first light. Hard riding across the harsh Nevada terrain got them there at about noon on Wednesday, January 4th. It was an unusual sight to see thirteen strangers ride into town on horseback together, wearing peacemakers and each toting rifles in scabbards. They also all wore the same style, dark colored, wide brim cowboy hats with rounded domes and the same type of long black riding coats. It was all part of Pinkerton's new excellence policy toward professionalism and discipline. This was Pinkerton's personal army. He was the general and the men were his lieutenants.

As the agents rode up to the marshal's office and dismounted, people on the streets stopped to look on. Shop owners up and down Main Street were peering out their windows wondering who these guys were and what intentions they brought with them to Carson City.

Pinkerton was the only one who entered the marshal's office. The other agents stood next to their horses. The marshal and Pinkerton introduced themselves to each other and then Pinkerton said,

"We are here to interrogate and possibly arrest this Billy Crane. I trust he is not aware that he's a suspect in this case."

"That's right Mr. Pinkerton. I have kept the contents of the letter we discovered a secret. My deputy doesn't even know about it. What's the plan now? Do you want me to arrest him?"

"No, I would appreciate it if you would lead me to him and we'll handle it from there. Where can we find him?"

"He's at the Mint working as a guard, the irony eh?"

"Well marshal, lead the way."

Once again the agents all mounted and then the marshal led the way to the Mint which was only about ten minutes away. When they arrived at the Mint, this time everyone went in. It was a sight to behold. The marshal met with Mr. Bonner, the person in charge, and told him that Pinkerton and he were there to see Billy Crane.

"Crane has guard duty up on the second floor today. I'll go up and get him," Bonner said.

When Bonner reached the second floor and found Crane, he told Crane that there were a few men downstairs who wanted to talk to him.

"Who are they?" Crane asked.

"One is Allan Pinkerton."

"Pinkerton? What's he doing this far west?"

"I have no idea. You best come with me. They want to ask you a few questions about the break-in."

"Sure thing," Crane said.

On the outside he acted cool but on the inside his heart was just two beats short of a coronary, at least that's how he felt as he also became light-headed. A guilty conscience will do that to a no-good scumbag.

When Crane reached the first floor, about six agents surrounded him. While he shook hands with Pinkerton with his right hand, one agent quickly grabbed the rifle out of his left hand and another swiftly removed the pistol from his holster. Crane looked on with a worried look now. His feelings on his inside were manifesting themselves on his outside. At first he thought, or one would say, hoped, that Pinkerton was there to get the scoop on the break-in since he was the only witness left alive. However, the way things were presenting themselves, it was looking more like he was a suspect. "But how could this be?" He wondered.

"Are we taking him back to the jailhouse for questioning?" The marshal asked.

"No marshal, your job is done here. Crane is going with us," Pinkerton said.

"Wait a minute, where are you taking me?" Crane asked.

"We're going on a journey and then we have some questions to ask you," Pinkerton responded.

With that, two agents grabbed Crane by the arms and led him to the front door. Bonner walked over to the coat rack on the wall by the door, picked up Crane's coat, and tossed it to him. Then Bonner asked the marshal what this was all about. The marshal told Bonner that Crane may have been involved with the hold-up.

"That can't be. There must be a mistake. He's one of my most trusted guards," Bonner said.

Pinkerton and his agents, along with their prisoner, all mounted their horses and quickly turned them around. They whipped the hindquarters of their steeds and galloped hard and fast to Reno with their heads down, shoulders forward and their long coats trailing behind them in the wind.

They arrived back at their train at about 7:00 p.m. Pinkerton had Crane brought into the plush coach car and sat him down on one of the leather chairs. Crane unbuttoned his coat. Pinkerton had one of the agents pour Crane a snifter of brandy. All of a sudden, things weren't looking so bad to Crane. He was being treated quite nicely. One of the agents lit up a fire in the potbelly stove to take the chill out of the car and the rest of the agents removed their coats and got comfortable. Then Allan Pinkerton asked Crane point-blank,

"How were you involved in this break-in and who's the mastermind behind all of this?"

"How was I involved? What are you talking about? Can't you see I was beat up by those outlaws? Hell, they even broke my nose."

"That's all I wanted to know. Button up your coat," Pinkerton said as he snatched the snifter from Crane's hand. Then Pinkerton told two of his agents to grab Crane and told two more to come along. At this point only one of Pinkerton's agents knew what was about to happen next. He was the one who brought the chickens.

"Where are you taking me?" Crane asked.

"To your new temporary home," Pinkerton responded.

They all stepped down off the plush coach car into the frigid night air and walked two cars down the railroad tracks to a freight car. One of the agents slid the heavy car door open. It was dark outside but even darker inside. Crane could see a chair in the middle of the car but that was all. Pinkerton told Crane to crawl up into the car and sit in the chair, so he did. Then Pinkerton and four agents climbed in as well. Pinkerton reached down and picked up a kerosene lantern, lit it and smiled with an evil look that would scare a rattler back into his hole. Three of the four agents couldn't believe their eyes. The other one knew what to expect. Crane looked around the car and felt like he was close to losing his lunch.

What Crane saw was a quasi-medieval torture chamber. There were several shackles chained to the back wall, blood splattered all over the other three walls, and a hangman's noose right above Crane's head and directly over the chair. Also, hanging on the wall were a bullwhip and several lariats. Pinkerton was going to shackle

Crane to the wall for the night and interrogate him in the morning but his curiosity got the best of him.

"Stand him up and tie his hands behind his back," Pinkerton ordered one of his agents. At this point all of the other agents gathered outside of the freight car to look in.

"Now Crane, I know you were involved with the break-in and you know who the leader of that gang is who murdered those innocent men and pulled off that heist, so I suggest you tell us right now what you know. Spill your guts man or we'll spill them for you."

"I have no idea what you're talking about, Pinkerton."

"Well Crane, I'm the judge and the jury in this trial. Justice will be served one way or the other. Put the noose around his neck and stand him up on the chair. When I say when, kick that chair out from underneath him. Look Crane, I'm losing my patience. Who is the leader of that gang?" Pinkerton asked as one of the agents followed Pinkerton's orders and positioned Crane to meet his maker at Pinkerton's command.

Crane began to perspire profusely. He was beginning to think that Pinkerton might be just crazy enough to actually hang him. He could see the determined look on Pinkerton's face and there was something about his eyes, something almost evil and quite frightening.

"OK, OK, I'll talk you mad man. His name is Brinkman. Brinkman's the man you want."

"You aren't as stupid as you look Crane. Where can I find this Brinkman?"

"I don't know."

"Kick that chair," Pinkerton ordered.

"Wait, wait, Brinkman has a boss."

"Who's that?"

"It's my cousin," Crane looked down and was depressed that he had to give up a kin.

"Speak up man, who's your cousin?"

"He's…"

Crane ratted out his cousin at this point. Pinkerton and the other agents were shocked at the revelation.

"Where can we find your cousin?" Pinkerton questioned.

"Topeka, Kansas," Crane mumbled as he looked down toward the floor.

"Take him down and shackle him to the wall. By the way Crane, I'm sorry about the stench in here. That chicken blood on the walls is starting to get a bit rank, don't you think?"

The other agents laughed as they followed Pinkerton's orders. A couple of them were convinced that Pinkerton was in fact going to hang the sap. Pinkerton was so into the moment that it was doubtful he even knew where he was headed with his interrogation.

When they all jumped out of the so called "torture car", Pinkerton walked beside the train and up to the steam engine and told the engineers to "Get this iron horse turned around. The next stop is Topeka, Kansas".

"We'll have to back up a few miles first to Wadsworth. We can turn around there," one of the engineers told Pinkerton.

"OK then, fire it up, and start heading east."

It was now January 4th. The trip from Reno to Topeka was about 1,500 miles. They figured they could get there in a day and a half. That would be sometime during the daylight hours on January 6th. Before the agents got some shut-eye, Pinkerton was still talking about that letter that was found on the dead guard's body. Where that letter came from was a perplexing mystery to the entire group. Oh everyone had their own theories alright, but nobody knew for sure.

He also mentioned that the pieces of the puzzles were beginning to form, as it were, a clear picture. Crane was going to jail for robbery and accessory to murder. He might even hang for his crimes. But the real trophy to Pinkerton now was the mastermind of the gang, plus Brinkman and his band of desperados. It became his personal crusade to take them all down.

News of the robbery and the five murders at the Carson City Mint was now appearing in every newspaper and gazette across the entire country: from the east coast to the west coast and from the northern borders with Canada to the southernmost tip of the state of Texas. And Pinkerton knew he was hot on the trail of these outlaws like Irish Wolfhounds closing the gap on a pack of wolves.

Back at the lodge in Abilene, Brinkman and his gang of killers were gloating over their successful mission. They got away with murder and $4,000,000 in gold. They made it back to Abilene on January 4th. The trip took a little longer since they took a train to Wichita and then rode their horses north to Abilene. Also, their passenger train traveled at a slower speed than Pinkerton's; plus there were passenger stops in addition to fuel and water stops along the way.

When they arrived back at their hideout, all four million dollars were put into Brinkman's safe behind his desk. He had already told them that they wouldn't get their share of the money until after their next big job which would end up doubling their current take. But just to keep the morale high, he gave each gang member $1,000 in spending money but told them to lay low for a few days until they got the lay of the land after their big heist. He jokingly told Rusty not to crack his safe.

The plan for the next several days was to gamble and pull a few corks at the lodge. Brinkman told his men that they could ride to town in twos but to stay out of trouble and away from brawls. Another thing he warned them about was to not get all liquored up and hook up with some floozy from the brothel. A slip of the tongue while sauced in a house of soiled doves could be devastating to the cause.

Brinkman already had his next job worked out and it was every bit as daring and the rewards as great as the last. He felt like he needed for the men to relax some before he rolled out his strategy for the next big heist.

During the late morning hours on Friday, January 6, 1882, Pinkerton's train pulled up onto a spur in Topeka. He told his men to stay on the train except for two of his detectives.

The first thing Pinkerton and his two agents did was to walk down to the marshal's office to inform him what he was up to. But when they arrived at the jailhouse, the only one there was a deputy marshal. The deputy marshal told Pinkerton that the marshal was in court over at the courthouse.

"Is the marshal a witness?"

"No sir, he's a spectator this morning."

"Perfect," Pinkerton said. "Come with us deputy. I want you to go into the courtroom and bring him out to me."

"Yes sir."

The courthouse was only one block down the street so it took them just a few minutes to reach it. The deputy did exactly what Pinkerton asked him to do. When the deputy walked out of the courthouse with the marshal, Pinkerton asked the marshal to walk over to a tree where they could be alone. He wanted to speak to him in private and didn't want the deputy to hear what he had to say. The other two agents stood with the deputy about thirty feet away.

They talked for about five minutes and then waited. The marshal told the deputy to go back to their office. Ten minutes later, the courthouse emptied and then the marshal went back into the courtroom and into the judge's chamber and told him that there was a detective out front from Chicago that needed to talk to him about a prisoner they captured.

The judge took off his robe and walked out to greet the detective. The judge was surprised to see that it was the famous Allan Pinkerton he had heard so much about. Pinkerton told the judge that they captured a criminal and they needed legal advice since they did some questionable acts to get him to talk. He told the judge that they were holding the prisoner in their interrogation car. Pinkerton said he wanted to show the judge the interrogation car and wanted his professional opinion before he moved on with the case.

The marshal, two agents, Pinkerton and the judge walked within twenty feet of the "torture car" and then Pinkerton told them to stop for a minute. There were two agents standing alongside of the car. When they saw Pinkerton give the signal, one of the agents slid open the car door and climbed into the car and the other one followed with his pistol drawn. One of the agents unlocked the shackles, stood Crane up, tied his hands behind his back and then gagged him. The last thing he did was to put a hood over his head.

Then the first agent climbed out of the car and the hooded criminal and the second agent followed. The judge started moving forward but Pinkerton grabbed his arm and said, "Wait, we want you to see something."

Pinkerton gave another signal and one of the agents removed the hood from Crane's head and Crane's eyes latched onto the judge's eyes and the judge's onto Crane's eyes. Pinkerton himself then stuck the barrel of his pistol deep into the back of Judge Robert Parker, Crane's cousin, and told him to quietly move toward the "interrogation chamber". The other agents moved Crane to the meeting car for the time being but not before the judge could see Crane's battered face. Parker wrongly assumed that it was the Pinkerton agents who beat Crane up so badly.

When Pinkerton and the group moved up to the torture car, Parker looked in. He saw the shackles, the blood on the walls, the bullwhip and the hangman's noose and quickly turned around, cowardly caved in, and said to Pinkerton,
"What do you want to know?"

CHAPTER TWELVE:

Back to Hays City

When Pinkerton obtained all the information he needed from the judge, he had Parker and Crane shackled to the wall of the "torture car" and slid the freight car door shut. Then he told the marshal that it was imperative that he keep everything to himself so that they could pull off a surprise ambush on Brinkman and his gang. The marshal agreed to do so.

Time was now of the essence. Pinkerton told the engineers to head to Abilene at full throttle. It was a ninety mile trip which would take just over two hours. That would put them in town around 1:30 in the afternoon.

While riding the rails west, Pinkerton had a meeting with his agents in the plush meeting car. There were no drinks poured on this trip and no idle jawing to pass the time away. Everyone needed their wits about them and it was time to start talking strategy on how to go about capturing or killing the most ruthless and now notorious gang in the west.

Now Pinkerton understood how this gang knew who and where to break those professionals out of prison. It was Judge Robert Parker who was able to assemble that information through his judicial networking. And what got Pinkerton all riled up, like a cougar returning to his deer kill in the Montana snow country and seeing a lone gray wolf dragging off his meal, was the fact that a federal judge, chosen by a president of the United States, could be so audacious as to scheme to rob a U.S. Mint. It was beyond his comprehension.

While the train was traveling wide open at full speed with a firebox producing extreme heat creating maximum steam pressure to turn the steel wheels and propelling the iron horse to Abilene, Pinkerton was laying out his last minute plans.

They knew these facts compliments of the judge: Brinkman was the on-site leader of the gang, he was the president of the local bank, the gang was staying in a lodge two miles west of Abilene near the Smoky Hill River and there were ten to twelve well-armed outlaws in the gang, all fugitives from the law. The plan was to waste no time, and ride out to trap the gang in their lodge, if in fact they were there. Pinkerton knew that it was like drawing to an inside straight to find them all there at one time. But he was gambling on lady luck because his pride was getting the best of him.

226

The train arrived in Abilene a few minutes early, about 1:15 p.m. to be exact, and pulled into a spur next to the old dilapidated stockyard loading area left over from the cattle town boom years of the late 60's and early 70's.

It was a sight to behold when thirteen men dressed in dark hats and long black riding coats rode their bay horses down the ramp exiting a large closed in freight car. The sound of fifty-two hooves pounding the wooden ramp was enough to turn heads two blocks away.

As per Pinkerton's policy, their first visit was to the marshal's office. When they all trotted down Main Street sitting tall in their saddles, Brinkman was across the street just strolling back to his bank after a long lunch with Kathleen. He spotted the riders and right away assumed the worst, that they were Pinkerton agents. In fact when he saw the heavy set man with a full facial beard limp into the marshal's office, he correctly identified him as Allan Pinkerton.

Now Brinkman changed his gait to a quick walk. For the first time ever, he was feeling the stress of an outlaw with the posse on his trail. He was a smart man and knew it was time to make a quick exit. He ran into the bank and told Rusty to come into his office.

"Look son, don't ask questions. Follow me out the back door and let's get on our horses and ride out to the lodge."

Rusty's curiosity got the best of him when he saw the worried look on Brinkman's face like he just saw a ghost climb out of its grave on Boot Hill.

"What's going on, Mr. Brinkman?"

"Pinkerton agents are in town, a whole army of them."

"Pinkerton agents?"

"That's right, let's ride!"

They rode hard and fast out to the lodge to warn the others, split up the loot and high-tail it out of their faster than the muzzle speed of a .44 exiting a Winchester '73.

Like ole Judge Robert Parker, the marshal broke down and told Pinkerton where to find Brinkman and the location of the lodge. But he pretended that he had no idea about Brinkman's involvement in the gang or that the lodge was a hideout for Brinkman's Professionals.

Pecos and Dakota were walking out of the saloon when they spotted the agents walking from the marshal's office across the street to the bank with their guns drawn. Dakota told Pecos to quickly duck back into the saloon. The saloon was on the same side of the street as the marshal's office so they were able to look out the saloon window and watch as the agents stormed the bank.

"Where's Brinkman?" Pinkerton asked the teller.

The teller looked up and was speechless when he saw the army of men entering the bank all pointing pistols forward. He didn't know if it was a hold-up or some outlaws coming to collect a debt.

"Speak up man, where is Brinkman?"

"He's in his office," the teller said.

Pinkerton signaled for three agents to bust through the door. When they did, they found the back door wide open and Brinkman gone.

"I'm Detective Allan Pinkerton. When did you last see Brinkman?" Pinkerton asked the teller.

"He just went into his office not more than five minutes ago, sir."

"Let's go men," Pinkerton ordered. "He's probably headed out to the lodge."

All the agents holstered their pistols and ran out to their horses, quickly mounted them and spurred them into a full gallop. They rode down Main street leaning forward in their saddles like a cavalry charge, continuously whipping the reins to the right and then to the left of their horses' hindquarters getting all they could out of their steeds.

Kathleen was standing at the newspaper press looking out the window also, watching and wondering what was going on. She saw two men run into the marshal's office and then within minutes run back out, climb on their horses and ride hard the opposite direction of the agents. It was Dakota and Pecos. The marshal told them that those guys with the long coats were Allan Pinkerton and his agents and they knew about Brinkman and the gang and they were out for blood. Well Dakota was smarter than your average cowpuncher and told Pecos to forget about the loot and said, "Let's both head south to Laredo, pronto." And so they did. They both thought it was better than swinging from a cottonwood tree.

Now Kathleen's curiosity was boiling over. She shut down the press and walked quickly over to the bank to ask Brinkman what was going on. She was shocked to find out from the teller that Pinkerton and his agents were looking for her foster father.

She then literally ran over to the marshal's office. When she opened the door, the marshal was standing at his desk. He had just taken off his gun belt and hung it on a wooden peg. Then right in front of Kathleen, he removed the marshal's badge from his vest and threw it on top of his desk.

"I have something pretty bad to tell you Kathleen, that I think you should know about your foster father."

Well the marshal spilled his guts about everything; Brinkman ordering the killing of her boss Jeff Porter, the deputy marshal, and the hanging of Nichols. He also told her about the gang Brinkman assembled, the robbery of the Mint and all those killings, and everything else he knew, including where the hideout was located.

"I thought that the guy who the vigilantes hung was Porter's killer," Kathleen said.

"No ma'am, it was Brinkman who ordered Porter to be killed. Porter stumbled upon your father's hideout and so Brinkman couldn't let him live. Brinkman lied about the guy who was hung for Porter's killing. He was really a Pinkerton agent trying to infiltrate their gang."

"I knew something wasn't right, I just knew it. Call it woman's intuition. But I had no idea it was this bad. What about Rusty? Is he part of the gang too?"

"I'm sorry, but I believe he is, Kathleen."

Kathleen was sickened. She sat down and slumped in the chair in front of the marshal's desk. It was obvious to see that she was experiencing major disappointment. She loved Rusty and knew that Rusty felt the same way about her. Then she looked at the badge on the desk top, and then up at the marshal and said,

"What are you doing?"

"I'm quitting. I knew too much and didn't do anything about it. I have a guilty conscience but not guilty enough to give myself up. I'm heading out of town and wish only the best for you, Kathleen."

Kathleen got up and stared at the marshal as he walked out of his office, left the door wide open, mounted his horse and rode the way of Pecos and Dakota. She ran both of her hands through her hair in a nervous gesture trying to figure out what to do. Then she spotted several rifles lined up on a rack on the wall. She ran over to get one, checked to see if it was loaded and then ran out to her horse and carriage, whipped the horse with her buggy whip and rode toward the lodge not knowing why or what she would do when she got there. Truth be known, she didn't want anything to happen to Rusty.

In the meantime, Brinkman had his gang assembled in their large meeting room. He told them about Pinkerton and that they didn't have a minute to spare. As he was counting out the money, the agents were already surrounding the lodge. As soon as Chan heard what was going on, he didn't care about anything else but making a clean getaway. So he opened the back door and a shot rang out. He ran back inside and closed the door and yelled, "They're here!"

"Damn!" Brinkman shouted. "Get to the windows, and start shooting. Bobby, you come upstairs with me. Bring you rifle and see if you can pick some of those agents off from up there."

The outlaws broke out the windows with the butts of their guns and started firing out into the woods as bullets were whizzing by their heads and hitting the inside walls breaking vases, busting lamps and shattering wine glasses.

All the outlaws were in the lodge except for Pecos and Dakota. The Kansas Kid, Arizona, Cole, Doc, Dane, Rusty, and Kenny were firing out of the bank of windows in the meeting room on two walls while Brinkman and Bobby were sending lead balls out the windows upstairs.

The fighting was fierce. Volley after volley went both ways. The first one to get hit was Cole. He took one in the neck and fell dead. Then Arizona took one to the head, stumbled back a few steps and fell backwards slamming against the floor. The bullets from all the repeating rifles outside were buzzing through the windows so fast now that the outlaws had to duck to keep from getting shot.

The one who didn't lower his head in time was Bobby on the second floor. He took one to the head right in front of Brinkman and was killed instantly. The guys downstairs heard two thumps from upstairs and thought Brinkman and Bobby were both shot. But Brinkman was still alive. He just tripped over Bobby's dead body,

Now, Dane, Doc, the Kid, and Kenny bunched up near three windows, kneeling down and dodging bullets. Chan was hiding in a pantry closet in the kitchen clinging to his meat cleaver ready to kill anyone who opened the door.

A fusillade of bullets was still flying through the windows. Then while holding one gun in his hand, Rusty reached down for Arizona's pistol. With a pistol in both hands and pointed forward, he shouted to Dane, Doc, the Kid, and Kenny,

"Throw down your guns right now!"

"What the hell are you talking about?" Kenny yelled as they all looked back at Rusty.

"I said throw down your guns, I'm a Pinkerton agent and you are all under arrest!"

They saw a look in Rusty's eyes like they had never seen before and knew that he was dead serious with his ultimatum.

Unfortunately, Brinkman was walking down the steps with a rifle and overheard Rusty's demand and his admission. Brinkman walked into the room and as soon as Rusty spotted Brinkman out of the corner of his eye, he swung his left arm and pointed that pistol on Brinkman and held the gun in his right hand on the other four. Brinkman held his rifle targeted right at Rusty's chest. It couldn't get any tenser in that room. Since no one was shooting anymore from the house, the Pinkerton agents ceased firing as well.

Brinkman said to Rusty,

"So you're a Pinkerton agent ehh? You sure had me fooled boy. I hope you know you aren't getting out of here alive, don't you?"

"That may be true Mr. Brinkman. But I don't think any of you are either unless you all give up. I know for a fact that Allan Pinkerton is one determined man and he's been disappointed once too many times in his past. I don't believe he will let any of you get away."

Just then while Rusty was looking at Brinkman, the Kid reached for his pistol and Rusty quickly shot him in the chest. But Rusty left his guard down and a rifle shot rang through the halls of the lodge and a body slammed to the floor. But it wasn't Rusty's body. It was Brinkman's. Kathleen had run past the agents and snuck in the back door and heard everything and shot her foster father in the back before Brinkman could put a slug into Rusty.

Rusty looked at Kathleen and Kathleen at Rusty and she said, "I know everything now."

"Not quite," Rusty said.

Then Rusty shouted out to Allan Pinkerton,

"Mr. Pinkerton, can you hear me?"

"I hear you. What do you want?"

"It's Agent Luke Barnes and I have prisoners in here for you."

Pinkerton looked at one of his lieutenants standing next to him and said, "Luke Barnes? I thought he was dead. By golly agent, there's your LB. Luke's the one who wrote that note and stuck it in that guard's pocket in Carson City. Come on, let's round up Luke's prisoners."

Luke, a.k.a. Rusty, held his gun on the three outlaws still alive while the Pinkerton agents entered the lodge. Allan Pinkerton was the first to enter followed by the rest. When Allan saw Luke, he shook his hand and grinned from ear to ear. Luke did the same. Doc, Dane and Kenny stood up and put their hands high into the air.

"Somebody found my note in Carson City, eh?" Luke commented.

"That's right, once we got the word, we acted fast," Pinkerton said

"It was a long shot but my only hope," Luke said.

"Tell me who these men are, Luke," Pinkerton insisted.

"Well, the one lying dead on the floor here is Brinkman, the ringleader of this group. I have no idea who his boss is but…"

"We do," Pinkerton interrupted. "He's Judge Parker."

"Out of Dodge City?" Luke asked.

"No, out of Topeka. We have him chained up in our holding car at the train station. I understand that the Parker we have is the brother of the judge in Dodge City. We also have Crane, the insider at the Mint. He's with the judge."

While Luke and Pinkerton were carrying on a conversation, one of the agents looked in the open safe and then on top of the desk and discovered what looked to be millions of dollars in gold certificates and greenbacks. It was the loot from the Mint alright. He picked up all the money and stuffed it in some saddlebags that were lying nearby.

Then Luke said, "Well when we get time, I have some more names for you. But for now, let me tell you who these three are. This tall guy with the handlebar mustache is Johnny Dane. He's the explosives expert who was broken out of the Huntsville Penitentiary. This short pudgy guy is Kenny Burkley. He's a sniper broken out of the Missouri Penitentiary. I believe you'll find his brother Bobby's body upstairs. And this clean cut fella is…"

Just then one of the Pinkerton agents interrupted and walked over to Doc, got face to face with him and said, "Let me guess, you are Doctor Eddie who was broken out of the Little Rock Penitentiary."

"Do you know this guy, Don?" Pinkerton asked.

Don got in Doc's face and said, "Yeah I know him. He's my younger brother, Doc Eddie Hawkens. I haven't seen him in over ten years but I kept up with his recent shady doings. Ma and pa would sure have been proud of you, Eddie."

Doc looked down in shame.

"Oh by the way Mr. Pinkerton, this is Kathleen, my fiancée. She saved my life when she put a bullet into the back of Mr. Brinkman."

Kathleen just realized she was proposed to and accepted it with a nod and a smile and then looked down with sorrow at her foster father lying there on the floor.

"Well round these criminals up men and take them to the train. Don, drag the bodies outside away from this lodge and then torch this place and burn the evil with it. When we get to town, tell the undertaker to come out and collect these bodies. Tell him to put them in cheap boxes and bury them on Boot Hill with no fanfare. Luke, I want you to come to our meeting car on the spur in town and give me a few statements. I want to hear what you've been up to since we lost contact with you early last year. You can bring Kathleen along with you if you want."

"I'll follow you into town," Luke said, "By the way Mr. Pinkerton, you'll find a Chinese cook by the name of Chan in the walk-in kitchen pantry. Don't take him lightly. He's a murderer like the rest. He'll be swinging a meat cleaver when you open the door."

"Thanks for the warning. Is that it Luke?" Pinkerton inquired as he gestured to two of his agents to fetch the cook.

"No sir, there's more. There are still two gang members missing. Their names are Dakota Wilson and Pecos Fransisco. They rode into town earlier today but they're probably long gone by now if they spotted you and your agents. And then there's two more you need to round up in town: The marshal and the telegraph operator. They both took their orders from Brinkman."

Pinkerton was taken aback at that revelation. "The marshal?" Pinkerton asked with astonishment. "He's the guy who told me where to find Brinkman and his lodge."

"Well, he probably got religion Mr. Pinkerton," Kathleen said, "but you won't find him nor Dakota and Pecos in town. They all rode out the road opposite to this lodge. They're long gone by now. You might still be able to capture the telegraph operator though. He might not be wise yet to what's going on."

"Well I'll have him send a wire to the three governors who hired us and tell them that this case is solved. Then I'll arrest the low-life and throw him in the freight car with the rest of his buddies."

When everyone arrived in town, Pinkerton did exactly what he said he would do and his agents continued to fill up the prisoner holding car with the captured outlaws.

One of the agents fired up the potbelly stove in the meeting car while the others congregated in the passenger car. Pinkerton wanted one agent with him when Luke and he sat down for a long chat with Kathleen at Luke's side. Pinkerton first asked Luke if he wanted a drink. Luke said no because he wanted to go over everything with a clear head. Pinkerton then led the discussion.

"First let me say Luke that I'm glad you're alive. I feared for your life when I hadn't heard from you in months."

"Yes, I feared for my life this whole journey, as well. I took a lot of risks but I put my trust in the Good Lord and He took good care of me. I truly believed He had plans for me."

"Does Kathleen know about you and your background?"

"No sir, not yet. But if you don't mind, Mr. Pinkerton, I'd like to start from the top and address both you and Kathleen at the same time."

"Go right ahead Luke, the floor is yours."

"Well Kathleen, my first job was as a locksmith for the Yale Company out of Connecticut. They're a fairly new company founded in 1868. I built all sorts of locks and knew their workings inside and out. I worked at Yale for three years. My objective was to earn enough money to go to a school of theology to become a minister. My father was a minister and I wanted to follow in his footsteps."

"A minister?" Kathleen questioned. "I haven't seen the inside of a church since I was eight years old."

Rusty looked at Kathleen, smiled, and then continued,

"I succeeded with my objective. I attended The General Theological Seminary of the Episcopal Church in Manhattan, New York. Their motto is Sermo Tuus Vertas Est which means 'Thy Word Is Truth'. I always loved that motto because that's exactly what I believed. During semester breaks and summer breaks, I continued to work at the Yale Company to finance my education.

Right when I graduated from the school of theology, my father wired me and told me that he wanted to build onto his church because his congregation was growing and he needed a larger building. He was frustrated that he didn't have the money. But he prayed, and he prayed hard. Well it was about that time that Allan Pinkerton visited the Yale Company looking for an honest person with locksmith experience who was interested in making good money by infiltrating a small gang of outlaws. The president of the Yale Company told Pinkerton to look me up since I was still living up east but making plans to move out west.

Well, I was daring, had locksmith knowledge, needed money to help my father out, and Mr. Pinkerton figured I was honest since I just graduated from a school of theology. So he met with me and hired me. He gave me an alias but I didn't like it so without telling you Mr. Pinkerton, I changed it to Rusty Blake."

"Well, that explains why I lost track of you."

"Yes sir. I can see now, that move was a foolish mistake on my part. Nevertheless, I did it not thinking of the potential consequences. The three outlaws who hired me to knock over several banks signed up with a larger gang called the Outlaws of Smoky Hill River. I know you heard of them and their demise."

"Yes I did," Pinkerton acknowledged. "Go on."

"We knocked over the Salina Bank first. We did it on Sunday. Since I was new in the gang, they kept me out of the planning loop. I had no way of knowing where we were headed or what the target was. They just took me along for the ride. So I couldn't get a message to you in advance.

However, I knew all the plans for our next heist which was the bank in Hays City. I was able to get a telegram off to you before we headed to Hays."

"I never received it, Luke."

"I figured as much for two reasons. First, I overheard the gang leader, Dead-eye, tell his pard to kill me after the safe was opened. Then after I was captured, convicted, and one day away from hanging without you showing up, I knew right then and there you never received the message. Sometime I'll tell you about my trial by a kangaroo court in a saloon in Hays City. I was waiting until the last minute before I sprung the news to the marshal that I was working for you. Truth be known though, they still would have hung me. Oh I probably should have told them earlier but I prayed on it and something told me to wait.

The Good Lord was really watching over me because I figured he saved my life four times: once from being shot and killed by Dead-eye's partner, again in the Hays City Mercantile Bank where the marshal or his deputy could have killed me, again from being hung on Main Street, and when Brinkman tested my safecracking skills. It was either open his safe or be dumped in the Smoky Hill River.

By the way, you probably heard that the town of Hays City was wise to the bank robbery. A floozy who became a murderer had a hand in that. You'll probably want to look her up later. She goes by the name of Diamond Lil and I'll lay odds that she's hanging out in San Francisco."

"Getting back to you Luke, was this when those outlaws broke you out of jail?"

"Yes sir, it was Dakota and Pecos. Those are the two outlaws who got away. They are a couple of the luckiest guys I ever laid eyes on. It was after that when I met Brinkman. I watched him build his gang. I'm sure you know about all the breakouts. I also know of three people he had killed. I'm sorry to talk about this in front of you Kathleen. Do you want to leave?" Luke asked.

"No, I want to hear everything."

"OK then. Brinkman had Jeff Porter, the deputy marshal, and your agent Nichols killed. A vigilante group made up of Brinkman's men hung your agent like he was a common criminal. I was sickened when they did that. But there was just nothing I could do at the time but pray for his soul and his family if he had one."

"Oh he had a family alright," Pinkerton said, "a wife and two daughters.

Tell me Luke, was the Northfield raid a test?" Pinkerton asked.

"Yes sir it was."

"I thought so," Pinkerton acknowledged.

"We didn't know it until it was over though, Mr. Pinkerton."

"I figured as much after hearing the story from the bank president up there."

"Well I believe you have everything except for one more thing. Brinkman's half-brother, Jacob Scott, the president of the bank in Virginia City, Nevada was in on it too. That's who traded the gold coins and bullion for certificates and greenbacks."

"Well, we'll send a wire to the marshal in Virginia City and have Scott arrested, Pinkerton said. "Now, what can I do for you Luke besides pay you the wages we owe you?"

"Remember I told you I went to work for you to help my father build onto his church?"

"Yes, I do, I'm anxious to meet your father, Luke. He sure did a good job raising his son."

"I would have loved for you to be able to meet him. But you can't. You see, he was the preacher killed in Hays City during the raid by the Outlaws of Smoky Hill River. If you would have received my telegram, he might still be alive today. What I need for you to do is to take this train to Hays City and meet with the marshal, his two deputies and the city council and explain to them who I am and that I want to add on to their church and become their minister. Can you do that for me Mr. Pinkerton?"

"You bet I can."

Kathleen was astounded at Luke's revelations. She had no knowledge of any of this, not in the least bit. Most of all, she was impressed with Luke's commitment to his faith and it really made her think about her own inner feelings and how she really had no one to turn to in times of trouble. She thought that maybe it was time for her to find the Lord as well. They say that the Lord works in mysterious ways. The events that unfolded in the flat lands of Kansas around the towns of the Smoky Hill River sure gave validation to that theory.

Well it all came to pass just as Luke wanted: everything was explained to the townspeople, Luke's name was cleared, and the church was enlarged. Kathleen and Luke were married, and Luke Barnes became the new Christian minister of Hays City.

It appeared that the Good Lord saved Luke's life to preach the gospel and follow in his father's footsteps. And on that momentous Sunday morning in Hays City, Kansas, at the startup of the dedication service for the newly remodeled church, with a packed house attending and his wife Kathleen sitting in the first pew, Preacher Luke Barnes said,

"Open up your Bibles to my father's favorite Psalm, the 23rd Psalm, the Psalm of David, and let's recite it together,

The LORD is my shepherd…"

THE END

EPILOGUE

After Pinkerton left Hays City, he and his men took the long train ride out to Nevada to collect one more outlaw in Brinkman's network of criminals, the president of the bank in Virginia City, Jacob Scott.

When Pinkerton returned to Chicago, he turned over the outlaws to the federal authorities. His self-esteem was at an all-time high. He felt that he finally redeemed himself and his detective agency from his failures in the 70's in their attempt to track down the James boys, Frank and Jessie.

However, there was still something churning his gut. And it was worrisome enough to him that he asked for a private audience with the President of the United States, President Chester Arthur.

President Arthur agreed to see him on Friday morning, January 27, 1882 at nine o'clock. It was snowing heavily in D.C. that morning and a blistering north wind was whipping up a virtual blizzard almost shutting down the capital city.

However, it was not about to deter Allan Pinkerton from meeting with the President on this day. He arrived at the White House at 9:10 a.m., ten minutes late for his meeting. But that couldn't be helped. He was having trouble finding a carriage driver who was willing to brave the elements to drive him from his hotel to the White House.

When Pinkerton walked up onto the porch of the White House, he kicked the snow off his boots and brushed the snow off his long black coat and top hat. The president had seen his carriage riding up the driveway so he met Pinkerton at the door. President Arthur welcomed him to Washington and then escorted him to his office where he had a fire roaring in the fireplace making the room nice and toasty.

They both sat down, the President behind his desk and Pinkerton in a chair in front of the desk. After some small talk of various natures, President Arthur got right to the point.

"Well Allan, congratulations on solving the Brinkman case. That Judge Parker and Brinkman had quite a criminal organizational network, didn't they? And they sure had a lot of bravado knocking over a United States Mint. I understand that many good men were murdered by that organization. I trust that the criminal justice system will find a way to hang the surviving outlaws, if they deserve such a fate, before vigilantes get their hands on them and employ their own type of justice. Nevertheless it's all over now and you can go about other business."

"Well Mr. President, that's what I wanted to talk to you about. I don't believe it is over."

"What are you saying Allan?"

"Sir, three men got away clean. But that's not why I am concerned. There are things that I found out in Northfield, Minnesota and in Carson City, Nevada that lead me to believe that we have a major criminal network on our hands."

"Well that's very disturbing to hear. It sounds like you have more work to do."

"Yes sir, Mr. President... that is a fact."

BONUS SECTION:

Actual Article on the Death of Jesse James Published April 6, 1882

This is the actual article obtained from the Library of Congress, that appeared in the Richmond Democrat, April 6, 1882. Jesse James was shot dead on April 3, 1882. Richmond, Missouri is 40 miles southeast of St. Joseph, Missouri by the way the crows fly. The article appeared on page 2 in columns 1 and 2.

NOTE: The article below includes "errors" in punctuation, grammar and spelling because it is exactly how it was printed in the Richmond Democrat.

Here then is the article in its entirety.

JESSE JAMES DEAD

The Notorious Outlaw no Longer a Terror to the Country

Shot by Bob Ford in His Own House at St. Joseph Last Monday

Between 9 and 10 o'clock on Monday morning last, Jesse James, the notorious bandit and outlay, was shot and killed at his residence in St. Joseph, by Robert Ford, of this vicinity and a son of Jas T Ford, who lives on a farm three miles north of Richmond. Bob will be recollected by every person here as carried on a Restaurant and grocery store for his brother John in the building now occupied by Pat Strader, and later they had a grocery store in the building now completed by W. H. Ballard.

It appears that Charley Ford, an elder brother, has been living with Jesse James since November last, at his residence in St. Joseph, but Bob, who is on the State Detective force, only went there a week before the tragedy. The particulars are given in the St. Joseph Gazette as follows:

There is little doubt that the killing was the result of a premeditated plan formed by Robert and Charles Ford several months ago. Charles had been an accomplice of Jesse James since the 3rd of last November and entirely possessed his confidence. Robert Ford, his brother, joined Jesse near Mrs. Samuel's home, mother of the James boys, last Friday a week ago and accompanied Jesse and Charles to this city Sunday, March 23. Jesse, his wife and two children removed from Kansas City, where they had lived several months until they feared their whereabouts would be suspected, in a wagon to this city, arriving here November 8, 1881, accompanied by Chas. Ford. They rented a house on the corner of Lafayette and Twenty-first streets, where they stayed till they secured the house 1318 on Lafayette street, formally the property of Councilman Ayleabury, paying $14 a month for it and giving the name of Thomas Howard. The house is a one-story cottage painted white, with shutters, and is romantically situated on the brow of a lofty eminence east of the city, commanding a fine view of the principal portion of the city, the river and railroads, and adapted as by nature for the perilous and desperate calling of James. Just east of the house is a deep, gulch-like ravine, and beyond that a broad expanse of open country, backed by a belt of timber. The house, except from the west side, can be seen for several miles. There is a large yard attached to the cottage and a stable where Jesse had been keeping two horses, which were found there this morning.

Charles and Robert Ford have been occupying one of the rooms in the rear of the dwelling, and have secretly had an understanding to kill Jess ever since last fall- A short time ago, before Robert had joined James, the latter proposed to rob the bank at Platte City. He said the Burgess murder trial would commence there to-day, and his plan was, if they could get another companion to take a view of the situation of the Platte City bank, and while the arguments were being heard in the murder case, which would naturally engage the attention of the citizens, boldly execute one of his famous raids. Charley Ford approved of the plan and suggested his brother Robert as a companion worthy of sharing the enterprise with them. Jesse had met the boy at the latter's house near Richmond three years ago, and consented to see him. The two men accordingly went to where Robert was and arranged to have him accompany them to Platte City. As stated all three came to St. Joseph q week ago Sunday. They remained at the house all the week. Jesse thought it best that Robert should not exhibit himself on the premises, lest the presence of three able-bodied men who were doing nothing, should excite suspicion. They had fixed upon to-night to go to Platte City. Ever since the boys had been with Jesse they had watched for an opportunity to shoot him, but he was always heavily armed, and was so watchful that it was impossible to draw a weapon without James seeing it. They declare that they had no idea of taking him alive, considering the undertaking suicidal. The opportunity they had long wished for came yesterday morning.

THE KILLING

Breakfast was over. Charley Ford and Jesse James had been to the stable, currying the horses, preparatory to their night ride. On returning to the room where Robert Ford was Jesse said: "It's an awfully hot day." He pulled off his coat and vest, and tossed them on the bed. Then he said, "I guess I'll take off my pistols, for fear somebody will see them if I walk in the yard." He unbuckled the belt in which he carried two forty-five caliber revolvers, one a Smith & Wesson and the other a Colt, and l aid them on the bed with his coat and vest. He then picked up a dusting brush with the intention of dusting some pictures which hung on the wall. To do this he got on a chair. His back was now turned to the brothers, who silently stepped between Jesse and his revolvers, and at a motion from Charley, both drew their guns. Robert was the quickest of the two. In one moment he had the long weapon to a level with his eye, with the muzzle not less than two, not more than four feet from the back of the outlaw's head. Even in that motion quick as thought, there was something which did not escape the acute ears of the hunted man. He made a motion as if to turn his head to ascertain the cause of the suspicious sound, but too late! A nervous pressure on the trigger, a quick flash, a sharp report and the well-directed ball crashed through the outlaw's skull. There was no outcry: just a swaying of the body, and it fell heavily backward upon the carpeted floor. The shot had been fatal and all the bullets in the chamber of Charley's revolver, still directed at Jesse's head, could not more effectually have becided the fate of the greatest bandit and freebooter that ever figured in the pages of a country's history. The ball had entered the base of the skull and made its way out through the forehead over the left eye. It had been fired out of a Colt's 45, improved pattern, silver mounted and pearl handled, presented by the dead man to his slayer only a few days ago.

Mrs. James was in the kitchen, when the shooting was done, divided from the room in which the bloody tragedy occurred, by the dining room. She heard the shot, and dropping her household duties ran into the front room. She saw her husband lying extended on his back, and his slayers, each holding his revolver in his hand, making for the fence in the rear of the house. Robert had reached the enclosure and was in the act of scaling it, when she stepped to the door and called to him, "Robert, you have done this. Come back." Robert answered: "I swear to God I didn't." They then returned to where she stood. Mrs. James ran to the side of her husband and lifted up his head. Life was not yet extent, and when she asked him if he was hurt, it seemed to her that he wanted to say something but could not. She tried to wash away the blood that was coursing over his face from the hole in his forehead, but it seemed to her "that the blood would come faster than she could wipe it away." And in her hands Jesse James died.

Charley Ford explained to her that "a pistol had accidently gone off." "Yes" said Mrs. James: "I guess it went off on purpose." Meanwhile Charley had gone back into the house and brought out two hats, and the two boys left the house. They went to the telegraph office, sent a message to Sheriff Timberlake, of Clay county, to Gov. Crittenden and other officers, and then surrendered themselves to Marshal Craig.

When the Ford boys appeared the the police station they were told by an officer that Marshal Craig and a posse of officers had gone in the direction of James residence, and they started after them, and surrendered themselves. They accompanied the officers to the house and returned in custody of the police to the marshal's headquarters, where they were furnished with dinner, and about three o'clock were removed to the old circuit court room, where the inquest was held in the presence of an immense crowd.

Mrs. James also accompanied the officers to the city hall, having previously left her two children, aged seven and three, a boy and a girl, at the house of Mrs. Turnal, who had known the James under their assumed name of Howard ever since they had occupied the adjoining house. She was greatly affected by the tragedy, and her heart-rending moans and expressions of grief were sorrowful evidence of the love she bore the dead desperado.

The Coroners jury in the case of the inquest over the body of Jesse James at St. Joseph, returned a verdict that he came to his death by a pistol shot, intentionally fired by Robert Ford. The boys are locked up in the St. Joseph jail, and it is said that Mrs. James and Mrs. Samuels were called before the Grand Jury on Tuesday to testify in the matter and that Ford boys will be indicted for murder in the first degree.

That concludes the article in the Richmond Democrat. But in case you are wondering the fate of Bob and Charley Ford. Then

FOR THE RECORD

Charley Ford (July 9, 1857 – May 6, 1884): Died at age 26

Deep depression after Jesse's death, terminally ill from tuberculosis, and a debilitating morphine addiction caused him to take his own life on May 6, 1884.

Bob Ford (December 8, 1861 - June 8, 1892): Died at age 30

Bob was shot to death in his tent saloon in Creede, Colorado by Edward O'Kelley who unloaded both barrels of a shotgun into Bob Ford. Bob died instantly.

Bibliography

Newspaper clippings in the Prologue and Author's Foreword
http://chroniclingamerica.loc.gov/

Bonus Section on the death of Jesse James
http://chroniclingamerica.loc.gov/

History of the Smoky Hill River and valleys
http://www.kshs.org/

Calendar of 1881
http://www.timeanddate.com/calendar/?year=1881&country=1

Calendar of 1882
http://www.timeanddate.com/calendar/?year=1882&country=1

Pinkerton Detective Agency timeline
http://www.pinkerton.com/history

Pinkerton Government Services
http://en.wikipedia.org/w/index.php?title=Pinkerton_(detective_a
gency)&oldid=640234497

Biography: Allan Pinkerton's Detective Agency and doings with the
James Boys
http://www.pbs.org/wgbh/americanexperience/features/biograp
hy/james-agency/

Allan Pinkerton
http://en.wikipedia.org/w/index.php?title=Allan_Pinkerton&oldi
d=637986658

Cooper (profession)
http://en.wikipedia.org/w/index.php?title=Cooper_(profession)&
oldid=638901629

Bibliography

Boot Hill
http://en.wikipedia.org/w/index.php?title=Boot_Hill&oldid=638
976294

Hays City newspaper article from April 18, 1878
http://chroniclingamerica.loc.gov/leen/sn84027670/1878-04-
18/ed-1/seq-1/

Colt M1877 pistol
http://en.wikipedia.org/w/index.php?title=Colt_M1877&oldid=6
38430397

Kangaroo Court
http://en.wikipedia.org/w/index.php?title=Kangaroo_court&oldi
d=638673000

Fricassee
http://en.wikipedia.org/w/index.php?title=Fricassee&oldid=6355
37239

Hangman's knot
http://en.wikipedia.org/w/index.php?title=Hangman%27s_knot&
oldid=625982911

Texas State Penitentiary at Huntsville
http://en.wikipedia.org/w/index.php?title=Huntsville_Unit&oldid
=626761512

Little Rock, Arkansas
http://en.wikipedia.org/w/index.php?title=Little_Rock,_Arkansas
&oldid=640128210

Missouri State Penitentiary
http://www.visitmo.com/missouri-travel/tour-missouris-1836-
state-
penitentiary.aspx?gclid=Cj0KEQiA2o6lBRCn_b7yppe98rQBEiQA
MpnYnW0rk8U2Qpf5VW9iy0S_nq_ZzHbCzQyGU1f21EY3r7oa
Aotw8P8HAQ

Missouri State Penitentiary
http://en.wikipedia.org/w/index.php?title=Missouri_State_Penite
ntiary&oldid=626027656

Anamosa, Iowa
http://en.wikipedia.org/w/index.php?title=Anamosa,_Iowa&oldid
=638373769

Anamosa State Penitentiary
http://en.wikipedia.org/wiki/Anamosa_State_Penitentiary

Arkansas Department of Correction
http://en.wikipedia.org/w/index.php?title=Arkansas_Department
_of_Correction&oldid=637883570

Carson City, Nevada
http://en.wikipedia.org/w/index.php?title=Carson_City,_Nevada
&oldid=638999158

James R. Mead
http://en.wikipedia.org/w/index.php?title=James_R._Mead&oldid
=605796320

George Bird Grinnell
http://en.wikipedia.org/w/index.php?title=George_Bird_Grinnell
&oldid=636680045

Hays, Kansas
http://en.wikipedia.org/w/index.php?title=Hays,_Kansas&oldid=
636866473

CPSIA information can be obtained at www.ICGtesting.com
Printed in the USA
LVOW11s2138120616

492181LV00003B/4/P